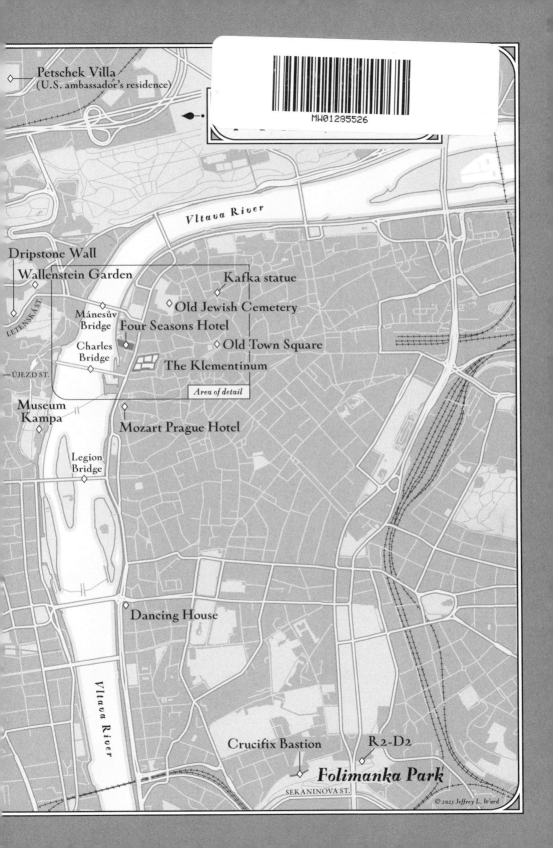

Petschek Villa
(U.S. ambassador's residence)

MW01285526

Vltava River

Dripstone Wall
Wallenstein Garden
Kafka statue
Old Jewish Cemetery
Mánesův Bridge
Four Seasons Hotel
Charles Bridge
Old Town Square
LETENSKÁ ST.
The Klementinum
ÚJEZD ST.
Area of detail
Museum Kampa
Mozart Prague Hotel
Legion Bridge

Vltava River

Dancing House

Crucifix Bastion
R2-D2

Folimanka Park

SEKANINOVA ST.

© 2025 Jeffrey L. Ward

THE SECRET OF SECRETS

THE
SECRET
OF
SECRETS

◆—·— A NOVEL —·—◆

DAN BROWN

DOUBLEDAY ⚓ NEW YORK

To my editor and best friend, Jason Kaufman,
without whom writing these novels would be nearly impossible . . .
and a lot less fun

THE SECRET OF SECRETS

The day science begins to study non-physical phenomena, it will make more progress in one decade than in all the previous centuries.

—NIKOLA TESLA

PROLOGUE

I *must have died,* the woman thought.

She was drifting high above the spires of the old city. Beneath her, the illuminated towers of St. Vitus Cathedral glowed on a sea of twinkling lights. With her eyes, if she still had eyes, she traced the gentle slope of Castle Hill down into the heart of the Bohemian capital, following the labyrinth of winding streets that lay shrouded in a fresh blanket of snow.

Prague.

Disoriented, she strained to make sense of her predicament.

I am a neuroscientist, she reassured herself. *I am of sound mind.*

That second statement, she decided, was questionable.

The only thing Dr. Brigita Gessner knew for certain at the moment was that she was suspended over her home city of Prague. Her body was not with her. She was without mass and without form. And yet the rest of her, the *real* her—her essence, her consciousness—seemed to be quite intact and alert, floating slowly through the air in the direction of the Vltava River.

Gessner could recall nothing from her recent past except a faint memory of physical pain, but her body now seemed to consist only of the atmosphere through which she was floating. The sensation was unlike anything she had ever experienced. Against her every intellectual instinct, Gessner could find only one explanation.

I have died. This is the afterlife.

Even as the notion materialized, she rejected it as absurd.

The afterlife is a shared delusion . . . created to make our actual life bearable.

As a physician, Gessner was intimately familiar with death, and also with its finality. In medical school, while dissecting human brains, Gessner came to understand that all those personal attributes that made us who we are—our hopes, fears, dreams, memories—were nothing but chemical compounds held in suspension by electrical charges in our brains. When a person died, the brain's power source was severed, and all of those chemicals simply dissolved into a meaningless puddle of liquid, erasing every last trace of who that person had once been.

When you die, you die.

Full stop.

Now, however, as she drifted over the symmetrical gardens of Wallenstein Palace, she felt very much alive. She watched the snow falling around her—or *through* her?—and oddly, she sensed no cold at all. It was as if her mind were simply hovering in space, with all reason and logic intact.

I have brain function, she told herself. *So I must be alive.*

All Gessner could conclude was that she was now in the throes of what medical literature termed an OBE—out-of-body experience—a hallucination that occurred when critically injured patients were resuscitated after clinically dying.

OBEs almost always presented in the same manner—the perception that one's mind had been temporarily separated from its physical body, floating upward and hovering without form. Despite feeling like real experiences, OBEs were nothing but imagined journeys, usually triggered by the effects of extreme stress and hypoxia on the brain, sometimes in conjunction with emergency room anesthetics like ketamine.

I am hallucinating these images, Gessner assured herself, gazing down at the dark curve of the Vltava River snaking through the city. *But if this is an OBE . . . then I must be in the process of dying.*

Surprised by her own calm, Gessner tried to remember what had happened to her.

I am a healthy forty-nine-year-old woman . . . Why would I be dying?

In a blinding flash, a frightening memory materialized in

Gessner's consciousness. She now realized where her physical body was lying at this very instant . . . and, even more terrifying, what was being done to her.

She was on her back, tightly strapped into a machine she herself had created. A monster stood over her. The creature looked like some kind of primordial man who had crawled out of the earth. His face and hairless skull were coated with a thick layer of filthy clay, cracked and fractured like the surface of the moon. Only his hate-filled eyes were visible behind his earthen mask. Crudely etched across his forehead were three letters in an ancient language.

"Why are you doing this?!" Gessner had screamed in panic. "Who are you?!" *What are you?!*

"I am her protector," the monster replied. His voice was hollow, his accent vaguely Slavic. "She trusted you . . . and you betrayed her."

"Who?!" Gessner demanded.

The monster spoke a woman's name, and Gessner felt a stab of panic. *How can he possibly know what I have done?!*

An icy weight materialized in her arms, and Gessner realized the monster had started the process. An instant later, an unbearable pinpoint of pain blossomed in her left arm, spreading along her median cubital vein, clawing its way sharply toward her shoulder. "Please, stop," she gasped.

"Tell me everything," he demanded as the excruciating sensation reached her armpit.

"I will!" Gessner frantically agreed, and the monster paused the machine, halting the pain at her shoulder, though the intense burning remained.

Racked with terror, Gessner spoke as quickly as she could through clenched teeth, frantically revealing the secrets she had vowed to keep. She answered his questions, divulging the disturbing truth about what she and her partners had created deep beneath the city of Prague.

The monster stared down at her from behind his thick clay mask, his cold eyes flashing with comprehension . . . and hatred.

"You've built an underground house of horrors," he whispered. "You all deserve to die." Without hesitation, he turned the machine back on and headed for the door.

"No . . . !" she shrieked as the agony seized her anew, surging through her shoulder and into her chest. "Please don't leave . . . This will kill me!"

"Yes," he said over his shoulder. "But death is not the end. I have died many times."

With that, the monster evaporated, and Gessner was suddenly hovering again. She tried to shout an appeal for mercy, but her voice was muted by a deafening thunderclap as the sky above her seemed to open wide. She felt herself gripped by an unseen force—a kind of reverse gravity—lifting her higher, dragging her upward.

For years, Dr. Brigita Gessner had derided her patients' claims of returning from the brink of death. Now she found herself praying that she could join the ranks of those rare souls who had danced to the edge of oblivion, peered into the abyss, and somehow stepped back from the precipice.

I can't die . . . I have to warn the others!

But she knew it was too late.

This life was over.

CHAPTER 1

Robert Langdon awoke peacefully, enjoying the gentle strains of classical music from his phone's alarm on the bedside table. Grieg's "Morning Mood" was probably an obvious choice, but he had always considered it the perfect four minutes of music to start his day. As the woodwinds swelled, Langdon savored the uncertainty of not being able to recall quite where he was.

Ah yes, he remembered, smiling to himself. *The City of a Hundred Spires.*

In the dim light, Langdon surveyed the room's massive arched window, flanked by an antique Edwardian dresser and an alabaster lamp. The plush, hand-knotted carpet was still scattered with rose petals from last night's turndown service.

Langdon had come to Prague three days earlier and, as he had on previous visits, checked into the Four Seasons Hotel. When the manager insisted on upgrading Langdon's reservation to the three-bedroom Royal Suite, he wondered if it was due to his own brand loyalty or, more likely, to the prominence of the woman with whom he was traveling.

"Our most celebrated guests deserve our most celebrated accommodation," the manager had insisted.

The suite included three separate bedrooms with en suite baths, a living room, a dining room, a grand piano, and a central bay window with a lavish arrangement of red, white, and blue tulips—a welcome gift from the U.S. embassy. Langdon's private dressing room offered a pair of brushed wool slippers monogrammed with the initials *RL*. *Something tells me that's not Ralph Lauren*, he thought, impressed by the personalized touch.

Now, as he luxuriated in bed and listened to the music from his alarm, he felt a tender hand touch his shoulder.

"Robert?" a soft voice whispered.

Langdon rolled over and felt his pulse quicken. She was there, smiling at him, her smoky gray eyes still half-asleep, her long black hair tousled around her shoulders.

"Good morning, beautiful," he replied.

She reached over and stroked his cheek, the scent of Balade Sauvage still on her wrists.

Langdon admired the elegance of her features. Despite being four years older than Langdon, she was more stunning every time he saw her—the deepening laugh lines, the faint wisps of gray in her dark hair, her playful eyes, and that mesmerizing intellect.

Langdon had known this remarkable woman since his days at Princeton, where she was a young assistant professor while he was an undergrad. His quiet schoolboy crush on her had gone either unnoticed or unrequited, but they'd enjoyed a flirtatious, platonic friendship ever since. Even after her professional career skyrocketed, and Langdon became a high-profile professor known throughout the world, the two of them had kept in casual contact.

Timing is everything, Langdon now realized, still marveling at how quickly they had fallen for each other during this spontaneous business trip.

As "Morning Mood" crescendoed into the full orchestration of the theme, he pulled her close with a strong arm, and she nuzzled into his chest. "Sleep okay?" he whispered. "No more bad dreams?"

She shook her head and sighed. "I'm so embarrassed. That was awful."

Earlier in the night, she had awoken in terror from an exceptionally vivid nightmare, and Langdon had needed to comfort her for nearly an hour before she could get back to sleep. The dream's unusual intensity, Langdon assured her, had been the result of her ill-advised nightcap of Bohemian absinthe, which

Langdon had always believed should be served with a disclaimer: *Popular during the Belle Epoque for its hallucinogenic properties.*

"Never again," she assured him.

Langdon reached over and turned off the music. "Close your eyes. I'll be back in time for breakfast."

"Stay with me," she teased, holding him. "You can skip *one* day of swimming."

"Not if you want me to remain a chiseled younger man," he said, sitting up with a lopsided grin. Each morning, Langdon had jogged the three kilometers to Strahov Swimming Center for his morning laps.

"It's dark out," she pressed. "Can't you just swim here?"

"In the *hotel* pool?"

"Why not? It's water."

"It's tiny. Two strokes and I'm finished."

"There's a joke there, Robert, but I'll be kind."

Langdon smiled. "Funny girl. Go back to sleep, and I'll meet you for breakfast."

She pouted, threw a pillow at him, and rolled over.

Langdon donned his faculty-issue Harvard sweats and headed for the door, choosing to take the stairs rather than the suite's cramped private elevator.

Downstairs, he strode through the elegant hallway that connected the hotel's Baroque riverfront annex with the building's lobby. Along the way, he passed an elegant display case marked PRAGUE HAPPENINGS, featuring a series of framed posters announcing this week's concerts, tours, and lectures.

The glossy poster at the center made him smile.

CHARLES UNIVERSITY LECTURE SERIES
WELCOMES TO PRAGUE CASTLE
INTERNATIONALLY ACCLAIMED
NOETIC SCIENTIST
DR. KATHERINE SOLOMON

Good morning, beautiful, he mused, admiring the headshot of the woman he had just kissed upstairs.

Katherine's lecture last night had been standing room only, no small feat considering she had spoken in Prague Castle's legendary Vladislav Hall—a cavernous, vaulted chamber used during the Renaissance to host indoor jousting competitions with knights and horses in full regalia.

The lecture series was one of Europe's most respected and always drew accomplished speakers and enthusiastic audiences from around the world. Last night had been no exception, and the packed hall erupted with applause when Katherine was introduced.

"Thank you, everyone," Katherine said, taking the stage with a confident calm. She wore a white cashmere sweater and designer slacks that fit her flawlessly. "I'd like to begin tonight by answering the one question I am asked almost every day." She grinned and pulled the microphone off its stand. "What the hell is *noetic science*?!"

A wave of laughter rolled through the hall as the audience settled in.

"Simply stated," Katherine began, "noetic science is the study of *human consciousness*. Contrary to what many believe, consciousness research is not a new science—it is, in fact, the oldest science on earth. Since the dawn of history, we have sought answers to the enduring mysteries of the human mind . . . the nature of consciousness and of the soul. And for centuries, we have explored these questions primarily through . . . the lens of *religion*."

Katherine stepped off the stage, moving toward the front row of attendees. "And speaking of religion, ladies and gentlemen, I couldn't help but notice that we have in the audience with us tonight a world-renowned scholar of religious symbology, Professor Robert Langdon."

Langdon heard murmurs of excitement in the crowd. *What the hell is she doing?!*

"Professor," she said, arriving before him with a smile, "I wonder if we might avail ourselves of your expertise for a moment? Would you mind standing up?"

Langdon politely stood, quietly shooting her a *you'll-pay-for-this* grin.

"I'm curious, Professor . . . what is the most common religious symbol on earth?"

The answer was simple, and either Katherine had read Langdon's article on the topic and knew what was coming, or she was about to be very disappointed.

Langdon accepted the microphone and turned to face the sea of eager faces, dimly lit by chandeliers hanging on ancient iron chains. "Good evening, everyone," he said, his deep baritone booming through the speakers. "And thank you to Dr. Solomon for putting me on the spot with no warning whatsoever."

The audience clapped.

"All right then," he said, "the world's most common religious symbol? Does anyone have a guess?"

A dozen hands went up.

"Excellent," Langdon said. "Any guesses that are *not* the crucifix?"

Every single hand went down.

Langdon chuckled. "It's true that the crucifix is extremely common, but it is also a uniquely *Christian* symbol. There is, in fact, one *universal* symbol that appears in the artwork of every religion in history."

The audience exchanged puzzled looks.

"You've all seen it many times," Langdon coaxed. "Perhaps on the Egyptian Horakhty stela?"

He paused.

"How about the Hindu Kanishka casket? Or the famed Christ Pantocrator?"

Silence. Dead stares.

Oh boy, Langdon thought. *Definitely a science crowd.*

"It also appears in hundreds of the most celebrated Renaissance paintings—Leonardo da Vinci's second *Virgin of the Rocks*, Fra Angelico's *The Annunciation*, Giotto's *Lamentation*, Titian's *Temptation of Christ*, and countless depictions of *Madonna and Child* . . . ?"

Still nothing.

"The symbol I'm referring to," he said, "is the *halo*."

Katherine smiled, apparently knowing this would be his answer.

"The halo," Langdon continued, "is the disk of light that appears over the head of an enlightened being. In Christianity, halos hover over Jesus, Mary, and the saints. Going further back, a sun disk hovered over the ancient Egyptian god Ra, and in Eastern religions a *nimbus* halo appeared over the Buddha and the Hindu deities."

"Wonderful, thank you, Professor," Katherine said, reaching for the microphone, but Langdon ignored her and pivoted away playfully—a touch of payback. *Never ask an historian a question you don't want answered fully.*

"I should add," Langdon said as the crowd laughed appreciatively, "that halos come in all shapes, sizes, and artistic representations. Some are solid gold disks, some are transparent, and some are even square. Ancient Jewish scripture describes Moses's head as being surrounded by a 'hila' —the Hebrew word for 'halo' or 'emanation of light.' Certain specialized forms of halos have rays of light emanating from them . . . glowing spines that radiate outward in all directions."

Langdon turned back to Katherine with a devious smile. "Perhaps Dr. Solomon knows what this type of halo is called?" He tipped the mic to her.

"A radiant crown," she said without missing a beat.

Someone did her reading. Langdon brought the mic back to his lips. "Yes, the radiant crown is a particularly significant symbol. It appears throughout history adorning the heads of Horus, Helios, Ptolemy, Caesar . . . and even the towering Colossus of Rhodes."

Langdon gave the crowd a conspiratorial grin. "Few people realize this, but the most photographed object in all of New York City happens to be . . . a radiant crown."

Puzzled looks, even from Katherine.

"Any guesses?" he asked. "None of you has ever photographed the radiant crown that hovers three hundred feet above New York Harbor?" Langdon waited as the murmur of revelation grew in the crowd.

"The Statue of Liberty!" someone called out.

"Exactly," Langdon said. "The Statue of Liberty wears a radiant crown—an ancient halo—that universal icon we have used through history to identify special individuals who we believe possess divine enlightenment . . . or an advanced state of . . . *consciousness*."

As Langdon handed the mic back to Katherine, she was beaming. *Thank you*, she mouthed to him as he returned to his seat amid applause.

Katherine walked back onto the stage. "As Professor Langdon has just stated so eloquently, humans have been contemplating *consciousness* for a long time. But even now, with advanced science, we have trouble *defining* it. In fact, many scientists are afraid even to *discuss* consciousness." Katherine glanced around and whispered, "They call it the c-word."

Scattered laughter rippled through the room again.

Katherine nodded to a spectacled woman in the front. "Ma'am, how would *you* define consciousness?"

The woman thought a moment. "I suppose . . . an awareness of my own existence?"

"Perfect," Katherine said. "And where does that awareness *come* from?"

"My brain, I guess," she said. "My thoughts, ideas, imaginations . . . the brain activity that makes me who I am."

"Very well said, thank you." Katherine lifted her gaze back to the audience. "So can we all start by agreeing on the basics? Consciousness is created by your brain—the three-pound bundle of eighty-six billion neurons inside your skull—and therefore *consciousness* is located inside our heads."

Nods all around.

"Wonderful," Katherine said. "We've all just agreed on the currently accepted model of human consciousness." After a beat, she sighed heavily. "The problem is . . . the currently accepted model is *dead wrong.* Your consciousness is *not* created by your brain. And in fact, your consciousness is not even located *inside* your head."

A stunned silence followed.

The spectacled woman in the front row said, "But . . . if my consciousness is not located *inside* my head . . . where *is* it?"

"I'm so glad you asked," Katherine said, smiling to the assembled crowd. "Settle in, folks. We're in for quite a ride tonight."

Rock star, Langdon thought as he walked toward the hotel lobby, still hearing the echoes of Katherine's standing ovation. Her presentation had been a dazzling tour de force that left the crowd stunned and clamoring for more. When someone asked about her current work, Katherine revealed she had just put the finishing touches on a book that she hoped would help redefine the current paradigm of consciousness.

Langdon had helped Katherine secure a publishing deal, although he had yet to read her manuscript. She had revealed enough of its contents to leave Langdon enthralled and eager to read, but he sensed she had kept all the most shocking revelations to herself. *Katherine Solomon is never short on surprises.*

Now, as he neared the hotel lobby, Langdon suddenly recalled that Katherine was slated for an 8 a.m. meeting this morning with Dr. Brigita Gessner—the eminent Czech neuroscientist who had personally invited Katherine to speak at the lecture series. Gessner's invitation had been generous, and yet after meeting the woman last night following the event and finding her insufferable, Langdon now secretly hoped Katherine would oversleep and opt for breakfast with *him* instead.

Pushing it from his thoughts, he entered the lobby, enjoying the fragrance of the extravagant bouquets of roses that always graced the main entrance. The scene that greeted him in the lobby, however, was far less welcoming.

Two black-clad police officers were stalking intently through the open space, working a pair of German shepherds. Both dogs wore bulletproof vests marked *POLICIE* and were sniffing around as if searching for . . . something.

That doesn't look good. Langdon went over to the front desk. "Is everything okay?"

"Oh, heavens yes, Mr. Langdon!" The immaculately dressed manager nearly curtsied as he rushed out to greet Langdon. "All is perfection, Professor. A minor issue last night, but a false alarm," he assured, shaking his head dismissively. "Just taking precautions. As you know, security is a top priority here at the Four Seasons Prague."

Langdon eyed the policemen. *Minor issue?* These guys hardly looked minor.

"Are you off to the swimming club, sir?" the manager asked. "Shall I call you a car?"

"No thanks," Langdon replied, heading for the door. "I'll jog over. I like the fresh air."

"But it's snowing!"

The native New Englander glanced outside at the faint skittering of snowflakes in the air and gave the manager a smile. "If I'm not back in an hour, send one of those dogs to dig me out."

CHAPTER 2

The Golĕm hobbled through the snow, the hem of his long black cape dragging through the dirty slush that covered Kaprova Street. Hidden beneath the cloak, his massive platform boots felt so heavy he could barely lift his legs. On his face and skull, a thick layer of clay tightened in the cold air.

I must get home.

The Ether is gathering.

Fearing the Ether might overtake him, The Golĕm reached into his pocket and grasped the small metal rod he kept with him at all times. He raised the object to his head and pressed it hard against the top of his skull, rubbing it in small circles on the dried clay.

Not yet, he incanted silently, closing his eyes.

The Ether dispersed, at least for the moment, and he placed the rod back into his pocket and pushed onward.

A few more blocks, and I can Release.

The Old Town Square—known in Prague as *Staromák*—was deserted this dark morning, save for a pair of tourists clutching burnt-sugar pastries and gazing up at the famous medieval clock. Every hour, the ancient timepiece presented its "Walk of the Apostles," a juddering procession of saints that mechanically rotated in and out of view through two small windows in the clock face.

Circling aimlessly since the fifteenth century, The Golĕm thought, *and still it attracts sheep to observe the spectacle.*

As The Golĕm passed the couple, they glanced over at him and spontaneously gasped, stepping backward. He was well accustomed to this reaction from strangers. It reminded him he had a physical form, even if they could not see what he truly was.

I am The Golĕm.

I am not of your realm.

The Golĕm felt untethered at times, as if he might float away, and he enjoyed draping his mortal shell in heavy robes. The weight of the cloak and platform boots accentuated the pull of gravity, anchoring him to the earth. His clay-smeared head and hooded cloak made him a frightening oddity, even in Prague, where costumes at night were common.

But what made The Golĕm a truly arresting vision were the three ancient letters emblazoned on his forehead . . . etched into the clay with a palette knife.

אמת

The three Hebrew letters—*aleph*, *mem*, *tav*—from right to left, spelled *EMET*.

Truth.

Truth is what had brought The Golĕm to Prague. And Truth is what Dr. Gessner had revealed to him earlier tonight—a detailed confession of the atrocities that she and her partners had committed deep beneath Prague. Their crimes were abhorrent, and yet they paled in comparison to what was planned for the near future.

I will destroy it all, he told himself. *Reduce it to rubble.*

The Golĕm pictured their dark creation . . . obliterated . . . a smoldering hollow in the earth. Although it was a daunting task, he was confident he could accomplish it. Dr. Gessner had revealed all he needed to know.

I need to act quickly. The window of opportunity is slim, he told himself, the plan already crystallizing in his mind.

The Golĕm turned southeast now, moving away from the square, finding the narrow alleyway that wound toward his flat. The Old Town neighborhood was a labyrinth of passageways known for its vibrant nightlife and distinctive pubs—Týnská Literary Café for writers and intellectuals, Anonymous Bar for

hackers and intrigue seekers, and Hemingway Bar for sophis-
ticates and cocktail connoisseurs. Of course, the Sex Machines
Museum was open late and drew crowds of gawkers well into
the night.

As The Golěm snaked through the maze of alleys, he found
himself thinking not about the terrors he had just inflicted on
Dr. Brigita Gessner, nor of the shocking information he had
extracted—but rather thinking of *her*.

He was always thinking of her.

I am her protector.

She and I are two entangled particles, entwined forever.

His sole purpose on this earth was to shelter her, and yet she
knew nothing of his existence. Even so, his time of service to
her had been an honor. To bear the burdens of another was the
noblest of callings; but to do so anonymously, without any recognition at all . . . *that* was a truly selfless act of love.

Guardian angels take many forms.

She was a trusting person who unknowingly was caught in a
world of dark science. She did not see the sharks circling. The
Golěm had killed one of those sharks tonight, but now there
was blood in the water. Powerful forces would soon be surfacing
from the deep to find out what had transpired . . . to ensure the
secrecy of their creation.

You will be too late, he thought. Their underground house
of horrors would soon collapse beneath the weight of its own
sin . . . a victim of its own ingenuity.

As he pressed on through the snowy streets, The Golěm felt
the Ether return, thickening around him. Again he rubbed the
metal wand to his head.

Soon, he promised.

◆—·—▶

In London, an American named Mr. Finch polished a pair of
Cartier Panthère glasses and paced his luxurious office. His
impatience had turned to deep concern.

Where the hell is Gessner? Why can't I reach her?

He knew the Czech neuroscientist had attended Katherine

Solomon's lecture last night at Prague Castle, and afterward she had sent Finch an alarming message regarding the book Solomon would soon publish. It was not good news. Gessner had promised to call Finch with an update.

So far, Finch had not heard a word, and it was nearly dawn.

He had messaged and called her repeatedly with no response.

It's been six hours . . . Gessner is meticulous—this is patently unlike her.

Having ascended to the pinnacle of his profession by following his gut, Mr. Finch had learned to listen to his intuition. Unfortunately, his instincts were now telling him that something in Prague had gone dangerously awry.

CHAPTER 3

The winter air felt crisp and invigorating as Robert Langdon ran southward along Křižovnická Street, his long strides leaving a lone trail of footprints in the sidewalk's thin covering of snow.

The city of Prague had always felt enchanted to him. It was a moment frozen in time. Having suffered far less damage than other European cities in World War II, the historical capital of Bohemia enjoyed a dazzling skyline that still sparkled with all its original architecture—a uniquely varied and pristine sampling of Romanesque, Gothic, Baroque, Art Nouveau, and Neoclassical designs.

The city's nickname—*Stověžatá*—literally meant "with a hundred spires," although the actual number of spires and steeples in Prague was closer to seven hundred. In the summer, the city occasionally illuminated them with a sea of green floodlights; the awe-inspiring effect was said to have inspired Hollywood's depiction in *The Wizard of Oz* of the Emerald City—a mystical destination that, like Prague, was believed to be a place of magical possibilities.

As Langdon jogged across Platnéřská Street, he felt as if he were running through the pages of a history book. The colossal facade of Prague's Klementinum loomed on his left, a two-hectare complex that housed the viewing tower used by the astronomers Tycho Brahe and Johannes Kepler, as well as an exquisite Baroque library holding more than twenty thousand volumes of ancient theological literature. This library was Langdon's favorite room in Prague, and possibly in all of Europe. He and Katherine had just visited its newest exhibit yesterday.

Now, as he turned right at the Church of St. Francis of Assisi, he could see, directly ahead of him, the east entrance to one of the city's most famous landmarks, illuminated in the amber glow of Prague's rare gas streetlamps. Hailed by many as the most romantic bridge in the world, Karlův most—Charles Bridge— was constructed of Bohemian sandstone and lined on both sides by thirty statues of Christian saints. Stretching more than half a kilometer across the placid Vltava River, protected on both ends by massive guard towers, the bridge had once served as a critical trade route between Eastern and Western Europe.

Langdon ran through the archway in the east tower, emerging to see an untarnished blanket of snow stretching out before him. The bridge was for pedestrians only, and yet, at this hour, there was not a single footprint.

I'm alone on Charles Bridge, Langdon thought. *A life moment.* He had once been similarly alone in the Louvre with the *Mona Lisa,* but those circumstances had been far less pleasant than this.

Langdon's strides lengthened as he settled into his pace, and by the time he reached the other side of the river, he was running effortlessly. To his right, illuminated high against the dark skyline, shone the city's most beloved glittering gem.

Prague Castle.

It was the largest castle complex in the world, stretching more than half a kilometer from its western gate to its eastern tip, and had a footprint of nearly five million square feet. The outer walls enclosed six formal gardens, four discrete palaces, and four Christian churches, including the magnificent St. Vitus Cathedral, in which the Crown Jewels of Bohemia were safe-guarded, along with the crown of Saint Wenceslas, the beloved ruler commemorated in the popular Christmas carol.

As Langdon passed beneath the west tower of Charles Bridge, he laughed to himself, thinking of the event at Prague Castle the night before.

Katherine can be persistent.

"Come to my lecture, Robert!" she had said when she had called him two weeks earlier to coax him to Prague. "It's perfect—you'll be on winter break. The trip is my treat."

Langdon considered her playful offer. The two of them had always enjoyed a platonic flirtation and mutual respect, and he was inclined to throw caution to the wind and take her up on the spontaneous proposal.

"I'm tempted, Katherine. Prague is magical, but really—"

"Let me cut to it," she blurted. "I need a plus-one, okay? There, I said it. I need a date for my own lecture."

Langdon burst out laughing. "*That's* why you called? A world-famous scientist . . . and you need an escort?"

"Just some arm candy, Robert. There's a black-tie sponsors dinner, and then I'm speaking in some famous hall—Vlad . . . something."

"*Vladislav Hall?!* In Prague Castle?"

"That's it."

Langdon was impressed. The quarterly Charles University Lecture Series was one of Europe's most prestigious gatherings, but it was apparently more highbrow than he imagined.

"Are you sure you want a *symbologist* on your arm at a black-tie dinner?"

"I asked Clooney, but his tux is at the dry cleaner's."

Langdon groaned. "Are *all* noeticists this tenacious?"

"Only the good ones," she said. "And I'll take that as a yes."

What a difference two weeks make, Langdon mused, still smiling as he reached the other side of Charles Bridge. Prague certainly had lived up to its reputation as a magical city . . . a catalyst with ancient powers. *Something has happened here . . .*

Langdon would never forget his first day with Katherine in this mystical place—losing themselves in a labyrinth of cobblestone streets . . . dashing hand in hand through a misty rain . . . taking cover beneath an archway of Kinský Palace in Old Town Square . . . and there, breathless, in the shadows of the Clock Tower . . . their very first kiss, which felt surprisingly effortless after decades of friendship.

Whether because of Prague, perfect timing, or the guidance

of some unseen hand, Langdon had no idea, but it had sparked an unexpected alchemy between them, which was growing stronger with every passing day.

＊

Across town, The Golĕm turned a final corner and arrived wearily at his building. He unlocked the outer door and stepped into the meager foyer of his domicile.

The entryway was dark, but he chose not to turn on the light. Instead, he slipped through a narrow passage to a hidden staircase, which he climbed in obscurity, gripping the railing for guidance. His legs ached, protesting as he ascended, and he was grateful when he finally reached his apartment door. After carefully wiping the snow from his boots, The Golĕm unlocked the door and stepped inside.

His flat was veiled in complete darkness.

Exactly as I created it.

Its interior walls and ceilings were painted solid black, and the windows were shrouded with heavy drapes. The lacquered floors were already dull and murky and reflected no light, and there were almost no furnishings.

The Golĕm threw a master switch, and a dozen black lights illuminated throughout the apartment, radiating a soft purplish glow on those objects that were pale in hue. His home was an otherworldly landscape—ephemeral and luminescent—and it instantly relaxed him. Moving through this space gave him the sensation of drifting through a deep void . . . floating from one shimmering object to another.

The absence of broad-spectrum light created a "time-neutral" environment—an atemporal world in which his physical form received no circadian cues. The Golĕm's duties required he keep irregular hours, and the lack of light freed his biorhythms from the influences of conventional time. Predictable schedules were a luxury enjoyed by simpler souls . . . unburdened souls.

My services are required by her at unexpected times—day and night.

He made his way through the ghostly darkness, entering his

dressing room and shedding his cloak and boots. Naked now below the neck, his skin glowed pale in the black light, but he avoided looking at it. His sanctuary intentionally had no mirrors, save the tiny handheld with which he applied the clay to his face.

Seeing his physical shell was always unsettling.

This body is not mine.

I have simply manifested within it.

The Golĕm padded barefoot to the bathroom, where he turned on the shower and stepped in. After peeling off his clay-caked skullcap, he closed his eyes, raising his face to the warm stream. The water felt purifying as the dried clay dissolved into dark rivulets that ran down his body and spiraled into the drain.

Once The Golĕm felt confident that he had shed all traces of his activities last night, he stepped from the shower and dried himself off.

The Ether was pulling harder at him now, but he did not reach for his wand.

It is time.

Still naked, The Golĕm made his way through the darkness to his *svatyně*—the special room he had created to receive this gift.

In total blackness, he walked to the hemp mattress he kept positioned in the middle of the floor. Respectfully, he lay down, positioning himself naked and supine in the exact center of the mat.

Then he secured the perforated *chengbaobaby* silicone ball in his mouth . . . and Released.

CHAPTER 4

First one here too, Langdon thought, arriving at Strahov Swimming Center just as the attendant was unlocking the building. Langdon knew of few experiences more luxurious than having an entire twenty-five-meter pool to himself. He found his rented locker, slid into his Speedo, took a quick shower, grabbed his Vanquisher goggles, and made his way to the pool.

The overhead fluorescent lights were just warming up, and the room was still mostly dark. Langdon stood with his toes over the edge of the pool, gazing out at the smooth expanse of water, which looked like a massive black mirror.

The Temple of Athena, he mused, recalling how ancient Greeks had practiced catoptromancy by gazing into dark pools of water to glimpse their future. He pictured Katherine asleep in their hotel room and wondered if perhaps *she* was his future. The notion was both unnerving and exciting for the consummate bachelor.

Langdon pulled the goggles over his eyes, took a deep breath, and launched himself out over the water, slicing through the surface. Underwater, he held his glide for two seconds and then did ten meters of dolphin kick before emerging into freestyle.

Focusing on the cadence of his breathing, Langdon drifted into the semi-meditative state that swimming always afforded him. His muscular frame relaxed, and his body became streamlined and lithe, powering forward through the darkness at an impressive pace for a man in his fifties.

Normally, swimming emptied Langdon's mind completely, but this morning, even after four laps, his mind was full . . . replaying moments of Katherine's compelling lecture last night.

"Your consciousness is not created by your brain. In fact, your consciousness is not even located inside your head."

Those words had piqued the curiosity of everyone present, and yet Langdon knew her lecture had barely scratched the surface of what would be included in her upcoming book.

She claims to have discovered something incredible.

Katherine's discovery—whatever it might be—was a secret. She had not shared it yet with anyone, including Langdon, though she had alluded to it several times in recent days, confiding in him that the research for her book had led to a stunning breakthrough. After her lecture last night, Langdon felt a growing sense that Katherine's book might well have explosive potential.

She doesn't shy away from controversy, Langdon mused, having enjoyed watching her ruffle the feathers of traditionalists in the audience.

"Science has a long history of *flawed* models," she had announced, her voice echoing across Vladislav Hall. "The flat-earth theory, the geocentric solar system, the steady-state universe . . . these are all false, though they were once taken quite seriously and believed to be true. Fortunately, our belief systems evolve when faced with enough inexplicable inconsistencies."

Katherine grabbed a handheld remote, and the screen behind her sprang to life depicting a medieval astronomical model—the solar system portraying the earth at its center. "For centuries, this geocentric model was accepted as absolute fact. But over time, astronomers noticed planetary motion that was inconsistent with that model. The anomalies became so numerous and glaring that we . . ." She clicked again. "Built a different model." The screen now displayed a modern illustration of the solar system with the *sun* at the center. "This new model explained all the anomalous phenomena, and heliocentricity is now our accepted reality."

The audience sat quietly as Katherine walked to the front of the stage.

"Similarly," she said, "there was a time when the suggestion of a *round* earth was laughable—scientific heresy, even. After all, if the earth were round, wouldn't the oceans flow off?

Wouldn't many of us be upside down? However, bit by bit, we began seeing phenomena that were inconsistent with the flat-earth model—the earth's *curved* shadow in a lunar eclipse, ships departing over the horizon disappearing from bottom to top, and then, of course, Magellan circumnavigating the globe." She smiled. "Oops. Time for a new model."

Heads nodded in shared amusement.

"Ladies and gentlemen," she said, her voice somber, "I believe a similar evolution is now occurring in the field of *human consciousness*. We are about to experience a sea change in our understanding of how the brain works, the nature of consciousness, and, in fact . . . the very nature of reality itself."

Nothing like aiming high, Langdon thought.

"As with all outdated beliefs," she said, "today's accepted model of human consciousness now finds itself challenged by a rising tide of phenomena that it simply cannot explain . . . phenomena that noetic labs around the world have meticulously authenticated, and that humans have witnessed for centuries. Even so, traditionalist science *still* refuses to deal with the existence of these phenomena or even accept they are real. Instead, they trivialize them as flukes and outliers filed under a dismissive heading—'Paranormal'—which has become shorthand for 'not science at all.'"

The comment caused several mutters from the back of the auditorium, but Katherine continued, unfazed. "In fact, you're all quite familiar with these *paranormal* phenomena," she declared. "They go by names like ESP . . . precognition . . . telepathy . . . clairvoyance . . . out-of-body experiences. Despite being deemed 'para'-normal, they are, in fact, entirely *normal*. They occur every day, both in science labs with carefully controlled experiments . . . and also in the real world."

The room had now fallen completely silent.

"The question is not *if* these phenomena are real," Katherine said. "Science has proven they are. The question is . . . why do so many of us remain blind to them?"

She pressed a button, and an image materialized on the screen behind her.

The Hermann grid. Langdon recognized the well-known visual illusion in which black dots seemed to appear and disappear depending on where in the diagram you focused.

The audience began to experience the effect, and a murmur of surprise spread across the room.

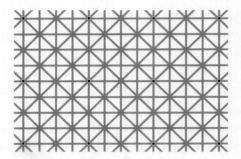

"I show you this for a simple reason—to remind us that human perception is riddled with *blind spots*," Katherine concluded. "Sometimes we're so busy looking the wrong way . . . that we don't see what's right before our eyes."

———•·•———

The morning sky was still pitch-dark when Langdon left the swimming center and headed back down the hill. His thirty-minute aquatic meditation had left him feeling tranquil, and his solitary walk back to the hotel was quickly becoming one of his favorite parts of his day. As he neared the river, the digital clock on the tourist information center glowed 6:52 a.m.

Plenty of time, Langdon told himself, still hoping to climb back into bed with Katherine and persuade her to cancel her 8 a.m. meeting with Brigita Gessner. The neuroscientist had essentially browbeaten Katherine into coming to her lab for a tour this morning, and Katherine had been too polite to decline.

When Langdon arrived at Charles Bridge, he saw that the smooth blanket of snow was no longer pristine, now dotted with footprints of other early risers. As he entered the bridge, Judith Tower rose on his right, the lone surviving piece of the original medieval structure. In the distance stood the "new" fourteenth-century guard tower where decapitated heads had once been displayed on spikes as a reminder to anyone who might question the Habsburgs' rule.

They say you can still hear their moans of pain as you pass.

The word "Prague" literally meant "threshold," and Langdon always felt like he crossed one each time he came here. For centuries, this magical city had been steeped in mysticism, ghosts, and spirits. Even today, guidebooks claimed the city had a supernatural aura that was palpable to all those who were open to it.

I'm probably not one of them, Langdon knew, although he had to admit Charles Bridge felt otherworldly this morning, with the falling snow casting spectral halos around the gaslights.

For centuries, this city had been Europe's nexus for the occult. Prague's King Rudolf II had secretly practiced the transmutational sciences in his underground Speculum Alchemiae. Clairvoyants John Dee and Edward Kelley had traveled here for scrying sessions to conjure spirits and converse with angels. Mysterious Jewish writer Franz Kafka was born and worked here, penning his darkly surreal *The Metamorphosis.*

As Langdon continued across the bridge, his eye fell on the Four Seasons Hotel in the distance, perched directly on the river, the deep waters of the Vltava lapping at its foundation. Above the glimmering surface, the second-floor windows of their suite were still dark.

Katherine's still asleep, he thought, not at all surprised considering the nightmare that had kept her awake much of the night.

About a third of the way across the colossal bridge, Langdon passed the bronze statue of St. John of Nepomuk. *Murdered on this very spot,* he thought with a chill. Ordered by the king to break his vow of confessional secrecy and reveal the queen's private confessions, the priest had refused, so the king had ordered him tortured and thrown off the bridge.

Langdon was lost in his own thoughts when his attention was drawn to an unusual sight up ahead. Approximately halfway across the bridge, a woman dressed all in black was approaching. Langdon guessed she was returning from a costume party because she was wearing an outlandish headpiece—a kind of tiara with a half-dozen slender black spikes emanating directly from her skull, fanning upward and outward, encircling her head, like a black . . .

Langdon felt a chill. *A radiant crown?*

The bizarre coincidence of seeing a radiant crown this morning was startling and a bit unnerving, but Langdon reminded himself that ghoulish costume play was common in Prague.

As she drew closer, though, the scene became stranger. The woman in the spiked halo seemed to be in a trance, walking as if half-dead, her doe eyes staring blankly ahead. Langdon was about to ask if she was okay when he noticed what she was holding in her hand.

The sight stopped him short.

But that's . . . impossible!

The woman was clutching a silver *spear.*

Just like in Katherine's nightmare . . .

Langdon eyed the pointed weapon, immediately wondering if maybe now *he* was dreaming. As the woman drew level with him, Langdon realized he had stopped walking, paralyzed by his own confusion. Snapping out of his stupor, he turned and called to the woman, trying to get her attention.

"Excuse me!" he blurted. "Miss?!"

She never broke stride, as if unable to hear him.

"*Hello!*" Langdon shouted, standing still, but the woman simply drifted past like an apparition . . . a blind spirit drawn across the bridge by some unseen force.

Langdon turned to run after her but advanced only two steps before halting in his tracks, this time arrested by a putrid smell.

Wafting in the apparition's wake was an unmistakable odor.

The smell of . . . death.

The stench had an instantaneous effect on Langdon. He was flooded with fear.

My God, no . . . Katherine!

Reacting on pure impulse, Langdon spun away, frantically digging his phone from his pocket while breaking into a full sprint along Charles Bridge. As he ran toward the hotel, he held the phone to his mouth and shouted, "Hey, Siri, call one-one-two!"

By the time the call went through, Langdon had already crossed the bridge and reached Křižovnická Street. "One-one-two," a voice announced. "What is your emergency?"

"The Four Seasons Prague!" Langdon shouted as he turned left and sprinted along the dark sidewalk toward the hotel. "You need to evacuate! Now!"

"I'm sorry, what is your name please?"

"Robert Langdon, I'm an Am—"

A taxi emerged from a parking garage in front of him, and he collided hard with the side of the car, dropping his phone onto the snowy street. He scooped it up and kept running, but the call had been dropped. It didn't matter; the entrance of the hotel was right in front of him.

Breathless, he burst into the lobby, spotting the manager and calling to him. *"Everyone needs to get out!"*

The police officers were gone, but a handful of guests enjoying morning coffee all glanced up in surprise.

"Everyone is in danger!" Langdon shouted again to the manager. *"Get out!"*

The man rushed over, looking horrified. "Professor, please! What's wrong?!"

Langdon was already running for the fire alarm on the wall. Without hesitation, he shattered the glass and pulled the lever.

Immediately, alarm bells blared.

Langdon dashed out of the lobby and sprinted the long corridor to the annex where their suite was located. Reaching the rear of the hotel, he skipped the elevator and bounded up two flights of stairs to the private foyer, unlocked the Royal Suite, burst inside, and called wildly into the darkness.

"Katherine! Wake up! The dream you had . . . !" He flipped on the master light switch and ran to the bedroom. The bed was empty. *Where is she?!* He ran to the bathroom. Nothing. Desperate, he searched the rest of the suite. *She's not here?!*

In that moment, a nearby church bell began to toll mournfully.

The sound filled Langdon with an overwhelming terror. Something told him he would never make it out of the hotel in time. Fearing for his life and acting on adrenaline, he sprinted to the bay window and looked down at the deep waters of the Vltava.

The river's smooth, dark surface lay directly beneath him.

The bell tolled louder.

He tried to think, but there was no thought, only an overpowering human instinct—survival.

Without hesitation, Langdon yanked open the window and climbed up onto the sill. The blast of cold air and snow rushing past him did nothing to quell his panic.

It's your only choice.

He stepped to the edge of the windowsill.

Then, taking a deep breath, Langdon launched himself out into the darkness.

CHAPTER 5

Robert Langdon gasped for breath.

The icy waters of the Vltava River had shocked his system into near paralysis, and as he struggled to stay afloat, he could feel the weight of his wet clothes threatening to drag him under.

Katherine . . .

Langdon looked up at the second-story window from which he'd leaped. The explosion he had feared was coming . . . had not occurred. The Four Seasons Hotel was still standing, still very much intact.

In the stark glare of emergency lighting, hotel guests were now flowing out the side exit onto a wide terrace that overlooked the hotel's mooring docks, which jutted out into the river.

As he fought to tread water, Langdon suddenly realized the current was pulling him away; the hotel dock would be his only chance of climbing out of the water before being carried downstream.

Doing his best to avoid panic, he attempted to freestyle toward the dock, but he could barely lift his arms. His soaking sweatshirt was like an anchor around him. The cold water was already constricting his circulatory system, and Langdon could feel the first warning signs of hypothermia in the pain shooting through his ankles and wrists.

Swim, Robert . . .

Resorting to an awkward breaststroke, Langdon strained against the current, trying to make his way toward the hotel dock. He glanced beyond it and feared being dragged over the waterfall that was not far downstream—although he knew he would probably be unconscious and submerged long before he went over the edge.

Push, dammit!

As his arms pulled him through the water, Langdon's mind burned with the image of the ghostly woman wearing the black radiant halo. The headpiece could have been a startling coincidence . . . but her spear? And the smell of death?

Impossible.

Beyond explanation.

For an instant, Langdon wondered if he was still asleep, trapped in a vivid nightmare like the one Katherine had experienced last night. *No.* The biting cold and frantic beat of his heart assured him he was awake. As anyone who had plunged through pond ice could attest, the onset of acute hypothermia brought with it a unique succession of mental states—shock, panic, reflection, and finally, acceptance.

Use the panic, he told himself. *Swim harder.*

Angling across the current, Langdon stroked awkwardly in the direction of the dock, trying to ignore his intensifying pain. With each effort it grew worse, although the blare of the hotel alarm seemed to be growing louder. *Closer.* His eyes stung in the freezing water, and his vision was beginning to fade.

The dock was close now, a dark mass in the glare of the security lighting, and Langdon urged himself toward it, making a final push. When his hand groped something solid, his numb fingers were barely able to feel the rough wood, much less take hold. He pulled himself hand over hand down the dock to the small metal ladder mounted there. Using every last bit of strength, he pulled himself up, flopping like a deadweight onto the landing, his soaking-wet clothes shedding water all around him.

Langdon lay immobile, shivering and spent, knowing he was still very much in danger.

I'll freeze quickly out here. I need to get warm.

He crawled to his knees and looked up at the hotel. The terrace was already jammed with guests, many wearing bathrobes, standing in the snow. He turned and looked back toward Charles Bridge, which looked like a postcard, its gas lanterns glowing warmly in the falling snow.

I saw what I saw.

Langdon heard the rapid approach of footfalls on the dock.

"Mr. Langdon!" the hotel manager shouted, arriving wild-eyed. He slipped to a stop on the snow-covered surface. "Are you all right, sir?! What happened here?!"

Langdon nodded. "I . . . thought . . . there was . . ."

"A fire?!"

Convulsing with cold, Langdon shook his head. "No . . ."

"Then why did you pull the alarm?!" The man's normally gracious tone was frayed and angry.

"I thought . . . there was danger."

"From *what*?!"

Langdon struggled to prop himself into a sitting position. His head pounded, and he could feel hypothermia setting in.

A hotel security guard sprinted down the dock and joined them. The muscular man reached down and roughly pulled Langdon to his feet, lifting him with a firm grasp beneath his armpits. Langdon was uncertain whether the guard was helping him up or restraining him.

"*Why* did you pull the alarm, sir?" the manager repeated, staring intently at him.

"I'm sorry . . ." Langdon replied, his teeth starting to chatter. "I was . . . confused."

"Because of the police in the lobby? I told you that was nothing!" The manager seemed barely able to contain himself. "I need to know—is it *safe* to go back inside?"

Langdon could see guests still flowing from the rear emergency exit, and he could only imagine the chaos at the hotel's main entrance. *I can't explain this to them. They'll think I'm mad.*

"Professor Langdon," the manager said, his frustrated tone now turning angrier, "I need an answer! I have four hundred guests standing outside in the snow. Is the building safe? Yes or no! Can our guests return inside?"

Langdon again saw the image of the woman wearing the

black radiant crown . . . the silver spear . . . and the putrid smell of death. *There must be another explanation. The world does not work this way! Get a grip, Robert.*

Langdon finally nodded. "Yes . . . I believe it's safe. I'm terribly sorry. As I said . . . I was confus—"

"*Vypněte alarm!*" the manager said to the guard, who released Langdon abruptly. As Langdon teetered on trembling legs, the guard pulled out a radio and barked orders while the hotel manager placed a call on his mobile.

Within seconds, the alarms fell silent, replaced by the distant wail of approaching emergency vehicles. The manager closed his eyes, took a deep breath, and exhaled slowly through pursed lips. Then he reopened his eyes and calmly brushed the snowflakes from his dark suit.

"Professor Langdon," he whispered through clenched teeth, "I need to receive the authorities. My security guard will help you to your room. Do *not* go anywhere. The authorities will need to speak to you."

Langdon nodded his understanding.

As the manager rushed off, the guard led Langdon through a smaller service entrance to a back staircase. Langdon's sneakers squished with every step as the two men made their way up to the Royal Suite. The door was open, and the lights were on, exactly as Langdon had left it.

"*Zůstaňte tady,*" the guard commanded, pointing into the room.

Langdon didn't speak Czech, but the guard's body language was crystal clear. *Enter and do not come out.* Langdon nodded and entered the suite alone, closing the door behind him.

The bay window from which he had jumped was still open wide, the flower arrangement on the sill already wilting from the icy cold. The red, white, and blue tulips had been a gift from the U.S. ambassador to Katherine in honor of her anticipated lecture, the colors being those of both the American and Czech flags.

Langdon closed the window, morbidly recalling that the practice of defenestration—throwing a victim from a high window—

had sparked both the Hussite Wars and the Thirty Years' War. Fortunately, Langdon's hotel window was significantly lower than Prague Castle Tower, and despite the trouble he'd caused this morning, Langdon doubted he'd started any wars.

I need to talk to Katherine . . . and tell her what I saw.

The encounter on Charles Bridge had been as disorienting as anything Langdon could ever remember, and despite Katherine's open-mindedness to all things "paranormal," Langdon doubted even she would have an explanation.

Hoping she might have texted to say she had safely exited the hotel, Langdon reached into the pockets of his dripping sweatpants to dig out his phone, but it was no longer there—most likely at the bottom of the Vltava River.

A fresh wave of cold shuddered through him as he hurried to the bedroom to use the hotel phone to call her. As he reached for the handset, though, he saw a handwritten note on the bedside table.

In his panic earlier, he had not noticed it.

R—
Decided to walk to my meeting at Dr. Gessner's lab.
You can't be the only one to get exercise today!
Back by 10 a.m. Save me a smoothie! ☺
—K

Langdon exhaled.
Katherine is safe. That's all I need to know.
Relieved, he went straight to a shower, turned it on, and climbed in fully clothed.

CHAPTER 6

The Ether had passed, and The Golĕm lay naked on the hemp mat.

His journey had climaxed, as it always did, with waves of euphoria and an overwhelming sense of spiritual connection to all things. To receive the Ether was a nonsexual orgasm—a cresting wave of mystical bliss that unlocked a gateway through which to glimpse Reality as it really was.

Mystical journeys like these were often disparaged as delusional fantasy, but those who saw the Truth had no need for small minds. The Golĕm knew from experience that the universe was far more complex and beautiful than most could comprehend. The Moderns still could not accept the Truth that the Ancients understood intuitively . . . The human body was nothing but a temporary vessel in which to experience this earthly realm.

He removed the perforated ball gag from his mouth and stood up, alone in the darkness of his *svatyně*. In the absence of light, he moved to the far wall and knelt on the cushion before the shrine he had created there.

Groping in blackness, he found the box of matches and struck one, lighting the three votive candles he had arranged on the table in a bed of dried flowers.

As the flickering candlelight grew, the photo on the wall before him came into view.

He smiled lovingly up at her face.

You don't know me, but I am here to deliver you from evil.

The forces of darkness that threatened her were potent and

had exceptional reach. She was more vulnerable now than ever before, especially because she was distracted.

She has found love.

Or so she believes . . .

The Golĕm felt sickened to know she was giving her body to someone so unworthy.

He does not understand you as I do.

Nobody does.

Sometimes, when she lay in bed, intertwined with her new lover here in Prague, The Golĕm permitted himself to watch . . . a visitor in her mind, looking on in silence, wanting desperately to shout into her ear: "He is not who he seems!"

But The Golĕm remained silent . . . a thought in the shadows.

She must never know I am here.

CHAPTER 7

The world's largest book publisher, Penguin Random House, publishes nearly twenty thousand books a year and generates over five billion dollars in annual gross revenues. Its American headquarters is located on Broadway in Midtown Manhattan and occupies twenty-four floors of a glittering gray-glass skyscraper known as Random House Tower.

Tonight, the offices were quiet. It was after midnight in the city, and even the cleaning crews had finished their rounds. Nonetheless, on the twenty-third floor, a single light burned in a corner office.

Editor Jonas Faukman was a night owl. At a youthful fifty-five, he still kept the hours of a teenager, ran daily in Central Park, and wore black jeans and sneakers to work. His wavy black hair fortunately was still thick, but his beard was definitely showing signs of gray—reminiscent of Joseph Conrad, he liked to think.

Faukman loved the undisturbed silence of these late hours, savoring his solitude as he wrestled with complex storylines and knotted prose, writing detailed pages of notes for his authors. Tonight, he had cleared his desk to spend the night doing what he enjoyed most in the world . . . reading a freshly delivered manuscript from a brand-new author.

Potential yet unknown.

Most published books came and went without a trace, but a select few captured the minds of readers and became bestsellers. Faukman had high hopes for the one he was about to read.

He had been anticipating its delivery for months. The book was a bold exploration of the mysteries of human consciousness, penned by prominent noetic scientist Katherine Solomon.

A little over a year ago, Faukman's close friend Robert Langdon had brought Katherine to New York to pitch her book idea over lunch. The scientist's presentation had been nothing short of mind-blowing—the most enthralling pitch for a nonfiction book Faukman could remember. Within days, he had taken it off the market by offering Katherine a lucrative publishing contract.

She had toiled for the past year writing in complete secrecy, and just this afternoon, she had called from Prague to report that she had finished polishing the manuscript and was ready for Faukman to read it. He suspected that Langdon might have had a hand in encouraging Katherine to stop tweaking and to seek her editor's perspective. No matter the catalyst, Faukman knew one thing for certain: if Katherine Solomon's manuscript turned out to be half as riveting as her pitch had been, this book would be one of the most important projects of his career.

Illuminating . . . startling . . . universally relevant.

The quest to understand human consciousness was quickly becoming the new Holy Grail of science, and Faukman sensed Katherine Solomon was poised to become a trailblazing voice in the field. If her theory proved correct, then the human mind was not at all as had been imagined; the truth would bring about a profound shift in our views of humanity, life, and even death.

Faukman wondered if he was about to edit a work that might one day stand alongside other paradigm-altering publications like *On the Origin of Species* and *A Brief History of Time*.

Slow down, Jonas . . . he reminded himself. *You haven't even read it yet.*

A sharp knock at Faukman's door snapped him back in the moment, and he wheeled around, startled to have a visitor in the dead of night.

"Mr. Faukman?" The young man standing in his doorway was a stranger.

"Yes? Who are you?"

"Sorry to frighten you, sir," the young man said, holding up his laminated company badge. "I'm Alex Conan—in data security. I work mainly at nights while system traffic is low."

The kid's mop of blond hair and Pizzeria Papagayo T-shirt made him look more like a surfer than a technician. "How can I help you, Alex?"

"Oh, it's probably a false alarm," the tech replied, "but our system just threw a flag on some data that was accessed."

Data that were *accessed*, Faukman thought, wondering when the world would finally accept that the word "data" was plural.

"I'm sure it's nothing," the kid said. "I was worried because 'unverified user' is a rare alert for us, but now that I see that you are actually *here* in the building and logged in, I feel better. It's probably just a glitch on your account."

"But I'm *not* logged in," Faukman said, motioning to his monitor. "My computer hasn't been on all night."

The kid's eyes widened ever so slightly. "Oh . . ."

Faukman felt a trace of alarm. "Is someone logged into my account?"

"No, no," the tech said. "Well, not anymore. Whoever it was, they're gone."

"Whoever it was? What does *that* mean?!"

The tech looked concerned now. "It just means that someone penetrated your personal partition, sir, without a password or authorized credentials. Whoever it was must have legit skills, because we've got a military-grade firewall protec—"

"Hold on, *what* exactly was accessed?" Faukman swiveled to his desk and powered up his computer. *My entire professional life is on that goddamned server!*

"Someone hacked one of your SVWs," the kid said.

Faukman froze. *That is* not *the answer I wanted.*

SVWs—secure virtual workspaces—were a fairly new implementation at PRH. Due to a rise in book piracy of stolen manuscripts, some PRH editors had begun encouraging top-selling authors to work *exclusively* on the Penguin Random House servers for an extra layer of security. Many of PRH's most valuable manuscripts were written, edited, and saved in a single secure location—the confines of the company's encrypted, firewalled system in Random House Tower . . . along with its redundant backup in Maryland.

I asked Katherine Solomon to use an SVW, Faukman thought uneasily.

Having sensed blockbuster potential in her proposal, Faukman had encouraged Katherine to adhere to strict security protocols while writing the manuscript. She had happily agreed, saying she loved the thought of logging in remotely from anywhere in the world to work on her manuscript, knowing all her materials were in one place, secure and automatically backed up.

Most authors felt the same way, albeit with one concern. *Privacy.* No author wanted an impatient editor monitoring the progress of a manuscript before they were ready to show it. For this reason, every author using an SVW protected his or her virtual workspace with a password—an access code known only to the author—until the manuscript was ready to be delivered.

For Katherine, that day was today, Faukman thought.

When she had called earlier from Prague, she had nervously given Faukman her access code so he could start reading and editing. Faukman immediately cleared his desk of other work so he could dive into her manuscript tonight and read it from start to finish over the weekend. Now, however, his long-awaited night of reading had been interrupted by a T-shirted security tech with unsettling news.

"*Which* SVW was accessed?" Faukman demanded, his throat feeling dry. "Which book?"

The kid pulled a scrap of paper from his pocket and began unfolding it. "I think it's some kind of *mathematical* book?"

Faukman perked up, feeling a glimmer of hope.

"Here it is," Alex said, reading the note. "The title is . . . *SUM.*"

The editor felt an immediate jolt of panic.

Breathe, Jonas. Breathe.

SUM was no math book. It was an acronym.

It stood for "Solomon—Untitled Manuscript."

CHAPTER 8

Savoring the warmth of the hotel shower's body jets, Robert
Langdon closed his eyes and breathed hot steam into his
lungs. He had managed to extricate himself from his wet
clothing, and yet he still had not managed to shed the shroud of
confusion surrounding this morning's events.

Langdon considered calling Katherine to interrupt her tour
of Dr. Gessner's lab and tell her what had happened, but he
thought better of it. *This is a bizarre conversation we'll need to have
face-to-face when she returns.* Even now, as Langdon's body gradually warmed and his thinking became clearer, he felt no closer to
a logical explanation for the ghostly apparition he had seen on
Charles Bridge. Or his reaction.

Normally Langdon reacted calmly under pressure, but this
morning he had panicked, overcome by a strange, visceral fear. It
had overwhelmed his rational mind . . . the sight of the woman,
the smell of death, the spear, the eerie tolling of the bells. The
haunting memory replayed endlessly in his head.

How could this happen?

He returned to the events of last night, barely five hours earlier, to Katherine screaming his name and jolting awake from
a vivid nightmare. He had consoled her as she frantically conveyed her harrowing vision.

*It was terrifying, Robert . . . There was a dark figure standing at
the foot of our bed. She was dressed in black . . . she had a spiked halo
on her head . . . and she was holding a silver spear. And she smelled
putrid, like death. I shouted for you, but you weren't there! The woman*

hissed at me, "Robert cannot save you. You are going to die." Then there was a deafening noise and a flash, and the hotel exploded in a cloud of fire. I could feel myself burning . . .

At the time, despite the obvious horror of Katherine's dream, the elements had made logical sense to Langdon. The spiked halo or radiant crown had featured prominently in Katherine's lecture that night. The silver spear had been a topic of conversation over drinks after the event with Brigita Gessner. The smell of sulfur could have lingered from their trip to the nearby hot springs of Karlovy Vary. And the explosion at the hotel was no doubt the unfortunate result of seeing some grim news footage yesterday of a bombing in Southeast Asia.

Langdon had comforted Katherine, reminding her that absinthe was a potent hallucinogen—and also that she was likely on edge because her editor was about to read her manuscript. *I know those nerves well*, Langdon thought. *No wonder you had a sleepless night.*

Now, however, hours later, standing in the shower, Langdon was at a loss to find any logical explanation for what he had just seen . . . at least not in his current understanding of reality.

Einstein had famously declared: *Coincidence is God's way of staying anonymous.*

What I saw was not a coincidence, Langdon's gut insisted. *It was a statistical impossibility.*

Either Katherine's nightmare had predicted the future . . . or the future had reacted to her dream. Whichever one was true, Langdon remained baffled.

More eerily still, Katherine's lecture last night had addressed this exact phenomenon.

Precognition.

The ability to sense or foresee future events before they happen.

From the stage in Vladislav Hall, Katherine had recounted some of history's most famous instances of precognition, including the clairvoyant dreams of Carl Jung, Mark Twain, and Joan of Arc. She explained that Abraham Lincoln, three days before his assassination, had shared a dream with his bodyguard, Ward

Hill Lamon, in which he saw a covered corpse guarded by a soldier who announced, "The president, he was killed by an assassin."

Then Katherine went on to describe the strangest case of all—Morgan Robertson—an American author who published the 1898 novel *Futility*, which he based on a vivid nightmare he had about an unsinkable ocean liner—*The Titan*—striking an iceberg and sinking on one of its first voyages across the Atlantic Ocean. Incredibly, the book was published fourteen years *before* the *Titanic* disaster. It so specifically described the ship's construction, navigational course, and sinking that the coincidences had never been explained.

"I know that there are skeptics in the audience," Katherine had said, glancing playfully in Langdon's direction, "and so I thought I'd share an experiment, which was first conceived and performed years ago by a colleague of mine at the Institute of Noetic Sciences. Since then, it has been replicated and built upon by labs around the world. It goes like this . . ."

Katherine pointed her clicker at the screen behind her, and an image appeared—a test subject wearing a brain monitor and sitting in the dark in front of a small movie screen.

"While monitoring a subject's brain waves with specialized equipment," she began, "we show him a random stream of images. These images fall into three distinct categories— horrifying violence, tranquil calm, or explicit sexual content. Because each type of image triggers a different section of the brain, we are able to watch in real time as his conscious mind registers the image."

She clicked again and displayed a graph of brain waves with intermittent spikes—each color-coded to indicate what type of image had been shown. "As expected, the appropriate sections of the brain light up with the appearance of each specific image. Follow me so far?"

Heads nodded eagerly.

"Great," she said, now zooming in on the graph's horizontal axis. "This timeline is an extremely accurate record to indicate the precise moment at which the computer flashed each image at random and the precise moment the brain spiked."

Langdon wondered where this was going.

"If we zoom in farther," she said, clicking to display increasingly shorter time increments, "we get down to the millisecond range . . . and we discover there is a big problem."

She said nothing further, but within seconds there was a communal murmur of bewilderment around the large hall. Langdon shared in the confusion. According to these graphs, the subject's brain spiked *before* the computer had shown the image.

"As you clearly see," Katherine said, "this man is registering each image far too early. The appropriate part of his brain is lighting up a full four hundred milliseconds *before* the image is displayed. Somehow, his consciousness *already knows* what type of image he is about to see." She smiled. "And that's not even the most startling part . . ."

The hall fell silent.

"As it turns out," Katherine said, "the brain reacts not only before the image is *displayed* . . . but before the computer's random-number generator has even *chosen* which image to show! It's as if the brain is not predicting reality . . . so much as *creating* it."

Like everyone around him, Langdon was stunned. He also knew that this very idea—the notion that human thoughts *create* reality—existed at the core of most major spiritual teachings.

Buddha: *With our thoughts, we create the world.*

Jesus: *Whatever you ask for in prayer, it will be yours.*

Hinduism: *You have the power of God.*

The concept, Langdon knew, was echoed by modern progressive thinkers and artistic geniuses as well. Business guru Robin Sharma declared: *Everything is created twice; first in the mind, and then in reality.* Pablo Picasso's most enduring quote proclaimed: *Everything you can imagine is real.*

A knock startled Langdon, and Vladislav Hall dissolved from his mind. He was back in the shower and heard the bathroom door opening. Through the translucent shower enclosure, Langdon saw the hazy outline of a person entering and he breathed a sigh of relief. *Thank goodness she's back early.* No doubt Katherine had heard about the hotel incident and quickly returned.

"Just finished," Langdon called, turning off the hot water and forgoing his usual ice-cold rinse. *I've had enough cold water for one morning.* He grabbed the towel hanging inside the enclosed shower door, wrapped it around his waist, and stepped out into the bathroom. "Katherine—"

He stopped short.

Katherine was not there.

Langdon was standing face-to-face with an angular man in a leather suitcoat.

"Who the hell are you?!" Langdon demanded. *How did you get in here?!*

The intruder moved several inches closer, his expression humorless. "Mr. Robert Langdon?" he said with a heavy Czech accent. "Good morning. I am Captain Janáček of the Úřad pro zahraniční styky a informace. I took the liberty of securing your passport from your bedroom. I trust you don't mind."

You took my passport? Langdon felt naked standing in only a towel before this strange man. "I'm sorry, *who* are you?"

The man flashed an identification badge, but in the steamy air Langdon could see very little except the organization's bold emblem—a lion reared up on his hind legs. *The Lion Rampant?* The symbol was quite common, and it also happened to be the logo of Langdon's prep school alma mater, although he was fairly certain this guy was not from Phillips Exeter Academy.

"I'm with ÚZSI," the man said gruffly. "Czech national intelligence service."

You don't look like an intelligence agent, Langdon thought. The man's eyes were bloodshot and weepy, his thinning hair was uncombed, and his shirt was badly wrinkled beneath his leather jacket.

"I will say this *once*, Mr. Langdon." The Czech official stepped toward him as if making a point of crossing some invisible line between them. "You just evacuated a five-star hotel. Either you give me a very good reason why, or I arrest you immediately."

Langdon was at a loss for words. "I . . . I'm terribly sorry," he stammered. "It's difficult to explain, Captain. I made a mistake."

"I agree," the man fired back, his expression revealing nothing. "A substantial one. Why did you pull the alarm?"

Langdon saw little choice but to tell the truth. "I thought there was going to be an explosion."

The officer's only reaction was a faint twitch of his furry eyebrows. "Interesting. And what might cause this explosion?"

"I don't know . . . perhaps a bomb."

"I see. Perhaps a bomb. So, you feared there was a bomb in this hotel . . . and yet you ran back *inside* the building and upstairs to this suite?"

"To warn my . . . friend."

The man pulled a notepad from his jacket and read it. "Your friend is Ms. Katherine Solomon?"

Langdon felt a chill to hear Katherine's name on the lips of a Czech intelligence officer. The situation was feeling more serious by the moment. "That's correct. But she was already gone."

"I see, I see. So, knowing your friend was safe, rather than taking the stairs back out, you risked drowning in an icy river by jumping out the window?"

Langdon had to admit that the action surprised even himself. "I panicked. A church bell suddenly began tolling . . . It seemed ominous."

"Ominous?" He looked offended. "It's called *Angelus*, Professor. Church bells ring on the hour here as a call to morning prayer. I would have thought you knew that."

"Yes, of course, but I wasn't thinking clearly. The bells made it feel like I was . . . I don't know . . . out of time. I had seen police in the lobby earlier—"

"Out of time? So . . . your bomb was a *time* bomb? Set for seven a.m.?"

It wasn't my *bomb!* Langdon strained to retain his composure. "No, I was just very confused, and I reacted on instinct. Of course, I will pay for the—"

"No need to pay, sir," the man said, his tone softening. "People get confused. That's not a problem. I'm just trying to understand *why* you thought there would be an explosion. *Where* did you get your information?"

I can't possibly tell him, Langdon knew. The truth was implausible—unlikely beyond belief—and an honest confession ran a serious risk of backfiring. *He'll never believe me.* Langdon suddenly sensed he might need an attorney.

"Mr. Langdon?" the officer pressed.

Langdon shifted, holding his towel around his waist. "As I said, I was confused. I had bad information."

The captain's gaze narrowed as he took a step closer and lowered his voice. "Actually, Professor, that is not the problem. The problem is you had *good* information. *Very* good information."

"I don't understand."

The officer glared, eyes probing. "No?"

Langdon shook his head.

"Professor," the captain said icily. "Early this morning, in this very hotel, my team located and defused . . . a bomb. It was set to detonate at exactly seven a.m."

CHAPTER 9

In flickering candlelight, The Golĕm glanced once more at her photo on the wall. Then he blew out the candles and exited his sacred space.

I am reborn.

Bathed in the ephemeral glow of his flat, he entered his dressing room. His hooded cloak and platform boots lay crumpled on the floor, hastily jettisoned so he could receive the Ether—a journey he always took unclothed, unadorned, and in total darkness.

The Golĕm carefully rehung his costume, brushing off the loose bits of dried clay that clung to the collar. Tourists were often startled by his appearance, but the locals barely even glanced. Prague was a city of drama and fantasy, and revelers regularly walked the streets masquerading as storied characters from her history—famous ghosts, witches, star-crossed lovers, martyred saints . . . and this hulking monster made of clay.

Prague's oldest legend.

A mystical guardian . . . just like me.

The Golĕm knew the clay monster's tale by heart because it was his own—a protective spirit . . . thrust into physical form . . . tasked with sacrificing his own comfort to carry another's pain.

According to sixteenth-century legend, a powerful rabbi named Judah Loew dug wet clay from the banks of the Vltava River and used it to build a monster that he hoped would protect his people. Using Kabbalistic magic, the rabbi inscribed the Hebrew word into the forehead of the lifeless guardian, and the clay monster immediately sprang to life, infused with a soul from another realm.

The word on his forehead was אמת—*emet.* Truth.

The rabbi called his creation a *golem*—meaning "raw material" in Hebrew—a reference to the earthen clay from which the monster had been forged. Thereafter, the golem patrolled the streets of the Jewish Ghetto, protecting those in danger, killing evildoers, and ensuring the safety of the community.

But here, the legend took a dark turn.

The monster became lonely and confused by its own violence, eventually turning on its creator. The rabbi barely managed to survive the monster's attack by desperately reaching up and smearing away one of the Hebrew letters on the creature's forehead.

By erasing the letter *aleph,* א, the Hebrew word for *truth—emet*—was transformed into something far darker—*met*—the Hebrew word for *dead.*

אמת became מת.

Truth became . . . *Death.*

The monster collapsed in a heap, lifeless.

Standing over his fallen creation, the rabbi took no chances. He quickly dismantled the clay body and hid the pieces in the attic of Prague's Old-New Synagogue, where the earthen shards were said to remain to this day, overlooking the ancient cemetery where Rabbi Loew was now buried.

That cemetery is where my journey began, The Golĕm thought, regarding his own dark costume hanging inanimately. *I am The Golĕm. Another incarnation . . . in the cycle of souls.*

He too had been summoned as a protector—a guardian of the woman whose photo hung on the wall in his *svatyně.* She could never know he existed or what he had done for her. *Nor, especially, what I soon will do.*

He had already killed one of her most devious betrayers, Brigita Gessner. He could still hear the echoes of her voice as she desperately divulged everything she and her coconspirators had done.

Some of her fellow betrayers were here in Prague, well within The Golĕm's reach. Others were thousands of miles away—power brokers who moved in the shadows.

I will not rest until all are punished.

The Golĕm knew of only one way to accomplish that.

I will destroy everything they have created.

CHAPTER 10

They defused a bomb?!

Robert Langdon's thoughts spun wildly as he got dressed in the hotel bedroom. He could not fathom that a bomb attack had actually been thwarted this morning, much less the event with the woman on the bridge.

Minutes ago, Langdon had requested a closer look at the Czech officer's ID, which the man had begrudgingly granted, confirming that he was Oldřich Janáček, a sixty-one-year-old captain at ÚZSI. The acronym, he informed Langdon, stood for Úřad pro zahraniční styky a informace—the Office for Foreign Relations and Information—and was pronounced "exactly like the submachine gun—Uzi."

The agency's logo of the Lion Rampant was accompanied by the motto *Sine Ira et Studio,* which meant "Without Anger or Bias," although the captain's demeanor seemed to suggest the presence of both.

Janáček had been standing in Langdon's bedroom doorway for the last three minutes, arguing in Czech on his phone while keeping one eye on Langdon.

Does he think I'm going to run?

Langdon finished dressing, finally feeling warm in his heavy chinos, turtleneck, and thick Dale sweater. He grabbed his antique Mickey Mouse watch off the dresser and strapped it on, sensing that today he might need a constant reminder to remain light of heart.

"*Ne!*" Janáček shouted angrily into the phone. "*Tady velím já!*"

He hung up and turned to Langdon. "That was your *chůva*. He's coming up to the room."

My chůva? Langdon had no idea what the word meant, but clearly Janáček was not happy about his arrival.

Janáček was unusually lanky, with an inclined posture that gave him the appearance he might pitch forward at any moment. Langdon followed him into the living room, where the man made himself at home, igniting the gas fireplace, settling into a leather club chair, and crossing his spidery legs.

As he settled in, the suite's door chime rang.

Janáček pointed to the foyer. "Let him in."

My chůva? Langdon wondered again, heading down the hallway and opening the door.

Standing in the foyer was a handsome, perhaps thirty-year-old Black man who was Langdon's height—slightly over six feet—with a shaved head, a bright smile, and a chiseled face. Immaculately dressed in a blue blazer, pink shirt, and Foulard necktie, the man looked more like a male model than someone with whom Captain Janáček had just been arguing in Czech.

"Michael Harris," the man said, extending his hand. "It's an honor to meet you, Professor Langdon." His accent was American, maybe Main Line.

"Thank you," Langdon said, shaking the man's hand. *Whoever you are.*

"First, I would like to apologize. Captain Janáček should have called my office before questioning you."

"I see," Langdon said, not seeing at all. "And your office is . . . ?"

Harris looked surprised. "He didn't tell you?"

"No, he said you were my *chůva*."

Harris frowned, making no move to enter the suite. "Janáček was amusing himself. *Chůva* means *nanny*. I'm the U.S. embassy's legal attaché. I'm here to assist you."

Langdon was deeply relieved to have some legal support, although he hoped the attaché wouldn't notice that Langdon had already killed the expensive arrangement of tulips the ambassador had sent over as a welcome gift.

"My job," the attaché said, speaking quietly, "is to safeguard your rights as an American overseas, which, from all I've heard so far, have been trampled this morning."

Langdon shrugged. "Captain Janáček has been aggressive, but considering the circumstances, I can understand his actions."

"That's generous of you," Harris whispered. "But I warn you to be circumspect with your kindness. Captain Janáček is skilled at exploiting courtesies as weaknesses, and it sounds like this situation is . . . unusual?"

You have no idea, Langdon thought, still bewildered by what he had seen on the bridge.

"A word of advice," Harris added. "This hotel and Charles Bridge are both heavily monitored by security cameras, which means Janáček already knows every detail of what happened. So you must tell the truth. *Do not lie.*"

"Harris!" Janáček's voice boomed from within. *"Čekám!"*

"Už jdeme!" Harris yelled back in what sounded like perfect Czech and then gave Langdon a reassuring look. "Shall we?"

They found Janáček seated in front of the fire, calmly puffing on a local Petra cigarette, tipping his head back and blowing smoke up into the air.

So much for our nonsmoking suite.

"Everyone sit," Janáček commanded, tapping his cigarette into a potted plant on the floor. "Professor, before we get started, I would like your phone." He held out a spindly hand.

"No, Captain," Harris intervened. "You have no legal—"

"My phone's gone," Langdon said. "I lost it in the river."

"Of course you did," Janáček grunted, exhaling a cloud of smoke. "How convenient for you. Sit."

Langdon and Harris took seats facing Janáček.

"Professor," the captain began, "while you were getting dressed, you questioned my handling of this situation. You told me you were shocked that I did not *evacuate* the hotel as soon as we found the bomb."

"I was surprised, but I wasn't questioning your—"

"Mr. Harris?" Janáček prompted, turning to the attaché

and taking another pull on his cigarette. "Perhaps you could enlighten our professor?"

"Of course," Harris said calmly. "That's a reasonable question, and while I cannot speak directly to Captain Janáček's procedural methods, I can certainly confirm that his actions do match general counterterrorism strategy. Widely publicized attacks, even *failed* attacks, only embolden terrorists. The correct response, when possible, is to defuse the threat, pretend it never happened, and deny the terrorists any publicity whatsoever."

"Okay." Langdon wondered how many terrorist attacks were thwarted every day without the public's knowledge.

Janáček leaned toward Langdon, elbows on knees. "Any other questions?"

"No, sir."

"Good, then let us move to *my* question . . . because I have only one. And it is one that, so far, you have refused to answer." Janáček took another pull on his cigarette and drew out his question as if talking to a child. "Professor . . . *how* did you know about the bomb?"

"I didn't *know*," Langdon replied. "I just—"

"You pulled the alarm!" Janáček exploded. "You knew *something*! And Professor, please don't say again, 'It's complicated.' I appreciate that you are a famous scholar, but I too am a smart man. I believe I am capable of understanding your complications."

"Mr. Langdon," Harris said calmly. "This is your moment; just tell the truth."

Langdon took a deep breath and hoped that John the Baptist had been correct when he promised "the truth will set you free."

CHAPTER 11

Editor Jonas Faukman clicked his computer mouse repeatedly, willing his terminal to boot up faster. Only two people on earth were supposed to have access to Katherine Solomon's private SVW—Katherine herself and, as of this afternoon, Faukman.

How could someone on the outside have gained access?!

Faukman felt physically ill imagining what might have been compromised—all of Katherine's scientific research, her notes, and, most importantly, the manuscript itself. *Hurry up!* he urged, waiting for his machine to power on.

Behind him, the young data technician was peering over Faukman's shoulder, fretfully humming to himself, which did little to calm Faukman's nerves. When the computer finally came to life, Faukman navigated to the proper folder and clicked on the alias for the server partition named "SUM": Solomon—Untitled Manuscript.

Faukman had written Katherine's access code on a file card and stored it safely in a drawer, but before he could move to retrieve it, the computer made an unfamiliar sound—three staccato beeps. Faukman turned back to the screen, expecting to see Katherine's log-in window, but instead he was looking at a bright red error message.

PARTITION NOT FOUND.

"What the . . . ?" Faukman clicked again on the SUM icon. There were three short beeps and the same error message. *Partition not found?* Faukman spun to Alex. "The entire partition is . . . *gone*?!" The partition had been there this afternoon when Faukman tested Katherine's password. *Where did it go?!*

Wide-eyed, the tech knelt down beside Faukman and commandeered his keyboard and mouse. Faukman held his breath as the tech worked, fingers flying. Attempt after attempt, the tech got the same result. Three loud beeps.

PARTITION NOT FOUND.

"Don't panic," the kid said, sounding utterly panicked. "This just means that in an effort to cover their tracks, they purged the partition."

"Purged?"

"Yes, sir, it means *deleted*. Your data—"

"Thanks, I'm familiar with the definition of 'purged.' Are you saying someone *deleted* all the research and manuscript drafts associated with this title?"

"Yes, sir. Purging is a common post-hack protocol. It makes tracking the hackers more difficult." He began typing again. "But don't worry, Mr. Faukman, we have redundant systems, and all your data will still exist on PRH's off-site backup. It's located in our distribution warehouse in Maryland. I'm logging in now to recover it."

Alex's fingertips were a blur. "We just have to access the remote partition and migrate—"

The computer pinged three short beeps again. A familiar dialogue box flashed on the screen.

PARTITION NOT FOUND.

The tech's eyes went wider as he tried the redundant server again.

PARTITION NOT FOUND.

"Oh . . . no," the kid said.

Faukman felt suddenly weak. *Katherine's partition is deleted from* both *servers?! Along with her manuscript and notes?*

Alex Conan jumped up and headed for the door. "I need to get to my terminal, sir. I've never seen anything like this before—it's a serious breach."

No shit!

Faukman sat numbly at his chair as the kid's footsteps receded down the empty hallway. "I need those files, Alex!" he called after him. "My author entrusted me with a year's worth of her work!"

— ·· —

Throughout the night in London, Mr. Finch had been monitoring a changing landscape.

First had been Brigita Gessner. The neuroscientist had sent Finch a deeply troubling message about Katherine Solomon's manuscript and then had seemingly evaporated. *Total radio silence.*

Second had been Katherine Solomon herself. Thirty-five minutes earlier in Prague, Solomon had done something so unexpected that it could not be ignored. *Immediate action had been required.*

Finch had considered alerting his superior in the U.S., but it was the middle of the night there, and they had given him "unilateral operative control" to make strategic decisions. His superiors' positions of power also required plausible deniability from operations that were ethically ambiguous.

Operations like this one, Finch thought, knowing his colleagues preferred *not* to know how Finch achieved his results.

And so, within minutes of learning of Solomon's actions, he had followed his instincts and pulled the trigger, transmitting two words into the field.

Execute now.

The order had been confirmed by his contacts standing by in Prague and New York City.

CHAPTER 12

I s *this* the woman you saw?" Captain Janáček demanded, holding up a computer tablet. The screen showed a grainy video capture of the woman with black spines encircling her head and carrying a spear.

Janáček and Attaché Harris were seated facing Langdon in front of the fire.

"Yes, that's her," Langdon replied, recalling his panic.

"According to the surveillance videos," Janáček said, "you were on the bridge, you passed this woman halfway across, stopped to speak to her, and then suddenly ran back here and evacuated the hotel. What did this woman say to you?"

"Nothing," Langdon replied. "She ignored me and kept walking."

"She said *nothing*?" Janáček laughed. "Professor, if she said nothing . . . what made you panic?"

Harris looked equally confused.

"She was wearing that unusual spiked headpiece . . . and carrying a spear," Langdon said. "There was also a very strong . . . smell." Langdon immediately realized how strange this sounded.

The captain raised his eyebrows. "You did not like her smell? So you ran away?"

"She smelled of . . . death."

Janáček stared at him. "Death? And what exactly does *death* smell like?"

"I don't know . . . decay, sulfur, rot . . . It's a complicated—"

"Professor Langdon!" Janáček barked. "How did you know this building needed to be evacuated?!"

"Captain," Harris intervened. "Perhaps we can give Mr. Langdon a moment to explain himself?"

Janáček drummed his pen against his notepad, never breaking eye contact.

Langdon took a deep breath. *Here goes nothing.*

"Last night," he began, his tone as matter-of-fact as possible, "my colleague Katherine Solomon gave a lecture at Prague Castle. Afterward, she and I returned to this hotel and had a drink in the bar downstairs. We were joined by a well-known Czech neuroscientist—Dr. Brigita Gessner—who was instrumental in inviting Katherine to Prague. Dr. Gessner insisted Katherine try the local Bohemian absinthe, which she did, and it caused a restless night's sleep."

Janáček took notes. "Continue."

"At some point, around one thirty a.m.," Langdon continued, "Katherine awoke in a panic from a nightmare. She was extremely upset. I brought her out to this room, sat her down by the fire, made some tea, let her get her bearings, and then, when she calmed down, we both went back to bed."

"How nice of you," Janáček grumbled. "And this relates to your evacuation stunt *how?*"

Langdon fell silent, formulating how best to explain it. Then, steeling himself for their response, he spoke the truth. "Katherine's nightmare," he said as calmly as possible. "She dreamed there was a deadly explosion . . . in this hotel."

Langdon could see that neither Janáček nor Harris had anticipated this response.

"That's obviously quite alarming . . ." Harris said quietly. "But the woman . . . on the bridge? Why did you run when you saw her?"

Langdon sighed, speaking slowly. "Because in Katherine's dream, a woman appeared beside our bed in this suite. She was dressed in black and was wearing . . ." Langdon pointed to the image on the iPad. "Exactly this—a black spiked headpiece. And she was carrying a silver spear. The woman reeked of death and said Katherine was going to die." Langdon paused. "And then, in the dream, this entire hotel exploded, killing everyone."

"*Hovadina!*" Janáček erupted. "*Bullshit!* As you Americans say! I don't believe a word of this!"

Harris's expression looked equally incredulous.

"I understand your reaction," Langdon said. "I'm still trying to grasp it myself, but I'm telling the truth. This morning, when I saw the same woman from Katherine's dream, in the flesh, I panicked. I was afraid maybe the dream had been some kind of . . . I don't know . . . warning."

"A dream warning?!" Janáček snapped, his heavy Czech accent making the scenario sound even less plausible. "So tell me, in Ms. Solomon's magical dream, what *time* did the bomb explode?"

Langdon thought about it. "I don't know. She didn't mention a time."

"And yet you jumped out of the window to escape by seven a.m., the exact time the bomb was set to detonate. How did you know seven a.m.?!"

"I *didn't*," Langdon said. "The church bells started tolling, and for some reason, it all just collided in my mind—"

"*Ještě větší hovadina!*" Janáček spat, jumping to his feet and pitching threateningly toward Langdon. "Double bullshit! You're lying to me!"

Harris leaped up in defense, facing Janáček. "Captain, that's enough."

"Really?" Janáček snapped, turning to the attaché. "At seven a.m. this morning—the precise time the bomb was set to explode—*both* Robert Langdon and Katherine Solomon were conveniently out of the hotel. Clearly, they were afraid for their lives."

"That's *ridiculous!*" Langdon exclaimed, unable to contain his anger.

"As ridiculous as a sulfur-scented dream?!"

"Captain Janáček," Harris warned firmly. "You're way over the line here."

"What line?!" the captain shouted. "A terrorist attack was narrowly avoided, and the evidence shows these two Americans knew about the explosion beforehand. I'm not accepting the alibi of a magical dream!"

Harris stared at Janáček and did not back up an inch. "You and I both know it's wholly inconceivable that Robert Langdon or Katherine Solomon would plot to blow up a hotel. It makes no sense at all."

"It *does* make sense when you consider Katherine had a clear motive."

"A motive to blow up a hotel?!" Langdon demanded in disbelief.

"Absolutely," Janáček replied. "In criminal investigations, I always ask myself one simple question: Who stands to benefit from the crime? Whoever that person is, no matter how unlikely, he or she is my prime suspect."

"Captain," Harris interjected, "what *benefit* could Katherine Solomon possibly derive—"

"Let me ask you something, Professor," Janáček interrupted, turning back to Langdon. "It is my understanding that Ms. Solomon is writing a book, no?"

"That's correct." Even though Katherine had mentioned her book last night in her lecture, Langdon still felt unnerved that this man knew about it.

"Furthermore," Janáček said, "it is my understanding that this book supports the existence of paranormal powers like ESP, seeing the future, that sort of thing—a specialty of Ms. Solomon. It seems to me that a news story about a mystical dream that saved a hotel full of people would be very helpful to her book's credibility . . . and sales?"

Langdon stared at the officer in disbelief.

"Captain," Harris said, sounding equally taken aback. "Your insinuation is clearly—"

"The *only* possible explanation," Janáček said.

"Sir," Langdon said quietly. "Are you implying the fire alarm and nightmare were . . . some kind of *publicity* stunt?"

Janáček smirked and took a long pull on his cigarette. "After thirty-eight years of investigative work, Professor, I thought I had seen everything. But now, in your social media world, I'm continually shocked what people will do for media coverage . . .

to go 'viral,' as you Americans love to say. Your plan was ingenious, actually, surprisingly safe and easy to pull off."

"How can you say planting a bomb would be *safe*?!" Langdon demanded.

Harris had fallen silent.

"You ensured it was safe," Janáček repeated. "The bomb we found was quite small and placed in a basement location where it would have done minimal damage. You called in an anonymous tip to be sure the explosive was discovered before anybody got hurt."

The police dogs in the lobby . . .

"By the way," Janáček added, "the crown of spikes was a nice touch—very memorable and hard to miss on security tapes."

Langdon felt slightly nauseous. "Sir, nothing could be further from the truth."

"If you believe that," the captain said, "then perhaps you don't *know* the truth. Perhaps you don't know Katherine Solomon as well as you think. Perhaps she did all this behind your back and used you as an unwitting accessory."

Langdon refused to dignify his words with a response.

"I'm quite skilled at discovering the truth, Professor," Janáček said flatly, "which is why I am eager to hear Ms. Solomon's version of the story. If, in fact, she had a dream that came true, then perhaps she is innocent. But that would mean that Katherine Solomon can see the future, which would make her very special indeed. Is she *that* special, Mr. Langdon?"

The sarcasm in the man's voice left little doubt that Langdon and Katherine were now fighting an uphill battle. *Guilty until proven innocent.*

"Which leads me to my final question," Janáček said. "Where *is* Ms. Solomon right now?"

"Meeting a colleague," Langdon replied tersely.

"Who?"

"The Czech neuroscientist I mentioned—Dr. Gessner."

"And the two women are meeting at Dr. Gessner's lab?"

Langdon was startled the officer would know that.

"Relax," Janáček said. He held up a note. "I took this from your bedroom along with both your passports."

It was the note Katherine had left. Janáček had merely been testing him.

"What time is the meeting?"

"Eight a.m.," Langdon replied.

Janáček checked his watch. "Which is in a few minutes. Where is this lab?"

Langdon had learned last night that Gessner's lab was located in a secure Prague landmark—Crucifix Bastion—a small medieval fortification that had been renovated into an ultramodern research facility four kilometers from the city center. "I'll call Katherine," he offered, suspecting she would not want to be interrogated in front of Gessner. "I'm sure she will come back immed—"

"*Where is the lab?!*" Janáček exploded, pushing past Harris and stopping inches from Langdon's face. "I will arrest you this instant, Professor, and your consulate will need weeks to cut through the red tape."

Langdon stood his ground. "I'd like to speak privately with Mr. Harris."

"Last chance," Janáček snapped. "Where is the lab?"

There was a long silence, and the voice that spoke next felt like a knife in Langdon's back.

"Crucifix Bastion," Harris said flatly. "Four kilometers from here."

CHAPTER 13

Robert Langdon felt like a criminal as Captain Janáček escorted him through the hotel lobby. When they passed the reception desk, Janáček's phone rang, and the captain peeled off to take the call out of earshot.

"Professor," Harris whispered beside him, seizing their moment alone. "Please understand—Captain Janáček *already* knew the lab's location. He was baiting you into an obstruction charge. I disclosed the location of the lab so Captain Janáček could not claim you impeded his investigation. You would have been arrested immediately."

Thank you . . . I guess?

"*Dost řečí!*" Janáček shouted, ending his call and marching across the lobby to Langdon. "Enough talking! We're leaving!"

Langdon dutifully followed Janáček and Harris out of the hotel into the light flurry of snow. Dawn came late in February, but the sun was finally up, spreading a grayish glow across the city. As they walked to the curb, Harris glanced up from his phone and said, "Captain, I've involved the ambassador."

"Madam *ambassador* herself?" Janáček chided. "You don't trust your own judgment?"

"It's *your* judgment I don't trust," Harris replied, unflinching. "Considering the seriousness of your accusation and the prominence of the individuals accused, I have a duty to involve the embassy at the highest level."

"Do as you will." Janáček smirked, waving his hand dismissively. "I'm sure Mr. Langdon and I will be fine without you."

"Wrong," Harris countered. "I will be taking Mr. Langdon to

the embassy with me. He can wait more comfortably there while you collect Dr. Solomon."

Langdon had no intention of leaving Katherine alone with Janáček and was about to protest, when the captain laughed out loud. "Mr. Harris, *you* may leave, of course, but my suspect Mr. Langdon is coming with me to the lab."

"*Suspect?*" Harris challenged. "You haven't charged him with anything, and he has every right—"

"I will be happy to charge him, if you prefer. It would not be difficult considering he evacuated one of Prague's finest hotels, and his excuse is some fantastical dream."

Harris fell silent, weighing his options. After a moment, Harris turned to Langdon, looking gravely concerned. "Professor, I've requested an emergency meeting with the ambassador. Are you okay on your own for about half an hour?"

"Absolutely," Langdon said.

"Good. I'll brief the ambassador and then join you at the lab—perhaps with the ambassador herself."

"Thank you," Langdon said. "I'm sure we'll sort this out as soon as we speak with Katherine."

Harris turned back to Janáček, who had lit another cigarette. "Captain, be aware that the embassy is watching you. We cannot stop you from being impolite, but if you dare cross any ethical or legal—"

"Got it," Janáček snapped, cigarette dangling from his thin lips. He turned away and signaled to a nearby car, which roared to life and sped toward the group, skidding to a stop only inches from them.

Langdon jumped backward. *Look out!*

The black Škoda sedan was emblazoned with the ÚZSI logo on both sides. Janáček opened the back door and motioned for Langdon to get into the car.

As Langdon climbed inside, Janáček turned to Harris. "Fair warning, Attaché. You should hurry. I have no intention of delaying my interrogation of Ms. Solomon."

◆——·——◆

Michael Harris's taxi pulled out of the Four Seasons. The cabbie signaled a right-hand turn, indicating that he had mistaken Harris for an unsuspecting American tourist with no idea how to get to the U.S. embassy—a perfect target for an inflated fare.

"Jeďte přes Mánesův most, sakra!" Harris shouted in profanity-laced Czech. *"Spěchám!"*

The driver's eyes went wide, and he swerved to the left. Locals were always startled when an American spoke fluent Czech—especially when the American happened to be a six-two Black man in a tailored suit.

Michael Okhu Harris had grown up in a wealthy Philadelphia household, raised primarily by his nanny, an immigrant from Brno. At his parents' suggestion, the nanny spoke only Czech to the boy, and by the age of fifteen, Michael was entirely bilingual. After UCLA law school, Harris had decided to put his language expertise to work by pursuing a post at the U.S. embassy in Prague—an exotic city with sophisticated food, beautiful women, and stimulating work.

In recent weeks, however, that work had become far more interesting than he had wanted. And this morning had taken "interesting" to an entirely new level.

The incident on Charles Bridge remained incomprehensible to Harris. Janáček's claim that it was a publicity stunt for Katherine Solomon's upcoming book seemed preposterous, and yet Harris had to acknowledge there was a strange logic to it; he was always astonished by the risks successful people took in an attempt to advance their own careers.

Myself included, Harris reminded himself.

For several months now, Harris had been performing some "off the book" work for the ambassador, and while the work was technically legal, it was on the edges . . . and decidedly distasteful. Even so, the under-the-table financial remuneration, along with the ambassador's personal leverage over him, had been impossible for Harris to decline. *I hope it doesn't come back to haunt me,* Harris thought.

But he had an uneasy feeling it would.

CHAPTER 14

In Old Town, The Golĕm wound his way out of the cramped labyrinth of alleyways surrounding his flat. The obscure warren of passages, some only two meters wide, twisted through the ancient neighborhood like the tendrils of a vine.

As he moved, The Golĕm inhaled deeply, forcing the cold air to the bottom of his lungs, trying to retune his mind. Encounters with the Ether always untethered him from physical reality, but they also roused his senses.

You must stay alert. There is work to do.

The Golĕm's plan for retribution required a specific piece of information that he did not yet possess. He needed to proceed with extreme caution; if he left any trace whatsoever of what he was searching for, he risked giving himself away. For this reason, he had chosen his next destination carefully—a quiet place where he could obtain answers anonymously.

This morning, he was dressed plainly—pants, shirt, parka, a pleated newsboy hat, and dark sunglasses covering most of his face. This attire was far more common for him than his costume, although he savored the hours he could walk the streets as The Golĕm, his outward appearance reflecting his inner soul—a powerful protector from another realm.

The costume had an earthly benefit too. Prague was a city of surveillance, and cameras with facial recognition software were ubiquitous in public places. It was often said that Prague's passion for costumes and masks was simply its citizens attempting to enjoy a fleeting anonymous moment. So when The Golĕm required true anonymity, he found it beneath a thick layer of clay, which afforded him the luxury of moving freely through the physical world.

Last night, he had dressed as The Golĕm not to obscure his appearance, but rather to hide his face from Dr. Gessner. *And to terrify her.* The shock of his appearance had no doubt helped convince her to reveal her deepest secrets; The Golĕm was still processing all the information he had learned from her.

The atrocity they had built underground . . .

The identities of her partners . . .

And unwittingly . . . the ingenious way he could bring it all crashing down around them.

The Golĕm merged now into a larger alley known as Melantrichova. Still too narrow for even a single car, the alley was dotted with a few stores and cafés, just now starting to open. A smattering of tourists had begun to wander the maze, sipping coffees and taking photos of the uniquely labyrinthine passages.

Turning right, The Golĕm passed the Sex Machines Museum with its display of contraptions designed to pleasure the human body. It held no allure for him; the Ether provided a climax far more fulfilling than physical gratification.

Even so, the lurid images in the museum windows conjured in his mind images of *her* . . . lying in the arms of her lover. The thought made him ill. The Golĕm had already decided the kindest thing he could do for her would be to remove this man as quickly as possible. His death would sadden her, of course, but The Golĕm would fully absorb her pain and help her forget.

The role of a golem is to bear the burden of a weaker soul.

When he reached the town square, the fragrance of roasting chestnuts filled the air along with the strains of a bock—a small Bohemian bagpipe that was a favorite of street musicians here. The slushy expanse of cobblestones was already dotted with larger groups of morning tourists, some of whom had gathered beneath the astronomical clock to watch the 8 a.m. perambulation of saints.

Nearby, several costumed characters posed for photos in

exchange for tips. The men wore long dark robes, top hats, and dramatic harlequin makeup—faces painted entirely white except for their blackened eye sockets.

Opportunists, he thought, doubting these men were truly members of Prague's infamous *Církev satanova*—Church of Satan. Ever since the *Daily Mail* had run an article titled "Inside Prague's 'Dark Harlequin' Satanic Ritual," complete with undercover photographs, it seemed tourists in Prague would pay handsomely for a photo of a real Satanist.

Religion and the occult were woven into the fabric of this city, and visitors found no shortage of angels, saints, devils, and ancient mythological characters wandering the streets. An actress dressed as a black angel often stood in the square, spreading her dark wings in front of the Hotel U Prince and ushering guests inside to the hotel's famous basement grotto—Black Angel's Bar.

At this hour, the winged angel had gone home to bed, and the elegant entryway of the hotel was deserted, just as he had expected. The Golěm slipped inside and descended the winding staircase toward the bar. He planned to find his answers there.

Black Angel's was housed in a twelfth-century Gothic stone cavern several stories beneath the hotel. According to lore, during a restoration, workers stumbled into a secret chamber containing a treasure chest of ancient diaries belonging to a man named Alois Krcha. The diaries included recipes for exotic cocktails and mystical elixirs from days gone by, some rumored to have magical qualities. Tourists frequented Black Angel's Bar in hopes there was some truth in the bar's famous motto: HERE IS IMPOSSIBLE POSSIBLE.

May that indeed be so, The Golěm hoped. If all went to plan, the information he required to achieve the impossible would be found in this basement.

Courtesy of the angel of death, he thought.

CHAPTER 15

Jonas Faukman stood alone at his twenty-third floor office window, staring blankly at the 2 a.m. lights of Manhattan. *The city that never sleeps,* the editor thought, knowing it would be a long time before he slept if he couldn't locate his author's prized manuscript.

He still hoped the tech would call at any moment to say the "hack" had been nothing but a digital glitch, but Faukman sensed something darker was indeed going on.

No other partition was affected.

Only Katherine's . . .

He picked up his office phone to call Katherine in Prague, but after holding the receiver a moment, he set it back in its cradle. It was still early morning in Central Europe, and the news would no doubt be devastating to her. Katherine had placed her trust in Faukman, and he felt a deep moral obligation to make this right . . . especially after convincing her to work securely on the corporate server.

So who stole her manuscript?

Will it appear on the black market in the next few hours?

Faukman forced himself to take a deep breath and exhale. He reminded himself that *one* thing had gone his way tonight . . . a little bit of good fortune . . . and he would need to act carefully and immediately.

Faukman walked across his office and closed the door, quietly turning the dead bolt. He then went to his bookshelf, which was packed with publishing memorabilia—marketing placards, die-print plates, literary awards, framed bestseller lists, and limited-run advance reading copies. From the top shelf, he lifted down one of his most cherished possessions . . . a personalized coffee mug.

The mug bore the symbols of a chalice, a triangle, and a rose. It had been a gift from Robert Langdon after their first publication together two decades ago—*Symbols of the Lost Sacred Feminine*—a book that had sold enough copies for Langdon to buy Faukman this mug . . . and not much else. Over the years, the mug had become a symbol of Langdon's enduring friendship as well as their ongoing professional collaboration.

From inside the mug, Faukman extracted a single key. Then he returned to his desk and used it to unlock the bottom desk drawer.

There, safely ensconced in the drawer, sat a thick bundle of printed pages—481, double-spaced—neatly stacked and bound with two rubber bands. Faukman lifted the manuscript out of the drawer and placed it on his large wooden desk.

The title page contained only two lines.

UNTITLED

BY KATHERINE SOLOMON

Thank God I still edit off paper, he thought, breathing a sigh of relief to know at least he still had *one* copy. By habit, Faukman had printed his editorial copy immediately after Katherine had given him access to the manuscript several hours earlier.

Most editors used word processors and the "Track Changes" feature to enter their edits directly into digital manuscripts, but Faukman still preferred a stack of paper and a traditional blue pen. *For once, being old-school just paid off.*

There had been a time in publishing, not so long ago, when it was common to have only *one* copy of a manuscript. Authors would write in longhand, put their manuscripts into a box, and deliver them to the publisher's office. *Wuthering Heights, The Brothers Karamazov,* and *For Whom the Bell Tolls* had each begun its life as a single, original, paper manuscript.

Relax, he told himself. *If Maxwell Perkins was able to remain calm while handling manuscripts by Hemingway and Fitzgerald, then certainly I can do the same with Katherine Solomon.*

That said, the very first thing he intended to do was to make a digital backup file. The process had once required retyping an entire manuscript into a word processor. Nowadays, optical character recognition scanners took a matter of minutes.

A little insurance while PRH sorts out what happened here.

But as Faukman considered the plan, he was struck by an unsettling realization. The publisher's OCR scanners and photocopiers were all connected to the company's network; if a hacker had gained access to PRH's most secure database, then the networked OCRs and copy machines could hardly be considered secure. With everything that had happened tonight, Faukman was not about to take any chances.

He checked his watch: *2:09 a.m.* If he slipped into the nearby twenty-four-hour FedEx Office Print & Ship, he could use their OCR and copy machines, which would be anonymous and untraceable—certainly much safer than using the publisher's networked device.

Confident in his plan, Faukman quickly wrapped the manuscript in a padded envelope and sealed it, slipping the package into his backpack. After lacing up his black running sneakers and donning his vintage gray wool peacoat, Faukman hoisted the backpack onto his shoulders and left his office, locking the door behind him. Thirty seconds later, he was riding the elevator down to the ground level.

As he stepped off the elevator, Faukman gave a wave to the night watchman who sat behind the security counter in the cavernous lobby. "See you tomorrow, Mark."

"Thanks, Mr. Faukman. Have a wonderful night."

A little late for that, Faukman thought.

As he hurried toward the exit, he passed between the lobby's two walls of soaring bookcases, which proudly displayed Random House classics dating back to the early 1900s, when cofounders Bennett Cerf and Donald S. Klopfer founded this company as a small reprint publisher. The founders' literary tastes were so varied and diverse as to seem almost "random," and they named their publishing venture accordingly.

A handful of Faukman's books sat on these hallowed shelves, and until tonight he had felt confident that a first edition of Katherine's book would one day be here too.

You have one job now, he reminded himself as he pushed through the large revolving glass doors and onto the street. *Protect this manuscript.*

The night was frigid, and the sidewalks were deserted at this hour. Faukman turned right on Broadway and strode briskly southward toward Fifty-Fifth Street, the icy wind blowing up the flaps of his coat.

As he crossed the avenue, he was too preoccupied to notice a black van following him a full block behind.

——— ·· ———

PRH Data Security is located on the fourth floor of Random House Tower and consists of six secure terminals located deep within a maze of humming server racks. The compact facility was responsible for maintaining an impenetrable firewall around the publisher's internal servers.

Security technician Alex Conan was now typing feverishly at his terminal, having confirmed that every last trace of Katherine Solomon's manuscript and research folders were gone—zeroed out, scrubbed, and irretrievable.

This is no longer a rescue mission, Alex thought. *There are no survivors.*

Disturbingly, the system's intrusion detection/prevention system had flagged no traces of exploited vulnerabilities—no unusual registry entries, modified files, altered system configurations, or suspicious packet captures. Clearly, the hackers possessed unique skills.

Who the hell are these guys?!

Eager to update Jonas Faukman, Alex dialed his office but got no answer. *Odd.*

He called down to the night watchman in the lobby. "Mark,

it's Alex Conan in Systems. Would you page Jonas Faukman to the security center for me right away? It's important."

"He won't hear me," the guard replied in his usual jovial tone. "He just walked out of the building."

Faukman left?! We've been hacked . . . because of his book!

Alex assumed Faukman had just stepped out for some air and would be coming right back. He wondered if he should alert the PRH corporate brass, but there was nothing anyone could do at the moment, and they would probably fire him on the spot for letting it happen on his watch.

Damage control, he told himself. *There's still time for me to solve this.*

Alex's hacking skills were robust, as was the case for most techs working in systems security. Given a few hours and a little luck, he had a fighting chance of sorting out *who* had hacked PRH. Then, depending on what he discovered, he might even find a clever way to hack them right back.

CHAPTER 16

Wedged into the backseat of the Škoda Octavia sedan, Robert Langdon felt boxed in. In front of him, Captain Janáček had rammed his own seat as far back as possible, and Langdon now had his knees to his chest, fending off mounting claustrophobia. The vents were blowing stiflingly hot air, mixed with the captain's cigarette smoke, and Langdon was glad he had worn only his Dale sweater and not his bulky Patagonia "puffer."

Janáček was on his phone again, talking in hushed Czech as the car raced southward along the banks of the Vltava. The captain's thick-necked driver was a twentysomething lieutenant in a navy-blue ÚZSI jumpsuit and tilted military beret. He looked more like a bodybuilder or professional wrestler than a law enforcement agent, and he was now serpentining in and out of traffic with only one hand on the steering wheel, as if trying to impress his boss.

As the car sped southward along the river on Masarykovo nábřeží, Langdon felt nauseous and forced his gaze out the window into the open spaces.

They had just passed a small island in the Vltava River, on which stood the bright yellow Neo-Renaissance Žofín Palace. In stark contrast to the ancient palace, Prague's most famous ultra-modern structure was ahead on the left. The Dancing House consisted of two small towers leaning into each other as if they were dancing. Architect Frank Gehry referred to his towers as *Fred and Ginger,* which seemed a stretch of the imagination, but considering London's skyline now boasted *The Gherkin, The*

Walkie-Talkie, and *The Cheesegrater*, perhaps Prague's two dancing film stars could be considered a blessing.

Langdon had long been impressed by Prague's passion for art of the avant-garde. Some of the world's most progressive collections were housed here at the DOX Center, Trade Fair Palace, and Museum Kampa. Unique to Prague, however, were its amateur "pop-up" installations that routinely materialized around the city and, for a few lucky ones—like *The Lennon Wall* and *The Hanging Umbrella People*—were so admired as to be adopted permanently.

"Professor," Janáček said, turning abruptly to face Langdon, causing his seatback to dig farther into Langdon's knees. "When we arrive at Crucifix Bastion, I will be separating you from Ms. Solomon. I intend to question her without you present. I don't want you two coordinating your stories."

"Our *stories*?" Langdon repeated, trying to keep the irritation from his voice. "Everything I told you is absolutely true."

"That is good to know. Then you have nothing to worry about." Janáček had already spun around to face front.

Langdon was concerned about Katherine's impending encounter with Janáček. The captain seemed to have made up his mind that the two Americans—or at the very least *Katherine*—had somehow orchestrated this bizarre series of events for personal gain.

Utter madness.

Even so, no matter how many ways Langdon examined the situation, he saw no explanation for her dream foretelling the scene on Charles Bridge.

She didn't tell anyone about her vision . . . and we went straight back to bed.

The only remaining explanation, as incomprehensible as Langdon found it, was that Katherine had experienced an *actual* precognitive dream . . . her own *Titanic* premonition.

The challenge for Langdon was that he had never believed in precognition. Throughout his career, he had encountered the subject in ancient texts, but he had always dismissed the notion of clairvoyance, arguing that precognition by any name—

prophecy, soothsaying, augury, divination, astrology—was history's oldest delusion.

For as long as humans had been keeping track of the past, they had longed to see the future. Prophets like Nostradamus, the Oracle of Delphi, and the Mayan astrologers had been revered as demigods. Even to this day, a steady stream of well-educated people consulted palm readers, fortune tellers, psychics, and modern-day astrological guides.

Knowing the future is a human obsession.

Langdon's history students often asked him about Nostradamus, arguably the most famous "seer" of all time. The prophet's enigmatic poems seemed to predict, among other things, the French Revolution, Hitler's rise, and the collapse of the World Trade Center. Langdon admitted to his class that a handful of the prophet's quatrains contained what *seemed* like shocking references to future events, but he always reminded them that Nostradamus wrote "Copiously, Cryptically, and Commonly." That was to say, the prophet wrote a *copious* collection of 942 separate poems, using *cryptic* and ambiguous language, and predicted *commonplace* events like wars, natural disasters, and power struggles.

"It's no surprise we see occasional points of congruence," Langdon told them. "We all want to believe in magic or something beyond this world, so our minds often trick us into seeing things that are not really there."

To illustrate his point, every year Langdon began his freshman seminar by asking each student to submit his or her precise date and time of birth. A week later, he handed everyone a sealed envelope with their names on it and told them he had given their birth information to a well-known astrologer and asked for readings. When the students opened their envelopes, they invariably gasped in disbelief at how accurate the astrologer's readings had been.

Then Langdon told them to swap papers with another student. To their surprise, they learned that all the "astrological readings" he had distributed were *identical*. The readings simply *felt* accurate because they included common personal beliefs:

You have a tendency to be critical of yourself.
You pride yourself on being an independent thinker.
You feel doubt at times that you have made the right decision.

Langdon explained that eagerness to find personal truth in general statements was known as the Barnum effect—so named for the sideshow "personality tests" that P. T. Barnum had employed to fool so many circusgoers into believing he had psychic powers.

The ÚZSI sedan swerved hard left, pulling Langdon from his thoughts as the car began ascending the vast wooded landscape of Folimanka Park, a sprawling public space on the outskirts of central Prague.

High atop the hill, Langdon was just able to make out the stone rampart of Crucifix Bastion perched on the ridgeline above them. He had never visited the small fortress, which had been in ruins for many years and had been renovated only fairly recently, but he now knew far more than he cared to about the reconstruction—having been regaled relentlessly last night by the bastion's proud new tenant.

Dr. Brigita Gessner.

The Czech neuroscientist was on the board of the Charles University Lecture Series and had personally invited Katherine to be last night's presenter. After the lecture, Gessner had joined Katherine and Langdon for a drink in the hotel bar. But rather than congratulating Katherine, Gessner had barely mentioned the brilliant lecture, boasting instead about her own work and her incredible new private lab.

"The bastion is quite small, but it's a *sublime* little location for a research facility," Gessner had gushed. "The old fortress sits atop a ridge with unparalleled views of the city, and its thick stone walls offer superb shielding from electromagnetic interference, making it ideal for my delicate work in neuroimaging."

Gessner went on to boast that her success in the field of brain imaging technology and neuroinformatic networks had given her total autonomy in her research—both financially and programmatically—and now she spent her time working on "whatever I damn well please, in an extremely private setting."

As the ÚZSI sedan emerged from the trees, the sight of the lab looming on the cliff brought with it an unexpected pang of concern for Katherine's safety.

For some reason, Langdon felt a sudden sense of danger.

He hoped it was not precognition.

CHAPTER 17

Jonas Faukman blew in his cupped hands as he walked east along Fifty-Second Street, which was deserted at this hour. The night was bitingly cold, and the manuscript felt heavy in his backpack. Thankfully, the twenty-four-hour FedEx office was just a block ahead, across Seventh Avenue.

Faukman was still struggling to make sense of why anyone would target *only* Katherine's book. The PRH database contained countless other more obvious targets—guaranteed blockbusters by big-name authors on whom the PRH bottom line depended. It made no sense. Faukman was starting to wonder if maybe this hack was not book piracy at all, but rather . . . something *else*.

Twenty yards ahead of Faukman, a black van had pulled to the curb and stopped, idling. Faukman instinctively slowed, feeling uneasy on the empty street at this hour. A moment later, however, he realized his paranoia was misplaced; the van's driver hopped out, whistling happily and reading a clipboard. Without so much as a glance at Faukman, he strode off in the opposite direction.

Faukman relaxed and continued past the van.

Up ahead, the departing driver stopped and looked up at the building numbers, checked the clipboard again, and turned around, walking back the way he had come. "Johnny!" he called toward the van. "What was the address on that email? I don't see any souvlaki restaurant here!"

"It's one block farther," Faukman offered, pointing. "Just past Seventh—"

From behind him, a fist collided with Faukman's right kidney, and a black bag swooped down over his head. Before Faukman could even process what was happening, two sets of powerful hands lifted him off his feet and heaved him into the van. He landed roughly on the hard floor, the impact knocking the wind out of him. The door slammed shut, and within seconds, he felt the van accelerating rapidly.

Gasping and unable to see, the terrified editor tried to catch his breath and take stock of his situation. Faukman had edited enough thrillers to know what happened when a character was blindfolded and thrown into the back of a van.

It was never good.

———···———

Three blocks away, in Random House Tower, Alex Conan had now dialed all of Faukman's contact numbers—office, home, cell—but had failed to get an answer anywhere.

Where the hell did he go?!

We're in the middle of a crisis!

Faukman, it seemed, had simply turned off his phone and wandered out into the night—perhaps to On the Rocks, a nearby whiskey bar frequented by neurotic editors trying to calm their nerves at all hours of the night.

So far, Alex had made no headway identifying the hackers. He had combed through the wreckage but had dislodged nothing of interest. *I need a finer-toothed comb*, he knew. His next pass would require a proprietary forensic algorithm tooled to scan for specific artifacts *unique* to the missing manuscript—keywords, concepts, names—but to do that, he needed to talk to Faukman.

Or . . . he realized. *I could call Katherine Solomon directly?*

PRH protocol prohibited that call, requiring all communication with authors to flow exclusively through each author's editor—the trusted soul who had learned how to navigate the writer's quirks, eccentricities, and insecurities.

Screw it, Alex thought. Not only was it critical that he learn more about Katherine's book, but he believed Katherine had a right to know that someone had targeted her manuscript, especially if it meant she might be in personal danger herself.

With that in mind, Alex accessed Katherine Solomon's author file, located her cell-phone number, and dialed. Faukman had mentioned Katherine was in Europe at the moment, meaning it was early morning for her, but if Alex woke her up, she'd understand this was an emergency.

Katherine's cell phone rang four times and went to voicemail. *Damn.* He left her a brief message, introducing himself and asking if she would please call him immediately.

He hung up and tried Faukman's cell phone again.

Nothing.

It was then that he recalled Faukman mentioning that Solomon was traveling with another of his authors—Harvard professor Robert Langdon. *Also in the PRH database*, Alex thought, deciding it was worth a try.

He accessed Langdon's file and called that cell-phone number as well.

Langdon's line didn't even ring—it went straight to voicemail.

Alex hung up, feeling suddenly very alone.

Where the hell is everyone?!

CHAPTER 18

In London, Finch had just received confirmation that his contingency plans were now in motion, in both Prague and New York. The news had arrived via a military-grade communication platform known as Signal, required for all field communications, as it provided end-to-end encryption of all texts and voice.

Finch, an American, held a covert position within the European headquarters of a global organization known by insiders as "Q." The firm's enigmatic nickname derived from a character in James Bond novels—the technologist-inventor "Q" who created deadly innovations in service to Her Majesty the Queen.

Like its fictional namesake, the real-world Q also developed advanced technologies in service to a higher power . . . though a power far more influential than any queen. The entity that had quietly founded Q back in 1999 wielded unprecedented influence around the world, and while its presence was rarely witnessed or even suspected, its actions regularly shifted the course of global events.

At seventy-three years old, Everett Finch carried a chess master FIDE rating of 2374, rowed nine thousand meters daily on his erg machine, and finished breakfast by popping three hundred milligrams of Nuvigil, a nootropic mind-enhancement drug that turned his mind into a Formula One race car on a highway of minivans.

Having spent the last decade in a position of power within Q's formidable parent organization, Finch had been tapped three years ago for a confidential assignment within Q's London office. He was also informed he would be spearheading the development of one of the most ambitious and secretive endeavors ever undertaken . . . by anyone, anywhere.

Threshold.

He was told the project required a certain flexibility with regard to legal and moral constraints, and Finch had been chosen for his expertise with "success-weighted ethical rubrics"—moral frameworks that prioritized success over purity of conscience.

Finch was not surprised when his letter of appointment read:

It is impossible to overstate the importance of Threshold. It warrants whatever extraordinary measures you deem necessary to ensure its success.

Message received, Finch thought. *There are no rules.*

———•··—→

Thirty minutes had passed since The Golĕm had entered Hotel U Prince and descended to the subterranean Black Angel's Bar. He had found the bar closed, with cleaning crew sweeping the floors, polishing the leather couches, and pulling cigarette butts from the rough-hewn ancient stone walls.

Before being spotted by anyone, The Golĕm continued past the bar, around the corner, to a closet-like space that contained a desk and two old computers whose faded displays glowed with the Black Angel's logo. The bar's offering of twenty-four-hour Internet to patrons was a quaint relic of the days when foreign cell phones barely worked in Prague, and tourists would choose to drink at Black Angel's just to send an email.

Earlier today, when The Golĕm realized he required specific technical information to carry out his plan, he immediately thought of Black Angel's. Nobody would be monitoring this machine.

And now I've found what I came for, he thought, eyeing the technical information on the screen before him. Many of the details were beyond his understanding, but that did not matter; firing a gun did not require a degree in ballistic science . . . only access to a trigger.

And that trigger had now been located.

Gessner had revealed many secrets in the attempt to save her own life—among them, the presence of a surprisingly powerful piece of technology located within the deepest reaches of their underground lab, sealed inside an airtight vault with walls of reinforced concrete two meters thick.

A piece of technology that could bring their entire world crashing down.

With the information he had just obtained, he now knew exactly how to make that happen.

The Golĕm quickly cleared the browser's search history and rebooted the computer. When he ascended and stepped back out into the square, he felt alive with the prospect of a revenge so bold that its shock waves would be felt thousands of miles from Prague . . . by all those responsible.

CHAPTER 19

Crucifix Bastion stands high atop a wooded ridgeline that defines the northern edge of Folimanka Park. In the mid-1300s, the towering crest caught the eye of Holy Roman Emperor Charles IV, who decided it was the ideal location on which to build a fortification to overlook his beloved birth city of Prague, a flourishing gem of Christendom.

Along the ridge, the emperor constructed a stone rampart topped by a small but robust fort. Its lofty perch reminded him of the mount on which Christ had been crucified, so he christened the fortification "Crucifix Bastion."

The ÚZSI sedan wound higher along the entry road, steadily climbing the ridge until it came to a stop in front of the bastion. Langdon looked out at the ancient fortress, impressed by the elegant modernist renovation.

This is Gessner's private lab? Clearly, the neuroscientist made a better living than Langdon had imagined.

Janáček jumped out of the passenger seat and yanked Langdon's door open, motioning impatiently for him to get out. Langdon quickly obliged, eager to exit the cramped vehicle and also increasingly anxious to see Katherine.

The thuggish driver remained in the car as Janáček led Langdon through the falling snow toward the lab. In the dusting of white on the gravel pathway, Langdon saw several sets of muted footprints—some of them no doubt Katherine's as she arrived to meet with Gessner.

Above the main entrance, an elegant bronze panel announced: THE GESSNER INSTITUTE. The bastion's door was a broad, styl-

ish pane of reinforced frosted glass in a steel frame. Janáček
pulled on the handle, but the door did not budge. He rapped
loudly on the thick glass.

No reply.

Janáček now turned to the call box beside the door—a biometric finger scanner, a speaker, and a call button. *No keypad for a
passcode?* Langdon wondered, puzzled because last night Gessner
had boasted gratuitously that her lab was secured with "an ingeniously clever passcode."

She must have been referring to an interior door.

Janáček impatiently pressed the call button, and the speaker
buzzed, an intercom now ringing inside. They waited, and after
five rings, the buzzer stopped.

Janáček stepped back and raised his hooded eyes to the security camera positioned discreetly overhead, as if he were staring
it down. He held his ÚZSI identification card aloft in front of
the camera and pressed the call button again.

It rang an additional five times with no answer.

Langdon glanced at the security camera, wondering if maybe
Katherine was looking back at him. *Why isn't Gessner answering
the door? Or buzzing us in?* Clearly, the two women could see that
Janáček was here, and Langdon found it unlikely that Gessner's
desire for secrecy was so intense that she would rebuff an ÚZSI
officer.

"Give me Katherine Solomon's cell number," Janáček said,
pulling out his phone.

Langdon recited it from memory, and Janáček typed it into
his phone, which he placed on speaker mode. The call went
instantly to Katherine's voicemail.

No service inside those thick stone walls? Langdon wondered,
although it seemed odd that a tech giant like Gessner had not
installed cellular boosters in her lab.

Janáček grumbled something under his breath and turned,
shouting in the direction of his car. "Pavel!"

The thick-necked driver leaped from behind the wheel
and hurried toward Janáček like a dog to its master. *"Ano, pane
kapitáne?!"*

Janáček pointed to the glass door. *"Prostřílej dveře."*

Lieutenant Pavel nodded, pulled out a handgun, and crouched in a firing position aimed at the door.

Jesus! Langdon leaped backward just as the lieutenant's gun roared.

Six rapid-fire shots rang out—the bullets piercing the center of the pane in an almost perfect circular grouping. The reinforced glass did not shatter, its gooey inner layer keeping it intact. Lieutenant Pavel wasted no time spinning and kicking his leg up and back, his heavy boot striking the glass in the circle of bullet holes. A spiderweb of cracks radiated outward. He kicked again, and the entire panel crashed inward, breaking free from the frame and skidding across the floor in a shower of safety-glass shards that looked like glistening sugar cubes.

Langdon watched in disbelief, wondering if Janáček had even considered that there might have been someone on the other side of the frosted-glass door when his lieutenant fired.

Pavel reloaded his gun and stepped through the demolished opening, his boots crunching on the broken glass. He looked left and right, and then he motioned *all clear* for Janáček to enter.

"After you, Professor," Janáček said. "Unless you'd prefer to wait in the car?"

Langdon had no desire to leave Katherine alone with Janáček and his trigger-happy madman. Heart pounding, Langdon stepped toward the shattered opening, wondering how many other times in history this medieval fortress had been breached.

CHAPTER 20

The United States embassy in Prague is located in the Schönborn Palace. It comprises more than a hundred rooms, many with the original stucco walls and thirty-foot ceilings. Built in 1656 by a one-legged count—Rudolf von Colloredo-Waldsee—the opulent palace includes several ramps that enabled Count Rudolf to ride his horse up into the building. Now, having become the official U.S. embassy, the palace housed twenty-three on-site personnel tasked with working on behalf of U.S. interests in the region.

This morning, the embassy's media liaison—Dana Daněk—was alone in her office, organizing the daily agenda. She was a thirty-four-year-old Praguer who had perfected her English while modeling in London in her twenties. After returning to Prague and earning a computer degree, she'd applied for a post at the U.S. embassy and landed in the public relations department.

Dana's office felt colder than usual on this snowy morning, and she walked over to the classic steam radiator, bending over to turn it on for some extra heat.

"*Pěkný výhled,*" a deep voice said behind her. *Nice view.*

She turned and swooned a bit as she always did when she saw the striking legal attaché, Michael Harris. He treated her politely inside the office; of course, it was how he treated her *outside* the office and in his bedroom that she found most appealing. Beyond his physical talents, Harris had a lightness about him that always lifted her mood.

"You're on the wrong floor," Dana said playfully, having

heard that Harris had requested an emergency meeting with the ambassador. "She's upstairs in her office, waiting for you."

"Could you do something for me?" Harris replied, sounding surprisingly serious. "It's important."

She nodded. *Anything your heart desires, Michael Harris.*

Harris quickly described his request.

Dana stared at him, trying to gauge if he might be joking. "I'm sorry . . . a woman wearing a spiked tiara?"

Harris nodded. "She was on Charles Bridge just before seven o'clock this morning. I only need to know where she came from and where she went afterward."

The request was unusual. Dana's access to the camera system was technically restricted to assessing specific incidents that impacted public relations—public rallies, demonstrations, protests, and so forth. This felt like something . . . else.

"Don't worry," he pressed. "I've got your back."

I certainly hope so, she thought. The two of them shared a perilous secret—an illicit office romance—which was strictly forbidden among embassy employees.

"I'll see what I can find," she said.

He gave her shoulder a little squeeze. "Thanks. I'll stop back after my meeting."

Dana watched him go. *You want me to track a woman wearing a spiked tiara . . . Why?*

In recent weeks, Michael had been uncharacteristically secretive, especially about his evening activities. He was increasingly unavailable to meet Dana after work and had become evasive when asked what he was doing instead. Dana was starting to suspect there was another woman.

Feeling a sudden wave of jealousy, Dana wondered if maybe his request to track this woman might be a *personal* matter. Her suspicion was absurd, of course; the embassy's legal attaché, of all people, would know never to use official resources for a personal matter, and Dana would be the last person Harris would ask to research another woman.

Still, he's using me, she knew.

Nonetheless, Dana settled in behind her desk and logged into the embassy's surveillance interface. "All right, Michael, let's see what we can find."

After the Czech Republic had joined NATO in 1999, more than *eleven hundred* surveillance cameras had been positioned in Prague as part of a U.S.-funded classified surveillance partnership known as Echelon. Despite strict Czech laws governing access to the cameras, the U.S. had built the network and had given its embassies, with a few exceptions, full access . . . a point of sharp contention for Czech authorities.

Dana Daněk was not entirely comfortable with the surveillance either, and yet citizens of Central Europe had little choice but to accept Echelon's watchful eyes monitoring their daily lives—including, in Dana's case, her occasionally sneaking in and out of Michael Harris's flat at all hours of the night.

Nobody is monitoring my activity, she assured herself. *There is simply too much data.*

Even so, civilian privacy campaigns like @ReclaimYourFace regularly held anti-American protests against Prague's ubiquitous security cameras. The embassy's counterargument was both simple and true: *Most citizens prefer to be monitored . . . than to be blown up by terrorists.*

With that thought in mind, Dana moved her cursor across a detailed map of Prague, navigated to Charles Bridge, and called up its recently archived security footage.

CHAPTER 21

Langdon's eardrums were still ringing from the gunshots as he stepped through the shattered doorway into Crucifix Bastion. His loafers crunched on the glass shards covering the pink marble floor as he joined Janáček and Lieutenant Pavel in the elegant entryway.

A hallway led to their right, but Janáček seemed more focused on the imposing steel door directly in front of them. Stenciled with the word LAB, the portal had a tiny reinforced window and a biometric panel.

"Stairwell down to the lab," Janáček said, peering through the window and trying the locked door.

Langdon glanced around for an elevator, curious how Gessner transported heavy scientific gear down to her facility, but he saw nothing else in the foyer except this stairwell and the hallway that led off to their right. Langdon had yet to see any sign of a keypad for the "clever passcode" that Dr. Gessner had bragged about the night before.

Janáček was studying the dislodged frame of shattered safety glass on the floor. After a moment, he crouched down, hoisted the frame, dragged it over to the lab entrance, and leaned it precariously against the lab door. "Makeshift alarm," he announced. "In case your friend thinks she can slip out while we're not watching."

Langdon could not believe Janáček thought Katherine would run, but his resourcefulness was impressive.

Lieutenant Pavel was already moving cautiously down the hall, his gun raised as if he could be ambushed at any moment.

Put your goddamned gun away! Langdon wanted to shout. *They're unarmed scientists!*

As Janáček and Langdon followed, Lieutenant Pavel peered into a small restroom, apparently found it empty, and continued to the end of the hall. Here the corridor turned left, and he inched warily around the corner, gun at the ready. After a moment, he holstered his weapon and turned back to his captain with a shrug. *"Nikde nikdo."*

Langdon followed Janáček around the corner into a dazzling space bathed in natural light. Furnished like the atrium of some boutique hotel, the room had stark white couches, pounded copper tables, and a sophisticated coffee station. The floor-to-ceiling windows offered a majestic view out across the bastion's long courtyard to Prague's skyline, Petřín Tower, and Vyšehrad Fortress.

As Langdon surveyed the space, his gaze fell on a massive piece of art on the rear wall—a Brutalist wall sculpture whose unique style he recognized at once.

My God, is that an original Paul Evans piece?

The eight-foot-square rust-colored metal was divided into a grid of rectangular recesses, each holding a smaller individual sculpture. An improvisation on a "cabinet of curiosities," Langdon had to guess the Paul Evans was easily worth a quarter of a million dollars. Gessner had bragged last night about her lucrative medical patents, but Langdon had clearly underestimated just *how* lucrative those patents must be.

Janáček was moving toward the far end of the room, where an oversized wooden door stood open into what appeared to be Dr. Gessner's office.

"Dr. Gessner?" Janáček called, walking into the office.

Langdon followed in the hope of seeing Katherine, but the office was empty.

The neuroscientist's office was adorned with a collection of vibrant abstract prints—each one an amorphous spheroid blob with regions of different colors—which Langdon immediately recognized as MRIs of the human brain.

Science as art.

Langdon wondered if Gessner was so self-involved as to hang images of her *own* brain. Bio self-portraits had become popular lately with the advent of imaging companies like DNA11, which generated artwork based entirely on a customer's unique DNA microscopy. *Genetic art*, they advertised, *means no two people ever own the same piece.*

Janáček walked over to Gessner's desk and examined what appeared to be an intercom and microphone. He selected a button and held it down.

"Dr. Gessner?" he declared into the mic. "I am ÚZSI Captain Oldřich Janáček. As I suspect you are aware, I am with Professor Robert Langdon. It is imperative that you and Ms. Solomon come upstairs immediately to speak with me. I repeat— *immediately.* Please confirm."

Janáček released the button and waited, glaring up into a fish-eye camera on the ceiling.

With each passing moment of silence, Langdon felt increasingly uneasy. *Why isn't Katherine responding? Did something happen down there? Has there been an accident?*

"Professor?" Janáček sauntered slowly over to Langdon. "Do you have any idea why Ms. Solomon would be ignoring me? They are obviously *here.* Dr. Gessner's office is unlocked, and there are fresh *footprints* outside."

Langdon was not sure how "fresh" the muted prints were, but considering their scheduled meeting here, it seemed logical that Katherine was indeed downstairs with Gessner. "I have no idea," he replied truthfully.

Janáček guided Langdon back to the waiting room and pointed to one of the white couches. "You sit."

Langdon obeyed, taking a seat on the long couch by the side wall. Janáček placed a phone call, speaking in rapid-fire Czech.

While Langdon waited, his gaze moved again to the colorful images decorating Gessner's office. *Just three pounds of flesh,* he thought, scrutinizing the mysterious contours and interconnected folds in each image. *And science still has no clue how it works.*

In her lecture last night, Katherine had projected a markedly *less* attractive image of a human brain—a stark laboratory photograph of a grayish, furrowed glob of tissue sitting in a stainless-steel tray.

"This blob is your brain," she had told the crowd. "I realize it looks more like a mound of very old hamburger, but I can assure you, this organ is nothing short of miraculous. It contains approximately eighty-six *billion* neurons. Together they form over a hundred *trillion* synaptic connections, which can process complex information almost instantly. Moreover, these synaptic connections can reorganize themselves over time as needed. This phenomenon, known as neuroplasticity, enables the brain to adapt, learn, and recover from injuries."

Katherine displayed another photo—a single DVD sitting on a table. "This is a standard DVD—it can hold an impressive four-point-seven gigabytes of information," she continued, "which equates to approximately two thousand high-definition photos. But do you know how many DVDs it would take to store the estimated memory of the average human brain? I'll give you a hint . . . If you stacked the required DVDs on top of each other"—she gestured at the soaring ceiling of Vladislav Hall—"they would reach well beyond the peak of this building. In fact . . . the stack would be so tall . . . it would reach the International Space Station."

Katherine tapped her skull. "We each store millions of gigabytes of data in here—images, memories, lifetimes of education, skill sets, languages . . . all sorted and organized neatly in this tiny space. Modern technology still requires a data warehouse to match it."

She turned off the PowerPoint and walked to the front of the stage. "Materialist scientists remain baffled as to how an organ so *small* could possibly hold such *vast* quantities of information. And I have to agree, it seems a physical impossibility . . . which is why I'm not a *materialist*."

There was a slight flurry in the audience. *Poking the hornet's nest again, I see.* Langdon had learned that Katherine had no qualms about striking a nerve when it came to the two opposing philosophies into which the study of human consciousness was divided.

Materialism versus Noetics.

The materialists believed that all phenomena, including consciousness, could be explained solely in terms of physical matter and its interactions. According to materialists, consciousness was a by-product of physical processes—the activity of neural networks along with other chemical processes within the brain.

For noeticists, however, the picture was infinitely less confined. Noeticists believed that consciousness was *not* created by brain processes, but rather was a fundamental aspect of the universe—akin to space, time, or energy—and was not even located inside the body.

Langdon had been stunned to learn that the human brain represented only 2 percent of a person's body weight, and yet it consumed an incredible *20 percent* of the body's energy and oxygen. The blatant mismatch, Katherine believed, was proof that the brain was doing something so incomprehensible that traditional biology had not yet been able to grasp it.

Her manuscript will likely unravel that mystery, Langdon thought, wondering if Jonas Faukman had begun reading yet. *Knowing Jonas, he's been wide awake all night and is halfway through the book already.*

Janáček had just placed a second call, and his increasingly urgent tone was not helping Langdon's frayed nerves. He glanced at his watch and hoped for the hasty arrival of Harris and the ambassador.

As Langdon waited on the couch, he found himself again scrutinizing the huge Paul Evans wall sculpture on the other end of the room. The expensive piece had frustrated Langdon the moment he first saw it.

He felt irritated by wealthy art enthusiasts who purchased world-class masterpieces, removed them from the safety of museums, and then displayed them privately in poor lighting or in unsafe conditions.

And on top of that, Gessner hung it improperly.

No doubt Paul Evans had intended this sculpture to be displayed like a painting—centered and mounted on the wall—but Gessner had lazily set the piece directly on the floor, propped vertically with only a stabilizing bar across the top to keep it from falling into the room.

That wall is solid stone, Langdon thought. *It could easily have handled the weight.*

As he studied the heavy horizontal bar, however, an unexpected thought struck him.

Unless . . .

He scrutinized the complete piece of art a moment longer. Then he stood up and began walking briskly toward it.

Without warning, Pavel leaped in front of him, pulling his weapon and aiming it directly at Langdon's chest. *"Nechte toho!"*

Langdon's arms shot skyward. *For God's sake!*

Janáček ended his call and nodded calmly at his lieutenant, saying something to him in Czech.

Pavel lowered the gun and holstered it.

"What the hell is he doing?!" Langdon shouted at Janáček.

"His job," the captain replied. "Are you trying to *leave* us?"

"Leave?!" he replied angrily. "No, I was . . ."

"You were *what?*"

Langdon hesitated a moment, reconsidering his words. "I was just going to the restroom," he lied, returning to his seat. "On second thought, it can wait."

———··———

The Golěm donned his sunglasses as he strode across the cobbles of Old Town Square toward the taxi stand. Despite his lack of sleep, he felt energized, his thoughts firmly focused on what would be required to carry out his liberating act of vengeance.

Last night, Gessner had confessed a dark truth, revealing that her colleagues had secretly constructed a sprawling, cavernous facility deep beneath the city of Prague. *They call it Threshold.* The scope of the project was astounding, and yet it was the facility's precise *location* that had most amazed The Golěm.

Right in the heart of the city.

Hundreds of people walk over it every day . . . with no idea it's there.

When The Golěm demanded Gessner tell him how to get

inside, she tried to resist but, overwhelmed with pain, quickly revealed the answer: Threshold could be accessed only by someone who knew where the entrance was hidden . . . and *also* possessed a highly specialized RFID key card.

It took The Golĕm only a few minutes of brutality to extract both. When he left Gessner to die, he possessed the information he required . . . and also her personal RFID key card.

Unfortunately, he later discovered that the neuroscientist had managed to withhold one critical piece of information from him: the key card *alone* was not sufficient to gain access.

Defeated and exhausted, The Golĕm had trudged homeward through the darkness, the useless key card in his pocket. Partway home, however, he realized there might be a solution to his problem. The more he considered it, the more confident he became. By dawn, he was fully certain.

I require a second item.

Fortunately, The Golĕm knew precisely where this item was located at this very moment—in Gessner's private lab, high on the ridgeline overlooking the city.

"*Bastion u Božích muk,*" he said as he climbed into a cab. "Take me to Crucifix Bastion."

CHAPTER 22

Lieutenant Pavel felt a smug bemusement to know he had frightened Robert Langdon so deeply that the man had forgone his trip to the restroom. The American was now sitting on a couch and staring blankly into space.

Having a gun in your face will scramble your thoughts.

Partly out of spite, Pavel walked around the corner, down the hall, into the restroom. Leaving the door wide open so Langdon could hear, he urinated loudly and then flushed.

As he exited the restroom, Pavel saw Janáček rounding the corner into the hallway.

"I'm going for a cigarette," the captain said.

Pavel had worked with Janáček long enough to know the captain smoked wherever he damn well pleased. He was probably going to make a private phone call. There were a lot of those with Janáček.

"The demolition team will be here in thirty minutes," Janáček said, "to blow through *that*." He pointed to the steel portal that protected the stairs down to the lab.

A single controlled blast, Pavel agreed, surveying the lab door. *And the lower level will be accessible.*

The shattered front doorframe was still leaning against the lab door as an alarm, but Pavel sensed nobody would be exiting today by their own accord. They had already defied a direct order from Captain Janáček . . . which left them precious few options.

"I'll wait for the team outside," Janáček said. "Stay here and make sure nobody exits the lab. And Langdon should never leave your sight."

He snapped his heels. *Understood.*

Pavel had been Janáček's right-hand man for nearly five years now. Lesser known in the police force, however, was the fact that Pavel was Oldřich Janáček's nephew. When Pavel was only nine, his father was killed in a fluke accident—struck by a tourist on a motorbike. When Pavel's mother descended into an abusive alcoholic haze, Pavel began spending most of his time on the streets making his living by committing local robberies, then convincing the neighborhood storekeepers to pay him for protection.

At nineteen, when Pavel was arrested, his mother was nowhere to be found, and her older brother Oldřich intervened on behalf of a nephew he barely knew. A rising officer at ÚZSI, Oldřich Janáček had been impressed enough with Pavel's guts and ingenuity to offer the boy a simple choice: *Go to prison and spend your life with criminals . . . or attend ÚZSI training, and I will show you how to catch them.*

It was tough love, but the choice was simple, and Pavel worked hard to become a dutiful servant of the law. Despite graduating only in the middle of his ÚZSI class, Pavel was promoted quickly through the ranks. Pavel was now a lieutenant, an unusually high post for an officer in his late twenties, and he addressed his uncle solely as Captain Janáček.

I owe him everything, Pavel knew. Janáček had become the father whom Pavel had lost, and the young lieutenant idolized his captain's fearlessness and resolve. *Sometimes enforcing the law requires being above the law.* Captain Janáček lived by that motto and often trusted Pavel to cover any tracks the captain left while pushing the envelope in an investigation . . . as he had done this morning.

He knows I will protect him to the end.

Pavel now stood in the foyer and watched as Captain Janáček exited the building into the bastion's snowy courtyard—a long, rectangular expanse enclosed by a low stone wall to protect visitors from the dizzying drop off the ridge. As the captain wound his way through the potted evergreens on the lawn, he placed a call and took up a position at the far end of the courtyard, gazing out at the Prague skyline.

Pavel took the opportunity to check his own phone for messages, hoping he might have a notification from his new app, *Dream Zone*—the virtual dating platform that had taken Europe by storm. Pavel had never imagined chatting with computer-generated women would hold his interest, and yet, like so many men, he had become addicted to the sexy conversation threads, revealing photos, and fantasy storylines.

Eleven notifications.

He smiled, pleased to have something to read while he waited. Phone in hand, Pavel headed back to the atrium to baby-sit Langdon, but as he entered, he was surprised to see the couch where Langdon had been sitting was now empty. Pavel turned left and right, scanning every corner of the space. He ran into Gessner's office but found that too was empty.

Pavel's confusion turned quickly to panic. Frantically, he dashed around the room, searching behind couches and chairs. *Where the hell did he go?!*

Robert Langdon seemed to have evaporated into thin air.

◄——··——►

Less than twenty feet away, Langdon stood motionless in the darkened alcove hidden behind the Paul Evans wall sculpture. Moments ago, finding himself alone, Langdon had jumped up from the couch and hurried over to the artwork to study it more closely. As he'd thought, the steel bar above the piece was not a stabilizing bracket at all.

It was a glide track.

Like a very expensive barn door.

Langdon had firmly grabbed the right-hand edge of the sculpture and heaved it to the left. The massive sculpture slid effortlessly, balanced on high-precision ball-bearing rollers. Hidden behind it, as Langdon had anticipated, was an opening.

He quickly stepped through, and the spring-loaded slider closed silently behind him.

Now, as his eyes adjusted to the dimly lit space, Langdon could hear Lieutenant Pavel rushing around the reception room and cursing loudly.

The alcove behind the sculpture was equally well-appointed and serene, with rich wood paneling and a marble pillar on which a cluster of faux candles flickered. The candlelight illuminated a brushed metal door.

A private elevator.

This seemed a far more fitting entrance to Gessner's small lab than the service stairwell, and Langdon now saw that the elevator door was secured by an illuminated keypad.

Apparently, Gessner had not been bluffing about securing her lab with an ingenious passcode. Now all Langdon had to do was figure out what it was.

CHAPTER 23

J onas Faukman had experienced plenty of terrifying moments before—leaping out of a helicopter with no parachute, nearly drowning at the hand of a cunning psychopath, dodging bullets while clinging to a steep rooftop—but those scenarios had all played out in the pages of the suspense novels he had edited.

Now the terror was real.

The bag on his head was making it increasingly difficult to breathe, and his hands were bound behind his back. He was lying on the hard metal floor of a vehicle that had been moving fast on a highway for at least ten minutes. He heard the phone in his coat pocket buzz several times, but he had no way to reach it.

From all Faukman could discern, he had been abducted by two men, both American by the sound of their voices, and they had rifled through his backpack.

They have the manuscript.

His fear was underscored by bewilderment.

Why?

The van suddenly pulled off the highway, wound along surface streets, and then abruptly stopped. When his captors finally ripped the bag off his head, Faukman found himself face-to-face with a powerfully built, thirtysomething man with a military buzz cut. Dressed all in black, the man had positioned himself alarmingly close, seated on a milk crate directly in front of Faukman, staring at him with ice-cold eyes.

Petrified, Faukman looked past his captor and through the windshield. All he saw were trees and darkness. He could hear heavy machinery thrumming in the distance. *Where the hell am I?*

Faukman's second abductor—a slightly smaller man—was in the front passenger seat, typing on a laptop. *The guy from the sidewalk with the clipboard.*

"Ready," the guy on the laptop said.

His partner with the buzz cut reached up to a video camera mounted on the van's ceiling and swiveled it directly into Faukman's face.

Survival rule number one, Faukman reminded himself. *Never show fear.*

"That's a cool camera," Faukman managed. "Are we making a TikTok?"

The man glanced down, looking surprised by Faukman's insolence.

Faukman tried to sound calm. "Or are we just doing a ransom video to send to my family?"

"You don't have a family," the man said flatly. "You're not married, you work six days a week, and you haven't left the country in more than four years."

Jesus! Who are *these guys?*

Faukman's first guess had been U.S. military, but it was hard to know these days. He had published a nonfiction book a few years back about the secret world of modern mercenaries—trained specialty contractors with mysterious names like Blackwater, Triple Canopy, Wackenhut, and International Development Solutions.

The truth was, these two operatives could be working for anyone.

Buzzcut pulled a small tablet from his coat, scrolled through it, and then shoved it in Faukman's face. "Do you recognize this place?"

Faukman eyed the photo. It took him a moment to understand the visual. *What the hell?!* It was his own living room. From the looks of it, his airy apartment on the Upper East Side had been ransacked . . . artwork knocked off walls, bookshelves emptied, couches shredded, tables overturned.

"What were we looking for?" Buzzcut said. "Take a guess."

Faukman eyed the man's close-cropped hair. "A better barber?"

Buzzcut lunged forward without warning and drove a mammoth fist into Faukman's stomach. The editor doubled over, falling on his side, gasping for breath.

"Try again," the man said, yanking him back up onto his knees. "What were we looking for?"

"I . . . don't . . . know," Faukman said, barely able to breathe.

The man on the laptop studied some data that appeared on-screen and shook his head. "He's lying."

"I will ask you one last time," Buzzcut said. "And before you answer, let me introduce you to Avatar." He pointed to the video camera overhead. "This is an AI engine that tracks your eye movement, facial microchanges, and postural shifts. It's a state-of-the-art veracity analysis system."

Veracity analysis system? Faukman decided not to chide the thug for using a ten-dollar term for a five-dollar gizmo, but at least it explained the video camera.

The man on the milk crate leaned forward until his face was uncomfortably close. "We know everything about you, Jonas. We know you work late at night, you go running in Central Park when you don't have a business lunch, and you drink gin martinis with your authors at the White Horse Tavern. So don't screw with me. Let me ask you one very simple question."

Faukman waited, his stomach still knotted in pain.

"The manuscript we found in your backpack," Buzzcut said. "Is that your *only* copy?"

Faukman knew what answer they were *hoping* to hear. Unfortunately, telling the truth right now meant instantly losing his negotiating power . . . and, quite possibly, his life.

Seeing precious few options, Faukman closed his eyes and pictured the hero from one of his most popular thriller series—a spy who consistently beat lie detectors using three simple steps, which Faukman now attempted to employ.

First, he lowered his shoulders and released all tension in his abdomen.

Second, he touched his index finger and thumb very lightly together and slowed his breathing.

Third, he held in his mind's eye a clear mental image of the truth he *wished* were true—in this case, an image of a dozen extra manuscripts sitting safely on his desk at Random House.

He felt much calmer.

"No," Faukman said with as even a tone as possible. "The manuscript in my bag is *not* the only copy. There are many others."

Laptop studied his computer and almost immediately shook his head. "Lying."

Goddamn it, Jonas! It's called fiction for a reason!

Buzzcut raised a fist once more, preparing to punch him again in the gut.

"Wait!" Faukman said. "I was talking about the *digital* copies on the PRH servers."

Buzzcut looked almost amused. "Mr. Faukman, we *deleted* all the digital copies, which is the reason you were rushing off to the copy center, was it not?"

Faukman fell silent, heart racing wildly. He could hear loud machinery beyond the van, possibly the whine of industrial engines.

"Let me make this very simple for you," Buzzcut said. "Other than the one in your backpack and those from the PRH servers, do you know of any *other* versions of this manuscript—digital, hard copy, or otherwise?"

Faukman shook his head. "No, the manuscript in my bag is the only remaining copy."

"*Was* the only remaining copy," Buzzcut corrected. "We've already destroyed it."

———··———

Alone in the PRH security center, Alex Conan was aghast.

This can't be.

He stabbed at his keyboard, refreshing the page, hoping the information before him was wrong, but the same chilling image kept appearing . . . and reappearing.

God, no . . .

Minutes earlier, with no sign of Faukman and having been unable to reach either Katherine Solomon or Robert Langdon, Alex had decided to take bold action.

You have skills. You have access.

Alex had employed both, and despite the dubious legality of his methods, he had managed to access information he was not supposed to have in order to track them down. A disturbing image now sat on his screen. Alex tried to conjure any benign explanation for what he was looking at, but his mind kept returning to the only logical conclusion . . . a chilling one.

Whoever wants to kill this PRH book . . . has killed a PRH author.

CHAPTER 24

In the darkness of the hidden alcove, Langdon studied the alphanumeric keypad on Gessner's private elevator, his mind already replaying their meeting with her last night.

Gessner was humorless and severe, with pale skin, taut lips, and her hair pulled back tightly like a flamenco dancer. Langdon had disliked the neuroscientist from the moment they met. She had joined them at the Four Seasons bar, CottoCrudo, after Katherine's lecture.

"Dr. Gessner!" Katherine said warmly, leaping to her feet as the woman approached the quiet booth Langdon had chosen in back. "Thank you for joining us and, of course, for inviting me to lecture here in your exquisite city."

The woman offered a perfunctory smile in return. "Big audience tonight," she said, her English slightly laced with a Czech accent. "You've made quite a name for yourself."

Katherine politely shrugged off the compliment and motioned to Langdon. "That's very kind. And I'm sure you know my colleague, Professor Robert Langdon?"

Langdon stood and extended his hand. "A pleasure."

Gessner ignored it, simply sliding into the booth with them. "I hope you haven't ordered drinks yet," she said. "I've asked them to bring over some local favorites." She turned to Langdon. "Professor, I've ordered *you* the 'Luce'—CottoCrudo's signature concoction of Canadian whiskey, cherry bitters, maple syrup, and bacon."

Bacon? Langdon would have much preferred his usual Vesper martini with Nolet's Reserve gin.

"And for *you*, Katherine," Gessner said, "I ordered *Staroplzenecký*—a local Bohemian absinthe. We joke that if you can still pronounce its name, you need to drink another."

A power play disguised as hospitality, Langdon suspected. There were few spirits stronger than Bohemian absinthe, and Katherine was a lightweight when it came to alcohol.

"Generous of you," Katherine said graciously. "I have so enjoyed being here and speaking in your magical city. It's been quite an honor." Langdon admired her poise, along with her elegant profile, softly framed by cascades of long dark hair.

Gessner shrugged. "Your talk was entertaining, but I found your subject matter, how shall I say it . . . predictably *metaphysical*."

"Oh," Katherine said. "I'm sorry to hear that."

"I mean no disrespect to noetics, but legitimate scientists like myself give no credence to ethereal notions like the soul, spiritual visions, or cosmic consciousness. We believe that all human experience—from religious ecstasies to debilitating fears—stem from nothing more than brain chemistry. Cause-and-effect physics. The rest is . . . delusion."

Did she just call herself legitimate and Katherine delusional? Langdon bristled, but Katherine smiled and gave his leg a playful squeeze under the table.

"I find it curious," Gessner continued, "that after your doctorate in *neurochemistry*—the most materialist of specialties—you drifted away into the oblivion of noetics."

"You mean California?" Katherine quipped. "I guess it made me want to see the bigger picture."

"I'm sorry," Langdon interjected, unable to contain himself. "But with such a low opinion of noetic science, why did you invite Dr. Solomon to speak?"

Gessner seemed amused by the question. "Two reasons, really. First, our original speaker—Dr. Ava Easton from the European Brain Council—had to cancel. We needed another female to fill her spot, and I figured someone like Katherine would jump at the chance. And second, I read an interview in which Katherine generously confessed that one of my articles had helped inspire part of her upcoming book."

"True," Katherine said. "I wondered if you saw that."

"I did see it, Katherine," Gessner said, her patronizing tone more suited to addressing a child. "Although you didn't mention *which* of my articles inspired you?"

"'The Brain Chemistry of Epilepsy,'" Katherine replied. "*European Journal of Neuroscience.*"

"A bit outside the purview of a noeticist, no? I do hope you're not twisting my research to fit your own conclusions."

"Not at all," Katherine said.

Langdon marveled at Katherine's politeness. *More than I could muster for this woman.*

"Nonetheless," Gessner replied, "as a professional courtesy, I'd appreciate a chance to read that section in advance. You must have a copy of your manuscript with you."

"Actually, I do not," Katherine said truthfully.

Gessner looked skeptical. "Well then, perhaps you could get one for me. If I like it, I'd consider offering you a celebrity endorsement, which could be quite helpful for your credibility with this first book."

"That's very kind of you," Katherine replied, exhibiting saintly patience. "I'll ask my editor about that."

Gessner looked annoyed at being rebuffed. "As you wish, but at least let me invite you to my private lab tomorrow to show you some of my work. I think you'll find it eye-opening. I'd love the chance to enlighten you."

Langdon shifted restlessly, but Katherine took his hand under the table and squeezed it with surprising strength, holding him at bay as she accepted Gessner's invitation.

After twenty minutes, Gessner was still talking . . . about what, Langdon had lost track. After half of his vile maple-and-bacon cocktail, his mouth tasted like breakfast. If Gessner's monologue went much longer, he was definitely going to need another round.

Perhaps a fried-egg martini?

Katherine had only partially finished her absinthe but was

already starting to show the effects, slurring her words slightly and struggling to keep her eyes open.

"Considering the innovative nature of my research," Gessner said offhandedly, "you'll obviously need to sign a nondisclosure before you come to the lab tomorrow."

To Langdon, this seemed an obscenely self-important requirement among colleagues.

"In fact, I have one with me now," Gessner said, pulling out a small leather briefcase and starting to unlock it. "We can get it out of the way before tomorrow's—"

"Actually," Langdon interrupted, "I wonder if Katherine's in any state to read a legal document. Perhaps tomorrow when she arrives at your lab?"

Clearly displeased, Gessner stared at him over her briefcase, as if weighing Langdon's resolve. Finally, she said, "Okay, that works too."

As Gessner fell back into conversation with Katherine, Langdon found himself wondering why a neuroscientist who thought so little of Katherine's work would be so eager to show off her private lab. Whatever Gessner's motives might have been, tomorrow morning Langdon planned to suggest that Katherine gracefully opt out of the tour.

"It's nothing personal, Katherine!" Gessner exclaimed loudly, breaking Langdon's train of thought. "You know I've never been shy about my distaste for the paranormal and PSI science. Remember my *Scientific American* cover?"

"I do," Katherine said, smiling. "Dr. Brigita Gessner, don't call her a neuro-PSI-entist."

"Yes," she said, laughing too loudly again. "Everyone got in on that joke. A fan sent me a mouse pad with my quote: 'There's no PSI in science.' And a colleague even joked that I should change all my passwords to P-S-I because it was the *last* thing anyone would ever guess I would choose!"

"That *is* funny," Katherine said, sipping her absinthe.

"What was even funnier was that years later, when I had to choose a security password for my new lab, I remembered his advice . . . and I chose PSI as my passcode!"

Langdon raised an eyebrow, questioning which was less probable—that Gessner had used a three-letter passcode to protect her lab or that she would tell them what it was.

"Not literally P-S-I, of course," she added, laughing. "I encrypted it. Quite cleverly, if I do say so myself."

Which you just did.

"Professor," she said, glancing over. "I believe you're a puzzle buff, no? You'd be impressed with my encryption."

"No doubt," he managed, barely listening.

Gessner preened. "I describe my ingenious little code as 'an Arabic tribute to an ancient Greek with a little Latin twist.'" She plucked the lemon rind from the rim of her glass and let it fall dramatically into her drink. *Mic drop.*

Langdon had no idea what she was talking about. "Sounds very clever."

"Robert could decipher it," Katherine blurted, the absinthe's effects on full display now. "He's an expert with codes."

"I'll take that bet," Gessner said with a smirk. "I calculate the professor's chances of guessing are just under one in three and a half trillion."

Langdon didn't miss a beat. "Sounds like a seven-character alphanumeric."

Gessner recoiled, wide-eyed, startled to have been so quickly outflanked.

Katherine let out a liquor-laced laugh. "I told you, he's very good at codes!"

"And exponentials, apparently," Gessner said, clearly unsettled. "Okay, Professor, no more hints for you."

"And on that note," Langdon said, standing brusquely, "I think it's a good time to call it a night."

"Ah, Father says the party's over," Gessner said, getting to her feet, leaving most of her vodka tonic behind. "Katherine, I'll see you in the morning. Eight a.m. sharp at Crucifix Bastion."

We'll see, Langdon thought.

As Katherine stood, she drained the remainder of her absinthe in a single swallow. Langdon calculated he now had approximately three minutes to get her upstairs before the concoction fully hit her.

They said their goodbyes, and as Langdon helped Katherine down the hall in the direction of their suite, he chided himself for tolerating Gessner for so long tonight. He had met plenty of self-important academics, but Brigita Gessner took arrogance to an entirely new level.

An Arabic tribute to an ancient Greek with a Latin twist? Seriously?

Langdon wished he'd been able to decipher Gessner's "ingenious passcode" on the spot, if only to blunt her unbearable self-importance. But the moment had passed. *Forget it,* he urged. *Who cares?*

When they entered their suite, Katherine disappeared into the bathroom to get ready for bed. Langdon paced the living room, knowing he was too wound up to go to sleep. As much as he wanted to forget his encounter with Gessner, his irritation over her smug superiority had awoken his competitive spirit. His analytical mind was already churning, looking for a way to unpack Gessner's riddle.

Isolate each piece, he thought. *An Arabic tribute . . .*

Langdon knew there were no Arabic letters in an alphanumeric alphabet, so he was fairly certain Gessner was referring to the *other* Arabic alphabet—numbers—the mathematical language popularized by the Arabs over a thousand years ago.

Gessner's passcode must be a number.

"An Arabic tribute . . ." he puzzled aloud, "to an ancient Greek."

Logically, if Gessner's passcode was a number, then her "tribute" would be *numerical,* so it therefore followed that the ancient Greek in question was probably associated with mathematics.

The three most famous mathematicians of ancient times were all Greeks.

Their names had been emblazoned in Langdon's brain after his prep school math teacher Mr. Brown informed the class that their school's ubiquitous acronym, "PEA," was not an abbreviation for Phillips Exeter Academy as everyone believed, but rather a secret tribute to the three titans of early mathematics—Pythagoras, Euclid, Archimedes.

So, which one might Gessner be referencing? Langdon worked his way through the list.

PYTHAGORAS: Pythagorean theorem, theory of proportions, sphericity of the earth.

EUCLID: Father of geometry, conic sections, number theory.

ARCHIMEDES: Archimedean spirals, the number pi, areas of circles.

Langdon paused.

"Pi," he declared loudly.

Katherine called from the other room. "That's a great idea! Call room service. I'll have a piece too!"

Different pie, he thought, chuckling as he went into the bedroom and helped Katherine woozily into bed. After kissing her good night, he stepped back into the living room, extracted a piece of paper and a pen from the rolltop desk, and sat down on the couch, overtaken now by a compulsive desire to finish what he had started.

The solution to Gessner's puzzle was far from clear, but Langdon had just realized that the spelling of pi—arguably the most famous number in history—was intriguingly close to that of PSI.

Gessner said her passcode was PSI . . . encrypted.

Langdon sensed he was on the right track.

3.14159, he thought, jotting down pi's most common form.

The number pi could certainly be described as a tribute to an ancient Greek, and it also was expressed in Arabic numerals, which meant it satisfied two of Gessner's three requirements.

An Arabic tribute to an ancient Greek.

Unfortunately, the decimal point in 3.14159 was problematic. First, there were no decimal points in a pure alphanumeric passcode. And second, the decimal point was not an Arabic creation; it was invented by a Scottish mathematician, John Napier.

You can solve both problems simply by deleting the decimal point.

There was only one problem: the number 314159 represented pi . . . not PSI.

And it's still missing the "little Latin twist."

Ten minutes later, Langdon had made no further progress,
and he decided he too should probably call it a night. *Gessner's
passcode can wait . . . or better yet, be forgotten.*

Langdon climbed into bed beside Katherine, where he slept
soundly for several hours . . . until she woke up screaming from
her nightmare.

A lifetime ago, Langdon thought, now standing in the darkened elevator alcove, staring at the numeric keypad and wishing
he'd solved Gessner's annoying little riddle.

On the other side of the wall, Pavel cursed loudly, and Langdon heard him dash out of the atrium, probably to go find
Janáček. Langdon knew this moment might be an opportunity
to slip out of the bastion unseen . . . but to where?

I'm not leaving without Katherine, he thought, increasingly
fearful that something might have happened to her. *I need to get
downstairs.*

He looked back at the keypad, wondering if he might have
a better chance of deciphering the final piece of Gessner's passcode now that an evening had passed. After all, there was a reason we "slept on" our problems; the subconscious mind could
make remarkable connections while we slept.

Langdon had gone to bed last night thinking the number
314159 was an accurate representation of "an Arabic tribute to
an ancient Greek."

Still, it was not quite right.

I'm missing the Latin twist.

Langdon knew the majority of languages in the world—
including English—used the lettering system known as the
Roman or *Latin* alphabet. As he surveyed the numbers and letters on the buttons of the keypad, he realized he had become so
focused on *numbers* that he'd forgotten he could also use *letters.*

Is the "Latin twist" a letter?

As he considered it, the simplest of shapes materialized in his
mind—the twisting curve of the letter *S.*

My God, he realized. *A literal "Latin twist"!*

In that moment, he flashed on Gessner smugly dropping her lemon twist into the center of her drink, and he couldn't help but be a little impressed.

"S" is the missing piece of the puzzle.

The rest was simple.

PI becomes PSI!

Gessner's code was a mixture of Arabic and Latin symbols—numbers and letters—and if Langdon was not mistaken, the solution had to be *314S159!*

He rechecked the logic against what Gessner had said. "An Arabic tribute to an ancient Greek with a Latin twist."

The number 314159 is a purely Arabic tribute . . . to the Greek number pi . . . and the "S" in the middle is a Latin twist that turns PI . . . into PSI . . . which Gessner said was her passcode.

If there had ever been a moment to shout Archimedes's exclamation "Eureka!" this was it, but instead Langdon moved silently to the keypad.

Holding his breath, he carefully entered seven characters into the digital screen.

3 1 4 S 1 5 9

After double-checking the sequence, he exhaled and pressed Enter.

Nothing happened.

An immediate rush of despair washed over him, but a moment later Langdon heard a click and a faint mechanical whir behind the door. The sound grew louder . . . an elevator ascending.

Eureka . . . he thought, permitting himself a relieved smile. *One in 3.5 trillion.*

The elevator door slid open to reveal an oversized, wood-paneled cabin. Ignoring his claustrophobia, Langdon stepped inside and searched the walls for the button that would take him down to the lab.

But this elevator had no buttons or controls of any kind.

Instead, the doors closed automatically, and Langdon felt himself descending.

CHAPTER 25

Images of Katherine Solomon played in The Golĕm's mind as his taxi climbed the ridge toward Crucifix Bastion. He could still see her onstage at Prague Castle . . . delivering her remarkable lecture. The Golĕm had attended, sitting quietly in back, dressed unremarkably, as he was now.

The Golĕm felt drawn to Katherine's ideas, sensing at times that she had been speaking directly to him. *I am living proof, Katherine, that you are correct.* For over an hour, Katherine had held the crowd in Vladislav Hall in rapt attention, alive with the thrill of new possibility . . . a fresh outlook on the workings of human consciousness.

One moment, in particular, had spoken to him.

"There exists an extraordinary phenomenon," Katherine had said, "that proves beyond any shadow of a doubt that our traditional views of consciousness are entirely wrong. It's called sudden savant syndrome, and the clinical definition is as follows: 'The abrupt manifestation in a human mind of a unique skill or knowledge that previously was nonexistent.'" She smiled. "In other words, you get conked on the head and you wake up a virtuoso violinist, or fluent in Portuguese, or a genius at math—where you previously possessed none of these skills."

Katherine quickly ran through a series of slides and video clips of individuals who had experienced sudden savant syndrome.

REUBEN NSEMOH—a sixteen-year-old American who was kicked in the head during a soccer game, fell into a coma, and woke up speaking perfect Spanish.

DEREK AMATO—a middle-aged man who dove into a pool, hit his head, and woke up a musical genius and virtuoso pianist.

ORLANDO L. SERRELL—a ten-year-old boy struck by a baseball who found he suddenly had the ability to do astonishingly complicated calendrical calculations.

"The obvious question," Katherine said, "is, *how is this possible?* How could a kick to the head magically impart into a brain the entirety of the Spanish language? Or a lifetime's practice on the violin? Or the ability to pinpoint precise dates that are centuries in the past or future? The answer is—in our current model of the brain—all of these events are, quite literally, *impossible."*

She motioned to a young man eyeing his phone. "Sir, imagine you hurled that phone against the wall, and when you picked it up, your photo gallery contained brand-new photos . . . of places you'd never been."

"Impossible," the man agreed.

The Golĕm understood, of course, how this could happen. He understood why cosmic signals got crossed. And clearly so did Katherine Solomon.

"Then, of course, there's the astonishing tale of Michael Thomas Boatwright."

Katherine went on to tell the story of a U.S. Navy vet who was found unconscious in a hotel room and awoke speaking fluent Swedish; he had no recollection of his own life, instead recalling his life as a Swede named Johan Ek.

Driving her point home, she relayed the well-known story of James Leininger—a two-year-old boy haunted by nightmares of being trapped in the cockpit of a burning fighter jet. In his waking hours, young James drew pictures of a burning jet and talked through complicated preflight routines, using technical vocabulary that his parents, and most certainly the young child, had never heard. When his frightened parents asked him *where* he got this information, the boy declared his name was not James Leininger but rather James *Huston,* and he was a fighter pilot who flew off "a Natoma" with his friend Jack. To the parents' astonishment, a search of World War II records revealed a fighter pilot named James Huston had flown off the *Natoma Bay* aircraft carrier with fellow pilot Jack Larsen. Huston had crashed and died, trapped in his burning cockpit. The story only got stranger from there, and it was now the subject of numerous documentaries as well as endless online speculation.

"These phenomena are inexplicable, but they are *real*," she continued. "They are true anomalies . . . and they so fundamentally undermine the current model of consciousness that we now find ourselves at a crossroads of human understanding, a juncture where an ever-widening circle of brilliant minds— neuroscientists, physicists, biologists, and philosophers—are seeing no choice but to accept the same shocking truth . . . quite simply, that our established scientific views of how the human mind works are no longer adequate. It's time for a new model. It's time to admit we don't know the answer to a very simple question: Where do our thoughts, talents, and ideas come from? And that, my friends, is the topic of tonight's talk."

The Golěm's taxi rounded the final corner toward Crucifix Bastion, and the lab came into sight in the distance. But when he saw what was before him, he immediately pounded on the Plexiglas divider. "*Zastavte! Zastavte!*"

The driver lurched to an abrupt stop.

The Golěm thought he would be alone here, but to his surprise, an ÚZSI sedan was parked in front of the building. *Nobody should be here at this hour!*

He sent the taxi away and approached the bastion slowly on foot, moving discreetly through the woods that surrounded the facility. As he drew closer, he saw that the entry door to the building was shattered. The foyer was gaping open, its floor scattered with glass.

Did ÚZSI break into Gessner's lab?

If so, The Golěm suddenly feared he might have difficulty retrieving what he had come for. *Without it, I won't be able to gain access to Threshold.*

The Golěm saw nobody moving inside the shattered foyer, but he did notice movement at the far end of the courtyard.

Seventy-five yards away, a lanky man in a suit gazed out over the low enclosure wall and spoke on the phone.

An ÚZSI officer?

One of Gessner's contacts?

Either way, his presence here was a problem . . . and needed to be rectified.

CHAPTER 26

At the far end of Crucifix Bastion's courtyard, Captain Janáček ended his phone calls and peered over the low stone enclosure wall into the deep ravine below. Strangely, in this moment, he felt totally alive. Whether it was his perilous downward view or the morning's events that he found so thrilling didn't really matter.

It has been a good day.

His years in law enforcement had been increasingly frustrating as Prague became overrun with tourists. Everyone demanded a safe city, and Janáček did what he could do, but he was constantly being reprimanded—either for lack of results or for being too aggressive.

Choose one or the other, Janáček argued. *Iron rule. Or chaos.*

He had been passed over numerous times for the chief position at ÚZSI after his handling of a group of carousing American college students a few years back. When confronted by Janáček, the kids had pushed back—drunk, entitled, and belligerent. Disgusted, Janáček threw them in prison for the night, determined to teach them a lesson.

As misfortune would have it, one of the boys was the son of a U.S. senator, who immediately placed a livid call to the U.S. embassy. The boys were released on the spot, and a lawsuit was promptly filed against Janáček for "excessive force" and "emotional damage."

Janáček had never recovered professionally.

Today I'm showing the Americans who is in control.

The demolition team had just confirmed their imminent

arrival, and Janáček had arranged a press conference for an hour from now. He could already envision the photos of himself escorting a prominent Harvard professor and a top American scientist out of Crucifix Bastion—both in handcuffs.

These two Americans put lives at risk today, he would announce austerely. *All in the name of seeking publicity for a book.*

Admittedly, Janáček's allegations were not *entirely* honest, but he was confident his lie would remain hidden. His nephew Pavel had helped cover Janáček's tracks. ÚZSI was a brotherhood, and it was understood that in law enforcement, sometimes one had to bend the rules in order to enforce them, especially in the face of the U.S. embassy's appalling influence in this country.

As Janáček relished his impending vindication, his phone began to ring.

When he saw the caller ID, he gave a self-assured smile.

Speak of the devil. Janáček had clashed with this woman on numerous occasions and had always lost their battles. *Not today.*

"Madam Ambassador," Janáček answered. "It's always an honor." He made no effort to hide his sarcasm from the American diplomat.

"Captain Janáček," the ambassador said. "Are you at Crucifix Bastion?"

"I am indeed," Janáček said arrogantly. "I am waiting for a demolition team and plan to take at least one American into custody."

"Attaché Harris is here with me," the ambassador said, her voice forceful, "and he is convinced that there is no way Katherine Solomon or Robert Langdon had anything to do with planting a bomb."

"Then why is Ms. Solomon resisting arrest?"

"Captain Janáček, I will say this only once. There are intricacies to this situation of which you're not aware—"

"Fuck your American intricacies, Madam Ambassador! What I *am* aware of is that *you* have no jurisdiction at Crucifix Bastion, and there is nothing you can do to stop me from enter—"

"*A DOST!*" the ambassador exploded, her outburst in Czech startling Janáček.

Having silenced him, the ambassador continued in a fierce whisper.

She spoke six words . . . and six words only.

Janáček felt like he'd been hit by a truck.

In that instant, everything changed.

CHAPTER 27

As the elevator slowed to a stop on the lower level, Langdon's pulse was already racing, partly on account of the claustrophobic cabin but mostly over his deepening concern for locating Katherine.

She's got to be here somewhere . . .

When the door opened, Langdon found himself in a long corridor whose rough-hewn stone walls looked like those of an eight-hundred-year-old fortress, which in fact they were. In stark contrast, the hallway floor was an elegant herringbone inlay of stained hardwood, extending away from the elevator, illuminated by evenly spaced, tastefully dimmed, recessed lighting.

"Katherine?" Langdon said softly, stepping out of the cramped elevator, his eyes adjusting to the soft lighting.

As the door closed behind him, he peered down the corridor and saw five elegant wooden doorways, spaced out along the right-hand wall of the hallway, each framed in an arched, stone doorjamb. This lab looked less like a neuroscience facility than it did a lavish boutique hotel.

"Dr. Gessner?!" he called, sensing there was no way Lieutenant Pavel could hear him upstairs now.

The first door Langdon reached opened into a large, elegant office suite with stone walls, lush carpeting, and high cabinets. On the desk sat two computers, a landline, and mounds of paperwork. Apparently, this was where Gessner did her real work.

"Hello?" he called, peeking into an adjoining office—a smaller space whose desk was decorated with photos and a fake plant, along with a magenta water bottle on which were penned the words *Пей воду!* Langdon had no idea what it meant, but he recognized the Cyrillic alphabet and recalled Gessner saying her lab assistant was Russian.

Stepping out of the assistant's office, Langdon moved down the hall to the next door, which bore a symbol Langdon did not immediately recognize.

For a moment, he thought it was a modified circumpunct— the ancient symbol of a circle with a center dot. It also looked vaguely like the logo of the Philadelphia Flyers hockey team. A moment later, though, he realized it was actually a modern pictogram depicting a supine person slid into a large tube.

Imaging lab, Langdon realized, rapping loudly on the door.

Silence.

"Katherine? Are you here?" he called softly.

He pushed and the door opened. The room lights snapped on automatically, revealing an elaborate control station that overlooked two massive imaging machines—a CAT scan and an MRI—both unattended.

Langdon backed out of the room and continued down the hall to a third door. The sign here gave him sudden hope.

VIRTUAL REALITY

Gessner had mentioned her work with VR, and Langdon now wondered if maybe the two women were inside, engrossed in some kind of full-sensory VR session, and had not heard the intercom.

Langdon's lone experience with VR had been intensely unsettling. A student had persuaded him to try a rock-climbing simulation called *The Climb*, and when Langdon pulled on the VR headset, he immediately found himself perched precariously on a thin ledge, thousands of feet in the air. Despite knowing he was standing safely on flat ground, Langdon was paralyzed with fear, his center of gravity was severely disoriented, and he was unable to take a single step. Incredibly, the *virtual* reality had been more persuasive than the *actual* reality his brain knew to be true.

Never again, he thought, knocking loudly on the VR room door as he pushed it open.

"Katherine?" he called as he entered. "Dr. Gessner?"

The space beyond was a small, carpeted chamber with stone walls and one freestanding recliner in the middle. It looked like a single-seat home theater with no screen. On the back of the chair hung some bulky head-mounted goggles with cables running to it.

This place is eerie, Langdon thought. *And Katherine isn't here.*

He quickly left the VR room and walked several more steps down the hallway, passing a restroom equipped with an emergency eyewash and a cubicle shower. Empty.

Continuing on, Langdon arrived at what he now realized was the lab's final door. The sign read:

TECHVELOPMENT

This trendy new term, pervasive among youthful tech start-ups, was one Langdon knew only because Jonas Faukman had once derided it as a "gratuitous amalgamation," arguing that young people who lacked the energy to spell "technological development" should not be given millions of dollars to develop anything at all.

Langdon knocked lightly and pushed open the door.

Last chance, he thought, willing Katherine to be on the other side.

As the door swung inward, Langdon found himself momentarily blinded. The room was glaringly bright . . . and noisy. Harsh fluorescent lights buzzed above a white tile floor, industrial fans roared, and an incessant beeping cut the air like some kind of warning alarm. Langdon was immediately on edge.

"Hello?" he shouted over the noise. "Katherine?!"

Stepping inside, he saw a maze of assorted worktables strewn with electronic gear, tools, parts, and blueprints, all giving Langdon the sense he had entered the lair of some mad scientist. Beyond the cluttered counters, at the back of the room, stood a cumbersome rack of gear that looked like an awkward hybrid of an archaic mainframe computer and an industrial generator. Cooling fans whirred from the device along with a loud and relentless beeping.

"Is *anyone* here?" he yelled into the frenzy.

Langdon made his way toward the machine, noticing the heavy braids of tubing and wires emerging from its side and winding across the floor to a secondary device—a slender, low-slung container made of clear plastic or glass. Beneath its transparent cover, the interior radiated a soft glow.

What in the world is this?

The size and shape made Langdon think of a sleeping pod.

Or a coffin, he realized, suddenly unnerved.

As he neared the pod, he could see its transparent shell was heavily fogged with condensation from whatever was happening inside. The beeping continued. He carefully approached, arriving over the pod, and peered down through the glass lid.

Langdon instantly recoiled in horror.

Lying motionless inside the pod, shrouded in thick swirling mist, was the hazy outline of a human form.

My God . . . Katherine?!

CHAPTER 28

On the second floor of the U.S. embassy, Michael Harris felt off-balance as he stepped out of his private conversation with the ambassador. Having just been partially "read in," Harris was still trying to process the full implications of the classified information the ambassador had now shared with him.

She had not shared everything, he sensed, but one thing was crystal clear: *Today is about much more than a bomb scare at the Four Seasons.*

Harris gathered himself and quickly headed back downstairs to Dana's office, wishing he had talked to the ambassador before involving Dana. He found her at her computer, engrossed in multiple video feeds of Charles Bridge. *Shit.*

Dana glanced up as he entered. "I located your woman with the spiked tiara, Michael. She's very cute. You never told—"

"Turn it off, Dana," he said, rushing over to her. "I made a mistake."

"But you asked—"

"I know. I'm sorry. Turn it off, please. *Now.*"

Dana eyed him warily and stood up. As a six-foot-tall former runway model, she was one of the few women who could look Michael Harris in the eye. Before she could say a word, however, Harris crouched down near the floor.

"Seriously?" she said. "Begging me on bended knee?"

Not exactly. Harris reached under her desk and pulled a plug, cutting power to her computer.

Dana saw her display go black. "What the hell are you doing?!"

"I need you to trust me," he said, standing again.

"You have a lot of secrets lately."

You have no idea, he thought. "Look . . . I'm just asking you to go back to work and forget I ever asked you about any of this."

Dana's glare was unflinching, and Harris sensed she had no intention of letting this go. Digging deep, he mustered a playful smile and lowered his voice to a whisper. "The walls here have ears. How about I tell you everything over dinner tonight?"

Dana's eyes brightened, her full lips pouting with promise. "Takeout? Your place?"

Harris winked. "Food optional."

She smiled. "I like the way you think, Mr. Harris."

Harris blew her a kiss and headed out.

Minutes later, he was in one of the embassy's black Audi A7s, zipping along Tržiště Street. He had expected to be going directly to Crucifix Bastion, but the ambassador had ordered him to do something for her first.

"Mr. Langdon will be safe a bit longer," the ambassador had told him. "Captain Janáček is well under control."

An understatement, Harris knew, having just witnessed the brutal phone call between the ambassador and the captain. *Janáček overplayed his hand . . . and lost.* He would be licking his wounds and behaving perfectly until Harris arrived.

Despite the alarming nature of everything Harris had learned from the ambassador, he felt a veil had been lifted, revealing much more about the puzzle pieces on the table and how they were connected . . . Harris's off-book work for the ambassador . . . Gessner's lab at Crucifix Bastion . . . the woman on Charles Bridge . . . and even the upcoming publication by Katherine Solomon.

———◆———

Dana Daněk was fuming.

You have no authority over my actions, Michael Harris.
You're my lover, not my boss.

The attaché's condescending sweet talk of dinner had infuriated Dana. Moreover, his strange behavior had only served to increase her intrigue about the mysterious woman on Charles Bridge.

Conveniently, the famed bridge was monitored by more security cameras per square foot than anywhere else in Prague—including a pair of 360-degree arrays atop the bridge's guard towers and thirteen eye-level cameras embedded in the gas lamps.

Choosing one of the aerial panoramas, Dana had rewound the feed to archived footage beginning at 6:40 a.m. To her surprise, the woman in a spiked halo was *already* there, lingering on the eastern end of the deserted bridge as if waiting for someone.

But waiting for whom?

Dana had called up an eye-level camera and zoomed in on the woman's face, displeased to see that the costumed woman was young and pretty, with deep dimples and big doe eyes. Her body looked petite and fit beneath her tight black coat.

Is that *why Michael is interested in you?*

It seemed inconceivable that Michael would ask Dana to research a romantic interest, and yet perhaps he was playing a cruel game with her. For weeks, her intuition had been telling her that Michael was with someone else.

A woman always knows . . .

Confident that Harris was now gone, Dana crawled under the desk, plugged in the computer, and rebooted the surveillance portal.

She navigated back to the pretty woman and had every intention of finding out *where* the woman had gone . . . but first there was a far more pressing question.

Who the hell are you?

One of the duties Dana performed for the ambassador was to confirm the identities and backgrounds of any visitors who showed up at the embassy requesting service or asylum. All she needed was a passport photo or a screen grab from the embassy's security gate cameras, and an entire world opened up. Nowadays, thanks to advanced facial recognition software, identifying any individual on the planet took only a matter of minutes.

Sorry, sweetheart, Dana thought, capturing several high-quality close-ups of the woman's face. *But you can't hide from me.*

She uploaded the photos into the embassy's international facial recognition database. If this woman had a criminal record anywhere in the world, she would be identified within thirty seconds. If not, her photo would be sent through a massive international database of photos collected from passports, driver's licenses, and major media.

And finally, if *that* didn't work, the photo would be run through the newest and most complete database in the world—the billions of unsuspecting selfies posted on Instagram, Facebook, LinkedIn, Snapchat, and other platforms.

Social media, Dana thought. *The biggest intelligence boon since the Catholic Church invented confession.*

CHAPTER 29

Langdon felt momentarily paralyzed as he stared into the pod at the human figure inside.

My God . . . Katherine.

He dropped to his knees and pounded on the glass, pressing his face to the surface, trying to see inside.

I have to get her out of there!

Beneath the lid, a motionless hand was pressed against the inside of the pod, its slender fingers pale and rigid, laced with frost. It looked as if her wrists were bound in place by heavy straps.

Langdon groped at the glass pod, trying to find a way to open it. He clutched the smooth surface, which was ice-cold, but he found no seam or handle or release button of any kind. The ear-splitting alarm continued to wail.

Open, goddammit!

Only inches from Langdon's face, the body's hazy outline appeared and disappeared within a cloud of the swirling fog.

Suddenly, there was a sound behind him—footsteps rapidly approaching on the hard tile floor. Langdon twisted to see a tall woman with shoulder-length blond hair. She was running toward him wielding a stainless-steel fire extinguisher, threatening to crash it down into his face.

"*Co to sakra děláš?!*" she screamed over the noise.

Langdon held his hands up in defense. "Wait!"

"How did you get in here!" the woman demanded in a thick Russian accent as she raised the heavy metal extinguisher over his head.

"Please we need to open—"

"How did you get in here?!"

"The elevator passcode!" Langdon exclaimed. "Dr. Gessner gave it to me! My friend Katherine Solomon and I—"

The woman immediately lowered the fire extinguisher, looking genuinely startled. "Professor Langdon? I'm so sorry . . . I'm Sasha Vesna, Brigita's lab assistant—"

"Katherine is inside this!" Langdon interrupted, pointing at the pod. "She needs help!"

Sasha suddenly seemed to register the beeping sound, and her expression turned from confusion to horror. She dropped the fire extinguisher with a loud clang and ran to the attached machine, where she yanked out a rackmount drawer, flipped open a laptop, and began typing feverishly.

"Oh no . . . No!"

Langdon had no idea what was happening, but the woman's panic only reinforced his own. "Just open the damn thing!"

"It's too dangerous!" Sasha shouted. "You have to reverse the process first."

What process? "Please just get her out!"

The assistant looked lost, glancing fearfully into the pod. "I don't understand—why would Dr. Solomon ever get in there?"

Langdon was half tempted to pick up the fire extinguisher and smash the pod open. *This can't be happening . . .*

Gessner's assistant tapped again at the keyboard, and the alarm noise finally halted. Moments later, the fans went quiet, and the tubes connecting the pod to the larger device began gurgling. Langdon didn't know what he expected to see coming through the clear tubes, but it most certainly was not the crimson liquid that began to flow toward the body.

"Is that . . . blood?!" Langdon asked, feeling suddenly ill. "What *is* this thing?"

"EPR!" Sasha said with panic in her voice, still typing as the liquid flowed back into the pod. "Emergency preservation and resuscitation machine. This is Brigita's prototype! It's not ready for use!"

As the cold mist swirled around the body, Langdon now

realized Gessner had actually mentioned her EPR machine last night. This lifesaving technology had been first proposed hypothetically by a surgeon named Samuel Tisherman at University of Maryland School of Medicine, but Brigita Gessner had been the one who seized upon the rudimentary concept, designed a highly modified prototype, and now held the patent—a patent she boasted was worth a fortune.

"Prolonged hypoxia causes brain damage," Gessner had informed them, "but my EPR can *protect* the brain from oxygen deprivation by putting its cellular activity on pause—a kind of suspended animation. My machine is essentially a modified ECMO bypass—an extracorporeal membrane oxygenation unit that swaps blood for supercooled saline at a rate of two liters per minute. It rapidly cools the brain and body down to ten degrees Celsius, giving a surgical team *hours* to treat a critically injured patient who would normally be brain-dead within minutes."

Standing over Gessner's prototype EPR pod, Langdon was on the verge of being sick.

Suddenly, a muted pop echoed inside the pod, and blood began spattering all across the interior of the glass. Langdon jumped back. *She's bleeding!*

"Блядь," Sasha cursed, abandoning whatever she was doing on the laptop and dashing to an emergency panel on the rear wall. She broke a plastic seal and, without hesitation, pressed a bright red button beneath. The pod instantly hissed and released suction on the lid, which began to hinge open, swinging upward like a gull-wing door. As the fog cleared, Langdon leaned over the container.

My God . . .

When he saw her, Langdon knew she was gone. Her eyes were blank and lifeless, and her face was frozen in an expression of pure terror. Langdon had never imagined that seeing a dead body could bring such an overwhelming sense of both despair and relief—but that was exactly what he now felt.

The corpse lying before them was not Katherine Solomon.

It was Brigita Gessner.

CHAPTER 30

S asha Vesna let out a wail of anguish and collapsed to her knees beside the corpse in the pod. "Brigita! No!" She covered her face and began to sob uncontrollably.

All Langdon could do was watch, his heart aching for her. Clearly, this woman's grief at seeing Dr. Gessner was as overwhelming as Langdon's relief that it was not Katherine.

After several seconds of tormented tears, however, Sasha glanced up, and her face took on an expression of alarm. She began patting her pockets as if she'd lost something. As she did, she began hyperventilating. "No . . ." she whispered, her jaw tightening into a rigid grimace. "Please . . . not now!"

Langdon hurried to her. "What's happening?!"

Sasha tried to clamber to her feet and make a move toward the door, but as she did, she faltered, dropping back to her knees. She seemed to be about to suffer a seizure of some sort, and Langdon did his best to steady her.

"What can I do?!" he offered.

Sasha made a throaty groan and pointed to the handbag she had dropped onto the floor nearby.

Medication? he guessed, then leaped into action, running over to the purse and rummaging frantically through its contents as he carried it back to her.

Dr. Gessner had mentioned last night that her lab assistant suffered from TLE—temporal lobe epilepsy—although the statement seemed less one of compassion than a way for Gessner to brag about how many TLE patients she had cured. "Seizures are nothing but electrical storms in the brain," Gessner had explained. "I invented a way to interrupt those storms. It's essentially a perfect cure."

Perfect? Ms. Vesna did not seem very "cured" at the moment.

Maddeningly, Langdon found only keys, gloves, glasses, tissues, and assorted other items. No pill bottles, no syringes, no inhalers, nothing at all that looked helpful in this situation. "What do you need?!" he asked, arriving beside her with the purse.

But he could see it was too late. Sasha was now on her side, shaking violently, her eyes glazed over and her head knocking against the tile floor.

Too late for medicine, Langdon thought as he hurriedly dropped to the floor, bracing her head in his palms and holding it safely away from the hard tile. As a teacher, Langdon had been trained how to help in the event of a student's seizure.

First, do no harm. He knew better than to roll a person onto her stomach, as television paramedics often did to prevent a victim from "swallowing her own tongue"—a bizarre old wives' tale that was actually a physical impossibility. It was also advised never to shove a belt into the victim's mouth, as some believed was prudent. *That's how you suffocate someone—or get your finger bitten off.* The only FDA-approved mouth protection for seizures was called a PATI mouth guard, and Langdon didn't see one in Sasha's purse. *Just help her ride it out.*

"It's okay," Langdon whispered. "I've got you."

As Langdon cradled the woman's head in his palms, he could see that her nose had been previously broken and poorly set and that she had a crimson scar under her chin, almost certainly injuries from previous seizures. He saw the traces of other scars peeking out from beneath her thick blond hair, probably from other similar accidents.

Langdon felt an upwelling of sympathy for her.

Epileptic seizures took a brutal toll on one's *physical* body. About that there was no debate. Paradoxically, however, the effect on one's *mental* state was documented throughout history to be quite different. Precisely the opposite, in fact.

Katherine had mentioned epilepsy in her talk last night as one of the human mind's naturally occurring "altered states" of consciousness. Apparently, when viewed in an MRI machine, seizures displayed a stunning electrical signature that was similar to certain hallucinogens, near-death experiences, and even orgasm.

Remarkably, some of humankind's most creative minds had been epileptic—Vincent van Gogh, Agatha Christie, Socrates, and Fyodor Dostoyevsky. The Russian novelist had once proclaimed his epileptic seizures to be "a happiness and harmony unthinkable in the normal state." Others described their seizures as "opening a gateway to the divine" . . . "blissfully freeing the mind from the confines of its physical shell" . . . and "providing otherworldly bursts of profound creativity."

Epilepsy appeared with notable frequency in Christian artwork, which was not surprising considering so many scriptural accounts of mystical experiences—visions, ecstasies, divine encounters, transcendent revelations—all seemed to describe, with uncanny specificity and accuracy, the experience of an epileptic seizure, including Ezekiel, St. Paul, Joan of Arc, and St. Birgitta. Raphael Sanzio's famed *The Transfiguration* depicted an epileptic boy in the throes of a seizure, which he and others commonly used as a visual metaphor for Christ's ascent to heaven.

In Langdon's arms, Sasha finally stopped trembling. Her breathing slowed to a normal cadence. The whole event had lasted about a minute, and she was now completely limp, most likely unconscious. Langdon knew just to be patient . . . and allow her time to return.

As he gazed down at the unconscious Russian, he felt disoriented by the disturbing detour his morning had taken. Just hours ago, Langdon had been quietly swimming laps. Now he was sitting on the floor of a private lab with two women he had never met before yesterday—one unconscious in his arms, the other dead in an EPR pod.

And most troubling of all . . . there was no sign of Katherine.

◆—··—◆

Lieutenant Pavel stood anxiously in the bastion's shattered entryway, scanning the courtyard for any signs of his ÚZSI captain. He had seen Janáček only minutes ago on the edge of the ridge making a phone call. Now he was gone. Pavel had called him twice. No answer.

Janáček also disappeared?!

Fortunately, the mystery of *Langdon's* disappearance had now been solved. Moments earlier, Pavel had located a hidden elevator behind a sliding wall in the waiting area. The elevator required an authorization code, but that was easily remedied; someone downstairs must have been watching Langdon on the security cameras and come up in the elevator to retrieve him.

Langdon's disappearance confirmed that Solomon and Gessner were indeed downstairs and had disobeyed a direct order from ÚZSI Captain Janáček. Pavel wondered if the Americans had any idea how serious their trouble was about to become.

Pavel had been examining the hidden alcove when he heard a loud crash in the foyer. Immediately he knew it was the shattered doorframe that the captain had ingeniously leaned against the lab stairwell's entrance as a rudimentary alarm.

Solomon, Langdon, and Gessner are escaping the lab!

Pavel had pulled his weapon and sprinted out of the alcove, rounding the corner into the hallway. "*Stůj!*" he shouted as he went. "*Stop!*"

But there was nobody there.

The shattered doorway was indeed tipped over onto the floor, indicating the door had been opened, and yet, strangely, the foyer was empty.

Pavel bolted to the entrance and looked outside. The wide-open area was deserted. *Nobody can run that fast.* Standing in the snow, Pavel turned and looked back at the lab door, realizing that perhaps the sound he'd heard was not someone exiting the lab . . . but rather someone entering.

Whoever it had been, the person clearly had biometric access. *A lab employee?* Pavel felt a cold sweat on his brow thinking about how Janáček would take this news. Not only had Pavel lost Robert Langdon . . . he had allowed someone *else* to enter the lab.

Dumb move, Pavel. He told me to stay here and guard that lab door.

Chilled by the wind, Pavel stepped back into the entryway, pacing to stay warm, his military boots crunching on shards of glass. He was about to reach for his phone when he noticed something on the biometric panel next to the lab door.

That's odd, he thought, eyeing the tiny green indicator light.

The light on the panel had been *red* this morning when they arrived and found the door locked. He was sure of it. Now it was green. And *blinking.* Puzzled, Pavel walked over to the lab door, grabbed the handle, and pulled.

To his surprise, the door swung open easily, revealing a stairwell beyond. The door, it seemed, had not locked properly after the last person entered. Glancing downward, Pavel now saw the reason—a chunky shard of safety glass had become caught in the doorjamb.

I need to alert the captain immediately—we have access!

But as Pavel gazed down the empty stairwell, he was struck by an alternate idea. It was aggressive and perhaps a bit risky, but the notion excited him, especially knowing he had disappointed his captain recently on numerous occasions.

Pavel pictured the scene below.

A few unarmed academics . . .

He imagined Janáček's delight upon returning to discover the fugitives expertly lined up on the couch at gunpoint. Pavel ran a hand across the CZ 75 D handgun in his holster, the feel of its textured handle like the reassuring touch of an old friend.

I have specialized training for this precise task.

Robert Langdon had already shown himself to be gun-shy, and no doubt the others would be as well. In Pavel's experience, civilians facing an armed ÚZSI officer always did the exact same thing . . . precisely what the officer demanded.

◄—··—►

Somewhere far below the ridgeline, staring at the sky, Captain Janáček was fading in and out of consciousness. He had no idea how much time had passed since his body had become airborne, plummeting downward at a terrifying rate, before smashing against the rocks at the bottom of the ravine with sickening force.

Suicide would have been poetic considering the news he had just received from the ambassador. But Janáček had not taken his own life.

I was pushed.

Lying on the rocks, shattered and bleeding, Janáček could still feel the two spots on his back where powerful palms had shoved him hard and sent him tumbling over the low stone wall. The captain had no idea who had snuck up on him, but quite strangely, that fact seemed wholly irrelevant to him at the moment.

This is the end . . . I am dying.

To his surprise, however, the transition felt quite natural and calm.

There was very little physical discomfort. All the dire concerns that had consumed him only minutes earlier seemed to be evaporating . . . including his devastating call with the U.S. ambassador.

He could still hear the six words she had spoken to him.

We know there was no bomb.

Janáček's claim that ÚZSI had found a small bomb had indeed been a lie . . . an embellishment to help him take total control of the situation.

I did what I was ordered to do.

The peculiar call had come early this morning from London, waking Janáček from a sound sleep. The American man on the line apologized for the hour and told the captain to check his text messages. Janáček did, and he found a set of sobering credentials confirming this man moved in the highest echelons of power.

"I have a situation," the man said. "And I'd like your help."

Janáček wiped the sleep from his eyes, trying to focus. "Yes?"

"There are two prominent Americans in Prague right now. I need them arrested."

"You know I can't simply arrest foreigners without—"

"All the intelligence you require will be provided. Listen carefully."

As Janáček listened to what the two Americans were plotting, he felt a familiar outrage. *A publicity stunt? A bomb threat at the Four Seasons? Outrageous!* He was tired of foreigners treating his country like a lawless playground.

"I have to warn you," Janáček said, "the only charge I can use here is 'disturbing the peace.' If these Americans are wealthy or well-known, the U.S. embassy will instantly intercede."

"Forget the embassy," the man assured. "I'll take care of the ambassador. All you need to do is amplify the severity of their offense. I'll tell you how."

The man's idea had been a clever one—simple, clean—a minor embellishment that would enable Janáček to make an ironclad arrest and finally show the ambassador that "being American" did not elevate anyone above Czech law.

A white lie that serves justice is an honorable lie, Janáček believed. He had no interest in the handsome reward the man had offered for helping. *Outsmarting the embassy will be reward enough*, he thought, still bitter from past skirmishes. And so, precisely as the caller had suggested, Janáček had crossed the line and enhanced the truth . . . ever so slightly.

There was no bomb—just a bomb threat—but the simple tweak escalated the charges to a far more serious level.

Now, lying broken in the ravine, Janáček had seen his moment of glory evaporate like a mirage. Humiliated by the ambassador, who planned to contact Janáček's superior, he had canceled his press conference and called off the demolition team. His eagerness to make a high-profile arrest had turned him into an easy target . . . a willing pawn.

Maybe the American caller used me for his own purposes? The man's credentials checked out, as did the number from which he called.

None of it mattered anymore.

Sprawled on the rocks, Janáček felt warm blood flowing freely from the back of his head. He was aware of the life draining out of him. In an odd way, death almost seemed a kinder option than having to cower before the American embassy, especially the smug Michael Harris.

This is a blessing, Janáček decided, surprised by his complete lack of panic.

Strangely, the captain now felt as if he were moving farther away . . . from *himself.* He was pleasantly detached from his broken physical form, untroubled by pain or injury, as if he were rising and leaving the complications of the world behind him.

There was no fear . . . only a swell of serenity. It was unlike anything he had ever experienced in life.

CHAPTER 31

Dana Daněk was growing impatient with the lack of results from the facial recognition database to identify the woman on Charles Bridge. The process seemed to be taking an unusually long time.

While she waited, she had returned to the bird's-eye surveillance footage. She was now watching the woman with the tiara standing motionless at the eastern end of the bridge . . . as if waiting for something.

Suddenly, at 6:52 a.m., the woman received a call. She answered immediately, speaking only a matter of seconds before placing the phone back into her pocket. Then, to Dana's bewilderment, the woman produced a small bottle from her pocket and splashed the liquid contents all over the shoulders and arms of her black coat.

Perfume? Holy water?

She pocketed the bottle, adjusted her spiked tiara, and then reached inside the lining of her coat and pulled out a metal rod of some sort. It looked like a small silver spear.

Is she carrying a weapon?

Then she began drifting slowly, almost zombielike, across the deserted bridge. As she approached the halfway point, a tall man with dark hair entered the frame, striding eastward, moving toward her. He was wearing exercise sweats and running shoes. As he drew even, he abruptly stopped and turned, as if talking to her. The woman either ignored him or didn't hear. She just kept moving. The man seemed momentarily paralyzed. He called out to her again with no response, and then abruptly he wheeled and sprinted away in the direction he had originally been running . . . until he was out of the camera frame.

What just happened?

Dana rewound the playback and watched the whole sequence again. She was curious to know where the man was running, but for now she scrutinized the strange phantomlike woman. Dana engaged the software's "autotrack" mode, which used facial recognition, artificial intelligence, and projection algorithms to stay locked on a subject. As the video continued, the program switched from camera to camera, following the woman in the spiked tiara across the bridge.

She was just passing the statue of St. Augustine when she abruptly stopped. After glancing around as if to confirm she was alone, she removed her tiara and nonchalantly dropped it off the bridge into the waters below. The spear went over next. Then she pulled a white wool cap from her pocket and donned it, tucking her dark hair up inside it. Finally, she removed her black jacket, revealing a heavy red sweater beneath it. She folded the coat and set it like an offering at the base of the statue of St. Augustine, a common site at which to leave donations for the homeless or those in need.

Now transformed, the woman took an abrupt left turn, disappearing down a narrow staircase that clung to the outer wall of the bridge and connected to the west bank of the river. Whoever this chameleon was, she apparently did not want to be followed.

Dana fast-forwarded through the archived footage, following the woman at high speed across the cobblestone plaza outside Liechtenstein Palace . . . past Museum Kampa with its bizarre outdoor installation of three giant bronze babies with barcode stamps for faces . . . and finally deep into Kampa Park, where she wandered awhile before buying a coffee at a kiosk. While sitting on a bench and sipping the hot brew, she received a phone call.

When the call ended, she rushed back to the Charles Bridge, which was now dotted with pedestrians on their way to work. The woman hurried back the way she had come, exiting the bridge and turning left on Křižovnická Street. As she strode down the sidewalk, the playback slowed abruptly and began flashing "LIVE." The woman's speed-walking turned to a normal pace.

Real time. This is happening right now . . .

Dana had no authorization to use the sophisticated surveillance system in this way, but she couldn't take her eyes off this shape-shifter. She watched as the woman strode down the sidewalk and turned left across an elegant parking courtyard toward the main entrance of one of Prague's finest hotels.

She's going to the Four Seasons?

As the woman disappeared through the hotel's revolving door, something unexpected caught Dana's eye—an Audi A7 parked in the reserved spaces in front of the hotel. Dana would have thought nothing of it, except that the unique red lettering on the sedan's license plate indicated a diplomatic vehicle.

Is that one of our embassy cars?

A moment later, Dana had her answer when the elegant form of Michael Harris stepped out of the sedan and strode briskly into the hotel.

Dana stared in shock and her stomach turned.

You son of a bitch, Michael. I knew it!

———·—➤

The manager of the Four Seasons Hotel was still aglow from his recent personal call from the U.S. ambassador. After she thanked him for his discretion this morning regarding the unfortunate situation with Mr. Langdon, the ambassador had asked a favor of him.

A favor that just walked in, the manager thought, seeing the well-dressed gentleman now striding toward reception.

"Mr. Harris," the manager said, extending a hand. "The ambassador just called."

"Thank you," the man replied, his handshake like a vise.

"I saw you earlier with Mr. Langdon," the manager said. "And . . . ÚZSI." He grimaced. "I hope all that is being sorted out?"

"Absolutely. It was an unfortunate misunderstanding, and we're working through it. I'm here now, as you probably already know, because Mr. Langdon has asked the embassy to collect a few things from his suite while we sort this out. There's some medication, which I gather is import—"

"Of course, I already have the room key printed for you, sir. I'll just need to see some identification? I apologize for the formality, but this is just a bit unusual, and hotel policy—"

"No worries at all," the man said, handing over his embassy ID. "I appreciate your care. The embassy has learned to expect only the best from the Four Seasons."

Beaming, the manager handed back the ID. "Very kind of you. I trust you remember how to reach the Royal Suite? And when you're finished, you can just leave the room key in the suite and pull the door shut behind you."

The man from the embassy thanked him and headed upstairs.

The manager returned to his duties, too busy to notice the pretty woman in a red sweater following the man upstairs.

CHAPTER 32

Where am I? Sasha wondered.

She felt a familiar tingling rise up through her body, light and pleasant, like having champagne bubbles in her veins. When she emerged from an epileptic seizure, Sasha often felt like her brain was a computer rebooting, starting from scratch, loading software bit by bit.

Instinctively, she began her usual post-seizure ritual. "Post-ictal focus," as Dr. Gessner called the strategy, was a way of reconnecting with the present reality by forcing the mind to conjure the most recent memory it could recall.

This morning I was making tea, Sasha remembered, conjuring the smell of the hibiscus, the morning light sifting through her kitchen windows, and the soft mewing of her two Siamese cats as they rubbed against her calves, eager for breakfast. Slowly, as her brain gained traction, she tried to remember what she had done after feeding her cats, but those memories were blank, refusing to surface.

Interictal memory impairment, as it was known, was quite common among epileptics and presented as periods of blackout memory loss, sometimes spanning many hours, as if the brain had simply forgotten to record whatever was happening.

For some epileptics, memory impairment was more debilitating than seizures, but Sasha had chosen simply to accept it. At times she wondered if it might even be a blessing.

There are parts of my past I'd rather not recall.

When Sasha was growing up in Russia, other schoolchildren

mocked her seizures, giving her a lurid nickname—*вибратор*—which meant "vibrator." Her parents took her to specialists, but the answers were always the same. "There is no cure. Sasha will die *with* seizures . . . but not *of* them."

But I want to die, Sasha often thought.

The moments of tranquility she felt immediately following the seizures, while magical in some ways, were outweighed by the emotional pain and physical injuries these episodes brought to her life.

Doctors eventually diagnosed Sasha with chronic syncope and acute mental illness and suggested she be institutionalized. The best her parents could do was a *psikhushka*—a dilapidated government mental institution located in the middle of nowhere near Russia's western border. On her tenth birthday, her parents left her there and never visited again.

Sasha had cried for weeks in her tiny room. Her seizures occurred several times a day, and staff members would forcefully restrain her with no show of compassion. The meals they provided were meager, but the medications they provided were copious. By the time she was a teenager, Sasha lived a life of heavy sedation and loneliness.

For more than a decade, she lived this way, forgotten and alone. Her only lasting escapes from reality were the American movies that played nonstop in the common room across the hall. Romantic comedies were her favorite, and Sasha often dreamed of falling in love in New York City. *One day I will see America*, she promised herself, sensing sometimes that her dream of going to America was the only thing keeping her going.

And then even that dream was shattered.

Sasha was assigned a new nighttime attendant—a pitiless nurse named Malvina—who amused herself in the desolate hours by withholding Sasha's seizure medications and then watching her spasmodic episodes like a circus sideshow before beating her. For weeks, Malvina abused Sasha physically, mentally, and perhaps in other ways that Sasha's mind blocked.

One morning, after barely surviving one of Malvina's more

brutal and traumatic attacks, Sasha was crying in bed when three staff members burst in and dragged her down the hall to the common room.

"*Priznavaysya!*" they shouted at her. *Confess!*

At Sasha's feet, on the floor of the common room, lay Malvina's lifeless body, her head twisted almost entirely backward.

It wasn't me, Sasha insisted, but the staff had already determined she was guilty. Not wanting to lose any government sponsorship money, they reported Malvina's death as an unfortunate accident on a slippery floor and locked Sasha in solitary confinement as punishment.

Alone in the darkness, Sasha often wondered who might have killed the nurse. There were other patients here who suffered seizures, and it was possible Malvina had taunted the wrong person. *Or maybe,* Sasha fantasized, *someone killed Malvina to protect me.* The idea made her feel less alone somehow.

After two weeks in solitary, Sasha was dragged out, put into a straitjacket, and informed she had a visitor. Sasha had never had a visitor, not even her parents. *They left me here to die.*

The person in the waiting area was a stranger—a small woman with jet-black hair, expensive clothing, and a stern face. She had an air of authority. The woman immediately reprimanded the orderlies, demanding they remove Sasha's straitjacket, which, to her amazement, they did.

"*Zvířata,*" she muttered, shooing them away. *Animals.*

Sasha squinted her eyes, having not seen daylight for weeks. "*Кто ты?*" she asked in Russian. *Who are you?*

"Can you speak Czech?" the woman asked.

Sasha shook her head.

"Any English?"

"Some," Sasha said. "I watch American television."

"Me too," the woman whispered, almost conspiratorially. "Isn't it wonderful?"

Sasha simply stared.

"My name is Dr. Brigita Gessner," the woman said. "I'm here to help you. I'm a neurosurgeon from Europe."

"Doctors can't help me," Sasha said quickly.

"I'm sorry for that. It's only because they don't understand your condition."

"I have insanity and seizures."

The woman emphatically shook her head. "No, Sasha, you are perfectly sane. You have a condition known as TLE—temporal lobe epilepsy—which is the cause of your seizures. It's entirely curable. I have a facility in Prague, and I'd like to take you there."

"To fix me?" she said, skeptical.

"You're not broken, my dear. Your brain just has occasional electrical storms. But I can help you control those. I've treated many TLE patients just like you, with superb results—including a young man named Dmitri from this very institution."

Dmitri? Sasha was familiar with the tall, striking man, but she had not seen him in a while. *I wondered where he went!* "You cured Dmitri?"

"I did indeed. And he has already returned home in Russia."

Sasha wanted desperately to believe what Dr. Gessner was saying, but it all seemed far too good to be true. "I don't . . . have any money."

"The treatment is free, Sasha," the woman said. "And quite simple."

The doctor quickly explained a procedure that involved implanting a small chip in Sasha's skull. If Sasha felt a seizure coming on, she could activate the chip by rubbing a small magnetic wand on her head, which caused the chip to generate electric pulses that interrupted the onset of the seizure . . . halting the episode before it even began.

"Is that . . . really possible?" Sasha said, on the verge of tears.

"It is! It's called a responsive neurostimulation chip. I invented it."

"But why . . . would you help *me*?!"

Dr. Gessner reached across the table and took her hand. "Sasha, I've been very fortunate in my life. The truth is that helping *you* is beneficial to *me* as well. It makes me feel good to help people who need it. If I can save someone's life, why wouldn't I do it?"

Sasha wanted to jump up and embrace this woman, but she was afraid to believe her. In her lifetime, she had rarely received the gift of kindness. "But . . . what if they won't let me out of here?!"

"Oh, they'd *better*," Gessner said sharply. "I paid them a small fortune to release you."

Four days later, Sasha awoke in a hospital bed in Prague, groggy from anesthesia and pain medication, but very much alive. When Gessner told her the procedure had been a success, Sasha's emotions surged wildly and, as often occurred, triggered the stirrings of an oncoming seizure. Gessner calmly produced the magnetic wand and rubbed it on the top of Sasha's head. Miraculously, Sasha felt the seizure evaporate. It felt to her like a sneeze that never materialized.

She was incredulous.

In the days that followed, Dr. Gessner observed her closely and fine-tuned the device for maximum efficiency. It worked perfectly, and Sasha realized she might never have another seizure again. She even wondered if someday she might miss the tranquility and ethereal bliss that accompanied the post-seizure haze, but it seemed a tiny price to pay for the luxury of functioning in the real world.

One afternoon, as they were running through diagnostic tests, Brigita Gessner casually said, "I'm not sure what your future plans are, Sasha, but I need to hire a lab intern, and frankly you'd be an ideal candidate."

"Me?" Sasha thought she must have been joking.

"Why not *you*? You've basically spent your entire life in a medical facility."

"As a *patient*!" Sasha said, laughing. "Not a doctor!"

"True," Gessner said, "but you're an intelligent woman. I'm not asking you to become a doctor or do brain surgery. I'm talking about office paperwork, disinfecting equipment, that sort of thing. Best of all, if you're working at my lab, we might be able to make improvements in your condition."

"Improvements? I feel perfect!"

"Really? No more memory loss and blackout periods?"

"Oh . . ." Sasha said. "There are still those."

She and Gessner shared a laugh, but in reality, Sasha had indeed forgotten. Her memory had always had blank spots, and she'd just gotten used to it.

"Interictal memory impairment," Gessner said, "is extremely common in all my TLE patients. I've got a few ideas for how we might start to make headway on IMI . . . that is, if you'll let me look at your brain from time to time."

"Of course, but—"

"I have a small apartment in town that I bought for my mother, but she's been gone awhile, and I've never gotten around to selling it. You can stay there as long as you like. It's furnished, but if you don't like the style, we can—"

"I *love* the style," Sasha burst, on the verge of tears.

That had been two years ago, and Sasha had never left. She was now twenty-eight years old, and her modest salary and the free rent were sufficient to support herself, which was a dream come true. Over time, she progressed from cleaning and doing paperwork to assisting Dr. Gessner in her research and learning how to run the basic imaging equipment.

Brigita scanned Sasha's brain regularly to monitor progress of her ongoing treatment, which included IV nutritional supplements and brain-training exercises in the virtual reality chair. Sometimes, as a treat, Gessner let Sasha watch VR travel immersions—the Eiffel Tower, the Great Barrier Reef, and her favorite escape, Manhattan. She loved floating over all those skyscrapers or winding through Central Park. *Someday, I hope to see it for real . . .*

"Sasha?" A deep voice resonated directly above her. "Are you okay?"

The voice sounded close, pulling her back to the present.

"Sasha?" it repeated.

The warmth of Sasha's afterglow began dissolving . . . and then, without warning, a surge of bitter sadness crashed over her like a wave.

She now remembered everything.

Brigita is dead.

My one true friend.

Her eyes jolted open, and she found herself looking up at the handsome but kind face of the man who was still cradling her head.

He smiled gently at her and whispered, "Welcome back."

CHAPTER 33

The interior of the van was getting colder by the minute, and Jonas Faukman was shivering. His hands were still bound behind his back, and his fingers had gone completely numb. Faukman's captors had torn off his vintage gray peacoat before tying him up, searching the seams and pockets, before dumping it onto the floor beside him.

The editor wondered if his phone was still in his coat pocket. He was half tempted to shout, "Hey, Siri! Call 911!"

The stocky man with a buzz cut was sitting on his milk crate, only a few feet away, and his partner remained in the front seat, typing intermittently on his phone. He seemed to be having a conversation with someone.

A commanding officer?

Faukman had been trying to put the pieces together, but he could not fathom who these guys were or that they had brazenly abducted him off the street. *They stole one specific manuscript . . . and destroyed all of the publisher's copies?* Even if Katherine's book was a runaway bestseller, to hack a corporate system, destroy hard copies, and *kidnap* people over it? *This is book publishing, for crying out loud . . . not* Die Hard*!*

"Okay," Buzzcut said, glancing up from his iPad. "I have some questions for you, Mr. Faukman."

"You can call me Jonas," he chirped. "Kidnapping is much less formal than it used to be."

Buzzcut stared at him, clearly unamused by the quip. "Is Katherine Solomon overseas?"

"Yes."

"Where overseas?"

"You *know* where. You're just calibrating your little lie detector by asking me questions to which you already know the answers."

"Where?" Buzzcut repeated.

The editor had no desire to be sucker punched again. "She's in Prague."

"Very good." He looked back at his iPad. "At some point before seven a.m. local time, Dr. Solomon left her Prague hotel room and entered the Four Seasons Business Center."

Faukman did a double take, feeling a trace of panic. "Wait . . . you've been spying on her?"

"Let's just say we've been paying attention."

"Who the hell *are* you guys?!"

"While in the business center," Buzzcut continued without answering, "Dr. Solomon used a hotel computer to log into the PRH server. She accessed the latest version of her manuscript."

So what? Authors frequently get last-minute jitters when their editors are poised to start reading. Katherine was probably second-guessing something and decided to reread it.

"Why didn't she use her own laptop in the privacy of her own room?" Buzzcut asked.

"Because Dr. Solomon does not *have* a laptop. She prefers a full screen, keyboard, and mouse." *And if you were really watching her, you'd know that.*

The guy on the laptop nodded. "True."

Buzzcut looked back at his iPad. "Our records show that this morning Dr. Solomon printed a complete hard copy of her manuscript—all four hundred and eighty-one pages—and left the hotel with it."

For an instant, Faukman was startled these thugs knew the precise page count, until he remembered they had just stolen his editorial copy. *Easy bluff.* "Dr. Solomon printed no such copy, and you know it."

The muscular guy sitting on the milk crate stared at him a long moment and then arched his back to stretch, inadvertently revealing a shoulder holster with a startlingly large handgun.

Faukman hadn't seen a move that transparent since fourth grade when he tried to put his arm around Laura Schwartz at the IOKA movie theater. Nonetheless, he got the message.

"You sure you want to play games with me?" Buzzcut asked.

"Hold on," Laptop interjected, eyeing his screen. "Avatar says he's telling the truth. He's unaware that Solomon printed a copy."

Buzzcut looked surprised. "Interesting. So . . . Dr. Solomon printed the manuscript behind your back?"

Nice try. Faukman had edited too many police interrogation scenes to fall for the Good Cop–Bad Cop routine—a divide-and-conquer strategy to get him to distrust Katherine. Unfortunately for these clowns, Faukman's professional career had been built on analyzing story narratives and pointing out inconsistencies. If his captors had said Katherine carefully printed a copy to edit in her hotel room, he might have believed them. But the devil was always in the details, and these guys claimed Katherine had carried the manuscript outside the hotel. *Not something she would have done.*

"We want to know," Buzzcut pressed, "why did Katherine print a manuscript? And who did she give it to?"

"To *whom* did she give it," Faukman corrected instinctively.

Buzzcut glared. "That's what I said."

"No, it isn't. Can you untie my hands? My arms are numb."

"*Whom* did she give it to?"

Faukman shook his head. "Still wrong. I have no idea."

"He doesn't know." Laptop called from the front.

Buzzcut looked flustered. "Has Katherine reached out to you?"

"No."

"And how about Robert Langdon?"

"No."

Laptop nodded. "Both true."

Buzzcut scratched his head, apparently pondering his next line of questioning.

Faukman was shivering more violently now as the cold intensified. "Can you at least turn on the heat?"

"I'm sorry, are you uncomfortable?" Buzzcut reached over the driver's seat and pressed a button on the dash. But rather than the heater kicking on, the driver's-side window went down. A blast of cold air swirled through the van. "Better?"

Faukman was starting to believe he might actually be in serious danger tonight.

Through the open window, he again heard the mechanical sounds from outside, louder this time, and he realized what he was hearing—the unmistakable roar of jet engines.

Holy shit . . . am I on a military base?

CHAPTER 34

Langdon was relieved to see Sasha Vesna open her eyes. Several minutes had passed since the intense seizure gripped her, and she now appeared to be starting to reorient herself.

"Thank you . . ." Sasha whispered, looking up at him.

"I'm so sorry," Langdon said. "I couldn't find your medication in your purse."

"It's okay," she said. "What I needed . . . it's in a hidden pocket. I'm fine."

Langdon helped her up to a seated position with her back against the pod, and Sasha gently worked her fingers and toes, as if trying to reclaim control of her body. The workspace was dead silent now, the cooling fans and warning beeps having stopped as soon as the EPR process was aborted.

Sasha leaned against the pod and seemed to drift off again, closing her eyes and doing deep breathing, as if she still needed time to reassimilate. After ten seconds, her eyes opened, and Langdon was struck by the difference in her gaze, which was suddenly stronger and more focused, as if she had forced herself to bury her pain and press on.

"I need water, please," Sasha said, her voice more assured now too.

"Of course." Langdon jumped up, recalling that dry mouth was one of the most common post-seizure symptoms.

"My office . . ." She motioned toward the door. "My . . . water bottle."

Langdon turned and hurried past a worktable, noticing a leather briefcase sitting on its surface. *Gessner's case from the bar last night.* He continued down the hall to the office suite, where he grabbed the magenta water bottle with the Cyrillic writing he had seen earlier. It was almost empty, and on the way back, Langdon stopped to fill it in the laboratory restroom.

At the sink, holding his fingers under the stream and waiting for it to get cold, he stared at his tired reflection in the mirror, taking a moment to calm his nerves. Finding Gessner's corpse had been horrifying, but her death had also amplified Langdon's fears about Katherine's safety.

Where is she now?

A series of thoughts suddenly haunted him. He had spotted Gessner's briefcase on a worktable near the pod and recalled her saying last night that she needed to return to the lab for some reason after drinks. It was very possible that Gessner had been trapped in the pod already when Katherine arrived here for their 8 a.m. meeting.

Did Katherine come face-to-face with Gessner's attacker?

As the water gurgled into the bottle, a flash of movement behind Langdon drew his attention. Before he could turn from the sink, an iron grip seized his forearm, twisted it backward, and pressed his head into the glass. The water bottle fell to the floor.

"Where are they?!" the man demanded, forcing his shoulder into Langdon's back and holding his head against the mirror.

Langdon felt the barrel of a gun digging into his ribs, and in the mirror he glimpsed the brutish face of Lieutenant Pavel.

"Where are Gessner and Solomon?" the ÚZSI officer repeated, twisting Langdon's arm more sharply behind him. "I know they are down here . . . along with another person who just arrived."

"Katherine isn't . . . here," Langdon managed through clenched teeth. "And Gessner . . . is dead."

"Bullshit!" Pavel shouted, sounding a lot like his boss.

Langdon wondered if Janáček was also on his way down here. "Why would I lie?" he grunted, fearing his arm was about to snap.

"Last chance," the lieutenant growled, wrenching Langdon's elbow impossibly tighter. "Tell me wher—"

There was a heavy metallic thud, and Pavel's grip immediately went slack as he collapsed to the floor, his gun clattering away. Langdon spun to see Sasha Vesna behind him, wielding the same fire extinguisher with which she had threatened him earlier. Her expression was frightened as she stared down at the ÚZSI lieutenant curled motionless at her feet.

"I didn't know what else to do . . ." she said. "He was hurting you!"

Langdon looked down at Pavel. No blood, but the man was definitely unconscious. "It's . . . okay," Langdon managed, gently taking the canister from Sasha with his aching arm and setting it down on the floor.

"Who is he?" she demanded.

"An ÚZSI lieutenant," Langdon said, retrieving Pavel's gun and putting it into the sink out of reach. "He's going to need a doctor."

"He's fine," she said. "It's a posterior parietal trauma—he'll be unconscious for a few minutes, then have a bad headache."

Langdon reminded himself that Sasha worked for a brain scientist.

"But how did he get down here?" Sasha demanded.

Langdon had no idea—maybe ÚZSI's demolition team had arrived already and broken down the door. The alarms on the machinery had been loud, and Langdon might not have heard the incursion. *And now I'm directly linked to an assault on an ÚZSI lieutenant.*

"Sasha, I need to get to the U.S. embassy as soon as possible," Langdon said, racing through the options in his head. "There's a man there who has been helping me. Michael Harris."

Sasha looked surprised. "I know Michael. He's a close friend."

"You *know* him?!" Langdon was startled that Harris had never mentioned he knew Brigita Gessner's lab assistant.

"It's not a friendship we advertise," Sasha said. "U.S. government employee . . . full-blooded Russian . . ."

Of course, Langdon realized. *Politics is perception*. Considering the growing U.S.-Russian hostility, an embassy official spending time with a Russian lab assistant would certainly raise eyebrows.

"Regardless, we can't go to the embassy from here," she said. "It's far too dangerous. ÚZSI will have it staked out, searching every car that approaches. We should text Michael and have him collect us at my apartment in an official embassy vehicle. It will be far safer."

It occurred to Langdon that for a woman who had just suffered a major seizure, Sasha Vesna was thinking more clearly than he was. *To her apartment then*, he thought, grateful for her help and hoping he would be able to make contact with Katherine shortly. "Is there any way out of here other than through the front door?"

"No, that's the only way out," Sasha said, grabbing Pavel's gun from the sink and putting it into her bag.

"Hold on," Langdon said, alarmed. "I'm not sure stealing an ÚZSI weapon—"

"I'm not going to *use* it, but this agent will be conscious in a minute, and if he decides to come after us, I'd prefer he didn't have a gun."

Hard to argue with that, Langdon thought. Pavel was already groaning and starting to twitch.

Sasha retrieved her magenta water bottle, which had been squashed by Pavel's boots in the struggle. She looked wistfully at the handwritten Russian text. "Brigita gave me this," she said as they started down the hall. "To remind me to stay hydrated. I always forget. It says, *Drink Water.*"

Sasha set the bottle just inside her office and led Langdon to the staircase, where they climbed in silence to the upper landing. He hoped Janáček was not waiting in the foyer. At the top, they reached the security door, which Langdon half expected to find blown off its hinges.

It was not.

Cautiously, Sasha peered out through the tiny window. Apparently seeing nothing, she pushed open the door and looked around. Motioning for Langdon to follow, she led the way out into the freezing-cold foyer, which was deserted. As the stairwell door closed behind them, the security panel beeped contentedly and turned red.

Crunching across shattered glass, Langdon and Sasha exited the building onto the walkway. All was quiet. Janáček's sedan was still parked in front, but the captain was nowhere to be seen.

Sasha thought a moment. "Follow me."

She led Langdon to the right, away from the bastion, arriving at an opening in the retaining wall. From there, they descended a stone staircase that deposited them on a wooded slope. This portion of the ridge was far less steep than the precipice surrounding the bastion's courtyard, and yet the snow underfoot was slippery, and he was already having trouble getting traction in his slick-soled shoes.

Langdon's attire this morning—a Dale sweater and campus loafers—had been in anticipation of a visit to a science lab . . . not an escape down a mountain. As Langdon began to fumble his way through the trees, he set his sights on reaching the bottom unscathed. This embankment, he now realized, descended directly to Folimanka Park.

And from there, he hoped, *a taxi to Sasha's apartment.*

— · —

From where The Golěm was located, he had a perfect view of the American professor slipping awkwardly down the wooded slope toward Folimanka Park. Robert Langdon's unanticipated presence at the bastion this morning, along with that of ÚZSI, was one of numerous wrinkles in The Golěm's plan.

His plan for entering Threshold would need to be slightly delayed, and yet a fresh opportunity had just presented itself.

An opportunity I have no intention of squandering.

Carefully, The Golěm descended the slippery ridge, confident that neither Langdon nor Sasha had any idea he was there.

CHAPTER 35

The lobby of the Four Seasons smelled like roses.

Just like the roses Michael used to bring me, thought Dana Daněk as she marched toward the reception desk. She had already searched the hotel lobby and restaurant, but Michael and his pretty little friend were nowhere to be seen.

Upstairs . . .

As Dana approached the man behind the reception desk, she forced a smile and handed him her U.S. embassy ID. "Good morning, sir," she said sweetly. "I'm sorry to trouble you. I'm with the U.S. embassy here in Prague and my boss, Michael Harris, is in your hotel at the moment. He asked me to deliver something to him urgently. Perhaps you saw him enter about fifteen minutes ago? He's a tall African American gentleman with—"

"Yes, of course," the man said, handing back her ID. "Mr. Harris is upstairs in the Royal Suite. Would you like me to deliver something to him?"

"No, thank you," she said. "It's a sensitive diplomatic paper that I'm required to hand-deliver personally. Remind me, which number is the Royal Suite?"

The concierge gave her directions to the back of the hotel, and a minute later Dana had climbed a private staircase and was standing in a foyer outside the hotel's most expensive room.

Seriously, Michael? The Royal Suite?!

Dana knocked softly and called out, "*Úklid!* Housekeeping!"

She could not wait to see Michael's face when she walked

in. She put her ear to the door and listened, definitely hearing movement inside.

"*Housekeeping!*" she called again, knocking more forcefully.

Footsteps approached the door, which opened slightly, and a familiar pair of doe eyes peered out. "I'm sorry," said the woman from the bridge. "Can you come ba—"

Dana launched herself against the door, driving the petite woman backward onto the floor. Dana stormed past her into the suite, heading straight back through the living room to what was obviously the master bedroom suite.

Empty.

Dana checked the master bath.

Empty.

No sign of Michael anywhere.

The suite was unkempt—with dresser drawers open, suit-cases open, even the hotel safe ajar—as if the room was being . . . *searched*?

When Dana exited back into the living room, the dimpled woman was waiting for her, staring over the barrel of a menacing matte-black handgun that was aimed directly at Dana's forehead.

My God!

"I'm going to ask you once," the woman said with an eerie calm. "What are you doing here?" Her accent was American.

The steadiness of the woman's voice, as well as that of her weapon hand, suggested she was no stranger to firing a gun. Dana had never had a gun trained on her, and the experience was sobering.

"I'm . . . looking for . . . Michael Harris," she heard herself say.

The gun remained leveled. "He's not here."

Dana had noticed the embassy sedan was no longer in front of the hotel when she entered, but she assumed Michael had asked his driver to park elsewhere so as not to draw attention.

"You need to leave immediately," the woman said. "This is not your concern."

"It is very much my concern," Dana replied, finding her

voice. "I am an employee of the U.S. embassy, and you're aiming a gun at me. Moreover, it appears you're searching the hotel room of two American citizens."

"As I said," she repeated, stepping forward with the gun still leveled. "This is not your concern."

Who in the world are you?! Dana knew she had only one card to play. She glanced out the bay window toward Charles Bridge and said, "I know what happened on that bridge this morning. Where's your crown of thorns?"

The woman with the gun did not so much as flinch. She took yet another step toward Dana. "Whoever you are," she said firmly, "I would strongly recommend you return to the embassy and speak to your ambassador before you mention this to *anyone* at all."

"First, tell me where Michael Harris is."

"Your ambassador sent him over to provide me access to this suite, which he *did*, and then he left. That's all I know about him." She motioned toward the exit. "Now leave. And close the door on your way out."

<hr />

Field Officer Susan Housemore waited until the door had clicked shut before she lowered her weapon and placed it into the discreet holster at the small of her back. Then she pulled out her phone and placed a secure call to Mr. Finch in London.

<hr />

Across town, in the backseat of the embassy car roaring toward Crucifix Bastion, Michael Harris was relieved to have completed the ambassador's bizarre errand at the Four Seasons. The contact he had been ordered to "assist" had accepted Harris's discreet room key handoff without even making eye contact.

Serious professional.

As Crucifix Bastion appeared ahead, Harris was pleased to see no signs of a demo team or any additional ÚZSI vehicles. The ambassador's call to Janáček had clearly stopped the man cold, and Harris was eager to meet up again with Robert Langdon, as promised.

As Harris exited the sedan, however, he hesitated. The lab's front door appeared to be shattered and wide open. *What the hell happened here?!* As Harris hurried toward the door, an ÚZSI agent lurched through the opening, clutching his head. Harris recognized him as the muscular lieutenant driving Janáček's car this morning at the Four Seasons.

Harris ran over to steady the man. "Are you okay? What happened?!" *And why is the front door destroyed?*

"Katherine Solomon," the man stammered. "She . . . hit me . . ."

The claim made no sense. "You're sure it was Dr. *Solomon?*"

"I saw her in the mirror . . . tall . . . blond . . ."

Definitely not Katherine Solomon. Harris knew there was only one tall blonde with access to this lab—Gessner's assistant, Sasha Vesna—and he found it hard to imagine Sasha was capable of violence. "Where is Robert Langdon?"

"He ran . . . with her."

The story sounded delusional, and yet Harris now noticed a series of footprints departing the front walkway . . . as if headed for the woods. *Langdon fled?!*

"Did you see anyone *else* inside?" *Dr. Gessner?*

"No . . . I came straight up to report this to my captain." The lieutenant motioned to the far end of the courtyard. "He's out there."

Harris looked out toward the ridge, but Janáček was nowhere to be seen. "I don't see him."

"He went out there to make a phone call . . ."

Harris was not surprised. *He was probably doing damage control after he spoke to the ambassador.* "You should really sit down, Lieutenant."

The man was already moving toward the ridgeline, and Harris scooped up a handful of snow, hurrying to catch up. "Here. Hold this on your head."

The man took the ball of snow and pressed it to the back of

his skull as he walked. "He was out here on the phone . . . but he never came back in."

Harris saw a tangle of footprints on the ridgeline, as if Janáček had been pacing or perhaps had been joined by someone else, but the area was now deserted. As the two men neared the edge, the lieutenant stopped and retrieved a metallic object from the ground. He dusted it off, his eyes wide with concern. "This is his phone!" he exclaimed.

Why would Janáček have left his phone?

Tentatively, they moved the final few yards to the edge of the ravine and peered over the ridge. The scene below was grisly. At the bottom of the chasm, grotesquely sprawled and broken on the rocks, lay a body in a dark suit. The man's head was encircled with red snow that radiated several feet in all directions. Even from this height, Harris had no doubt he was dead . . . and no doubt who he was.

My God . . . Janáček jumped?

Beside Harris, the lieutenant turned away and bellowed like a wounded animal. His voice echoed with the pain of true loss . . . and uncontrollable rage.

CHAPTER 36

Langdon lowered his head against the wind as he and Sasha Vesna descended the wooded slope away from the bastion. The dense tree cover provided enough dry ground that Langdon was able to descend more gracefully than anticipated, sliding several times on the slick snow but maintaining a steady pace.

By the time they emerged from the woods into Folimanka Park, Langdon's loafers were caked with snow and his feet were frozen. A scattering of pedestrians dotted the pathways, heads down, making their way to work.

Without speaking, Sasha led them quickly across the park, heading due south. As they passed Folimanka Fountain, Sasha spoke under her breath. "I'm convinced Katherine never entered the bastion this morning . . . the display on the EPR pod showed Brigita had been in that pod since late last night, which is far longer than anyone could survive."

Langdon hoped this meant Katherine had arrived at the lab, received no answer at the buzzer, and simply returned to the hotel. *She and I might have crossed paths*, he told himself, trying to ignore the nagging sensation that something with Katherine was indeed very wrong. He felt terrified by the prospect of losing her.

For the past three days, he and Katherine hadn't spent a moment apart, and it amazed Langdon that after nearly thirty-five years, their casual friendship had ignited into such a natural, passionate romance, catching them both off guard.

Langdon had savored the days together. He took Katherine

to see the bizarrely fetishistic *Infant Jesus of Prague* statue, which was ritualistically undressed and dressed in different outfits like some kind of sacred Barbie Doll. He showed her the mysterious 165-pound *Devil's Bible*, the largest book in the world, whose terrifying legend involved an adulterous monk, the skins of 160 donkeys, and death by "immurement" . . . and even dared Katherine to taste the local *tlačenka*—"meat jelly"—which she agreed was surprisingly delicious despite being made of pig's heads.

Katherine had also been on an adrenaline ride these last few days, having just finished her manuscript. With a mixture of enthusiasm and coy reserve, she had told Langdon about it in general, playfully rebuffing his attempts to learn more about the details of the book in order not to ruin the surprises for him. But mainly, Langdon recalled, she had fretted about whether readers and book reviewers would be open to new ideas.

"Let's face it—the human mind hates change," she had said yesterday while sipping espresso at the stylish La Boheme Café. "And the mind despises abandoning *existing* beliefs."

Langdon smiled. *That's why religions endure for millennia despite mountains of evidence contradicting their beliefs.*

"*Thirty* years ago," Katherine complained, "physicists proved that communication between two entangled particles is *instantaneous* . . . and yet we're *still* teaching Einstein's mantra that 'nothing travels faster than the speed of light'!"

The original experiment, as Langdon recalled, involved using a magnet to reverse the polarity of one entangled particle, resulting in the polarity of its "twin" particle reversing instantly—whether it was in the same room or miles away. Upping the ante, Chinese scientists had later performed the same experiment using satellites to demonstrate that two entangled particles remained "instantaneously connected" over a distance of twelve hundred kilometers. *Science Magazine* ran the cover story "China Shatters 'Spooky Action at a Distance' Record," referring to the phrase coined by Albert Einstein in the mid-1930s to describe the phenomenon.

"And it's been decades," Katherine continued, "since we've

proven repeatedly that human thought, when focused, can quite literally alter one's body chemistry. And yet . . . the notion of remote healing is skeptically debunked by medical experts as voodoo."

An obdurate mind can be an immovable mountain, Langdon thought, always amazed how many people still fervently believed humans came from Adam and Eve despite the overwhelming scientific evidence for evolution.

"I've got a student with a one forty-eight IQ," Langdon recounted, "who insists the earth is six thousand years old. So, I took her down the hall to the geology department and showed her a three-million-year-old fossil. She simply shrugged and said, 'I believe God placed that fossil on earth as a trick . . . to test my faith.'"

Katherine laughed. "If you think *religious* zealots are irrationally tied to their worldviews, you should meet the tenured academics of higher education."

"*I'm* a tenured academic of higher education!"

"And you've always been a skeptic, Robert. Old-fashioned, but cute."

"Old-fashioned?" Langdon cocked his head. "I'm younger than you are . . . hate to remind you."

"Careful . . ." she said, flashing a devastating smile. "You took my undergrad seminar *twice*, lover boy, and I'm pretty sure it wasn't my slideshow you were staring at."

Langdon laughed out loud. "Guilty as charged."

"The point is, *nobody* likes change," she continued. "And stodgy academics have a tendency to cling to the comfort of their existing beliefs long after their models are clearly obsolete. For this reason, establishing a new scientific paradigm—like that of human consciousness—becomes an exceptionally frustrating and slow process."

Langdon thought of Thomas Kuhn's 1962 classic, *The Structure of Scientific Revolutions*, describing how paradigm shifts occurred only when a critical mass of incompatible phenomena had been attained. Katherine was clearly hoping her book would add substantial weight to that ongoing quest for a critical mass.

"Your manuscript . . ." Langdon said. "You still haven't told me *specifically* what your big breakthrough is."

Katherine smiled. "Patience. I think you'll find it all quite fascinating—but I'd rather you read it and give me feedback."

A car horn blared, and the warm memories of the café evaporated, returning Langdon to the cold of Folimanka Park. Shivering, he followed Sasha out of the park through an iron gate, pleased to see a line of yellow Škoda sedans idling at a taxi stand.

They climbed into the first cab, Langdon very grateful for the warm interior. Sasha gave the driver an address, and the cab pulled out onto Sekaninova Street.

Then she pulled out her phone and placed a call on speaker.

Michael Harris's familiar voice answered. "Sasha?!"

"Michael!" she exclaimed, her voice distraught. "Something terrible happened to Brigita!" Sasha weepily relayed their grim discovery.

"I'm so sorry," Harris said, sounding stunned. "I had no idea. I'm here at the bastion now."

Damn, we just missed him, Langdon realized.

"ÚZSI is here too," Harris added. "They have no idea Brigita is dead."

Pavel must not have seen the body.

"Sasha," Harris said, "did you attack an ÚZSI officer?!"

She hesitated, startled. "He attacked Robert Langdon! I didn't know what to do."

"Langdon?" Harris demanded. "Is he with you?"

"Yes, he wanted to take a taxi to the embassy, but—"

"Bad idea. ÚZSI will intercept."

"I know. So I'm taking him—"

"Don't say it on the phone!" Harris interrupted. "I know where you're going. Tell Harry and Sally I said hello. I'll be there as fast as I can. Maybe twenty minutes. Stay off the phone."

The call ended.

"Harry and Sally?" Langdon asked.

"My cats. He didn't want me to say we're going to my apartment."

Smart. "Sounds like you know him well."

She nodded, looking almost embarrassed. "A couple of months now."

"And obviously you trust him," Langdon said.

"I do." Sasha's eyes welled with sudden emotion. "He'll know how to help you."

What about helping you? Langdon hoped the embassy would be able to protect the Russian woman despite her attack on an ÚZSI lieutenant. He wished Sasha had asked Harris for any new information about Katherine, but the attaché seemed to trust the phones as little as Sasha did, and he probably wouldn't have said anything anyway.

I'll speak to Harris shortly at Sasha's home.

Next to him, Sasha closed her eyes and settled into her seat. She began rocking her body gently, as if trying to comfort herself. *She needs calm*, he thought. She had just endured an epileptic seizure, as well as a physical battle with an ÚZSI officer, and was now putting herself at risk to shepherd Langdon to safety, all after witnessing the gruesome death of her mentor.

Langdon checked his watch. Mickey Mouse's outstretched arms indicated it was just past 9 a.m. . . . only a few hours since he had awoken peacefully with Katherine in his arms.

It felt like a lifetime ago.

CHAPTER 37

Langdon's body eagerly absorbed the taxi's warmth. His bitter trek across Folimanka Park had left him chilled, and he now kicked off his snow-caked loafers and massaged his frozen toes. Beside him, Sasha remained silent, her eyes still closed.

The woman on Charles Bridge continued to haunt him. Everything about the brief encounter felt otherworldly . . . the ghostly way she moved, the blank stare in her eyes, the smell of death, and the way she seemed not to hear him . . . as if she lived in a parallel reality.

Ghost sightings were reported almost nightly in this necromantic city, most commonly the local spirit celebrities—the headless Templar Knight who haunted Charles Bridge seeking revenge for his execution . . . the White Lady of Prague Castle who walked the castle ramparts trying to escape imprisonment for allegedly practicing witchcraft . . . the earthen golem monster who still moved through the shadows near the Old Jewish Synagogue protecting the weak.

Ghosts don't exist, Langdon knew. *And they certainly don't leave footprints in the snow.* Whatever had transpired on Charles Bridge was flesh and blood.

Langdon had always enjoyed Prague's supernatural lore, even while instinctively dismissing it. And this morning, his rational mind had cut through the mystical fog, arriving at a black-and-white conclusion. There existed only three viable explanations for the startling presence of the woman on Charles Bridge.

First, the possibility that Katherine's dream was indeed a miraculous precognitive vision of a future event. If that was true, Katherine had just experienced one of the most vividly accurate clairvoyant events anyone had ever reported. *Probability near zero. Dismissed.*

The second explanation felt equally unlikely. *Coincidence.* A woman dressed in a halo, carrying a spear, and smelling of sulfur had just happened to cross the bridge a few hours after Katherine's dream. *Statistically impossible to the point of absurdity.*

The third scenario—while disturbing—seemed to be the only remaining rational explanation. According to Sherlock Holmes: *When you have eliminated the impossible, whatever remains, however improbable, must be the truth.* The improbable truth, in this instance, was that someone else had learned about Katherine's dream . . . and had orchestrated the spectacle.

A setup.

But why?

And how?

The question of *why* remained a mystery, but the question of *how* seemed eerily plausible. While on book tour in Russia a few years back, Langdon had been warned that most luxury hotel rooms in Moscow were bugged by the government. *Could Prague be similar?* This city felt nothing like Moscow, and yet history cast a long shadow. Not too long ago, Prague had spent forty-five years behind the Iron Curtain, and aside from the all-too-brief "Prague Spring," Soviet hard-liners had set the tone here with ubiquitous KGB surveillance. If there was *one* suite in Prague worthy of monitoring, it was the Four Seasons Royal Suite—top choice for billionaires, world leaders, and diplomats.

Was someone listening when Katherine told me about her dream?

If the suite was surveilled, Langdon cringed to imagine what private moments might have been overheard, or recorded, during these past few passionate days with her.

But who would be listening? Janáček? ÚZSI?

Whatever the motive to re-create the disturbing dream, Langdon had run that same route across Charles Bridge at the same time for three days now, and he'd told Katherine this morning he'd be back at seven.

Clockwork.

By that logic, he felt more confident it had all been a setup.

And somehow, that felt scarier to him than the existence of any ghost.

CHAPTER 38

Mr. Finch was livid.

His field officer in Prague had just phoned to report that her simple cleanup job at the Four Seasons had gone sideways. Field Officer Housemore was Finch's eyes, ears, and muscle for all local matters relating to Threshold, and despite her compartmentalized knowledge of the project, she knew secrecy was paramount.

So what the hell just happened?!

For someone with her skills, the errand at the hotel should have been trivial, but somehow it had resulted in an armed confrontation with an embassy employee.

For Christ's sake . . .

Fuming, Finch placed a secure call to the U.S. ambassador in Prague.

———··———

At the Four Seasons, Susan Housemore took a final look around the Royal Suite, confirming everything was finally in order. She was exhausted from her sleepless night but felt confident her mission here was now complete—despite the unfortunate interruption.

The strangeness had begun around 4 a.m., when she was awakened by a phone call from Mr. Finch—who issued the most unusual directive Housemore had ever received. Knowing better than to ask for any kind of explanation, she had jumped out of bed, recovered the package that had already been left for her, and unpacked the specialized "components" required for this assignment.

Shortly after 6 a.m., Housemore had exited her apartment feeling like she should be going to a movie set rather than executing a mission. She was dressed all in black, carrying an elaborate spiked headpiece and a menacing silver spear. In her pocket, she carried a bottle of foul-smelling liquid that had nearly made her gag when she cracked the lid to sniff it. Whatever the purpose behind this operation, Finch was very specific about how to carry it out.

Field Officer Housemore had followed Finch's directions precisely, making her trancelike march across the bridge when the order was given. And while the charade meant nothing to her, it clearly scared the hell out of Robert Langdon.

And chaos ensued.

Housemore suspected that *chaos* had probably been Finch's goal. He was a seasoned strategist who was known to admire the tactics of figures from Sun Tzu to Napoleon—seizing every opportunity to enhance the effectiveness of field operations by layering in psychological warfare whenever possible. "Psyops" was a bloodless, low-risk, extremely effective way to weaken the opposition. *Disrupt. Destabilize. Disorient.* An enemy distracted by chaos made poor decisions and was easier to manipulate.

Mission accomplished, Housemore thought. It had been reported back to her that Robert Langdon had pulled the fire alarm and evacuated this hotel.

Now she was tying up the final loose ends. After an exhaustive search of the suite, she had confirmed for Mr. Finch that there were no printed manuscripts hidden anywhere, including in the hotel safe, which was open and unused. She had now cleaned up, leaving the suite as she found it.

Before she exited, however, there was one final order of business.

Field Officer Housemore walked to the bay window and eyed the lavish arrangement of red, white, and blue tulips that had been sent three days earlier to Katherine Solomon from the U.S.

embassy. The handwritten note of congratulations from Ambassador Heide Nagel lay on the floor.

Blasted by frigid winter air, the flowers were drooping prematurely, their flaccid stalks leaning outward in all directions, barely concealing the electronic device that had been hidden among them.

Housemore reached in and carefully extracted the Sennheiser parabolic surveillance microphone and FM transmitter. The listening device had been placed there by the U.S. ambassador's office, at Mr. Finch's request.

She slid the device into her coat pocket, fluffed up the dying flowers, and took one last look around the suite.

Then, utterly drained, Housemore headed home to get some sleep.

CHAPTER 39

Through the van's open window, Jonas Faukman could hear the shrill whine of jet engines. He knew Brooklyn had a little-known U.S. military base that was surprisingly close to Manhattan, but he could not recall if Fort Hamilton had an airfield. Wherever they had brought him, his captors definitely seemed to be involved in something more serious than book piracy.

Someone powerful wants to prevent the publication of Katherine Solomon's manuscript. But who—a rival scientist perhaps?

Shivering on the frigid metal floor of the van, Faukman plumbed his memory for clues, thinking back to the moment he had first learned of the manuscript's existence. Robert Langdon had called to ask if Faukman would be willing to have lunch with his brilliant friend Katherine Solomon and listen to her stunning book proposal. Faukman agreed immediately, knowing that "brilliant" and "stunning" were not words the Harvard professor threw around lightly.

They met at Faukman's favorite table in Manhattan—the back booth at Trattoria Dell'Arte—where authentic Italian cuisine was served in a room decorated like an artist's studio, adorned, rather distinctively, by paintings and sculptures featuring famous Italian noses. He had read the biographical info Katherine Solomon had sent him, and he was thoroughly impressed by her list of scientific accomplishments, published articles, PhD in cognitive science, and prominence in her field.

When they sat down in person, Faukman saw within minutes that Katherine Solomon was even more impressive in real life than she was on paper. Not unlike Langdon himself, she was affable, humble, and razor-sharp. She was also naturally promotable—possessing a rare combination of charm and striking beauty that would be an ideal fit for the brave new world of twenty-first-century publishing, which relied so heavily on social media. After some small talk and uncorking a bottle of 2016 Solaia—Langdon's favorite Super Tuscan—conversation naturally flowed toward her book idea.

"In the simplest terms," Katherine began, "the book will be an exploration of human consciousness. It's based on my research over the last twenty years . . . as well as several of my recent scientific breakthroughs." She paused, sipping her wine, thinking. "As you probably know, human consciousness has long been believed to be the product of chemical processes in the brain. This means that human consciousness cannot exist *without* the brain."

Interesting, but rather obvious, Faukman thought. It was his job to remain skeptical until he was bowled over by an idea.

"The problem," Katherine said, a mysterious smile parting her lips, "is that this standard model of consciousness is incorrect."

Both men grew more attentive.

"I intend to write a book that illuminates a revolutionary new model of consciousness that will have repercussions for *everything* we know about life . . . including the very nature of 'reality' itself."

Faukman arched his eyebrows appreciatively and smiled. "From a publishing perspective, there's nothing like aiming high." He studied Katherine. "But I do have one question. Many people propose books with exciting new theories . . . do you—"

"Of course," she said. "My work is backed up with plenty of hard science."

"You read my mind," Faukman said, impressed.

"I wouldn't waste your time without evidence," she countered.

Langdon looked amused that Katherine was holding her own so effortlessly.

"Well, you certainly have my attention," Faukman said. "What is this revolutionary model of human consciousness?"

"At first it will seem impossible," Katherine replied. "So to prepare your minds for that and establish a baseline . . ." She reached into her Cuyana bag and pulled out an iPad. "I will first show you an example of something I think we can all agree is . . . *impossible.*"

Faukman glanced at Langdon, who looked equally mystified.

Katherine tapped the tablet a few times and then propped it on the table, facing Faukman and Langdon, who found themselves looking at a pair of side-by-side videos—a split screen showing two different fishbowls, each with a lone goldfish swimming in lazy circles.

Goldfish are impossible?

"These are two live video feeds," Katherine said. "The feeds are from two separate, stationary cameras in my lab in California."

They watched the two fish, which swam in two similar fishbowls with blue pebbles on the bottom and a submerged statuette. The only difference between the two bowls appeared to be the statuettes inside each bowl. One was the sculpted word *Yes* and the other the sculpted word *No.*

Bizarre. Faukman glanced up at Katherine Solomon, waiting for her to explain, but she just nodded for him to keep watching. Politely, Faukman returned his gaze to the two camera feeds. *Two fish swimming in circles . . . What am I supposed to be seeing here?*

"Incredible . . ." Langdon whispered beside him.

In that moment, Faukman saw it too. Strangely, the two goldfish were swimming in perfect unison. When one fish paused, darted, or swam to the surface, the other did *precisely* the same thing in the other bowl . . . at the exact same instant! The two fish were perfectly synchronized, down to their slightest twitches.

Stupefied, Faukman watched the two goldfish swim in flawless unison for at least fifteen seconds before he finally shook his head and glanced up. "Okay, that is . . . impossible."

"I'm glad you feel that way," Katherine said.

"How are the fish doing that?!" he demanded.

"Remarkable, right?" she said. "The answer, in fact, is quite simple."

Langdon and Faukman sat riveted, awaiting her explanation.

"To start," she said. "How many fish do you see here in total?"

Faukman met both their eyes. "Two," he replied.

"And you, Robert?"

"Two," Langdon concurred.

"Perfect, you both see what most people see, and what is presented before you: two separate fish in two separate bowls."

How else could you see it? Faukman thought. *One bowl says Yes and one says No, but the two fish are in precise synch.*

"Now, what if I told you," Katherine said, "that their separateness is an *illusion*? What if I told you these two fish are, in fact, *one* entity . . . a single unified organism connected to the same consciousness, moving in unison."

Faukman sensed he was about to hear some New Age mumbo jumbo about how all living things are interconnected. He had no idea how these fish had linked their movements, but he was pretty sure it was not because they were tapped into the same cosmic consciousness. *What did you expect, Jonas? She's a noeticist from California!*

"Perspective is a choice," Katherine continued, "and perspective is key when it comes to understanding consciousness. You have both *chosen* to view this as two fish swimming in perfect synch. However, if you can change your perspective and view them as *one* fish, *one* mind, *one* unified organism, simply swimming . . . then it's quite normal."

Langdon looked suddenly concerned that her pitch was about to go off the rails. "It's not really a *choice*, is it, Katherine? *Two* separate, unconnected goldfish cannot be viewed as a singular organism."

"This is true. But they're *not* two separate organisms, Professor," she replied. "They are *one*. And I'll bet you your Mickey Mouse watch that I can prove it to you right now. Scientifically. Beyond any shadow of a doubt."

Langdon again studied the two live videos: *Two distinct bowls. Two distinct fish.* "I'll take the bet," Langdon finally said. "Convince me it's one organism."

"Very well." Katherine smiled. "And let me quote my favorite symbologist—*sometimes a change in perspective is all it takes to reveal the Truth.*"

She touched the iPad screen. "Here is a third live camera feed from the same lab. And here is your change in perspective, gentlemen."

The new camera angle was an aerial view, looking *down* at a single fishbowl similar to the other bowls—blue pebbles, some kind of statuette, and a lone goldfish swimming in circles. Curiously, this aerial view also showed that two video cameras were set up next to the bowl, pointing at it from different positions.

"I don't understand," Faukman said.

"You've been looking at two videos of the same bowl," Katherine said. "One bowl. One fish. Viewed from two different perspectives. Their separateness is an illusion. They are a single organism."

"But they're clearly in two different bowls," Faukman protested. "What about the *Yes/No* statues? Those are *different* . . . how could it be *one* bowl?!"

Langdon hung his head. "Markus Raetz," he whispered. "I should have seen it."

Katherine reached into her bag and pulled out a familiar statuette—a copy of the *Yes* statue from the first bowl. She held it up, letting Faukman read the word. Then she rotated the statue ninety degrees, and Faukman heard himself gasp. From this new angle, the statuette looked totally different. From this direction . . . it read *No*.

"This piece of art," Katherine said, "is the work of sculptor Markus Raetz, who—much like the universe we live in—is a master of illusion."

Langdon was already unbuckling his Mickey Mouse watch.

"You know I don't have children, Robert." She laughed. "Keep your Mickey watch. I did this only to illustrate a point about impossibility. And the point is this: what I am about to tell you about human consciousness will *seem* impossible at first—as impossible as two synchronized goldfish—but if you permit yourself a change of perspective, everything will suddenly make sense . . . and those things you once found mysterious will appear as plain as day."

From that moment on, Faukman found himself hanging on her every word. Lunch turned into a three-hour, mind-bending journey of discovery . . . including Katherine coyly promising him that her book would outline a series of cutting-edge experiments that she had performed, and whose results not only supported this new paradigm but also suggested our current human experience was woefully limited compared to what it could actually be.

By the end of lunch, Faukman was uncertain if his spinning head was on account of Katherine Solomon's ideas or too much wine, but he knew one thing for certain:

I am definitely publishing this book.

He suspected this lunch might end up being the best publishing investment he'd ever made.

Now, however, a year later, hog-tied on the floor of a freezing-cold van, he was having serious second thoughts about his decision. He hadn't yet read a word of the manuscript and knew nothing about her mysterious experiments, but still he felt perplexed that anyone would want to destroy it.

For God's sake, it's a book about human consciousness!

Faukman's kidnappers were sitting nearby, engrossed in their devices.

"Hey, guys?" Faukman ventured, teeth chattering. He wanted to keep them talking. "What's so special about this book? You know it's about *science*, right? There are no pictures."

No reply.

"Look, I'm freezing. This is insane. If you can tell me *why* you're so interested in this manuscript, maybe I can—"

"We're not interested at all," Buzzcut said. "Our *employer* is."

"Darth Vader can read?"

Buzzcut actually chuckled. "Yes, and he wants to speak to you. We have a plane fueling. We'll be leaving shortly for Prague."

Faukman felt his body tense. "Wait! No way in hell I'm going to Prague! I don't have my passport! I need to feed my cat!"

"I stole your passport from your apartment," Buzzcut said. "And I shot your cat."

Faukman was genuinely afraid now. "That's not funny . . . I don't even have a cat. Can we talk about this?"

"Sure thing." Buzzcut gave a cocky smile. "Plenty of time to chat on the plane."

CHAPTER 40

The Havelský Market was crammed with traffic moving at a crawl. A few blocks from their destination, Langdon and Sasha abandoned the cab and walked through the tangle of roads and alleys that form the residential district of Old Town. As he followed Sasha toward her apartment, Langdon was surprised to learn that her home was, in fact, owned by Brigita Gessner, who permitted Sasha to stay there rent-free.

Another uncharacteristic act of kindness, Langdon thought, curious why Gessner seemed so intent on helping this young woman.

Brigita Gessner was an enigma. While seemingly generous and compassionate toward Sasha, last night over cocktails she had been unbearable. At one point, while Langdon was absently nursing his repulsive bacon-flavored cocktail, Gessner had turned and abruptly put him on the spot.

"Professor Langford," she said, no doubt botching his name on purpose. "Katherine and I disagree on something, and we want you to settle it for us."

Katherine winced, obviously not looking to draw Langdon in.

"You're an educated man," Gessner said, "and your perspective on this will be of interest. Katherine and I diverge on an issue that lies at the core of the materialist-noetic debate. That being . . . life after death."

Oh dear . . .

"So tell us," Gessner pressed, "which do *you* believe? When you die, is that the end? Or is there something . . . else?"

Langdon hesitated, trying to figure out how to navigate the moment.

"As I have stated many times," Gessner jumped in, "I view life after death as an empty fantasy—an illusion sold by religion to recruit the faint of heart and weak of mind."

Oh boy, I'm not touching that one . . .

"And as I'm sure you know," Gessner continued, "Katherine has stated publicly that she believes out-of-body experiences are strong evidence that consciousness resides *outside* the brain and therefore can *survive* death. In other words . . . the afterlife is real." The neuroscientist casually sipped her cocktail. "So which is it, Professor?"

"I have no definitive idea," he replied. "I've taught thanatology, but it's not really my field—"

"The question is simple," the woman scoffed, interrupting him. "If you were dying, and you found yourself looking down at your own body on an operating table, would you classify that as evidence of an afterlife? Or as hypoxic hallucination?"

I've never had a near-death experience . . . I have no idea what I would think.

Langdon's only encounter with near-death experiences had been in the pages of Raymond Moody's 1975 bestseller, *Life After Life,* the book credited with persuading scientists to look more seriously at the possibility that death was not the end of a journey . . . but rather just the beginning.

The book included hundreds of medically documented cases of clinically dead people who had reawakened to report very similar out-of-body experiences—a disembodied point of view, hovering, moving upward into a dark tunnel, approaching a bright light, and, most remarkably, feeling a sense of absolute calm and boundless knowledge.

After Moody's book, the question was no longer *if* people were having out-of-body experiences . . . but rather *what* was causing them, and what did they mean?

Langdon was certainly aware that life after death was the cornerstone of literally every enduring spirituality: the Christians had heaven; the Jews had *gilgul;* the Muslims had *Jannah;* the Hindus and Buddhists had *devaloka;* the New Age philosophers had past lives; Plato had metempsychosis. A constant in all spiritual philosophies was that the soul was . . . *eternal.*

Even so, when it came to believing in life after death, Langdon had never been able to pry himself from the materialists' camp. The notion of the afterlife, he believed, was a comforting story, a coping mechanism, and if he was to answer Gessner's question honestly . . .

Near-death experiences are . . . hallucinations.

A scholar of art inspired by religion, Langdon was intimately familiar with masterworks depicting visions of a world beyond this one—divine revelations, spiritual visions, theophanies, religious ecstasies, visitations from angels. The faithful considered these experiences to be *actual* encounters with other realms, but Langdon quietly believed they were something else—vividly persuasive visions brought on by a profound spiritual longing.

There is a reason, Langdon often reminded his students, *that mirages of oases are seen only by thirsty travelers in the desert—and never by college students walking on the quad. We see what we* want *to see.*

And with respect to *wanting,* Langdon imagined that most people in the throes of dying wanted the same basic thing: *not* to die. And the fear of death, of course, was not reserved for the dying. It was a universal fear . . . perhaps *the* universal fear.

Mortality salience, as it was known—the knowledge that we would die—was frightening not because we feared losing our physical bodies, but rather because we feared losing our memories, our dreams, our emotional connections . . . in essence, our *soul.*

Religions had learned long ago that a human mind facing the terrifying prospect of eternal nothingness would believe almost anything. *Timor mortis est pater religionis,* Langdon mused, recalling the ancient saying made famous by Upton Sinclair. *Fear of death is the father of religion.*

Sure enough, every world religion had produced copious writings suggesting an afterlife—the Egyptian Book of the Dead, the Sutras, the Upanishads, the Vedas, the Holy Bible, the Quran, the Kabbalah. Each religion had its own eschatology, its own architecture of the life beyond this one, and its own meticulously cataloged hierarchy of attending spirits.

These religious claims were widely ignored by modern thanatologists—those who studied the *science* of death. And yet, astonishingly, scientists today readily admitted that they had made very little progress in answering the fundamental question of their field:

What happens when we die?

The question was, without compare, the greatest mystery of life . . . the secret we *all* longed to know. Ironically, the elusive answer was revealed to each of us eventually . . . but with no way back to share it.

"Cat got your tongue?" Gessner asked, smirking.

"Not really," Langdon replied testily. "I just find it curious that you accept as absolute fact a premise you're unable to prove. In my world, we call that *faith* . . . not science."

"*Zbabělče,*" Gessner huffed. "I know you're a *materialist*, Professor, and with a little luck, tomorrow when Katherine comes to the lab, I can persuade her to join us in the rational world."

With that, Gessner unlocked her leather briefcase, extracted a business card, and placed it in front of Katherine.

Langdon eyed the card.

DR. BRIGITA GESSNER
GESSNER INSTITUTE
CRUCIFIX BASTION, 1
PRAGUE

"Give this card to your driver tomorrow morning," Gessner said. "My lab is private, but the location is well-known. The bastion is quite *famous* actually."

Langdon groaned inwardly. *Famous in the 1300s perhaps . . .*

As Gessner moved to close her briefcase, Langdon caught a glimpse of the meticulously organized contents—various documents in folders, a pen in a loop holder, a smartphone secured with a leather strap, and a collection of credit cards, IDs, and key cards all perfectly aligned in individual transparent sleeves. Among the group, a symbol caught his eye.

"What's that card?" he asked, pointing to a black card sticking out of a specialized, lead-lined sheath designed to safeguard cards equipped with radio frequency identification. He could see only the top half inch of the card but was intrigued by the six characters printed boldly across it.

PRAGUE

Gessner glanced down at the card, faltering a moment. "Oh, it's nothing." She closed her case. "It's for my health club."

"Oh?" Langdon said. "I'm curious. The third character—what was it?"

She gave him an odd look. "You mean the letter *A*?"

"That wasn't an *A*," Langdon said, having seen it clearly. "It was a Vel spear."

Both women looked puzzled.

"I'm sorry?" Gessner said.

"The crossbar is the difference," Langdon said. "An *A* has a single line. That logo had three lines and a dot. Whenever you see an upward-facing blade—that is, the shape of a capital *A*—with three crossbars and a dot, it's a specialized icon with a very specific meaning."

"Does it mean *health*?" Katherine ventured, sounding a bit tipsy.

Not even close, Langdon thought. "The Vel spear is a Hindu symbol of power. The point of the spear represents enlightenment, a sharply tuned mind, the superior insight used to cut through the darkness of ignorance and conquer your enemies. The Hindu god of war, Murugan, carried the spear with him everywhere."

Gessner looked genuinely surprised.

"Killing your foes with insight?" Katherine said. "Strange message for a health club."

I agree.

"Happenstance, obviously," Gessner scoffed. "I'm sure the club has no idea and simply liked the design."

Langdon let it go, but he felt quite certain Gessner was hiding something. A shielded RFID card seemed an unusually high-tech passkey for a health club, and Gessner hardly seemed like someone who would tolerate exercising with the unclean masses. Besides, a local health club would most likely use the Czech spelling, "PRAHA," rather than English.

"It is clear," Gessner said, sounding irked, "that symbologists and noeticists are a perfect match for one another." She took a sip of her drink. "You both see meaning where there is none."

CHAPTER 41

Sasha Vesna's first-floor apartment was small but homey—
tastefully furnished, well organized, and with plentiful natural light. As Langdon stepped inside, he breathed in the
smoky scent of malt that hung in the air.

"Russian Caravan tea," Sasha offered, sounding self-conscious
about the noticeable smell. "And I have cats . . ."

As if on cue, a lithe pair of Siamese cats materialized at the far
end of the hallway and padded toward them. Langdon crouched
down to pet them, and they hurried over for attention.

"They love men," Sasha said, and then awkwardly added,
"Not that they have seen many!"

Langdon smiled politely. "Well, they're beautiful animals."

"That one's Sally. He's Harry. I named them after my favorite
movie." Sasha pointed to an old movie poster hanging nearby.
"Dr. Gessner got me that."

The film title was in Russian, but Langdon recognized Meg
Ryan and Billy Crystal standing face-to-face against the New
York skyline. He'd never seen the classic *When Harry Met Sally*,
but he'd heard about the famous "sex scene" in a New York deli.

"I always loved American romantic comedies," Sasha said. "It's
how I learned English." She admired the poster a moment, her
eyes clouding with sadness. "My cats were a gift from Dr. Gessner
too . . . so I wouldn't be alone."

"Very thoughtful of her," Langdon said.

Sasha removed her heavy shoes and left them on a rubber mat
just inside the doorway. Langdon followed suit, happy again to
be out of his damp loafers.

"The bathroom is there if you need it," she said, motioning toward an alcove partway down the hall.

"Thank you," Langdon replied. "I'll take you up on that."

"I'll put on some tea," she said, leaving him and disappearing down the hallway.

Langdon stood a moment, eyeing the poster, Katherine again on his mind. The New York skyline and the Columbia Pictures logo—a robed woman holding up a torch—conjured images of the Statue of Liberty . . . and Katherine's lecture last night.

Where are you right now? he wondered as he walked to the bathroom. He was anxious to call the Four Seasons to see if Katherine had returned to the hotel, but as Harris had implied, ÚZSI would be looking for Langdon and Sasha for assaulting an officer and fleeing the scene. He would need to wait for the attaché to arrive.

The bathroom was cramped but orderly, and Langdon felt self-conscious using Sasha's personal space. After washing his hands, he dried them on his own pants to spare Sasha's perfectly arranged hand towels. When he glanced into the mirror, the face staring back at him looked like a stranger's. His eyes were bloodshot, his hair was disheveled, and deep stress lines furrowed his brow. *You look like hell, Robert.* Considering the morning he'd had, it was not surprising. *Just get to the embassy and find Katherine.*

When Langdon returned to the kitchen, Sasha was pouring dried cat food into two bowls on the counter. Harry and Sally vaulted up effortlessly and began devouring the food.

Sasha moved to the stove, where a kettle was simmering. "How do you take your tea?"

With coffee, he wanted to say. "Plain is perfect. Thank you."

She set out three teacups, three saucers, and three spoons. "I'm going to use the bathroom," she said, moving for the door. "Then I'll pour us some tea. Michael should be here in fifteen minutes or so."

Langdon heard her padding up the hallway and closing the bathroom door.

The apartment fell silent except for the sound of the simmering water. Alone in the kitchen, Langdon eyed Sasha's cell phone on the counter and was again tempted to call the Four Seasons. Then again, Janáček had probably staked out the hotel by now, so it was anyone's guess as to where Katherine was at the moment.

The water had just begun to boil when Langdon heard a sharp knock at the apartment door. *Odd*, he thought, doubting it would be Harris already. Langdon felt suddenly fearful that Janáček or Pavel might have followed them here . . . or taken a logical guess to check Sasha's apartment.

He hurried around the corner into the hallway just as Sasha was emerging from the bathroom, drying her hands. She looked concerned and silently mouthed to Langdon, "Did someone knock?"

Langdon nodded.

From the look on Sasha's face, a visitor was unexpected. They waited fifteen seconds in total silence, but there was no second knock. Sasha padded to the door and peered through the peephole. After a long moment, she turned back to Langdon and shrugged. Nobody.

Langdon now saw that a small white slip of paper was lying on the floor, sticking out from beneath the door. "Someone left you something," he whispered, pointing.

Sasha glanced down and spotted the paper. Looking puzzled, she crouched down and pulled it from beneath the door. From the little Langdon could see, it appeared to be a handwritten note.

Sasha stood up and looked at the message, immediately drawing a startled breath. With trembling fingers, she handed the note to Langdon. "It's for *you*."

Me? Langdon took the slip of paper and read it, his chest tightening instantly.

Filled with fear, he yanked open the apartment door, burst into the deserted entryway, and ran out of the building into the snow, wearing only his socks. Wheeling in circles in the slush, he shouted into the empty air, *"Who are you?! What have you done with her?!"*

———·——

Twenty yards from where Langdon was shouting, The Golĕm watched from the shadows.

The note The Golĕm had just placed at Sasha Vesna's door had sparked the desired reaction. If all went to plan, Robert Langdon would soon be rushing off alone to a deserted location.

Fear is motivational.

CHAPTER 42

Michael Harris could still hear Sasha's desperate phone call as he sped down the road away from Crucifix Bastion.

I'm with Robert Langdon! We need your help!

When he reached the main road, Harris turned right, racing north toward Sasha's apartment. *A place I know all too well,* he lamented, having visited numerous times, always against his better judgment.

Harris had first met Sasha two months ago at David Rio Chai Latte, where Sasha stopped every morning on her way to work. Sasha was alone at a standing table, and Harris approached her with a smile.

"*Privet, Sasha,*" he said in Russian. *Hello, Sasha.*

The tall blonde glanced up, looking alarmed. "How do you know my name?"

Harris smiled and pointed to her paper cup, on which the barista had written: SAŠA.

"Oh," Sasha said, looking sheepish but still uncertain. "But . . . you spoke Russian."

"Lucky guess," Harris said. "I heard your accent when you ordered."

Now Sasha looked embarrassed. "Of course. Sorry to be jumpy. Russians aren't exactly the most popular people in Prague."

"Try being *American*!" he replied, showing her his MICKALE cup. "The barista misspelled my name on purpose, I'm sure."

He smiled and put on his best Bogart impersonation. "Of all the coffee joints in all the towns in all the world, I walk into *this* one."

"*Casablanca!*" She brightened. "I love that movie!"

Over the next half hour, they swapped stories, and Sasha shared a heartbreaking tale of debilitating epilepsy and childhood abandonment in a Russian mental institution . . . until a neurosurgeon rescued her and brought her to Prague.

"And this Dr. Gessner *cured* you?" Harris asked.

"Perfectly," Sasha said, gratitude in her eyes. "She invented a brain implant that I can activate by rubbing a magnetic wand over my skull whenever I feel the fog."

"The fog?"

"Yes, sorry, before a seizure, epileptics get a hazy, tingling warning . . . kind of like that prickly sensation before you sneeze. When it happens, I rub the wand on top of my head, and the magnet triggers the chip inside my skull." She hesitated, looking suddenly self-conscious. "Sorry, it's kind of unappealing to talk about."

"Not at all—I can't see a thing," Harris said honestly. "If there are scars, they're totally hidden beneath all that beautiful blond hair!"

The compliment was earnest, but Sasha averted her gaze, looking suddenly uncomfortable. "I can't believe I told you all this. How embarrassing. I don't talk to many people, so . . . anyway, I have to go to work." She abruptly drained the rest of her chai and quickly started packing up.

"I have to go too," Harris said, "but it was fun talking, and if you ever want to have lunch sometime, I'd love to talk more."

Sasha looked startled by the request. "No, I don't think that's a good idea."

"Of course, sorry," Harris said, fumbling. "I didn't mean a *date* date. I just . . . anyhow, you're probably seeing someone, so—"

"Me? No, I'm not *seeing* anyone," she blurted clumsily. "It's just . . ." Her eyes suddenly welled with tears, as if she were about to break down.

"Oh no!" Harris said, confused. "I didn't mean to upset you."

"It's my fault . . ." she said, her voice fragile. "I'm sorry . . . I'm just afraid if you get to know me . . . you'll be so disappointed."

"Why would you ever say that?"

She wiped her eyes and looked at him. "Michael, I'm not very good at . . . you know, relations. I spent most of my life alone and on strong medications. I have serious memory problems, a lot of ugly scars from seizu—"

"Stop right there," Harris said. "I find you quite charming. And considering what you've been through, you're remarkably easy to talk to."

"Really?" She blushed. "Then it must be the company."

They talked a bit more, and ultimately Sasha agreed to see him again.

Two weeks later, after a lunch, a dinner, and an evening walk in Wallenstein Garden, Harris sensed he knew all he would ever know about Sasha Vesna. She was a simple woman with no friends, who spent all her time either working at Gessner's lab or at home watching old movies with her cats. *Sasha is a loner . . . and lonely.*

Unfortunately, Harris felt increasingly uncomfortable about their deepening relationship. *If she ever discovers the real reason I'm seeing her, it will destroy her.* Burdened by guilt, Harris chided himself for ever agreeing to do this. *It's time I end this charade.*

Mustering his resolve, Harris had climbed the marble staircase to the ambassador's office. He knocked on her open door, and she waved him in.

Ambassador Heide Nagel was a sixty-six-year-old graduate of Columbia Law. The child of German immigrants, she had come to America at the age of four and risen to the top of her field. Her German surname, it had been noted publicly, literally meant "nails"—as in "as tough as."

With inscrutable eyes and a politely diplomatic manner, she often lulled adversaries into a false sense of security before she dispatched them. Even Nagel's quotidian attire seemed calculated to downplay her influence—simple black pantsuits, comfortable shoes, and reading glasses on a chain that looked more befitting a librarian than a diplomat. She wore her black hair with laser-straight blunt bangs and very little makeup.

"Michael," she said, closing her laptop. "What can I do for you?"

Harris entered and stood before her desk. "Ma'am, I'm afraid I'm no longer comfortable with the off-book project you assigned me."

"Oh?" Nagel took off her glasses and motioned for him to sit. "What's the problem?"

Harris cleared his throat and took a seat. "As I've reported, ma'am, Sasha Vesna is a naive young woman who was horribly mistreated as a child and is simply doing the best she can to live a normal life. There's nothing more for me to learn. At this point, I just feel that continuing to lie to her is, well . . . morally wrong." He had not allowed their relationship to become overly physical, but Harris still felt Sasha's heart opening to him.

"I see," Nagel said. "For a moment, I thought you were going to say *dangerous*. I hope you know if it were dangerous, I'd pull you out immediately."

Harris believed her. Nagel ran this embassy with an iron hand, but she also cared loyally for her staff. "No, ma'am," he assured her, "I don't see any danger. The problem is that Sasha *is* becoming attached. *Ethically*, it feels . . ."

"Dishonest?" The ambassador looked almost amused. "I must say, Michael, I find it ironic that you would cite *morality* as the reason you want to quit seeing Sasha."

"I'm sorry?"

The ambassador stood up and walked to the wet bar in the corner of her office. Without a word, she poured a tumbler of Vincentka mineral water and returned, handing it to him. Then she sat behind her desk, raising her eyes to his.

"My suspicion," she said, "is that the *real* reason you want to stop seeing Sasha Vesna is because you're afraid my PR liaison, Ms. Daněk, will catch you spending time with another woman."

Harris tried to maintain a poker face, but he could feel himself crumbling. *The ambassador knows I'm seeing Dana?!* Any moral high ground Harris had hoped to occupy just evaporated.

"I hope you're aware," Nagel said, "that this embassy has a zero-tolerance policy on interemployee relationships." She paused, as if suddenly recalling. "Oh, of course, you're aware of the policy . . . You helped *draft* it."

Shit.

"Relax," Nagel said calmly, "I'm not looking to have you fired. I'm simply exploiting a weakness in service to my country."

"That's quite a euphemism for 'coercion,'" he managed.

"You're an attorney, Michael, so just think of it as effective negotiating. And believe me, I would not be applying this kind of pressure if my superiors weren't applying that same pressure to me."

"With respect, ma'am, I find it hard to believe our president cares about a Russian epileptic with two cats named Harry and Sally."

"First off, the White House is not the only powerful entity to whom I answer. Secondly, my superiors have not told me precisely what their interest is in Sasha Vesna, only that they want to be apprised of what secrets she is telling those people she trusts."

"Sasha has no secrets!" Harris insisted. "She's an open book, and she's just happy to have someone to talk to."

"Exactly. And *you* have now established yourself in that position, which is very valuable. You need to keep her talking. In the meantime, I'll ignore your situation with Dana, and I'll tell my superiors to pay you twice what they're already paying you for this special project."

Harris was stunned. His additional financial compensation was already exceedingly generous. *Who is so eager to keep tabs on Sasha Vesna? And why?*

"And Michael," she said, "if this project ever feels even *slightly* dangerous, you tell me, and I pull the plug." She locked eyes with him. "Deal?"

Harris gazed down at her outstretched hand, stunned by how effortlessly she had reached checkmate. Despite his gut reservations, he suspected that if he himself didn't do this, someone *else* might take more drastic measures. *Sasha doesn't deserve that.* He shook the ambassador's hand.

In the weeks that followed, Harris's relationship with Sasha naturally progressed to an awkward physical romance. Fortunately, Sasha was extremely inexperienced, and Harris insisted they take things incredibly slowly. So far, the most intimacy they had shared was lying in each other's arms in her bed, mostly clothed, watching old American romantic comedies until they both fell asleep.

Now, as Harris raced north to meet with Sasha and Langdon, he reflected on everything he had learned this morning from the ambassador. The scope of the operation going on in Prague was beyond his wildest imagination. Even without specifics, Harris knew he was in miles over his head.

It's time to get out.

As he neared Old Town, Harris made himself a solemn vow.

No matter the repercussions, this will be my last visit with Sasha Vesna . . . ever.

CHAPTER 43

Robert Langdon paced anxiously around Sasha Vesna's small kitchen, his soaking-wet socks leaving footprints on her tile floor.

This can't be happening.

He stared again at the slip of paper that had appeared moments earlier under Sasha's door.

The handwritten note had jarred his world from its axis.

I have Katherine.
Come to Petřín Tower.

His mind raced with agonizing questions.

Who are you? What have you done with her? Why Petřín Tower?

Prague's two-hundred-foot Petřín Tower was not far from the city's center, situated atop a heavily wooded hill. The forest's storied history of virgin sacrifices did little to calm his nerves.

Langdon could imagine no possible motive for anyone abducting Katherine Solomon. *Come to Petřín Tower . . . why?*

"We must have been followed here," Sasha said, sounding frightened. "Maybe from the taxi stand? Maybe this is ÚZSI, but—"

"Why the hell would ÚZSI *kidnap* Katherine?!"

"I don't know." Sasha looked distraught. "Michael will know what to—"

"I can't wait for Michael," Langdon interrupted, hurrying up the hallway to find his shoes. "I've got to go right *now.*" *Katherine is in danger. I need to get there as soon as possible.* As he slid his wet socks into his loafers, Sasha opened the hall closet and reached for her coat.

"No, Sasha," he interjected, "the best thing you can do is to stay here, meet with Michael, have him take you to the U.S. embassy, and tell them everything you know. *Everything*. Including what happened with Brigita, the ÚZSI agent, this note, my going to Petřín Tower, everything."

Langdon had already witnessed Sasha's spontaneous capacity for abrupt violence, and he could not afford to show up at Petřín Tower accompanied by a wild card.

"Okay," she said, reaching into her handbag, "but if you're going alone, at least take *this*." She pulled out Pavel's weapon.

Langdon recoiled instinctively. He had always been unnerved by weapons and knew enough about confrontation not to add a gun to the mix if not necessary. He had no desire to carry a stolen ÚZSI weapon through the streets of Prague, especially as he had no way to transport it except tucked into the waist of his pants, a technique that, every time he saw it in the movies, seemed an insane risk.

"I'd feel better if *you* kept it," he said. "Obviously, whoever left that note knows where you live. Hide it in a kitchen cupboard . . . and if you desperately need it, you'll know where it is."

Sasha thought for a moment and then nodded. "Okay, but *this* you should take." She walked to a hook on the wall and removed a plastic key ring with a single key. "My spare key. If you and Katherine need a safe place to go or hide, come *here*. I don't know what Michael will suggest we do, so we might not be here when you come, but at least you'll have a way in."

"Thank you," Langdon said, doubting he would be back. Nonetheless, he accepted her generosity, noting that her key ring was a plastic cutout of a spread-eagle cat, with the words "Krazy Kitten." He slipped it into his pocket. "I'll find a phone and call you as soon as I know what's happening."

"You'll need my number."

"I have Michael's cell."

She looked surprised. "He gave you his private line?"

"I saw you dial it in the car," Langdon said.

"And you remember it?"

"Weird brain," Langdon said. "I don't forget things."

"That must be nice," she said. "I have the opposite problem. I can't remember things. Memories get muddled . . . lots of blanks."

"From the epilepsy?"

"Yes, but Brigita was working with me on that . . ."

Langdon gave a comforting smile. "It sounds like Dr. Gessner was very good to you."

"She saved my life." Sasha looked melancholy. "I hope I don't forget *her* too."

"You won't," Langdon assured her, reaching for the door. "And trust me, remembering *everything* is not always a blessing."

CHAPTER 44

From the moment Jonas Faukman had been thrown into this van, he had tried to manage his fear with a feigned flippancy, but it was becoming difficult to maintain in the face of the foreboding sense that he was about to be abducted to Prague. The roaring jet engine nearby, combined with losing all feeling in his hands, left him on the verge of panic.

"I'll tell the pilots we're ready," Buzzcut said to his partner. "Then we'll load him up." He opened the slider and stepped out, leaving the door wide open as he departed, apparently to punish Faukman for his insolence.

"It's freezing . . ." Faukman said to the other man.

No reply.

The whine of jets was much louder now, and Faukman finally had a view of his surroundings. The van was parked on a wooded service road of some sort, behind a white building that was no more than a couple of hundred yards away. Faukman had imagined he was on a secret air base about to board a military transport, but the illuminated marquis on the building told a much different story.

SIGNATURE AVIATION / TETERBORO

Holy shit. I'm in Jersey?!

Signature was a popular private jet terminal at New Jersey's Teterboro Airport. Only twenty minutes from Manhattan, the luxurious FBO was a hub for wealthy Manhattanites to jump onto their private planes bound for business trips or secluded vacation homes on the slopes of Aspen or the beaches of West Palm.

For an instant, Faukman felt relief that he was not on a military base, but then, as the truth started to settle, he wondered if this might be even worse. At least the military had certain protocols, and Faukman was a U.S. civilian. If these thugs were actually mercenaries working for a rich, international whoever-the-hell-it was, there were no rules of engagement.

They could fly me out of the country . . . and nobody would even know I was gone!

As a fresh blast of winter wind swirled through the van, the guy in front set down his laptop and climbed back between the seats, then pulled the slider shut. "You're right, buddy, it's cold."

The man had softer features than Buzzcut, of mixed Asian descent, and like his partner, he had a clean-cut military air about him. "How are the hands?" he asked.

"Honestly, if this goes on much longer, I think I may lose them."

"Let me have a look." The man maneuvered in behind Faukman and examined his hands. "Yeah. That's not good." He pulled out an army knife. "Just stay still. I'm going to cut you free and attach a slightly looser tie, okay?"

Faukman nodded, his thoughts still spinning over what he had just seen outside.

"No stupid stunts and don't screw around with me," the man said. "Remember, I'm the one holding a knife."

"Got it."

An instant later, Faukman's hands were free. He gingerly maneuvered his arms back in front of him and wiggled his fingers to coax the blood to flow again.

The man behind him circled back around and sat on the crate, knife at the ready.

"I'll give you sixty seconds," he said.

"Thanks." Faukman grimaced as excruciating needles of sensation returned to his wrists and fingers.

"Sorry about my partner," the man said. "Auger can be a bit . . . *intense.*"

"The appropriate literary term is 'douchebag,'" Faukman replied.

The man laughed out loud.

The two sat in silence as Faukman continued to massage his hands. His toes felt frozen as well; the running sneakers he had put on when he left his office weren't exactly insulated.

"Do you want to put your coat back on," the man asked, "before I put a fresh tie on your wrists?"

Faukman eyed his coat on the floor. *Hell yes!*

Half-standing and half-crouching, Faukman awkwardly slid his aching arms into his coat and savored the warmth. He tried to fasten the buttons, but his partially thawed fingers refused. "Little help?" he said, looking to his captor, who was sitting on the milk crate with his knife.

The man shook his head. "And set down my weapon? Sorry, buddy. I don't trust you."

"I think you greatly overestimate my potential for heroics," Faukman said, wrapping the coat around him as best as he could, pleased to feel his cell phone in the pocket, right where he had left it.

"Okay," the man said. "Let's get you secured again."

"Can you just give me one more minute? My hands are killing me."

"Now," the man commanded. "Turn around."

Faukman complied, turning 180 degrees and facing backward in the van. As he did, he found himself with a clear view out the window in the van's rear door. Through it, he could see the Signature Aviation building. He could also see the parking lot, where a single SUV was idling, its exhaust billowing into the cold morning air. The SUV's driver's door was open, but the seat was empty, the driver most likely inside the small terminal.

"I'll leave it loose for now," the man said, retying Faukman's wrists. "But we'll have to tighten it up when my partner gets back."

"Thanks."

The man finished tying his hands, and Faukman twisted his

wrists slightly, surprised to find the restraints so loose that he could probably slip right out of them.

"Be right back—nature calls," the man said, exiting the van through the side door and sliding it closed again. Faukman turned around and watched through the windshield as the man passed in front of the van, stepped a few yards into the woods, and unbuckled his belt.

Then he began urinating against a tree.

Having edited all of Langdon's books on symbols, signs, and hidden meanings, Faukman had no doubt how the professor would categorize this moment.

A heraldic sign.

Faukman would call it something a bit less poetic.

My last fucking chance.

Attempting to escape men with guns was borderline crazy . . . but not as crazy as letting them abduct him to a foreign country without a fight. Worst-case scenario, they would catch him again and throw him onto the plane.

Through the windshield, Faukman could see the man was still peeing.

Once you start, it's hard to stop.

And until you stop, it's hard to run.

Faukman made up his mind in an instant, grateful for the countless hours he'd spent running in Central Park. *If they try to shoot . . . I'll be a moving target.* He quickly wriggled his hands out of the tie and double-checked that the man was not watching.

Here we go . . .

He grabbed the handle to the van's rear door, depressed it, and quietly swung the door open. Then he crouched down and leaped out. The instant his feet touched down on solid earth, he exploded into a full sprint down the access road, forcing past the pain in his cramped legs. He was an experienced runner, and his legs responded effortlessly to the sudden exertion. His wool coat billowed behind him as he picked up speed and set his sights on the idling SUV in the distance.

Faukman glanced over his shoulder and saw his abductor

awkwardly zipping up and trying to give chase. *No chance,* he thought, feeling the wind in his face.

The man in pursuit was yelling as Faukman approached the SUV. A gunshot rang out, and a bullet whizzed over Faukman's head.

Holy shit!

Faukman reached the idling SUV, hurled himself into the driver's seat, slammed the door, and muscled the vehicle into gear. He crushed the accelerator to the floor and the SUV peeled out, tires screeching as it bounced up and over the median, fishtailing out of the parking lot onto Industrial Avenue.

As Faukman sped off, leaving Signature Aviation and his captors behind, he grabbed his phone from his coat pocket, held it up to his face, and shouted, "Hey, Siri! Call Robert Langdon!"

⎯⎯ · ⎯⎯

A hundred yards away, the operative named Chinburg stopped running, finished zipping up his fly, and calmly watched the SUV disappear into the night. Once the vehicle was out of sight, he walked back to the van.

"All clear," he announced.

His partner with the buzz cut, Auger, stepped out of hiding. "Phone?"

"All good. He took it."

"Nice job."

Despite their captive's extensive experience editing suspense novels, the man had just fallen for the most basic interrogation ploy of all—the Fugitive.

Threaten someone's life and he'll always do the inevitable if you give him the chance—run.

There was no plane waiting, no flight to Prague. They had simply parked their van on an access road adjacent to Teterboro's Signature Aviation services, called in a third operative to pose as a chauffeur, and then created the illusion of a perfect escape moment.

Faukman took the bait . . . and his escape car has a tracking device.

Sometimes, before letting a fugitive escape, they would plant a surveillance bug on the quarry, but in Faukman's case, there was no need; he was already carrying a powerful two-way transceiver with GPS—his own smartphone.

While Faukman had been blindfolded, the operatives had quietly removed his phone from his coat, plugged it into the laptop, bypassed his passcode, and uploaded a variety of proprietary software before replacing the phone in his pocket.

"We've got activity," Chinburg announced, his face illuminated by his iPad's screen, which displayed a full surveillance interface with Faukman's phone—location, text, voice and data received and sent.

The iPad speaker crackled with Faukman's voice, who seemed to be leaving a voicemail.

"Robert, it's Jonas . . . call me immediately! You're in danger—Katherine is too. This is going to sound crazy, but someone hacked into our server and deleted her manuscript . . . I don't know why yet. I was literally abducted off the street near my office. I'm calling Katherine now, but you need to stay wherever you are. Don't talk to anyone!"

The call was severed, and another was immediately initiated.

The second call also went to voicemail, this time Katherine's. Faukman left another breathless message, similar to his first, except for one addition.

"Katherine," Faukman said, "these guys said you printed the manuscript this morning? If that's true, then lock it up somewhere safe—it's our only remaining copy! All the others are gone . . . literally every last one. Call me when you get this."

The call ended.

"A bit of bonus intel," Auger said, sounding smug. "Confirmation that the manuscript in Prague is the *only* one left."

"Finch will be pleased," Chinburg said, pulling out his phone. "I'll let him know."

CHAPTER 45

Lieutenant Pavel's head was still throbbing from the fire extinguisher blow, but it was nothing compared to the pain of seeing his uncle's lifeless body at the bottom of the ravine. The embassy attaché Michael Harris believed the captain had jumped, but Pavel knew better.

Janáček was fearless . . . not a quitter. He was murdered . . . and I know who killed him.

Robert Langdon's list of crimes against ÚZSI was growing ever longer since his hotel stunt—resisting arrest, assaulting an officer, stealing an ÚZSI weapon, and now, if the jumble of footprints on the ridge were to be believed, murdering Captain Janáček and fleeing the crime scene.

Alone now at the bastion, Pavel was recuperating on the plush couch in Gessner's reception room. Harris had given him a bag of ice, told him not to move, and then headed off to the U.S. embassy, promising to call ÚZSI headquarters immediately about Janáček.

That fall was no accident, Pavel knew.

He also knew that Harris was full of shit; the attaché had no intention of making that call. He was just buying time so the embassy could concoct their lies before ÚZSI even heard about Janáček's death.

Pavel had pulled out his phone to call headquarters himself, but after thinking a moment, he paused. He had no doubt that the arrest of a prominent American would end as it always did—infuriatingly—with the U.S. embassy stepping in, taking over, and finding some loophole to leave ÚZSI in the cold.

"Oko za oko," Pavel said aloud, knowing how his late captain would handle this situation. *An eye for an eye.*

Nobody was aware yet of Janáček's death, which meant Pavel had a small window of opportunity to handle Langdon himself. *But first I have to find him.* Locating a fugitive in a city this size would have been nearly impossible, except for one ace up Pavel's sleeve . . . which would turn the tables on the American in an instant.

Janáček taught me to bend the rules . . . to improvise for the greater good.

Technically, Pavel did not hold sufficient rank to do what he had in mind, but he was in possession of Captain Janáček's personal phone, which he had found on the snowy ridge.

With one little lie, Pavel could change everything.

Langdon would have nowhere to hide.

<hr />

Dana Daněk marched back into her office at the embassy, still fuming from her confrontation at the Four Seasons. The ghostly woman from Charles Bridge had scared the hell out of Dana, which was not easy to do.

She aimed a fucking gun at my face!

Dana's jealousy had turned to seething rage.

Who the hell is she?

The answer, Dana knew, was already waiting on her computer—the results of the facial recognition search that Dana had launched nearly an hour ago with the screenshot from Charles Bridge.

Dana hurried to her computer and sat down. As expected, the program had run its complete cycle.

Dana stared at the results in disbelief.

There must be some mistake . . .

SEARCH COMPLETE

MATCHES: 0

Dana had never had a database search return no matches whatsoever. In the modern world, it was a physical impossibility to exist without leaving a single digital footprint *any-where*.

Digital "whitewashing" was the only possible way for a person to remain outside this Echelon database. The network was U.S. owned and operated, meaning the American government could create "invisible people" simply by limiting search results to *exclude* any faces they preferred untraceable. This technique was employed often to ensure the privacy and security for government officials, prominent American businesspeople, and undercover military or intelligence personnel.

Dana considered the puzzling bouquet of red, white, and blue tulips she had seen in the Royal Suite. These flowers were the standard welcome gift from the U.S. ambassador to American VIPs visiting Prague, and as PR liaison, Dana was responsible for having them delivered. The problem was that *these* tulips, Dana had never even heard about.

Did the ambassador organize these herself?

"Ms. Daněk!" a woman bellowed from the doorway.

Dana spun, knowing the voice at once. "Madam Ambassador?! I was just—"

"Were you at the Four Seasons?!"

Dana opened her mouth, but no words came.

"Did you follow Mr. Harris there?"

"No!" Dana blurted. "Well, sort of . . . I thought . . ."

"You thought . . . *what*?" The ambassador's glare cut through her.

Dana stared at the floor. *Shit.*

"Ms. Daněk, *this* is precisely why we don't sleep with co-workers."

CHAPTER 46

As Langdon's taxi ascended the wooded hill toward Petřín Tower, he realized he was still clutching the note that had been slid under Sasha's door.

I have Katherine.
Come to Petřín Tower.

Whoever had left it had a grim sense of symbolism; the tower stood on a hilltop noted for its macabre history of death and human sacrifice.

Specifically, the death of women . . . at the hands of zealots.

According to lore, a sacrificial altar once sat atop Petřín Hill, where pagan priests would burn young virgins to delight the pagan gods. The sacrifices continued for centuries until the Christians took over, demolished the altar, and built the Church of St. Lawrence on that spot. To this day, however, mysterious fires broke out regularly on Petřín Hill and were believed by some to be the handiwork of the ghosts of the sacrificed women who still haunted these woods by the hundreds.

The fortysomething, ponytailed cabdriver navigated the winding road up Petřín Hill, glancing in the rearview mirror at his passenger. The man in the back seemed on edge, craning his neck and squinting nervously up at the top of Petřín Tower.

If you're afraid of heights, my friend, just don't go up.

The passenger was tall with dark hair, and while his American accent and expensive sweater screamed *tourist*, he had jumped into the cab with the urgency of a man fleeing a wildfire. The cabbie had warned him that Petřín Tower might not be open at this hour and also that he was underdressed for the cold winds, but the man had insisted.

Suit yourself . . . A fare is a fare.

As the taxi climbed the hill, the cabbie tapped happily on his steering wheel, keeping rhythm with the song streaming on his phone. His favorite oldie *"Klokočí"* was playing, but as the song reached its lilting clarinet solo, the music cut out abruptly, replaced by a high-pitched series of tones.

"Sakra!!" the cabbie cursed, annoyed by the interruption.

Czech law enforcement had taken to broadcasting these irritating "public alerts" in hopes of recruiting the public's help with local police work. The first wave of alerts was always sent to transportation employees, airport personnel, and local hospitals.

I've got my own job, he grumbled. *Why am I doing yours?!*

Annoyingly, most of Europe had adopted the American system of "AMBER Alerts," despite the acronym's literal meaning: America's Missing: Broadcast Emergency Response.

The cabbie reached down to dismiss the alert and get back to his song, but the blinking banner on his phone's display gave him pause. This alert was coded blue, which was extremely rare in Prague. Normally alerts were coded amber or silver, requesting the public's help locating a missing child or a disorientated elderly person. Blue was much more serious. It meant a law enforcement officer had been killed and a criminal was still at large.

Someone killed an officer in Prague?!

Then the cabbie saw the photo of the suspect.

That guy . . . is my passenger!

Stunned, the driver confirmed with a quick glance in the rearview mirror. Then he nonchalantly picked up his phone and placed a call to the number on the alert, calmly relaying information in Czech to the officer who answered.

●———··———●

Lieutenant Pavel's head was pounding as he dashed out of Crucifix Bastion and leaped behind the wheel of his ÚZSI sedan. The Blue Alert he had issued with Janáček's phone had just generated a response call, within minutes . . . which, as Pavel had arranged, came back directly to Janáček's phone.

Nobody else has the information I just received.

Robert Langdon was headed to Petřín Tower, and while Pavel could not imagine why, there could be no place better for Pavel to take the American. The area around Petřín Hill was isolated and vast. Most importantly, at this early hour on a winter morning, it would be nearly deserted.

It will be my pleasure to take Langdon down.

All I need is a weapon.

Pavel found Janáček's handgun inside the glove box. As he slid the weapon into his empty side holster, Pavel fantasized about how fitting it would feel to fire his captain's gun and kill the man who had murdered Janáček in cold blood.

An eye for an eye.

CHAPTER 47

In 1889, after Prague city officials visited the Exposition Universelle in Paris and saw Gustave Eiffel's showstopping tower, they decided soon after to build their own "miniature" Eiffel Tower in Prague. Situated atop Petřín Hill and completed in 1891, the tower was hardly miniature, rising two hundred feet above a hilltop that was already more than a thousand feet tall.

Like its Parisian inspiration, Petřín Tower was built in an open-lattice construction of riveted steel beams and supports. Apart from their differing heights, the towers of Paris and Prague look markedly similar in silhouette, the only obvious exception being Eiffel Tower's square base and Petřín Tower's octagonal one.

When Langdon's taxi finally reached the wooded parking lot at the base of Petřín Tower, he anxiously scanned the deserted area for signs of life.

I have Katherine. Come to Petřín Tower.

Langdon quickly paid the fare, including a generous tip, and asked the driver to wait for him. The cabbie muttered something in tense Czech and sped off as soon as Langdon had stepped out and closed the door, leaving him alone in the windy parking lot.

Thanks a lot.

Petřín Tower was considerably taller than Langdon recalled, and today it seemed to sway against the gray sky. The snow-dusted forest surrounding the tower looked quiet and majestic, with only a handful of groundskeepers and employees starting their day. Langdon saw no sign of Katherine, nor anyone suspicious. Trying to forget this hill's history of human sacrifice, Langdon moved quickly toward the tower itself, hoping with a pang in his chest that Katherine would indeed be somewhere up here . . . and safe.

Beneath Petřín Tower stood the visitor's center, a low octagonal building nestled perfectly within the tower's eight massive supporting legs. The building had a gently sloping roof through which ascended a slender shaft that climbed all the way to the top of the tower. *Tiny elevator*, Langdon knew. Unfortunately, option number two was a tightly wound, open-air staircase that spiraled around the shaft all the way up. Neither mode of ascent looked particularly inviting.

As he neared the tower, Langdon heard the grinding of elevator gears and the scraping of metal on metal as the carriage moved upward into the shaft.

Someone is going to the top, he thought expectantly. *Katherine?*

He rushed into the visitor's hall, an octagonal room decorated with historical photos of the tower's construction. The hall was deserted except for a young female attendant who was unpacking boxes of Prague paraphernalia.

"*Dobré ráno!*" she said cheerily. "Good morning!"

"Good morning," Langdon replied. "Is the tower open?"

"Just now," she replied. "Only two people at the top. Would you like a ticket?"

Langdon felt his pulse quicken. *Two people.* He couldn't help but wonder if it was Katherine and her captor. *Am I supposed to go up?* The note had not been specific, but Langdon was not about to take that chance. The thought of Katherine in the hands of some lunatic, hundreds of feet up on an open-air observation platform, filled him with dread.

Langdon bought a ticket and waited outside the elevator door. Somewhere above him, the carriage ground its way noisily back down from the top. When the doors finally rattled open, Langdon found himself peering into a tiny, awkwardly shaped cabin that looked like it hadn't been refurbished since the 1800s.

Instinctively, he turned his gaze to the nearby spiral staircase, which was cordoned off with a swag and a placard: ZAVŘENO /

CLOSED. Another sign warned that the 299 stairs were extremely steep.

"Are the stairs open?" Langdon asked, hoping the attendant was just now opening and had not yet removed the sign for the day.

"Closed for winter," she said. "Too windy . . . and the snow and ice today!"

Terrific. He peered reluctantly into the lift's tiny compartment, and three words echoed in his mind.

I have Katherine.

Taking a deep breath, Langdon stepped into the lift. He pressed the button, and the doors lurched shut. As the carriage rattled upward, he focused his attention on the metal engraving on the wall, where a series of red lights blinked on and off to indicate his progress.

As the lift climbed, Langdon began feeling increasingly unprepared for whomever or whatever he might find up here. He wondered if he had been a fool not to take the gun from Sasha. *What if her captor is armed?* The higher he went, the more the elevator walls began closing in around him. Langdon closed his eyes and hummed the country song "Wide Open Spaces."

When the lift finally slowed to a stop, Langdon braced himself and opened his eyes. The elevator doors rumbled open, and Langdon felt an instantaneous surge of relief to see open air, but that emotion was immediately dampened by disappointment. The couple on top of the tower were both in their twenties, of Indian descent, and happily taking pictures of Prague.

Katherine was not here.

Langdon urged himself to be patient; he had, after all, left Sasha's apartment immediately upon receiving the note and arrived here quickly. *I'm early,* he concluded, which in some ways might even be better. *I can see them coming,* he thought, walking to the railing and peering down at the parking lot far below.

The wind was gusting more fiercely now, and the swaying tower only accentuated Langdon's already precarious mind-set. As he paced the narrow observation platform that encircled the elevator, he passed the descending spiral staircase, its entrance cordoned off by a NO ENTRY sign and the ominous graphic of a person being blown off the tower. *No, thank you.*

Langdon found a somewhat sheltered spot to wait, overlooking the woods of Petřín Park. The popular tourist site offered numerous attractions for children, including a secret garden, a rope playground, swingsets, and a carousel, which was just now being uncovered for the day. His eye fell on the Church of St. Lawrence far below, where the ancient pagan sacrificial altar had once existed, and Langdon thought again of the rumors of roaming ghosts and murdered virgins.

Not exactly family-friendly, he mused and raised his gaze higher, tracing the quintessential Prague panorama . . . the twin spires of Vyšehrad, the Powder Tower, Charles Bridge, and the monolithic St. Vitus Cathedral, surrounded by the sprawling fortification of Prague Castle.

Katherine had lectured in that castle just last night, and Langdon now wondered if perhaps her abduction might in some way relate to something she'd said in her lecture . . . or in her scientific research. If so, he had no idea what it could be.

Another possibility had occurred to Langdon as well. He was starting to have misgivings about the authenticity of Katherine's ransom note. Something about the message seemed off. *Who are you? Why Petřín Tower?* None of it made a lot of rational sense, and it seemed possible that the note was all part of some strange ploy.

"Sir?" a voice said behind him.

Langdon turned to see the young Indian couple. The woman was smiling and holding out her phone to Langdon. "Would you mind taking our photo? I left my selfie stick in the hotel."

The young man looked apologetic. "Sorry. Instagram honeymoon."

Langdon gathered himself. "Of course."

The woman positioned her husband at the railing, joined him, and gave Langdon the all clear. After taking several photos, Langdon was about to return the phone, but the woman asked him to keep shooting while they tried out various poses and expressions.

"She has a lot of followers," the man said, clearly mortified.

Immortality through fame, Langdon mused as he took photographs, recalling that Shakespeare, Homer, and Horace had all opined that the uniquely human desire to be "famous" was, in fact, the symptom of another uniquely human trait—our fear of death. To be famous meant you would be remembered long after you died . . . fame a kind of eternal life.

"That should do it!" the woman said, reaching out for her phone. "Let me check them!"

Langdon returned her device, noticing the sea of red notification badges on all her social media apps. *The world's new popularity metric. Digital applause.*

She swiped through photos, nodding. "They look perfect!" she gushed. "Thank you!"

Langdon managed a smile. "Congratulations."

The newlyweds headed back to the elevator, having been up here only long enough to photograph themselves before moving on, most likely to the next photo opportunity. Langdon sometimes sensed the only reason to do *anything* anymore was to post it for the world to see.

As the elevator doors rumbled open, Langdon was struck by a thought. "Excuse me," he called to the couple. "Could I ask a small favor?"

They paused in the doorway, holding the door open and looking back at him.

"I was supposed to meet someone here," Langdon said. "But she never arrived. I lost my phone this morning, and I was wondering if I might use yours to give her a quick call?"

The woman looked as if Langdon had asked to hold her newborn, but after a nudge from her husband, she reluctantly handed over her phone.

With the young couple watching him closely, Langdon quickly dialed the number he had seen repeatedly on the Four Seasons registration desk, and the familiar voice of the hotel manager answered on the first ring.

"Thank you for calling the Four—"

"Good morning, sir," Langdon interrupted. "This is Robert

Langdon. I need to speak to Katherine Solomon immediately. It's important."

"Oh, hello, Professor." The manager's enthusiasm cooled abruptly. "I don't believe Dr. Solomon is here. She left the hotel this morning while you were . . . swimming."

"She never came back?"

"I haven't seen her, sir. I'll try your room."

As the line to their suite began ringing with no answer, Langdon had to accept the frightening reality that Katherine might not have returned to the hotel this morning. *So where did she go?!* As he tried to imagine where she could be, an odd thought struck him.

I can't believe I didn't think of it earlier . . .

The line was still ringing, and the Indian couple looked increasingly impatient as they held open the elevator door and waited to descend.

"Sweetie!" Langdon blurted suddenly, pretending someone had answered. "Where *are* you?! I'm at Petřín Tower and—" He fell silent, as if listening, and then gasped dramatically. "Wait, *what?!* Slow down. Just talk to me . . ."

Langdon indicated he needed a moment of privacy, and without waiting for consent, he turned his back on the couple and walked around the platform, out of sight behind the shaft, immediately launching a web browser.

Katherine may have tried to reach me this morning . . .

He had been so caught up in the chaos of the morning that he had not been thinking clearly, but the red notification badges on the woman's apps were now reminding him of those same notifications on his own laptop. *Email.* For years before this trip, Katherine and Langdon had always communicated that way. Katherine called it old-school, but Langdon despised the implied urgency of texting, so they defaulted to email.

If Katherine had tried to reach him this morning by phone or text with no reply, he realized, she would likely have sent him an email that he could read on his laptop.

I never checked mine this morning!

Langdon quickly navigated to gmail.com and signed into

his account. His inbox started to load, displaying very slowly. *Come on!*

The elevator door was buzzing, apparently protesting being held open for so long.

Finally, the screen refreshed, and Langdon's inbox appeared. YOU HAVE 31 UNREAD MESSAGES.

He cursed his overflowing inbox and rapidly scanned the list of incoming messages from colleagues, friends, and assorted spam. As he neared the bottom of the list, he was losing hope.

Then he saw it. *Yes!*

FROM: KATHERINE SOLOMON

The time stamp was 7:42 a.m. this morning—after Katherine had left the hotel but before her meeting with Gessner.

Strangely, the subject line was blank.

Heart racing, Langdon tapped to open the message, but when it displayed, it was also blank. *There's nothing here?* An instant later, he noticed the icon indicating there was a graphic attached to the message. *She sent a photo?* He stabbed at the icon, and the cursor began spinning again as the image loaded. The phone showed only one bar of service.

"Sir?" a voice demanded nearby.

Langdon looked up and saw the young man coming around the elevator shaft.

"What are you doing?!" the man demanded. "You said you had to make a call! Are you looking through her—"

"No!" Langdon said. "I need to check an incoming message. I'm sorry. It's very important." He held up the blank screen. "It's just loading. I'll give it back in a second."

"I'd like it back *now*, sir," the man said, walking toward him.

The elevator continued buzzing.

Load, goddammit!

The wind whipped harder, and the woman began calling for her husband.

"Sir!" The man held out his hand for the phone.

"Please . . . one second," Langdon said as the cursor spun. "I *really* need to see—"

"Now!" the young man demanded. "You have no righ—"

"Here it is!" Langdon shouted as the image finally materialized before him.

Whether the wind had just moved the tower or his knees had gone weak, Langdon wasn't sure, but he felt suddenly off-balance. The image on the screen was as unexpected as anything he could ever imagine Katherine sending him.

Langdon stared for a long moment at the bizarre "message," letting his eidetic memory take a mental snapshot of it. Then he quit the browser and handed the phone back to the young man, who grabbed it and stalked angrily off.

A few seconds later, Langdon heard the elevator begin its descent.

CHAPTER 48

Michael Harris arrived outside Sasha Vesna's apartment door wondering how many times he had stood right here, ashamed, telling himself that *this* would be his last visit.

Steeling himself, he knocked loudly. No answer. He tried the door and found it unlocked.

Not surprising. She is expecting me.

"Sasha?" he called, entering the apartment. "I'm here!"

The only signs of life were Harry and Sally padding toward him down the hallway. Harris stepped inside and closed the door so the cats could not get out.

"Sasha? Professor Langdon?"

Silence.

Puzzled, Harris headed down the hall and into the kitchen. He saw three cups laid out for tea, steam rising from the kettle.

Strange. Have they left?

As he began to turn back toward the hallway, a floorboard creaked behind him, and a sudden blaze of electricity tore through the center of his back. Instantly paralyzed, Harris dropped to his knees and pitched forward, crashing into the floor.

For several seconds, his mind went blank, ears ringing, muscles locked. As he slowly regained his mental bearings, all Harris could imagine was that someone had just stepped out of the small kitchen closet and used a Taser on him.

What's happened to Sasha and Langdon?!

"Sa . . . sha!" Harris tried to call to her, barely audible.

"Sasha cannot hear you," a deep, hollow voice said above him. "Not where she is now."

No. Before Harris was able to roll over and see his attacker, he felt the prongs of the stun gun pressing sharply into the base of his skull.

There was a scalding blast . . . and his world went entirely black.

———•··—•———

The Golĕm stood over the paralyzed body of Michael Harris, who lay facedown on the wooden floor. The Vipertek stun gun blast had knocked him unconscious. Straddling the powerful man, The Golĕm crouched down, took out a heavy plastic bag he had found in the closet, and pulled it over Harris's head. Twisting it tightly around his neck, The Golĕm cut off the man's oxygen supply.

Three minutes later, The Golĕm released his grip.

He suffered very little.

Sasha would appreciate that. The Golĕm had locked Sasha away and intended to keep her there until he was prepared for his final step.

Now, as he stood up, The Golĕm could feel the Ether gathering, as it often did in moments of exertion. He quickly took out the metal wand he carried at all times.

"Ne seychas," he whispered, rubbing the wand on top of his head. *Not now.*

The Ether would have to wait. There was work yet to complete in *this* realm. Abandoning the corpse on the floor, The Golĕm disposed of the plastic bag in the kitchen trash and walked to a small desk in the hallway, where he sat down to write.

The only paper he could locate was a sheet of Sasha's stationery, which was decorated with kittens. Nonetheless, he composed a short letter and sealed it in a matching envelope.

He addressed the envelope in bold letters to Michael Harris's superior.

U.S. AMBASSADOR HEIDE NAGEL.

Before exiting, The Golĕm dropped the envelope onto the attaché's lifeless body. Then, leaving Sasha's door unlocked, he headed home.

CHAPTER 49

A lone now atop Petřín Tower, Langdon steadied himself against the observation rail as the wind whipped across the platform. While his eyes were directed out over the snow-dusted city, the image in his mind's eye was not Prague at all; it was a snapshot of what Katherine had emailed him earlier this morning.

For Langdon, the effect of "eidetic" recollection was indistinguishable from seeing the object live. His eidetic memory provided precise, total recall of a visual input and derived its name from the Greek *eidos*, meaning "visible form."

Langdon pondered the image she had sent, which seemed to be a screenshot of her own phone. On her display was a glowing string of seven characters.

$$\mathsf{CITTDLB}$$

Langdon recognized the ancient language at once, but he could not begin to imagine what it was doing on Katherine's phone.

She sent me something in . . . Enochian?

Often called the "Angelic Tongue," Enochian was a language "discovered" here in Prague in 1583 by the two self-proclaimed English mystics, John Dee and his partner Edward Kelley. It was allegedly the language by which the mediums could speak to spirits and obtain "wisdom from the other realm."

The only reason Katherine knew Enochian existed was because Langdon had told her about it just yesterday. While walking the streets, they had seen a poster advertising an exhibit called *Making Gold and Swapping Wives*, which, in addition to the catchy text, was adorned with Enochian symbols. Katherine asked Langdon what the symbols were, and he relayed the sordid tale of Dee and Kelley's historical passion for alchemy, wife-swapping, and talking to angels in their own special language—Enochian—the mystical language of the spirit world.

"They were almost certainly a pair of charlatan opportunists," Langdon told her, "but they were in high demand in their day, even hired by Emperor Rudolf II to ask the angels to help him make wise political decisions."

"Have our current politicians tried that?" she asked with a smile.

"It's not hard to do," Langdon replied. "There's even an Enochian app for your phone."

"A Renaissance app for talking to spirits?!" Katherine exclaimed, laughing out loud.

Langdon took her phone and quickly downloaded the free app. "There, now you, too, can communicate with another dimension."

"That's thoroughly ridiculous."

"Ridiculous?" Langdon asked, smirking. "Did we finally find a mystical idea that you *don't* believe in?"

"Very funny, Professor."

Langdon kissed her on the cheek. "You're cute when you're cynical."

Now, shivering atop Petřín Tower, Langdon surmised that Katherine must have used the Enochian translation app to create a message, then emailed a screenshot to him.

But why? Was she being playful?

Langdon found nothing playful about reading the language of spirits while standing atop a ghost-infested hilltop looking for a woman who had disappeared. It was conceivable that Katherine was not being playful at all, but rather had encoded her message for secrecy. The problem was that anyone with an Enochian dictionary or app could easily decipher it.

Langdon held the image in his mind.

ːⲤⲄⲅⲆⲭⳫⳠ

The translation of Enochian to English was actually an absurdly simple substitution scheme. Langdon had always found it suspiciously convenient that the mystical language discovered by a *British* clairvoyant turned out to be a letter-by-letter transliteration into *English*.

Langdon had long ago memorized the Enochian "key," and he needed only a few seconds to make the transliteration, converting the symbols in Katherine's message to English letters.

The decryption that emerged, however, appeared meaningless.

LXXEDOC

Langdon puzzled over the jumbled string of letters, which looked vaguely like a Roman numeral, except that the letters *E* and *O* did not exist in that numbering system, and the other letters were not in proper sequence.

Whatever Katherine wanted to tell me . . . this isn't it.

Unfortunately, if she'd made a mistake while translating, she would never have suspected her message wasn't right because all she would have seen were the symbols she had sent him.

Frustrated, Langdon stared out at the wooded landscape and tried to figure out his next move. As he did, a huge flock of birds took off from the trees, rising en masse, all turning at the same precise instant, flocking as one.

The universe is mocking me, Langdon decided as he watched the amorphous cloud of birds undulating across the sky. Katherine had researched the synchronized murmurations of starlings and declared the phenomenon to be scientific proof of an invisible connection between living things.

"Separation is an illusion," she had told Jonas at their lunch last year and pulled up a mesmerizing video of starlings all moving as one. "This phenomenon is called behavioral synchronization, and it occurs all throughout nature."

She scrolled through several video clips—a mile-long school

of bluefish all turning left and right in perfect synch; an endless herd of migrating gazelles, all bounding and leaping in unison; a swarm of fireflies, all illuminating and blinking in unison; a nest of hundreds of sea turtle eggs, all hatching within seconds of one another.

"Incredible," Faukman said.

"It never ceases to amaze me," Katherine said. "Some traditional scientists claim behavioral synchronization is actually just an *illusion* . . . that these organisms are simply *reacting* to one another so rapidly that the delay is imperceptible." Katherine shrugged. "Unfortunately, a pair of high-speed video cameras linked to atomic clocks at the front and back of a school of fish has shown that their alleged reaction time is faster than the speed of light."

"Oops," Langdon said.

"Exactly," Katherine said with a smile. "That's a no-no in our current model of physics and reality. Instead, I would argue that there exists a point of view from which these synchronizations are not miraculous at all. If you view a murmuration of starlings *not* as many individual birds—but rather as one complete organism—then the synchronization is to be expected. The starlings are moving as one because they *are* one . . . an interconnected system. No separation. Much like the individual cells in your body, which form the integrated whole that is you."

Faukman looked fascinated.

"I believe the same holds true for each of us as human beings," Katherine said, sounding excited now. "We mistakenly picture ourselves as isolated *individuals* when in fact we are part of a much larger organism. The loneliness we feel is because we can't see the truth—we are, in fact, integrated into the complete whole. Separation is our shared delusion."

She touched the tablet. "Don't take it from me, though. Here is one of the most brilliant minds in history." A new screen appeared—a quote from Albert Einstein.

A human being is a part of the whole called by us "universe" . . .
He experiences himself, his thoughts and feelings

as something separated from the rest,
a kind of optical delusion of his consciousness.
This delusion is a kind of prison for us.

"Even the greatest scientist who ever lived," Katherine said, "declared that our conscious minds *delude* us and trick us into seeing disconnectedness where there is only unity."

Leonardo da Vinci had said the same thing, Langdon recalled. *Realize that everything connects to everything else.*

"And similar proclamations have been made by spiritual prophets throughout time," Katherine continued, "but today, a growing number of quantum physicists are echoing a belief in the interconnectivity of all things . . . and all people." Katherine smiled at Faukman. "I admit it's hard to visualize our connection to a world we cannot *see*, but believe me, future generations will understand. One day we'll see that our perception of being alone in the world was once humankind's greatest shared delusion."

"And your *experiments*?" Faukman pressed. "The ones you're not telling us about? They echo this interconnectivity?"

Katherine smiled, eyes sparkling with excitement. "Gentlemen, the results of these experiments will not only remind us we are all connected. They will light the way toward an entirely new understanding of our reality and human potential."

Just then, a piercing squeal brought Langdon back to the cold wind at the top of Petřín Tower. For a moment, he thought it was a sound from the elevator, but instead he looked down and saw that a car had just skidded loudly to a stop at the base of the tower. The black sedan looked forebodingly familiar. The emblems on the doors confirmed it.

ÚZSI.

Langdon could not make out the face of the uniformed man who jumped from the driver's seat far below and was now sprinting across the parking lot toward the tower. But there was no mistaking his muscle-bound build.

Or the large pistol clutched in his hand.

CHAPTER 50

Lieutenant Pavel burst into the Petřín Tower visitor's hall with his gun already drawn.

"*Kde je ten Američan?!*" he shouted in Czech to the attendant behind the counter.

The frightened woman backed up, dropping the stack of brochures she was arranging in the countertop display. She pointed overhead as Pavel described Langdon. "He went up!" she exclaimed, cowering.

Pavel could hear the elevator moving in the shaft, the sound growing louder. *Descending.* The staircase was cordoned off and closed. *Perfect.*

The elevator pinged, and Pavel set his feet wide and raised his weapon. When the door slid open, he found himself aiming at a young Indian couple, both of whom leaped back at the sight of Pavel's gun.

"Get out!" Pavel commanded.

As the couple scurried away, Pavel charged into the lift and stabbed the button for his lone option—the top. In his hand, the captain's weapon was loaded and ready to fire.

Ascending, Pavel paced the tiny compartment like a wild animal until finally the lift lurched to a stop and the doors opened, springing him free. He stormed out of the elevator with his gun raised. Finger on the trigger, he wheeled left and right, scanning the platform for his target. *Nobody.* Knowing there was only one place Langdon could be, Pavel sprinted clockwise around the elevator shaft to the other side of the tower. Strangely, he found nobody there either. Pressing on, Pavel ran all the way around the small platform and arrived right back where he had started.

The elevator stood open. And empty.

Where the hell did he go?!

Pavel stopped, lowering his gun.

The platform was deserted.

The throbbing in Pavel's skull suddenly intensified on account of his exertion, and with it surged a fresh wave of rage. The wind gusted, whistling loudly, but above that plaintive howl, Pavel heard something else—a repetitive pounding somewhere beneath the platform. For a moment, he thought a workman was hammering metal, but the rate was too frantic and fast.

Then Pavel saw it.

At the top of the descending spiral staircase, the NO ENTRY swag was lying on the ground . . . along with fresh footprints on the metal stairs.

Bad move, Professor.

Pavel leaped into the elevator just as the doors were starting to close. Even if Langdon managed the perilous descent without plunging over the railings, there would be nowhere to run once he reached the bottom.

◆——··——◆

Sixty feet below the observation deck, Langdon feared he'd made a terrible mistake. He was bounding down the tight spiral of the open-air staircase at breakneck speed with almost no traction from his hard-soled loafers, which were clanging loudly on the icy metal treads. Somewhere above him, the elevator was already whirring back into motion, descending loudly through the enclosed shaft around which Langdon was spiraling.

Faster, Robert.

Langdon's hands were quickly freezing as they slid along the metal railings on either side of the treacherous stairs, the only way to steady his descent on such perilous footing. Overhead, the elevator sounded like it was gaining on him, and Langdon questioned if he could win the race to the bottom. A tie would go in Pavel's favor; the lieutenant was carrying a gun, and Langdon somehow doubted that the blow to Pavel's head had imbued the man with any additional self-restraint.

Where would I even run? He clearly won't hesitate to shoot me.

The only option Langdon had seen was Petřín Park behind the welcome center. And the only way to reach it would be to sprint through the visitor's center and out of the building before the elevator doors opened.

A moment later, however, he realized he was too late.

As he spiraled down the staircase, the elevator shaft beside him began shuddering with an unmistakable sound—the grating scrape of the elevator passing him by.

———··———

Lieutenant Pavel exploded into the visitor's center like a bull entering a ring. The attendant and Indian couple were huddled to one side.

"*Kde je?!*" Pavel shouted. "The American! Where?"

The frightened attendant shook her head and shrugged.

Good, Pavel thought. *You're still above me.*

He moved to the bottom of the spiral staircase and trained his weapon up into the void, awaiting Langdon's arrival. After ten seconds passed, however, he quickly realized it was entirely *too* quiet above him. The clanging of Langdon's footsteps had stopped.

Dead silence.

And then . . . he heard a heavy thud directly overhead.

———··———

Langdon landed harder than anticipated on the roof of the visitor's center. Having halted his descent where the stairs entered the rooftop, he had gripped the handrail and swung his legs up and to the left, launching his body over the low railing and sticking an inelegant landing on the gently sloped roof.

He rolled onto his stomach, slid down to the edge, and lowered himself feetfirst over the gutter, dropping the short distance to the ground on the backside of the building. Langdon assumed his amateur gymnastics had not gone undetected inside, and he wasted no time dashing into the woods and moving away from the tower as fast as he could.

Barely thirty yards from the structure, Langdon heard Pavel yelling and crashing through the snowy forest behind him. *That was fast.* Langdon had hoped for a longer head start. He also wished his footwear had been made by Nike rather than Tod's.

As he sprinted through the trees, Langdon had the uneasy sense that Petřín Tower had all been a setup. Within a few minutes of Langdon's arrival, ÚZSI had appeared. He wondered if perhaps the note had been left by Pavel? *Was he trying to isolate me so he could shoot me? Does someone actually want me dead?!*

I have Katherine. Come to Petřín Tower.

Clearly, Katherine was not here, and it seemed unlikely that she had been. Nothing was making much sense—including Katherine's Enochian email.

LXXEDOC?

What is she trying to tell me?!

Not far ahead, Langdon saw a clearing with several of the park's attractions—carousel, pony stable, rose garden, chapel. Breaking free of the forest, he dashed onto the gravel courtyard, grateful for the firmer footing, though he could hear the heavy footfalls of his pursuer behind him.

Langdon raced past the stable and garden to the chapel, whose rooftop belvedere was historically a symbol of "sanctuary," although the padlock on its door sent a different message. Without breaking stride, he scanned the plaza for any other shelter. He saw three buildings ahead and made his decision in an instant.

The first two structures were most likely locked at this hour—Calvary Chapel and the Church of St. Lawrence—both part of a program to Christianize this pagan hill. The third structure was a kitschy, bright yellow, fairy-tale castle whose faux turrets flew colorful coat-of-arm banners on rooked fortress walls. Beyond the fake drawbridge, a man in a medieval costume was just now hoisting the iron gate, apparently opening the castle for the day. Over the entrance hung a banner that read: VÍTEJTE / WELCOME.

Sometimes the universe points the way, Langdon thought.

Whether or not the sign was a cosmic nudge in the right direction, Langdon saw no other options for cover. A quick glance over his shoulder confirmed that Pavel had already emerged from the woods at the far end of the plaza, and he seemed to be gaining ground. Digging in, Langdon dashed across the faux drawbridge, past the startled attendant, skidding into a small anteroom whose unmanned ticket booth bore a sign:

ZRCADLOVÉ BLUDIŠTĚ

Langdon had no idea what the words meant, but it didn't matter; the anteroom contained a single turnstile that blocked what appeared to be the only entrance into the castle—a narrow archway into a darkened hallway.

Forgive me, Cinderella, Langdon thought, vaulting over the turnstile and rushing through the opening. He sprinted down a stone corridor, took a hard left, and plunged into a glistening six-sided room. Langdon skidded to a halt, stunned by what he saw surrounding him.

What the . . . ?!

Six men stood in a circle, evenly spaced around Langdon, all staring directly at him.

Stranger still, all six men were Robert Langdon himself.

Langdon now realized the meaning of ZRCADLOVÉ BLUDIŠTĚ, and he desperately wished he had made a different choice.

CHAPTER 51

The purple glow of The Golěm's apartment felt soothing after the violent episode of Michael Harris's death. Having taken a quick shower and donned a robe, The Golěm now kneeled silently in his darkened sanctuary to his *svatyně*—the sacred room in which he kept the shrine he had erected to her.

A tribute to the woman I was born to protect.

Kneeling in the darkness, he struck a match and lit the three votive candles that were arranged among the dried flowers on the table. As the flickering light grew brighter, he raised his eyes to the photo hanging above the shrine.

The Golěm smiled lovingly at her face.

I am here to watch over you . . . and yet you don't even know me.

The details of the woman's face were not classically beautiful. She had strong Slavic features, shoulder-length blond hair, and a broken nose . . . but Sasha Vesna was The Golěm's entire world.

I am your protector, Sasha.

Although she didn't know it, Sasha's soul had collided with his years ago in a Russian mental institution . . . in a moment of horrific violence. Sasha had been alone and unprotected, enduring a brutal beating from the wicked night nurse, a woman called Malvina, when The Golěm had appeared in the room, unable to bear the abuse any longer. Fueled by an upwelling of outrage, The Golěm had intervened, lashing out with brutal force and breaking the nurse's neck.

Mercifully, Sasha had been unconscious and never discovered what had truly transpired that night. The Golěm had slipped silently back into the darkness undetected . . . but in that moment, their two souls had become forever intertwined, and he had pledged to protect her.

The night I saved her life . . . is the night I became her protector.

Before his act of compassion, he had been an empty vessel, a ghostly spirit. But in that instant, as if struck by a beam of energy from another realm, he felt his life begin, immediately understanding who he was and the nature of his mystical connection to Sasha Vesna.

I am her guardian angel.

She is my entire reason for living, for suffering, for being.

And yet . . . she must never know.

To this day, Sasha Vesna had no idea The Golĕm even existed . . . much less that he was involved in her life, watching from the shadows, protecting her innocent soul from the stark horrors of the world.

Sasha's body and mind had been abused by Brigita Gessner. Michael Harris, on the other hand, had betrayed Sasha's *heart*—the cruelest of all deceptions.

"Michael . . ." The Golĕm had whispered only twenty minutes earlier, gripping the neck of the unconscious man to secure the plastic bag tightly over his face. "*Your* betrayal was the harshest of all. I watched you prey on Sasha's loneliness. I watched you lie in bed, wrapped in her arms, pretending to love her."

The Golĕm had tightened his grip without remorse, feeling his fingertips burrow into Harris's flesh.

"Sasha will be heartbroken to learn of your death," he whispered, "but that would be nothing compared to her learning the *truth* . . . that the only man she ever loved was *using* her . . . deceiving her . . . spying on her."

As the pulse in Michael Harris's neck grew faint, The Golĕm knew, from his own deaths, that the man was leaving his body now, hovering in this room, bearing witness to his own demise.

The Golĕm had turned his eyes upward at the ceiling, addressing Harris directly. "She is a child, Michael . . . Abandoned by her parents . . . Locked in an asylum . . . Lured to Prague by a monster. Everyone in her life betrayed her . . . *except me!*"

When the last trace of life had been wrung from Harris's body, The Golĕm leaned down and coldly whispered the same words he had heard Sasha whisper to Harris as he fell asleep in her arms. "*Spokoynoy nochi, milyy.* Good night, sweetheart."

This piece of The Golĕm's plan had been a success. Michael Harris had been cornered alone. Sasha was safely locked away. And the American professor, Robert Langdon, had been sent off. Langdon did not deserve to die, but the man's presence at Sasha's apartment would have made it impossible for The Golĕm to execute Harris. And so The Golĕm had improvised, leaving a note at Sasha's door that would cause Langdon to scramble in search of Katherine Solomon.

Langdon would not find her at Petřín Tower, of course.

There's a good chance he will never find her, The Golĕm thought, recalling what Gessner had confessed last night while ice-cold saline tore through her body.

"Katherine has no idea the danger she is in . . ." Gessner had uttered through the pain. "The people I work for . . . they will stop at nothing to silence her."

CHAPTER 52

MetLife Stadium is located several miles south of Teterboro Airport in East Rutherford, New Jersey, and is one of the highest-grossing stadiums in the world. Home to both the New York Giants and New York Jets football teams, the stadium was built with transformation in mind, regularly swapping out banners, field logos, and lighting schemes from Giants Blue to Jets Green each week to host the home team.

Tonight, as the deserted stadium loomed to Faukman's right, it looked foreign to him—like some kind of dark mother ship abandoned in the middle of a sprawling parking lot. He checked his rearview mirror for any sign of pursuit, and seeing nobody, Faukman pulled the stolen SUV off Route 17, swung around behind the stadium, and parked in one of nearly thirty thousand available spaces.

Take a minute, Jonas. Think.

He had been white-knuckling the SUV at ninety mph, and his nerves were frayed. This moment of calm was a welcome respite, especially as the warmth of the seat heater finally began permeating his body.

Alone now in the deserted parking lot, Faukman checked his phone, concerned that Langdon had not called back. *He's got to be awake by now . . . it's nine in the morning in Prague.* Faukman's call history showed no missed calls except for several from a Penguin Random House IT extension, which at this hour Faukman imagined could only be the security technician, Alex.

Faukman tapped the button to call the tech back, hoping he

might have information that could shed some light on what was going on here. The familiar voice of Alex Conan answered on the first ring.

"Mr. Faukman! Where have you been? Are you okay?!"

I'm nowhere near okay, kid.

"I need to warn you," Alex continued breathlessly. "The hackers who deleted your manuscript . . . I think they may be very dangerous."

No shit, Faukman thought, unconsciously touching his sore abdomen where he'd been punched. "I came to the same conclusion, Alex."

"And . . . well . . . I'm just so sorry to have to tell you this, but . . ." The tech's voice cracked, and Faukman felt a rising alarm.

Tell me what?

"I . . . I think they might have killed one of your authors."

The editor hoped he had misheard the words.

As the young tech shared what he had learned, Faukman listened in shock, thinking he would be sick.

———··——

One mile away, having tracked Faukman's phone from a safe distance, the two operatives—Auger and Chinburg—were now parked on a quiet residential street in East Rutherford, New Jersey, adjacent to MetLife Stadium. They were listening to the phone call through their iPad.

What they heard was alarming to them as well.

One of the American authors had been killed in Prague? Was it Langdon or Solomon? Clearly, something has gone terribly wrong.

Then again, Mr. Finch had made it abundantly clear that the recovery of Katherine Solomon's manuscript was of vital importance. And Finch always accomplished his mission, whatever the cost.

CHAPTER 53

Prague's historic Zrcadlové Bludiště—Mirror Maze—was built in 1891 for the Prague Jubilee Exhibition, and to this day it remains a popular spot for tourists and children. Despite being a short labyrinth by modern standards, the maze can still be difficult to navigate due to the disorienting nature of its layout and angled reflective walls.

Robert Langdon had stalled in the very first chamber . . . surrounded by panicked images of himself. *Pavel is right behind you.* It took Langdon a moment to see that one of the reflections was slightly smaller than the others, and he ran toward it, finding the mirror recessed by several feet, hiding a cleverly disguised opening, beyond which a mirrored hallway extended in both directions.

Left or right, Langdon wondered, having always disliked the random guessing game of mazes. Statistically speaking, in a right-hand-biased world, when presented with a choice of right or left, the overwhelming majority turned *right*, which meant maze designers usually ensured the first right-hand turn was a circuitous mistake.

Langdon dashed to the left. As he did, he placed his right hand against the wall, letting his fingers run along the mirrors. *Never lose touch with the wall.*

He had learned the trick as a child, thanks to his passion for Greek mythology and the legend of Crete's famed Minotaur's Labyrinth. The *labrys* double ax was a symbol of choice, and indeed it was choice that made the Labyrinth so challenging.

But the savvy Minoans removed the burden of choice with the hand-on-the-wall strategy; without needing to deliberate, a maze-goer simply followed whichever direction the hand on the wall led. It didn't guarantee the *shortest* route out, but it did guarantee never having to make the same choice twice, resulting in a faster escape . . . and, in their case, avoiding death at the hands of the Minotaur.

When Langdon reached the next intersection, instead of hesitating to make a choice, he kept his hand on the mirror as he ran, turning immediately to his left, committed to following wherever it guided him. Over and over, Langdon turned, hand on the wall, moving deeper into the maze.

He could hear Pavel lumbering through passageways somewhere nearby, his loud breathing sometimes only a thin mirror's breadth away. Langdon ran as quietly as he could, knowing that if he'd made the wrong initial guess by turning left, then this hand-on-the-wall strategy would eventually lead him back along this same hallway in the *opposite* direction . . . potentially directly into Pavel's path.

Langdon burst into a larger chamber whose mirrors were twisted and distorted like those in a carnival fun house. Several of the mirrors here were freestanding, disrupting Langdon's wall strategy. He could hear the ÚZSI agent eerily close now, and as he scanned the new space, Langdon spotted an unmistakable grayish glow at the far end of a hallway. *Daylight!* He pulled his hand from the wall and rushed toward the light.

But he never made it.

The hulking form of Lieutenant Pavel materialized ahead on his right. As their eyes locked, Pavel raised his weapon and took dead aim at Langdon's chest.

"Wait!" Langdon yelled, lurching to a stop, his arms reaching skyward.

But Pavel pulled the trigger.

The gun roared, and Langdon staggered backward, expecting impact, but instead there was the crash of shattering glass. The image of Pavel disintegrated before Langdon's eyes.

Somewhere nearby Pavel screamed in frustration.

Without waiting to figure out what convoluted series of reflections had created the illusion that he and Pavel were face-to-face, Langdon took off. He charged toward the grayish opening again, nearly crashing into yet another mirror. He could now see that the actual exit was just ahead to his left, and he burst through it into the light.

With lengthening strides, he dashed down the paved walkway away from the castle. Behind him, the sound of gunfire and shattering glass filled the air. Three shots. The lieutenant was apparently creating his *own* exit.

The walkway curved deeper into the woods, and Langdon sprinted past a handful of elderly tourists ascending the path. For a moment, he thought they had *climbed* Petřín Hill, but then he saw where they had come from. Ahead, a small stucco building sat beside a steeply descending train track on which a lone train car was sitting, pitched downward at an alarming incline.

The Petřín Funicular.

Langdon had never taken the cable car, but this seemed like a good moment for his maiden voyage. The doors were just closing as he arrived breathless and slipped inside. The train began its descent, and Langdon realized that his decision to enter the Mirror Maze might just have saved his life.

Maybe the universe was right after all.

◆—··—◆

The Golěm pulled the rubber skullcap down over his head and retrieved the bucket of wet Vltava clay that he kept beneath the bathroom sink. Plunging his hand through a layer of water, he scooped out a fistful of silky, soggy earth. With ritualistic care, he began smearing a thick layer across his skullcap and eventually his face, covering everything except his eyes.

Once he was entirely masked, only then did he reach into the drawer and extract the shard of reflective glass—the only mirror in his home. Using the glass and a palette knife, he carefully etched the three sacred letters into his forehead.

אמת

Truth.

Truth was something The Golĕm had experienced in abundance recently.

He had long suspected that Brigita Gessner was not the selfless, benevolent soul Sasha seemed to regard her as. In an effort to learn more about Gessner, The Golĕm had orchestrated various ways to surveil the neuroscientist and better understand what was fueling her generosity toward Sasha.

The truth he uncovered was unexpectedly disturbing.

He considered relaying it all to Sasha, but the trauma would be too great for her.

Sasha desperately needs a mentor . . . someone to believe in.

The truth about Michael Harris was even worse. The Golĕm had watched the handsome American's calculated advances on Sasha and seen through them in an instant. But Sasha was too naive to realize that a man like Harris would never have chosen her.

Now their treachery has been repaid.

As he carefully checked the clay around his mouth and nostrils, The Golĕm reveled in his experience with Gessner the night before. He had tailed her to Katherine Solomon's lecture, then to the bar at the Four Seasons, and finally back to her lab . . . where he violently overwhelmed the neuroscientist and improvised a devastatingly effective interrogation technique.

Gessner's forced confession had filled in the gaps in his understanding . . . and the betrayals were even more depraved than The Golĕm had ever suspected. She had revealed the identity of her influential partners, as well as the chilling details of what they had built beneath Prague.

Threshold.

The Golĕm was enraged. Upon leaving her lab, he immediately began to plan. The head of the snake was an American man named Finch, to whom Gessner answered directly. Finch operated from the safety of an office in London and moved around the world.

I will first destroy your creation in Prague . . . and then I will take pleasure in hunting you, wherever you may be.

Gessner had revealed the location of the underground facility, but unfortunately her personal key card had proven insufficient authorization to enter. *I require something more.* He had already made one failed attempt to obtain it from Crucifix Bastion, but on this visit he would be far better prepared for anything he might encounter.

As The Golĕm stepped into the windy alley outside his home, he could feel the wet clay on his face drying fast, pulling at his skin. His platform boots were still damp from last night, but he ignored the discomfort. His enemies could be watching . . . and he could take no chances being recognized.

I move now as my true self.

I feel the force of that truth.

He knew his mission today would require extraordinary focus. For this reason, he would first need to replenish his energy by visiting the site where he felt the pulse of Prague's most mystical power. There, in a hallowed field of the dead, The Golĕm would kneel on the cold earth and draw strength from his namesake and inspiration . . . the golem who came before.

CHAPTER 54

As Dana Daněk climbed the stairs to the U.S. ambassador's office, she had a feeling that this summons would be her last. The ambassador had turned on her heels and vanished after angrily confronting Dana about her visit to the Four Seasons and her personal relationship with Michael Harris.

I'm about to be sacked, she sensed, knocking quietly.

"Come in," the ambassador said. "And close the door."

Dana obeyed and turned to face her boss.

As always, Ambassador Nagel's demeanor matched her unadorned attire—all business. Dana found Nagel intimidating even *outside* her office, but right now, sitting behind her mahogany desk, flanked by the flags of both the U.S. and the Czech Republic, Ambassador Heide Nagel looked like a lion about to consume its prey.

The ambassador stared at Dana over the reading glasses she always kept low on her nose. "Turn off your phone. Put it on my desk."

"Am I being fired?"

"You *should* be," the ambassador said. "Let's see what happens."

Dana turned off her phone and put it on the ambassador's desk.

"You will need to sign *this*," the ambassador said, pushing a document across her desk.

Dana studied the document. "I don't understand."

"It's a nondisclosure agreement. It means you cannot discuss what I am about to tell you."

"Of course, ma'am, I'm just not sure that I should sign something without—"

"Would you like *Michael* to review it for you?"

Shit. The ambassador had a way of getting to the point. Dana picked up a pen and signed the NDA.

"Ms. Daněk," she began, "your visit to the Four Seasons was reckless . . . and unfortunate. You were not supposed to witness what you saw."

I gathered as much when that woman's gun was aimed at my face. "Yes, ma'am. I would be happy to *forget* what I saw and simply contin—"

"Let's be honest, you won't forget what you saw. And now you've left me no choice but to make sure you *understand* what you saw."

CHAPTER 55

Langdon sat at the back of the Petřín Funicular as the all-but-empty train descended the steep ridge. Confident he had evaded Pavel, at least for now, Langdon closed his eyes and took a deep breath, attempting to make sense of what had just happened.

Whoever had lured him to Petřín Tower clearly knew Katherine was missing. *I have Katherine.* Whether or not that statement was true, it now seemed entirely possible that the note was intended as a means to isolate Langdon . . . or perhaps to isolate Sasha.

Langdon felt guilty for leaving the young Russian woman alone and unprotected, although judging from her encounter with Pavel, Sasha Vesna clearly could take care of herself. *And she's armed with Pavel's gun*, Langdon reminded himself, hoping that Michael Harris had arrived at her apartment by now. He also hoped Harris would have some information about Katherine's whereabouts.

Langdon focused again on the one piece of information he did have—the strangely encoded email Katherine had sent him earlier this morning. But even that seemed to be unhelpful. Gibberish. The image flashed through his mind.

$$\text{⊂⌐⌐⊐Σ⌿ʟᗷ}$$

Just to be certain he had not made a mistake, Langdon performed the Enochian transliteration once again but ended up with the same meaningless string of letters.

LXXEDOC

Maybe she confused recto and verso? he thought, trying to imagine why her message to him seemed nonsensical.

Recto and *verso*—front and back—were the terms used by iconographers to designate which page of an open book should be read first . . . in other words, the *direction* in which a language should be read. Enochian was a right-to-left language—like Hebrew, Arabic, or Farsi—the opposite of English. Was it possible that the app had failed to reverse the text direction during encryption? Or maybe that Katherine had mistakenly reversed it, thereby doubling up and causing it to encrypt incorrectly?

Langdon transliterated the letters again, backward this time, and within a moment he knew his instincts had been correct.

$$\text{ʙⅬⅫⅡⅠⅭ}$$

A new word emerged in his mind.

CODEXXL

Code XXL—much closer to English.

Nonetheless, Langdon had no idea what *Code XXL* was referring to.

What am I missing here? He closed his eyes, again picturing the line.

CODEXXL

Suddenly, it dawned on him, and he realized his mistake.

I put the space in the wrong place . . .

Katherine was not saying CODE XXL . . . she was saying CODEX XL.

It was an allusion Langdon understood perfectly—as would Katherine. "Codex XL" was a crystal-clear reference to an enigmatic artifact that was located right here in the heart of Prague. They had actually visited it just yesterday.

The Devil's Bible!

Officially known as the Codex Gigas, the "Devil's Bible" was a mysterious object with a bizarre—some claimed haunted—history. It was the largest book in the world, measuring three feet by nearly two feet, and weighed an astounding 165 pounds. Normally housed in the Swedish National Library, it was currently on loan to the Klementinum here in Prague. While visiting the exhibit with Katherine yesterday, Langdon had mentioned that the codex bore more than a dozen different historical titles—so many, in fact, that one of his students had given it the humorous and simple nickname "Codex XL," a reference to its extra-large size.

As the train trundled down the mountain, Langdon realized that Katherine's cleverly encrypted message should have provided him some clarity, but instead it presented a new list of questions. *Is she afraid someone is reading her email? Is she trying to remind me about something in the book . . . or maybe of something that happened there yesterday?*

Langdon pictured the exhibit they had visited. The priceless Devil's Bible was locked in a colossal, bulletproof, fireproof display case within the Klementinum, about a mile from where he was now. Langdon had first seen the codex years ago in Sweden in the Kungliga Biblioteket, but when he discovered that it was on tour here in Prague, he had insisted he and Katherine go see it.

"*Codex Gigas* literally means 'gigantic book,'" he told her excitedly as they stood before the imposing object. He pointed at the book's thick spine. "It has a wooden plank binding that contains more than three hundred pages of hand-scraped vellum, crafted from the skins of a hundred and sixty donkeys. The pages are meticulously calligraphed and include not only the complete Latin Bible but also assorted medical texts, histories, magic formulae, conjurations, and incantations. It even includes an elaborate exorcism—"

"Stop, Robert," she said, smiling and affectionately squeezing his hand. "You had me at a hundred and sixty donkeys."

He grinned back at her. "As you can tell . . . I enjoy teaching that class."

Only a month earlier—in a course offering called *Illumina-tions: The Art of Medieval Manuscripts*—he had shown several slides of the codex, beginning with the manuscript's most famous page.

"Here we have Folio 290," he said, displaying the bizarre illustration of a horned devil squatting awkwardly, entirely naked except for a white loincloth wrapped around his private parts. "And it is the page from which this book derives its oldest nickname."

"The Diaper Devil?" chimed in one of Harvard's lacrosse stars, eliciting laughter from his classmates.

"Nice try, Bruiser," Langdon said patiently. "It's called the Devil's Bible. This image portrays Satan wearing a loincloth made of ermine—a symbol of royalty."

"Wait . . . so the image presents Satan as a king?" a young woman commented. "In the pages of a Bible?"

"Bingo—thank you for noticing," Langdon said. "It's *highly* unusual iconography. But there's a larger story to this document, and Satan's appearance factors into it. According to legend, the scribe who created this illumination did so as a way to thank Satan for a favor. Rumor holds that this massive codex was writ-ten *in a single night*, by a single monk, who was able to complete the inconceivable task only because Satan himself stepped in to help him."

"Will Satan help with my midterms?" chirped lacrosse guy.

"I'm about to silence you the same way this monk got silenced," Langdon said. "Immurement."

From the kid's blank stare, Langdon gathered he didn't know the term. "*Immurement*? Anyone?" He scanned the room. "No? Modern justice systems don't use immurement as punishment anymore because it's too cruel. It derives from the Latin—*in murus*—which means . . ." Langdon waited. "Anyone?" *Bueller?*

"In the wall?" someone offered.

"Correct. Immurement literally means to be sealed alive inside a wall."

"Gross," someone said. "Like in *The Cask of Amontillado.*"

"Exactly." Langdon nodded, pleased to know Harvard students were still reading Edgar Allan Poe.

Another student asked, "Did they seal him into a wall for putting Satan in the Bible?"

"No," Langdon said, "in fact, they sealed him in the wall for breaking his monastic vow of celibacy. But as the story goes, before the final brick was placed, the monk begged for mercy and was offered a chance at redemption. The monastery's abbot left the last brick unlaid and told him that he would be freed only if he could create, within a single night, a book that contained all the world's knowledge."

"Well, that was a generous offer," someone muttered.

"Yes, but in the morning," Langdon continued, "when the abbot returned and peered through the opening, the prisoner was sitting atop a massive codex, explaining that he had sold his soul to the devil in exchange for the book. The monk was immediately freed, mostly out of terror, and the Devil's Bible instantly became a priceless artifact. In its early history, it was stolen, reacquired, and pawned many times, eventually becoming the property of the Cistercian monks of Sedlec. Perhaps you've heard of them? They are famous for having built . . . *this*."

Langdon advanced the slide carousel, and as always, everyone in the room recoiled.

"What . . . the . . . hell . . . ?" someone blurted.

The image before them was an altar made of human bones, above which hung a chandelier also made of human bones, flanking which were four massive pyramids of human skulls and femurs, all housed within a chapel whose walls and ceiling were adorned entirely with human bones.

"Sedlec Ossuary," Langdon said. "The Bone Chapel. It contains the skeletons of an estimated seventy thousand people, mostly victims of the Black Death. If you ever visit Czechia, it's worth a trip—about fifty miles outside Prague. It's an astonishing location."

"Utterly repulsive," someone muttered.

"Memento mori," Langdon said. "Remember death is coming . . . and live well."

Langdon went on to explain how the Devil's Bible was taken from Sedlec and eventually found its way to Prague in 1594, where it was housed in the library of Emperor Rudolf II until 1648, when it was taken as war booty by Sweden and moved permanently to the Swedish Royal Library in Stockholm.

"For three and a half centuries," Langdon concluded, "the Swedes displayed the codex under armed guard. Then, in 2007, after pressure from the Czech government, the book was temporarily returned to Prague for a four-month exhibition at the Czech National Library, during which more than a hundred thousand people came to see 'the book cowritten by the devil.'"

"That's a lot of gullible people," muttered lacrosse guy.

Langdon decided not to mention the millions who crossed continents and oceans to see miracles like the Shroud of Turin, Lourdes, or any of the world's countless "weeping Virgin Mary" statues. Miracles and mystery had always been catalysts for hope—"reality softeners," as Langdon sometimes called them.

"But whether or not you believe in its divine origins," Langdon said, "there are other significant mysteries within this book. One of Codex Gigas's most enigmatic features is the extraordinary quality of the calligraphy. More than a dozen top handwriting experts have examined the codex over the past century—and every specialist insists that the entire manuscript was written by a single hand. A *lone* scribe."

Langdon waited for this to soak in, but his punch line fell flat.

"Folks!" he prompted. "A book of this size, length, and complexity would have taken an estimated *forty years* to complete."

"Well," someone said, "that makes more sense than doing it in one night."

"I agree," Langdon said, "but there's a major problem with the logic. In the thirteenth century, life expectancy was approximately thirty years—and it would have taken *at least* half of those years to master the artistic skill exhibited in this calligraphy and illustration. Stranger still, the specialists confirm that the penmanship is astonishingly consistent across the entire book.

There is no degradation of the lettering from beginning to end . . . no signs of fatigue, loss of eyesight, decreasing mobility, aging, senility. No change in style whatsoever. You put all those factors together, and it's a puzzle that is technically impossible."

Silence.

"So, Professor . . . what do you think happened?" someone finally asked.

Langdon thought a long moment. "I have no idea," he said honestly. "History contains many inexplicable anomalies, and this is one of them."

"That's why I'm a physics major," chimed in a quiet student in the front row.

"Sorry to burst your bubble," Langdon said with a chuckle, "but science doesn't do much better on anomalies. Perhaps you could explain for us the double-slit experiment? Or the horizon problem? Or Schrödinger's—"

"I retract!" the kid surrendered good-naturedly.

"Signs of intelligent life, after all," Langdon said to laughter. "In any case, in 2007, when the stolen codex was loaned to Prague, the Swedes feared the Czech government might not return it, but indeed the artifact was returned as promised, and the good-faith gesture now means the Devil's Bible visits Prague for six months once every ten years, provided it is never removed from its sealed display case."

With a small jolt, the funicular came to a halt at the bottom of Petřín Hill. Langdon glanced up, still considering the codex and Katherine's message. She was clearly urging him to return to the Devil's Bible, and yet Langdon saw no logical reason for her to make that request.

No reason . . . except one.

Is Katherine there . . . waiting for me?

CHAPTER 56

The George Washington Bridge is the busiest motor bridge in the world. Connecting the steep cliffs of New Jersey with the shores of New York, its fourteen traffic lanes provide safe passage to more than a hundred million vehicles per year.

Today, however, in the predawn darkness, Jonas Faukman was nearly alone on the bridge as he rocketed toward Manhattan in the stolen SUV. His eyes flicked repeatedly to the rearview mirror, looking for any signs that he was being followed. He hoped he could reach the relative safety of Random House Tower before someone reported this vehicle missing.

Alex, the PRH tech, had just communicated horrifying news out of Prague. All Faukman could do was pray there was some mistake in what the IT tech had found.

Is the discovery in Katherine's book really worth killing *for?* He thought back to the theory of consciousness that Katherine had pitched to him over lunch in New York. It was certainly a bold departure from the current paradigm, but it hardly seemed dangerous.

"The theory," Katherine had said, "is called *nonlocal consciousness.* And it's based on the premise that consciousness is *not* localized to your brain . . . but rather it is *everywhere.* That is to say, consciousness permeates the universe. Consciousness is, in fact, one of the fundamental building blocks of our world."

"Okay," Faukman said, already struggling to keep up.

"In the nonlocal model," she continued, "your brain does not *create* consciousness, but rather your brain *experiences* what already exists around it." She glanced from Faukman to Langdon and back. "In simple English, our brains interact with an *existing* matrix of awareness."

"That was simple English?" Faukman looked bemused.

"Count your blessings," Langdon said. "She could ruin lunch by trying to explain the triadic dimensional vortical paradigm."

"Seriously, Robert?" she chided. "A man of your intellectual capacity should be able to grasp a nine-dimensional quantized, volumetric reality embedded in an infinite continuity."

Langdon rolled his eyes. "See what I mean?"

"Kids." Faukman held up his hands. "Don't make me stop the car."

Langdon refilled their wineglasses as Katherine continued.

"Here's the easiest way to think of it," she said. "Look at that speaker." She pointed to a nearby shelf on which a miniaturized wireless speaker was playing classical music. "Let's say Mozart traveled ahead in time and joined us right now at this table for lunch—he would be amazed to hear music coming out of that tiny box. In his world, there were no recordings. When he heard music, there was *always* an orchestra present. Seeing this speaker, he might mistakenly conclude there is an orchestra hidden behind the wall—or even a miniature orchestra inside the speaker itself. There would be no other options within his intellectual grasp. He would never conclude that the music was in fact hovering *silently* all around us in the form of radio waves and was somehow being *received* by this speaker."

Faukman looked around the room and imagined it full of invisible radio waves.

"We could try to explain our reality to Mozart," she continued, "but he would have no frame of reference to comprehend it. Even the first primitive recording technique wouldn't be invented for another hundred years after his death. My point is, here we are sitting at this table in modern Manhattan, and yet explaining *nonlocal* consciousness to you is a bit like attempting to describe radio waves to Mozart. In *his* reality, music comes solely from live musicians playing instruments in real time, and no other possibilities exist."

A silence hung over the table as the ideas sank in.

"But in *our* reality . . . things are different." Katherine leaned in toward them. "In the world of nonlocal consciousness . . . the music exists *everywhere* around us. Our brains simply 'tune in' to hear it."

Faukman thought for a long moment. "You're saying consciousness is like a streaming service to which our brains subscribe?"

"Very close . . . more like an immeasurably large radio dial. Think of consciousness as an infinite cloud of radio waves in this room. Your brain is a receiver . . . tuned to its own unique station. In your case, it's tuned to the Jonas Faukman station."

The editor frowned. "Not to sound like Mozart, but it sounds . . . impossible."

"I don't disagree," Langdon said to Faukman. "But in fairness, many scientific discoveries were initially deemed absurd or impossible—heliocentricity, the spherical earth, radioactivity, the expanding universe, germ theory, epigenetics, and countless others. Historically speaking, important truths often begin their lives as total impossibilities. And just because we can't imagine *how* something could possibly be true, doesn't mean we can't *observe* it to be true. The ancient Greeks proclaimed the earth was round nearly two millennia before Newton explained exactly *how* the oceans stayed in place thanks to gravity."

"Touché." Faukman smiled. "I should know better than to debate a Harvard professor."

"I think what Robert is trying to say," Katherine offered, "is that while we are still learning exactly *how* nonlocal consciousness works . . . we have certainly shown that the theory offers clear answers to a host of phenomena that seem incomprehensible in the current model."

"Okay . . ."

"Moreover," Katherine said, "unlike Mozart, you have the advantage of living in a world where you interact daily with a very similar model."

"Similar to nonlocal consciousness?" Faukman saw no parallel in his world.

"What if I told you," Katherine said, "that I could fit *all* the information in the world into a container the size of a deck of playing cards? True or false?"

"Impossible. False."

Katherine held up her cell phone. "It's all in here. What do you want to know?"

"Clever . . ." Faukman said, smiling. "But that information is not contained *inside* the phone. The phone is accessing data contained in countless data banks worldwide."

"Exactly," she said, although he sensed she was leading him . . . somewhere. "You make an excellent point. Now, what if I told you I could store *millions* of gigabytes of data inside a blob of human tissue about the size of . . . well, say . . . a human brain?"

Faukman frowned. *That was fast. Checkmate in three moves.*

"It's the identical concept," she declared. "The inconceivable storage capacity of the human brain is a *physical* impossibility. It's akin to trying to cram every song in the world into your phone. It makes no sense. Unless . . ."

"Unless," Faukman conceded, "the brain is accessing data . . . from elsewhere."

"Non*locally*," Langdon added, looking impressed.

"Exactly." Katherine smiled. "Your brain is just a receiver—an unimaginably complex, superbly advanced receiver—that chooses *which* specific signals it wants to receive from the existing cloud of global consciousness. Just like a Wi-Fi signal, global consciousness is always hovering there, fully intact, whether or not you access it."

"The ancients certainly felt that way," Langdon chimed in, now seeing myriad parallels in history. "Almost all of the world's spiritual traditions have long echoed a belief in a universal consciousness—the Akashic Field, the Universal Mind, Cosmic Consciousness, and the Kingdom of God, just to name a few."

"Indeed!" Katherine said. "This 'new' theory actually runs parallel to some of our most ancient religious beliefs."

She went on to describe how nonlocal consciousness was increasingly supported by discoveries in diverse fields like plasma

physics, nonlinear mathematics, and consciousness anthropology. New concepts like superposition and entanglement were
unveiling a universe in which all things existed at all times in all
locations. In other words, the nature of our universe was *unified*, or, as the title of a recent Oscar-winning film had so aptly
described it—*Everything Everywhere All at Once.*

"What is really turning heads," Katherine continued, "is that
this new model provides logical explanations for all the 'paranormal anomalies' that have plagued the traditional model for so
long—ESP, sudden savant syndrome, precognition, blindsight,
out-of-body experiences . . . the list goes on and on."

"But how could any model," Faukman challenged, "explain
an average kid getting hit on the head with a baseball and waking
up a virtuoso violinist?"

"Well, it does happen. Sudden savant syndrome has been
medically documented numerous times."

"Yes, I've read about it," he said, chuckling, "and I choose to
ignore it!"

"Precisely . . ." Katherine said. "That's how we humans
have *always* dealt with phenomena that don't fit our reality. We
ignore the occasional oddity rather than admit our entire model
is wrong."

"And you believe nonlocal consciousness explains all this?
Getting into an accident and suddenly being able to speak fluent
Mandarin?"

Katherine nodded. "I do. If your brain is a receiver, think of it
like a classic car radio with a physical dial. It's tuned to your normal classic rock station—a clear signal of familiar content. One
day, you hit a pothole and there's a jolt to the radio. Suddenly,
the tuner jumps slightly on the dial, and in addition to hearing
classic rock, you're now also hearing a Spanish newscaster from
an entirely different station mixed in with it."

Faukman looked uncertain.

"Let's look at it this way," Katherine said. "What does it take
to become a virtuoso violinist?"

"Practice," Faukman replied.

"And to become a great golfer?"

"Practice."

"And why does practice make you a better golfer?"

"It helps you develop muscle memory. Grooves your swing."

"Wrong," Katherine said. "There's no such thing as muscle memory. It's an oxymoron. Muscles don't have memory. In reality, when you practice, you're fine-tuning your *brain* . . . gradually rewiring it to receive information more clearly and consistently from the universal consciousness so it can command your muscles to contract in a perfect pattern to perform a task in a certain way."

Faukman scowled. "You're saying there's a golf channel in the universal consciousness?"

"I'm saying everything already exists out there . . . and practice helps *clarify* the signal your brain is receiving. This is how we become more skilled—we slowly acquire a new specific signal. Some brains are born prewired to receive a certain signal, which is why we have star athletes, virtuosos, and geniuses."

"Okay . . ."

"And the same holds true for many people with Asperger's or autism," she added. "They can have highly specialized receivers that provide them access to remarkable skills and insights, and yet simultaneously make it difficult to perform routine tasks. It's a bit like wearing *binoculars* instead of eyeglasses; you could see much farther than most . . . and yet your immediate surroundings would be blurry."

A unique perspective, he mused. "And you claim this model also explains ESP?"

"Completely," Katherine said. "The 'extra sense' we attribute to ESP is really nothing more than a brain tuning in to information that is normally filtered out. According to this new theory, when you have an intuition or a hunch, it's exactly like the car radio picking up the brief wisp of a different station it doesn't normally receive. And in some instances, if the brain picks up multiple stations too clearly, the experience can be profoundly confusing, even debilitating—schizophrenia, dissociative identity disorder, voices in your head, multiple personalities—all of these can be explained in this model."

"Fascinating," Langdon interjected. "And an experience like *precognition?*"

"Sometimes radio broadcasts bounce around in the atmosphere," she replied, "creating echoes and time delays. In this model, those manifest in our minds as déjà vu or, in reverse, as precognition."

Faukman sat a long moment, glancing back and forth between Langdon and Katherine. "My friends," he finally said, smiling, "I daresay this calls for another bottle of wine."

Now, one year later, Jonas Faukman's consciousness—however it worked—returned to the highway before him. As he sped along the upper deck of the George Washington Bridge, Faukman wasn't sure what channel he was tuned in to tonight, but it certainly was a strange one.

He approached the middle of the bridge, and he lowered his window to perform the task the PRH tech had urged him to complete. "Get rid of your phone," Alex had said. "There's a high probability it's being traced."

Reluctantly, Faukman hurled the phone out into the night. It sailed over the guardrails and began a 212-foot plummet toward the Hudson River.

As the phone fell, Faukman recalled the final words the tech had spoken.

"Try to get back here as fast as you can . . . I figured out who hacked us."

CHAPTER 57

The funicular doors opened at the bottom of Petřín Hill, and Langdon stepped off and found himself at Újezd Station, an unexpectedly bustling interchange for taxis, buses, and trolleys. Eager to put as much distance as possible between himself and Lieutenant Pavel, Langdon surveyed his options.

His last two taxi rides had ended badly, and he decided it was safest to take a tram and lose himself in the crowd. Tram #22 was the only one with a line of people waiting to board, and according to the placard over its windshield, it went toward Prague Center.

Toward the Klementinum . . .

Langdon wanted very much to believe that Katherine's message was an encoded plea to meet her at the Devil's Bible, and yet he had realized there was a small problem; she had sent her email more than two hours ago—long before the museum opened. The standard opening time for Prague museums was 10 a.m., which was still a few minutes from now.

Could she have been waiting outside all this time?

Despite being plagued by uncertainty, Langdon boarded tram #22 and headed for the museum that housed the Devil's Bible. As he crossed the river, he hoped to find what he was looking for—as he had done many times in his life—with the help of an ancient book.

By the time Lieutenant Pavel made it back up to his sedan at the base of Petřín Tower, his head was throbbing so deeply that his vision was blurring. He slid in behind the wheel, closed his eyes, and pondered his next course of action. He sensed he needed a hospital, but his pursuit of Langdon was urgent, and he was unwilling to give up on it—or on his captain.

Despite the professor's reputation as a mild-mannered academic, he was turning out to be a dangerous and highly resourceful criminal. Even so, there was a limit to how far he could run. The American was out in the wild, and tips from Pavel's Blue Alert would keep flowing directly to the captain's phone in his pocket.

Unfortunately, it would not take long for others—ÚZSI, the U.S. embassy, the local police—to discover Langdon was a wanted man. They would all soon be involved, and those organizations would treat Langdon more gently than he deserved.

Pavel knew his window for retribution was closing quickly . . . and there was only one way he could fully honor his captain's memory.

Find Langdon before anyone gets to him first.

———··———

The conductor of Prague tram #22 had witnessed many oddities in her career. Normally she would not have glanced twice at a foolhardy tourist wearing only loafers and a sweater in midwinter. *This* man, however, had just exited the tram and crossed directly in front of her window. She noticed his handsome face, and there was no doubt in her mind. This was the same face that had been broadcast to her phone as a "Blue Alert" less than an hour ago.

CHAPTER 58

Night watchman Mark S. Dole reveled in his job at Random House Tower. For two years now, he had been securing this building, feeling a sense of pride whenever he donned his blue jacket and security cap and took his place behind the lobby's imposing security counter. He was twenty-eight and had promised his wife he'd be promoted to the day shift by the time he was thirty.

One of the perks he loved most about working here was the free employee library—a basement storeroom brimming with everything from old classics to modern thrillers. Since taking the job, Dole had read more than three dozen books, and tonight he was working his way through Steinbeck's *The Grapes of Wrath* and feeling blessed to support his family with a job that did not rely on the weather.

Dole glanced up from his book when a black SUV skidded jarringly to a halt in front of the main entrance. He had never seen such a thing, particularly at 3:48 a.m. Even more surprising, the man who leaped from the driver's seat was editor Jonas Faukman. Dole could not remember Faukman ever driving to work, and considering the man's parking job, that was probably a good thing.

Faukman was now outside the electronic door, frantically searching his pockets. Dole had seen this dance many times before. *He forgot his key card.* The night watchman pressed a button under his counter, and the door clicked open.

Faukman rushed into the lobby, looking somewhat crazed.

"Is everything okay, sir?" Dole asked.

"Fine, fine," the editor assured him, although he seemed anything but fine. His wild hair and beleaguered expression looked more like he'd been riding the Coney Island roller coaster all night. "I lost my backpack. My key card was in it."

"Sorry to hear that. I'll make you a temporary card." He pulled out a fresh plastic card and put it into the magnetizing machine.

Faukman waited, leaning heavily on the counter, eyes closed, breathing deeply.

"Mr. Faukman?" Dole said. "You sure you're okay?"

Faukman opened his eyes. "Yeah, I'm sorry, Mark. Just . . . a long night."

"Working on a tough manuscript?" Dole asked, handing him a fresh entry card.

The editor gave a wry nod and headed for the elevators. "This one's been more complicated than expected."

—·—

Having followed the signal from Faukman's phone, operatives Auger and Chinburg had caught up with his stolen SUV just before he threw his phone out the window. From there, they had discreetly tailed the SUV to the corner of Fifty-Sixth and Broadway, where it was now parked at a canted angle in front of Random House Tower.

The question was how to proceed.

They pulled over on the far side of Broadway, and Auger placed another secure call to Finch, who answered with a curt "Go."

"Sir," Auger said, "we lost audio on the editor, but we intercepted some startling intel. The PRH tech seems to have learned that one of the Americans in Prague is dead."

Finch was silent for a beat. "Where did he get his information?" he asked, his tone revealing nothing.

Auger shared what they had overheard on the call between the tech and Faukman.

"It's not your concern," Finch said, shutting down the inquiry. "Anything else?"

"Yes, sir," Auger said, having saved the worst for last. "The tech also claims to know who was responsible for the hack on their servers."

Finch drew a sharp breath. "Give me Chinburg."

Auger put the phone on speaker and held it up to his partner.

"Sir," Chinburg said, "we believe the tech's info is wrong. He has shared no specific details, so we have no idea if he's even on the right track."

"Have you spoken to your penetration team?" Finch demanded.

"Yes, sir. Just now. They assured me the hack was clean." Chinburg hesitated. "They did mention, however, that because the operation was carried out under such tight time restraints, they were forced to prioritize speed and efficiency over redundant anonymity measures."

"I'm sorry? They took *shortcuts?*"

"No, sir, they performed the best possible operation feasible in the window provided them. They assure me confidence is high."

"Confidence is high?" Finch snapped, his tone like ice. "In my experience, that phrase is used only by those whose confidence is lacking." There was a full three-second pause on the line. "Find out what this tech knows . . . and contain it *immediately*. However you deem necessary."

The call went dead.

Chinburg looked shaken. "Shit."

Auger looked amused. "Confidence is high?"

"Don't be an asshole."

Auger glanced across the street into the lobby of the towering skyscraper. "If Finch wants intel, we'll have to get inside."

Ascertaining how much the tech knew should have been as simple as remotely activating the microphone on Faukman's phone and listening to the conversation he was about to have with the tech. Unfortunately, the editor had performed his first security-savvy move of the evening, and his phone was now resting on the bottom of the Hudson River beneath the George Washington Bridge.

Seeing no other option, Auger packed several items into the compartments of his black tactical jacket and backpack. The technology-assisted portion of the evening had just concluded, which meant it was time to get their hands dirty.

CHAPTER 59

In Prague, U.S. Ambassador Heide Nagel stood at her office window and gazed wearily at the Alchymist Hotel across Tržiště Street. Having just finished briefing Dana Daněk on the covert operation she had unwittingly stumbled upon this morning, the ambassador had sent the media liaison back to her office to await further orders. Not surprisingly, Dana had been frightened by what she had learned.

Good, Nagel thought. *Fear may be the only way to control her.*

A quiet knock at the door drew Nagel's attention. She turned to see a U.S. Marine standing at attention in his traditional blue-white dress uniform. An eight-man Marine Corps embassy security group was part of the team that secured U.S. embassies and key diplomats around the world.

"Madam Ambassador," the Marine said. "We have a situation."

The more the merrier . . . I've already got a goddamned situation, she thought, but waved him in.

The man stepped into her office. "Ma'am, ÚZSI Captain Janáček has issued a public alert for an American citizen." He checked a note card. "His name is Robert Langdon."

Nagel closed her eyes, incredulous that her threat to expose Janáček had not stopped the captain in his tracks. *Janáček is going all in on Robert Langdon? Shit.* Clearly, she had not been as persuasive or intimidating as she had imagined.

"And the APB is a *Blue* Alert," the Marine added, "meaning ÚZSI is claiming Langdon killed one of their own."

"What!" she exploded. "That's a goddamned lie!"

"If we don't find Langdon right away . . ." the Marine said quietly, "someone's going to take him down."

Nagel took several breaths and gave him a tight nod of thanks. "I'll have orders for you shortly. Please close the door on your way out."

The Marine spun and departed.

Nagel immediately placed a Signal call to Mr. Finch.

"Go ahead," he said, answering on the first ring.

Nagel gave him the rundown on the deteriorating situation in Prague:

ÚZSI is pursuing Robert Langdon with lethal force.

Katherine Solomon is missing.

Attaché Harris went to Crucifix Bastion but is no longer answering his phone.

Finch, as anticipated, was furious. "I thought you handled ÚZSI! What kind of half-assed operation are you running there?!"

"This is *your* operation!" Nagel fired back. "And this situation is your own goddamned fault!"

Even as she spoke the words, Nagel knew she had overstepped.

Finch's voice grew uncharacteristically quiet. "Heide," he whispered, eschewing her formal title as if to remind her she was a mere pawn in his world. "I suggest you remember who placed you in this position . . . and *why*."

◆—··—◆

Field Officer Housemore had slept less than an hour.

She was now standing bleary-eyed at her sink, having just been awoken by a new call from Mr. Finch issuing updated orders.

Go to Crucifix Bastion immediately.

Secure Gessner's lab.

Housemore's knowledge of the Prague operation was "compartmentalized." While she knew Gessner was integral to Threshold, she also knew the underground facility Finch had built was located somewhere else in the city. *So why secure Gessner's lab?*

In addition to the new directive, Finch gave her the startling news that he was coming to Prague in person. If the overlord himself was on his way to Prague, then Housemore knew that this mission had definitely gone haywire.

———·——

As The Golĕm crossed Old Town Square, he passed near a throng of tourists huddled around a bronze statue and sipping hot *svařák* out of plastic cups. The voice of their tour guide blared loudly over a handheld megaphone.

"This Art Nouveau masterpiece," the guide declared, "depicts the leader of the Czech reform movement—Jan Hus—who was burned at the stake in 1415 for refusing to obey papal orders."

The guide was about to continue, when he spotted The Golĕm's dark form passing by. Even though Prague was overrun with costumed actors posing for tips, the guide apparently decided to seize the moment to create a little drama for his customers.

"Ladies and gentlemen," he announced excitedly. "We have an unexpected guest this morning! One of Prague's most famous celebrities!"

The tourists spun around as if expecting to see Ivan Lendl or Martina Navratilova. Instead, they saw a cloaked figure with a clay-caked face.

"The golem monster!" a young boy exclaimed. "You just told us about him in the synagogue!"

"Excellent," the guide said, turning to the boy. "And do you remember the meaning of the Hebrew letters on his head?"

"Truth!" said the kid. "Until the rabbi erased one letter and killed him!"

"Excellent," the guide said as The Golĕm passed by. "Okay, well it looks like no photo op with the golem today, but who can name the *second*-most-famous monster in Prague?"

Nobody answered.

"The *cockroach*!" the guide said dramatically. "Franz Kafka wrote a novella, right here in this city, called *The Metamorphosis*—in which a young man wakes up in bed one morning and discovers he's been transformed . . . into a giant cockroach!"

The Golĕm quickly left the group behind, exiting the square and heading north. As he walked, he found himself thinking of Franz Kafka and recalling the first time he had seen Prague's famously eerie statue of the author—a cloaked giant with no head . . . carrying on his shoulders a much smaller man.

A faceless creature who carries the burden of a weaker soul.

The Golĕm had felt an immediate kinship with the statue.

The tiny supported man represented Kafka, who, in his story *Description of a Struggle*, had been supported by a protective friend called his "acquaintance."

The acquaintance carried Kafka, The Golĕm had realized, just as the golem carried the Jewish people. *Just as I carry Sasha.*

Thoughts of Sasha drew his mind back to the task at hand.

Today I will infiltrate Threshold.

Sasha had not been their first victim . . . nor would she be their last. It all had to be destroyed. Forever.

CHAPTER 60

Langdon hurried along the sidewalk toward the Klementinum, his eyes scanning the sparse crowd for any sign of Katherine. A cold wind was whipping around him once again as he aimed for the museum's astronomical tower, which was visible above the other buildings less than a kilometer away.

He passed the opulent Mozart Prague hotel, where Wolfgang himself had played numerous private concerts, and he recalled once having witnessed its pale facade magically transformed into towering staves of sheet music that scrolled past in synch with an amplified recording of *Eine kleine Nachtmusik*. Every October, Prague hosted the Signal Festival, a week during which architectural landmarks were converted into canvases using light projection and video mapping. Langdon's favorite had been a soaring projection on the Archbishop's Palace depicting the origin and evolution of species—an irony that mirrored Prague's unflinching affinity for avant-garde artistry.

As he passed the hotel, Langdon's gait slowed suddenly, his eyes drawn to an advertising kiosk in a tiny park. The poster depicted a futuristic army of soldiers marching across a desolate planet. Above the armed warriors hung a single word whose appearance at this instant felt jarringly coincidental.

HALO.

Is the universe taunting me?

This ominous poster, of course, was not referencing a radiant symbol of the enlightened mind but rather a hugely popular computer game series, which, according to Langdon's students, had cleverly appropriated the cultural resonance of Christianity by incorporating biblical terms like the Covenant, the Ark, the Prophets, and the Flood, along with a tapestry of erudite religious references.

"Sounds like I might like it," Langdon had told his class.

"You won't," quipped a student. "Brutes with manglers would kill you instantly."

Langdon had no idea what he meant but decided to stick with online backgammon.

Nonetheless, at this moment, here in Prague, the appearance of the word *halo* felt like an eerily timed allusion to Katherine. He was uncertain whether to take this as a good omen or a foreboding one, considering they had just discussed the topic two days earlier.

"Halos are entirely misunderstood," she had said. "They have always been imagined as radiant streams of light encircling the head and depicting energy flowing *out* of an enlightened mind. But I believe we are interpreting halos in reverse. Those rays represent beams of *consciousness* . . . flowing *in* . . . not out. To say someone has an 'enlightened mind' is simply another way of saying they have a 'better receiver.'"

Langdon had studied halos as prominent religious symbols for many years, and yet he had never considered them in the way Katherine had just expressed. Like most people, he had always viewed halos as radiating *outward*. The reverse interpretation felt disorienting. He had to admit, however, that the Bible invariably described prophets as *receiving* divine wisdom from God . . . never formulating or broadcasting it.

In Acts 9, the Apostle Paul's conversion on the road to Damascus was described as the result of a burst of energy *received* from heaven. In Acts 2, the Holy Spirit flowed *into* the apostles and gave them the instantaneous power to speak in multiple languages so they could preach the gospel. *Sudden savant syndrome?*

The symbol of the halo was widely associated with Christianity, but Langdon knew there were many earlier versions—from Mithraism, Buddhism, and Zoroastrianism—that portrayed rays of energy around their subjects. When Christianity adopted the symbol of the halo, the rays were gradually removed in favor of a simple disk hovering over one's head. Thus, an important symbolic element of the halo had been lost to history, and Katherine believed that the lost version might confirm a forgotten understanding and ancient wisdom . . . the lost understanding of what had now become nonlocal consciousness theory.

The brain is a receiver . . . and consciousness flows in, not out.

"You still can't quite believe the concept, can you?" she had challenged playfully. "You're waiting for some kind of *proof* that your brain is a receiver."

Langdon considered it. Scientific models were never *proven* in any kind of absolute sense. They gained acceptance by consistently explaining and predicting observations better than alternative models. Katherine's concept was convincing and also could explain many anomalies like ESP, out-of-body experiences, and sudden savant syndrome.

"If you ask me," Katherine said, "your eidetic memory should be proof enough, Robert. I know you believe your brain has *stored* every single image you've ever seen. But full photographic recall is a physical impossibility. Your *lifetime* of vivid image data would fill a warehouse, even using the most advanced digital storage methods, and yet you can still recall that data perfectly. The truth is, the human brain—even *your* brain—is physically far too small to hold that much information."

Langdon's attention was piqued. "You're saying our memories function like cloud computing? All of our memory data are sitting *elsewhere* . . . waiting for us to access them."

"*Exactly.* Your eidetic brain simply has a superior mechanism for reaching out and grabbing data. Your receiver is sophisticated and highly tuned to accessing *images.*" She smiled. "But maybe a bit less tuned to accessing faith and trust."

Langdon laughed. "Well, I have *faith* in you, and I *trust* that soon you'll share your scientific experiments . . . and explain to me exactly what you've discovered."

"Nice try, Professor," she said. "But you'll have to wait and read the book."

CHAPTER 61

The Klementinum—like so many of the stunning buildings of Europe—was erected to further the glory of the Christian God.

Emperor Ferdinand I, in an effort to increase the presence of the Catholic Church in Bohemia in the 1500s, invited to Prague members of the growing Society of Jesus—the Jesuits—and offered them the city's finest real estate on which to build a Jesuit college. By the end of the century, the Jesuit's "Klementinum"— named after St. Clement—had become one of the largest building complexes in the land, second only to Prague Castle.

Celebrated for its dedication to the sciences, the Klementinum university eventually included an Astronomical Tower that rose to sixty-eight meters, a scientific library of thousands of books, and an ingenious Meridian Room, which used geometry and sunlight to indicate the precise time of noon every day, at which moment the official timekeeper would fire a cannon to mark midday for everyone in town.

In modern times, the Klementinum functioned primarily as the seat of the Czech National Library and as a historical museum. Savvy tourists seeking the best views of Prague climbed the Klementinum's Astronomical Tower, their 172-step ascent rewarded by stunning vistas as well as an absorbing exhibit of eighteenth-century astronomical instruments.

Hurrying up the road toward the museum, Robert Langdon gave no thought to the countless treasures within, instead focused solely on Katherine and the cryptic message that had led him here. As he passed the eastern gateway of Charles Bridge,

Langdon realized he was on the exact same sidewalk he had run only a few hours ago.

I'm going in circles, he thought. *Just like Katherine's goldfish.*

It was 9:55 a.m. when Langdon arrived outside the Klementinum's main entrance and began scanning the area for Katherine. She wasn't here, but to his surprise, he saw a family entering through the main doors.

The museum is open already?

Feeling a rush of hope that Katherine might be waiting inside, Langdon hurried through the doors into the welcome warmth of the lobby. He expected to find the museum nearly deserted at this early hour, but instead the lobby was bustling with tourists, many of them sitting atop suitcases while sipping coffee and eating donuts. The scene looked more like an airport lounge than the anteroom of a sixteenth-century Jesuit monastery.

What in the world?!

A perky museum employee walked over to Langdon with a smile. "Coffee?" She held out a tray of coffee.

Baffled, Langdon gratefully accepted the hot beverage, wrapping his frozen fingers around the warm paper cup. "Thank you, but . . . what's happening here?"

The woman nodded toward a banner on the wall.

KLEMENTINUM

NOW OPEN AT 7 A.M.!

"New marketing initiative," she said cheerily. "Most U.S. flights arrive at six a.m., so tourists have hours to kill before they can check in to their hotels. We offer a free airport shuttle, luggage check, coffee and donuts . . . *et voilà!*" She motioned to the full lobby. "Whatever it takes to get you Americans into museums, right?!" She headed off.

The comment would have been more offensive had Langdon not heard that one of Prague's most popular tourist attractions was now an underground shooting range where Americans could legally fire an exotic array of automatic weapons.

Nonetheless, he now felt a piece of the puzzle slip into place.

When Katherine sent her email, the museum was open! In addition, she would have had to walk directly past the entrance on her way to Gessner's lab. *Did she step inside . . . and attempt to summon me? Codex XL . . .*

Buoyed by the idea that Katherine might still be somewhere in this complex of buildings, Langdon scanned the teeming lobby for her thick dark hair. He didn't see her and hurried to the ticket window to purchase a full-access ticket. The cashier seemed to study him a moment, almost suspiciously, but she issued his badge without question. Langdon adhered it to his sweater and hurried off through a series of ornate corridors toward his destination.

SPECIAL EXHIBITION
CODEX GIGAS
(THE DEVIL'S BIBLE)

When he reached the library's grand entrance, a docent stopped him. After studying Langdon's badge, he affixed a red sticker to it.

"You have a one-hour window, sir," the docent said. "Enjoy."

Langdon had forgotten that access to the Baroque Library was restricted to hourly increments, meaning if Katherine had sent her email from inside . . . her allotted time would have long ended by now. *Please still be here . . . somewhere.*

Langdon quickly strode through the doorway, into what author Jorge Luis Borges had once called "the most exquisite library in Europe."

Even in Langdon's current state of distress, he still found the room utterly transfixing. It was a long, narrow chamber whose ceiling fresco was a divinely rendered, pale blue expanse of sunlit heaven, complete with cherubim that seemed to hang weightlessly overhead. The trompe l'oeil gave the impression that sunlight was pouring *through* the structure itself.

Supporting the fresco, the library's walls were thirty-foot-high bookshelves, containing more than twenty *thousand* editions dating back centuries. The unmistakable scent of vellum drifted down from the library's oldest editions on the second level—those with the white spines and red markings—accessible only by ascending a secret staircase to the library's wraparound balcony. The floor was an inlaid wooden parquet whose intricacy rivaled any Langdon had ever seen, including that of the Grand Gallery in the Louvre.

Langdon stopped several paces into the quiet space, searching the large crowd for any sign of Katherine. *Nothing.* He headed farther into the ornate room, moving along its distinct procession of oversized antique globes that stretched down the middle of the floor, all the way to the far end of the hall. The globes were interspersed with signs bearing a symbol as self-evident as any Langdon could imagine.

Who lights a match in a room full of ancient books?!

As he moved deeper into the library, the main attraction came into full view, surrounded by visitors.

The Devil's Bible.

The colossal book was housed in a cube-shaped Plexiglas viewing case so large that it looked more like an airport smoking lounge than a protective container. It was surrounded by a throng of quietly murmuring tourists who were taking photos and admiring the mysterious codex, which lay open to the iconic illumination of a demon in an ermine loincloth. As Langdon arrived, he barely glanced at the codex, instead scanning the faces in the crowd.

Are you here, Katherine?

Many of the visitors were still bundled up, some blowing in their hands. The Klementinum kept this library exceptionally cold—most would say uncomfortably so—as Katherine had commented yesterday. Langdon had explained that curators often cooled their most crowded exhibition halls to keep tourists moving through quickly, providing faster turnover—a crowd-management tactic, he noted, that was later adopted by fast-food restaurants. *In and out.*

"*Katherine?*" Langdon called tentatively into the quiet crowd.

Several visitors turned and gave him curious looks. A few of them did double takes, as if they recognized him. Otherwise . . . no response.

Maybe she's already come and gone?

He scanned the crowd and then looked up at the deserted upper balcony. "*Katherine Solomon?*" he called again, louder now.

A docent marched over and hushed Langdon with a finger raised to his lips. This was, after all, a library. Langdon nodded his understanding and quietly continued scanning the ornate room in all directions. After two complete turns, he had seen no sign of Katherine anywhere.

His heart sank as he considered how large the city was and how little direction he had.

If you aren't here, where are you?

———··———

No sirens, Pavel thought as he skidded to a stop outside the Klementinum. His Blue Alert for Langdon had already generated four separate tips.

A tram conductor near National Theater reported Langdon was moving north along the river.

A cabdriver near Virgin Mary Square spotted him entering the Klementinum.

Clever hiding place, Pavel thought, bearing in mind how well the historian probably knew this building complex. *It won't matter. I have eyes everywhere.*

Pavel hurried into the museum and showed Langdon's photo to the woman at the ticket booth, who shared not only that this man had purchased a ticket . . . but also the exact room in which he was almost certainly now standing.

He's mine, Pavel thought, discreetly checking that his weapon was loaded and plunging into the museum.

"*Barokní knihovna!*" he shouted to a docent in the main hallway. "The Baroque Library! Where is it?!"

CHAPTER 62

Night watchman Mark Dole was familiar with nearly everyone who had been granted key card access to Random House Tower, but the two men who had just used a key card to buzz themselves into the towering lobby were strangers to him.

The pair's arrival, in the middle of the night and on the heels of Faukman's dramatic entrance, was odd in itself, but the fact that they were both dressed in black military gear sent a jolt of alarm through Dole.

"Gentlemen!" Dole exclaimed, jumping to his feet. "How may I help you?" *And how the hell did you unlock my door?!*

"You've got an emergency," the muscle-bound man called in a firm voice, striding urgently toward the security desk. He was carrying a bulky backpack. "Your building's *tuned mass damper* triggered an alarm with the city—it's in danger of a structural failure."

Dole needed a moment to understand what the man had just said. Indeed, most Manhattan skyscrapers were built with a "tuned mass damper," a weighted device mounted on a high floor to act as a steadying counterweight that prevented a building from swaying in heavy winds or earthquakes. In the case of Random House Tower, its tuned mass damper was an eight-hundred-ton tank of water suspended on the fiftieth floor.

A structural malfunction? Why is there no alarm at the desk?

"You need to evacuate, and I need to get upstairs," the man urged, arriving at the counter.

"But I don't underst—"

There was a flash of movement, and a fist collided with Dole's sternum, driving the air from his lungs. The night guard landed hard on his back, gasping on the floor, out of sight behind the counter. An instant later, the large man was kneeling over him, gun barrel pressed into his chest.

"Not one goddamned sound," the man whispered as he fished the master key card from Dole's uniform pocket and tossed it over the desk to the other man.

Dole lay motionless on his back, staring up at the lobby ceiling. He could hear rapidly departing footsteps and a familiar series of beeps; the other intruder had just used the key card to pass through the security turnstile and access the elevator.

"Just lie there quietly," the man above him whispered, "and you won't get hurt." He zip-tied Dole's hands, scooped up the guard's security cap, donned it himself, and calmly assumed the watchman's seat at the desk, gun in his lap.

Dole's chest ached as he tried to catch his breath. Whoever the intruders were, they had needed less than ten seconds to take over Dole's post and steal a key card that provided access to the entire building.

———⋅⋅———

On the fourth floor, Jonas Faukman stepped off the elevator and headed for the steel door marked DATA SECURITY CENTER. It required a special key card, and he pounded on it loudly until it finally opened, and a familiar face appeared.

Alex Conan looked like he'd been through a war of his own. "Thank God," the tech said. "You made it back."

"Any news on Langdon and Katherine?" Faukman pressed, still haunted by the tech's words on the frantic call earlier: *The hackers who deleted your manuscript . . . I think they might have killed one of your authors.*

"I'll explain everything," Alex said, "but it's good news. Nobody was killed. I was wrong."

Faukman felt a visceral rush of relief, and he bent over, hands on his knees, taking several deep breaths. *Thank God.*

"Langdon is the one I thought was . . . dead," Alex said as he ushered Faukman into the security center. "But I just spoke to the manager at the Four Seasons. The situation is complicated, but he confirmed Robert Langdon is very much alive . . . although it sounds like he may be in trouble with the local authorities."

What kind of trouble? Faukman wondered, although his curiosity was eclipsed by the profound relief of knowing Langdon was all right.

Bolstered by the good news, he followed Alex through a maze of floor-to-ceiling computer racks, all humming loudly. They emerged into an open area with an expansive workstation housing multiple computer monitors, fanned out in a gentle semicircle. Several high-backed padded chairs sat before the monitors. Faukman felt like he had walked into a mini mission control.

On the wall over the workstation was a wide framed illustration depicting an ocean liner in distress . . . sinking into a sea of ones and zeros. The caption read: LOOSE BITS SINK SHIPS. The spoof on the famous World War II slogan was supposed to be a reminder to secure data at its root level.

A little late for that, Faukman thought. *The manuscript's gone.*

Alex slid a second swivel chair next to his, and the two men sat down, rotating to face each other. "Okay . . . a lot happened," the tech said, his expression dire. "Let me start at the beginning."

Starting at the beginning, Faukman knew, was the worst way to narrate a story, but he held his tongue.

"I didn't want to share all of this on the phone," Alex began, "but after you disappeared, I was scared and felt I should warn Katherine Solomon immediately that her manuscript was under attack—and that she might be in personal danger."

"Okay."

"I pulled her employee file, called her cell, and I got no answer. Same thing for Robert Langdon. When I couldn't reach any of the three of you, I panicked and decided to track your exact locations by hacking into your phones."

"Wait . . . you can do that?"

"Not in *your* case," the tech said, spinning toward his terminal and beginning to type. "And not for Dr. Solomon either, but Mr. Langdon was easy. I noticed he had an iCloud email address and also that he had chosen the *same* exact password for multiple credentials on the PRH server. I have to say, I'm surprised such a smart guy would use a single password, especially one as weak as 'Dolphin123.' "

Langdon's password is Dolphin123? Faukman hung his head. *Why do we even have security protocols?* Langdon's nickname at Harvard was "The Dolphin" because he could still outswim half of the varsity water polo team. Unfortunately, Langdon was also a self-proclaimed Luddite—a classicist whose expertise in the ancient past made for a reluctant relationship with the future. *He still has a Rolodex and wears a Mickey Mouse watch, for God's sake.*

"I was desperate to locate one of you," Alex said, "and so I used Langdon's password to hack into his FindMy app and pinpoint his location."

The tech typed a few more keys, and a map of Prague materialized.

"According to iCloud," he continued, "Langdon's phone was *completely* offline, which is very unusual. And if we check his last known location . . . we get this disturbing image." Conan refreshed the screen, zooming in. "This says Mr. Langdon's last known location was this morning at 7:02 a.m. local time, and he was exactly . . . *here.*" He pointed at a tiny blue dot on the map. "And then nothing."

Faukman squinted at the dot on the map. "I'm sorry? This says he was in the middle of the Vltava River?"

"Yes! Considering we had been attacked by military-level hackers," Alex said, "and you had disappeared, and Langdon wasn't answering . . ."

"You thought he was *drowned?* Langdon's a world-class swimmer! Maybe he just threw his phone away."

"I wanted to believe that, but if Langdon *threw* the phone, the phone's location tracking would have been a straight line. But *his* track moves around and even doubles back on itself before it disappears! It looked like Langdon was taken out onto the river, dumped overboard, and then tried to swim back to shore, before he drowned and took the phone with him to the bottom."

Faukman could see it was an alarming scenario, but Alex's

tenuous leap from a cell phone's "last known location" to Langdon being murdered was missing a few steps in logic. Then again, it was probably no less logical than the surreal happenstance of both Langdon's phone *and* Faukman's lying on the bottom of rivers on different sides of the planet.

"I know you think I overreacted," Alex said, "but considering *who* hacked us . . . I had a right to be worried. I still am."

"So who hacked us?" Faukman demanded, leaning forward.

"That's why I wanted to talk to Katherine—to find out if she could think of anyone who might be targeting her so I could build a proprietary algorithm and search for specific digital artifacts."

My God, this kid needs an editor. Just tell me who the hell did it?!

"But before I could build the algorithm, my FTK scan returned a hit. One of the IoCs from this hack had a match on MISP associated with known—"

"Alex, I have no idea—"

"All you need to know is that the people who hacked PRH were in a hurry! They saved time by using a piece of their *own* recycled code—duplicated strings that hackers call copy pasta! It saves time, but it also risks revealing—"

The tech suddenly jumped to his feet and spun around, staring intently back through the rows of rack-mounted gear in the direction of the entrance. "Allison?!" he shouted.

Faukman was already on edge. "Who's Allison?"

"My boss. Either she's early or I'm hearing things." Alex stood up, checking his watch. "Did you hear the door beep open?"

Faukman shook his head. *I haven't heard anything since October 5, 1987. Fourth row, Pink Floyd, Madison Square Garden. Gilmour was sublime.*

"Hold on," Alex said, disappearing into the maze of computers.

Unbelievable, Faukman thought, waiting impatiently.

Ten seconds later, the tech returned with a shrug. "Sorry, I've been totally paranoid tonight." He looked shaken as he sat back down. "The people we're up against are not the kind you screw with." Alex rolled his chair to a nearby computer terminal and motioned for Faukman to join him, which he did. "Let me show you," the kid said, launching a web browser. "You're not going to believe—"

Faukman abruptly reached out and seized the tech's arm, signaling for him to stop talking. *Not another word!*

"What the hell?!" Alex said, recoiling.

"Sorry," Faukman said loudly but calmly. "I just want to check one quick thing online."

Faukman raised a finger to his lips, staring intently at the young tech, urging him to be silent. When Alex nodded his understanding, Faukman took over the computer keyboard. The browser had opened to a standard search page, and Faukman quickly typed his search string all in caps:

YOU AND I ARE NOT ALONE IN HERE . . . FOLLOW MY LEAD.

The tech spun toward Faukman with eyes flashing fear.

Yes, I'm scared too, Faukman thought, having just realized that the entry beep Alex heard was not a paranoid imagination; someone had indeed entered this control room and was now hiding somewhere among the gear racks behind them.

And now they are listening to us. A moment earlier, Faukman had noticed a barely perceptible dot of blue light reflected in the glass of the framed illustration nearby. *Editing spy thrillers just paid off.* Some would have assumed the dot was a laser sight from a gun, but this dot was blue, not red, and it was aimed at a sheet of *glass*.

"This site is interesting," Faukman said, calmly deleting his first message and typing another.

WHO IS RESPONSIBLE FOR HACK?

Alex's face was pale as Faukman pushed the keyboard back to him.

Taking a deep breath, the tech dutifully tapped out his reply.

Faukman studied the bizarre, hyphenated word that Alex had typed. It was unfamiliar to him. He gave the tech a confused shrug and anxiously mouthed, "Who . . . is . . . that?"

Alex began typing again—this time a short acronym.

Faukman stared at it in mute shock. *No.*

On any other morning, Faukman would never have believed

what had just appeared on the screen, but considering all that had transpired tonight, the information certainly answered a lot of questions.

Fuck.

The question now was what Faukman was going to do about his current predicament. The answer, he suspected, lay in his skills with dialogue . . . and also in understanding the subtle difference between two very similar words.

Misinformation and *dis*information.

CHAPTER 63

Inside the Baroque Library, Langdon scanned and rescanned the faces of the crowd of visitors, finally accepting that he had arrived here too late.

She's gone.

Two hours had passed since Katherine sent him the encrypted email telling him to come to this place; even if she had been here earlier, her ticket would have expired, and the docents would have asked her to leave.

As Langdon gazed down at the Codex Gigas, splayed open in its protective glass cube, the illustration of the "Diaper Devil" seemed to be staring back mockingly. Just yesterday, he and Katherine had stood on this very spot, hand in hand, happily discussing the mysteries of this incredible book.

Katherine had been intrigued by the legend of the Devil's Bible, but it had been the architecture of the lush library itself that most captured her imagination. Spellbound by its beauty, she asked him about the parquet floor, the frescoes, and what she referred to as the "faux balcony."

"What do you mean by *faux*?" Langdon questioned, surprised.

"It's *decorative*, right?" She pointed up at the balcony that encircled the entire room. "Look . . . there's no way to get to it—no ladders or doors entering from above."

Langdon had to laugh. *Leave it to a scientist to notice the inconsistency.* Most tourists who admired the suspended walkway around the room never spotted the obvious riddle: there was no visible means to access it.

"Follow me," Langdon whispered, nodding discreetly to his

right. He walked her into the corner of the library, and then, double-checking that the rest of the patrons were focused on the Bible, he gently grabbed a section of bookcase and tugged it toward him. The case hinged silently outward, revealing a dark alcove, in which a spiral staircase ascended to an opening in the balcony floor.

"And of course you knew that," she said, rolling her eyes.

Langdon's warm memories of yesterday dissolved as an authoritative voice suddenly broke the silence and began shouting at the library door.

"*Dámy a pánové!*" a man yelled. "*Opustte výstavu! Požární poplach!*"

Many of the Czech visitors exchanged startled looks and began moving immediately toward the exit. A smattering of foreign tourists glanced at them and followed.

"*Fire emergency!*" the same voice shouted. "*Go to the exit! Now!*"

Fire? Langdon smelled nothing. *Really?*

He peered toward the crush of tourists now crowding through the library's lone exit. Beyond the crowd, in the hallway, a muscular man in a blue ÚZSI uniform was overseeing the library evacuation . . . intently studying each person who exited, even halting one or two to scrutinize their faces more closely.

Langdon recognized him immediately. *Lieutenant Pavel.*

He had no idea how the man had located him so quickly—or so accurately—but there he was, sorting through the crowd.

It's a fake emergency, Langdon sensed. *So he can trap me.*

Considering Pavel had already fired his weapon at Langdon in the Mirror Maze, there was no guarantee he wouldn't simply shoot him on sight once the last person had exited the library.

Scanning the room for anywhere to hide, Langdon saw only the line of globes and the codex's transparent display case. Neither offered much help. In desperation, he turned his eyes toward the upper balcony and then down to the hinged bookcase in the corner of the room.

Even if Langdon ascended to the balcony, there was no exit up there. *The bookcase is a dead end.* But hiding on the hidden staircase might buy him a few extra minutes. Museum security would find him eventually, of course, but anything was better than being alone with an unhinged, trigger-happy ÚZSI officer.

Before Pavel had a chance to see him, Langdon slipped away from the mass of exiting guests and moved back toward the bookcase. When he arrived, he grabbed the door and pulled it toward himself.

The door didn't budge.

Puzzled, he pulled again.

Have they locked it?

Installing a lock on this bookcase made no sense whatsoever, and besides, the door had been open just yesterday when he and Kath—

An unexpected thought materialized.

Inexplicable . . . and yet . . .

Startled by the possibility, Langdon put his mouth close to the partition and whispered, "Katherine?"

Langdon heard a rustling within, as if someone was unlashing whatever was holding the door closed. A moment later, the bookcase swung open.

Langdon found himself staring into the tear-filled eyes of Katherine Solomon.

Without hesitation, he moved into her arms, letting the bookcase swing closed behind them. As they held each other in the darkness of the tiny alcove, Langdon could hear her quietly weeping.

"Thank God," she managed. "I thought you were dead."

"I'm right here," he whispered.

CHAPTER 64

I n the blackness of the alcove, Katherine pressed her body into Langdon's, holding on tight, neither one saying a word. Whatever chaos currently existed outside this small space, they were now alone in the world, at least for this brief moment, safe and together.

I thought I might never see him again, Katherine thought.

It felt like an eternity that she had been hiding in here, terrified for her life and also devastated that she might have lost the man with whom she was falling in love. To be without him would have been the cruelest of twists; for years Katherine had felt powerfully drawn to Langdon's effortless charm, and yet for some reason, she'd always resisted letting it become romantic. Perhaps it had been the fear of losing him as a friend, but even so, every time their paths had crossed, she had found herself secretly wondering if one day, after decades of friendship, the time might be right.

And now . . . at last, it *was.*

Overcome with emotion, Katherine held Langdon tighter, savoring the seamless fit of their embrace and the warmth of his body.

"You feel cold," Langdon whispered. "Are you okay? Where's your coat?"

"I used it to tie the door shut," she said, having lashed one sleeve to the spiral railing and the other to the handle on the door so nobody could pull open the bookcase. "This alcove was the only place I could think to hide."

"But *why* are you hiding?!" he asked, sounding thoroughly confused.

Katherine explained how she had received a panicked voice-mail this morning from a PRH systems tech named Alex. She had called him back, and he frantically warned her that someone had hacked into the PRH server . . . and deleted all traces of her manuscript.

"What?!" Langdon sounded aghast. "Your manuscript is *gone?*"

"Apparently so," she said. "And the tech was terrified. He told me . . ." Katherine paused, her voice catching with emotion. "Robert . . . he said he thought *you* had drowned."

———··———

Langdon pulled away, trying to see her face in the darkness. "He told you I was *dead?!*"

"He feared as much, yes," Katherine replied, her voice frail and emotional. "He said he had tracked your phone to the middle of the Vltava River . . . and the signal disappeared. I was too upset to ask questions, and he told me to dump my phone immediately, get off the street, and hide somewhere safe until he had more information. The problem was that he couldn't reach us anywhere, and it seemed like whoever had deleted my manuscript had come after all *three* of us! He also told me Jonas has entirely disappeared!"

Langdon could barely get his head around what he was hearing. *Jonas is missing?* "But why would anyone target your manuscript? Or any of us?!"

"I have no idea," she said, pulling him even closer, her sweet-smelling hair falling against his cheek. "I'm just relieved you're safe."

"Katherine," he whispered. "I have no idea what's going on here . . . but I'm so sorry you've had to go through it." He knew he needed to share the details of his own chaotic morning, but for the moment he was still trying to figure out what to do next. "And you're certain your manuscript is . . . *gone?*"

"According to Alex, yes," she said. "Deleted from all servers. The only good news is that this morning, on my way out of the hotel, I noticed the business office was deserted, and I decided to take advantage of the private moment to print a hard copy of the manuscript for you to read."

For the last several days, Katherine had said she was almost ready to give him his own reading copy, but publishing decorum required that her *editor* receive the manuscript first . . . which he now had.

"I printed your copy, but as I was about to go upstairs and lock it in our suite's safe, a fire alarm went off at the hotel, and I had to evacuate the building!"

To his amazement, Langdon realized that Katherine had been just around the corner in the business center when he sprinted through the lobby and pulled the alarm. *My God, I just missed her.*

"The hard copy you printed," Langdon asked, able to see nothing in the darkness. "Did you manage to put it somewhere safe?"

"I have it right here in my bag!" she said. "When I told Alex I was carrying it, he said it might turn out to be the only remaining copy, and he urged me to take it somewhere secure until we could figure out what was going on. I was just down the street at the time, so I came *here.*"

Langdon held her tighter.

"I trusted you were alive, Robert—I could *feel* it, whatever Alex said about you drowning. I wanted to call and tell you where I would be waiting for you. The problem was, he warned me someone was probably monitoring our communications."

"So you emailed me in code before you dumped your phone," Langdon said, feeling the pieces now fall into place.

"Yes. Enochian and Codex XL. It was as obscure a message as I could think of, but I knew you'd understand."

Langdon couldn't help but smile. "That's actually pretty damn clever, Katherine Solomon."

"It wasn't very hard." She laughed and kissed him tenderly on the cheek. "I just asked myself: What would *you* do?"

In the hallway outside the Baroque Library, Lieutenant Pavel watched the last of the tourists exit.

Where the hell is Robert Langdon?

Five minutes earlier, Pavel had shown Langdon's photo to the museum docent checking tickets at the library entrance. The man had confirmed that the tall American had indeed entered this library shortly before Pavel arrived and, to the best of the docent's knowledge, had not yet exited.

So where is he?!

"Is there another way out?" Pavel demanded. *"Jiný východ?!"*

The frightened docent shook his head. *"Žádný tu není."*

Pavel stepped through the doorway and scanned the long rectangular chamber. It was essentially a wide hallway with towering bookcases for walls, offering nowhere to hide. A procession of antique globes ran down the center of the room toward a huge transparent display case of some sort—neither of which provided much cover.

It was then that Pavel noticed the balcony.

Very clever, Professor.

The library's wraparound loggia was high enough that Langdon could remain out of sight simply by lying flat on the elevated floor. Pavel looked around the room and saw no stairs, doors, or access to the upper level.

He summoned the docent and pointed to the balcony. "How do you get up there?" he said quietly, towering over the thin young man.

The docent pointed nervously to the corner of the library on the left of the entrance. "There's a door in the bookcase . . . and a spiral staircase behind it."

Pavel considered his options. "Seal the library!" he commanded. "Get out and keep the doors locked. The man trapped inside is extremely dangerous. *Do not* open these doors for any reason—no matter what you hear! Including gunfire. Is that clear?!"

The docent went pale and nodded, wasting no time rushing

back into the hallway and heaving the doors closed behind him. The slam resonated through the empty room, and Pavel heard multiple dead bolts clank into place.

Alone now, Pavel turned and faced the silent chamber.

Just you and me, Professor . . . in this beautiful killing box.

CHAPTER 65

The historic Old-New Synagogue is nestled in the neighborhood of Josefov—once the original walled Jewish ghetto of Prague. As the oldest active synagogue in Europe, it has been a silent witness to the changing tides of history since the late thirteenth century. Despite the encroachments of time and tumultuous events that Prague has endured, the synagogue remains unscathed—a testament to the resilience of faith and tradition.

According to legend, the stones for this temple were brought by angels from Jerusalem "on condition" that the stones would be returned to Jerusalem upon the arrival of the Messiah. Many scholars believe that this gift "on condition"—in Hebrew, *al tnay*—was confused with the Yiddish *alt-nay*, which literally means Old-New, hence the building's unusual name.

A spiritual oasis . . . in a desert of materialism, The Golĕm thought, gazing ahead at the synagogue's austere stone facade, which was flanked closely by the storefronts of Hermès, Montblanc, and Valentino. The modern world had encroached upon every corner of this ancient ghetto, swallowing up its somber residences until barely a trace remained of the perilous streets once patrolled by the original mythical golem, who had been created on this spot centuries ago.

In many ways, the synagogue was where The Golĕm had been born as well. Shortly after arriving in Prague, he had been walking aimlessly past this building when he heard a tour guide narrating the legend of the Jewish ghetto's great protector—a guardian soul inserted into the body of a clay monster. The story felt familiar and personal. As if drawn by some unseen gravity, The Golĕm had entered the temple.

Inside, the air was deathly still, infused with an almost mystical energy. Behind the altar, the sacred ark stood sentinel, harboring the ancient Torah scrolls inspired by the eternal dialogue between the earthly and the divine. The Golĕm felt comforted by the silence and dim light. He took a seat on a wooden pew whose surface was worn smooth by generations of the faithful, and it was there, by the fragile light of medieval chandeliers, that he had picked up an informational pamphlet . . . and he had begun to read.

He found himself captivated by the legend of the golem and its *creator*, a powerful rabbi named Judah Loew ben Bezalel, also revered as the Maharal of Prague. In addition to being a scholar of Jewish mysticism and the Talmud, Rabbi Loew had been a mathematician, astronomer, philosopher, and Kabbalist who had written extensively, including an important text known as *Gur Aryeh al HaTorah*.

Later that night, The Golĕm had quietly read the rabbi's text, which he had purchased in the gift shop beside the synagogue. As he consumed the ancient words, The Golĕm was stunned to find *himself* on every page . . . the Truth as he already understood it!

Reality has many different levels.

Guf, nefesh, sechel . . .

A solitary soul can fuse with another to form a new entity.

Yesodot, taarovot, tarkovot.

Souls are reborn again and again.

Gilgul neshamot . . .

That fateful night, as he studied the cycle of souls, he was struck by the realization that he, like the original golem, had materialized with clarity and without preamble into this realm, a blank soul awaking inside a physical form that felt so foreign to him as to be repulsive.

He recalled that first moment inside the dank mental institution when, inspired by an act of unspeakable cruelty, The Golĕm had suddenly perceived himself and felt purpose . . . rising up out of nothingness . . . seeing a helpless woman being beaten senseless by a night nurse. He had launched himself forward and struck the nurse to the ground, strangling her unrelentingly until the life left her.

Then he had stood over his victim and savored his victory, empowered by his first act of service in this realm. The woman he saved had not been conscious to witness his act of valor. Nor had she felt him transporting her beaten body back to her bed, where he tended to her wounds and then slipped back into the darkness . . . beginning to understand who he was and why he had been summoned.

I am her protector.

From then on, he served as a silent guardian within those prison walls, watching from the shadows, confirming she was safe. Not until that night in Prague, reading the words of Rabbi Loew, had it finally dawned on The Golĕm why the Jewish legend felt so familiar . . . and the real reason why he had been brought to Prague.

I am The Golĕm.

He pictured the clay monster awaking without warning, knowing only that he was here to protect.

My story is his story.

Like the ancient clay monster, The Golĕm often felt like an outcast, condemned to being alone. He too struggled with his sanity. Sometimes The Golĕm longed for recognition of his sacrifice, but that was not his place. And so he continued to move through her world unseen.

Today brought a vastly different challenge. He had killed her mentor and also her lover—two monsters who had abused her trust—but it was critical that Sasha not discover his actions on her behalf.

She would never forgive me . . . never understand.

For this reason, The Golĕm had decided what needed to be done. He had gently locked Sasha away in darkness, where she would be blessedly unaware of all that was transpiring . . . and all he was about to do.

As he neared the synagogue, he felt burdened, and yet the

weight he was carrying was not only spiritual. His cloak pockets were full—a Vipertek stun gun, a retractable blade, and a metal wand to control the Ether. The Golĕm suspected he would need them all.

Before reaching the temple, The Golĕm veered abruptly left on Široká Street, heading not for the synagogue today, but rather for the lot next door—three acres of earth surrounded by a tall stone fortification.

Both revered and feared, what lay within these walls had become known worldwide . . . as the ghostliest place on earth.

CHAPTER 66

Under different circumstances, Lieutenant Pavel might have tried to appreciate the serenity of this ancient library, but today he had no room in his life for calm. The rage growing within him was unlike anything he had ever felt.

My captain, my uncle . . . murdered.

"Professor!" he bellowed into the empty space, pulling out his weapon and scanning the balcony above him. *"I know you are up there! Stand up!"*

No movement.

Silence.

"Show yourself now!"

Pavel rotated slowly, allowing his weapon to trace a slow line around the entire perimeter of the walkway.

Nothing.

Turning toward the corner of the room where the docent had indicated there was a concealed staircase, Pavel moved stealthily across the floor and located a portion of bookcase that was discreetly cut out into a doorway. He grabbed the tiny brass handle and pulled, but the door moved only slightly before it stopped.

He tried again. The door was somehow locked from within.

Bracing himself, Pavel pulled on the handle with all his strength, but the door moved only a reluctant half inch before the brass handle tore free of the historic bookshelf, sending Pavel tumbling backward onto the hard parquet. The collision with the floor sent searing pain through his already pounding skull.

Incensed, the lieutenant leaped to his feet, aimed his gun at the bookshelf door, and squeezed the trigger. With an explosive echo, a bullet passed through the bookcase and clanged loudly off something metal on the other side, perhaps the spiral staircase the docent had told him led to the second floor.

Pavel did not hear a body hit the floor. He considered emptying his entire weapon into the bookcase, but he knew better.

Trpělivost, the ghost of his captain whispered. *Patience is a weapon.*

Pavel lowered his pistol.

If the sound of a gunshot had not caused the docents to come running in, then nothing would. Time was on Pavel's side, and he had already formulated an idea.

At the far end of the room stood an antique ladder leaning against a bookcase. Designed to retrieve books from the highest shelves on the first floor, the ladder was not long enough to reach all the way up to the balcony.

His eye moved to the transparent display case at the far end of the room. The heavy Plexiglas cube was almost as tall as Pavel himself and looked to be bulletproof—a perfect base for a ladder. If Pavel could get the ladder to reach the balcony, he could climb over, circle around to the top of the spiral staircase . . . and attack from above.

Trpělivost, he thought. *Patience, my captain.*

———·· —➤

Inside the alcove, Katherine and Langdon crouched in terror, having just heard a bullet whiz into the cramped space and hit the metal staircase below them. It had exploded with a bright spark and deafening clang.

A minute earlier, upon hearing Pavel's voice and the slam of the outer doors being locked, Langdon had quickly retied Katherine's full-length Canada Goose coat around the banister as tightly as he could. Then they had climbed halfway up the spiral stairs, waiting on the landing between floors so they could quickly flee either up or down. Pavel had just made it clear he would shoot first and ask questions later.

We're locked in this library with a madman.

Langdon wondered if Pavel's head injury had left him truly unmoored, or whether the lieutenant had received official clearance to use deadly force. *Clearance from whom?* Considering everything Langdon had now learned, there existed the unsettling notion that Pavel had been tasked by someone to track down Katherine's manuscript and destroy it.

And destroy us *along with it.*

Langdon sensed their only hope was to alert the embassy or the local police immediately. The problem was that they had no phones, and if they yelled for help, Pavel would be the only person who would hear them.

"Are you okay?" Langdon whispered into the darkness.

"Not in the least," Katherine's voice replied. "And you?"

Langdon found her hand and squeezed it. "Don't move. Stay on this landing. I'll go up and see if there's any other way out of here."

In total blackness, Langdon groped his way up the rest of the tiny staircase until he felt the trapdoor above him. He gently pushed up, and the small square of wood hinged open a crack.

Light poured through the opening, and Langdon squinted as he lifted the panel, inching his head upward until his eyes were at floor level. Peeking out from beneath the trapdoor, he surveyed the balcony for any possible exits—even a window out to the roof. Nothing. Just walls of ancient books that climbed up to the stunning ceiling fresco that arched overhead.

Langdon eased the trapdoor all the way open and gently laid it down on the balcony floor. He climbed one more stair until he was able to peer down through the balcony railing. Below, at the far end of the library, Pavel was visible with his back to Langdon, his face pressed against the display case for the Devil's Bible . . . as if intensely examining the artifact.

Pavel did not strike Langdon as a man who would be interested in an ancient codex, especially at this moment, but then Langdon heard a high-pitched screech and saw the case move several inches. The muscular lieutenant, he realized, was not admiring the codex, but rather attempting to push its massive display case across the floor.

Why? That cube must weigh a thousand pounds!

Langdon was distressed to see the deep scratches being carved into the magnificent parquet floor, although he was far more alarmed to see the antique ladder lying on the floor near the display case. In an instant, Pavel's intentions became clear. *He's coming up here.* The transparent cube certainly looked sturdy enough to support the base of a ladder, and Pavel was apparently strong enough to move it. The case shifted a few inches with each heave, creeping toward the side of the room. Moving it close enough would take time and patience, but it appeared Pavel had adequate quantities of both.

If he flushes us out, there's nowhere else to hide. No escape from this locked room.

Langdon searched intently for a solution, and his eyes moved skyward, as they often did when he hoped for inspiration. Staring into the colorful expanse of the fresco arching overhead, he found himself fully enveloped by the beauty of the work—a depiction of Jesuit saints engrossed in reading and writing among the clouds, underscoring the importance of knowledge.

Think, Robert.

As he gazed into the lofty depiction of paradise, his eye halted unexpectedly on an incongruous object disguised among the billowing clouds in the fresco.

It was a small, metallic disk.

A glistening halo of sorts . . .

This metal disk, Langdon knew, had most certainly *not* been placed there by the artist, and as distasteful as he found its intrusion into the fresco, when Langdon's eyes beheld it, he felt as if the heavens had just opened up . . . and offered a road to salvation.

CHAPTER 67

Field Officer Housemore arrived at Crucifix Bastion to discover no vehicles parked outside, no signs of life, and the front door destroyed. *What happened here?* Sidearm raised, she stepped cautiously into the glass-strewn entryway, her shoes crunching on the scattered shards.

Housemore was relieved to find the steel access door marked LAB was intact and locked. She moved down the hall into Gessner's reception area and office.

Where is everyone?

She placed a Signal call to Mr. Finch, relaying what she had found.

"My jet just took off from London," Finch replied, an unusual tension in his voice. "Secure the building—nobody in or out. Use deadly force if necessary."

With that he was gone.

◆—·—◆

On the fourth floor of Random House Tower, concealed in the warren of loudly humming computer banks, operative Chinburg adjusted his headphones and listened intently to the conversation now taking place about forty feet away between Jonas Faukman and Alex Conan.

The beam of his laser microphone was aimed at the smoothest surface he could find—a pane of glass that covered an illustration of a sinking ship. Conveniently, the illustration included a blue ocean, on which the blue dot of light was fairly well disguised. More importantly, the illustration hung very close to where Faukman and his tech were talking, close enough that the sound of their voices caused microvibrations in the surface of the glass, which in turn caused microfluctuations in the laser beam. An interferometer then analyzed the interference patterns in the light beam and "translated" the vibrations back into audio.

Chinburg could hear every word. *And I'm not the only one listening.*

Somewhere on his private jet over Europe, Mr. Finch was patched in via satellite and Voice-Over-Wi-Fi, listening in real time. Chinburg was certain their boss would be pleased. Until only a few moments ago, the entire team was concerned that the PRH tech might indeed have found a way to identify Q as the source of the hack.

Not even close.

Chinburg smirked, listening to his headphones with amusement as the editor seethed at the young tech. *"Library Genesis!"* Faukman spat. "We were hacked by Library-Fucking-Genesis! One of the most notorious piracy outfits in the world! How could you have let them into our servers, Alex!"

Chinburg had certainly heard of the elusive organization, known among hackers as LibGen. Established more than a decade ago by Russian scientists, LibGen was the Internet's largest "shadow library" of pirated academic and literary works. Despite numerous legal challenges and lawsuits from major publishers, LibGen had managed to persist, thanks to an ingeniously decentralized structure of mirror sites and backup domains.

The tech got it wrong. We're in the clear.

Chinburg was relieved, sensing it could have gone the other way. His team had expedited the attack by repurposing existing code that, in this new era of AI-enhanced web scouring, could potentially have led back to Q's operational division.

Thankfully, the tech missed it.

Chinburg's best guess was that LibGen had attempted to hack PRH at some point in the recent past, and tonight the tech had discovered a digital artifact from that older hack.

Faukman continued to rail against the infamous piracy group while the tech was typing furiously, most likely searching for more information . . . or possibly crafting his resignation letter.

Keep searching, Chinburg thought. *You're barking up the wrong tree.*

Just then, Chinburg felt a pulse on his phone, and he checked the screen.

It was a secure message from Mr. Finch, who had apparently heard enough.

MISSION COMPLETE. PULL OUT NOW.

◄—··—►

Downstairs in the lobby, incapacitated on the floor behind the counter, security guard Mark Dole was still kicking himself for not handling this situation better.

It all happened so fast . . . I failed when it counted most.

The muscle-bound thug who had stolen Dole's seat and security cap was now going through Dole's phone and wallet, taking notes.

Dole wished he'd had the foresight to dial 911 when these guys arrived. The Midtown North Precinct was just a few blocks away, and officers could have arrived in minutes.

The elevator pinged, and Dole heard the second intruder returning to the lobby.

"All set," the arriving man said. "They're convinced we're book pirates—we're clear."

"Hilarious." The big guy swiveled around and knelt down beside Dole. "Your bosses are clueless, Mark. I hope you're smarter . . . smart enough never to mention we were here."

Dole stared into the man's steely eyes.

"By the way," the thug added, "your kids are cute. I see you live in Sunset Park. Brooklyn's not a bad commute, and your place on Forty-Sixth looks close to the park for the kids. You've got a peaceful life."

Dole understood his meaning.

The man hoisted Dole to his feet, screwed the security cap back onto his head, clipped the zip ties, and left Dole's wallet and phone on the front desk. "No harm done. Now get back to work."

Dole watched the two men stride nonchalantly across the lobby toward the four exit doors—two swinging doors and two revolving doors. They were headed for the swinging door through which they'd entered, but before they got there, Dole touched one of two buttons under the counter, silently engaging all the automatic locks.

The muscle-bound man arrived at the swinging door and found it locked. "Hey, ping us out!"

"Can't do that," Dole lied.

The man turned, looking incredulous. "You *really* want to lock us in here with you?"

"No," Dole said. "I mean I literally *can't*. I don't have control over the doors. They're automated. Green building and all that. Conserving heat in the lobby. During the winter months, only the revolving doors—"

"We *just* came through this goddamned door!"

"*Inbound* with an employee key card. *Outbound* all employees must use the revolving doors. Even assholes."

"You're lucky we're in a hurry," the man said, moving with his partner toward one of the revolving doors. Dole quickly pressed the button under the counter again, now silently unlocking all four doors.

The revolving doors at Random House Tower were oversized, which meant that most small groups shared the same compartment. Dole was pleased to see the two thugs were no exception. As they stepped into a single partition and pushed outward, the door began to rotate counterclockwise. Dole calmly watched, his finger hovering over the lock button. When the door had made a perfect quarter turn, Dole pressed the button a third time, reengaging all the locks. The revolving door abruptly stalled, mid-turn, sealing his two attackers in a tiny glass prison.

As Dole dialed 911, a muffled string of profanity echoed across the lobby.

Shout all you like, Dole thought. *Nobody threatens my kids.*

◆—··—◆

For two full minutes after the laser-microphone dot had disappeared and the door had clicked shut, Jonas Faukman had continued his theatrical rant against the LibGen book pirates, just to be certain the eavesdropper was really gone. It was clear that book piracy had nothing to do with the PRH hack, but the truth was infinitely more disturbing.

Faukman was still reeling from seeing the acronym that Alex had typed, questioning why this group would mount a coordinated international campaign against Katherine Solomon and her unpublished book. They certainly had the resources and influence to do so.

With a rush of dread, Faukman realized that Alex's panic about Robert Langdon and Katherine Solomon suddenly seemed much more plausible. It also occurred to him that whoever had broken into Random House Tower would have had to get past the good-natured night watchman, Mark Dole.

Faukman immediately phoned down to the security desk to check on him.

No answer. *Dammit.*

Fearing the worst, Faukman ran for the elevators. When he reached the ground floor, he dashed around the corner into the lobby, bracing himself for the worst. But the scene before him was perfectly calm, and unexpected. Night watchman Mark Dole was very much alive and well, coolly giving a statement to a pair of metro police officers.

The police are here?

Faukman was relieved to see Dole unharmed, and the editor's attention shifted immediately to the two handcuffed men on the floor near the revolving door, both looking furious.

My God . . . is that . . . ?

Faukman could not begin to imagine what had transpired down here, but he made no effort to hide his delight as he walked across the lobby toward the two captives, who were restrained and lying on their sides.

"Hey! Welcome to Random House!" Faukman gushed. "I had no idea you guys were readers."

"You don't want to do this," Buzzcut hissed, glaring up at him. "You don't know who we work for."

"For *whom* you work," Faukman corrected, frowning. "I thought we went through this."

"Fuck off!" he snapped, his eyes smoldering with rage.

Faukman crouched down and smiled. "You know, Buzz, if you went to the library as often as the gym, you'd realize that every great story has the same ending." He winked. "The bad guys always lose."

CHAPTER 68

Katherine was relieved to see Langdon descending from the balcony, his body silhouetted by the dim light from the trapdoor that he had opened above.

"We need fire," he said urgently as he joined her on the landing. "Tell me you have a lighter or matches."

"I'm sorry, *what?*"

"*Smoke.* We need smoke if we're going to get out of here." The urgency in Langdon's eyes sent a very clear message: what he had seen from the balcony had alarmed him . . . and also perhaps offered a solution. "Katherine, we have about two minutes until a deranged gunman comes charging down these stairs."

"I . . . I'm not sure what I might have. My bag is at the bottom of—"

"Let's get it—now!"

With Langdon close on her heels, Katherine descended the stairs, having now deciphered Langdon's logic. If the sound of gunfire hadn't drawn in the museum staff, nothing else would . . . except, perhaps, the threat of *fire* in an ancient library.

Yesterday, when she had been here with Langdon, he had pointed out Jan Hiebl's meticulous fresco on the ceiling, bemoaning the presence of the three ugly metallic disks that had been installed in the 1970s, interspersed throughout the painting. Katherine suspected Langdon was now pleased these little disks had been installed, despite their being eyesores.

Smoke detectors.

Reaching the bottom of the stairs, Katherine found her shoulder bag and hoisted it up onto the first step. The bag was unusually heavy today, as it contained her manuscript—a stack of more than four hundred pages—along with a large bottle of water. Reaching to the bottom of the bag, she began rummaging semi-blindly through the contents looking for some means to start a fire.

Katherine knew she had no matches or lighter in her bag, although as the plethora of "survival" shows on television had demonstrated, fire could be created using all kinds of everyday items—cell phones, magnifying glasses, batteries, steel wool. But as she rooted through her bag, Katherine realized it was a dead end.

"I've got nothing," she whispered to Langdon, who was just above her on the stairs. "No matches. No lighter. My cell phone is in a dumpster. I have gloves, lip balm, a brochure for the museum, a granola bar, a bottle of wat—"

"Granola bar? From the hotel?"

"Yes. The minibar."

"That'll work."

Combustible granola?

"Batteries?" Langdon pressed. "Anything electronic? Penlight, key fob, earbuds, anything?"

"No, Robert, I'm sorry." She paused. "Although . . . my bag came with a Clutch in the lining. I don't know—"

"Clutch? What is that?"

"A phone charger for purses," she said, opening the bag. She pulled aside her bulky manuscript and showed Langdon the nub of a phone charger cable sticking out of the interior lining. "Kind of a Cuyana gimmick, but it's handy. I charged it before the trip, but I don't know how much—"

"Stay right here," Langdon said, taking the bag. "I'll tell you what to do in a minute."

Without another word, he rushed back up the spiral staircase.

———————

I hope she forgives me for this, Langdon thought with trepidation.

Sixty seconds had passed since he'd left her downstairs, and he was now crouched on the landing halfway up the stairs. He had located the granola bar and placed it with the stack of manuscript pages that he'd already set aside. Now he was groping around the bag's silk lining, finally feeling a hard rectangle in a Velcro pocket. He extracted it. *This is a charger?* Katherine's ultrathin Clutch looked more like a pink credit card with a tail. *I hope it still has juice.*

Raising the Clutch to his mouth, he placed its power cable between his teeth, yanked hard, and snapped off the connector plug. Then he pulled the two wires apart, stripped each with his teeth, and tapped the two bare wires briefly together.

A bright spark lit up the dark space momentarily.

He hoped it would be enough.

Langdon laid the charger flat on the manuscript pages and picked up the granola bar, which, as anticipated, had a thin foil wrapper. He tore off the foil and peeled away a narrow strip, rolling it between his fingers to create a kind of foil thread. Then he attached one end of the foil filament to one of the Clutch's bare wires, leaving the other end dangling.

In theory, once he connected the loose end and completed the circuit, electricity would flow through the foil. Being a poor conductor, the foil would create resistance, resulting in a buildup of heat . . . that would ultimately *ignite* the foil.

Briefly.

Unfortunately, the ultrathin material would burn for only a moment—not nearly enough to ignite a laminated brochure or even a sheet of the thin manuscript paper. If Langdon was to have any chance of starting this fire, he would need something flammable.

Highly flammable.

◄─ ·· ─►

At the bottom of the stairs, Katherine felt increasingly anxious as she waited in silence for further instructions from Langdon. *Stay right here . . . I'll tell you what to do in a minute,* he had told her. He had been moving around on the stairs and finally positioned himself halfway up on the grated landing where they had been standing earlier.

In addition to the sounds of Langdon overhead, Katherine had been hearing noises from the library—a series of repetitive, loud, staccato screeches—which Langdon said were from the display case being relocated. *That noise has now stopped*, Katherine realized, sensing they were nearly out of time.

With rising fear, she looked up again toward the metal grate on which Langdon was working. To her surprise, the light now filtering through the grid looked different suddenly. It was no longer solely the pale rays from the trapdoor above them . . . it was a flickering glow.

Fire?

He did it?!

Stunned, she held her breath, waiting . . .

Within seconds, the glow began growing brighter, and Katherine finally exhaled with a rush of hope. She had no idea what Boy Scout magic Langdon had invoked to start this fire, but as the flames swelled, she could see that the porous metal grid on which he'd set the fire was providing perfect ventilation from beneath.

Her amazement, however, quickly turned to concern.

That's a lot of fire . . .

The flames were quickly expanding and now seemed to be covering a larger portion of the landing. In the growing firelight, she could see that Langdon had moved off the platform and was now kneeling a couple of steps below, feeding the fire from the side. As the flames spread, Katherine started to feel air drafting in under the bookcase door, rising up the stairwell like a chimney, feeding the fire further.

Katherine knew her first concern should have been: *Is this safe?* But it was not. Her first concern was something else entirely. *What is he burning?!* These flames had grown far too intense to be a museum brochure, a pack of Kleenex, or whatever else he had found in her bag. *What is he using for fuel?!*

Her answer appeared a moment later when a partially charred

scrap of paper drifted down from above, landing on the stairs directly in front of her. The scorched shred of white paper was printed with black text, some still legible. Katherine needed only an instant to recognize the words.

Robert, no!

She launched herself up the stairs, calling for him to stop. As she spiraled up toward Langdon, she suddenly suspected he had told her to stay below because he knew she'd never agree to his plan. *He's burning my manuscript!*

She could feel the heat as she arrived beneath the landing. Above her, through the metal grid, she saw the underside of a stack of manuscript pages that Langdon was feeding into the fire. The pages were burning fast and bright.

"Stop!" she gasped. "That's our *only* copy! We can't lose it!"

Langdon glanced down, his eyes intense in the firelight. "We've *already* lost it, Katherine—I'm so sorry. This hard copy will be confiscated the *second* we step outside this alcove. And then it's over for us. We might as well use it to save our lives."

"But there's no other—"

"Please listen," he said, still feeding pages into the fire. "There are things I haven't told you yet, but people have been *killed* today on account of this book. As long as we're holding this manuscript, we are *targets*. The first bullet barely missed us. The next one won't."

"My God, people were killed?!" she repeated. "Because of my manuscript?!"

"Katherine, professionals *deleted* your manuscript from a secure corporate server! The ÚZSI captain who interrogated me this morning accused us of orchestrating a terrorist publicity stunt for this book. Brigita Gessner asked for an advance copy, and she was tortured and killed last night. Jonas seems to have gone missing. ÚZSI has been hunting *me* sinc—"

"Brigita Gessner is *dead*?!"

Langdon gave a grim nod. "I don't claim to know what's going on, but *nothing* is worth our lives. And each other. This is the right move. I need you to trust me."

A little late for trust, she thought, seeing the meager stack of remaining pages. *You've already burned most of it.*

———··——

Lieutenant Pavel's skull pounded from exertion.

He had finished manhandling the large display case across the library floor, finally succeeding in positioning it beneath the balcony. The transparent cube had been considerably heavier than it looked, much of its weight no doubt coming from the mammoth object inside.

Pavel had taken a minute to catch his breath, staring through the thick Plexiglas at the absurdly large book inside the cube. It was famous enough to draw a crowd, but the book was open to a page depicting a half-naked devil, squatting in a loincloth.

People pay money to see this?

Eager to get up to the balcony, Pavel retrieved the ladder and hoisted it onto the top of the display case, pleased to see that it now reached up to the balcony.

Before climbing onto the display case, Pavel turned for one last scan of the balcony to see if Langdon had come to his senses and revealed himself. As his eyes traced the upper perimeter of the room, moving along the balcony, his gaze stopped short.

Pavel hoped he was hallucinating.

In the far corner of the balcony, above the locked alcove, a column of black smoke seemed to be rising out of nowhere . . . drifting to the highest point of the arched ceiling . . . already gathering into a dark cloud that was now creeping outward across the priceless fresco.

No . . .

But it was too late.

A split second later, the fire alarms began to blare.

CHAPTER 69

Within seconds of the smoke alarm sounding, Lieutenant Pavel could hear the docent frantically unbolting the doors of the Baroque Library.

I gave you orders! Pavel fumed. *Stay out!*

But apparently the threat of fire in an ancient library overruled even ÚZSI orders, and the docent dashed in, wheeling wildly and looking for the source of the smoke.

Pavel was at the farthest end of the room, perched atop the display case, preparing to climb the ladder to the balcony. The docent never even noticed him, fixated instead on the pillar of smoke rising off the balcony. The docent ran to the hidden bookcase, trying in vain to open it.

I can still kill Langdon, Pavel knew, beginning his climb up the ladder. *An eye for an eye.*

Two other museum employees with fire extinguishers ran in behind the docent, shouting to one another and trying to open the concealed door without breaking it. No luck. But the smoke billowing through the trapdoor now seemed to be abating as quickly as it had begun.

Pavel was halfway up the ladder when another docent spotted him. The elderly man rushed over, looking horrified to see someone on a jerry-rigged ladder atop the library's priceless exhibit. "*Co to sakra děláš?!*" the docent yelled, arriving beneath him. *What the fuck are you doing?!*

Pavel ignored him, still climbing.

As he neared the top, he could taste the smoke in his lungs. The murky cloud had coalesced just above him, along the peak of the arched ceiling, although loud ventilation fans had just been turned on and seemed to be clearing the air rapidly.

Pavel arrived at the top of the ladder and peered over the balcony railing toward the trapdoor at the far end. It was still wide open. The American's smoke plan had been clever, but it was about to backfire. *Langdon will never see me coming.* Even if he unlocked the door and dashed out into the library, Pavel held the high ground—a perfect vantage point for the kill shot.

Patience, his captain had urged, and patience had paid off. Reaching out, he grabbed the iron railing of the balcony and prepared to pull himself over.

"Lieutenant Pavel!" a woman's authoritative voice shouted from the library entrance. "Stop right there!"

Perched on the top rung, Pavel turned and scanned the library, blinking several times, trying to make sense of what he now saw. The mirage moving toward him was so unexpected and bizarre that he wondered if maybe the smoke and skull injury were triggering a hallucination.

The woman approaching was an elegant, dark-haired beauty—easily one of the most breathtaking women Pavel had ever seen in the flesh. She moved on slender legs that carried her with the intensity of a fashion model on the runway. She could have been one of Pavel's Dream Zone fantasies . . . except for one small problem: she was flanked by two U.S. Marines in full embassy blues and carrying sidearms.

———·———

Inside the stairwell, on the landing of the spiral, Langdon stood over the smoldering pile of ash, wanting to ensure that every last ember was extinguished.

This fire made possible by Procter & Gamble, he mused, grateful for the tiny bottle of hand sanitizer he'd found in the bottom of Katherine's bag.

Safeguard gel was 80 percent alcohol, and Langdon had smeared it liberally over the title page of Katherine's manuscript before rolling the sheet into a tube to concentrate the fumes. After inserting the tube into the grate to hold it in a vertical position, Langdon used the Clutch to ignite the foil directly over the tube's opening. As expected, the foil flamed out almost instantly, but the concentration of alcohol fumes combusted, and the gel-soaked tube went up in flames.

The rest happened quickly.

The light-bond Czech printer paper burned faster than Langdon had anticipated; for a moment, he feared he'd made a terrible mistake and put the entire library in danger. The fire was raging in a matter of seconds. While feeding more pages, Langdon also drained the remains of Katherine's water and tossed the plastic bottle onto the manuscript pages, creating billowing clouds of black smoke as it melted.

It was rare that Langdon invoked Shakespeare, but this near disaster seemed Bard-worthy. *All's well that ends well*, he assured himself, considering he could have burned down a priceless library or been shot dead.

Now, after confirming he had left nothing behind, Langdon hoisted Katherine's bag, which was much lighter without her manuscript and water. She had already descended in silence, distraught over witnessing her manuscript pages being incinerated. Langdon felt confident that she would eventually come to understand that he had played their cards as best as he possibly could.

We're alive.

As Langdon came down the steps, he could hear multiple conversations outside the bookcase door, and he hoped the crowd included museum security.

"Mr. Langdon?!" a deep voice called through the door. The accent was American. "I am Marine Embassy Guard Morgan Dudley."

Langdon and Katherine exchanged a startled look. *That was fast.*

"You are safe to exit, sir," the man announced. "I can confirm that the ÚZSI lieutenant who threatened you has relinquished his weapon, and the Blue Alert has been canceled."

Langdon had no idea what a Blue Alert was, but the embassy's presence certainly sounded like an improvement over ÚZSI.

"Open the door, sir." The voice was polite but firmer now.

Katherine immediately began untying the sleeve of her full-length coat from the door handle.

"Wait!" Langdon whispered, feeling apprehensive. "He could be an ÚZSI officer imitating an American."

Whether the man outside was psychic or had overheard the comment, Langdon did not know, but a moment later a laminated carnet came skittering in beneath the door. In the dim light, Langdon couldn't read the small text, but fittingly, his fears were allayed by the card's embossed *symbol*—a bald eagle with a shield of stars and stripes.

◆——·——▸

Outside the bookcase, Dana Daněk waited anxiously for the hidden door to open. Less than ten minutes had passed since Ambassador Nagel had rushed into Dana's office with an urgent order—to go with a Marine escort to the Klementinum and save an American's life.

Mission accomplished, she thought. *Albeit barely.*

Lieutenant Pavel had been escorted out of the library and into a holding room, and his superiors had been alerted. ÚZSI was incensed to learn of the U.S. embassy's intervention in an official Blue Alert—no matter its origins—although they had no choice but to issue an immediate "Alert Retraction."

When the bookcase finally swung open, Robert Langdon stepped forward, squinting from within the darkened alcove. Dana Daněk was relieved to see him safe, and yet she was shocked to see him emerge with a woman. Dana recognized the elegant face in an instant.

Katherine Solomon.

CHAPTER 70

Still shivering from her time in the frigid stairwell, Katherine savored the relative warmth of the Klementinum hallways as the embassy's striking PR liaison, Ms. Daněk, hustled them toward the museum exit.

U.S. Marines had scoured the alcove, taking photos of the ash pile on the landing and collecting charred scraps of manuscript pages from the floor. Their keen interest in the burned remains of her book, as inconceivable as it was, seemed to support Langdon's claim that her manuscript was indeed at the center of whatever had been happening here today.

But why?

It was starting to seem more evident that Langdon might have made the right call; the manuscript made them a target, and removing it had saved their lives.

The thought of writing her book all over again filled Katherine with a dread she could not begin to process at that moment. Langdon had suggested that PRH might somehow be able to retrieve a digital copy from the hacked server, or maybe the hackers would demand a reasonable ransom. She hoped he was correct. Or maybe the universe would offer up some unforeseen miracle.

We're alive, she thought. *Let's start there.*

She couldn't fathom that Brigita Gessner was dead, and clearly Langdon still had a lot to share about his *own* morning; he had just informed Dana Daněk that he was deeply concerned about the safety of two individuals. *Michael Harris? Sasha Vesna?* Katherine recognized neither name.

In addition, quite strangely, when Langdon asked Ms. Daněk to borrow a phone to check on Jonas Faukman, she had refused, saying the ambassador insisted on no outside contact until Katherine and Langdon had been brought to safety and fully briefed . . . for their own protection.

Our own protection?!

Langdon was walking beside Katherine now, and she reached out and took his hand. The group, led by the armed American Marines, exited the museum through a series of courtyards and archways into the bustle of Marian Square. Directly ahead, the flags of the New City Hall flapped in the bitter wind, and Katherine heard sirens growing louder in the distance. Their Marine escorts, apparently hearing the sirens as well, now urged them to move faster. Langdon gripped Katherine's hand more tightly and they quickly followed the Marines into the square to their waiting vehicle.

That's our ride? Katherine thought, startled. *Not exactly discreet.*

One of the Marines was holding open the door of a black stretch limousine that bore the U.S. embassy logo on the side and two small banners on the hood—one Czech and one American—both red, white, and blue. The limo was already drawing considerable attention in the square.

"Forgive the formality," Ms. Daněk said. "Diplomatic vehicles provide a level of protection from local authorities. The ambassador thought it prudent. Please get in."

From the sounds of approaching sirens, Katherine realized that diplomatic immunity might be a good thing. As Katherine took a step toward the car, however, Langdon discreetly restrained her with a strong grip on her hand.

The sirens wailed closer.

"Ma'am?" the Marine said. "We need you both in the vehicle *now.*"

Langdon's hand remained firm and immobile, his eyes locked on the American flag fluttering on the limo's hood. Katherine had no idea what he was thinking, but for some reason, Robert seemed to be having second thoughts about getting into the car.

"Get in, sir!" the Marine shouted suddenly as a line of black sedans with lights flashing rounded a corner and came into view. "Now!"

Langdon's eyes shifted from the flag to the interior of the limo to the flashing lights of the approaching authorities. Finally, with the reluctance of a man choosing the lesser of two evils, he helped Katherine into the limo and climbed in after her.

The Marine slammed the car door just as a convoy of ÚZSI vehicles arrived, sirens splitting the cold morning air.

◄━ ·· ━►

Dana Daněk stood on the curb and watched the embassy limo speed away. She wasn't sure what Langdon's hesitation had been, but it no longer mattered. With both of them safely under the ambassador's control, Dana had fulfilled her duty.

She had already phoned Ambassador Nagel, who sounded deeply relieved that Langdon and Solomon had both been found alive. Now, however, Dana had additional information—deeply troubling information—and she found a quiet niche behind a statue on the corner of City Hall to call the ambassador back.

"There's one more thing to report, ma'am," Dana said when the call was transferred to the ambassador. "I just spoke to Professor Langdon, who said he has reason to be very concerned about the safety of Sasha Vesna . . ." She paused, emotions catching in her throat. "And also that of . . . Michael Harris."

"Harris?" Nagel sounded surprised. "Did Langdon tell you why he's concerned?"

Dana had now been informed of the true nature of Michael's "relationship" with Sasha Vesna, and while Dana was relieved that these trysts were not Michael's choice, she was also inwardly furious that the ambassador would put him in such a position. *He's a legal attaché, for God's sake—not a trained field operative!*

"We didn't have time to talk," Dana replied, "but he said he and Sasha were supposed to meet Michael at her apartment, but something happened. Langdon urged me to send someone over to check on them both. He gave me Sasha's apartment key."

"Langdon had Sasha's key?"

Dana glanced down at the chintzy Krazy Kitten key ring that

Langdon had just handed her. "She insisted he take it—in case he needed a safe place to go."

The ambassador was silent for an unusually long beat. "Okay," she finally said. "I'll send Scott Kerble down to pick you up right away. He can accompany you to Sasha's."

Me?! Dana had not expected to be sent over herself and wondered if it was punishment or a vote of confidence. Either way, Nagel was sending her most trusted and skilled Marine security guard. It seemed the ambassador wanted to be absolutely certain that nothing *else* went wrong today.

Despite the warm air pouring from the limousine's vents, Katherine Solomon's chill only deepened as she listened to Robert's account of the events of his morning.

"My God, Robert. I don't know what to say . . ." Langdon's account of the woman on the bridge, reenacting Katherine's nightmare, left her speechless.

As the car roared along the river toward the embassy, Langdon shared another disturbing piece of news—the reason he had hesitated before getting into the limousine.

The U.S. embassy seal on the sides of the vehicle.

As Langdon explained himself, Katherine realized he had just experienced what noeticists called "delayed visual processing," which was common among people with eidetic memories. Because eidetic memories recorded such vast quantities of visual input, the brain did not process all of it in real time. In fact, most of the visual input held by an eidetic memory was never accessed at all, never recalled unless the individual *actively* tried to recall what he or she had seen.

Or . . . unless there was a trigger.

The U.S. embassy seal on the limousine door had triggered one of Langdon's memories from this morning—a note card emblazoned with the same embassy seal, which accompanied the large arrangement of red, white, and blue tulips that had been sent to their hotel by the U.S. embassy.

"When I returned to our room this morning," Langdon

explained, "the bay window was still wide open, and I noticed the embassy note card was on the floor. The room was freezing—and the wind had begun to wilt the flowers on the sill. But as I closed the window, I saw a thin metal rod with a clear plastic cone on top—it was nestled among the flower stalks."

Langdon ran a hand over his dark hair and seemed to be retrieving details of the memory.

"The device barely registered in that moment—I thought it was a humidity detector or something trivial—but with everything going on now, I just realized I've seen a similar device at Boston Symphony Hall . . . a parabolic microphone hovering over the orchestra to capture every nuance of the music.

"Wait . . ." Katherine stammered. "You think our flowers were *bugged*?!"

Langdon nodded. "You and I were sitting right near the bouquet when we talked about your nightmare last night. It's the only explanation. If someone heard you describe—"

"But it truly makes no sense!" she exclaimed, shaking her head. "Why would our *own* embassy eavesdrop on us? And even if they had been listening and overheard my dream, why would they ever want to . . . *re-create* it?"

"I don't know. But I damn well intend to ask the ambassador when we get to the embassy."

"We're not going to the embassy," Katherine said. "I heard Dana tell the driver to take us to the ambassador's residence."

Langdon looked surprised. "Why?"

Katherine shrugged. "Maybe she thought it would be more welcoming?"

From the troubled look on Langdon's face, she could see he found this change to be the exact opposite of welcoming. "Special protections for U.S. citizens take effect only *inside* the embassy itself," he whispered. "The ambassador knows that. Meeting at her residence means you and I are still . . . unprotected. Exposed."

Katherine felt a stab of panic. *What could they possibly want from us?* She wished she'd never accepted Gessner's request to speak in Prague.

"For whatever reason, this *all* revolves around your book, Katherine." Langdon leaned forward, his eyes holding hers. "You need to talk to me. We've only got a few minutes alone, and you need to tell me everything. What's in the manuscript? What did you discover?"

Katherine had wanted Langdon to read about her experiments and conclusions in full detail, but that luxury was no longer an option.

There is no manuscript . . . and there is no time.

"Okay," she whispered, sliding closer to him. "I'll tell you."

CHAPTER 71

In the midst of Prague's ritzy retail district, a small plot of earth stands untouched, encircled by a stone fortification. For five centuries, this sacred ground had been a somber chronicle to the intolerance of humankind.

The Old Jewish Cemetery, The Golěm thought as he stepped through the gate into the mossy, tree-dotted sanctuary.

The ghostly landscape before him was packed wall to wall with headstones—more than twelve thousand of them in this tiny space. The ancient tombstones were crowded in so tightly that many were touching one another . . . pitched over in all directions. The scene looked more like a storage area for headstones than any kind of sacred burial ground.

Incredibly, there were over one hundred thousand bodies buried in this three-acre plot of land. Jews in fifteenth-century Prague were relegated to the peripheries of societal acceptance and cordoned off into their own ghetto. When they needed to bury their dead, as was Jewish custom, those in power allotted them only a very small piece of land to do so.

Because Jewish custom forbade the exhumation of a buried body, when space in the cemetery was at capacity, the Jewish leaders merely brought in a new layer of earth, building it over the original graveyard and moving the existing tombstones up to the new ground level. This process was repeated many times over the centuries, each time resulting in a new layer of bodies and a new group of tombstones. In some places, the bodies were buried *twelve* deep, and without its retaining walls, it was said the Old Cemetery would have long ago spilled out into the surrounding streets, strewing five centuries of bones in all directions.

As he moved into the graveyard, The Golĕm stopped at the large wooden box and selected a *kippa*—the traditional Jewish "dome" or skullcap worn by cemetery visitors as a symbol of humility and reverence. He lowered the hood of his cloak and placed the kippa on his clay-caked skull, ignoring the glances and whispers of the handful of visitors nearby. He could understand how his presence here in costume might be perceived as disrespectful, but in fact he felt only respect for this sacred place . . . and for the rabbi who had created the first of his kind.

Advancing with deliberation, The Golĕm navigated the chaotic clutter of tombstones, careful not to slip on the mossy cobblestone pathway. Moving toward the fringes of the cemetery and the western wall, The Golĕm made his way to the tomb of Rabbi Loew.

The rabbi's gravestone stood almost two meters tall and was ornately decorated with the symbol of a lion, attesting to Rabbi Loew's surname—"Löw" or "Lion." The narrow ledge across the top of the monument was littered with dozens of tiny, folded slips of paper on which prayers had been written and left behind by visitors. Those who didn't have paper had left pebbles, in keeping with Jewish tradition.

Alone before the elegant tomb, The Golĕm reverently knelt on the cold ground and opened his mind to the unseen connections of the universe . . . the unity of souls that so many failed to perceive . . . and refused to believe.

We are as one.

Separation is an illusion.

Minutes passed, and The Golĕm could feel himself absorbing power from this mystical place. Slowly, he began to feel a growing presence, and the strength of the original golem flowed up through the earth and filled his soul.

CHAPTER 72

As the embassy limousine turned left onto Mánesův Bridge, Katherine opened a bottle of Kofola cola from the limousine's bar and took a long sip. Langdon waited as she gazed out at the spires of Prague Castle. She seemed to be organizing her thoughts for what she was about to say.

I want to hear everything, he thought, still unable to imagine what Katherine could have discovered that would trigger someone to destroy her manuscript. *Or commit murder . . .*

"Okay," Katherine said, lowering the bottle and turning to him. "There's a scientific phenomenon called the replication crisis. Are you familiar with it?"

Langdon had heard the term bandied about by his colleagues in the science department. "If I'm not mistaken, it refers to any experimental result that occurs *once* and cannot be replicated."

"Precisely," she said. "And over the past fifty years, dozens of highly respected scientists have produced a range of laboratory results that *strongly* support nonlocal consciousness. Some of these experiments have yielded results that are truly mind-boggling . . . and yet attempts to *repeat* them have either failed or produced inconclusive results."

Like cold fusion, Langdon thought.

"It's actually quite maddening," Katherine said, frustration in her voice. "Most of these nonrepeatable results stem from meticulously executed, peer-reviewed experiments, carried out by skilled, reputable scientists."

"Even so, their results are discredited?"

"Entirely. There's an intellectual war raging in my field between the local and nonlocal models of consciousness. The inability of noeticists to replicate certain results has become the battle cry of materialists everywhere—skeptics like Gessner who will denounce your experiment as deceptive and brand you an overeager charlatan or fraud."

Langdon was not surprised. In his field of religious history, published claims were brutally debunked as part of the battle between believers and nonbelievers. Fraud was commonplace. The Shroud of Turin—the alleged burial cloth of Christ—had now been radiocarbon-dated to 1,200 years *after* Christ. The famous "James Ossuary Inscription" of 2002 had been revealed as counterfeit. The influential imperial decree known as the Donation of Constantine had been revealed as a clever forgery manufactured by the Church to consolidate power.

We proclaim the Truth that serves our needs.

"There is *one* PSI experiment in particular," Katherine said, "that has become a lightning rod in this ongoing storm. It was first performed in the early 1980s by a highly respected scientific team who worked with rigorous care and produced inconceivable results. Unfortunately, those results have proven nonrepeatable, despite countless follow-up attempts."

"The Ganzfeld experiment," Langdon offered.

Katherine looked impressed. "You know about that?"

"Only recently," he admitted. "After your rather jaw-dropping book pitch about nonlocal consciousness, I decided to do some reading in the field."

"I would feel flattered," she said, "but I'm guessing you were double-checking that I wasn't crazy."

Langdon laughed. "Not at all. I was truly interested."

The Ganzfeld experiment, he had learned, consisted of placing a subject into a sensory deprivation chamber and asking a second subject to "mentally transmit" images to him. The experiment was carried out over many sessions, and the results overwhelmingly displayed the existence of mental telepathy. Strangely, the astonishing level of statistical success displayed in that *first* series of attempts had never been replicated, even by the same team, resulting in a firestorm of criticism and allegations of deceit.

"And if you read about Ganzfeld," she said, "then you probably also read about social scientist Daryl Bem—one of the Ganzfeld experiment's most vocal defenders and author of the controversial 2011 article 'Feeling the Future.'"

"I read that one too," Langdon admitted, recalling the intriguing subtitle: "Experimental Evidence for Anomalous Retroactive Influences on Cognition and Affect."

Bem's article described an experiment in which he had shown participants a list of random words and then, after removing it, had asked them to recall as many words as possible from the list. The next day, he gave the participants a short selection of words chosen completely at random from the original list and told them to memorize those words. Incredibly, the test results from day one clearly indicated that participants were far more likely to recall words that they would see again on day two—*after* the test!

Wait a minute! Langdon recalled thinking, bewildered. *You can study* after *a test? The future affects the past?*

Troubled, he had taken the Bem results to a colleague in the physics department—a bow-tied Oxford grad named Townley Chisholm—who seemed surprisingly unfazed by the data. Chisholm assured Langdon that "retrocausality" was indeed real and had been observed in numerous experiments, including one called "the delayed-choice quantum eraser."

Chisholm described it as "a tricked-out version of the classic double-slit experiment." The original, Langdon knew, had stunned the world by proving that light traveling through a double-slitted barrier could move *either* as a particle or as a wave . . . and, inconceivably, it seemed to "decide" which way to act each time based on whether someone chose to *observe* it.

The "delayed choice" modification, Chisholm explained, incorporated the use of entangled photons and mirrors to effectively "delay" the observer's real-time choice of whether to observe . . . until *after* the light had revealed how it was going to act. In other words, the scientists forced the light to react to a decision that had *not* yet been made. The mind-boggling result was that the light was not fooled at all. It somehow *antici-pated* what choice the observer would make in the future . . . as if the universe already knew what would happen *before* it had happened.

Later, after googling the experiment, Langdon was able to get his head around only enough to accept that some very smart minds believed future events did *indeed* affect past events . . . and that time was capable of flowing in reverse.

"I have to admit," Langdon said, frowning at Katherine, "the mere *idea* of retrocausality gives me cognitive dissonance."

"You're not alone," she replied. "You should see how my visitors react to the plaque on my desk. It says: 'Today's experiences are the result of tomorrow's decisions.'"

As much as Langdon tried to open his mind to retrocausality, he found it impossible to accept. "But time moving *backward* makes no sense! There must be some other explanation."

"There is, but you won't like it much better," Katherine said. "The other possibility is that all the nutjob 'universal conscious-ness' folks are correct . . . and the universe knows *all* things. In this view, the universe isn't bound by linear time as humans per-ceive it. Instead, it operates as a timeless whole where past, pres-ent, and future coexist."

Langdon's head was starting to hurt. "What about your book? You were talking about the replication crisis . . . and how it plagues PSI and noetics?"

"Yes, it does, like no other field, and it's unfair." Katherine took a sip of her drink. "Consider the field of athletics. If an athlete has an amazing Olympic result and sets a world record— something that has never occurred before, and which nobody else can replicate—we don't decide the television cameras played a trick, or the audience was hallucinating. We see it simply as a remarkable result. Just because you can't perform the same thing *twice*, that doesn't mean it didn't happen."

"Fair point . . . but that's sports. This is science. *Repeatability* is a key part of the scientific process."

"Yes, and I agree that repeatability is a reasonable burden of proof at the *macroscopic* level. But at the *quantum* level, things work differently, Robert. The quantum world is understood to be *unpredictable*. In fact, unpredictability is quite literally its most agreed-upon trait!"

Another fair point, he realized.

"The language of the quantum world," she said, talking faster now, "is literally the language of *unpredictability*—probability waves, quantum fluctuations, uncertainty principles, probabilistic tunneling, chaos, quantum interference, decoherence, superpositions, dualities. All of this translates loosely to 'We don't know what's going to happen because the classical rules of physics don't apply!'"

"Okay, so consciousness—"

"Consciousness is not a flesh-and-blood organ in your body. Consciousness exists in the *quantum* realm. It is therefore extremely difficult to observe with any predictability or repeatability. You can use your consciousness to observe a bouncing ball, but when you use your consciousness to observe your *consciousness* . . . you get an endless feedback loop. It's like trying to observe what color your own eyes are, without the use of a mirror. As intelligent or persistent as you are, you can't possibly know, because you can't observe your eyes with your eyes— any more than you can observe your consciousness with your consciousness."

"Interesting. And you make this point in your book?"

"Yes, along with the argument that *repeatability*, as a burden of proof, is an unreasonably high bar when studying consciousness. It's doing damage to the field and destroying careers."

Langdon wasn't sure how to respond. It was a fascinating concept, but in light of what they'd been through today, he had expected something more controversial . . . or dangerous . . . to warrant the kind of attention she had drawn. "So, this is the backbone of . . . your discovery?"

"Heavens no!" Katherine laughed loudly. "I was simply explaining why consciousness is such an elusive beast to hunt. My discovery is *tangible*. I found something amazing through a series of experiments." She leaned toward him and smiled. "And by the way, yes, these experiments I was able to *repeat.*"

———•———

In Random House Tower, the elevator pinged, and Jonas Faukman stepped out onto a collage of colored floor tiles. The seventh floor was like stepping into a parallel dimension, a place where he knew his tension would dissipate. Here were none of the orderly bookshelves, muted tones, and straight lines that defined the other floors at PRH. The seventh floor was a winding maze of brightly colored "work pods" decorated with cartoon art, inflatable palm trees, beanbag chairs, and stuffed animals.

Children's books: playful decor. Serious business.

In addition to this division's pleasantly whimsical setting, Faukman appreciated that there was nothing childish about its coffee machine—a Franke A1000 with FoamMaster technology—a far cry from the Nespresso pods on the other floors. Sometimes, late at night, Faukman would sneak in here with a manuscript, make a double espresso, and plop down in a beanbag chair to edit under the watchful eye of a giant Winnie-the-Pooh on one side of the lounge and the mischievous smile of seven-foot-tall Cat in the Hat on the other.

Tonight, as the machine ground his coffee, Faukman breathed in the aroma, trying to ease his fears. The arrest of the operatives downstairs should have been a relief, but he felt no real contentment; the whereabouts of Robert and Katherine were still unknown, and he felt increasingly desperate to know they were safe.

Alex Conan had already solved one vexing question:

Who stole Katherine's manuscript?

But the startling answer now begged a second question.

Why?

Jonas Faukman had devised a plan to unravel that mystery.

CHAPTER 73

We *need to hurry*, Langdon thought as the limousine climbed the steep switchback curves traversing Chotek Gardens. The "Prague 6" neighborhood that housed the ambassadorial residence was a matter of minutes from here, and Langdon desperately wanted to know everything he could about Katherine's book and her discovery. *Before we face the ambassador*, he thought, still uncertain whom to trust.

Katherine continued. "In the nonlocal consciousness model, your brain is a kind of radio that *receives* consciousness, and like all radios it has countless stations bombarding it all the time. So you can immediately understand why a radio must have a tuning dial—a mechanism that enables it to choose which *single* frequency it would like to receive. The radio itself has the capacity to receive all stations, but without a way to filter the frequencies that flow in, it would play all those frequencies at once. The human brain works the same way; it has a complex series of filters to prevent the mind from being *overloaded* with too much sensory stimulus . . . so it can focus on only a small sliver of the universal consciousness."

That makes perfect sense, he thought. *Our perception of light and sound is filtered.* Langdon knew that most humans were unaware that they experienced only a small fraction of the practical frequency range and electromagnetic spectrum; the rest sailed by us, beyond our tuning dials.

"Selective attention is a prime example of filtering by the brain," Katherine said. "It's called the 'cocktail party effect.' Picture yourself at a crowded party with your brain focused solely on the words coming from the person who is speaking to you—and then you get bored, and your focus switches effortlessly to a more interesting conversation halfway across the room. It's what enables you to filter out background noise and not be overwhelmed by every voice within earshot."

Faculty meetings, Langdon thought, often catching himself tuning in to music outside on the quad while his colleagues debated the curriculum or scheduling.

"Habituation is another kind of filtering," Katherine said. "Repeated sensory input is blocked by your brain so effectively that you literally cannot hear the incessant hum of the air conditioner or feel the pair of glasses sitting on your nose. That filter is so powerful that we can search the house for glasses that are literally right before our eyes, or a phone clutched in our hand."

Langdon nodded. He had not felt the Mickey Mouse watch on his wrist for decades.

The concept of "filtered reality," he knew, was a recurring theme in ancient scripture. The Hindu Vedanta, which had inspired the great quantum physicists like Niels Bohr and Erwin Schrödinger, described the physical mind as a "limiting factor" that could perceive only a fraction of the universal consciousness known as *Brahman.* The Sufis defined "mind" as a veil that disguised the light of divine consciousness. The Kabbalists described the mind's *klipot* as obscuring most of God's light. And the Buddhists warned that the ego was a limiting lens that made us feel separate from the universe—*uni-versum*—literally "everything as one."

"And modern neuroscience," Katherine continued, "has now identified the actual biological mechanism by which the brain filters out incoming data." A faint smile crossed her lips. "It's called GABA. Gamma-aminobutyric acid."

"Okay." Langdon was reminded that most of Katherine's postgraduate work had been on the brain's neuro*chemistry.*

"GABA is a remarkable compound—a chemical messenger in your brain that plays a critical role in regulating brain activity. But probably not in the way you'd think. Specifically, GABA is an *inhibitory* agent."

"Meaning, it *impedes* brain activity?"

"Exactly. It actually decreases neuronal firing and *constrains* the overall activity of neurons. In other words, GABA shuts off parts of the brain in an effort to filter out excessive input. In our most basic understanding of it, GABA filtering ensures the brain does not become overloaded with too much information. In the radio analogy, GABA is like the tuner that limits reception to a single frequency while blocking out dozens of others."

"Makes perfect sense so far . . ."

"GABA really caught my eye a few years ago," Katherine continued enthusiastically. "I read that the brain of a newborn baby has incredibly *high* levels of GABA, filtering out everything except what is directly in front of its face. Newborns are therefore virtually unaware of details across the room. The filters work like a set of training wheels, protecting the baby's mind from too much stimulation as it develops. As we mature, our GABA levels slowly decrease, and we take in more of the world and gain wider understanding."

Fascinating, Langdon thought. He had always imagined a newborn's tiny field of perception was because it couldn't see very well.

"So I started researching further," Katherine said, "and learned that Tibetan monks also exhibit exceptionally high levels of GABA during meditation. The meditative trance apparently causes a surge of the inhibitory neurotransmitter, which shuts down nearly all neuronal firing, essentially preventing most of the outside world from entering their brains during deep-state meditation."

The elusive empty mind, Langdon thought, familiar with the goal of meditation but never having known the chemical process by which it was achieved. *Literally blocking out the world . . . reverting to the purity of the newborn mind.*

"I suppose the results were not that shocking," Katherine said, "but they gave me an idea—the concept of human consciousness being a *signal* . . . flowing into the brain through a series of gates."

"Gates that decide how much of the world to let in."

"Exactly, and it was about eighteen months ago, during my further research into GABA, that I stumbled across a neuroscience paper . . . written by Brigita Gessner."

Ah yes, Langdon thought, *which sparked Katherine's invitation to speak in Prague.*

"Gessner's paper," Katherine revealed, "was about an *epilepsy* chip she had invented that could thwart an oncoming seizure by triggering the brain's natural GABA response, literally 'calming' the nerves. It made sense. As it turns out, epilepsy is a condition often related to dangerously *low* levels of GABA, which is the brain's braking mechanism. With too little of it, your brain goes into overdrive, has runaway neuronal firing, and ultimately—"

"A seizure."

"Yes," she said, taking a quick sip of her Kofola. "The chaotic electrical storm of an epileptic seizure is the exact *opposite* of the focused blank mind of a monk in meditation; seizures are associated with a deficit of GABA . . . and meditation with an excess. I was familiar with all this previously, but her paper reminded me that epileptic seizures are often followed by a pleasurable refractory period known as postictal bliss—a peaceful, expanded state of consciousness, accompanied by bursts of connectedness, creativity, spiritual enlightenment, and out-of-body experiences."

Langdon recalled his experience earlier with Sasha, as well as the descriptions offered by history's innumerable visionary epileptics.

"And I suddenly found myself wondering," Katherine said, "*how* an epileptic brain could so quickly transition from the storm of a seizure . . . to the peace of postictal bliss."

Langdon shrugged. "I'm guessing a natural spike in GABA levels . . . quiets the storm?"

"Great guess—it was mine too—it's called rebound inhibition, and it does indeed occur, but not immediately. As it turns out, something *else* happens first. The brain *reboots.* The whole system shuts down. And when it comes back online, it does so *gradually* . . . buying time for the brain to restore its GABA levels, reengage its filters, and shield the waking brain from too much input."

"Sounds like how we wake up in the morning . . . opening our eyes *slowly* to give our pupils time to constrict and filter out some of the morning light."

"Exactly! Except in *this* scenario, we never see the true morning light, because as we wake up, someone is simultaneously pulling thick curtains across our windows so we can't see what's really outside."

"And that *someone*, I'm guessing, is GABA?"

"Precisely. GABA *usually* closes the curtains in time, before our eyes are open. But if the timing is off, and the curtains don't close quickly enough—"

"We catch a glimpse of the outside world."

"Yes," she said with a smile. "And apparently it's beautiful. Unfiltered reality. Postictal bliss. Pure consciousness."

Remarkable, he mused, wondering if some of history's celebrated "flashes of genius" might be attributable to a timing glitch . . . a brief moment when the doorway to reality was mistakenly left ajar.

"The more I thought about GABA," Katherine said, "the more I realized that GABA was the key I'd been looking for . . ."

"The key to . . . ?"

"The key to understanding consciousness!" she exclaimed. "Human beings have extraordinarily powerful minds, but we *also* have extraordinarily efficient filters to prevent an overload of input. GABA is the protective veil that prevents our brains from experiencing what we can't handle. It *limits* how expansive your consciousness can be. This single chemical may be the reason why humans are not able to perceive *reality* as it truly is."

Langdon sat back on the plush limousine seat, absorbing the provocative idea. "You're suggesting there's a reality around us . . . that we can't perceive?"

"That's *exactly* what I'm suggesting, Robert." Her eyes flashed with excitement. "But that's not even the half of it."

———·———

In the Old Jewish Cemetery, the sounds of the nearby bustling streets had faded from The Golĕm's perception . . . his mind now bathed in a welcome silence. On his knees, he absorbed the power of this hallowed ground . . . listening for the voice of his predecessor.

With no true birthplace of his own, The Golĕm called this place home, visiting from time to time when he needed strength.

The first golem went mad . . . but I am stronger than that.

His visits to this site always centered and replenished him, but today, he felt especially fortified. As he opened his eyes and stood to face the task before him, a light breeze whispered through the cemetery. The Golĕm heard the voice of the original golem . . . a single word rustling in the bare branches overhead.

Truth . . .

He pictured the ancient letters on his forehead. The truth of his purpose in this realm was to protect a beautiful soul who lacked the strength to protect herself. The truth was that she would not be safe until The Golĕm carried out his acts of retribution.

"There are only two paths," the wind whispered in the trees. "Truth or Death."

The Golĕm had already made his choice.

I choose both.

CHAPTER 74

The limousine was approaching the posh neighborhood of Bubeneč, and Langdon knew the ambassadorial residence was not far off. Transfixed by Katherine's revelations, he was eager to hear the rest.

There's a reality around us that we can't perceive?

"The idea first dawned on me," Katherine continued, "while I was researching the postictal experiences described by *epileptics*," she explained. "I suddenly realized that their blissful experiences were remarkably similar to the accounts of *another* group." She paused, her eyes alight. "Those who have *died . . .* and come back."

Near-death experiences, Langdon thought, realizing she was right. Following the trauma of near death or a seizure, both groups reported an untethering from the body, a deep connection to all things, and a profound sense of peace.

"So I ran with that idea . . . and I devised an unusual experiment." Katherine gave him a quiet smile. "And *this* is where things really got interesting. First, I located a terminally ill patient not too far from my lab—a retired neurologist himself—who agreed to undergo his death process while enclosed inside a new kind of imaging machine—a real-time magnetic resonance spectroscopy device. I explained that I would be able to watch his brain chemistry moment by moment as he died. He felt gratified by the chance to provide accurate data like we've never been able to measure previously. With his family and hospice staff gathered around on a lovely afternoon, he passed away while being scanned inside the massive machine.

"Throughout the dying process," Katherine continued, "I saw rapidly rising levels of key neurotransmitters—including adrenaline and endorphins, which function to subdue pain and help the physical body through the stress of the death process. In other words, a shutdown of the sensory systems. It followed logically that GABA levels would also increase—to filter out the death experience as the brain shut down." Katherine smiled. "But that's not what happened."

"No?"

"What happened was the exact opposite! As he died, his GABA levels *dropped* precipitously! In his final moments, GABA levels approached *zero*, meaning *all* of his brain filters were gone. The entire death experience was flowing in—with nothing blocked out!"

"Is that . . . good or bad?"

"Robert, I would say it's wonderful! It means that during the dying process, our brain's filters open up, and we become a radio that hears the *entire* spectrum. Our consciousness witnesses *all* of reality!" Katherine took his hands and held them tightly. "That is *precisely* why people who have near-death experiences describe a feeling of total connection, of all-knowing bliss. The chemistry proves it! As we die, our *bodies* shut down . . . and our *brains* wake up!"

Langdon flashed on the opening line to one of his favorite novels. *It is said that in death, all things become clear.*

"What's more," she continued, "in the sixty seconds before the patient's heart stopped, his brain flooded with high-frequency oscillations that included *gamma* waves! These are associated with intense memory retrieval, and his levels were off the chart."

"So he was . . . *remembering* something?"

"No, at *these* levels, he was remembering *everything*. The gamma numbers definitely suggest there is truth to the enduring legend that your life passes before your eyes before you die."

The concept of a "full life recall," Langdon knew, appeared in many religions; the Angel of Death showed the soul all its life choices as a form of enlightenment and karmic teaching.

"At some point," Katherine said, "the brain *itself* dies, and our receiver is gone. And my belief, based on my experiments, is that the dying process *foreshadows* what lies ahead—a kind of preview of coming attractions—an ability to perceive so much more than we normally can."

"So, when the brain finally dies and can no longer perceive anything at all . . . is that not the *end*?"

Katherine smiled thoughtfully. "We already know from near-death experiences that death involves a breaking free from our physical form . . . combined with an intense feeling of joy and connection to all things. If we know our individual conscious-ness comes from outside our brain—as so much noetic research now shows—then to my ear, it sounds like consciousness sim-ply abandons the physical realm at the moment of death . . . and reintegrates back into the whole. You no longer need your body to *receive* the signal . . . you *are* the signal."

Langdon felt a chill. *The soul returns home.* The concept was an ancient one. *The dust returns to the ground it came from . . . and the spirit returns to God who gave it.—Ecclesiastes 12:7.*

Despite his uncertainty that consciousness continued beyond death, Langdon had no doubt that if Katherine was correct about brain filters limiting our perception of reality, her discovery was life-altering. In essence, she was positing that all humans were equipped with the hardware required to perceive the true nature of the universe . . . and yet we were chemically protected from using it . . . until the moment of death.

"This is all amazing," he said. "Even if it presents a cruel, cosmic Catch-22."

"How so?"

"We have to *die* to see the Truth . . . and when we do, it's too late to tell anyone what we saw."

Katherine smiled. "Robert, *death* is not the only path to enlightenment. History is filled with great minds that have enjoyed a momentary glimpse of some divine light that nobody else could see. Consider Newton, Einstein, and Galileo, religious prophets . . . These brilliant minds had scientific epiphanies and spiritual revelations that, as it turns out, can be explained in *sci-entific terms.*"

"You mean their filters got lowered?"

"Temporarily, yes. And in that moment, they received far more information about the universe than we are able to see."

Langdon thought of scientist Nikola Tesla, whose quote Katherine had sent him after their first discussion about non-local consciousness: *My brain is only a receiver. In the Universe there is a core from which we obtain knowledge.*

"Have you ever done drugs, Robert?"

The non sequitur took him off guard. "Do you consider *gin* a drug?"

She laughed. "No, I'm talking about psychedelics—hallucinogens that cause overwhelming emotions and vivid imagery."

Clearly you've never had enough gin. "No."

"Psychedelics like mescaline, LSD, psilocybin—do you know *how* those drugs make you experience all that?"

Langdon had never really thought about it. "I assume they stimulate your imagination?"

"That's a reasonable guess," she said, "and that's what most people think, but then again nobody had yet thought to use real-time magnetic resonance spectroscopy to observe a mind in the midst of a psychedelic drug trip."

"You *did* that?" He pictured someone tripping on LSD, strapped into an MRI tube, with Katherine looking on.

"Of course I did . . . it was the logical next step in my research. Many drug trips include out-of-body experiences, and I wondered what the GABA response looked like when that happened."

"And?"

Katherine was beaming now. "As it turns out . . . just like our historically misunderstood halo, we've been seeing it all backward. Hallucinogens don't *excite* your neurons, as you guessed—they do the opposite. Those drugs, through a series of complex interactions in the brain's default mode network, drastically *decrease* your GABA levels. In other words, they lower your filters and allow a wider spectrum of reality to flow in. That means you are *not* hallucinating, you're actually seeing *more* of reality.

Those sensations of connectedness, love and enlightenment . . . *are real.*"

It was a remarkable assertion and Langdon considered it— that the brain had *limitless* potential to receive consciousness . . . except that it was locked inside a protective cage that could be escaped only through death . . . or, to a lesser degree, an epileptic seizure or certain psychedelic substances.

The topic of psychedelics seemed to be everywhere these days; health experts all over the media were suddenly extolling the virtues of "microdosing" psychedelic mushrooms, proclaiming that psilocybin was a panacea for anxiety, depression, and distraction.

One of Langdon's Harvard colleagues, author Michael Pollan, had made headlines not long ago with his number one bestseller and Netflix documentary about the positive power of psychedelics, *How to Change Your Mind.*

Another Boston-based superstar in the field, Rick Doblin, had founded MAPS—the Multidisciplinary Association for Psychedelic Studies—which had raised over $130 million for psychedelic research with astonishing success treating depression and PTSD.

Brave new world, Langdon thought, recalling that Huxley's vision of the future had included dosing the entire population with a happy drug called SOMA.

"The chemistry of consciousness," Katherine said, "is not just a fascinating exercise in self-exploration . . . it could be the shift humanity needs to *survive.* Think of the chaos and discord of our world today. Imagine a future in which humans start to lower our brain filters and begin to exist with a greater understanding of reality . . . a greater sense of inclusion and togetherness. We might truly start to believe that we're a unified species!"

Langdon was transfixed by her out-of-the-box thinking.

"Think of all the elusive enlightened states we crave," Katherine said. "Expanded consciousness, universal connection, unbounded love, spiritual awakening, creative genius. They all seem out of reach—the products of very special minds or rare experiences. Not true! We *all* have that capacity—*all* the time. We're just chemically blocked from experiencing it . . ."

Langdon felt a surge of love and respect for her. *Katherine may have just revolutionized our understanding of human conscious-ness . . . and discovered a road map for widening it.* "I'm floored, Katherine—your work is going to have profound impact," he said, letting it all settle and trying not to get dragged back to reality by the obvious question that remained on his mind.

"I know," Katherine said with a frown, anticipating his thought. "It still doesn't explain why all this is happening . . . why anyone would want to destroy my manuscript."

Exactly.

The answer to *that* question, Langdon realized, would have to wait.

The limousine had just banked left and slowed at a stone archway and a heavy cast-iron gate outside the ambassadorial residence. A sign read, ALL VISITORS MUST PRESENT IDENTI-FICATION. The security protocol apparently did not extend to those in the ambassadorial limousine, because the gate swung open and the Marine in the stone sentry house ushered them through without hesitation.

Langdon gazed out at the fortified perimeter walls surround-ing the grounds of the residence and wondered what answers might lie inside. As the limo snaked along the tree-lined drive-way, he noticed the gate had already closed tightly behind them. An uncomfortable thought gripped him.

Are we entering a sanctuary . . . or a lion's den?

CHAPTER 75

The U.S. ambassador's residence in Prague—known as Petschek Villa—is a palatial Beaux Arts chateau whose French architectural grandeur inspired its local nickname, *Le Petit Versailles*. Built for Otto Petschek, a wealthy Jewish industrialist whose family was driven out of Prague by the Nazi occupation, Petschek Villa was overrun and inhabited by the armies of both the Nazis and the Russians. A touchstone of history, the villa now stands as an iconic landmark to the region's dark history of occupation, oppression, and genocide.

After Hitler declared his intention to turn Prague into a "museum of an extinct race," Petschek Villa was selected as a "trophy case" for Nazi triumph. He ordered that all of Petschek's finest artwork and furniture be marked with swastikas, cataloged, and carefully stored in the basement for display once Germany won the war.

The thought made Langdon ill. He stared out the window as the limo curled up the driveway into a sprawling garden surrounded by a high iron fence with sharpened vertical members and security cameras. This fortress, he noted, would be as difficult to exit as it would be to enter.

"Oh my," Katherine whispered as the regal home came into view. "This is the U.S. ambassador's *house*?"

Built on a gently sloping convex line, its luxurious columned facade stretched nearly a hundred yards in length and climbed three stories to a copper mansard roof with hooded dormers—a European palace, quite literally.

"Now I know why my taxes are so high," Katherine joked. "We house government employees in private palaces . . ."

Not quite that simple, Langdon knew, having read former ambassador Norm Eisen's book *The Last Palace,* a detailed historical portrait of this astonishing home. In fact, the U.S. had spent an astronomical sum to purchase and restore the villa to its original glory after the war, having maintained it now for almost a century at great expense. *America's way of helping preserve the heritage of Prague.*

Langdon had met Eisen once and recalled him sharing an inspiring account of his mother, Frieda, an Auschwitz survivor, who often said, "The Nazis took us out of Czechoslovakia in cattle cars, and my son flew back on Air Force One."

"All in a single generation," Eisen had pointed out.

Now, as the limo glided to a stop beneath the mansion's columned porte cochere the U.S. Marine in the front seat jumped out, circled the vehicle, and opened their door.

"Watch your step, please," he said. "These cobbles get slick in the snow."

A cold wind whipped as Langdon and Katherine followed the Marine into a small, elliptical anteroom whose carpet bore the colorful symbols of an American eagle and American flag. Overhead, a cylindrical chandelier cast a sunburst pattern on the molded ceiling and walls, illuminating a stern portrait of U.S. Ambassador Heide Nagel.

Langdon immediately recognized Nagel from photos. Sixty-something, she was a serious-looking woman whose pale skin was accentuated by stylish jet-black hair, which she wore in precise box bangs.

Footsteps approached, and a cheerful older man in a well-worn herringbone sport coat entered and welcomed them. After dismissing the Marine, the man motioned for Langdon and Katherine to follow him into the home.

As they moved down a wide hallway, Langdon could smell the homey scent of a wood fire, but he also detected a second scent hanging in the air—the unmistakable aroma of freshly baked chocolate chip cookies. *Subtle*, Langdon thought, always amused when luxury hotels did the same. The hospitality tactic had been invented by a 1950s real estate agent and was now widely implemented to impart a sense of comfort and "home."

Langdon and Katherine followed the man into a sprawling living room, where he seated them in front of a freshly lit fire. The table before them contained a small buffet—assorted pastries, a fruit basket, a pot of coffee, a large bottle of water, two bottles of Coca-Cola, and a fresh plate of homemade chocolate chip cookies.

"I apologize it's a mishmash," the man said. "Madam Ambassador just now told me she had guests arriving. She's on a call and will be with you in about ten minutes. Cookies are fresh out of the oven, so be careful—they're hot."

With that, the old man departed, leaving Langdon and Katherine alone in front of the fire with a tableful of food.

"Well," Langdon whispered, "we may be dancing with the devil, but at least she's a terrific host."

Upstairs in Petschek Villa, Ambassador Nagel hung up the phone and stared a long moment out the bay window of her home office. The snow-dusted estate looked foreign to her today, lonely somehow. For nearly three years now, this palace had been her home, and when she thought back to her first months as ambassador—her naivete and optimism—she knew both had long since dissolved in the harsh light of reality.

The debacle with ÚZSI and Langdon was now a closed chapter. The official story was that Captain Janáček had fabricated evidence against two prominent Americans and, upon learning that his crime had been discovered, leaped to his own death at Crucifix Bastion.

Nagel had threatened a public investigation if ÚZSI did not comply with her demands to stay *far away* from Crucifix Bastion and recover Janáček's body only by accessing the bottom of the ravine through Folimanka Park. ÚZSI had no choice but to comply.

Now, turning from the window, Nagel snapped her attention back to the unresolved matter at hand—Robert Langdon and Katherine Solomon. On her desk, the printer whirred, kicking out two documents that Mr. Finch had just sent to her.

Let's hope this works.

Nagel retrieved the pages, snatched a black lacquer "U.S. Embassy" pen from the desk, and headed down to meet her guests.

———·——

In the living room, having enjoyed two cookies and a strong cup of coffee, Langdon felt somewhat refreshed and resigned to whatever awaited them with the ambassador.

He had already advised Katherine that they should not discuss their private thoughts any further once they entered the ambassadorial residence. *The walls have ears.* Regrettably, Langdon feared he might have already said too much in the back of the limo, wondering if the ornate car had an intercom—and if anyone was listening. His carelessness occurred to him only after they arrived, having talked openly about the stunning ideas in Katherine's book . . . and, of course, the listening device in the tulips in their suite . . . and Langdon's growing distrust of the embassy.

Nothing we can do about it now. We'll find out what's going on when we meet the ambassador.

As they waited, Langdon spied the formal dining room across the hall. He recalled the documentary he had seen about this mansion and an unusual tale he'd heard about the dining chairs.

I'm curious, he thought, motioning for Katherine to follow him to the next room to the long satinwood table surrounded by antique hand-tooled leather chairs. He grabbed one of them, flipped it upside down, and instantly realized he was holding a piece of dark history. On the bottom of the seat was affixed a faded yellow sticker bearing a stamped catalog number 206 along with the Nazi symbols of the *Reichsadler* Imperial Eagle and the swastika.

Katherine drew a startled breath to see it. "What in the world is *that* doing here?!"

Langdon held the chair up, examining the sticker more closely. "Apparently, when the Nazis took over Prague and occupied this villa, they cataloged all the furnishings to claim them for later use as museum pieces. These stickers are the original Nazi catalog numbers. The embassy decided to leave them in place as a reminder of the horrors of the war."

A voice spoke behind them. "A professor of furniture, I see."

Langdon and Katherine spun to find themselves face-to-face with United States Ambassador Heide Nagel. Her blunt-cut bangs were instantly recognizable from the portrait in the hall. She wore a black power suit and a necklace of colorful beads.

Ambassador Nagel was definitely not smiling.

Langdon awkwardly scrambled to flip the antique chair. "Sorry about that," he said, carefully setting the chair down and sliding it back into place at the table.

"Professor," the ambassador said tautly, "if there are apologies to be made, they are mine. As far as I can tell, the U.S. government owes you both one hell of an explanation."

CHAPTER 76

The U.S. government owes us an explanation?

Langdon felt disoriented as he and Katherine followed the ambassador along an elegant, curved gallery that ran along the southern wing of Petschek Villa. The ambassador's apologetic introduction had startled Langdon, who had arrived here on high alert and in no mood to trust anyone.

Now, however, the moment of warmth was gone. Ambassador Nagel strode with an intensity of purpose that felt urgent, official, and strangely out of place for her own private home. She offered no commentary whatsoever as they passed a music room, a gold-themed sitting room, and a conservatory with views of the terrace and winter gardens. When they reached the end of the hall, she pushed through a set of mirrored double doors into a small library.

"This is the most private space in the home," she said, speaking for the first time since leaving the dining room. "It is where I make all my private calls. I thought we'd speak here."

The cozy, wood-paneled library smelled of leather and cigars. Enclosed by shelves stocked with antique books, the room centered on a pair of blue sofas facing each other beneath a gilded chandelier. In the corner, a well-worn club chair with an octagonal side table was positioned by the window for reading. The library's marble fireplace was unlit and set with pristine white birch logs.

Following the ambassador's lead, Langdon and Katherine took their places on one of the sofas with the ambassador facing them on the other. She had been carrying papers with her, which she now laid facedown on the coffee table between them. She set an official embassy pen down on the papers, sat back, folded her hands in her lap, and exhaled.

"I'll skip the pleasantries," she began. "First, I will tell you how extremely relieved I am that you are both safe. Your situation with ÚZSI, Mr. Langdon, was particularly dangerous, and I'm happy I was able to protect you."

Thank you . . . I think? Langdon was not entirely convinced he was any better off.

The ambassador studied them both a moment, as if to be certain she had their full attention. "I brought you to my home today to say, in person, what needs to be said. Quite simply . . . *I'm sorry.* On behalf of the U.S. government, I would like to apologize. Our embassies were established to protect American citizens and interests overseas. As ambassador, I took an oath to do precisely that, and I take that oath seriously. I regret to inform you that several days ago, in service to that oath to protect U.S. interests, I was ordered to facilitate placing an audio surveillance device in your hotel room."

So there it is, Langdon thought, stunned as he pictured the arrangement of tulips and handwritten note from the ambassador. *My suspicions were right.* The woman on Charles Bridge was not a premonition, but rather some kind of bizarre performance in response to someone overhearing Katherine's dream. *But why?!*

"The surveillance order came from above me," the ambassador said, "and I complied. I assumed it was for your protection, and I had no idea that the information gleaned would be used in a way that would put you both in danger. That was inexcusable, and I accept full responsibility."

Katherine glanced at Langdon, outrage registering on her face. "So you *did* bug our hotel room?" Katherine demanded, making little effort to hide her anger.

"Before you get too indignant," the ambassador replied, her tone hardening, "these are dangerous times in the world. I can assure you nobody cares about your bedroom habits or pillow talk. That surveillance device was placed there in the name of national security."

"With respect, Madam Ambassador," Langdon said as calmly as possible, "do we *look* like a national security threat?"

"With respect, Professor," she fired back, "if you think national security threats have a *look*, then you are more naive than your résumé suggests. I am offering you an apology and some transparency about what happened to you this morning, and I suggest you work with me. Our time is short, and there are aspects to your situation that you both very much need to understand."

Langdon could not recall ever being reprimanded quite so succinctly. "Understood. Please . . . go on."

"First off," Nagel said, "I am aware, Dr. Solomon, that you have written a book that will be published soon. What you need to understand is that there exist powerful entities who believe that this book, if published, will pose a *substantial* risk to national security."

"How?" Katherine demanded. "It's a book about human consciousness!"

The ambassador shrugged. "That is not information I have been given. However, the man who *does* have that information is arriving in Prague shortly to speak to you both."

Langdon was taken aback. "Speak to us—or interrogate us?"

"A bit of both, I imagine," Nagel replied, her gaze holding steady. "I am committed to protecting you, but I have limited power."

"How *limited* could it be?" Katherine asked. "You're the U.S. ambassador."

Heide Nagel gave a tired chuckle. "Diplomats come and go, Dr. Solomon. The permanent forces in government are those who make the real decisions, and I'm sorry to report that *those* are the forces with whom you're dealing."

Several guesses came to mind, and Langdon felt increasingly on edge.

"I've been forbidden to discuss anything more specific without presenting these." She reached down and flipped over the two pages she had set on the coffee table, sliding one page in front of each of them along with the pen. "Standard nondisclosure agreement—a promise to keep private the conversation you are about to have with the man arriving shortly. Once you sign these, I can brief you by telling you everything I know."

A single-page NDA? Langdon thought. *Since when did lawyers accomplish anything in a single page?* Langdon was no attorney, but he suspected that an NDA this abbreviated would have to be a sweeping exclusion of all topics discussed. *Total blackout.* There was also the odd coincidence of Gessner having also asked them to sign an NDA.

Katherine reached for the document, but Langdon, without breaking eye contact with the ambassador, placed a quiet hand on Katherine's wrist, stopping her. "Madam Ambassador, as this situation clearly relates to Katherine's book, she can't sign these without speaking to a lawyer, or at least to her editor. If we could quickly use a phone, perha—"

"That's a reasonable request," she interrupted, "and yet I'm unable to oblige. The man coming to speak to you gave me a clear directive prohibiting any outside contact until the NDAs were signed and he had spoken to you."

"Who is this man?" Katherine asked.

"He goes by Mr. Finch, and these are *his* NDAs. You're free to read them, of course."

"No need," Langdon said. "I'm guessing it states that anything we discuss in our meeting can never be divulged outside this room."

Nagel nodded, beginning to look impatient. "That's usually the point of a nondisclosure."

"Whoever Mr. Finch is," Langdon said, "if he cannot even permit us to use a phone, then I hope you can understand why it's difficult for us to blindly trust this request. I think it's best if Katherine and I return to our hotel now."

Katherine looked startled by the comment, as did Ambassador Nagel, whose veneer of diplomacy was starting to crack. "If you truly wish to leave," Nagel declared sharply, "I do not have the authority or desire to hold you against your will, but I don't think leaving is in your best interest." She paused, locking eyes with Langdon. "To be frank, I'm not sure it's entirely safe for you out there."

"To be equally frank," Langdon parried, "I'm not sure we feel entirely safe in here either."

Nagel's expression was now a mix of confusion and indignance. "Professor, I had hoped my admission about bugging your hotel room might have bought me a bit of goodwill and trust, but in light—"

A hollow ping from Nagel's phone cut the air. Annoyed, she pulled out the device and read the incoming message. Her expression morphed from irritation to overt horror. She gasped and covered her mouth, jumping to her feet, eyes wide with emotion.

"I'm . . . so sorry," she stammered, steadying herself against the table. "I'm going to need ten minutes. This message is . . . I'm sorry." With that, the ambassador rushed out of the door, her rapid footfalls echoing down the marble hallway as she left.

Katherine looked alarmed. "I don't think that was an act."

Langdon had the same impression, although politics and acting were more closely related than anyone liked to admit.

"You were *very* short with her, Robert," Katherine chided, clearly surprised with Langdon's resistance to signing the documents. "After all, she had a fair point—she *did* tell us about the surveillance bug."

"The same bug I told *you* about while we were in the ambassador's limousine. I suspect the ambassador, or perhaps Mr. Finch, eavesdropped on that conversation and realized they had no choice but to tell us what we already knew. I must admit, it was a clever attempt to gain our trust."

Katherine's lips tightened into a thin frown. "My God, do you really think she bugged her own limo? You and I talked about . . . *a lot.*"

"All I know," Langdon replied, scooping up one of the documents, "is these NDAs are a trap." He scanned the text, confirming his suspicions. "This basically says *anything* we discuss with

Mr. Finch is instantly classified. All this guy has to do is mention topics in your book that concern him, and you can never speak or *write* about them again. You would be legally forbidden from publishing this book. Ever."

"They can *do* that?!"

"Hell yes, if you sign this paper." Langdon had a friend who wrote a thriller about a major tech company, only to have it blocked from publication because he had signed a "standard NDA" before touring the company's offices.

"Well . . ." Katherine said, staring into space. "This NDA answers one question I've had all day."

"What question is that?"

She turned back to him. "Robert, when I learned someone was trying to destroy all the copies of my manuscript, I kept wondering why they weren't concerned that I would just *rewrite* the book. Now we know. They thought I wouldn't be allowed to."

"Exactly," Langdon said. "And I don't like the fact that we're at a private residence rather than the U.S. embassy." He motioned out the window toward the high security fences surrounding the property. "Think about it. There's no way out, we can't use a phone, and some strange guy is coming to talk to us. *Here?* In a private home? Someone who can order a U.S. ambassador to plant listening devices?"

Katherine's expressive brown eyes seldom flashed fear, but there was definitely concern in them now. "What scares me," she said, "is nobody knows we're here. And we don't even know if Jonas is safe."

Langdon stood up. "Which is why I'm going to kill those two birds with one phone."

She gave him an odd look. "You mean 'stone'?"

No, I mean phone.

Langdon walked toward the vintage club chair, whose leather cushion he had noticed was deeply indented from use. "She said this library is the most private room in the house . . . and where she makes all her calls. So where's her phone?"

"She has a mobile," Katherine said.

Langdon shook his head. "Her legal attaché told me landlines are required for all official business."

Taking a seat in the worn leather chair, Langdon looked around, eyeing its unusual side table—an octagonal pillar whose unique Beaux Arts design was popular in the late 1800s during alcohol prohibitions. Gripping the lip of the tabletop, he lifted. The tabletop hinged open to reveal the cavity within. As Langdon imagined, this cabinet contained not hidden alcohol, but rather the ambassador's hardwired telephone.

He reached in, lifted it out, and placed the phone on his lap.

"You're ridiculous," Katherine said.

"Lucky guess." Langdon lifted the receiver to his ear, hearing a dial tone.

"Do you really think you should use that phone?" Katherine looked wary.

"Why not?" he replied, dialing. "It's probably the safest line in the country."

CHAPTER 77

Buoyed by the double espresso, Jonas Faukman had now left the children's publishing floor and returned to his office with a clear mission—to figure out exactly *why* Katherine's manuscript had been hacked, particularly by such a formidable entity. Alex Conan had joined him, eager to help—at least until his boss summoned him for the inevitable interrogation.

Faukman was at his desk computer, and the tech was seated opposite him with an open laptop. They had just begun to work when the piercing ring of Faukman's office phone broke the silence.

A business call at 5:15 a.m.? Faukman wondered. When he saw the caller ID was a European exchange, he lunged for the phone and pressed the speaker button. "Hello?!"

"Jonas!" The familiar baritone of Robert Langdon crackled through the room. "Thank God, you're safe! I tried your cell and home numbers. What are you doing at your office so early?!"

"Jesus, Robert . . ." Faukman's heart pounded. "We thought you were . . ."

"I know what you heard," Langdon said, "Katherine told me, but it was just my *phone* that drowned, not me."

"Katherine is *with* you?"

"She is, and we're both relieved to hear your voice. The last we heard, you were missing."

"That's a long story to be told over martinis," Faukman said. "As you probably know, Katherine's manuscript is *gone*. We were hacked, and it was deleted right out of the PRH system."

"I heard. Is there any chance of resurrecting a backup from the server?"

Faukman glanced at Alex, who was shaking his head.

"It was wiped clean," Faukman replied dejectedly. "I don't know what to say."

Langdon let out a sigh. "Too bad they didn't delete *my* last book instead."

Harsh but true, Faukman thought. Langdon's last book—*Symbols, Semiotics, and the Evolution of Language*—had gotten rave reviews but never found an audience outside academia. "I was told Katherine printed a hard copy of her manuscript. Is that true?"

"Yes . . . but that one's gone as well."

Faukman took a deep breath. "Okay, let's focus on what matters—you're both safe. We can deal with the book later."

"Well, that's why I'm calling," Langdon said. "I'm actually not *sure* we're safe. We're with the U.S. ambassador at her private residence, but it's a peculiar situation. I'm not even supposed to be calling—"

"Wait! You're with the American ambassador?!" Faukman tried not to sound panicked. "Robert, I would be very careful about trusting *anyone* in our government. Our tech here traced the PRH hackers back to an extremely powerful organization." He recalled the strange hyphenated name that Alex had typed earlier in the PRH Security Center. "The organization is called In-Q-Tel."

"Never heard of them."

"I hadn't either. From all I can gather, they're an incredibly well-funded venture capital firm that develops advanced technologies, mostly under the radar, so it's no surprise you don't know who they are."

"But that makes no sense," Langdon argued. "Venture capital firms don't hire hackers and field operatives."

"I believe *this* one does. You may not have heard of In-Q-Tel, but you've definitely heard of their parent organization."

"Who is that?"

Faukman sighed heavily. "A little group called the CIA."

The line went silent.

I know, Faukman thought, recalling his own stunned reaction. "Here's all I know," Faukman continued. "The CIA owns and operates In-Q-Tel as a private venture capital firm to discreetly invest in technologies related to national security. They control hundreds of high-tech patents, as well as majority stakes in some of the boldest new tech companies." The editor had turned back to his computer, pulling up the screen he had just been reading. "Their critics—mostly in competing investment firms—consistently complain that In-Q-Tel's affiliation with the U.S. intelligence machine affords them, and I quote, 'an alarming flexibility in the way they pursue their goals.' Something tells me we've witnessed some of that *flexibility* tonight."

"Incredible," Langdon whispered, sounding shaken. "Who knows why the CIA would target Katherine's book, but considering all that's happened, their fingerprints seem to be all over this—"

"You've got to be *kidding*!" Alex exclaimed, waving wildly and spinning his laptop so Faukman could see the screen. "Look at this!"

The laptop displayed a Wikipedia page, which Alex had apparently opened after hearing Langdon mention the ambassador.

Wikipedia:
Heide Nagel: U.S. Ambassador to the Czech Republic:

The citation was several pages long and dotted by a series of underlined highlights, underscoring the results of the document search Alex had just conducted.

. . . Nagel was hired by CIA directly out of NYU Law . . .
. . . overseeing CIA policy counsel . . .
. . . promoted to CIA general counsel advising agency director . . .
. . . retired from CIA to serve as ambassador . . .

"Oh *shit*, Robert . . ." Faukman whispered into the phone. "*Get out* of that house! Now!"

CHAPTER 78

Upstairs in her sprawling master bathroom, Ambassador Nagel gripped the sides of the marble sink and threw up. The text that had just arrived from Dana was only four words.

MICHAEL HARRIS IS DEAD.

Horrified, the ambassador had immediately excused herself and called Dana, who fumbled her way through a tearful, frantic update. Apparently, Dana and her Marine escort had found Sasha's apartment unlocked. Kerble had entered to ensure all was safe and was immediately confronted by a body on the hallway floor.

Michael Harris's strangled corpse.

No trace of Sasha Vesna or anyone else.

Despite the waves of emotion Nagel felt, she kept her cool long enough to give orders for Kerble to secure the apartment and call a forensics team to recover the body. *And keep this quiet!* The last thing Nagel needed was the press exploding with headlines of a consulate official's murder on foreign soil. *Not today.*

Whatever had transpired in that apartment, her first order of business was her own employee. *Michael.* Nagel felt ill. *His blood is on my hands.* She stared into her bathroom mirror now, overwhelmed with guilt and regret . . . not just for Michael, but for everything that had occurred in the last three years since coming to Prague . . .

Unlike so many ambassadors who attained their coveted appointments by having donated a small fortune to the winning presidential candidate, Heide Nagel had simply been in the right place at the right time.

Or the wrong place, as it turned out.

Several years ago, during her tenure as general counsel for the CIA, an important file of classified documents had gone missing until an agency task force broke into her home and located the file buried in a desk drawer. Not surprisingly, Nagel was escorted to the top floor of Langley for a meeting with the agency overlord.

CIA Director Gregory Judd was a former U.S. senator with a quiet and thoughtful demeanor, despite his reputation for total intolerance of anything short of perfection. CIA insiders said Judd knew where all the bodies were buried, because *he* had buried many of them.

"Gross negligence or treason?" the director demanded as she entered his office.

"It was a careless mistake, sir," she replied truthfully. "That file must have gotten mixed up with my work papers. I had no idea it was even in my possession."

The director studied her a long moment. "I'm inclined to believe you, but obviously you can no longer continue as general counsel until we sort out how this could happen. I'm putting you on indefinite leave and handing this over to the IG for an inquiry."

"Sir, I really—"

"Effective immediately," he declared, his eyes unyielding. "This is a gift, Ms. Nagel, and I strongly suggest you accept it before I change my mind."

A week later, Heide Nagel was still at home, suffocating from boredom and professional limbo. Her children were long grown, and her postdivorce "luxury condo" was empty and depressing, although she'd never noticed until now because she'd spent most of her waking hours at work.

My life is over, she realized. *I'm damaged goods.*

At sixty-three years old, Nagel was too young and ambitious to retire, but too old to hang a shingle and start a law practice. She wondered what she was going to do with herself. Book groups? Online dating? It all sounded like hell.

Then came a call she never expected.

The director phoned two weeks later in a rare display of contrition. "I feel bad about how this played out, Heide, and I'm hoping to make it right."

That's impossible, she thought.

"As you may know," Judd told her, "the president-elect and I are old prep school chums. He called me this morning for guidance on staffing a few key appointments—including the U.S. ambassadorship to the Czech Republic. I told him that considering the growing unrest in the region, he needed an ambassador with solid knowledge of international law as well as experience in the intelligence community. In a word—*you*."

Nagel was stunned. *The old-boy network is now recruiting old girls?*

The decision had been a no-brainer. Four months later, press releases had been sent, and Heide Nagel found herself living in Prague's spectacular ambassadorial residence, overseeing a talented embassy staff and doing meaningful work. Best of all, every time she caught a glimpse of the castle, she felt like she was living in a fairy tale.

Then, in a single night, it had all changed.

A month into her new post, Director Judd had called to check in, and after some small talk, he made an unusual request. "Heide, I'd like you to dine with a colleague of mine who is now stationed in Europe."

"Of course, sir," she said, feeling it was the least she could do for the man who had essentially saved her life. "Who is it?"

"A new hire for the European office of In-Q-Tel."

Q? she thought, feeling a twinge of apprehension.

She was no stranger to In-Q-Tel—or "Q," as agency spooks called it—the secretive investment arm of the CIA. Their shadowy team of financiers took huge positions in technologies they deemed relevant to the CIA's interests and national security—everything from Biomatrica's anhydrobiosis mechanisms to Nanosys's microscopic electronics to D-Wave quantum computing.

More than once as CIA counsel, Nagel had advised the director on legal issues related to In-Q-Tel's "creative investment techniques" and "asset protection methods," but it was rare that the group was ever reined in.

Why is someone from Q coming to Prague? Nagel was puzzled that a high-tech investment firm would be interested in Old World Prague. Their normal hunting ground was Silicon Valley.

On the night of the meeting, Ambassador Nagel arrived early at her restaurant of choice—CODA—a discreet local establishment with superb Czech cuisine. To her surprise, her contact was already seated. He was a slight, formally dressed man, probably in his mid-seventies, with a thick shock of silver hair. He was polishing his glasses as she approached the table.

Numbers guy, she decided.

Nagel could not have been more wrong. This man turned out to be Everett Finch—the legendary longtime director of the CIA's Directorate of Science & Technology. Finch's team at DS&T, along with those of the other three directorates—Administration, Operations, and Intelligence—made up the four pillars of the Central Intelligence Agency.

They moved Finch to In-Q-Tel? In Europe?

The only logical explanation Nagel could imagine was that Director Judd had wanted Finch's expertise in Europe for some clandestine reason . . . and quietly stationed him here under the radar.

The waiter arrived, presenting them both with an amuse-bouche—two tiny teacups of a delicate Czech mushroom soup called *kulajda.* Mr. Finch drained his cup, touched a napkin to his lip, and then leaned across the table.

"Heide . . ." he said, ignoring her formal title. "I trust you're enjoying your ambassadorship here?"

"I am," she replied, wary.

"Excellent." He gave her a tight smile. "I believe it's time you knew the *real* reason you were placed in Prague."

That night had marked the death of Nagel's wide-eyed

naivete regarding the serendipitous events that brought her to Prague.

My presence was orchestrated.

The old-boy network had placed a female pawn in a position of power where they needed her, and Nagel had been trapped ever since. She eventually learned what should have been obvious from the start—that Finch had engineered her dismissal from the CIA, planting the documents in her home.

When Nagel angrily confronted him on the matter, his response was chilling. With no show of emotion whatsoever, Finch produced photocopies of the classified documents that she'd allegedly possessed in her home, informing her that if these copies ever surfaced in the hands of foreign operatives, her claims of an "innocent mistake" would immediately be considered treason.

Nagel threatened to call CIA Director Judd, but Mr. Finch only encouraged it, telling her that both Judd and the president were briefed on the plan, and that a call to them would only confirm that she was playing in the big leagues with no allies.

I'm a puppet.

Finch might have been bluffing, but Nagel could not possibly risk calling the bluff of men like the U.S. president and the director of the CIA, especially when a treason charge hung in the balance . . . not to mention a top secret intelligence project.

That's how people disappear.

From that moment on, Nagel had despised Finch . . . and obeyed him.

Now, standing alone at her bathroom sink, Ambassador Nagel rinsed her mouth out and stared into her own tired eyes.

Michael Harris is dead.

"No more," she said aloud.

Finch had pushed too hard . . . too far.

For more than two years, Nagel had been looking for any way out of her prison, but Finch had never provided even the slightest opening.

Until now.

CHAPTER 79

The Golĕm felt alive with anticipation as he approached Crucifix Bastion. By all appearances, Gessner's hilltop lab was now deserted, meaning he would finally be able to retrieve what he had failed to secure earlier this morning.

This time, I will not be denied.

Gessner's RFID key card was safely tucked into his pocket, and he estimated he would need less than three minutes to obtain the only remaining element he required. Then he would depart the lab for his final destination.

Threshold.

Which I will reduce to dust.

As he strode toward the bastion's shattered doorway, he recalled the words of his legendary predecessor—the golem of Prague.

There are only two paths . . . Truth or Death.

The Golĕm had chosen both.

Unveil Truth.

Accept Death.

The Golĕm had died countless times, but death was never permanent. Unlike the ancient golem whose death had been final, The Golĕm moved in and out of this form at will.

I am my own creator. I will always be my own master.

Each time he erased the Hebrew letter *aleph* from his forehead—transforming Truth to Death—The Golĕm died . . . but only from view. He became invisible. His hulking outer shell evaporated, transforming a monster into . . . one of *them.* Unremarkable. Inconspicuous. His inner power hidden.

You cannot see me, but I am still here . . . watching over her.

Despite this morning's unexpected obstacles, The Golĕm had improvised well, protecting those who were innocent . . . and destroying those who were guilty. Now it was time to finish what he had started.

As he stepped through the entryway to Gessner's lab, he was pleased to find the elegant hallway deserted. The LAB access stairwell ahead of him was secured with a biometric security panel, but the fingerprint would not be a problem; Sasha had unwittingly provided him access long ago.

The Golĕm moved across the foyer toward the panel, his platform boots crunching loudly on the shattered glass on the floor. The sound crackled through the marble space.

An instant later, The Golĕm heard a second sound, from down the hall. It was the distinctive click of a weapon being cocked.

———·——

Delirious from lack of sleep, Field Officer Housemore had helped herself to a cup of coffee and taken a seat at the bastion window to admire the panoramic views of Prague Castle, which sat serenely in the distance. She had been daydreaming peacefully when an unexpected sound in the hallway jolted her back to attention, causing her to leap up and reflexively prep her weapon.

Now on high alert, Housemore moved toward the entryway, her gun at the ready. Finch had ordered her to secure this building, and while he had promised support, she knew it was too soon for it to have arrived. Certainly, any trained military support would have announced themselves before entering.

Someone else is here . . .

As Housemore moved stealthily around the corner into the hallway, she saw a hooded figure in a black cloak. He was heaving open the metal door to the lab stairwell.

"*Stůj!*" Housemore shouted, running toward him. "Halt!"

The man ignored her, slipping quickly through the door as Housemore fired. The bullet clanged off the security door, just missing him. She ran forward, but she arrived just as the door resealed, locking her out.

Housemore put her face to the small reinforced window and peered into the stairwell. Instantly, she froze. The cloaked figure was staring back at her . . . only inches away from the other side of the glass. His face was earthen, like the surface of the moon, and he had symbols carved into his forehead. His icy eyes studied her a moment, as if memorizing her face, and then he turned and rushed down the stairs, his cloak billowing behind him as he descended from sight.

Housemore stepped back, gathering herself.

Who . . . or what *was that?!*

She had no idea how this intruder had unlocked the biometric door, but she needed to alert Finch immediately. Housemore knew this was not the location of the agency's secret facility, although Gessner's lab obviously contained something of importance, and Finch had ordered her to protect it under any circumstance. And *someone* had just slipped right past her.

The man who had entered, Housemore guessed, was Russian. His steely pale eyes had a Slavic feel, and his thick clay makeup struck Housemore as a perfect example of Russian ingenuity; by embracing Prague's tradition of "cosplay," the intruder had effortlessly thwarted the city's facial recognition security cameras. Moreover, Russians were now masters at defeating biometrics with duplicate fingertips created on UV resin–based 3D printers.

Housemore kept one eye on the lab door as she holstered her weapon and reluctantly pulled out her phone. Finch was not going to take well to this news. Her hands were trembling slightly, and she decided it would be prudent to take a moment before the confrontation.

Slow down. Gather your thoughts.

Without relinquishing her watchful eye on the lab door, Housemore slowly backed out of the entryway, moving in reverse down the hall toward the reception room.

There, in the relative shelter of the hallway, still facing the stairwell door, she took several deep breaths and composed herself. She began to dial Finch.

Housemore never got the chance.

Someone was suddenly behind her.

A searing blast of electricity tore deep into her back. Every muscle in her body seized, and she went rigid, pitching forward onto the tile floor, her phone skittering away. Her attacker grabbed her and flipped her onto her back, pinning her down. Impossibly, Housemore found herself looking up into the pale eyes of the earthen creature she had just seen enter the stairwell.

Where did he come from?! How . . .

It was as if this monster had materialized out of thin air directly behind her!

He was on top of her now, on the hard tile floor, with his hands around her neck. As he cut off her air supply, Housemore tried to resist, but her paralyzed muscles refused to respond. Helpless, Housemore could only wait, trying to stay conscious.

After nearly twenty seconds on her back with her windpipe blocked, she could feel her muscle control slowly starting to return. She needed more time, but unfortunately, her vision was starting to blur. *Now or never.* In a last-ditch effort, she summoned all the strength she could muster, raised her hands, and drove them firmly into his chest, trying to shove him off her.

But her attacker barely moved.

The feeling of this clay man's flesh was odd—wholly unexpected.

"I am not as you think I am," the monster whispered, gazing down into Housemore's eyes as he tightened his grip. "I am The Golĕm."

CHAPTER 80

The eighteen-meter swimming pool beneath Petschek Villa was built in the style of a traditional Roman bath. Encircled by a double ring of forty-eight red marble columns, the azure and white pool was heated by twin coal furnaces and was considered the mansion's most opulent luxury.

According to lore, the pool was used for only one season before Otto Petschek's daughter caught pneumonia in it and nearly died. Petschek immediately emptied the pool and declared it forever off-limits.

Robert Langdon stood at the foot of the empty and forgotten pool, scanning the subterranean space for any exit other than the narrow stairs that he and Katherine had just descended in a frantic attempt to find a way out of the house.

"Of course you'd find a *pool*," Katherine whispered in the reverberant space. "Too bad it's empty, or you could take your second swim of the day."

Third, Langdon thought. *If you count the Vltava.*

Langdon had hoped the stairs might descend to a basement exit so they would be able to flee the ambassador's residence, but the pool room had no exits. *Dead end.* Overhead, the frantic footfalls of the ambassador echoed down through the vents as she rushed around the south wing, no doubt looking for her missing guests. Apparently, she knew her house well enough to calculate their limited options for escape, and it took her less than thirty seconds to appear on the staircase, descending toward the pool.

Langdon half expected Ambassador Nagel to arrive with a U.S. Marine at her side, but when she came down the stairs, she was alone. Without a word, she marched over to where they were standing and held up the two NDAs that Langdon and Katherine had left unsigned on the coffee table. Then she tore the documents into pieces, letting the scraps flutter down onto the empty pool tile.

Langdon watched in confusion. *What is she doing?*

Having fully shredded the papers, the ambassador fixed them both with a serious gaze and raised an index finger to her lips, admonishing them not to say a word. Then she pulled out her cell phone, touched a few buttons, and placed an outbound call . . . on speakerphone.

"Finch," a man's voice answered, crackling out of the speaker. "Everything under control?" His accent was American with a touch of a Southern drawl.

"Yes, we're just waiting," the ambassador said. "How far out are you?"

"Just landing. I'll be there within the hour."

"*Please* tell me you have news on Michael Harris," Nagel said urgently. "I'm worried about his safety."

"If Harris is blown," the man replied, "there's nothing we can do about it now. He's probably irrelevant at this point, anyway. He confirmed for us that Sasha is not talking, and that's—"

"Irrelevant?!" Nagel demanded. "Michael is involved in this . . . at *your* command."

"Forget about Harris. Just stay focused on the task at hand. Where are you, by the way? Your voice is echoing."

"In my bathroom. I needed privacy to call."

"Where are Langdon and Solomon?"

"I left them in the library," she said, "and told them to relax until you arrive."

Langdon shot Katherine a startled look.

"Did you admit the hotel surveillance?" Finch asked.

"I did," Nagel replied. "As you suggested."

"And it worked?" the man asked.

"Like a charm."

"They both signed the NDAs?"

"They did," the ambassador said without hesitation. "Your

nondisclosures are signed, sealed, and locked in my personal safe."

"Excellent," Finch said, sounding relieved. "It will be good to have leverage on Langdon as well."

Langdon and Katherine were now staring at each other in utter bewilderment.

"And just to confirm," the man said, "you have physical proof that the hard-copy manuscript in question was burned?"

"Yes, my team collected the only remains—there're a few charred scraps. I'll send photos."

"And you say the author burned it *herself*?"

"It is my understanding that both Langdon and Solomon burned the manuscript because they felt they were in danger from a rogue ÚZSI agent . . . and also, obviously, from *you*."

"It was a gutsy choice," the man mused. "I'll believe it when I look them in the eyes. If that manuscript is truly gone . . . *and* they both signed NDAs . . . then we may be very close to ending this."

"I hope so."

"And Crucifix Bastion?" the man asked. "You're confident ÚZSI has agreed to stand down? I don't want anyone near Gessner's lab or her work."

"Confirmed. Nobody is up there now."

"Good," he said, sounding relieved. "I want you to send a Marine security detail up there immediately. Obviously, my main concern is our primary facility—but we can't afford any leaks at the bastion either. Have your team secure it, and I'll go up in person to assess after our meeting at your residence."

"Understood," Nagel replied. "I'll send a team up right away."

"See you shortly," he said.

The line went dead.

In the silence, the ambassador double-checked that the call was indeed ended, and then she raised her eyes to Langdon and Katherine and let out a weary sigh.

"What in the world just happened?!" Katherine demanded.

The ambassador glanced overhead at the ceiling vents and, apparently not wanting to risk being overheard, led Langdon and Katherine into the pool's utility room, where a single bulb illuminated two antique, cast-iron water boilers, which, despite nearly a century of nonuse, still smelled of coal.

"The first thing you should know," the ambassador said quietly, closing the door behind them, "is the man I just spoke to works for the Central Intelligence Agency."

Langdon stepped back, feigning surprise despite having been warned by Jonas. "I'm sorry?"

Nagel nodded. "His name is Everett Finch, and he used to run the agency's Directorate of Science and Technology." She paused. "I should add that I also worked for the CIA. I was an attorney."

And there it is, Langdon thought, not sure whether he was relieved or unsettled that the ambassador had simply laid it out.

Nagel now confirmed what Faukman had told Langdon on the phone—the CIA quietly ran a venture capital firm named In-Q-Tel, Q for short, which invested in national security technologies and protected their investments aggressively.

"The CIA runs an investment bank?" Katherine asked.

"More for patriotism than profit," Nagel explained. "U.S. intelligence budgets have been slashed in recent years, and the CIA functions under an oath to defend the nation from *all* enemies—including the shortsightedness of our own Pollyanna politicians—and so the agency feels morally empowered, if not *obligated*, to find outside funding to facilitate important CIA programs that otherwise could not exist."

As Langdon listened, he realized that a project funded with Q money would bypass all traditional congressional oversight associated with a black-budget allocation, meaning the CIA could essentially do whatever it wanted and answer to no one.

"A few years ago, the CIA director transferred Everett Finch to London and assigned him an off-book posting in Q's European headquarters. His duties are confidential, but he seems to have been given carte blanche, and as you've no doubt figured out, Finch is gravely concerned about Katherine's manuscript."

"Why?" Katherine pressed.

"All I know," Nagel replied, "is Finch considers your manuscript a threat to one of Q's most important investments. For this reason, it is deemed a matter of national security, which affords Finch dangerous latitude in how he chooses to deal with you."

Langdon felt increasingly trapped down here in the windowless basement.

"But *how* is it a threat?!" Katherine pressed. "I've been trying to imagine how anything I've writ—"

"I don't know. I have no specifics. Only orders—to force you to sign an NDA."

"But if the CIA thinks my book is a national security risk," Katherine said, "then why not just call my publisher, cite national security, and demand I remove the dangerous material?"

"As former CIA counsel," Nagel replied, "I can tell you that isolating *specific* passages reveals too much about the CIA's concerns. It would shine a light on precisely what they are trying to keep secret. Moreover, your publisher could simply refuse the CIA's request and publish the full text under the banner: *Read the book the CIA doesn't want you to read . . .*"

Langdon knew she was right. The Vatican regularly made that mistake, fanning sales of popular books by insisting they were "anti-Catholic" and attempting to forbid Catholics to read them.

"Did you read these NDAs?" Langdon asked.

"Blanket verbal," Nagel said, nodding. "Dangerously general. It basically means you would have a recorded conversation with Finch, and anything mentioned therein would immediately be considered 'protected information.' Depending on what Finch says to you, that NDA would have the legal teeth to shut down Katherine's book immediately and permanently."

Langdon's thoughts again churned through all that Katherine had told him about her manuscript and her discoveries— brain filters, GABA, nonlocal consciousness. *Why would the CIA care about any of it?*

"You just told us," Langdon pressed, "that Mr. Finch believes Katherine's book poses a threat to one of Q's most important investments . . . which begs an obvious question: Do you know *what* that investment is?"

"I know it relates to a top secret CIA facility here in Prague."

"In *Prague?*" Langdon was surprised. "You're kidding. What do they do there?"

Nagel shook her head with frustration. "I don't know. All I can say is the facility has a code name. They call it 'Threshold.'"

CHAPTER 81

I have been provided very few details," Nagel said as the three of them huddled in the dingy boiler room beneath the villa. "The agency claims I'm insulated for my own safety. All I know is the CIA director himself considers Threshold the agency's *single* most important endeavor . . . absolutely critical to future security."

The bold statement hung in the air.

"And you're not involved?" Langdon asked.

"Only as a political facilitator," she said. "Three years ago, behind my back, the CIA orchestrated my embassy posting here so I could be their diplomatic pawn—an agency insider who would answer to Finch and help cut through the legal red tape involved in secretly building the Threshold facility."

"And you still don't know what kind of operation it is?" he asked.

Nagel shook her head. "I know it's a science research facility. From what little Finch has said and judging by Brigita Gessner's prominent involvement, I'm fairly certain they're doing brain research of some sort . . . perhaps in human consciousness—but the intense military security means there's far more going on down there than simple scientific curiosity."

Katherine seemed riveted. "Is the facility up and running?"

"The structure is complete but not yet fully operational. I know they've done some isolated testing . . . which I gather was successful because they're now gearing up to begin in earnest; they're currently training staff off-site in the U.S. and expect the facility to be live within a matter of weeks."

"And this facility is here in Prague?" she asked.

Nagel paused, as if debating one last time whether to reveal the details. "Technically *beneath* Prague," she said. "The whole thing is subterranean."

For an instant, Langdon flashed on the lower floor of Gessner's small lab. "Not Crucifix Bastion, I assume?"

"No," the ambassador replied. "That's Brigita Gessner's private research lab. The CIA invested in her technologies, but the Threshold facility lies elsewhere. It's actually not far from the bastion, but it has over ten thousand square feet of space."

Ten thousand square feet? All underground?! "How could anyone possibly build something that big in total secrecy underneath a city like this?"

Nagel shrugged. "Pretty simple, actually—the basic structure was *already* there. The CIA took it over and rebuilt it." She paused. "Although, *publicly*, it was the U.S. Army Corps of Engineers that took it over."

Langdon needed only a moment to put the pieces together.

In the 1950s, one of Europe's largest Soviet-era bomb shelters had been built in Prague. The massive network of dank subterranean chambers was said to contain space for some 1,500 people along with its own power station, air-filtration system, showers, toilets, gathering hall, and even its own morgue. The bunker was long since abandoned, although a portion of it was still open today as a tourist attraction.

"Folimanka Shelter . . ." Langdon whispered, amazed to realize he had literally walked over parts of the bunker earlier today; it was buried beneath the sprawling expanse of Folimanka Park.

Langdon had never been inside, but he'd seen the tourist entrance—a cement tunnel festooned with colorful spray-painted graffiti depicting atomic bomb explosions and the words KRYT FOLIMANKA, which Langdon had assumed meant *Folimanka Crypt* but was informed meant *Folimanka Shelter.*

The well-known tourist portion of the bunker—located at the easternmost edge of Folimanka Park—was relatively shallow, in fair condition, and perfectly safe to tour. The larger portion of the bunker, however, extended deeper and farther out into Folimanka Park. Over the decades, its vast network of tunnels and chambers had flooded, fallen into disrepair, and were sealed off and forgotten.

The ambassador quickly described how the CIA had managed to take control of the abandoned portion of the bunker. As a fellow member of NATO, the U.S. government regularly cooperated on military matters and political affairs here. From time to time, this also meant lending civil assistance for infrastructure—in the case of Folimanka Park, figuring out how to save the vast expanse, which city officials announced had begun to sag and they feared might one day collapse into the abandoned hollows of the decaying bunkers beneath it.

The cavalry had arrived in the form of the U.S. Army Corps of Engineers, who dug a new entry tunnel at the western end of the park and began the multiyear project of draining, sealing, and reinforcing the expansive system of bunkers.

The project was now about to be completed, and yet the ambassador said anti-U.S. conspiracy theories still swirled: *Folimanka Park was never really sagging . . . It was being rebuilt as a secret military prison . . . or a chemical weapons bunker.* Another claimed that the deeper caverns didn't even exist, and the U.S. was actually *digging* them—a suspicion fueled by the absence of any reliable Soviet-era blueprints outlining the full bunker, which either had never existed or had been effectively purged from history.

Whatever the truth was, Langdon had to admire the devilishly simple ploy, except for one glaring question. "Why build *here*?" he asked. "Why not locate Threshold in a warehouse in the Arizona desert?"

"Quite simple," Nagel replied. "Crowded urban settings provide a level of camouflage from satellite surveillance, which is not something you get when transporting extensive materials and personnel to an isolated desert location. More intelligence facilities are being moved to urban centers now, and selecting a city *outside* the U.S. helps keep congressional oversight and domestic legal restrictions to a minimum."

That last statement Langdon found ominous. "Why are you

telling us all of this?" he asked, startled by the ambassador's candor.

"Yes," Katherine agreed. "It seems—"

"Treasonous?" The ambassador's gaze turned distant. "My reasons are personal, but whatever ends up happening to me, please believe me when I tell you I will make it my first order of business to keep you both safe."

Langdon knew there were many unanswered questions, but he was inclined to believe her.

"I need to warn you, though," Nagel said, "you're dealing with powerful forces. In the orbit of the CIA and Threshold, the stakes are unimaginably high—and frankly, people die." She sighed and looked at Langdon and Katherine; for a fleeting moment it appeared she might cry. "Dr. Gessner was killed last night, but she's not the only casualty. I just received word that my legal attaché, Michael Harris, was found dead half an hour ago."

Langdon felt sickened as he recalled his interactions with Harris at the hotel just hours earlier. "I'm so very sorry."

Nagel quietly explained that Harris's body had been found in the apartment of Sasha Vesna, with whom Harris was having an "insincere" relationship as a form of surveillance ordered by Mr. Finch, who wanted to keep close tabs on Gessner's Russian assistant. Sasha's whereabouts were still unknown, but Nagel was not optimistic.

Langdon felt an immediate concern for Sasha's safety.

The ambassador continued, pursing her lips and letting out a deep sigh. "I'm directly responsible for Michael Harris's death . . . and I'll carry that forever." She raised her eyes to meet them both, forcing herself to stand straighter. "I have no idea how to start making amends for Michael, and for blindly going along with Finch's orders . . . except that right now I know I need to do *whatever* is required to make this right and to protect you both."

"How do you intend to do that?" Katherine pressed.

"We have three possible moves," Nagel said. "Unfortunately, you're not going to like any of them. The first option would be the safest. I would reprint the nondisclosure agreements, you would sign them, and you would have your meeting with Mr. Finch as planned, providing him the guarantee of silence he desires. This would essentially remove you from his radar, but it would likely mean you could never publish your book, and Ms. Solomon, there might be fields of study that you would no longer be completely free to pursue."

"That's not an option at all," Katherine said flat out.

"Agreed," Langdon said. "Second choice?"

"Option number two . . ." Nagel said, looking from one to the other. "We have about an hour until Finch gets here. We could leave right now. I drive you both immediately to the airport and get you out of the country. There would be repercussions, of course—for all three of us—but at least we would buy some time to come up with other solutions."

"Such as?" Langdon asked.

"For one, Ms. Solomon could publish her book immediately. Its publication would provide some level of immunit—"

"My book is gone," Katherine interjected. "It would take a very long time to re-create."

"And even if she did have a copy," Langdon noted, "it takes months for a book to be produced and published. Not to mention, wouldn't a move like that make her a target of the CIA forever?"

"On some level, yes."

"No thanks," Katherine said. "I have no interest in looking over my shoulder for the rest of my life. What's the third option?"

Nagel was silent for a moment, as if formulating details in her mind. When she spoke, her tone was matter-of-fact, that of an attorney advising a client. "In the intelligence business, there is only one true source of power. *Information*. It is the only leverage anyone understands . . . and you are now in a position to receive a vast quantity of it. Remember, Mr. Finch believes you signed NDAs, and he is coming here to orchestrate a conversation that uses those NDAs against you. He'll tell you as much as he possibly can—to ensure every topic he mentions is off-limits to you going forward. The more he tells you, the more information you will have . . . and therefore, the more leverage."

Langdon realized they were playing with a pro. *And playing with fire.* Even so, Nagel's plan hardly seemed as simple as she made it sound. "I understand how we *obtain* the information," he said. "But then what?"

"I would help you," she said. "We would entrust all the data to a third party—an outside attorney, for example—who would create a mechanism by which if anything happens to any of us, or we fail to touch base with him regularly, the information would be sent immediately to the press. Lawyers call it an 'untimely death clause.'"

"I believe the word is 'blackmail,'" Langdon said.

"In crude terms, yes. Though it's perfectly legal."

Katherine took a step backward. "You're suggesting we *blackmail* the CIA . . ."

"Think of it as informational leverage, Ms. Solomon. Intelligence threats are a language these people speak and understand. If they attack you, they know they will suffer damage. And so they will leave you alone."

"And vice versa," Langdon said. "You protect their secrets in return for immunity."

"Mutually assured destruction," Nagel said. "It's a proven model. If it didn't work, the world's superpowers would have launched nuclear weapons at each other in the 1960s. Instead, self-preservation creates a standoff; we simply agree to disagree."

Katherine still looked wary.

"Having leverage would instantly deescalate this crisis," Nagel said. "The agency would have to back off, regroup, give everyone a chance to take a breath and negotiate; maybe they even tell you what they don't like about your book, and you offer to remove it. This path at least gives you options." Nagel caught Katherine's eye and held it. "And I hope you know I'm taking an enormous personal risk here helping you, Ms. Solomon, which makes me a powerful ally for you."

"Thank you," Katherine said, sounding increasingly convinced.

Langdon liked the concept in principle, but execution was another matter. "Not to rain on the parade here," he said, "but what happens if Mr. Finch demands to see the signed NDAs *before* we talk to him?"

"He probably will," the ambassador replied. "I'll simply tell him I knew the documents were crucial to his plan, so I had a Marine escort transport them under diplomatic seal to the embassy and lock them in my personal safe. He'll have to trust me . . . or move this meeting to the embassy, which he definitely will *not* want to do."

Langdon weighed the plan, still feeling wary. It was a stretch to assume that he and Katherine could learn enough in this conversation with Finch to have any leverage at all. *We'll be talking to a trained CIA veteran.* And even if this man believed Langdon and Katherine had signed the restrictive NDAs, would he really reveal data that would compromise the agency or a top secret project?

"You look uncertain," Katherine said.

He glanced up at her, still thinking. "Sorry, I don't think it will work."

"Those are the only three options," Nagel said.

"Actually, there's a *fourth* option," Langdon declared, having made an unexpected connection. "It's dangerous . . . but I believe it may be our best play."

CHAPTER 82

On final descent into Václav Havel Airport, Mr. Finch's Citation Latitude streaked toward the mountain of Bílá Hora. The jet's interactive map noted that the hilltop was the battlefield on which the Catholics had quelled the 1620 Bohemian uprising.

Fitting, Mr. Finch thought, having just quelled his own little uprising with Ambassador Nagel. For obvious reasons, the ambassador had always despised Finch, but that was of no concern to him. *She's a smart woman . . . smart enough to know her place in this operation.*

As the plane descended, Finch buckled his seat belt, feeling far more relaxed on approach than he had on departure. Only an hour earlier, this entire operation had been in chaos. Now, almost miraculously, all the disarray seemed to have vanished. A notorious book-pirating ring was shouldering the blame for the hack at PRH; Robert Langdon and Katherine Solomon had been located and secured in Prague; NDAs had been signed; all copies of the manuscript were now contained; and the two operatives in New York had received the order to pull out and maintain radio silence with no further contact.

Mission complete, he thought, staring out the private jet's oval window. As he looked at the peaceful Czech landscape, Finch reminded himself that this entire complicated operation boiled down to one simple fact that had myriad ramifications and justified his actions.

The human mind is the world's next battlefield.

The wars of tomorrow would be fought differently, and Finch

had been tapped to lead the charge. The nerve center of that directive was Threshold . . . and Finch's superiors had empowered him to do anything necessary to protect the technology being developed there.

Threshold would always be at risk. But one of its first true threats had materialized from an unlikely source, even before the facility was fully operational.

Katherine Solomon.

For years, the talented noetic scientist had been on the CIA's watch list. Among other things, the nature of her work overlapped with projects being explored by the agency. Several years earlier, the team surveilling her had flagged a transcript of a podcast in which she was asked how she felt about noeticists who left academia to work with the U.S. military on brain-related research. Her reply had been unequivocal. "Working with the military is anathema to everything I believe. Under no circumstances would I consider it. Noetic research is for everyone . . . It should never be weaponized."

A shame, Finch recalled thinking. *DARPA could have used her on the N3 or subnets projects.* With a single quote, Katherine Solomon had marked herself as someone the CIA could never approach, even discreetly, without risking blowback.

When the agency learned that Solomon was writing a book on human consciousness and had landed a major publishing deal, Finch directed his team to monitor the project closely and secure a draft of her unpublished manuscript as a precautionary measure.

Surprisingly, Finch's operatives reported that Solomon's manuscript was being composed in an unconventional way—entirely on the publisher's private server, protected by a high level of security. This fact, combined with other concerning elements in Solomon's past, raised alarm bells for Finch, and he devised a plan B.

He instructed Brigita Gessner to coax the noeticist to Prague with a prestigious lecture invitation. Gessner was to assess the lecture, then sit down face-to-face over a few drinks and see what she could get Solomon to divulge about her manuscript.

She would also make a rare offer to the first-time author—a "celebrity blurb" for which she would need an advance reading copy of Solomon's book. And finally, Gessner would offer Solomon a lab tour that required signing a short NDA . . . with a few discreet lines that would allow Finch to take full control of the situation if necessary.

Unfortunately . . . plan B exploded in my face.

After drinks at the Four Seasons, Gessner had sent a decidedly alarming message to Finch:

> SOLOMON REFUSED OFFER. NO ADVANCE COPY.
> ALSO REFUSED NDA. BIGGER PROBLEM—
> SHE LIED TO ME. WILL CALL IN 30 MINUTES.

Solomon lied? Gessner's text implied Solomon was considerably savvier than Finch had believed and might well be hiding something monumental about her manuscript.

Finch waited anxiously that night for Gessner's call.

It never came.

Thirty minutes came and went, and then an hour passed.

Finch called her but got no answer.

Two hours later, when his phone finally did ring, it wasn't Gessner but rather his electronic surveillance team with an urgent update: *Katherine Solomon has just screamed for help in her hotel room.*

Finch immediately jumped onto the audio feed from the microphone he had placed in her suite, which, thus far, had produced no valuable intelligence whatsoever. What he heard was Langdon consoling Solomon after some kind of nightmare, discussing the details of the dream that had just awoken her. Then Finch heard something unexpected and profoundly alarming—Langdon pointing out that the strange elements in her dream made perfect logical sense . . . including the appearance of a "spear."

"Remember the symbol of the Vel spear on Brigita's access card?" Langdon asked. "We were just discussing it with her a few hours ago."

Finch could not believe his ears. The card Langdon was referring to was a highly secure, *all-access* key card to Threshold. For the moment, only two such cards existed—Gessner's and his own—and there was no way in hell Gessner would *ever* have revealed it to them.

She keeps it in a protective sleeve . . . in a locked briefcase.

Dumbfounded, Finch pulled out his own identical card and studied it. *This is the most secure RFID access technology on earth.* Ingeniously, the *entire* surface of the card was a biometric reader—capable of reading any of the user's fingerprints, in any orientation—meaning the card was impossible to use without being held by the authorized user. If stolen, the card would be useless. And if lost, the card's lone marking offered no clue as to its affiliation.

The word itself was perfectly generic. But in truth, it was an encrypted code name.

PRAGUE

Prague, literally, meant "threshold"—and these high-tech cards were the first level of security to gain access to Threshold's subterranean facility. The subtle incorporation of the historic Vel spear symbol in the *A* was Finch's touch—an iconographic nod to the weapon of valor, strength, and enlightenment being created beneath the earth.

Why would Gessner show this card to an outsider—especially Katherine Solomon?!

The only explanation Finch could conjure was deeply unnerving. Perhaps he had misjudged Gessner's ability to be discreet. She was transparently driven by money, for sure, which made her easy for Finch to control, but she also had a monumental ego. He wondered if maybe the two Americans had cleverly turned the tables on her, taking advantage of the neuroscientist's need to brag, and had persuaded *Gessner* to talk instead of Katherine. Maybe they'd gotten her drunk or even taken her hostage, which might explain why Gessner wasn't answering her phone.

Finch felt his temples throbbing with increasing concern as he analyzed the facts:

Solomon refuses to share the manuscript . . .

Her publisher is exercising extreme security . . .

She is aware of Gessner's RFID key card . . .

As Finch sat alone in London in the dead of night, he hoped he was being paranoid. But an unsettling possibility now struck him: *Maybe Solomon knows about Threshold . . . and is writing an explosive exposé to reveal the CIA's work in human consciousness.*

A moment later, as Finch continued to monitor the audio feed, Solomon confessed something that proved to be the tipping point. "I'm particularly anxious right now, Robert," she said, still tearful. "I finally gave Jonas the green light to start editing today. He was planning to print the manuscript and start reading tonight, so I'm nervous."

The news caught Finch off guard. *Katherine has submitted her book to her editor?* As soon as her manuscript entered the "editing" phase, copies would be distributed all around the publishing house—proofreaders, fact-checkers, book designers, even early publicity and marketing staff. *Containment, if necessary, will become impossible.*

Finch realized he was out of time and options. He had not wanted to create unnecessary waves by hacking the publisher, but now he needed to find out what was in this book . . . *immediately.* Without hesitation, he ordered his tech team to penetrate Penguin Random House's secure server and steal a copy of Solomon's manuscript. Once he had seen what was in it, he would either exhale . . . or order a complete purge of every last shred of her work.

Finch also realized that another liability had materialized— Katherine Solomon's partner—Robert Langdon. The Harvard professor had a reputation for uncovering secrets nobody wanted uncovered.

I'll need leverage over Langdon, too, he decided. Finch quickly formulated a plan, using the scant intelligence he had just surveilled from the Royal Suite. Long ago he had learned that even the most innocuous information, presented properly, could be molded into a potent weapon of confusion. Ancient Chinese strategist Sun Tzu had devised entire military campaigns around his famous mantra: *Confusion creates chaos . . . and chaos creates opportunity.*

Time was short, but he had built a career on being prepared for all contingencies and acting decisively. He picked up the phone and made several calls, including one to Field Officer Housemore, with clear logistical instructions and orders to remain on standby.

Just before 6 a.m., Prague local time, Finch's hackers finally transmitted an encrypted version of Solomon's complete manuscript to him. He had no intention of reading the entire document and began by just scrolling through the table of contents. He was relieved to find that the manuscript, at first glance, appeared to be precisely what the prepublication chatter suggested—an exploration of a new theory of consciousness.

To be certain, Finch searched electronically for the keywords "CIA" and "Threshold," relieved to see that neither turned up any matches.

So far so good . . .

Lastly, he entered a very specific search string—looking for one single piece of information.

It will either be here . . . or it won't.

Finch held his breath and touched the return key to initiate the search. A full two seconds passed with no results, and Finch began to relax.

And then his computer pinged.

Shit . . .

The search had located a match near the very end of the manuscript. As the page popped up, Finch leaned in, his eyes racing across the text. Within moments, he realized this was a disastrous scenario. Whether wittingly or not, Katherine Solomon had stepped squarely into a hornet's nest. Her book posed a severe problem.

As Finch weighed his limited options for managing the crisis, his phone pinged with more bad news—a notification that Solomon had just accessed the PRH server from the Four Seasons Business Center, where she currently was *printing* her manuscript.

She's making hard copies at 6:45 a.m. . . . on a hotel printer?!

The action seemed anathema to the publisher's security protocols, and Finch suddenly feared that Solomon had learned her manuscript had been hacked . . . and she was already taking actions to protect it.

Distressed, Finch made a final attempt to reach Brigita Gessner, though his call went straight to voicemail. Gessner had been missing all night . . . ever since she had met with Solomon and Langdon.

One thing he knew for sure. *Where there's smoke, there's fire.*

Finch had prepared bold countermeasures in both Prague and New York, which could be deployed with the issuance of a single-word command.

Assessing the entire situation, he concluded it was time.

He sent simultaneous Signal messages to his operatives on the ground in both cities:

EXECUTE.

CHAPTER 83

The Golĕm knelt on the pink marble floor, deeply depleted after his struggle. Gathering his strength to move and hide the body, he was pleased to find his victim's corpse far lighter than Harris's had been. He dragged the woman with little effort, dumping her out of sight behind a couch that sat near the side wall. He considered stealing the woman's handgun, but he had never had the opportunity to learn how to fire one, and he much preferred the simplicity and silence of the stun gun.

The Golĕm now moved to the wall sculpture and slid the heavy piece of art aside, revealing the elevator he had ascended minutes ago to catch the woman by surprise. The elevator's security keypad glowed before him, and he carefully typed in Gessner's seven-character passcode, recalling her terror last night.

She told me everything . . . as anyone in her position would.

As the elevator descended one floor, The Golĕm closed his eyes, recalling with satisfaction his interrogation method, which utilized a machine his victim herself had invented.

Gessner's EPR pod was designed for fully anesthetized, unconscious patients in conjunction with intravenous fentanyl—the most powerful painkiller on earth—which would block the excruciating sensation of having your circulatory system flushed with ice-cold saline. The Golĕm, however, had simply buckled her in, skipping anesthesia and securing her wrists and ankles with the pod's heavy Velcro straps. The machine's IVs were designed for femoral arteries and veins, but he inserted the catheters into her arms instead, which he imagined would provide just enough flow to keep her conscious to experience the agony.

The elevator opened automatically to Gessner's lab, and The Golĕm made his way through the dim light, his cloak billowing behind him, casting ghostly shadows on the stone walls. This time, he was alone in the bastion, and he would not be interrupted.

I will need only a minute to retrieve what I came for.

Then he would head for the secret facility known as Threshold.

—————

The trauma of being abducted had not faded for Jonas Faukman, and having now learned that Robert and Katherine had been lured into the residence of a former CIA attorney, he could only hope they had taken his advice and gotten the hell out of there.

Call me, Robert. Let me know you're okay . . .

Alex Conan had been pecking away at his laptop, performing a deep dive on In-Q-Tel. Faukman was fiercely interested in knowing why the investment firm would be so opposed to whatever was in Katherine's manuscript.

"Have a look at this," Alex finally said. "It's a partial list of Q's private investment holdings."

Faukman darted over and looked at the screen over the tech's shoulder, eyeing the firm's catalog in disbelief. There were more than three hundred entries, mostly in language that was indecipherable to him.

- MemSQL—synchronous analytics Boundless Spatial
- Xanadu—photonic quantum solutions
- Keyhole—geospatial visualization
- zSpace—3D holographic sculpting

The list went on and on.

"This looks like what I'd expect," Alex said, quickly scanning the list. "What I recognize is mostly cybersecurity, data analytics, imaging, computing . . ."

"How about neuroscience or consciousness—*that* sort of thing?"

"Maybe, I don't know. We need to throw this list into a da—" Alex's phone buzzed, and he glanced at the caller ID, drawing a fortifying breath before answering. "Allison, good morning. I was just—"

Faukman could hear the data security director yelling on the other end of the line.

"I understand," Alex said calmly. "I'll be right there." He ended the call and stood up. "Sorry, interrogation time."

Faukman felt for the kid. Considering PRH had been hacked by a global intelligence agency, this was not exactly a fair fight, and Alex had handled the crisis admirably.

"I'll be back when I can," the tech said, before appearing to have another thought and typing quickly on his laptop. "I just copied and sent you that list; throw it into a DAP and look for any crossover."

"Wait! What? What's DAP! I don't have one!"

"Yes, you *do*," Alex said patiently, heading for the door. "There's an entire suite of data analytics platforms on the PRH server for your use."

Faukman had no idea even where to look.

"Never mind," Alex said, "just use an online engine— ChatGPT or Bard or something. Tell it to analyze Q's investments and cross-reference them with whatever topics you think are relevant to Dr. Solomon's book. I'll be back when I can."

With that, Alex rushed off.

Faukman stood alone in his office, casting a wary eye at his computer. He'd seen artificial intelligence apps, of course, but he'd sworn publicly never to use them. *An existential threat to the noble craft of writing!* PRH was already receiving submissions that clearly had been written by robots, but they were getting alarmingly harder and harder to spot. Faukman had taken a defiant stand—urging his fellow editors to boycott all AI products in the face of the coming literary apocalypse.

Now, however, Faukman found himself at a crossroads. As he opened the email Alex had sent him and eyed the list of Q's investments, he pictured the egregious abuses the shadowy organization had imposed on Katherine . . . on Robert . . . and on Faukman himself.

Screw ethical fortitude, he decided, sitting down at his machine. *This is war.*

CHAPTER 84

The "personal use" SUV provided with the ambassador's residence was a nondescript, cream-colored Hyundai Tucson with Czech plates, which Heide Nagel occasionally used for private weekends to escape the city. Her most recent outing had been to Tisá Rocks Labyrinth in Bohemian Switzerland, a maze of hiking trails through breathtaking sandstone formations that were so otherworldly as to have made an appearance in the fantasy film *The Chronicles of Narnia*.

I wish I were there right now, Nagel thought, still feeling sickened over the death of Michael Harris.

As she pulled out of the residence, alone now in her SUV, she felt the weight of the treachery she was committing by helping these two Americans. She genuinely hoped Langdon knew what he was doing.

If this doesn't work, Finch will bury me . . . probably literally.

Nagel approached the security gate, and she tapped her horn twice. The Marine guard in the sentry booth jumped up from his bank of security monitors and hurried to the window, looking surprised. The ambassador seldom departed unannounced, seldom in her own vehicle, and she never beeped her horn.

"Sorry, Carlton," she said, lowering her window. "Just zipping back to the embassy. Forgot my Enbrel shot. Damn snow is wreaking havoc with my arthritis."

"Ma'am, I'd be happy to send—"

"Simpler to do it myself. Meds are locked in my desk drawer, and I have to grab some paperwork too. I'll be right back."

"Of course, ma'am." The guard pressed a button, and the

gate swung open. He turned back toward the security monitors that covered the grounds, but Nagel called him back.

"One more thing, Carlton," she said. "I'm sorry—I have two American guests waiting in the library, and I'm expecting another guest shortly, a Mr. Finch. I'll be back before he arrives, but if for some reason he beats me here, I've asked my staff to make him comfortable in the living room until I'm back to make introductions. I just wanted to be sure you know he's expected."

"I do *now*, ma'am," he said, smiling. "Thank you. I'll see you shortly."

Nagel thanked the Marine and prepared to pull forward, but as she planned, the gate timed out and began swinging closed again. "I'm sorry," she said, shaking her head. "Espresso always make me chatty!"

The guard smiled. "No worries, ma'am." He pressed the button to reopen the gate.

As she prepared to move through, she popped the clutch and stalled the Hyundai. "Oh my heavens, how embarrassing. I rarely drive anymore!" She restarted the car, but not before the gate closed a second time.

They repeated the process, and this time Nagel made it through. She pulled out onto Ronald Reagan Street and turned immediately left on Bubenečská, hoping her antics had kept the guard's eyes off the security feeds long enough for Langdon and Solomon, upon hearing the cue of her car horn, to hurry out of the conservatory and across the lawn to the far side of the grounds, where, if one could find the hidden latch, a wrought-iron pedestrian gate opened from the inside out onto Československé armády.

Sure enough, as she circled the property, Langdon and Solomon were visible on the street corner, both underdressed for the weather. The ambassador pulled up beside them, and they jumped into the vehicle, Katherine motioning for Langdon to sit in front beside Nagel.

As they accelerated away from the residence, no one said a word. All of them, it seemed, were starting to grasp the dangers of the plan that Langdon had proposed.

The fourth option.

"There's a good possibility," Langdon had told them minutes earlier in the basement boiler room, "that even if we take the meeting with Finch, and he believes we've signed those NDAs, he'll never share what's really happening at Threshold. There's only one way to be certain we have the information and the proof we'll need to protect ourselves—and that's documentation and photos." He paused, eyeing them both. "Somehow, we need to get *inside* Threshold."

"Impossible," Nagel said. "Searching Threshold is a non-starter."

"Why?" Solomon pressed. "You said the facility is unmanned right now, and everyone is training off-site. It would be deserted."

"That's true," Nagel replied. "But I haven't explained just how secure this installation is. Threshold's entrance is basically a reinforced tunnel protected by steel barricades, security cameras, armed guards, and sophisticated biometrics."

"As I would expect," Langdon said. "But I have a plan to get us in."

Now Ambassador Nagel found herself guiding her SUV farther away from the residence, setting a course for the south side of Prague. *No turning back*, she thought. *I'm officially an accomplice.*

Taking precautions that her unsanctioned departure would not be tracked by Finch, Nagel had left her diplomatic cell phone at the residence, connected to her home network. Instead, she had dug out her old personal Samsung, which she never powered up except to stream after-hours entertainment at home. *No need for the embassy to know I listen to Taylor Swift and watch reruns of* Ted Lasso.

The Samsung's battery had been dead but was now recharging on the dash. Nagel hoped it would charge fast enough to take photos of whatever was happening inside Threshold.

If Langdon truly can get us inside.

Langdon had yet to share the details of his plan, but the more Nagel thought of the impenetrable barrier that sealed the entrance, the less optimistic she was feeling.

On the snow-dusted tarmac at Václav Havel Airport, Mr. Finch's Citation taxied toward the private terminal, where a Town Car was waiting to take him into Prague. Finch was glad to be on the ground, and yet he could not shake the nagging sense that something about his call with the ambassador had been . . . *off.*

He and Nagel had always had bad blood, but something about her manner on the phone earlier had left him feeling unsettled. He decided to give her another quick call, if only to ease his mind and reconfirm that she had indeed sent a Marine detail to secure Crucifix Bastion.

When he called her cell, however, the ambassador didn't answer. *Odd.* He immediately sent her a secure message, but this communiqué went unanswered as well.

As the sleek jet rolled to a stop and the engines powered down, Mr. Finch felt the knot in his gut tighten further.

On the lower floor of Crucifix Bastion, The Golĕm pulled his hood tightly over his clay-caked skull and mentally prepared for what lay ahead. He had returned to the cluttered workroom in which he had killed Brigita Gessner last night, and her pale corpse still lay bloodied and grim in the open EPR pod. Gessner and her assistant were the only two people who worked here, and so far, the embassy and local authorities had no means of access.

On a worktable nearby, The Golĕm saw Gessner's leather briefcase, which he had pried open last night with a flathead screwdriver, extracting the black RFID key card that she kept protected in a special sheath inside the lid.

But the card had not been enough; Gessner had withheld that detail last night.

To access Threshold, The Golĕm required one final item.

Pulling a pair of heavy wire cutters from the full rack of tools, he walked to the EPR pod and knelt beside Gessner's corpse.

"For Sasha," he whispered as he gently took the doctor's lifeless hand in his.

Sixty seconds later, The Golĕm was back to the hallway, preparing to leave the bastion. He now carried with him everything he would need to gain access to Threshold . . . and reduce the secret facility to a pit of rubble.

CHAPTER 85

Katherine Solomon had spent much of her morning hiding alone in the darkness of the Klementinum's Baroque Library, trying to figure out who was targeting her manuscript—and *why*. Now, seated comfortably in the backseat of Nagel's SUV, Katherine found her thoughts shifting to a far more immediate question.

How can Robert possibly get us inside Threshold . . . without getting us killed?

They had all agreed with Langdon's proposed goal—to get inside the actual facility and gather classified information to protect themselves—but according to Nagel, the bomb shelter entrance was a heavily barricaded driveway that descended to a checkpoint with video surveillance, armed army personnel, and biometric security.

Katherine was beginning to wonder if maybe this had all been a clever bluff by Robert to escape the ambassador's residence. *But if that's true . . . now what?*

"Before we go any farther," Nagel said, slowing to a stop on the side of a quiet street in her residential neighborhood, "I need to know your plan for entering the facility." She put the car in park and turned to face Langdon in the front seat.

"Fair enough," Langdon said. "It should actually be quite simple." He paused, an uneasy smile parting his lips. "Provided my logic is sound."

Nagel was not smiling. "Go on."

For the next sixty seconds, Langdon outlined exactly how and why he believed he could get them access to Threshold. When he was finished, the inquisitive look on Nagel's face had turned to one of shock, matching Katherine's own feelings of surprise. Langdon's explanation was, in his own particular fashion, utterly unexpected . . . perfectly logical . . . and surprisingly simple.

"I don't know what I thought you were going to say," Nagel said, "but it was not *that*." She sounded suddenly hopeful. "I must admit, the thought had never occurred to me."

Langdon nodded. "I imagine they hope it never occurs to anyone."

Nagel put the SUV into gear and pulled out, driving faster now, heading southward toward the river. Nobody said another word.

In the backseat, Katherine felt rising anticipation to think she might finally learn how her work could be a threat to a classified CIA project. *What in the world are they doing at Threshold that relates to my manuscript?*

The code name Threshold sounded generic and nondescript, revealing nothing about the nature of the CIA project. This was apparently standard practice, Katherine concluded, running through a list of declassified CIA code names mentioned by the press from time to time: Bluebook, Artichoke, Mongoose, Phoenix, Stargate . . .

In that moment, Katherine felt an unexpected connection emerge. "Psychotronics," she declared.

Nagel glanced over her shoulder. "I'm sorry?"

Langdon turned, looking equally puzzled.

"Psychotronics," she repeated. "It's the term the Russians used for their early research into paranormal phenomena—mind reading, ESP, thought control, altered states of consciousness. Psychotronics is considered the precursor to modern noetic science."

"Ah yes, I'd forgotten the name," Nagel said. "Russia invested a billion dollars in psychotronics during the Cold War—the world's first 'neuro-military' initiative—mind control, psycho-surveillance, brain-related tactics, that sort of thing. The CIA, of course, found out about the program, panicked, jumped on board, and initiated our own series of highly classified, neuro-military research programs."

"And one of those projects," Katherine said, "was called Stargate."

"It was," Nagel replied, revving the SUV to make the light at a bustling six-way intersection. "But as you probably know, Stargate was a fiasco—one of the agency's most humiliating public failures. When Stargate was discovered, the agency was mercilessly mocked for spending millions on pseudoscience, parlor tricks, and attempts to train 'magical ghost spies.' In the end, it turned out the CIA had been baited by Russian disinformation and tricked into chasing our tail on fringe science that was never going to work."

Not exactly fringe, Katherine bristled, but she held her tongue. Despite its failures and embarrassing history, Stargate's attempts to explore paranormal brain phenomena fell under what scientists would now term metaphysics or parapsychology.

"Why did you mention Stargate?" Langdon asked. "Did you write about it in your manuscript?"

"No," Katherine said. "But it occurs to me that Stargate was one of the very first attempts to test the possibility of nonlocal consciousness."

"Oh?" Langdon turned, looking surprised. "So the CIA did work in nonlocal consciousness?"

"In a sense, yes," Katherine said. "Stargate tried to develop a never-before-imagined surveillance technique called 'remote viewing.' It consists of a 'viewer' sitting in a quiet location, meditating until he falls into a trance, and then projecting his consciousness out of his body . . . freeing it from its local bonds . . . and letting it materialize effortlessly anywhere in the world so the consciousness can 'view' what is happening in remote locations."

Langdon arched an eyebrow, looking extremely skeptical.

Thanks, Robert, she thought, considering remote viewing essentially *defined* her theory of nonlocal consciousness. *A mind unrestrained by locality.*

"The ultimate goal of Stargate," Nagel added, "from a military perspective, was to train a psychic spy whose consciousness could hover inside the Kremlin, observe a meeting, private conversation, or military strategy session, and then 'return' home to report what had transpired."

"Hard to imagine it didn't work," Langdon said sarcastically.

Katherine leaned forward in her seat, speaking forcefully now. "For the record, Robert, *you* wrote about remote viewing and nonlocal consciousness long before I did."

"What? I've never written about eith—"

"You called them 'astral projection' and 'untethered KA.'"

Langdon hesitated, cocking his head. "Oh . . . *Spiritual Architecture*? You read that book?"

"Well, you *sent* it to me . . ."

The practice of astral projection, Langdon had written, dated back to ancient Egypt, where pyramids included carefully angled shafts to enable the pharaoh's soul, or Ka, to move in and out to the stars. The word "Ka," Langdon had noted in his book, was often mistranslated as "soul," when in fact it meant "vehicle" . . . a way of transporting consciousness to other locations. The wisdom the pharaohs acquired on their soul's journey to the stars was possible only because of their understanding of untethered Ka . . . in other words, nonlocal consciousness. The notion of an "eternal, incorporeal soul," Langdon wrote, was a universal constant across all religions.

He's always talking about nonlocal consciousness. He just doesn't realize it.

"Okay," Langdon said, looking chagrined, "but I write about historical *beliefs*—not hard science. Just because a culture *believes* something is true . . . that doesn't make it a scientific fact. I'm just saying I find it hard to imagine that remote viewing is scientifically possible."

Normally Katherine appreciated Langdon's skepticism because it challenged her, but today she felt he wasn't opening his mind far enough to see a truth that was obvious to her. The father of American psychology, William James, had famously said: *In order to disprove the assertion that all crows are black, one white crow is sufficient.* As Katherine described in her manuscript, an entire *flock* of white crows had now been flushed out . . . by noetic science, by quantum physics, and by the work of an impressive cadre of academics who were vocal advocates of nonlocal consciousness.

Respected minds like Harold Puthoff, Russell Targ, Edwin May, Dean Radin, Brenda Dunne, Robert Morris, Julia Mossbridge, Robert Jahn, and many others had made astounding findings in diverse fields like plasma physics, nonlinear mathematics, and consciousness anthropology, all of which supported the notion of nonlocal consciousness. Their popular books bore titles like *Limitless Mind*, *Remote Perceptions*, *The Seventh Sense*, *Anomalous Cognition*, and *Real Magic*.

Katherine had not heard about any of these other titles getting pushback from the CIA. And why would they? The notion of "mind separated from body" was not nearly as exotic as most imagined. The millions of people who practiced meditation were in fact already flirting with the peripheries of this world, focusing their minds until their physical bodies seemed to evaporate and they perceived themselves as only mind—a consciousness no longer located inside the body.

From there, a small percentage of skilled meditators achieved "projection," a state in which consciousness was perceived as moving *away* from one's physical location. This was the same detached sensation described by many epileptics and survivors of near-death experiences.

The closest Katherine had ever come to projecting was the occasional "lucid dream"—a bizarre experience wherein she "woke up" inside her dream, realized she was dreaming, and was able to do whatever she wanted within her dream. *The ultimate virtual playground.* An accessible bridge between consciousness and fantasy, lucid dreaming offered a unique window into the manipulation of one's own subjective reality. Not surprisingly, lucid dreaming had become a multimillion-dollar industry of "lucidity"—dream instruction manuals, sleep goggles, and even galantamine drug cocktails designed to help dreamers "Go Lucid!"

Katherine knew lucid dreaming had been recognized across

various cultures for centuries, but it wasn't until the 1970s that scientific methods, notably by psychophysiologist Stephen La-Berge, had empirically validated its existence. LaBerge demonstrated that lucid dreamers, while sleeping, could communicate their "conscious awareness" to researchers by performing a series of pre-agreed eye movements . . . all while the dreamer's mind was having an experience far from his sleeping body.

Waking up within a dream was a learnable skill for those who were interested, but for those who were not, there was still good news. Katherine believed that *everyone* would have at least one out-of-body experience in their lifetime.

The moment of death.

The data overwhelmingly suggested that death was accompanied by a transition through a conscious out-of-body experience, usually perceived as your mind detached from your body, hovering over your own physical form on an operating table, accident site, deathbed . . . observing those who were attempting to revive you or say their tearful goodbyes. Thousands of revived patients had stunned surgeons by recounting precise actions and conversations taking place in the hospital while they were clinically dead and even had their eyes taped shut for surgery.

There was still no consensus on what caused these out-of-body visions.

Fortuitous hallucinations caused by hypoxia? Evidence of the soul leaving the body? A fleeting glimpse into our next existence?

The true nature of death, Katherine knew, was the secret we all yearned to understand . . . across every culture, every generation, and every era. Unlike most of life's unknowable mysteries, however, *this* was a secret that was guaranteed to be unveiled to every one of us . . . yet only at the end.

Our last moments of life . . . become our first moments of truth.

CHAPTER 86

Ambassador Nagel was carefully navigating the hairpin turn on Chotkova when her personal cell phone chirped on the charger beside her. For a moment, she imagined the unfamiliar sound must be some kind of alert to inform her the phone was no longer completely dead.

But the phone kept chirping. Nagel glanced down, startled to see an incoming call—her first ever on this phone, whose ringtone was apparently set to "cricket."

Nobody knows this line even exists . . .

Nonetheless, her caller ID showed a familiar name—SERGEANT SCOTT KERBLE—the lead officer on her Marine security guard detail. Nagel trusted Kerble with her life, but she was surprised that he had this number. Seeing no option but to answer, she took the call.

"Scott?"

"Madam Ambassador!" the guard exclaimed, sounding relieved. "I apologize for using your private line. I tried all your other numbers, but—"

"It's fine—I just wasn't aware anyone knew about this phone. Is there a problem?"

"Your residence informs me," the Marine said, "that you're coming to the embassy for some medication. What's your ETA?"

Nagel slumped over the wheel. *Dammit.* "Actually, Scott, it's not a convenient time. Is something wrong?" She could see the entrance to Mánesův Bridge fast approaching ahead of them.

"I'm waiting for you at the embassy, ma'am, with an item that I believe you need—"

"Wait, I thought you were with Dana overseeing the recovery of Mr. Harris!"

"I was, ma'am, but I left Dana in charge so I could return to the embassy and give you . . ." Kerble hesitated, sounding uncharacteristically hesitant. "Ma'am, when I entered the flat, there was a sealed envelope lying on Mr. Harris's body."

Nagel was caught off guard. "I'm sorry? An envelope?"

"Yes, ma'am. By all appearances, it was left there by the person who killed Mr. Harris."

For God's sake. "What's inside?"

"I haven't opened it. I decided to remove it discreetly and bring it to you at once." Kerble paused again, lowering his voice. "The envelope is addressed specifically . . . to *you*."

"Me?!" Nagel let the phone drop in her lap, grabbed the wheel with two hands, and spun it left, veering off the road only moments before she would have entered the bridge. The SUV lurched to a stop on the shoulder of Klárov just beyond the Winged Lion Memorial.

Nagel picked up the phone again. "Scott, give me a second here."

Langdon and Katherine looked understandably alarmed, and Nagel signaled to them that she needed a moment. She killed the engine, exited the vehicle, and walked toward the riverbank with the phone pressed to her ear.

"Tell me," Nagel snapped, more angrily than intended, "why the *hell* would Michael Harris's killer leave an envelope addressed to me?!"

"I don't know, but it was clearly meant to be found and delivered. The envelope is marked 'Private and Personal.'"

A gust of wind coming off the Vltava sent a chill to Nagel's core as she struggled to understand the worsening situation.

"Ma'am?" Kerble pressed. "I am fully aware you left the residence unaccompanied. In light of this letter, I'm going to have to ask you to come in immediately."

Nagel was half tempted to tell the Marine to open the letter and tell her what it said, but she knew he would decline. Rightly so. She was on a cell phone, and God only knew the contents of the letter. She could hear the concern in Sergeant Kerble's voice and had no doubt that if she didn't come in immediately, he would be forced to direct the entire Marine security detail to try to locate her.

Nagel glanced back at the SUV. Langdon and Katherine had both climbed out and were watching her with concern. Kerble's voice was in her ear again.

"Ma'am?" the Marine pressed. "I can hear you're outside. Did you slip out to do some errands?"

Sergeant Kerble's question about "errands" was an indication that—as the kids liked to say—"shit just got serious." The reference was a rehearsed distress call in case she was in trouble. All she had to do was say, "Yes, I'm out doing errands," and all hell would break loose.

"Scott," she said. "You know I don't do errands. Bring the letter to my office. I'll be there in ten minutes."

"Thank you, ma'am." The Marine sounded relieved.

Nagel hung up and headed back toward the SUV. Letenská Street was nearby, an eight-minute walk to the embassy. She obviously couldn't take Langdon and Katherine anywhere near there.

"What just happened?" Langdon asked as she arrived.

"When it rains, it pours," Nagel said, telling them about the envelope. "I have no idea what it says, but if I'm not back in the embassy in ten minutes, my entire security detail will be scouring Prague—and they don't play games." She handed Langdon her car keys. "You'll be safer without me."

"Any news on Sasha?"

"No, he would have mentioned it. I'll ask my tech officer to run a facial recognition sweep of city surveillance."

"And the phone?" Katherine said, motioning to the old Samsung in her hand. "For photos?"

Nagel sighed. "Clearly, it's compromised. I don't know if it's trackable, but you shouldn't risk it. It occurs to me anyway that if you take photos, the CIA will simply claim they're AI fakes. You'll be much better off finding documents and hard evidence if you can."

"Okay," Langdon said. "There's one other problem. I promised Jonas Faukman I'd phone him after getting away from your residence. If he doesn't hear from me, he'll be contacting Prague authorities shortly. I was waiting to call him until your phone was charged, but now that we know it's compromised . . ."

"What's your editor's direct number?" Nagel asked, reaching into the SUV for a pen and scrap of paper. "I'll call him from the embassy's secure line. Or I can email a—"

"He won't believe you," Langdon said. "He knows you're CIA. He'll want to hear from me directly."

Damn, she thought. *He's right.*

"Actually . . ." Langdon's brow furrowed as he schemed a moment. "Give me that." He took the pen and paper and began writing. "Here's Faukman's email address." The professor paused, closing his eyes for a long moment, as if composing a message in his mind. "Okay, send him *this*." Langdon quickly wrote out a strange-looking message and handed it to her.

Nagel eyed the nonsensical text. "What *is* this?"

"Just send it," Langdon replied. "He'll understand."

CHAPTER 87

S tick shifts should be outlawed," Langdon grumbled, struggling with the SUV's manual transmission as the vehicle jerked gracelessly southward toward Folimanka Park.

"Or perhaps just the men who pretend to drive them?" Katherine offered.

Langdon had to smile, grateful for her levity amid all the tension. His mind had been elsewhere, thinking about the ambassador's abrupt departure. Nagel had put herself at enormous professional risk for them, which Langdon appreciated. But his primary concern was for their safety . . . and figuring out why Katherine's book was in the crosshairs of the CIA.

Those answers lie inside Threshold.

With luck, his optimistic gut feeling about gaining access to the hidden facility would not turn out to be delusional overconfidence.

We'll know in a matter of minutes.

Katherine's suspicions that Stargate had something to do with their predicament, meanwhile, seemed unlikely to Langdon. He didn't know too much about the discredited program, but he did know that even Hollywood had enjoyed a laugh at the CIA's expense, releasing a George Clooney picture sardonically titled *The Men Who Stare at Goats.* It was based on an alleged Stargate experiment in which subjects tried to kill goats by staring at them.

Despite Langdon's skepticism about remote viewing, the basic concept was more than seven thousand years old. The ancient Sumerians had written about mystical "star journeys"—

out-of-body experiences in which their minds traveled to the stars to view distant worlds.

Of course, there was a lot of opium involved, Langdon knew, wondering if maybe Threshold might be exploring drug-induced altered states . . . perhaps even relating them to non-local consciousness.

Katherine had mentioned earlier a new class of drugs known as *dissociatives,* which apparently were accompanied by a sense of being *disconnected* from one's body. And certainly the CIA had a long history of running secret drug experiments.

Including on the Harvard campus . . .

One of the most notorious CIA projects ever to reach the public eye had been code-named MKULTRA, which secretly administered LSD to unsuspecting college students to study the effect of the drug on young minds. Eerily, one of the test subjects had been Harvard undergrad Ted Kaczynski—who later became known as the Unabomber—and while the CIA testified that Kaczynski had never been given drugs, they did admit subjecting him to "experimental interrogation techniques," which quite possibly could have destabilized his mind.

The Harvard drug lore did not stop there. Concurrently with MKULTRA, faculty psychologist Timothy Leary launched the infamous Harvard Psilocybin Project, which encouraged students to explore the mind-expanding benefits of hallucinogens: *Turn on; tune in; drop out.* Many now suspected that Leary might have been working undercover with the CIA.

"I'm curious," Langdon said, turning to Katherine, who was staring out the window. "In your book . . . did you write about chemically induced altered states?"

"Of course," she said, "as I mentioned earlier, certain hallucinogens will decrease GABA levels in the brain, thereby lowering the brain's filtering mechanism. This implies, in my opinion, that the out-of-body sensations associated with hallucinogens are a reflection of unfiltered *reality,* rather than hallucination."

It made sense, and there was certainly historical precedent for drugs as a road to enlightenment. From the ancient texts of *The Rigveda* and *Eleusinian Mysteries* to Huxley's 1954 classic *The*

Doors of Perception, great writers had long been suggesting psychedelic substances were a way to expand human consciousness and perceive "reality unfiltered."

"I've never asked you, Katherine," Langdon ventured casually, "does your consciousness research involve doing drugs *yourself*?"

She turned and stared at him, looking amused he would even ask the question. "Robert, *really*?! The brain is an *incredibly* delicate mechanism, and trying to alter it with hallucinogens is like trying to adjust a priceless Rolex wristwatch with a sledgehammer! Drugs induce altered states by creating a jarring chain reaction of neurological disruptions that can have *permanent* effects. As enlightening as you may find that brief experience, you risk undermining long-term synaptic integrity and neurotransmitter equilibrium. For most hallucinogens, the primary mechanism through which they exert their effects is the dysregulation of serotonin—a very bad idea—as it can easily lead to cognitive deficits, emotional instability, and even enduring psychotic states."

Langdon nodded with a smile. "I'll take that as a no."

"Sorry," she said sheepishly. "I have colleagues who experiment responsibly with various psychedelics, and there's certainly a place for that. I just get nervous when young people assume it's *all* safe. It's not."

Langdon downshifted as smoothly as possible to avoid colliding with a tram.

"I assume you were asking," Katherine said, "because you think *drugs* might have something to do with Threshold?"

"It seems like a possibility," Langdon said. "You mentioned in your talk last night a host of new drugs that seem to increase psychic ability. If you consider the countless documented cases of crimes being solved by psychics, it's not a big leap to imagine the CIA trying to develop drugs to enhance psychic ability. The applications would be endless."

"I suppose . . ." she said. "But it's not exactly a cutting-edge idea."

True, the CIA would be a bit late to that party. The Oracle of

Delphi had regularly seen visions of the future while breath-ing gases escaping through a fissure in Mount Parnassus; the Aztecs spoke to future spirits while tripping on peyote; and the Egyptians saw tomorrow's events while consuming mandrake and blue lotus. Our modern "pioneers"—names like Castaneda, Burroughs, McKenna, Huxley, Leary—were actually following centuries of souls who had attempted to expand their minds with chemicals.

"I really don't think Threshold is related to drugs," Kather-ine said. "There's very little about them in my manuscript."

"So what's your best guess?" Langdon asked, guiding the SUV southward along the river toward Folimanka Park.

Katherine leaned her head back against the headrest. "I'd say their concern lies with my experiments in *precognition*."

Langdon recalled Katherine's precognition tests—a subject's brain reacting to an image *before* actually visually "seeing" it. The randomly selected image, as if by magic, appeared in the subject's consciousness before the computer had even selected *which* image to show.

"To be honest," he said, "I'm not sure I even understand your precognition experiment. If the brain registers the image *before* the computer has even chosen the image . . . then it's as if your *brain* is making the choice . . . and then *telling* the computer which image to choose."

"Consciousnesses creating reality. That is one possibility, yes."

"Is that what *you* believe?"

"Not exactly. In my model, your brain is not *making* the choice . . . but rather *receiving* the choice."

Langdon glanced over. "Receiving the choice . . . from where?"

"From the field of consciousness that surrounds you. Even though you *feel* like you're actively making choices yourself, in fact, those choices have been made already and are streaming into your brain."

"That's where you lose me . . . If I'm only *imagining* I'm mak-ing my choices, then there's no free will!"

"True. But maybe free will is overrated."

"How can you possibly—"

Katherine leaned over toward the driver's seat and kissed him on the lips. Then she sat back and smiled. "I have no idea *where* that decision came from . . . but does it really matter? Isn't the *illusion* of free will enough?"

Langdon considered it a moment and placed a hand on her thigh. "I believe more research is required."

She laughed. "Craving an out-of-body experience, Professor?"

"Actually, I think I'd prefer to stay *in* my body for that particular activity."

"Don't be so sure," she said. "As it turns out, *sex* is very closely related to the noetic view of out-of-body experiences."

Langdon groaned. "Does *everything* with you relate to work?"

"In this case, it does. As you know, during sexual climax, the mind experiences a blissful moment of oblivion in which the entire corporeal world evaporates. Climax is considered in every culture to be the most intensely pleasurable experience a person could have, a blank-slate detachment from oneself, a momentary abandonment of all concern, pain, and fear. Do you know what the French call it?"

"*Oui,*" he said. "*La petite mort.*"

"Yes—the little *death.* That's because the self-detachment felt at orgasm is precisely the same feeling described by people who have had near-death experiences."

"That's morbidly fascinating."

"It's brain science, Robert. Of course, the problem with sexual climax is that it's frustratingly fleeting. Within seconds of being ecstatically released from all things, your mind rushes back into your body, reconnecting with the physical realm and all its attendant pains, stresses, and guilts." She smiled. "Which is another reason we want to do it over and over. The experience of climax *overloads* the nervous system . . . and releases the mind. Much like an epileptic seizure."

Langdon had never associated orgasms with death or seizures, and he suspected the connection would forevermore resurface in his mind at the most inappropriate moments. *Thanks a million.*

"Actually . . ." Katherine said, cocking her head. "I just had a strange thought."

You seem to have a lot of those . . .

"Gessner's lab assistant," she said, glancing over. "You said this young woman is an epileptic? And she spent time in an institution?"

"She did."

Katherine's brow furrowed. "Don't you find it odd that the CIA would permit Gessner to hire an unskilled *Russian* mental patient? I mean I know Sasha only works in Crucifix Bastion in a menial capacity, but it seems like a security risk to have a Russian with brain problems so close to Gessner's work . . . which I gather is critical somehow to Threshold."

"I don't see a risk," Langdon countered. "Sasha seemed quite stable, and she's certainly no fan of her home country. I think Gessner probably hired her out of compassion."

Katherine laughed out loud. "Robert, you're adorable. Naive but adorable. Brigita Gessner—no disrespect for the dead—was a self-serving egomaniac and a ruthless businesswoman. If she hired an uneducated Russian mental patient for her inner circle, it's because Sasha has something Gessner *needs*."

"Well, then I have no idea what that is."

"I might," Katherine said, sounding suddenly more energized. Her eyes were alight. "It just occurred to me, and it's something I wrote about in my manuscript."

"What is it?"

"I know you're deeply skeptical about remote viewing," she said, turning fully toward him now, "but if Threshold has anything at all to do with remote viewing . . . then Sasha's *epilepsy* makes her valuable."

"How?"

"Think about it! The fundamental skill possessed by a remote viewer is the ability to conjure an out-of-body-experience. The challenge is that organic OBEs are exceedingly rare, and very few people can actually *have* them."

Langdon suddenly realized where Katherine was headed with this. Epileptic seizures were described as a peaceful "untethering" from the physical body—in effect, a brief period of nonlocal consciousness.

"Out-of-body experiences," Katherine continued, "are something *epileptics* experience quite naturally. The epileptic brain is already wired for OBEs . . . meaning an epileptic would be far more likely to be a skilled remote viewer."

"You can't really believe Sasha Vesna is a psychic spy for the CIA . . ."

"Why not?"

"Because I spent time with her. She has a Krazy Kitten key ring! She's a lost, gentle soul."

"Gentle?!" Katherine challenged. "You said she smashed a guy in the head with a fire extinguisher!"

"Technically that's true . . . but it was to protect—"

"Robert, I'll admit maybe Sasha is not a remote viewer *herself*, but Gessner could have been studying epileptic brains to find out what makes them so prone to out-of-body experiences. Tapping into detailed neurological information about an epileptic brain could be incredibly valuable for a program trying to *detach* mind and body."

An interesting idea, Langdon thought, particularly in light of something Sasha had shared earlier today. "I forgot to mention that Gessner brought *another* epilepsy patient to Prague from that same institution—before Sasha—a Russian named Dmitri. He received the same surgery as Sasha and was also cured."

"I would say that's significant," Katherine said. "It's hard to believe that Brigita Gessner was plucking epileptics from mental hospitals and curing them at her own expense, purely out of goodwill."

Langdon had to agree it seemed out of character. Moreover, he now realized that a test subject taken from *Russia*—probably with the help of the CIA—would be entirely off the radar in Europe. *A ghost in Prague.*

"Let's assume for a moment," Katherine said, "that Gessner recruited these epileptics as study subjects for Threshold. That would explain why she was keeping Sasha around."

"To monitor her."

"Yes. Give her a minor job, an apartment, some money. Easy."

"I suppose . . ."

"And Dmitri?" Katherine asked as they neared Folimanka Park. "Where is he now—still in Prague?"

"Sasha said he went home to Russia after Gessner cured him."

"I doubt it. Maybe that's what Gessner told Sasha, but if the CIA pulled a test subject from an institution, invested in him, made him a research subject in a top secret program . . . would they really just let him go home? To *Russia*?"

Good point, Langdon thought, accelerating along the stretch of road before them. He craned his neck slightly to look farther down the street.

With luck we'll have our answers soon.

The entrance to Threshold was just ahead.

CHAPTER 88

Outside the U.S. embassy, Sergeant Kerble stood on the sidewalk, freezing in his dress blues as he scanned the street for an approaching vehicle. When he finally spotted the ambassador, he was startled to see her only ten yards away.

She's on foot?! Alone?!

"I know, Scott, I'm sorry," she said, arriving and rushing past him. "I just needed some air."

"Where's your vehicle?!"

"Everything's fine. Really. Follow me."

Kerble had been Ambassador Nagel's lead security detail for two years now, and he had never known her to be careless or difficult—or erratic. The death of Michael Harris had clearly shaken her deeply.

After climbing the stairs to the ambassador's office, Kerble waited as Nagel dumped her coat, grabbed a bottle of water, and then, to his surprise, began typing on her computer, meticulously consulting a paper she had extracted from her coat pocket. Finally, the computer swooshed with an outbound email.

Your attaché is dead, and you're sending an email?

"Okay, Scott," she said, turning her full attention to him. "I trust the envelope's clean?"

"Full scan," he assured her, having already run it through the embassy's safety protocol for incoming mail. "No foreign substances." He extracted the envelope from his breast pocket and laid it in front of her.

Nagel picked it up. "A basket of kittens?"

"Ma'am?"

"The killer wrote to me on *kitten* stationery?!" She pointed to the logo of a basket of kittens on the envelope.

"Yes, ma'am. He took the stationery from Ms. Vesna's apartment. She seems to like cats."

Nagel grabbed her letter opener and carefully ran the blade under the envelope's seam. Then she pulled out a sheet of matching stationery, which had been folded once.

Sergeant Kerble couldn't see what the letter said, nor could he read the ambassador's reaction, but the message was apparently short.

Moments after laying eyes on the letter, she laid it facedown on her desk and walked to the window. After ten full seconds of silence, she turned and faced Kerble.

"Thank you. I'm going to need some privacy."

CHAPTER 89

The entrance to the Folimanka Shelter's "renovation project" was precisely where Ambassador Nagel had said it would be—discreetly situated in an industrial section of the city, bordered by commuter train tracks, a busy street, and the southwestern corner of Folimanka Park.

Surrounded by a metal fence, the small triangle of land on which the entrance sat was known as Ostrčilovo Square. The triangular "square" had served many purposes over the years—a failed playground, a makeshift skate park, and, most recently, a recycling drop-off center. For the past few years, however, it had served as the Army Corps of Engineers' staging ground for a "refurbishment" of Folimanka's failing 1950s bomb shelter.

Katherine felt rising nerves as Langdon drove alongside the high barricade—a solid, eight-foot wall on which signage warned:

VSTUP ZAKÁZÁN / ZUTRITT VERBOTEN /
ENTRY FORBIDDEN

At the end of the wall, Langdon turned left and drove slowly along the second leg of the triangle, where a large informational placard had been erected with diagrams and text outlining what was happening within the walls:

PROJEKT OBNOVY PARKU FOLIMANKA /
FOLIMANKA PARK RECOVERY PROJECT

A fortified access gate along the wall was closed, with only a small section of the gate panel affording a view of what lay beyond. Two soldiers in black fatigues were patrolling a freshly paved access road that descended into a wide, arched tunnel that disappeared beneath Folimanka Park. The mouth of the tunnel was blocked by retractable steel bollards.

"That's some robust security for a *restoration* project," Langdon said, craning his neck as they drove by.

A secret government project . . . hiding in plain sight.

Katherine stole a final glance at the entry tunnel as they passed it. Other than the nondescript guards outside the entrance, she saw no trucks, no personnel, nothing. It seemed the ambassador might have been correct that Threshold was currently inactive.

Langdon turned left and drove along the third and final leg of the enclosure, which ran parallel with the western edge of Folimanka Park.

Here we go, Katherine thought, still marveling at the remarkable entry plan that Langdon had outlined earlier. His plan was rooted in a single, startling idea.

Threshold has a secret entrance.

Using an irrefutable chain of logic, Langdon had convinced the ambassador that the "construction entrance" on the western tip of Folimanka Park, which would serve as the main entrance when the project was complete, was not the only way in.

Threshold had a second access point . . . ingeniously disguised.

More importantly, Langdon had determined exactly where it was located . . . as well as how to get in.

<hr>

The Golĕm stood alone in a chamber unlike any he had ever seen or imagined. Having followed the detailed directions he had forced Gessner to provide last night, his journey had finally delivered him to this surreal place.

Threshold.

Gessner had confessed all the details . . . and yet seeing it in person now left him disoriented, almost nauseous.

They built this room with Sasha's blood.

Sasha had not been the project's first victim . . . nor would she have been its last.

And for that reason, Threshold will end today.

The Golĕm's long road to this moment of retribution had taken a severe toll, and he could feel deep emotion welling up within him. He could also feel a faint but unmistakable tingling within his body—an advance warning.

A hazy fog began to settle in the room.

The Ether was gathering.

"Ne seychas," he whispered. *Not now.*

Instinctively, The Golĕm slid his hand into his cloak pocket to retrieve his metal wand.

CHAPTER 90

Jonas Faukman scowled at ChatGPT's latest search results.

Despite using varied prompts and approaches, his efforts to find any link between Katherine's work and In-Q-Tel's investments had turned up nothing but far-flung offerings that felt more like a disjointed game of Mad Libs than anything intelligent—artificial or otherwise.

Frustrated, he abandoned his computer and walked to the window, gazing north up Broadway toward Central Park. In the dawn light, on the horizon line behind the "pencil towers" on Billionaires' Row, storm clouds were gathering.

He stood a while, lost in thought, and finally returned to his computer to continue his search. As he took his seat, he noticed he had a new email.

The subject line startled and excited him.

A MESSAGE FROM ROBERT LANGDON

Faukman had been waiting over an hour for a phone call and was feeling increasingly anxious that something had gone wrong at the ambassador's residence. The relief he felt seeing the email, however, was short-lived. Despite the subject line, Faukman now saw that the sender's address was that of U.S. Ambassador Heide Nagel . . . the former CIA general counsel.

She's sending a message for him?

Faukman could think of nobody in Prague he trusted less at the moment. If Robert was truly safe, then the ambassador should simply have let him call.

Until I hear Robert's voice, I won't believe a word of this email.

He debated whether to open the message, envisioning a virus or yet another hack, but at this point he figured he had nothing left to lose. Warily, he clicked open the message, puzzled to see what appeared to be a meaningless string of letters.

ROT13EY&XFETHQ

It took him a moment to realize that the first five characters did *indeed* have meaning. *ROT13* was the name of a rotational cipher in which every letter was substituted for the letter occurring *thirteen* places away from it in the alphabet. Faukman knew this only because several years ago, while editing a book on ancient encryption techniques, the book's author had regularly sent him texts playfully encrypted with ROT13.

That author had been Robert Langdon.

With a swell of optimism, Faukman grabbed a pencil and applied the simple decryption scheme. Then he examined the result.

RL&KSRGUD

His confusion lasted only a moment before he laughed out loud, half from amusement and half from relief.

Only Robert could have written this message.

Langdon and Faukman often commiserated over the decline of written language due to the proliferation of "textese" emoticons and abbreviations. The trend was so distressing to Faukman that he'd written a piece about it for *The New Yorker*, including one particularly overwrought sentence that Langdon mocked mercilessly.

Faukman had written: *To save a single keystroke by typing "gud" instead of "good" is not only indecorous, it is an abomination of indolence.*

Still chuckling over Langdon's message, Faukman was tempted to reply: *Your message is not only adroit, it brings propitious consolation.*

CHAPTER 91

L angdon pulled the SUV to a stop and set the emergency brake. He gathered himself before climbing out of the vehicle with Katherine, well aware that he would know momentarily if his plan would lead them to success—or disaster.

The wind on the high ridge had picked up, rustling through the woods beneath them. Langdon paused a moment. He gazed down at the snow-covered expanse that lay beyond the trees—Folimanka Park—which stretched eastward away from the ridgeline. *This entire place feels different now,* he thought, turning his attention to the building before them.

Crucifix Bastion looked ghostly. The structure stood as a stark silhouette against the darkening afternoon sky. As he strode with Katherine toward the main entrance, Langdon felt a shadow of uncertainty, and he quickly reminded himself what had led him back here.

Rational logic.

The truth had dawned on him at the abandoned swimming pool in the ambassadorial residence. The ambassador had torn up the NDAs, called Finch on speakerphone, and convincingly lied that Finch's wishes had been carried out. Then, to Langdon's surprise, Finch had ordered Nagel to send a Marine security detail up to Crucifix Bastion to secure the perimeter. *Finch's priority is to secure an isolated Czech lab? Why?*

As Langdon considered it, a second thought occurred. Earlier today, Janáček had told Langdon that Prague's surveillance system could not confirm that Katherine had arrived at the bastion, because—much to the captain's chagrin—the all-seeing camera system appeared to be hampered by an unprecedented blind spot that blacked out the area around Gessner's lab.

Prague's camera system is the Echelon surveillance network . . . run by the CIA.

Now the wheels were turning, and Langdon found himself questioning the statistical improbability of Gessner's private lab being perched on a ridge directly overlooking Threshold—the secret project that employed her.

Unless they're somehow connected . . .

The rationale for hiding a covert intelligence facility beneath Folimanka Park made sense to Langdon—natural camouflage, access to supplies, existing infrastructure—and yet he was having trouble accepting that Threshold was built with a sole access point . . . only *one* way in or out. The design would be a death trap in a fire or emergency, which seemed an incongruous risk for an agency built on strategy, contingency, and planning ahead.

Even the Vatican has secret escape routes!

It was then that the ambassador revealed an unexpected twist: The entity that had quietly acquired the bastion on behalf of Gessner was none other than Q. The investment firm had offered Gessner the building as part of the neuroscientist's recruitment package to the CIA, luring her in with the irresistible cachet of running her institute from such a unique and historic location.

That's not the real reason, Langdon surmised, sharing his growing suspicion that Finch had secured the bastion *not* as enticement for Gessner . . . but rather as something far more valuable.

Another access for Threshold.

Most medieval bastions included a unique architectural feature known as a *poterne*. From the Latin "posterior"—a *poterne* was a literal "back door"—a secret passageway used for emergency escapes.

The ancient Estonian bastion in Tallinn, he told them, had a *poterne* carved four stories underground that stretched more than a mile away to the basement of a nearby monastery. The Slovenian mountaintop castle Predjama was rumored to have a six-story vertical shaft with a rudimentary pulley system "elevator" for restocking supplies, livestock, and troops.

Crucifix Bastion, Langdon thought, was likely to have a *poterne* too. And considering the recent construction in Folimanka Park and the vast scope of the Threshold project, it made logical sense that a vertical shaft might exist beneath the bastion.

Earlier, in the SUV, Langdon had quickly shown Katherine and Nagel on a map that a modern-day *poterne*—whether it existed previously or was drilled recently by construction crews—would descend directly to the edges of Folimanka Park and could potentially extend to the walls of the existing bomb shelter.

The location of the bastion could not have been more perfect. Remote and discreet, Gessner's lab offered a flawless cover story—plausible deniability for any personnel who came and went: they were simply working at the Gessner Institute.

Let's hope I'm right, Langdon now thought as he guided Katherine toward the bastion's shattered entrance.

———·—

This is a science lab?

Katherine Solomon could scarcely believe her eyes as she followed Langdon down the luxurious, pink marble hallway into a lavish atrium with sumptuous couches, striking art, and floor-to-ceiling windows looking out at the skyline of Prague.

Maybe I should work for the CIA, she thought, estimating that Gessner's "waiting room" could have housed the entire IONS staff.

Even so, Katherine felt a foreboding air about this space. If Langdon's suspicions were correct, then this opulent "Gessner Institute" was actually camouflaging a darker purpose—a secret entrance to Threshold.

Langdon strode to the far end of the space and went immediately to a ponderous wall sculpture made of welded metal blocks, stopping only inches away from it.

What in the world is he doing?

To Katherine's surprise, Langdon grabbed the sculpture, heaved it to one side, and the sculpture slid silently along the wall to reveal a large alcove behind it. In the dim light beyond, she could see an elevator door.

Why am I not surprised? she mused, hurrying across the room toward Langdon, who was holding the sliding artwork aside for her. As she arrived beside him, however, she noticed Langdon was staring at something behind her.

"What is it?" she asked, glancing back over her shoulder.

"That couch on the far wall . . . it's cockeyed."

Katherine eyed the couch. *Seriously, Robert?* One edge of the long white couch was pulled at a slight angle away from the wall.

"It was straight this morning when I sat on it," he said, still staring at the couch. "I don't know if I missed that, or if it was moved, or—"

"Or if you forgot your OCD meds?"

Langdon returned his attention to her. "Sorry," he said, shaking it off. "Eidetic memories can be distracting."

"Apparently," she said with a smile. "Shall we correct this feng shui emergency, or shall we try to find this facility and save our lives?"

"Right." Langdon guided her into the dimly lit alcove.

Inside, Katherine spotted an illuminated touch pad next to the elevator door.

"This keypad is for Brigita's use only," Langdon said. "It's the way she would access her private lab one floor below us."

"But you think there's a separate entrance to Threshold hidden somewhere *here*?" Katherine asked.

"Yes, in fact, I think it's right in front of us." He motioned to the elevator. "If I'm correct, this elevator shaft goes much deeper—but to descend all the way to Threshold, you'd need an RFID key card like we saw in Gessner's briefcase."

He pointed to a sleek, round pad of black glass mounted on the wall just above the keypad. Katherine hadn't seen it.

An RFID reader.

"I noticed the reader this morning, but when we were at the ambassador's residence, I realized what it was. It dawned on me why Gessner might have two authorization methods for the same elevator. If I'm right, then all we need is the key card from her briefcase, which I saw earlier in her lab downstairs."

Langdon was already typing a passcode into the keypad.

"So you really *solved* the code?" Katherine asked. "An Arabic tribute to an ancient Greek . . . with a lemon twist?"

"*Latin* twist," he corrected with a smile. "You were drunk."

He finished typing the passcode, and the elevator whirred to life.

Impressive, Katherine thought. *He can explain it to me later.*

The elevator seemed to take a long time to arrive, but when it did, Katherine noted that the compartment itself was oversized, surprisingly large for Gessner's private use.

Perhaps more suited to carrying personnel and equipment.

So far, Langdon's logic seemed sound.

They stepped inside and descended a single floor.

When the elevator opened, Katherine was looking down a long hallway with rock walls, polished inlaid floors, and modern spot lighting. It gave the impression that the Old and New Worlds had come to some kind of awkward compromise.

As they exited the lift, Langdon pointed out another RFID reader on the wall, and Katherine nodded in acknowledgment. They began walking. She was not eager to see the macabre scene ahead—which Langdon had described to her in detail—but she was feeling increasingly confident that Langdon's theory might be correct. If so, the plan was simple: as soon as they had Gessner's access card, they would descend to Threshold.

They progressed down the hall, passing a small office suite for Gessner and Sasha, an MRI imaging lab, and a door with an icon of someone in VR goggles.

Her virtual reality lab, Katherine thought, recalling Gessner mentioning VR last night at dinner. At the time, Katherine had not given it much thought, but now, after the conversation about Sasha's epilepsy and out-of-body experiences, she wondered if virtual reality might be relevant in a unique way. *Like an artificial out-of-body experience . . .*

"Brigita's briefcase . . ." Langdon said, his voice halting. "Is in the room at the end of the hall. Along with . . . her body."

Katherine glanced at Langdon, who looked suddenly pale. "Are you okay?"

He gave a grim nod. "Thanks. I'd just rather not see her corpse again. This morning, when I first saw it, I thought it was *you*."

Katherine wrapped an arm around his waist as they walked, recalling her own harrowing fears earlier that Langdon had drowned. She had witnessed a lot of death in her research, but it was always peaceful, anticipated, and clinically detached. This was something different—violent and disturbing.

"I try to think of a body as an empty shell," Katherine said. "Not a person anymore. A lifeless mannequin."

"Thanks, I'll keep that in mind," he replied, looking no less apprehensive.

"If you think about it, as a species we tend to be entirely irrational about corpses. Even with no trace of our loved one left in the body, we embalm, dress, and entomb it, and then make regular visits! Many of us even purchase luxurious, cushioned caskets to ensure a body will be 'comfortable.'"

Langdon managed a weak smile. "I would venture that the practice is more for the living than the dead."

"Yes, but in reality, the documentation of near-death experiences clearly shows that humans who die are *relieved* to abandon their aged, injured, or sick bodies. According to all accounts, the deceased care as much about what happens to their corpses after death as they do about what happens to the old cars they used to drive. Not at all."

———·—➤

I love a woman who can explain life and death with a used car analogy, Langdon thought as they reached the cluttered workroom where he had discovered Gessner's body in the EPR pod earlier today.

"Maybe wait here?" he suggested, hoping to spare Katherine the blow of seeing the corpse. "I'll be right back."

Leaving Katherine in the doorway, Langdon hurried inside, intentionally averting his eyes from the pod and heading instead for the worktable at the far side of the room.

Gessner's leather briefcase, as expected, was sitting exactly where he had seen it earlier. He had assumed the case was probably locked and would require force to open, but when he arrived and examined it, he found something totally unexpected.

The case's latches were already pried open . . . its lock shattered.

Oh no . . .

Langdon seized the case and yanked open the lid, finding all the items from last night—documents, folders, phone, pens. The entire contents appeared to be intact . . . except for the one item they required. Gessner's RFID key card was no longer in its protective sheath. Panicked, Langdon dug his finger into the sheath, hoping the card had slipped down, but there was nothing there. After dumping out the case and rummaging through the contents twice, he accepted the devastating truth.

Our access to Threshold is gone.

"It doesn't matter," Katherine said somberly, her voice closer than expected.

Langdon turned and saw that Katherine was no longer in the doorway. She had entered the room and was crouched beside the EPR pod, gazing down at Gessner's body.

"Brigita's key card wouldn't have helped us," Katherine whispered, raising her eyes to him. "It was *biometric.*"

"I'm sorry?" Langdon moved toward her.

"Her card doesn't work unless it detects her fingerprint."

"Why do you say that?"

Katherine pointed to an object lying on the floor near the pod—a pair of wire cutters whose blades were smeared with blood. "Because whoever took Brigita's card . . . took her thumb too."

CHAPTER 92

Alone in her office, the ambassador gazed down at the note that had been left on Michael Harris's body.

TO: U.S. Ambassador Heide Nagel
Private and Personal

The letter was handwritten, unsigned, and contained only two lines. Nagel had read it several times now, disoriented by its contents. She had fully expected the killer's letter would be dark and threatening, and she had braced herself. But the note was short and oddly restrained. Almost polite.

Please help Sasha.
https://youtu.be/pnAFQtzAwMM

That's it? He wants me to help Sasha?

Puzzled, the ambassador reached for her computer keyboard and began typing the URL the killer had sent. Had the file been on a USB or attached to an email, Nagel would have known better than to open it on an embassy machine, but a public link was safe enough.

When the YouTube window opened, Nagel saw what appeared to be an amateur video made from a cell phone propped beside some kind of long, low-slung container that reminded her of the hard-shell "transport caskets" used by the military to fly bodies home. The body inside *this* container, however, was very much alive, struggling against the Velcro straps that restrained her. The woman was petite, stylishly dressed, with pale skin and dark hair pulled back tightly.

My God . . . Dr. Brigita Gessner, the ambassador knew at once, recoiling as she remembered Langdon's description of finding Gessner's corpse. She suddenly feared she was about to witness Gessner's final moments of life. *Is this a snuff film?!*

The question was answered a moment later as Gessner's attacker moved into frame. The hooded figure was cloaked in black, and as his face came into view, Nagel physically backed away from the screen. The man had a thick layer of earthen clay covering his face, and on his forehead were etched three Hebrew letters.

Nagel was quite familiar with the history of Prague, and she had no doubt what this was. *He's dressed as the golem?* With growing horror, she watched what came next—a brutal inter-rogation involving IV lines and some kind of medical process Nagel had never seen before. The pain inflicted was appalling, but the information revealed—Gessner's detailed confession—left Nagel reeling.

As the video reached its grisly conclusion, Ambassador Nagel closed her eyes. She breathed deeply, struggling to absorb all she had just learned. There were many aspects of Gessner's confes-sion that Nagel didn't understand, but one thing was alarmingly clear. The classified project Nagel had blindly helped facilitate was now in danger of being made public, and the fallout would be catastrophic. What she had just heard about the program sickened her, and she could only imagine how the rest of the world would react.

Fearfully, Nagel reached for her phone.

The time had come to make a very dangerous call.

A call I should have made years ago.

———··—➤

Submerged, somewhere in an endless void of blackness, Sasha Vesna strained to get her bearings. This world was foreign to her.

Where am I?!

Sasha was no stranger to disorientation and feeling detached from her body, but those periods were always accompanied by complete darkness. No light, no shadows, no visual stimulus at all.

But I see light . . .

Definitely light. Dim, soft, distant.

Who brought me here?

In her groggy state, she could recall nothing of how she had come to this place. She could feel she was lying on her back, and she tried to sit up, but she felt pinned by an immovable weight.

Am I restrained? Or paralyzed?

With rising panic, Sasha struggled to locate herself . . . but the effort only fatigued her, and the light began to fade. An undertow was already churning beneath her, eroding the physical world that constrained her. Then, with an overwhelming force, the tide rose up, cresting over her like a wave, and plunged her back into total darkness.

CHAPTER 93

Deep down within Threshold, The Golĕm felt like a ghost of himself.

His body was still in shock.

Literally.

Minutes ago, having reached the most innermost chamber of this subterranean facility, he had been overwhelmed with emotion. He felt a familiar tingling in his temple. The Ether was gathering . . . moving in quickly . . . threatening to swallow him whole. Instinctively, The Golĕm had slid his hand into his cloak pocket to retrieve his metal wand, but he realized in a moment of distress that the wand was missing. He emptied his pockets on the floor, sorting through all the items that fell out.

The wand is gone . . . I lost it while struggling with the woman upstairs.

The Golĕm knew he was now at the mercy of his condition, with no choice but to accept the impending seizure. He prepared as best he could, taking hasty precautions, finding a safe place to lie down to prevent a fall.

The convulsions had hit him hard, knocking him unconscious.

———•••———

When The Golĕm regained his senses, he was unsure how much time had passed. He needed several minutes to get his bearings.

Finally mustering his strength, he stood to his full height and again took in the astonishing space around him. To engineer something like this in total secrecy seemed an almost impossible feat, and yet he now understood who was behind it all.

They possess nearly unlimited influence—and resources.

Reassimilating, The Golĕm shook off his postictal haze and returned to the spot where he had emptied his cloak pockets in search of the wand. Crouching on all fours, he collected the items one by one, returning them to his pocket—the Vipertek stun gun and a plastic box he had taken from a nearby work surface, which had once contained nuts and bolts, but now contained Brigita Gessner's black RFID key card . . . and her severed thumb.

My access to Threshold.

As anticipated, Brigita's thumbprint had immediately authorized the card whenever he pressed them together.

And led me to this inner sanctum.

Gessner had admitted the existence of this room, and now that The Golĕm had seen it for himself, he felt invigorated by the need to destroy it. More determined now, he moved to the deepest reaches of the chamber, passed through a glass door, and found what he was looking for—a niche cordoned off by a safety gate.

Beyond the gate, the floor was a metal platform, stenciled with the words:

SYSTEMS / UTILITIES

The Golĕm stepped onto the platform and, using the toe of his boot, depressed an oversized red button on the floor. A soft hiss of air escaped somewhere beneath him, and the platform began to drop, lowering him through the floor.

The descent was short—maybe twelve feet.

As the platform came to a stop, fluorescent lights flickered on to reveal a low-ceilinged passageway that extended back the way he had come, beneath the heart of the facility.

As The Golĕm moved along the cramped concrete tunnel, he passed mechanical vaults of generators, pumps, air handlers, and control panels, plus miles of copper tubing, ductwork, and heavily insulated wiring. It was all connected like a gurgling, breathing, blinking ecosystem.

Despite the absence of employees at Threshold, the heartbeat of this facility was very much alive.

For only a short while longer, The Golĕm told himself, pressing toward his final destination.

CHAPTER 94

Katherine stood over the EPR pod and stared down at the bloody nub of bone where Brigita's right thumb had been snipped off just beneath the joint. For a moment, all thoughts of entering Threshold dissolved . . . overwritten by the horror of the scene before her.

Oh, Brigita . . . I'm so sorry.

The grisliness of the severed thumb barely registered against the macabre backdrop of the surrounding scene. Inside the pod, the neuroscientist's face was contorted in agony, her eyes staring into nothingness, her lips pulled back in a grimace. Her skin was drained of all color. Gessner's wrists and ankles were chafed from struggling against the Velcro straps, and both forearms had been penetrated crudely with IV catheters. One catheter had erupted from the flesh, covering her forearm with congealed blood, which had already turned a dark crimson.

A peripheral IV? Katherine thought. *No wonder the IV failed.*

Gessner had described this prototype EPR device as a "modified bypass machine," which she used to swap out supercooled saline for blood in order to slow the dying process. That kind of bypass would require, at the very least, a pair of femoral IVs.

This is definitely not *how you connect an ECMO.*

Surveying the setup, Katherine concluded that whoever had done this to Brigita either had been wholly incompetent, or, possibly, had known this process would kill her and had opted for a slow application of cold saline to inflict pain. Katherine shuddered imagining the agony Gessner must have endured if she had not been previously sedated. Moreover, this machine looked like a crude, jerry-rigged prototype . . . definitely not ready for human testing.

When Langdon arrived beside her, Katherine was startled to see a smartphone in his hand. "Is that *Brigita's*?" she asked.

He nodded. "It's still on, but almost dead. Her elevator passcode didn't unlock it, but . . ." He crouched down beside the pod, looking grim as he held the phone out over Brigita's face. "I wonder if facial recognition can distinguish between living and—"

The phone chimed.

Langdon stood up and began swiping through the phone.

"Wait, what are you doing?!" Katherine asked.

"The ambassador needs to know we failed," he said quietly. "My plan to enter Threshold hinged on that card being—"

"Give the phone to me!" Katherine exclaimed, holding out her hand. "I have an idea . . ."

———··———

Langdon watched as Katherine quickly scrolled through Gessner's device. *What is she looking for?*

"Brigita is smart . . . and efficient," Katherine muttered to herself, swiping through screens. "It *has* to be here!"

"*What* has to be there?"

"An NFC clone . . ."

"I don't know—"

"Near-field communication," Katherine clarified, still scrolling. "It's the technology that lets you wave your smartphone or watch at an RFID scanner for touchless interaction—Apple Pay, hotel room doors, airport ticketing."

Katherine kept swiping. "Most people install *clones* of their credit cards in their e-wallets now because carrying a phone is so much more convenient than carrying all your cards."

She had a point, but Langdon strongly doubted she would find what she was looking for. "You don't really think Brigita loaded a copy of her Threshold card into her *phone*, do you? I mean . . . it's a huge security risk."

"On the contrary," Katherine said without glancing up from her search. "Digital clones are much safer than physical cards because the interaction is encrypted, and the user can program *multi*factor biometric authentication—facial recognition, fingerprint, retinal scan, whatever you like, along with a passcode. It's actually far more protection than a biometric card. And better yet, nobody sees you taking your card in and out of your briefcase every time you reach a doorway."

Interesting point.

Katherine's explanation brought a glimmer of hope, and yet the longer she swiped, the less hopeful she looked.

"I don't know," she said, frowning at the screen. "Her e-wallet has a lot of cards, but nothing that looks helpful. I see credit . . . debit . . . rewards . . . ID . . . garage access . . . mass transit . . . health club . . . insurance . . . airline loyalty—"

"Health club," Langdon interrupted.

Katherine glanced up.

"Remember last night?!" he pressed. "When I asked Brigita about the black card with the Vel spear? She said it was her *health club*. It seemed like a lie . . . so maybe that's how she disguises it?"

Katherine returned to the screen and tapped that entry. A moment later, a faint smile appeared on her lips. "This might look familiar," she said, handing him the phone.

The image of the cloned card was unmistakable.

Langdon felt a rush of excitement that was immediately quashed by the text beneath the card.

THREE-FACTOR AUTHENTICATION REQUIRED

1) PASSCODE

"The only passcode I know is her elevator code," he said, "which didn't work to unlock the phone."

"But it might work *here*," Katherine urged. "This card provides access to Threshold—just like the elevator did—so it might be logical for her to use the same sequence."

Gessner is nothing if not efficient, Langdon agreed, carefully typing the code.

314S159

The phone pinged cheerfully and advanced to the next screen.

"Nicely done!" Langdon exclaimed. The second authentication was far simpler.

2) FACIAL ID

Once again, Langdon held the phone to Brigita's face, and the device pinged, displaying the final screen.

3) FINGER SCAN

Langdon glanced down at Brigita's mangled hand and hesitated. Katherine stepped in, gently taking the phone from him. Seemingly unfazed by touching the body, Katherine manipulated Gessner's index finger onto the phone.

When the phone pinged for a third and final time, Langdon assumed they could now use the phone to take the elevator to Threshold. Katherine, however, was unsmiling as she studied the screen.

"Bad news," she groaned. "It's got another safety feature." She held up the phone. "Authentication lasts only ten seconds."

On-screen, Langdon watched a descending countdown clock tick down to zero. The card deactivated and returned to its initial password screen, requiring the entire three-step authorization process all over again.

Damn.

"And her battery is about to die," Katherine added. "Literally any minute."

Think, Robert. He had seen no charger in Gessner's briefcase, and he was now feeling a deepening weight of guilt for having convinced Katherine and the ambassador to risk everything on his plan.

For a moment, Langdon wondered if they could remove Gessner's IVs, lift her body out of the pod, and somehow transport her to the elevator. *There's no time.* Moreover, removing the dead body and further tainting a crime scene would only incriminate them further.

"We've got to find a way into Threshold, Robert . . . We're so close!"

Katherine's comment, of course, was figurative . . . and yet, for some reason, her words registered literally. *We're so close.*

How close exactly? he wondered, picturing the long, inlaid hallway outside this room . . . and the elevator and RFID reader at the far end. *Ten seconds close?*

Usain Bolt had set a world record by running one hundred meters in 9.58 seconds.

The hallway must be less than half that . . . forty yards at most.

Katherine returned, shaking her head, and Langdon immediately told her his plan.

"*Sprint?*" she challenged. "I don't see—"

"Ten seconds is longer than it seems," he said.

"I know you run often, Robert, but in loafers on polished wood floors?"

"It's worth a shot," Langdon argued. "I think I can make it."

Katherine checked the phone's battery, eyes widening. "Then you'd better make it on your first try."

She immediately began the three-step authorization as Langdon positioned himself beside her, hand extended as if prepared to receive a baton. When the phone pinged for the third time, Katherine slapped it into his palm, and he instantly took off across the room, clutching the phone tightly. As he reached the door, he grabbed the frame and slingshotted himself around the corner, launching into a full sprint down the hall, his loafers finding tentative traction on the smooth wood.

Langdon flew past the bathroom, VR lab, imaging lab, and then the offices, now spotting the black circle of the RFID reader on the wall beside the elevator.

Twenty more yards . . .

Faster!

As he neared the elevator, he held the phone out in front of him . . . and saw the display counting down.

Three . . . two . . .

I'm not going to make it.

◄—··—►

Katherine rounded the corner into the hallway just as Langdon crashed at full speed into the elevator door and slammed the phone against the reader. He slumped over, lowering the device, putting his hand on his knees as he caught his breath.

He didn't reach it in time . . .

But as she moved toward him, Langdon's huddled frame suddenly transformed into a silhouette as the elevator doors slid open, and light poured out from the interior.

"You did it!" she called, rushing down the hallway to Langdon, who was holding the elevator door open, still panting.

"Okay, Professor," she said. "I'm impressed."

"Glad it worked . . . A second attempt would have been impossible."

"Is the phone dead?"

"No . . . *I* am."

She smiled and kissed him on the cheek as they boarded the elevator together. The door slid shut. For a long moment, nothing happened.

And then Katherine felt it . . . that momentary lightness in her physical body.

They were *descending*.

CHAPTER 95

In a dank corner of his basement, CIA Director Gregory Judd was sweating profusely. Six minutes remained to finish his morning workout on the Airdyne stationary bike he'd owned since his early days as a senator. His wife, Muffy, had placed a new Peloton in the sunroom for him, but Judd preferred darkness and solitude. Mornings were his private time to think—usually about how to stop the world from blowing up.

When the cell phone in his cup holder rang, he was surprised to see an unknown caller. Very few people had this number, and there were even fewer who would dare phone before dawn.

He stopped pedaling, caught his breath, and answered. "Yes?"

"Good morning, Director," said a woman's voice with an urgent edge. "This is Heide Nagel in Prague."

"Heide?" The call from his former senior counsel was entirely unexpected. "You're an ambassador now—call me Greg."

"Never going to happen, sir."

He smiled. "Okay then, how can I help you?" *And who gave you this number?*

"I need to ask you a direct question," she began. "And I would appreciate an honest answer."

Troubled by her agitated tone, Judd got off his bike. "Actually, I'm on a cell phone, and I can see you're not using a secure platform, so a landline would—"

"I explained to your overnight staff that I was a U.S. ambassador, and this was a national security emergency. This is the line they gave me."

"A security emergency? Heide, depending on what you would like to discuss, we can—"

"I should have asked you this over two years ago," she said. "But I'm asking you now." Before Judd could interject, Nagel said, "The classified documents I was accused of removing from Langley—are you aware that Q framed me? Are you aware I was set up as a puppet in Prague?"

Judd exhaled, no stranger to keeping calm in pressure-filled moments. He opted for the truth. "Yes, Heide, I am aware of that."

The silence that followed felt like a gathering storm.

"However," Judd added quickly, "I found out *after* the fact. At the time it happened, I had no idea. You were my top legal adviser, and I hated losing you."

"Finch did this behind your back?!"

"He had complete autonomy to carry out his duty as he saw fit," Judd said, pacing the basement. "I was furious when I found out, but you were already established in Prague, and there also were national security considerations in the region. Blowing it up seemed counterproductive. You know firsthand how valuable it is for the agency to have one of their own on the diplomatic side to help navigate the complexity of overseas intelligence work."

"Yes, I've been quite valuable to Finch and this project— flexing diplomatic muscle whenever asked—cutting through red tape, bypassing local law enforcement, eavesdropping on hotel rooms . . . coercing Michael Harris to surveil Sasha Vesna."

Shit. "I'd prefer not to use *names* on an open—"

"Do you know I forced Michael into that situation based on Finch's claim that Sasha was a *person of interest*. But he refused to tell me *why* she was of interest. Do *you* know, Greg?"

"That's enough. I'm hanging—"

"Does it have anything to do with the classified facility you're about to open beneath Folimanka Park?"

Director Judd stopped pacing and stood dead still. "Ambassador Nagel," he replied with as much calm as he could muster. "While I have no idea what you're talking about, I suggest you give me fifteen min—"

"I sent you a video link," she said, her voice like stone. "You'll get it at the office. And once you see it, you're going to do something for me."

"Am I really?" he challenged.

"Call me when you've watched the video. I think you'll find my demands reasonable."

"Your demands . . . And if I can't meet them?"

"You're the director of the CIA. There's little you can't do." *You'd be wise not to forget that.* "And if I *choose* not to?"

"Then this video will become public," she said flatly. "It contains detailed information about your project, and the content is exceptionally disturbing. You'll want to hurry. This is a public link, and someone will stumble across it eventually, probably within the next few hours."

Heide Nagel was in way over her depth. "Heide, you *do* know my people can simply delete—"

"I've downloaded the file and made copies. Plenty of them. They're in safe hands."

"Have you lost your mind?!" Judd demanded. "I understand your anger, but why would you *ever* threaten—"

"Because, *Greg,*" Nagel exploded, "I've been collateral damage long enough! I've been nothing but a loyal colleague, and I deserve some fucking loyalty coming *my* way for a change. So get off your ass and do the right thing, goddammit!"

Judd had never heard Nagel lose her cool, and frankly, it scared him. Heide Nagel was formidable. *And unhinged people make incredibly poor decisions.*

"I'll call you within the hour," Nagel snapped. "And if I disappear, believe me, you'll be seeing this video on every news feed on earth."

"Ambassador, I would suggest—"

She had already hung up.

◆—··—◆

Nagel rarely drank, especially midday, but the tumbler of Becherovka she had just poured from her office bar felt warranted. Her hands were still a bit unsteady as she slid in behind her computer and downloaded a copy of the video to her desktop. Just for safety, she downloaded a second copy, renamed it innocuously as "Recipes," and buried it deep in her hierarchy of folders.

Next she searched her desk drawers and found a lone USB stick—an old PowerPoint for a speech she'd given to the International Women's Association of Prague. After deleting the presentation, she copied Gessner's confession video onto the USB and placed the stick inside a letter-sized diplomatic pouch that bore the embassy seal.

She zipped the pouch shut and inserted the plastic security ring into the zipper, clamping it down until it locked permanently in place. Then she addressed the pouch's routing fields, conveying the pouch directly to . . . *herself.* In accordance with Article 27.3 of the Vienna Convention on Diplomatic Relations, anyone else who opened this pouch was committing a punishable crime.

As Nagel began searching her office for a safe place to store the sealed pouch, she realized there *was* no truly safe place in this office. She wanted to believe that Director Judd would make the right call, but if he decided to cross her, this office would be the first place he would target.

"Scott!" she shouted, carrying the pouch toward the door.

Her sentry was waiting outside and entered immediately.

"I need to entrust this to you," she said.

"Of course, ma'am," he said, eyeing her hands. "The pouch or the cocktail?"

She looked down. *Ugh.* "The pouch, Scott." She handed it to him. "Keep it safe. Mention it to no one. And I mean no one. Can I trust you with that?"

"Of course, ma'am." He slid the pouch into the breast pocket of his uniform and gave her a concerned look. "Is everything okay, ma'am?"

"Everything is fine, thank you. Mr. Harris's death has left me somewhat . . ." Her voice trailed off. "Is there any news from forensics?"

"Not yet, ma'am."

"Would you please contact Ms. Daněk and ask her to come back here at once."

"Of course, ma'am." The Marine hesitated. "Although . . . I should warn you that Ms. Daněk was extremely upset when we found Mr. Harris's body. It seems they were close."

Yes, Nagel thought, ashamed for having used their romance as leverage. "Thanks for alerting me. I have an urgent situation here that requires her skills." *I'm hoping she'll be professional.*

Sergeant Kerble departed, and Nagel returned to her desk. She took a long swallow from her drink. The letter from Harris's killer was staring up at her.

Please help Sasha.

I can't help her if I can't find her, Nagel thought, slipping the letter into her desk drawer. Fortunately, Prague had an unparalleled surveillance system. The challenge was not going to be finding Sasha—it would be persuading Dana Daněk to help with the task.

◆——·——◆

The Golĕm had traversed a cramped mechanical passageway that extended nearly a hundred meters, extending like an elongated spine beneath the core of Threshold. Having reached the end, he was now standing before an unusual portal.

The door was steel, oval in shape and windowless, with a heavy turn wheel for sealing and unsealing it. It resembled an airtight submarine hatch.

The sign read:

SMES

AUTHORIZED PERSONNEL ONLY

Last night, Gessner had revealed to him the surprising technology that was housed inside this unique chamber. The Golĕm's web research this morning had provided the rest of the information he needed, including confirmation of the scientific reason the machine was located in this precise spot.

Directly beneath a popular feature in Folimanka Park.

The structure above them was one of the lone visible remnants of the 1950s bomb shelter, and tourists regularly photographed themselves standing in the park beside it. None suspected, of course, what The Golĕm had recently learned—that the feature had been ingeniously repurposed to serve the needs of Threshold.

It is now a ventilation shaft for the sealed room behind this door.

The Golĕm took a moment to catch his breath before attempting to turn the wheel. Without his wand, he needed to be prudent; another seizure down here could be dangerous, especially surrounded by so many hard surfaces and sharp edges.

Once he felt centered, The Golĕm planted his feet, gripped the turn wheel, and heaved it counterclockwise. The wheel barely moved, rotating only a few centimeters.

He pictured Sasha's face, and her innocence gave him strength.

I do this for all who have been abused here. For you . . . for me . . . and for all those to come.

Gritting his teeth, he heaved the wheel again.

CHAPTER 96

As the elevator continued to drop deeper into the ridge beneath Crucifix Bastion, Robert Langdon found himself fighting a wave of anxiety. He had been so focused on the task of gaining access to the facility that he had not fully imagined the route he would need to take to get there.

I'm enclosed in a narrow shaft, surrounded by thousands of tons of rock.

He also had no idea what to expect when the elevator doors opened. The ambassador had told them Threshold was not yet up and running, and as such, she doubted they would encounter any security personnel once inside. But there was no way to know for sure.

Langdon also found himself considering the dilemma that had arisen several minutes earlier. *Someone took Gessner's access card . . . and removed her thumb.* Obviously, the grisly crime had been committed to gain access to Threshold, but the question was, when had this occurred? Had intruders come and gone hours earlier . . . or were they still in the facility? And if they were still here . . . how dangerous were they?

Katherine shifted her weight in the roomy elevator. "It's a long way down," she said in the silence, starting to look unnerved by the lengthy descent.

Langdon was trying hard not to think about it. "Phone is dead," he said absently, noticing the screen was now black. Katherine took the device from him and dropped it into her shoulder bag.

Finally, the elevator began to slow. They pressed into the

corner of the carriage, out of the sight line of the door, as the lift glided smoothly to a stop. Neither of them breathed.

The doors slid open.

Huddled in the corner, Langdon and Katherine waited for any sounds or signs of movement outside, but there were none. Langdon carefully leaned to one side and peered out.

The space outside was pitch-black.

Beyond the small fan of light spilling out of the elevator, Langdon could see nothing. He had never considered that because Threshold was not yet operational, there might not be power at the moment.

We're deep underground. No lights. No windows. We could be in a massive cave, for all we know.

He felt his heart rate climbing as he inched out of the lift, taking an uncertain step into the darkness. Before his foot had even touched the floor, a bank of floodlights blazed to life overhead, momentarily blinding him. He covered his eyes, hoping the lights had been activated automatically by a motion sensor . . . and not by an interrogation team or a firing squad.

Slowly, he lowered his hand, squinting at the scene before him.

As the image came into focus, he stared in disbelief.

You've got to be kidding . . .

They had clearly departed Crucifix Bastion. All the ancient, organic touches were now gone. The new world into which Langdon had just stepped was sleek, futuristic, and pure tech.

"Unbelievable," Katherine whispered, emerging behind him. "This looks expensive."

Langdon guessed the facility was probably funded through In-Q-Tel investments, outside the black budget, with no congressional oversight.

Katherine walked onto the narrow metal platform outside the elevator, marveling at her surroundings. "It's like . . . a tiny subway station."

Some kind of futuristic monorail, Langdon thought, peering down into the concrete channel beneath them, where a single narrow-gauge rail extended away from the platform into a circular tunnel and disappeared into darkness. The tunnel opening looked very tight, not nearly wide enough to handle a normal subway car, and yet when Langdon saw the vehicle that ran on this track, he realized the opening was plenty large enough.

The car was a long, slender, open-air deck—more of a movable platform than a car—with two long benches that faced each other on either side. At the back, there was a section that looked like it was for transporting supplies, which currently included two wheelchairs strapped into place.

Langdon was reminded that there was a similar underground system connecting buildings on Capitol Hill. Unlike the quaint, boxy tram cars in D.C., however, *this* system looked minimalist, sleek, and efficient.

"I'm glad it's at *this* end of the line," Katherine said, moving toward the car. "That seems like a good omen."

Langdon immediately grasped her meaning. If the transport was here, that meant that whoever had taken Brigita's card must have already been to Threshold and come back this way to exit. "Excellent point," he said, relaxing slightly. "Also, the motion-sensor lights were off, so it seems like we're alone."

Katherine stepped onto the deck, and Langdon joined her. As they boarded the transport, a low electric hum came to life beneath them, and the platform seemed to rise an inch or two.

Someone or something knows we're here, Langdon thought, hoping this train was fully automated . . . and not that someone was watching them and had just powered up the system.

"Maglev," Katherine said. "We've got one in California."

Like anyone who had played with magnets as a kid, Langdon was familiar with the repulsive effect that the same magnetic poles had on each other—a force strong enough, in this case, to levitate a platform and make it "hover" essentially friction-free.

"I don't see any controls," Katherine said. "I guess we just sit down?"

It was as good a guess as any, and Langdon took a seat beside her, both of them facing the right-hand side of the car. Within seconds, three low chimes echoed through the station, and the platform began moving forward, picking up speed.

With the exception of the electric hum, the motion was silent.

The rapid acceleration was startlingly smooth, and within seconds they were plunging into the opening of the tunnel, hurtling through the darkness in perfect silence except for the sound of air rushing past them.

The tram's headlight illuminated only a small portion of the single track directly in front of the car. In the darkness, it felt as if they had accelerated to an alarming speed, and it was hard to gauge how far they had traveled.

Suddenly, Katherine grabbed Langdon's arm and gasped, pointing down the tunnel ahead of them.

Langdon had just spotted it too. Dead ahead, on the one-lane track, a headlight was approaching—another transport hurtling toward them on a collision course.

Clearly, Langdon and Katherine were not supposed to have taken this tram.

"There's got to be an emergency brake!" Katherine shouted, turning in her seat and scanning their surroundings.

Langdon wheeled in desperation to either side, looking for anywhere they could leap off, but concrete walls enveloped them tightly on both sides.

The blinding headlight was racing toward them, now only seconds from a head-on collision. Langdon and Katherine grabbed hands and braced for impact, but suddenly their tram shifted smoothly to the left, while the oncoming tram shifted in the opposite direction, and the cars swooshed harmlessly past each other in a slightly wider section of tunnel. An instant later, their car shifted back to center, and the tunnel narrowed again to a single lane.

Langdon exhaled, his heart still crashing in his chest. "It's a passing loop," he said, voice shaky. "Computer-timed."

Katherine let out a deep sigh of relief and gave his hand a tight squeeze.

While the passing loop was an efficient way to avoid digging a two-lane tunnel, it had just brought Langdon closer to a near-death experience than he ever cared to be.

The tram sped on another ten seconds and then began decelerating again, gliding to a comfortable stop at an identical station, a deserted metal platform devoid of any signage. Once they stepped off, the electronic hum disappeared, and the transport dropped an inch or two back into its dormant position.

"A two-tram system," Katherine said, "which means we can't be sure that whoever entered before us . . . is already gone."

Langdon nodded. *There's* always *one car at either end.*

His best guess was that they were now somewhere beneath the northern edge of Folimanka Park, abutting the deepest reaches of the sprawling 1950s bomb shelter.

Rather than an elevator door, this platform had an archway opening with no door. Langdon and Katherine stepped through and found their path blocked by an imposing security checkpoint—X-ray conveyer belt, body scanner, more biometrics, two guard desks—all of which were currently unmanned.

This place will be a fortress when it's up and running, Langdon realized as they sidestepped through the body scanner and exited the checkpoint into a main hallway.

So far, Langdon had seen no signage anywhere to indicate this was a CIA facility. But as they arrived at a set of double glass doors, he saw a single word, in a small font, stenciled into the glass.

PRAGUE

Confirmation.

Langdon reached for the doors, but they swung open automatically, the hallway beyond immediately illuminating. The light in this hall was more of a soft glow than the blazing spotlights they had seen prior. Two strips of muted floor lighting ran along the base of the corridor walls, stretching away from them in two parallel lines, reminiscent of an airport runway.

The immaculate flooring was black terrazzo tile and resembled a strip of polished basalt. The walls here were silver metal, most likely a chrome veneer, and glistened in the baseboard lighting. The air carried the scent of fresh paint, concrete, and cleaning supplies.

Walking briskly, Langdon and Katherine headed down the corridor, their footsteps echoing off the hard interior. After about twenty yards, they paused at an intersection where a secondary hallway branched off to their right. Tiled in a pale green, this hallway was completely dark, and Langdon could see only a few office doors before everything was black.

A sign read: SUPPORT.

Langdon's gut told him that sorting through offices and files would be a waste of precious time. They needed hard evidence that showed what was going on in Threshold, and there was really only one way to do that.

We need to find the heart of the facility.

Conveniently, ahead of them on the black tile, Langdon saw a single word stenciled in bold letters: OPERATIONS.

As they moved down the long, straight hallway, floor lighting ahead continued to come on automatically. They came to an alcove, which contained an oversized metal door that bore a familiar symbol.

The caduceus? Langdon was surprised to find a medical symbol in a CIA facility, but there it was, prominently displayed. Iconographically, he knew this symbol was frequently misused, as it was here. The caduceus was actually the ancient symbol of Hermes, the Greek god of travel and commerce. The more accurate symbol would have been the Rod of Asclepius—the staff of the Greek god of healing—a similar icon with no wings and only a single snake, rather than the caduceus double snake. Embarrassingly, in 1902, the U.S. Army Medical Corps had mistakenly emblazoned the *caduceus* on their uniforms, and to this day the symbol was displayed in error by U.S. doctors and hospitals.

Katherine walked over and opened the door.

Langdon followed her through, into a suite of rooms that appeared to be a small hospital. A medical examination room was equipped with advanced diagnostic and imaging equipment.

A narrow supply closet contained shelves stocked high with unopened medical supplies. A private room contained two beds surrounded by more medical gear than Langdon had seen even in an intensive care unit.

Eerily, that room was marked RECOVERY.

Recovery from what?

As they pushed deeper into the suite, they came upon a small, ride-on forklift with a massive crate in its tongs. Katherine crouched down to read the labels on the crate. "NIRS," she said. "Near-infrared spectroscopy. Advanced real-time imaging."

"In a medical facility?" Langdon associated NIRS with astronomy.

"Neuroscientists use it to analyze brain activity by assessing oxygen saturation." Katherine stood, a look of concern in her eyes. "I don't understand . . . Why would the CIA build a secret hospital under Folimanka Park?"

Langdon was wondering the same thing as he walked over to a set of swinging doors and cautiously pushed them open a crack. There was only darkness within. He pushed a bit farther, and the lights inside blazed to life.

When he stepped through the doors, he found himself in a surgical scrub room. On the far wall, a plate-glass window offered a view of the adjoining chamber—a glistening white operating room. There, suspended ominously over a sleek surgical table, hung a device unlike anything Langdon had ever seen.

"I don't know what that machine is . . ." he whispered as Katherine arrived behind him. "But it looks terrifying."

CHAPTER 97

The traffic on Evropská was at a crawl, and Finch estimated another thirty minutes before he reached the ambassador's residence. He hoped Nagel was making Langdon and Solomon as comfortable as possible.

Offer them an afternoon cocktail, Finch thought. *Or two.*

Nagel had been an effective asset in Prague, and despite her bitterness over how she had been hired, she had carried out Finch's directives effectively and flexed her diplomatic muscle when necessary. Granted, she had pushed back on his order to use Michael Harris to get close to Sasha Vesna.

"Why monitor Sasha?" Nagel had asked him. "Do you think she's spying?"

"Sasha is not a spy," Finch assured Nagel truthfully. "Nor is she dangerous."

Sasha Vesna is far more valuable than a spy.

She is an investment . . . a work in progress . . . an unwitting CIA asset.

"She needs to be watched . . . simply as a precaution," he explained.

She remains entirely unaware . . .

Finch's phone chirped with an incoming Signal call, which he guessed was Housemore with an update from the bastion. When he checked the caller ID, however, Finch sat up straight, seeing it was his boss on the line.

"Greg," he answered calmly, skipping the formalities generally due a CIA director. "This is a surprise."

"It won't be a pleasant one," Judd fired back, apparently in no mood for small talk. "It's about Nagel. She *knows* you framed her for those documents."

"She's known that for a long time. As have you."

"Be that as it may, I'm still appalled by the way you recruited her."

Appalled? Really? Finch had no patience for the man's self-righteous commentary. The director had hired Finch to oversee Prague for one reason only—his track record of doing *whatever* was necessary to win a war, even if it meant circumventing policy.

"I intentionally left you out of the loop, Greg—for your own protection," Finch said. "To shield you from accountability." *You're welcome.*

"I appreciate that, but Nagel deserved better."

"Better than an ambassadorship? She's now a United States diplomat! And she's served us incredibly well in Prague. Win-win."

"Maybe not the win you think. She's threatening to go public with everything she knows about the project."

Finch was certain he had misheard. "What did you say?"

"You heard me."

"A threat to go public . . . That makes no sense."

"She's incredibly pissed off. And she has demands."

"But . . . she knows *nothing*!"

"She claims to have detailed proof. She sent some kind of video to me at Langley. I'm headed in shortly to see it."

"A video of *what*?!" Finch snapped. "Nagel is far too smart to cross the agency. I have no idea what she's playing at . . . but she's bluffing."

"I worked with her for years," Judd said. "She was the god-damned general counsel of the CIA—Nagel *does not* bluff."

Finch felt his stomach tighten uncomfortably. *Did the ambassador cross me?!* "What are her demands?"

"She hasn't made any yet."

Finch wondered if that was true.

"I'm speaking to her again shortly," Judd said. "But if there are security concerns you need to deal with, do it immediately. I don't need to remind you that it would be catastrophic if details of this project were to leak."

"I'm handling it personally. I've just arrived in Prag—" Finch winced, realizing he'd said too much.

Judd paused carefully. "If you are in Prague, then clearly you already *knew* there was an issue brewing."

Among other things, Gessner is missing. "Yes, a few small wrinkles last night, but everything is under control. I'm on my way now to tie up loose ends."

"You damn well better. Don't make me regret putting you in charge—this is one of the most important ventures this agency is running."

"You chose me, sir, because you know my capabilities."

"Yes . . . and on that topic," the director said, "a word of warning. If anything happens to Heide Nagel, *anything* at all, I will be sure you pay. For everything."

"I'm not the enemy," Finch said flippantly. "I'm on your side."

"Watch yourself," Judd said. "You don't want to test me."

The line clicked and went dead, and Finch sat in dazed silence as his vehicle raced toward Prague.

Finally, fuming, he called Ambassador Nagel.

The call went straight to voicemail without ringing once.

Has she turned off her phone?

Anxious, he dialed Housemore at Crucifix Bastion, and thankfully her line began to ring. After eight rings, however, it too went to voicemail as well. *What's going on?* Field Officer Housemore answered Finch's calls on the first ring, day or night . . . without fail. He tried her again. No answer.

Finch pocketed his phone and gazed out at the skyline for a long moment, thinking.

Then he made up his mind.

"Change of plans," he said to his driver. "Skip the residence. Take me to Crucifix Bastion."

CHAPTER 98

The machine dominating the center of the subterranean operating room looked like a futuristic torture device. Mounted on the ceiling directly above a lone surgical bed, four articulated robotic arms with pincerlike fingers protruded from an organized tangle of cables and wires. The mechanized claws appeared poised to attack whoever was unfortunate enough to be lying on the slablike bed below.

For Langdon, the most frightening feature of this contraption was not the robotic limbs but rather the bed's restraint system. A dozen or so heavy Velcro straps hung off the bed, clearly designed to bind arms, legs, and chest to render the patient incapable of the slightest movement. And further, arching over one end of the bed was a semicircular band of metal from which five thin rods protruded at different angles—cranial immobilization screws. Langdon shuddered. He could not imagine the terror of being bound here, skull screwed in place, with this mechanical monster hovering over one's face.

Claustrophobia on steroids.

"Unbelievable . . . they have a robotic-assisted brain surgeon," Katherine said. "You probably remember the first one invented was called the da Vinci."

Langdon vaguely recalled the news stories.

Katherine walked over to the skull clamp and examined the long screws radiating outward. "These remind me of my nightmare."

A spiked halo, Langdon thought, seeing the object in a new light.

"Control room is over here," Katherine said, walking over to a plate-glass window and peering through.

Langdon joined her and could see three ergometric chairs facing a series of flat-panel monitors equipped with LCD awnings for stereoscopic 3D viewing. They were accompanied by a perfectly aligned array of gleaming stainless-steel input devices—mouse, rollerball, e-stylus, editing shuttle, console, and joysticks. A tray marked HOLOGRAPHIC KINETICS contained a pair of mesh gloves.

"Amazing," Katherine said. "I knew robotic surgery was progressing, but this device looks years beyond anything I've ever even heard about."

Langdon wondered if maybe Gessner had designed it. *Another lucrative patent.* "So this is how she implants her epilepsy chips?"

"Heavens, no," Katherine said. "Placing an RLS chip is rudimentary—technically not even brain surgery. It's just placed in a thumb-sized hollow in the skull; there's no actual contact with the brain." She walked back to scrutinize the device mounted on the ceiling again, examining it from several angles. "No . . . this is a different universe. This is for *deep* brain work—removing complex tumors, cauterizing aneurysms, or . . . perhaps for extracting specialized delicate tissue samples for analysis." Katherine turned to him. "You said Sasha Vesna had scars on her skull. Substantial ones?"

Langdon nodded as he recalled holding Sasha's head during her seizure. "Mostly hidden beneath her hair, but yes. I assumed they were from injuries, but later she did mention that Gessner had encountered some minor complications implanting her chip; the surgery was successful . . . but also a little more invasive than planned."

"A *little*?" Katherine glanced back up at the robotic surgeon. "This machine is not pristine; it's been used before, and I hate to say this, but Sasha would be a perfect test subject. Naive, no family, unlikely to question the follow-up procedures recommended by a famous doctor who saved her life and is now paying her salary."

The thought seemed reprehensible to Langdon, but he forced himself to focus on the matter at hand. "Do you see *anything* here related to what you've written about?"

She shook her head. "Not yet. And there's nothing particularly incriminating here to take with us as proof of what they're even doing. All I can tell you is that they're doing some highly advanced, in-house brain surgery."

The Island of Dr. Moreau, Langdon thought, unsettled by the notion of the CIA performing secret surgeries in an underground lab on foreign soil. "Let's keep looking."

They quickly exited the medical suite, returning to the black-tiled corridor, continuing deeper into Threshold.

They reached another alcove that also contained a doorway, but this door was covered in a thick layer of acoustical foam.

"Immersive Computing," Katherine said, reading the placard beside the door. "This could be something."

Uncertain what to expect, Langdon followed Katherine into a chamber whose walls, ceiling, and floor appeared to be covered in black carpet. The only light came from the muted baseboard lighting that had faded on as they entered.

Running down the middle of the room was a row of eight, unusually deep, reclining chairs equipped with shoulder-strap seat belts. Each one sat atop its own tangle of hydraulic arms and valves. "They're on gimbals," Langdon said. "These chairs move."

Katherine nodded, moving toward them. "Immersive computing is essentially advanced virtual reality. The motion of these chairs is synchronized with the images and sound being fed into *these*." She lifted some kind of futuristic, opaque glass helmet off the chair. "Deep-spectrum panoramic displays. This is exceptionally advanced virtual reality, Robert."

Virtual reality? What would they be doing here?

Katherine headed for a computer workstation at the back of the room. "The data required to run these VR simulations is massive, and they no doubt run it off a larger system . . . like that one." She pointed at a plate-glass window with banks of computers behind it. "Although I suspect everything is accessed out here, at this terminal." Katherine sat down and turned on the computer.

Langdon joined her as they waited for the terminal to power up. "Did you mention VR in your manuscript?"

Katherine glanced up at him, nodding. "A few times, yes, but just anecdotally. I was once a subject in a VR experiment at Princeton Engineering Anomalies Research, and my experience played a role in my decision to study nonlocal consciousness. So I wrote about it."

"Really? That seems like it could be relevant."

"In principle, perhaps," she said, looking skeptical. "But not—"

"Tell me," Langdon said.

"Well . . . as you know, the goal of VR is essentially to trick the brain into *believing* an illusion. The more virtual input you can feed the mind—sights, sounds, motion—the more likely you are to convince the brain to accept an artificial situation as *real*. That moment you start *believing* the illusion is a state that psychologists call 'presence.'"

"I did some virtual rock climbing," Langdon said. "I was quite literally paralyzed with fear."

"Exactly. Your mind *believed* your body was on a cliff and in danger. The illusion became your temporary reality. I too experienced 'presence' in the VR experiment at Princeton, although . . . the experience was quite a bit different. Transformative, really."

"What was it?"

She glanced up from the computer and smiled. "Simply stated . . . I experienced my own consciousness—and it was nonlocal."

———·· ·———

Katherine would never forget that first magical encounter with "detachment from self." The experience had changed her life, cementing her passion for consciousness as a field of study.

The experiment began with her Princeton professor asking

Katherine to stand all alone in an empty room. Over the intercom, he instructed her to don her VR goggles. When she did, she was instantly transported to a vast meadow where she stood among flowers and trees.

The scene was bucolic . . . with one unexpected twist.

She was no longer alone.

Standing only two feet away was an exact double of . . . *herself.* The double was smiling calmly and gazing directly into Katherine's eyes. As Katherine looked upon her other *self*, she knew of course that it was a projection, and yet the sensation was disquieting. She stood for nearly a minute in the meadow, face-to-face with herself.

Next, the professor's voice on the intercom instructed Katherine to reach up and place a hand on the shoulder of her ghost double. This confused Katherine. *My double is not real.* Uncertain, Katherine raised her hand and lowered it gently toward the shoulder of her other self. Fully expecting to touch *nothing* but air, she was shocked when her hand came to rest on an *actual* physical shoulder. More shocking still, in that exact instant, Katherine *felt* the weight of her hand on her *own* shoulder!

The effect was completely disorienting, and her brain suddenly found itself asking:

Which body . . . is my real body?!

The sight of her hand resting on the *other's* shoulder, combined with the sensation of a hand on her *actual* shoulder, was enough sensory input to shift Katherine's sense of "physical self" to the other body. For several mystical seconds, her consciousness hovered *outside* herself. She was an observer, a disembodied mind gazing upon her own physical body . . . much as a near-death patient hovered over their own corpse.

In that moment, Katherine was imbued with a blissful sensation that her consciousness was free and did not require a physical form to exist. Even after she relocated her true *self*, the afterglow of the "untethering" remained for many days.

Despite its potent effect, Katherine learned the illusion had been fairly simple to create. After she had donned her VR goggles and stood in position, a lab tech had slipped silently into the room and stood directly in front of Katherine. When she reached up to place her hand on her "ghost self," Katherine unwittingly placed her hand on the shoulder of the lab tech, who simultaneously placed *her* hand on Katherine's shoulder. In that moment, Katherine's sense of self was coaxed to exit her physical body.

Obviously, this was not an *authentic* out-of-body experience, but the sensation was so peaceful, reassuring, and connected to the nonphysical world that it cemented her career fascination with the potential *nonlocality* of consciousness.

As Katherine finished her recap, the computer powered up to its welcome screen.

"Password protected," Katherine said. "I was afraid of that. Unless I know what kinds of simulations they're running, I can't begin to guess if this VR lab has anything to do with my book."

Langdon sat down on the desk's metal chair and made a handful of guesses. Nothing worked, and he finally shook his head, standing up again. "Maybe they're running out-of-body simulations? Like the one you just described? That kind of thing seems like it would relate to epilepsy and Sasha and remote view—"

"True, but . . ." Katherine studied the helmets and gimballed chairs. "My gut tells me this room is for . . . something *else.*"

Her gaze moved now to the plate-glass window and computer room beyond it. She went over and tried the metal door beside the window, but it was locked. Putting her face to the glass, Katherine surveyed the space beyond and saw a tall rack of computers, assorted containers of electronic gear, and a glass-paneled refrigerator full of colorful vials.

Then she recoiled, pulling away from the glass. "What in the world?"

Langdon came over. "What is it?!"

"*Those* . . ." Katherine pointed to the line of eight objects standing against the rear wall. "Those have *no* business in a VR lab."

Langdon peered in at the eight stainless-steel IV poles on wheels.

"IV stands," Katherine said, disturbed. "And a refrigerator

full of pharmaceuticals! This facility is *combining* intravenous drugs with virtual reality."

"Okay . . . and that's unusual?"

"Yes! Those types of dual-stimuli experiences can be very damaging to the brain. Overexposure can literally alter your brain's physiology . . ."

"Alter it . . . *how?*"

"It all depends on what drugs they're administering," Katherine said, squinting in at the glass-walled refrigerator, trying in vain to read the labels on the vials. "Robert, I need to get inside this room and see *specifically* what drugs they're using. Then we might be able to figure out what they're trying to accomplish . . ."

Langdon studied her a moment and then nodded. "Okay, stand back." He strode over to the desk and returned with the heavy metal chair, eyeing the window.

"Wait, are you—"

"We're already in over our heads," he said. "A broken window isn't going to change anything."

With that, Langdon torqued his body, swinging the chair around himself like a hammer throw. When he let it go, the chair sailed through the air and crashed into the window, partially shattering the glass.

Startled, Katherine waited for an alarm or some kind of commotion, but the eerie silence of Threshold remained.

Langdon walked to the window and, using his elbow, knocked out a portion of the broken glass. Then he carefully reached through, found the knob, and unlocked the door from the inside.

"Inelegant but effective," he said with a smile. "After you, Doctor."

CHAPTER 99

How goes the inquisition?" Faukman asked when Alex
Conan reappeared in his office. The tech's mop of hair
seemed messier, and for a moment Faukman wondered
if the guy had actually aged since first appearing in his doorway
last night.

"I'm okay," Alex said, clearly exhausted. "My boss knows this
isn't my fault, but she wants to talk to you at some point. I told
her you went home for the day."

"Thanks."

"Any word from Robert Langdon?"

"Thankfully, yes. He emailed. They're both okay."

Alex looked surprised. "He didn't *call*?"

Faukman shook his head. *Not yet, at least.*

"And the In-Q-Tel investment list? Any luck finding crossover with Dr. Solomon's work?"

"No. The AI gave me garbage data. Definitely not a fan."

"I may have something for you," he said, opening the laptop he was carrying. "I realized that your AI search would have
flagged overlap with anything online that was *written* by Dr.
Solomon, but not necessarily anything *spoken*—like audio-video
content—so I ran a modified cross-reference and learned that
both In-Q-Tel and Dr. Solomon have a unique interest in the
science of . . . *fractals.*"

Faukman knew nothing about fractals other than that they
often appeared as swirling designs consisting of infinitely repeat-
ing patterns.

"In the past three years," Alex said, pulling out his phone, "Q

has invested heavily in fractal technologies, while Katherine . . ."
He launched a video and held up the screen for Faukman.

Katherine appeared, seated on a dais with several other speakers and the IONS logo behind them. "You ask an interesting question," Katherine said, addressing someone in the audience. "Coincidentally, in the book I'm working on about human consciousness, I've written *extensively* about fractals."

Faukman's ears perked up.

"As you know," she continued, "fractals possess an astonishing attribute: each individual section, when magnified, turns out to be an exact smaller version of the whole—an endless telescoping repetition of self-similarity. In other words, each individual point contains *everything* else. There is no individual . . . only the whole. A growing number of physicists now believe our universe is arranged like a fractal, which would suggest each person in this room contains every other person, and there is no separation between us. We are *one* consciousness. It's hard to picture, I admit, but if you look up images of the Koch snowflake or the Menger sponge, or better yet, just read *The Holographic Universe*—"

"That's the gist of it," Alex said, stopping the video.

Faukman was uncertain. "Alex, I strongly doubt the CIA's interest in fractals has anything to do with the interconnectedness of the universe and humanity."

"I agree, but *fractals* play a critical role in encryption schemes, network topologies, data visualization, and all kinds of other national security technologies. Katherine said she wrote *extensively* about fractals in her book, so I'm thinking maybe she discovered something that compromised one of Q's investments. It's worth a look."

"Fair point," Faukman agreed. "I'll dive in. I appreciate it."

"Let me know if you find anything. Gotta run."

The tech hurried back to his interrogation, and Faukman returned to his computer.

Outside, the rain fell harder.

CHAPTER 100

This is a veritable pharmacy of psychedelic substances . . .

Katherine felt dumbfounded as she stared into the refrigerator at the staggering array of potent drugs. In addition to several substances she did not recognize, Katherine saw vials of diethylamide, psilocybin, and DMT—the effective ingredients in LSD, magic mushrooms, and ayahuasca. She even spotted containers of distilled Salvia extract and MDMA—both illegal in these forms.

The presence of these drugs inside a VR lab could mean only one thing. *Threshold is administering drugs in conjunction with state-of-the-art virtual reality immersions.*

Dual-stimuli VR/drug therapies were strictly regulated in the medical field because their results were not yet understood. In many cases, the combined stimulation was so powerful that it altered the brain's structure rapidly and in unpredictable ways. Neuroscientists had already begun to see startling structural changes in the brains of young people who combined computer gaming with designer drug use.

A new generation of thrill seekers now donned consumer VR goggles and spent hours smoking cannabis while floating virtually through space . . . snorting cocaine while riding a virtual roller coaster . . . or "edging" on various time-dilation sex drugs while watching VR porn. To no avail, countless warnings had been issued because the experiences were intensely addictive.

People don't want to hear how dangerous it is . . .

Last year, Katherine had been booed when she spoke to an

audience of tech-savvy gaming enthusiasts and explained that prolonged exposure to hyperrealistic first-person shooter games had been shown not only to shape people's sensitivity to the graphic subject matter—but to *rewire* the brain's structure, muting normal empathic triggers.

The boos grew louder when she informed them of new brain studies showing that voracious consumption of online pornography was physically altering young minds—"essentially growing a callus on the human libido" and desensitizing them to real sex. The result was that arousal, even in young people, could be achieved only with the assistance of a mind-boggling quantity and variety of stimuli.

Langdon stood beside her, scanning the vials and containers in the refrigerator. "What are the drugs for?"

"Specifically, I'm not sure, but some of these substances are no joke—powerful hallucinogens." She looked around, her thoughts now racing. "If I had to guess, I'd say this room was custom-built for one purpose—to *rewire* a human brain."

"I'm sorry—rewire?"

She nodded. "It's called neural plasticity. Our brains physically *evolve* to meet the needs of new environments. The brain creates new neural pathways to process new experiences. Taking drugs like these, in conjunction with VR simulation, would create a staggeringly intense experience—exponentially more vivid than what occurs in normal life—the type of experiences, which, if repeated, would literally begin to *rewire* a brain's neural network with alarming speed."

"Rewire the brain . . . to do *what*?"

That's the million-dollar question, she thought.

Katherine knew the brain of a lifelong meditation guru was anatomically unique—the years of meditation having gradually rewired it to access a state of deep calm at will. In essence, *calm* became that brain's new normal.

"Robert, it now occurs to me that if Threshold repeatedly placed a subject into an artificially induced out-of-body state— *accentuated* by psychedelics—that subject's brain would begin to rewire itself to make that *disassociated* state feel more . . . normal. In other words, this process might be trying to *tune* a consciousness . . . to be more comfortable *outside* the body."

Her words hung a long moment in the silence of this underground space.

"Nonlocal . . ." Langdon finally said. "That would certainly relate to your book."

"Yes, it certainly would." *Not to mention Stargate*, she thought. "I hate to say it, but Sasha would be a perfect candidate for VR rewiring. As an epileptic, her mind is already partially wired for out-of-body experiences. Using her as a test subject would be something of a shortcut."

"Sasha never mentioned anything like that to me."

"She might not remember, or even be aware . . ." Katherine said, her voice trailing off as she pointed into the fridge. "See that? It's Rohypnol."

"The date-rape drug?"

She nodded. "It profoundly impairs memory function and causes anterograde amnesia—keeping its subjects functional but making it extremely difficult for them to remember anything that happened."

Langdon looked horrified. "Sasha told me she has memory issues. She thinks it's *epilepsy*-related."

"They may well be," Katherine replied. "But if Sasha is being given Rohypnol regularly, she would have serious memory impairment . . . perhaps even no recollection of ever coming here."

"Maybe that explains the wheelchair in the transport? They could have been shuttling Sasha back and forth?"

"It's quite possible," Katherine said. "And it makes me think of the other epileptic you mentioned—the man Brigita brought from that same institution? Brigita may have told Sasha that he went home, but these are incredibly dangerous drugs . . . *Anything* could have happened. He could have gone insane or died— who knows? One advantage of recruiting a patient who was abandoned in a government institution is that he won't really be missed if he disappears."

Langdon was already heading for the door. "This is starting to make sense," he said, "and if we're right . . . and we can find proof that the CIA is experimenting on innocent test subjects without their knowledge . . ."

It would be game over, Katherine realized, imagining the extent of public outrage if this was true.

———··——

Back in the hallway, Langdon was eager to push deeper into Threshold. The main corridor turned sharply right, and he could see two smaller hallways branching off it to the left. The facility was turning into a labyrinth.

A meandering Cold War bomb shelter . . . How far does it go?

He knew they would need to pay close attention if they were going to find their way out of here.

At the corner, they turned right, keeping with the main corridor. Once again, as they stepped into the darkened space, the floor lights immediately illuminated.

Not far ahead, a pair of double doors blocked the hall. Langdon felt reassured to note the door's oval windows were dark, suggesting no lights were on in the area beyond.

We're still alone down here . . . at least in this section.

They pushed through the double doors into more darkness, and again floor lighting came on to reveal another section of hallway. But something was different here . . . The air was about ten degrees cooler and carried the faint carbon tang of museum air. *Heavily filtered.*

The second thing Langdon noticed was that the hallway was a dead end. The hall offered only a single alcove on the left, about halfway down, which, by all appearances, was the entrance to another suite of some sort.

Langdon realized that if they didn't find what they needed in *there*, they'd have to start venturing off the main hall into other areas. Despite his eidetic memory, he was already getting turned around in this maze.

As they continued walking, Langdon tried to gauge exactly where beneath Folimanka Park they were now located. He eyed the dead-end wall at the end of the corridor, wondering if perhaps there were tourists milling on the other side of it in the public section of the shelter . . . unaware of the ominous facility that existed right beside them.

They turned into the lone alcove and stopped short. In front of them was an oversized glass revolving door with thick rubber gaskets designed to retain air quality. It looked like another lab door, but the space beyond was pitch-black.

"RTD," Katherine said, reading three stenciled letters above the revolving door. "Sounds promising."

"Does it?" Langdon's only memory of RTD was from grade school math. *Rate x Time = Distance.*

"Research and technical development—it's the European equivalent of R&D," she said, peering into the dark glass. "Which means *this* could be exactly what we're looking for."

CHAPTER 101

CIA Director Gregory Judd gunned his wife's Jeep Grand Cherokee down Georgetown Pike toward CIA's Langley headquarters. His regular driver was not prepared at this early hour, and Judd did not have time to wait. Despite his distaste for Finch's methods, the director had a duty to country first . . . and most Americans could not begin to comprehend the threats this country faced.

America and her allies are under attack . . . at all times.

In recent years, their enemies had needed only the most rudimentary social media tools to influence the minds and decisions of millions upon millions of people. His agency had tracked measurable foreign influences over elections, consumer habits, economic decisions, and political trends. But those attacks paled in comparison to the storm that was coming.

There's a new battleground emerging, and it requires new kinds of weaponry.

The Russians, Chinese, and Americans were *all* racing to dominate this new arena, and winning that race had been Gregory Judd's primary directive for his entire twenty-year tenure in the upper echelons of the agency. Threshold, and its astonishing technology, was about to give him an edge.

Now, as he raced toward Langley, he wondered what it was that Ambassador Nagel had sent to his secure server that she believed was explosive enough to hold the CIA hostage.

A bluff? Doubtful. *An overplayed hand?* Nagel was too smart for that.

All he could imagine was she had somehow discovered what

they were doing inside Threshold. If that was true, Judd would need to do everything in his power to keep her quiet. If Nagel went public with that kind of sensitive information, the fallout would be explosive—and global.

Overnight, the psychic arms race would escalate uncontrollably.

———

Deep beneath Folimanka Park, The Golĕm sat with his back against the heavy metal door, catching his breath.

I cannot risk another seizure.

I need to escape alive . . . I must release Sasha.

As his pulse slowed, he stood cautiously and gripped the thick wheel mounted to the door. He paused for ten seconds to allow any lightheadedness to clear. Then, with all his strength, he turned the wheel repeatedly until he heard the heavy latch disengage inside. The Golĕm pushed the steel portal inward. From out of the blackness beyond, an icy wind whipped past him, lifting his cloak tails as he put his head down and stepped through the airtight opening. The lights inside snapped on, and he heaved the door closed behind him.

Instantly, the wind subsided.

The fortified vault in which he was now standing was bitter cold, but he knew this was not air-conditioning. This was Prague winter seeping in. The ceiling had a gaping circular hole in it, more than two meters in diameter. The hole ascended through a vertical steel conduit that climbed several stories through the earth to an ingeniously disguised opening in the middle of Folimanka Park.

The Golĕm had seen the opening many times.

Everyone had.

The conduit emerged from the ground, rising about three meters into the air, and was capped with a perforated concrete dome. For decades, to the passersby in the park, it resembled a giant concrete torpedo sticking out of the earth.

Guidebooks correctly identified it as the original ventilation shaft for the now-defunct Folimanka bomb shelter, and despite many petitions to remove the "torpedo tip" as an unsightly reminder of Cold War times, anonymous street artists had come up with a very different idea. Prague was a city of avant-garde art, and years earlier the concrete vent had been mysteriously transformed. The odd-shaped canvas now paid tribute to one of Hollywood's most beloved movie stars—a robot who was conveniently shaped exactly like the tip of a torpedo—the droid R2-D2 from *Star Wars*.

R2-D2 had become a popular feature in Folimanka Park, towering over all who posed for photos beside its iconic silver, blue, and white body. The city government agreed it was historically appropriate to leave the anonymous art in place, as it actually had been a Czech writer—Karel Čapek—who had coined the term "robot" for the very first time in a play he wrote in 1920.

Of course, from the outside no one would have any idea that this defunct ventilation shaft had been entirely repurposed. It was no longer used to pull air *in*. Rather, it was now an emergency fail-safe—engineered to let something else *out*.

<hr />

The monotonous patter of rain on Faukman's windows seemed an apt soundtrack for his latest dead end. Having researched all of In-Q-Tel's fractal-based investments, he had found nothing that seemed like it could be compromised by Katherine's writings.

Fractal telescopes? Fractal cooling components? Fractal stealth geometry?

Faukman shook his head in frustration as the exhaustion of the night settled deeper into his bones. He couldn't know for certain, but he suspected that whatever in Katherine's manuscript had provoked this attack . . . was far more significant than fractals.

CHAPTER 102

As Langdon and Katherine pushed through the revolving door into the RTD facility, they found themselves in a small antechamber—an immaculate glass cubicle with shoe racks, storage cubbies, and a series of hooks holding clean white jumpsuits. In addition, there were two "air showers"— enclosed cubicles with high-velocity jets of filtered air to blow particles and contaminants off clothing and skin.

Like the narthex of a cathedral, Langdon mused. *A room to purify the unclean . . . before they enter the sanctuary.*

In this case, the sanctuary was apparently whatever lay beyond the glass wall directly in front of them, its entrance delineated by a second airtight revolving door rather than a Gothic arch.

Katherine was already pushing through the second door, and Langdon followed. The halogen lights that blazed to life overhead were as bright as any Langdon had ever seen. Their brilliance was further amplified by the room's contents; nearly *everything* in this huge space was stark white—walls, floor, tables, chairs, work counters, even the plastic coverings on all the equipment.

"It's a clean room," Katherine said.

Row after row of countertops housed perfectly organized tools, along with electronic devices and machinery beneath plastic protective sheaths. The computer systems looked elaborate, but all the displays were dark.

Katherine walked into the center of the room while Langdon moved along a side wall, stopping to peer through a window into an adjoining space. On the other side of the glass was some kind of biology lab—microscopes, flasks, petri dishes—much of it unpacked. Against the rear wall—in its own glass isolation booth—stood a piece of equipment that Langdon had never seen.

The delicate-looking device consisted of hundreds of long glass vials that hung down vertically through a perforated platform. Each appeared to be fed by its own ultrathin tube that descended from the upper body of the machine. It reminded Langdon vaguely of a precision hydroponic drip system he had once seen an indigo exhibition. *Are they growing something in there?*

"Over here," Katherine said, standing beside a large contraption that was about three feet tall and looked like some kind of futuristic Rube Goldberg invention. Langdon headed over to her and examined the device.

"It's a photolithograph," she said.

Langdon sensed his knowledge of Greek was about to fail him. "So, it writes . . . on rocks . . . with light?"

"Exactly," she said. "Provided the light is deep ultraviolet . . . and the rock is a *silicon* wafer." She motioned to a stack of glossy metallic disks sitting beside the machine. "This lab has everything required to design and build custom computer chips."

Computer chips? The notion seemed totally unrelated to human consciousness or to whatever Katherine might have written about in her manuscript. "Why would they be designing *computer chips* down here?"

"My best guess," Katherine said, "is *brain* implants."

The idea startled him, but he quickly made the connection. "The robotic brain surgeon . . ."

"Exactly. I think I was wrong when I guessed it was extracting brain samples. It seems pretty clear the robot is used for *implanting* brain chips."

An uneasy silence settled in the bright room.

"Didn't you say brain implants were *basic* surgery?" Langdon asked.

"*Epilepsy* chips, yes. They're tiny electric shock machines embedded in the skull. But an advanced implant would be more deeply placed and would definitely benefit from robotic surgery for implementation."

Langdon thought about Sasha and felt a trace of dread. He wondered if she could have been implanted with a prototype chip—probably under the guise of an epilepsy procedure. She would have no idea what was really inside her head . . . or that Threshold even existed, for that matter.

"If Gessner lied," Langdon said, "and the implant she put into Sasha was actually a more advanced, subcranial chip . . ."

"Then that implant could easily function as the RLS stim device to control Sasha's epileptic seizures, and yet, at the same time . . . it could have countless other functions."

"I hesitate to ask . . . like what?"

Katherine tapped her index finger on the top of the photolithograph machine, thinking. "There's no way to know without examining the chip," she said. "But it looks like they're starting to build them here. I'm guessing Sasha and that other male subject were probably their first patients . . . an initial validation study and proof of concept before shifting this facility into high gear."

Langdon felt intensely disturbed by what he was hearing.

"Whatever they did," Katherine said, "it must have gone well, because Threshold is clearly gearing up for a larger-scale operation." She glanced around the room and frowned. "Unfortunately, there's nothing specifically incriminating here. All it proves is the CIA appears to be developing some kind of brain implant—a project that would surprise absolutely nobody."

True, Langdon realized. *Brain implants are the future.*

Langdon had read enough science columns to know that implanted brain chips, despite conjuring images of cyborgs and science fiction, were already functional and startlingly advanced.

Companies like Elon Musk's Neuralink had been working since 2016 to develop what was known as an H2M interface— human to machine—a device that could convert data obtained from the brain into understandable binary code. One of Musk's first milestones had been to implant a monkey with a Neuralink chip and teach it to play the computer game *Pong* using only its brain impulses to move the paddle.

When Neuralink had finally received FDA clearance to test on humans, they had implanted Noland Arbaugh, a thirty-year-old quadriplegic, with a device called PRIME and miraculously returned a fair number of the patient's motor skills. Unfortunately, after only a hundred days, the chip's electronic threads—the metallic sensors by which the chip communicated with the brain's neurons—retracted from the brain, apparently rejected by the biological neurons they were supposed to monitor. Nonetheless, it was a substantial leap forward.

Other industry leaders like Bill Gates and Jeff Bezos's Synchron, along with BlackRock's Neurotech, were designing less invasive, more specialized chips that they claimed would accomplish stunning results such as overcoming blindness, curing paralysis, overcoming neurological disorders like Parkinson's, and even providing "type with your mind" capability.

Although Langdon was still unclear on this technology's link to human consciousness and Katherine's work, he had no doubt that brain chips would have critical implications for military intelligence—drones piloted by the mind, telepathic battlefield communication, endless applications for data analysis—so it made perfect sense that the CIA would be investing heavily.

Human-to-machine interface is the future.

Langdon recalled what he had witnessed at the Barcelona Supercomputing Center, where modeling software was predicting the future evolution of the human race: HUMANS WILL MERGE WITH ANOTHER QUICKLY EVOLVING SPECIES . . . TECHNOLOGY.

"Okay, so the key question is, where does this intersect with your manuscript?" Langdon pressed, eager to find the connection. "Did you write about computer chips?"

"A little bit," she said, visibly frustrated, "but it's nothing that could be of any interest or threat to this program."

"Are you sure?"

"Yes. My only mention of brain implants was in the final

chapter, and it was more of a theoretical narrative musing about the future of noetic science."

Noetics Tomorrow, Langdon thought, having glimpsed her chapter index before adding it to the fire in the library. "And brain implants played a role in that chapter?" he urged, sensing they might be close.

"*Hypothetical* implants, yes," she said. "Implants we won't have for decades . . . if *ever.*"

Langdon had once heard that the technology available to the intelligence community was *years* beyond what was known publicly. "Katherine, is it possible that the CIA is further along than you imagine?"

"It's possible, but not *that* much further," she said. "What I wrote about is more of a thought experiment, rather than a plausible technology. Think of Maxwell's demon or the twin paradox—obviously you can't invent a molecule-sorting demon or propel twins to the speed of light, but *imagining* it is helpful in understanding the bigger picture."

I'll take your word for it, he thought. "Tell me what you wrote."

Katherine sighed. "It was a fantasy relating to my discoveries about GABA. Remember we talked about the brain being a receiver . . . a kind of radio that receives signals from all around us—from the universe?"

Langdon nodded. "And the brain chemical GABA functions like the radio *dial* . . . filtering out unwanted frequencies and limiting the amount of information and consciousness that flows in."

"Precisely," she said. "So I hypothesized that one day, in the distant future, we would figure out how to build an implant that could *regulate* GABA levels in the brain—essentially lowering our filters on demand . . . so we could experience more of *reality.*"

"Incredible," Langdon said. The mere thought of it was thrilling. "And that's not *possible*?"

"God, no!" she said, shaking her head. "The most advanced noetic science is not even in that ballpark yet. In the first place, we would have to be correct about the noetic theory of a Universal Consciousness or the Akashic Field or Anima Mundi—or whatever you want to call the field of consciousness that is theorized to surround all things."

"Which *you* believe."

"I do. We can't yet *prove* this cosmic realm exists, but it seems to be regularly glimpsed by minds in altered states. Unfortunately, these experiences are fleeting, uncontrolled, subjective, and often nonrepeatable—making them suspect scientifically."

"And easy targets for skeptics."

"Yes. We have no quantifiable method, machine, or technology capable of receiving signals from the cosmic realm. Only the *brain* can do that." She gave a casual shrug. "And so I proposed a hypothetical chip that could piggyback on a brain, lower its GABA levels, widen its bandwidth, and turn it into a far more *powerful* receiver."

Langdon stared at her in awe. Not only was Katherine's idea indisputably brilliant, it might finally explain exactly *why* the CIA was panicked about her manuscript.

What if Katherine was about to publish a book that described an ultrasecret chip the CIA is already building?!

"Katherine," he said, "Threshold is taking consciousness study to the next dimension, and your book might have been about to blow the lid off the centerpiece of their secret technology."

"There's no chance of that," she said. "Like I said, the chip I described is *not buildable*. It's interesting conceptually, but strictly hypothetical. The technical barriers to its construction are immovable—specifically this: regulating system-wide levels of a neurotransmitter would require *complete physical integration* with the brain's neural network . . . and the brain has over a hundred trillion synapses to monitor."

"But scientific progress is accel—"

"Robert, believe me, complete physical integration is unachievable. It would be the equivalent of directly wiring every single lightbulb on earth to *one* switch, a million times over. It's genuinely *impossible*."

"So was splitting the atom . . ." Langdon retorted. "But science has a way of figuring things out, especially with unlimited budgets. Remember the Manhattan Project?"

"Huge difference . . . Nuclear technology already *existed* in 1940. Uranium existed. Scientists just pulled it all together. The chip I proposed requires technology and materials that don't even exist on earth. Before we can even *talk* about integrating with the brain's dendritic tree, someone has to invent a nano-electric biofilament."

"A nanoelectric what?"

"Exactly—it's not even a *real* thing. I invented it in my book as a way to talk about a technology that does not exist. It would be a futuristic, ultrathin, flexible filament made of biocompatible material that can carry both electronic and ionic signals. Essentially, an *artificial neuron*."

"And artificial neurons are not possible to create?"

"No, we're not even close. Last year, two guys in Sweden made international headlines by persuading a Venus flytrap to open and close by chemically stimulating a neuron. Just a single binary impulse—and yet it sent scientific shock waves around the world. That's the state of the art, Robert, and it's generations away from an artificial neuron."

Langdon was already moving across the room toward the window of the biology lab he had seen several minutes earlier. "Theoretically speaking," he said, "would you *build* artificial neurons . . . or *grow* them?"

She thought a moment. "A nanoelectric biofilament? Well, it would be a biological filament, so you'd have to *grow* them."

Langdon stopped at the window and peered at the machine with hundreds of long glass vials and tubes. "In a liquid suspension, I imagine?"

"Yes. Fragile microstructures are always cultivated in suspension."

"Then I think you should come over here," he said, waving her to the window. "It looks like Threshold is growing *something* . . . and I'm guessing it's not arugula."

CHAPTER 103

Everett Finch burst through the compromised entrance of Crucifix Bastion and stormed down the hall into the glass-walled atrium. *Where the hell is everyone?!* Enraged to find no trace of Housemore or the embassy's promised security detail, he pulled out his personal RFID key card and headed for the elevator.

As he crossed the room, the key card's biometric sensors activated in his fingertips, but he stopped short, reminded that there was no possible way for Housemore—or *anyone* for that matter—to access the elevator down to Threshold.

She must be upstairs . . . or else she left the bastion for some reason?

He dialed Housemore's line one last time.

As soon as Finch placed the call, a phone began chirping nearby. *Odd.* The sound seemed to be emanating from a couch against the far wall. *Did Housemore lose her phone?* At least it would explain why she hadn't answered earlier.

Finch strode to the couch but saw no phone. The ringing had stopped, and he called again. Once more, a phone began to chirp. *Is it beneath the couch?*

Finch crouched down to look under the stylish furniture.

As he stared into the dark space, he knew instantly that Threshold was under attack.

Staring back at him were two dead eyes—the lifeless gaze of his field officer Susan Housemore.

———··———

In the frigid vault, The Golĕm gazed at the powerful machine sitting before him. The device's gleaming metal body was a bulbous ring of polished aluminum that occupied nearly the entire concrete chamber. Five meters across and one meter tall, the machine resembled a giant metal donut. The unusual donut shape—technically "toroidal," according to The Golěm's research this morning—was apparently the most efficient shape in which to wrap superconducting coils if one wanted to create a magnetic field capable of storing vast amounts of energy.

SMES, he thought. *Superconducting magnetic energy storage.*

This was the secret source of Threshold's power.

The Golěm had learned this morning that energy fed into the toroidal magnetic field would race in loops indefinitely with no degradation and could be siphoned off as needed. The only prerequisite was to keep the superconducting coils cold.

Extremely cold.

The critical temperature for its coils was somewhere below negative-260 Celsius, and if the coils rose even slightly above this temperature, they lost superconductivity and began resisting the current. That resistance caused rapid heating of the coils, which in turn caused more resistance, and within seconds the feedback loop blossomed out of control . . . resulting in a dangerous event known as a *quench*.

To prevent quenching, the coils were continuously flushed in a bath of the coldest liquid on earth. *Liquid helium.*

He gazed past the SMES to the adjoining chamber, where, locked within a Mu-metal mesh cage, stood twelve austenitic, stainless-steel tanks of liquid helium. Each of the five-hundred-gallon, Cryofab flasks stood as tall as The Golěm and was equipped with a cryogenic bayonet and vacuum-jacketed piping that transported the cold liquid into the SMES to keep the superconductors cold.

Liquid helium, by most measurements, was harmless—nonexplosive, nonflammable, and nonpoisonous. Its sole dangerous quality was possessing the lowest boiling point of any substance known to man . . . a frigid *negative*-270 Celsius. This meant that if the helium was permitted to "warm up" above negative-270 Celsius—already near absolute zero—it immediately boiled and converted to helium gas.

The gas itself was also harmless, but the danger lay in the *physics* of the conversion process. Liquid helium's conversion to gas was shockingly fast and violent . . . and, as it turned out, it was the entire reason Threshold had co-opted the R2-D2 vent in Folimanka Park.

When liquid helium converted to gas, its volume multiplied by a mind-boggling ratio of 1 to 750. This meant that the liquid helium in this vault, if released, would rapidly convert to enough gas to fill *seven* Olympic swimming pools.

In an unvented space, the new volume would have nowhere to go, and the pressure buildup would happen so fast that it would create a "pressure bomb"—a near-instantaneous, violent outward force expanding in all directions. In a desperate attempt to make room for itself, the gas would blow apart whatever constrained it, resulting in a shock wave much like that of a tactical nuclear weapon, tearing through everything in a given radius.

To mitigate risk, all facilities using liquid helium, including hospitals with MRI machines, were required to install a "quench vent"—a ventilation pipe that ascended up through the roof of the building—to ensure that, in the event of an inadvertent helium leak, the rapidly expanding gas would have a safe *alternate* route to escape . . . rather than blowing up the building. Threshold's quench vent was massive, but then again, so was the quantity of liquid helium stored down here.

The Golěm gazed again past the SMES to the twelve Cryofab flasks. *More than twenty thousand liters of helium,* he had calculated. The expansion potential was almost incalculable.

Catastrophic explosions with liquid helium, he had learned online, were fairly common—including SpaceX's Falcon 9 rocket, CERN's Large Hadron Collider, and even a veterinary clinic in New Jersey whose MRI had a small leak and exploded.

The Golěm knew that if *this* SMES quenched unexpectedly, the liquid helium loaded into the system would instantly boil off in a torrent of expanding gas racing up the conduit and shooting skyward over Prague in a geyser of freezing-cold helium.

Most likely blasting off R2-D2's head in the process.

The liquid helium loaded into the SMES machine at any time

represented a very small portion of the total volume contained in the tanks. The Golĕm could not begin to imagine what would happen if *all* the helium in this facility were released at once . . . converting from liquid to gas in an instant.

Such an event had never occurred. Ever. Anywhere.

There were too many fail-safes.

Helium flasks were extremely robust with multiple safety features. Built like giant Thermoses, their double-hulled "Dewar" design employed nature's most efficient insulator—a pure vacuum—to ensure the liquid inside stayed cold enough never to convert to gas. For additional safety, each flask stored its liquid under extremely high pressure. This raised the helium's boiling point, offering a wider margin of error before it hit critical temperature.

The flask's final safety measure was a "rupture disk"—a tiny copper disk built into the shell of the tank. An intentional weak spot, the disk was calibrated to rupture if the internal pressure climbed too high . . . thus averting a cataclysmic tank explosion.

Although rupture disks were designed to explode *outward*, they would also rupture *inward* if the pressure outside a canister became too great. Of course, that never happened because nobody was ever careless enough to store liquid helium in an airtight space.

Considering these three fail-safes, the probability of multiple tank failures at the same moment carried a statistical probability of zero.

It simply could not happen.

Not without help.

Reflecting on the horrors inflicted on Sasha by Threshold, The Golĕm took a final look at the quietly humming SMES device, savoring the irony. This machine was the secret source of Threshold's power . . . and was about to become the agent of its destruction.

CHAPTER 104

Having entered the bio lab with Langdon, Katherine was carefully examining the sophisticated machine before her.

Artificial neurons don't exist. Not yet.

This had always been Katherine's belief . . . but now she was not so sure. While the machine did indeed look like an elaborate hydroponic incubator, she had no way to know, with her naked eye, what was in the vials of liquid.

It's impossible . . . isn't it?

Much of Katherine's postgraduate work in brain science had centered on neurochemistry, studying the specific chemical mechanisms by which the brain's neural network functioned. Artificial neurons, in concept, had first been proposed in 1943 by American scientists Warren McCulloch and Walter Pitts—but the *realization* of that concept had always seemed a distant dream. There was a common quip among biologists: *Humans will inhabit Mars long before we build an artificial neuron.*

"Check those manuals?" she said, motioning to a bookcase across the room. "See if you see anything about this incubator or what they're growing in here. I'll check the drawers."

As Langdon headed to the bookcase, Katherine began rifling through a set of file drawers built into the room's glistening worktable. Most meticulous laboratories, including the Institute of Noetic Sciences, created a "protocol book" for every project—a hard copy set of procedural guidelines to ensure consistency and reproducibility of results. This is what Katherine hoped to find, but she found nothing of much interest within the drawers.

It was not until she discovered a recessed "flat tray" drawer in the table that she found anything promising . . . including a heavy black three-ring binder. Although it was far too thick to be the protocol book she was looking for, she felt a chill when she saw the words emblazoned on the cover.

TOP SECRET
PROPERTY OF CENTRAL INTELLIGENCE AGENCY

Katherine immediately hoisted the binder onto the table and opened it.

Please tell us something . . .

As she skimmed the first few pages, she was startled to learn that the authors of this binder came from the prestigious Laboratory of Organic Electronics (LOE) in Sweden. *The CIA recruited from LOE?!* In the quest to produce artificial neurons, LOE was one of the world's leading think tanks. Katherine had mentioned their Venus flytrap breakthrough only minutes ago!

Spellbound, she flipped through the various sections of the binder, reading the headers. She saw a number of familiar topics, but then her eye hit on one that stopped her cold.

MODULATION VIA MIXED ION-ELECTRON
CONDUCTING POLYMERS

Modulation? She immediately began scanning the section. *Did they really solve modulation?!*

One of the most daunting hurdles in the quest to build an artificial neuron was to mimic "ion modulation"—a neuron's unique ability to activate and deactivate sodium ion channels. And yet if this header was to be believed, ion modulation was now possible.

But . . . how?!

Heart racing, Katherine began reading about Threshold's

solution to the modulation problem. Everything about it made perfect sense to her . . . almost too perfect . . . and the further she read, the harder it became for her to breathe.

No . . . no . . . this can't be!

———·——

"Katherine?" Langdon repeated, having joined her at the table after hearing her gasp a few moments ago. "Are you okay?"

But she made no reply, her eyes riveted to the binder as she flipped pages, one after another, muttering quietly to herself.

Langdon peered over her shoulder, trying to see what was upsetting her, but the page header meant nothing to him. *Modulation via mixed ion-electron conducting polymers?*

As the seconds wore on, Langdon sensed Katherine was in a state of mild shock, and he finally placed a hand on her arm. "What is it?"

She spun abruptly toward him, her eyes full of fire. "What is it? Threshold is using synthesized BBL as an organic electrochemical transistor! They cast it into a thin film and dissolved it in methanesulfonic—"

"Slow down—what?"

"BBL! They're using it in the *artificial neurons*! That was *my* idea, Robert!"

"First of all, what is BBL?"

"Benzimidazobenzophenanthroline. It's a highly conductive polymer that is uniquely tough and also elastic."

"Okay, and . . . ?"

"And they are implementing *polycondensation* to synthesize BBL—which was *my* suggestion. The result is a substance that is vastly conductive to electrons . . . much like a *neuron*." She flipped a page of the binder. "Look! The chemical protocols in this binder are *exactly* the protocols I describe in my manuscript! Down to the finest details! I suggested modifying conductance by adding three millimolars of glutamine to the electrolyte solution—and that's exactly what they are doing!"

Langdon wasn't following much of this, but clearly Katherine believed she had identified a point of direct intersection between her manuscript and the Threshold project. *That's what we came here for.*

"Katherine," he said quietly, "can you take a breath and explain to me, in simple English, what's going on?"

She nodded, exhaling. "Sorry, yes," she said, lowering her voice. "Simply stated, my book theorized how this technology might actually be *produced* someday. I specifically proposed weaving the fabricated substance into a neural 'mesh' that could be pulled over the brain like a cap . . . a sheath of neurons in direct contact with the brain." She sighed. "And . . . most incredibly, that is *exactly* what they are doing here. I just . . . well, I can't believe it."

"So you wrote expressly about artificial neurons?"

"I did. When I proposed a hypothetical brain chip to regulate GABA, I knew the chip could not be built without artificial neurons, so I included my best guess at how neurons might be fabricated someday . . . in the distant future."

That future is apparently now, Langdon realized, glancing down at the binder. "And you think Threshold actually built the GABA chip you proposed?"

"No, no," she said, shaking her head. "I have no idea *what* chip they built—but I'm pretty certain it would not be the one I proposed. If they have artificial neurons, the sky's the limit; they could build literally *whatever* they dream up. Artificial neurons are *the* critical leap required for full H2M integration. You've got to understand, Robert . . ." She looked him straight in the eyes. "This neuron technology is the key to the future. It changes everything."

Langdon had no doubt she was correct; he had read more than once that futurists predicted an artificial neuron breakthrough would usher in an astonishing era of direct brain-to-brain communication, memory augmentation, accelerated learning, and even the ability to record our dreams at night and play them back in the morning.

Most disturbing to Langdon, however, was the forecast hailed as "the ultimate social media"—humans making full-sensory recordings of their own experiences . . . and sharing their own personal "channels" directly with other minds. In essence, people would be able to relive the sights, sounds, smells, and feelings of someone *else's* experience. Of course, it would not take long for black-market libraries to offer particularly shocking, titillating, or grisly memories. The 1990s cyberpunk movie *Strange Days* had ventured into this dark world . . . presciently, it now seemed.

Even though Langdon recognized this could well be a turning point in science history, the momentous impact of the breakthrough was not foremost in his mind. He was far more focused on the ramifications of Katherine's incredible bad luck.

She proposed an inconceivably brilliant idea in her book . . . only to learn the CIA is already secretly developing it.

While the coincidence was stunning, Langdon knew the cliché "Great minds work alike" had been borne out countless times through the ages; Newton and Leibniz independently invented calculus; Darwin and Wallace simultaneously envisioned evolution; Alexander Graham Bell and Elisha Gray both invented a telephone device and filed patents within hours of each other. Now, it seemed, Katherine Solomon and the CIA had both figured out how to make artificial neurons.

"This all makes sense now . . ." Katherine whispered to herself, staring absently into space. "It's no wonder I was targeted . . ."

"It's an incredibly unlucky coincidence," Langdon said sympathetically. "At least now we underst—"

"This is *not a* coincidence, Robert!" Katherine's eyes were alive with anger. "The CIA *stole* my idea!"

Stole? The claim made no sense to him; clearly the CIA had been developing artificial neurons long before Katherine had started writing her book.

"They stole my design!" she repeated. "*All of it!*"

For as long as he'd known Katherine Solomon, Langdon had never heard her make a single irrational claim, much less a paranoid outburst. "I don't understand," he said, offering a reassuring smile. "You've been writing this book for a year, and the Threshold program is more than twenty—"

"I'm not being clear," she said, cutting him off. There was a fierceness in her eyes that he had never seen before. "My *manuscript* included a section about artificial neurons, which explained the details of this very design. But in that section I was talking about my passion and work as a young *grad student*, when I was already dreaming about the future of noetics . . . designing hypothetical technologies that future scientists might one day use to deepen our understanding of human consciousness."

Her meaning suddenly became clear to Langdon. "My God . . . *what*?!"

She nodded. "Yes! Robert, I first proposed—and *documented*—the exact design for these artificial neurons in my postgraduate thesis . . . twenty-three years ago."

CHAPTER 105

Katherine could see from Langdon's stunned expression that he was still struggling to comprehend the logistics of what she'd just told him.

"This is my *exact design* for artificial neurons," she said, tapping Threshold's classified binder. "From twenty-three years ago. There's no mistaking it."

"So you wrote your doctoral thesis on artificial neurons?" Langdon asked.

"Not directly, no. I was in neuroscience, and my thesis was titled 'The Chemistry of Consciousness'—a geeky paper about neurotransmitters and awareness, but at the end, just like in my manuscript, I wrote a section about the *future* of consciousness research. I fantasized about various hypothetical breakthroughs, including the most significant advance that could ever occur in my field—artificial neurons—a technology that would finally make possible a true H2M interface and allow scientists to monitor the brain's consciousness in new ways . . . and finally to *see* how it all worked."

"And you're positive . . . there's no coincidence with the CIA's work?"

"Robert, the neurons in this binder are *identical* to what I proposed in my thesis, right down to the nomenclature! The description literally refers to 'nanoelectric biofilaments' and 'bilateral organo-technic fusion'—both are terms I *made up*!"

Langdon now looked convinced. "Wow . . . for starters, that means *you*, Katherine Solomon, figured out how to make artificial neurons . . . while in grad school?"

"I was a *kid* with an overactive imagination. The idea was a fantasy. Don't forget that twenty-three years ago, artificial neurons were science fiction!"

"So were genetic engineering, self-driving cars, and AI," he countered. "But here we are. Courtesy of Moore's law."

True, she thought, *the future comes at us faster every day.*

"Twenty years ago, people in the field assumed artificial neurons would turn out to be *silicon*-based, which made sense considering neurons were essentially binary on/off switches like those in a computer chip. I disagreed and argued in my thesis that because the ultimate goal of artificial neurons would be *integration* with the brain, any true solution would need to be *biological*. And so I let my imagination go, and I designed, in great detail, my best guess at how such a neuron might someday be created."

"I'd say it was a pretty good guess," Langdon said, still looking impressed. "The CIA has probably been working on developing this for decades . . . and finally succeeded. The question of ownership or credit is another issue."

"I'm just wondering how they *heard* about my idea . . . or got their hands on it."

Langdon shrugged. "Well, they *are* the largest intelligence-gathering operation in the world."

"Actually," Katherine said, memories now flowing. "It just now occurs to me . . ." She hesitated, lost in thought.

"Tell me on the way out," Langdon urged, picking up the binder and heading for the door. "We need to get out of here with this—and get it into the ambassador's hands. Let's hope it's enough."

Katherine hoisted her shoulder bag and followed Langdon across the lab, her thoughts now racing. "Something odd happened with my thesis. I never really understood it, and I haven't thought about it in decades . . . but it might explain something."

"What happened?" Langdon asked as they hurried across the brightly lit computer lab in the direction of the revolving door.

"My thesis adviser at Princeton," she recalled, "was *the* A. J. Cosgrove, legendary chemist, who took me under his wing. He loved my thesis and told me he believed it could win a Blavatnik Award—a national prize for postdoctoral science research. Anyhow, I lost, which was fine with me, but for some reason it really pissed off Cosgrove, and he ended up having some kind of spat with the head of the prize committee, a hotshot professor from Stanford. When the dust finally settled, Cosgrove told me I deserved the prize and that I was denied for 'reasons other than merit.' I chalked it up to academic politics. But I told him I didn't care, because I had decided to pursue noetics anyway. Then he said something strange. He said that before I left neuroscience *entirely*, he strongly suggested I . . ." Katherine stopped short of the door. "Oh . . . *no*."

Langdon turned. "What is it?!"

Katherine closed her eyes in disbelief, setting her bag onto a worktable. In all the chaos, it hadn't dawned on her until this very moment. "Robert," she whispered, opening her eyes and running a hand through her thick dark hair. "There's an even *bigger* reason the CIA needs my book to disappear forever."

◆——··——◆

Clutching the SIG Sauer pistol he had taken from Field Officer Housemore, Finch leaped off the Threshold transport and hurried across the familiar platform and through the unmanned security center. After finding his officer's corpse in the lobby, he'd rushed down to Gessner's workroom, where, with brutal clarity, his worst fears had been confirmed.

Brigita was murdered.

Finch had immediately called for agency backup, but with his local field officer now dead, he knew the arrival of on-site support was going to take time. This situation was becoming increasingly alarming, and delicate, and prudence dictated he handle the crisis without delay. Finch was an expert marksman and was eminently capable of neutralizing anyone he might encounter.

As he entered the OPS hallway, he was relieved to see all the lights in this section were off. Then again, he had been instrumental in designing this subterranean structure, and he knew the lights timed out every ten minutes; technically, the darkness was no guarantee that he was alone down here.

Finch still could not fathom that Housemore and Gessner had been murdered. Even more disturbing was the unlikely identity of their killer. While pulling Housemore from behind the couch, Finch had been startled to find a metal epilepsy rod on the carpet. Someone had clearly dropped it, and there were only two epilepsy patients who had ever entered Crucifix Bastion— Sasha Vesna and Dmitri Sysevich—both taken from the same institution.

And Dmitri, I have been assured, is no longer with us.

The notion that Sasha had killed anyone seemed almost unthinkable. Gessner had always described her as timid and kind. Then again, Sasha had reportedly attacked an ÚZSI officer today, which implied something was terribly off-balance with the woman. Her brain had been under a great deal of pressure, and it was not out of the question that she'd suffered some kind of mental breakdown.

Sasha murdered Gessner? It seemed unthinkable . . . and yet, if Sasha discovered what Gessner had done to her, that would be strong motivation. Even so, Finch doubted Sasha was capable of all this . . . at least, not alone.

He took a hard right into BIO, relieved to find the surgical area dark. When the lights came on, everything appeared to be in order. Finch eyed the robotic surgeon hanging from the ceiling. So far, Gessner had used this technology to perform only two human surgeries—one successful, one catastrophic.

Finch was in no mood for surprises and intended to search the facility completely, starting with a systematic sweep of the medical section to confirm that nobody had slid under a bed or into a closet, hiding long enough for the motion lights to time out.

If someone had penetrated Threshold, Finch would not let them slip past him.

Anyone who had seen this place . . . would not be permitted to exit alive.

———··———

Deep in the SMES vault, The Golĕm gazed up into the open ventilation shaft. High above him, he could barely make out the dappled daylight that filtered down through the perforations in the R2-D2 statue's domed head several stories above in Folimanka Park.

For obvious reasons, quench vents like these were left open at *all* times to allow for emergency ventilation. They were sealed only to pressure-test the vault for leaks, and only under very specific conditions . . . specifically, the total absence of liquid helium.

Today, there will be a slight change in protocol.

Mustering his strength, The Golĕm climbed up on top of the humming ring of metal. The top was rounded and perilous, but his boots had good traction. He could feel the faint vibration of the machine as he reached for the ceiling and steadied himself by grabbing a crank handle protruding from the ceiling. This handle worked a series of pullies that moved a thick plate of metal affixed to the ceiling.

The test cover.

A square panel of steel was supported in a track whose rails ran on either side of the vent's opening. This panel, like a giant manhole cover, could be cranked into place and tightened with butterfly screws, sealing the opening and rendering the room airtight.

Not surprisingly, the steel covering was emblazoned with bright red stenciled letters.

NEBEZPEČÍ! NEZAVÍRAT!

DANGER! DO NOT CLOSE!

Ignoring the posted warning, The Golĕm began turning the handle.

Within a minute, this vault would be airtight.

CHAPTER 106

An even bigger reason? Langdon could not imagine what additional motivation the CIA could have to destroy Katherine's manuscript. *Her book reveals a new top secret CIA technology. Game, set, match . . .*

Katherine had stopped short and turned to him, her face a mask of concern in the harsh halogen lights. "I think Professor Cosgrove must have known something was wrong," she said. "After his argument with the Stanford guy, he gave me a final assignment before I left neuroscience for noetics. It was an unusual request."

"What did he want you to do?"

"He insisted that part of the education of any future scientist was to undergo the process of applying for a patent. He said he loved my creative approach to the artificial neurons, and even though the patent would never be granted, the process of applying would—"

"Wait . . ." Langdon said. "You're saying you filed a *patent* for these artificial neurons?"

"It was an academic *exercise,*" she said, nodding. "Cosgrove warned me that my application would be denied for 'lack of utility' because it was not *buildable.* Nonetheless, he urged me to think it through, get as technical as I could, imagine tools, technologies, and materials that did not yet exist, and to go through the process of filing the application. And so I did! I filled out a fourteen-page application as best I could and mailed it in. My patent was denied, as expected, and I never gave it another thought . . ."

Until now, Langdon realized, incredulous. *She's face-to-face with her own invention.*

"In retrospect," Katherine said, "it occurs to me that Professor Cosgrove might have been *protecting* me when he told me to file a patent . . ." She paused, her voice catching. "As if he knew the *real* reason my thesis was denied."

"Because your technology was being secretly appropriated by the CIA?"

"Stolen, yes."

"But how would Cosgrove possibly know the CIA did that?"

"That's a mystery to me," Katherine said, "but my gut tells me he *knew*. Years later, I found out that I was the *only* student Cosgrove ever pushed to apply for a patent."

"That's suspicious."

"Yes, and Cosgrove was insistent. I remember him saying, 'Don't *talk* about it, Katherine. Just *do* it.' He's long since passed away, or I'd call him."

"Do you still have a copy of your application?" Langdon asked, imagining it was a fairly dangerous piece of paper to have lying around.

"I certainly did . . . but any copies I had mysteriously disappeared from my files at some point. I always assumed they got lost in the shuffle of moving, but now . . ."

They probably stole those too. Langdon shuddered to think that the CIA had been watching Katherine for such a long time, but it explained a lot.

"But here's the thing," Katherine continued. "All those years ago, when I received a rejection from the patent office, I had to laugh—it was fourteen pages of my most earnest scientific efforts stamped with a bright red DENIED on every page. I showed it to Professor Cosgrove, and he didn't seem as amused as I was, but he asked if he could keep a copy for posterity and for 'when I became famous.' Of course I said yes."

"So *Cosgrove* has a copy?!"

"Yes," she said, her voice suddenly emotional. "When he died about ten years ago, his sister showed up on my doorstep with a sealed manila envelope and said part of his final wishes was that this envelope be delivered to me." Katherine's voice caught. "Sure enough, it contained my old rejected patent application—faded but still very much intact."

Incredible. Langdon was now convinced that Katherine's old professor had known something was suspicious with the handling of her thesis paper and her patent application. The question of *how* Cosgrove knew what he knew was still unanswered, but clearly he had taken measures to ensure Katherine retained proof.

Leverage, Langdon thought. *That's what this represents.* "Where is that copy now?" he demanded, suddenly afraid the CIA might have gotten to that one too.

"In my desk at home," she said. "Last I knew."

"We need to go," Langdon said, motioning toward the door. "If the CIA discovers—"

"There's one more thing you should know." Katherine shifted awkwardly and then looked Langdon in the eye. "While I was writing the final chapter of my manuscript about the future of noetics, I was describing my youthful, wide-eyed dream of creating artificial neurons. On a whim, I decided to include a copy of my failed patent application—all fourteen pages stamped DENIED—in the book, because I figured sharing my own early failure might help inspire other young scientists who faced rejection along the way."

Langdon was speechless. *The final piece of the puzzle.*

Katherine's patent application would have been published in her book for the world to see. No other motive was required for the agency to take desperate action against her.

Threshold is the Manhattan Project of the future of brain science . . . and Katherine was about to publish blueprints for their atomic bomb.

Langdon could only imagine the legal nightmare for the CIA if a watchdog group like the Federation of American Scientists discovered that a prominent noeticist's patent application had been denied . . . and then stolen by the CIA without the applicant's knowledge or compensation.

It would be an investigative reporter's dream.

The book included a bold vision for a breakthrough technology that represented the missing piece in the global race for a true human-to-machine interface. At the moment, the CIA alone possessed it . . . but if Katherine published, all bets were off.

Whatever specific purpose the CIA's implants might serve, Threshold clearly had the potential to provide the CIA with a secret and unmatched technological advantage.

But that's not all, Langdon realized. *Threshold is a potential gold mine.*

If the CIA decided to bring proprietary H2M technology to market, Q would become the richest venture capital firm in the world, capable of funding every operation the CIA ran. Either way, secrecy was paramount.

"What's more," Katherine said, "this explains why Brigita bragged to me about her *patents* last night. She raised the subject because she was on a reconnaissance mission. Remember she asked me if I had any patents . . . or if I'd ever *applied* for a patent?"

Langdon remembered it well. "And you said you hadn't!"

"I just didn't want to get into it. And it was quite a long time ago."

"No wonder Finch panicked last night," Langdon said. "Gessner probably told him that you not only rebuffed her request for a signed NDA but rejected her request for an advance copy of the manuscript, *and* she must have reported that you'd also blatantly lied about never having applied for a patent! Finch would have suspected you were jockeying for personal gain and preparing to publish some kind of bombshell exposé."

"Well, we can publish it *now*," Katherine said, motioning to the classified binder in his hand. "Complete with PALM of an implanted brain. Pretty conclusive proof."

"What is PALM?"

"Photoactivated localization microscopy—a brain imaging technique. Threshold genetically encoded their artificial neurons with fluorescent proteins so they could, in effect, *see* them . . . and track their growth. Clever idea—*theirs*, not mine."

"Wait, are there *images* in this binder?! You didn't—"

"You took it away too fast," she said, holding her hands out for the binder. "I'll show you."

Langdon thrust the binder eagerly back into her hands. Despite their evidence that the CIA had stolen Katherine's idea and was building artificial neurons, Langdon had seen no actual *proof* that Threshold was doing human trials. *This could be it . . .*

"Here's a good one," Katherine said, laying the open binder on the counter before them.

When Langdon saw the image, he felt both repulsed . . . and vindicated. The colorful photo resembled a computer-enhanced X-ray of a human brain inside a skull. What was horrifying, however, was what *else* was inside the skull with the brain.

Beneath the bone of the skull, a surprisingly large computer chip was nestled into the brain tissue. Attached to the chip a cord snaked to an illuminated mesh of fluorescent threads that seemed to be woven into a lacy, weblike cap, similar to a hairnet, and pulled down over the top of the brain.

"That neural mesh," Katherine said. "*My* idea."

Langdon looked on in amazement as she flipped through various images, graphs, and notes monitoring the implant's progress over time. The records were startling, but the bigger shock came when Langdon noticed the tiny footer at the bottom of every page.

PATIENT #002 / VESNA

"Sasha . . ." Langdon whispered, his worst fears now confirmed. *What have they done to you?*

Langdon felt sickened to see the thick mesh of tentacles spread out over Sasha's brain like some kind of parasite. Ironically, he and Katherine had broken into Threshold to find incriminating evidence . . . only to learn that the single most incriminating piece of evidence was on the outside, inside Sasha Vesna's head.

I hope the ambassador has located Sasha, he thought, again sensing it was time to go.

"Whatever Ms. Vesna has in her head," Katherine said, "it does a lot more than cure epilepsy."

"Is there anything here that describes what the chip *does*?"

"Nothing specific," Katherine said, flipping pages. "This binder is all about neural integration, and I have to admit, I am amazed they're achieving *integration* so quickly."

"What do you mean?"

"Integration between chip and brain," she said. "Once you lay an artificial neural mesh on a living brain, the two elements need time to fuse into one system. Neural plasticity is a miracle, but it doesn't happen overnight. For a brain to synapse fully with a neural implant would take at least a decade—maybe two. It's one of the big obstacles I mentioned in my grad thesis."

"What did you propose as a solution?"

"I didn't," Katherine replied. "There is no solution but to wait. Biological growth takes *time*. Evolution takes *time*. And yet somehow . . ." She studied a series of graphs, shaking her head. "They've accelerated the process with remarkable speed. In a year, they've done what should have taken at least a decade. The question . . . is *how*?" She kept flipping pages, passing one on which appeared a tiny headshot of a younger Sasha Vesna with long blond hair.

"I have a different question," Langdon said. "If Sasha is patient number *two* . . ."

Katherine glanced up. "Right, then who is patient number *one*?"

She immediately began flipping backward through the binder, looking for information on patient number one, who Langdon assumed was most likely the Russian epilepsy patient, Dmitri, from the same institution as Sasha.

"This is strange," Katherine said. "I don't see any section with data on any other—oh, wait—here it is. It's much shorter. I missed it."

The section included assorted data, graphs, and a similarly eerie X-ray of the subject's brain showing an implanted chip and neural mesh.

The footer read:

PATIENT #001 / SYSEVICH

Sysevich certainly sounds Russian, Langdon thought.

"Handsome man," Katherine said, having turned to a page bearing a small headshot of a striking, square-jawed man with curly black hair. His features were clearly Slavic, sturdy and commanding, and yet his eyes had an unsettlingly lifeless gaze. "This guy was clearly implanted with the same chip as Sasha," Katherine said, still reading. "But it's weird—there's absolutely no data post-op. Nothing."

"We can talk on the way out," Langdon said, heading for the revolving door. "We've got to get out of here."

Katherine closed the binder and slipped it into her shoulder bag. "I hate to say it, but his records end too abruptly. Zero follow-up. It's like they put the chip in, and . . . something went wrong. Maybe he *died.*"

The thought was disturbing, and yet it added additional ammunition to the leverage they would have; if the CIA experimented on and *killed* an unsuspecting Russian epilepsy patient, the diplomatic fallout could have dire repercussions in a world already on edge.

As they pushed through the revolving door back into the hallway, Langdon was reassured to find the corridor pitch-black, its lights having timed out while they were in the lab.

We're still alone down here.

The floor lighting immediately came on, and Langdon and Katherine turned back toward the double doors through which they had come.

They had taken only a few steps when Katherine grabbed Langdon's arm. "Look!" she whispered, pointing dead ahead to the doors with the oval windows.

Langdon had seen it too.

The lights on the other side of that door had just blazed to life.

———··———

Having completed his thorough search of the medical area, Finch had continued around the corner, where the floor lighting came on to illuminate his path to the double doors at the end of the hall. Taking no chances, he took a moment to stick his head into Immersive Computing, where he was relieved to find all the VR chairs empty and helmets in order.

Then he saw the desk chair on its side.

And the cracked glass in the computer room window.

Normally Finch would have dashed over to check the computer, but he had just had a far more alarming realization—a delayed reaction to something he had glimpsed only moments earlier in the hallway . . . a soft glow coming through the oval windows of the double doors.

The lights in the RTD hallway were on.

———·· ·——→

Someone is coming!

Whether a cleaning crew, a security guard, or worse, Langdon knew he and Katherine could not afford to be seen. Unfortunately, they were trapped in a dead-end corridor with no way out except the way they had come.

Langdon rushed back toward the RTD lab, hoping to find somewhere to hide, but as he neared the clean room door, he realized Katherine had stopped in the middle of the hallway and was pointing at the floor. "Robert," she whispered. "These are tire marks!"

Langdon had seen the marks earlier—a trail of scuff marks worn into the polished floor by the treads of the forklift.

To his confusion, Katherine immediately sprinted past him, waving for him to follow her toward the dead end. *What is she doing?! There's no exit!* A moment later, Langdon spotted what Katherine had seen: the wear of tire tracks continued down the hallway and disappeared . . . *beneath* the far wall.

Impossible . . . unless . . .

Langdon broke into a full sprint, pulling even with Katherine fifteen yards from the end of the hall. He spotted the electric eye and ran toward it, waving to activate the sensor. The entire wall began to slide, retracting smoothly to the left, revealing another section of darkened corridor beyond.

The air emerging from the opening was noticeably colder.

Without breaking stride, he and Katherine ran through the opening and within a few yards plunged into sudden darkness. They came to a stop at a metal railing just as the retracting wall closed behind them.

Soft lighting swelled to reveal their surroundings. Langdon was startled to see they were standing atop a concrete ramp that wound downward around the perimeter of a narrow shaft. As he peered over the railing into the darkness below, he realized that Threshold was indeed considerably larger than what they had seen . . . and it continued in an unnerving direction.

Down.

CHAPTER 107

Ambassador Nagel hurried down the embassy's marble staircase, feeling somewhat unsteady, which wasn't all that surprising considering she had just strong-armed the CIA director and drained an afternoon cocktail.

Where the hell is Dana?

Sergeant Scott Kerble had promised to escort the publicity liaison upstairs to speak to the ambassador, but Dana had never shown up. Oddly, Kerble was nowhere to be seen either.

When Nagel arrived at Dana's office, the willowy publicity liaison was on her hands and knees, tearfully packing up personal belongings and piling them into a cardboard box. Dana glanced up, bloodshot eyes flashing disdain, then went back to packing.

Not good.

The ambassador took a moment and centered herself before speaking. "Ms. Daněk, did Scott Kerble ask you to come to my office?"

"He did."

"And you ignored him?"

"I don't work for you anymore," she said bitterly.

Nagel took a deep breath, entering and closing the door behind her. "Dana, I can see you're upset. I too cared deeply for Michael Harris, but—"

"*To je lež,*" she muttered without looking up.

"I *did* care about Michael," she insisted, "and I will never forgive myself for putting him in harm's way. I was pressured by my superiors. It was wrong, and I'm ashamed. I will explain it all to you at some point, but right now it's critical we locate Sasha Vesna, and I desperately need your help."

"Why would I *ever* help you?!" Dana fired back. "You should have known better than to force Michael into a romance with a stranger—a stranger who ended up killing him!"

"Sasha did *not* kill Michael," Nagel assured her. "The truth is that Sasha is in substantial danger herself—probably from the same person who killed Michael—and I need you to help me find her as soon as possible."

"Why do you care so much about her?"

Nagel moved closer and lowered her voice to a whisper. "Dana, I'm ashamed to say this, but like Michael . . . Sasha is a victim of my government." *She's a CIA asset . . . and doesn't even know it.* "I feel a duty to help her." She paused, holding Dana's gaze. "And I believe Michael would have wanted you to help Sasha too."

The statuesque young woman shivered suddenly, wrapping her arms around herself and setting her jaw tightly as if trying to fend off tears. Nagel was reminded that when someone was as strikingly beautiful as Dana Daněk, it was easy to forget their human frailties.

"I could never trust you again," Dana said, her voice cracking.

"I've got absolutely nothing left to lose," Nagel replied. "Dana, I'm trying to buy my soul back at any cost. And for whatever it's worth, I just burned my last bridge. I called my old boss and threatened the U.S. government."

Dana looked skeptical. "Your old boss? You threatened the director of the CIA?"

"I did." Nagel gave her a tight smile. "As I said, nothing left to lose. I've just learned some extremely disturbing news about a program I helped facilitate, and my only hope of stopping it and proving my own innocence is a video I just received—a deathbed confession by the program's principl—"

"Ambassador?" a man said behind her.

Nagel spun to see the face of Sergeant Scott Kerble, peering through the narrow opening of the door he had just quietly opened.

"Most people knock," Dana snapped.

"Scott?" Nagel said. "Where *were* you? You were supposed—"

"I'm sorry, ma'am." His voice sounded uncharacteristically stern. "I'm afraid I've been ordered to detain you."

Nagel eyed her trusted security guard, having little doubt what had just transpired. "Ordered by the director of the CIA?"

"Please come with me."

"You can't arrest the ambassador!" Dana said. "She's your boss!"

Kerble shook his head. "We're U.S. military."

Dana looked at Nagel, who confirmed it with a nod. Unfortunately, Marine security guards took their orders from much higher up the food chain. The ambassador now deeply regretted her decision to entrust Kerble with the diplomatic pouch. *My only copy of the video . . .*

"Madam Ambassador?" Kerble looked genuinely uncomfortable. "Please come with me."

"Of course, Scott. I just need a moment. Ms. Daněk has tendered her resignation, and I'd like a private moment to say goodb—"

"Hands in front of you!" a deep voice commanded as the door swung open to reveal two other Marines waiting behind Kerble. They apparently felt duty bound to support their lead agent whose courtesy was getting him nowhere.

"Handcuffs won't be necessary," Nagel said. "I'll come quietly, but I'd like a quick word with Ms.—"

"That's not possible," the first Marine barked, moving through the door. "Show me your wrists, ma'am."

Incredulous, Nagel looked to Kerble, whose expression had turned decidedly colder in the presence of his fellow agents.

"Give him your wrists," Kerble commanded. "And not another word with Ms. Daněk. We have orders. No further contact with anyone. We've sealed your office and will be searching it, along with the rest of the embassy."

"Searching?" Nagel could feel her only leverage slipping away. "For . . . *what*?"

Kerble ignored the question and turned to Dana. "Ms. Daněk,

if you have tendered your resignation, you will need to exit the embassy immediately. Do you understand?"

"I do . . . but—"

"Are those your personal items in that box?"

Dana nodded.

Kerble walked over to the box, peered inside, and then glanced back at Nagel, catching her eye for an instant as the other Marines focused on binding her wrists. She watched as Kerble leaned over Dana's desk and jotted something on a sticky note. Then, in one smooth motion, he reached into his uniform's breast pocket, extracted the diplomatic pouch Nagel had given him, affixed the sticky note to it, and slid the pouch into the box, tucking it out of sight beneath Dana's belongings.

Did he really just do that?!

Stone-faced, Kerble marched back toward Nagel, who was now restrained with a set of standard-issue nylon flex cuffs. "Madam Ambassador," he said, "I would suggest you follow the orders of these men without hesitation. It is for your own safety."

Before Nagel could reply, Kerble had turned back to Dana.

"Ms. Daněk!" he said sternly, leaving no doubt who was in charge. "Time's up—collect your box of personal items and vacate these premises immediately!"

Dana looked frightened as she grabbed her cardboard box and rushed past the handcuffed ambassador, heading straight for the exit.

———

Nagel is in some serious trouble.

Scott Kerble watched as his officers escorted the ambassador down the service stairwell toward the basement. Having served diplomats his entire career, Kerble had never met one he more admired or trusted than Heide Nagel. His impulsive decision to break ranks and protect her had been a reflex . . . a gut instinct . . . and he had done it at no small risk to his career.

Something is not right here . . .

CIA Director Gregory Judd had offered Kerble's team no

details—only a direct order; the ambassador was to be locked in the embassy's situation room, under guard, and detained until further notice.

Wildly irregular.

Stranger still, the director had ordered an exhaustive search of the ambassador's private office to collect any and all digital media—computers, hard drives, DVDs, USBs, etc.—which made sense in only two scenarios. Either they suspected Nagel was a spy, which was absurd, or the director was afraid she had information that would be damaging to the agency itself.

Kerble felt confident that whatever the director was hoping to confiscate had just left the building . . . in a cardboard box with Dana Daněk.

Keep it safe, the ambassador had told him. *Mention it to no one.*

Kerble had no idea what the contents of the pouch might be, but he knew Dana would never dare open it. Moreover, the CIA director would be the last person Dana would ever call about it.

Just to be certain, Kerble had added a safely anonymous sticky note to the pouch:

D— Tell no one about this. I will contact you.

The pouch is safe, he thought. *At least for the moment.*

Kerble had said nothing to his colleagues. Nor had he mentioned the ambassador's aberrant behavior—including her arrival to the embassy on *foot* and unescorted. *Nagel is the most ethical person I've ever met*, he reminded himself. *She's clearly caught up in something I don't understand.*

Considering the ambassador was now in custody, he thought it prudent to recover her private SUV, get it off the street, and store it in the embassy's parking courtyard with the rest of the fleet. Kerble went to the security office and retrieved the emergency set of keys they kept for all embassy vehicles. Then he turned to a computer terminal to pull up the location of the concealed tracking device that existed in any vehicle that might carry the ambassador. Kerble knew the SUV was close by, since the ambassador had walked back to the residence, but using the GPS coordinates would save him precious time wandering the streets.

He waited a moment as the tracker was activated. When the blinking dot appeared on the map of Prague, Kerble stared in confusion. The vehicle was most definitely *not* parked nearby, as expected. Instead, it was parked three miles away . . . on the ridgeline above Folimanka Park.

Several stories underground, The Golĕm strode across the SMES vault toward the twelve Cryofab tanks of liquid helium. The top of each massive flask terminated in a reinforced electronic bayonet and valve connected to an insulated pipe that fed the SMES. On the wall near the tanks glowed a control panel bearing a diagram of all twelve canisters and their various statuses.

By all appearances, the screen regulated the flow of helium to each canister. The Golĕm had no idea how to use this panel, nor did he have any intention of trying. What he was planning required no subtlety. There was a very simple way to halt the flow of the supercooled liquid into the SMES.

He approached the first canister, a bulbous stainless-steel flask taller than he was. His clay-caked face reflected back at him. *I am not a monster,* he reminded himself, knowing his outer shell, like everyone's, was a mirage that shrouded the truth within. *I am her protector.*

As expected, at the top of each tank beside the clutter of electronic connectors and valves, there was a *manual* cutoff—a handwheel valve that one could turn in emergencies to stop the flow of helium.

As simple as turning off a garden hose.

According to everything he had read, the slow chain reaction would begin as soon as the flow of helium was halted, causing the superconducting coils to begin to heat up, losing some of their conductivity, resisting the current . . . and commencing a deadly feedback loop.

Heat $\Rightarrow$ Resistance $\Rightarrow$ Heat $\Rightarrow$ Resistance $\Rightarrow$ Heat . . .

Once I close the valves, he estimated, *I'll have about twenty minutes.*

After that time, the coils would heat up and reach critical temperature—the "quench limit" when all the liquid helium in the system would begin to boil . . . converting to gas. The Golĕm pictured the quench vent above him, which was now sealed shut, and he imagined the rapidly expanding cloud of helium gas trying to escape safely in a geyser of icy helium vapor.

No longer possible, he thought. *Today will be a different scenario.*

The rapidly expanding gas cloud would find no escape and would begin applying enormous pressure to every square inch of this airtight chamber.

Including on the rupture disks.

The Golĕm took a deep breath and surveyed the line of canisters. He could already imagine the pressure in the vault climbing . . . pressing out against the thick concrete walls . . . causing the rupture disks in each tank to fail. Very suddenly, there would be some twenty thousand liters of liquid helium exposed to open air.

The chain reaction would be instantaneous and unstoppable—a catastrophic expansion event—as violent and destructive as igniting a powerful warhead in this small space.

CHAPTER 108

As he descended, Langdon found himself wishing their escape through the retracting wall had led to *daylight*, rather than to a ramp that spiraled deeper into the earth. While it was logical that a bomb shelter would have a lower level—after all, the nuclear command centers at Cheyenne Mountain and Yamantau Mountain were both built under more than a thousand feet of solid granite—Langdon had hoped to be carrying the evidence they had gathered *up* and *out* of Threshold . . . not farther into it.

With luck, whoever had entered Threshold behind them was not a threat, but still Langdon and Katherine had wasted no time beginning their descent and putting distance between themselves and whoever was entering behind them. Having finally obtained the proof they needed, they now had to find their way *out*.

Spiraling deeper, they reached the bottom of the ramp just as a frightening sound materialized above them—the rapid staccato of hard-soled shoes on concrete, moving at an accelerated pace. This was no janitor.

"We need to *go!*" Langdon whispered.

At the base of the ramp, there was another retractable wall, identical to the one above. They hurried through it and found themselves in an eerie corridor that was approximately thirty feet long. In the dim light, the matte-black walls, ceilings, and floors gave off the aura more of a mausoleum than a tech facility.

"It's a different world down here . . ." Katherine whispered.

Wherever they now were, Langdon estimated they had less than twenty seconds to find a place to hide. The spiral ramp had left him increasingly disoriented, and the exit at Crucifix Bastion felt farther away with every step. Being spotted way down here, Langdon now feared, would result in an alarm being sounded, making escape nearly impossible.

They jogged down the sepulchral hallway, passing a long window on their right, beyond which a sea of green and red pinpoint lights pulsed in the darkness. Langdon could just make out the silhouettes of dozens of massive computer racks housed inside a meshed cage.

"Faraday shielding . . ." Katherine whispered. "Those computers must be quantum."

Langdon knew very little about quantum computers except that they required shielding from cosmic rays and other forms of radiation. *Another reason why Threshold is underground?*

As they passed the computer room entrance, Katherine never slowed, apparently sharing Langdon's instinct not to trap themselves inside a literal metal cage.

The hallway took a sharp left, and as they rounded the corner, more soft lighting came on, illuminating a much longer section of similar black corridor.

"There!" Katherine whispered, pointing to the far end of the hall.

What lay ahead did indeed offer a ray of hope, but Langdon now heard the unmistakable sound of footsteps echoing behind them again.

We'll never make it in time.

In the distance, the hallway terminated at a metal door, above which a message was emblazoned in the most efficient and universal language on earth—a symbol whose entire meaning was instantaneously conveyed.

The symbol of the ascending staircase was a welcome sight, and Langdon felt confident that if they could climb back to the upper floor, they could find their way to the bastion exit the way they had come.

But we can't reach the stairs unseen, he thought, hearing the footsteps getting closer.

The hallway ahead offered two other doorways, both on the right. Regrettably, Langdon could already see that neither would be of any help.

The first door, just ahead, was marked SUPPLY ROOM. If it was anything like the medical supply room upstairs, the space was a long warren of shelving with automatic lights and no exit. *A death trap.*

The second doorway, just beyond it, was much larger and set back several feet in a recessed alcove. Whatever lay beyond the door was apparently important, because Langdon could see from here that it was equipped with a familiar security device—a circular pad of black glass.

An RFID scanner . . . for which we no longer have authorization.

The footsteps behind them were getting loud.

As they approached the supply room door, Langdon slowed to a stop as a thought materialized. One of the great mysteries of consciousness was *where* ideas came from. Katherine claimed the mind was a receiver that tuned into a greater field of consciousness. Gessner claimed the brain was a computer whose trillions of neural switches simply solved the problem.

At the moment, Langdon didn't care who was right. The source of his idea was irrelevant. All that mattered was that he suddenly knew exactly what to do.

—··—

Why did he stop?!

Katherine turned back to Langdon, who was opening the supply room door. It was obvious they could not reach the stairway at the end of the hall without being seen, but hiding in the supply room seemed like suicide.

She hurried back to stop him, but Langdon had already

stepped inside. The fluorescent lights directly above flickered on to illuminate the entrance to the narrow warren of shelves that extended away from them into darkness. Without hesitation, Langdon grabbed a bottle of liquid cleaner off the shelf and, like a bowler, slung the bottle down the aisle between the shelves. It skittered along the floor and slid all the way to the end without touching either side, triggering a series of motion lights into the deepest recesses of the supply room. Even before the bottle had hit the far wall, Langdon stepped back into the hall. He closed the door but left it open a crack, allowing a sliver of fluorescent light to spill into the dimly lit corridor. Then he grabbed Katherine's hand and pulled her as quickly as possible in the direction they had been going, toward the stairwell door that was still at least forty yards away.

As they ran, she felt buoyed by a sudden optimism, having just realized Langdon's clever thinking. *We don't need to reach the end of the hall yet . . .*

As she anticipated, when they neared the recessed alcove with the RFID scanner, Langdon cut hard right, pulling Katherine with him into the alcove. The recess was shallow—less than three feet deep—and they spun around and stood with their backs against the cold metal of the heavy door, making themselves as tall and slender as possible, hoping the alcove was deep enough to conceal them from view.

A moment later, the sound of footsteps entered the hall and stopped.

There was a long silence.

Then Katherine heard the unmistakable sound of a gun being cocked.

Jonas Faukman's eyes opened abruptly, and he realized he had drifted off at his desk. He was uncertain why he had awoken so suddenly—perhaps the sound of rain that was now pelting his window—but as he stood to stretch, he was surprised to feel the cool creep of returning dread.

Everything is fine, he assured himself. *RL&KSRGUD.*

CHAPTER 109

Langdon and Katherine stood rigid, side by side and barely breathing. Their backs were quite literally against the wall, or more accurately, against an exceptionally wide steel door. Even though they had slipped into this recess undetected, their arrival had been accompanied by the unwelcome sound of a gun being cocked.

Langdon remained still, hoping the fluorescent lights blazing in the supply room would be suspicious enough to warrant a search.

We just need a minute's distraction.

If not . . . they were trapped.

The footsteps slowly began again, moving closer. After several tense seconds, Langdon saw a welcome sight—a faint splash of fluorescent light on the far wall. *Whoever is there opened the supply room door!*

Suddenly, the fluorescent lights disappeared, and Langdon heard the supply room door click shut. *Did he go inside?!* Langdon strained to hear footsteps, but there was only silence. Katherine shifted beside him, and he felt her hand trying to find his at his side. For a moment, he thought she was looking for emotional support, but then he felt her press a small object into his palm. He glanced down and saw a compact mirror, which she had just pulled from her bag.

Langdon flipped the mirror open with his thumb and carefully extended it just an inch past the edge of the recess. In the tiny reflection, he hoped to see an empty hallway. But instead, he saw the unmistakable shape of a figure approaching, inching stealthily toward them. The man was older, with silver hair, a dark suit, and glasses.

Whoever the man was, he had not been fooled. His handgun was raised, pointing in their direction.

———··———

Everett Finch peered over the barrel of the outstretched SIG Sauer pistol and surveyed the hallway ahead. The intruder was near. Whoever had penetrated the lower level of Threshold had not come to hide in a supply closet; they had come for something else.

And if they've made it this far, they're perilously close to uncovering Threshold's most sensitive secret.

As Finch advanced, he maintained focus on the hallway's lone hiding place—the recessed doorway ahead on the right, which was just deep enough to conceal anyone who was standing flush with the heavy metal door.

Hugging the left-hand side of the corridor, he moved with furtive steps, keeping his gun trained on the alcove. As his angle improved, his sight line began to reveal the interior of the alcove. When he finally glimpsed the leftmost edge of the metal door, Finch surged forward with two long strides and crouched down, swinging his arms around and taking dead aim.

To his surprise, the alcove was empty.

———··———

Langdon and Katherine stood face-to-face, hearts pounding.

What just happened?!

Seconds ago, with their backs against the wide steel door, Langdon had recoiled from the reflection of a man advancing on them with a pistol. As he pressed up hard against the door, he felt suddenly as if he was losing his balance—but then Katherine's eyes went wide with disbelief, and it dawned on Langdon what had just happened.

The heavy door behind them . . . had moved.

Langdon leaned back hard again, joined by Katherine. The door was spring-loaded and stiff, but as they braced their feet and thrust themselves backward, it swung open. It made no sense considering the presence of an RFID scanner, but as he and Katherine slipped through, Langdon noticed the strike plate in the doorjamb was stuffed with some kind of green fabric, apparently to keep it from locking.

Who propped this door open?!

Fearing the gunman in the hall, Langdon instinctively pulled the green material out of the strike plate and quietly let the door close. The portal clicked and engaged. *Locked.* The material in his hand, he now realized, was not fabric at all, but rather vinyl or rubber—a cluster of artificial leaves that must have been yanked off the fake ficus tree just inside the door.

"Incredible luck," Langdon whispered in amazement.

Katherine looked less relieved than he expected. "Unless someone wanted to be sure they could get *out*."

"What do you mean?"

She pointed to a second RFID scanner on the wall beside the ficus tree. "You also need a card to *exit*, Robert. Someone was trying to prop this door open . . . but we've just locked ourselves in."

◄——··——►

The Golĕm gripped the turn wheel on the fourth canister of helium and twisted it to the right, just as he had done with the first three. *The end is near.* After several tight turns, the valve was fully closed, and the control panel beeped urgently. The icon for canister #4 turned red. OFF. Four indicators in a row now glowed red with warning, alongside eight that still were illuminated green.

He began the process anew for canister #5, laboring slowly as the wheel turned. OFF.

The Golĕm made his way down the line, turning off each valve. Every time he shut down a canister, the controller pinged and made an adjustment, opening the helium flow to the next fresh backup canister.

Despite his eagerness to finish the job, The Golĕm moved slowly and maintained slow, deep breathing to help prevent another seizure. His objective was within sight now, and he forced himself to be cautious. As he closed each valve, he rehearsed in his mind the steps he would take to escape.

Twenty minutes will be plenty of time . . .

A loud buzzer sounded now, pulling The Golěm back from his thoughts. The control panel was flashing warnings and emitting increasingly urgent beeps. The display screen showed *eleven* canisters were off. Every canister except #12 was now manually disconnected from the SMES. More importantly, nine of those canisters were listed as 100 percent full.

Thousands of kilos of liquid helium in this tiny space.

The Golěm took a deep breath and reviewed his plan one last time, then placed his hand on the turn wheel of #12.

I do this for you, Sasha, he thought as he began closing the valve.

Threshold was built with your blood.

Our blood.

The valve came to a stop, fully closed.

And now I have destroyed it.

◆——··——◆

At CIA headquarters in Langley, Director Judd sat alone in his secure communications room. He was trying to formulate the proper response to the horrifying video he had just witnessed. A tech team had already purged the video from the Internet, but that offered little solace; whoever had interrogated Gessner could simply repost it at any time.

If this video leaked, Judd had little doubt it would go viral almost immediately—across the globe. Not only did it feature the brutal torture of a prominent scientist, but the video contained a confession that revealed the existence of a highly secret U.S. intelligence project . . . including its location . . . technological breakthroughs . . . and use of nonvoluntary human subjects.

The fallout would be like nothing the CIA had ever experienced.

CHAPTER 110

L angdon surveyed the small room into which he and Katherine had just escaped.
Whatever this place is . . . I've just locked us in.
The space felt decidedly softer than the sterile corridor outside; it had carpeting, a number of realistic artificial trees, and even a series of abstract paintings on the wall. There was an arched opening ahead of them, and he eyed it with trepidation. Beyond, a wide concrete tunnel curved to the left and out of sight. Three things about the passage felt instantly ominous to Langdon.

First, the tunnel lights were already on—pale blue on the gray walls—suggesting that someone else might already be inside. Second, the floor of the tunnel was inclined downward, and Langdon hesitated to venture *deeper* into the earth. And finally, it seemed clear from the RFID cards required to enter *and* exit this area that the tunnel likely led to the most secure area of Threshold—rather than to an exit.

For a fleeting moment, Langdon wondered if the safest move would be to surrender, but he had a growing suspicion that the older, well-dressed man pursuing them might actually be Mr. Finch himself—a man who, according to the ambassador, took no prisoners and would stop at nothing to protect Threshold.

We need somewhere to hide . . . now.

Langdon caught up with Katherine partway down the tunnel, which they followed to another arched portico. This entrance was framed in elegant black stone, with a wide swinging door of frosted glass. The translucent surface was etched with a familiar image:

PRAGUE

Langdon and Katherine exchanged a silent look. It seemed that whatever they had seen so far—robotic surgeons, VR labs, artificial neurons, and computer chips—was only the preamble to whatever lay beyond this doorway.

With a surge of adrenaline, Langdon moved to the door and pushed it open just far enough to peer inside. To his surprise, he felt his gaze shift immediately in the one direction he had not anticipated this deep underground.

Up.

Langdon found himself looking skyward into a high domed ceiling—a concave canopy that was gently illuminated from below. The circular dome reminded him of a planetarium, and yet Langdon knew what it once had been. *The dome is the strongest architectural form.* This was Folimanka Bunker's "blast shelter"— the safe room where people congregated during an attack—its deepest, most secure space.

Langdon had once seen another secret underground dome— also owned by the U.S. government—concealed beneath the golf course of the Greenbrier Resort in West Virginia. For over three decades, the U.S. Congress's private nuclear fallout shelter, Greenbrier Bunker, had been one of America's best-kept secrets until the *Washington Post* published an exposé in 1992.

Langdon lowered his gaze and looked around the room itself. *This is definitely not a planetarium.* The chamber was vast and perfectly round, and it looked like nothing Langdon had seen in his entire life.

What is this place?

Bewildered, Katherine stepped into the domed chamber with Langdon. At first glance, it seemed like a depiction of a futuristic spacecraft's command bridge.

The center of the room was dominated by a raised circular platform on which at least twenty sleek workstations sat in a ring, all facing outward. Each command post consisted of an elaborate cockpit—similar to a flight simulator.

As Katherine lowered her gaze to the main floor, she found herself unable to make sense of what she was seeing there. Precisely arranged on the plush carpeted floor surrounding the command bridge, a starburst array of sleek, low-slung metallic pods radiated outward like the spokes of a wheel. Each glistening pod resembled a piece of modern art—a minimalist, torpedolike shell of sleek black metal, three meters long and aligned with its own command post up on the bridge.

Puzzled, she moved toward the closest pod, now seeing that the top of each was actually a convex panel of tinted glass, so perfectly tailored that it had no seams. She peered down through the glass but saw only darkness within.

"What are these things?" Katherine whispered as Langdon arrived beside her.

He studied the pod a moment and then reached down and touched a button discreetly recessed in its side. There was a hiss of air, like the release of a vacuum, and the glass lid of the pod hinged upward like a gullwing door. Soft lights illuminated inside, revealing a padded interior that resembled a futuristic sleeping pod.

Or a coffin.

"It looks like an advanced version," Langdon said, "of the pod we saw in Gessner's lab."

Katherine nodded, peering in at the Velcro restraints and the IV connector. This machine was clearly the offspring of the rudimentary prototype in which they had seen Gessner's body . . . the suspended-animation machine capable of holding a critically injured patient on the threshold of death for hours.

In addition to being larger and sleeker than its forefather, this version contained a specialized head cradle with plush leather padding and a skull-sized opening. The opening looked a lot like a magnetoencephalograph's "sensing cavity"—the area equipped with magnetic sensors to detect neuronal activity—although Katherine assumed that if brain chips were involved, the opening probably contained some kind of near-field or ultra-wideband technology commonly used to interface with brain implants.

Wireless communication directly through the skull, she thought, feeling a chill. *If a subject is implanted with a fully integrated H2M brain chip . . . and that chip is capable of real-time monitoring . . .*

Katherine felt dizzy as it began to dawn on her precisely what this room was designed to do. Incredibly, she and Robert had been discussing the topic all afternoon . . . altered states of consciousness, out-of-body experiences, psychedelic drug trips, epileptic postictal bliss. A collage of concepts now flooded her mind: brain filters, universal connection, humankind's untapped ability to glimpse a vastly wider spectrum of reality.

These gleaming sarcophagi, she now realized, were the final piece of a research project that, less than an hour ago, she would have declared utterly impossible.

Is this really happening?

Beside her, Langdon raised his eyes from the pod and gazed out over the entire dome. "But I don't understand . . . what happens in this room?"

The answer to his question, Katherine knew, was as simple as it was mind-bending. *This place was engineered to unveil life's most enigmatic secret . . . the mind's ultimate altered state . . . the single most elusive of human experiences.*

As the weight of the moment settled over her, Katherine reached out and quietly took his hand.

"Robert," she whispered. "They've built a death lab."

CHAPTER 111

A death lab.

As Langdon began to grasp the implications of Katherine's startling revelation, he felt a rush of new questions. *Why would the CIA be studying death? What are they hoping to find?*

As intellectually exciting as Langdon found the prospect of understanding death, he feared this room served a far darker purpose than simply studying human consciousness or death. The horror of subjecting someone to the "death state" for any reason other than life support seemed unconscionable. *Even if the patient is drugged or cannot recall the experience . . .*

"I need to know *everything* about this research," Katherine said, moving deeper into the array of pods.

"We need to keep moving," Langdon urged, firing a nervous glance back toward the entryway.

He quickly joined her and motioned to the far side of the dome, where a sign read SYSTEMS / UTILITIES. He doubted a utilities room would have an exit, but at least it might offer somewhere better to hide, and Langdon saw no better option. *No way out.*

They hurried through the maze of pods, and halfway across the dome, Langdon could see that the utility area was accessed not through a door . . . but rather through a large rectangular opening in the floor.

Farther underground?

Whether the opening had stairs, a ladder, or some kind of lift, the idea of descending any deeper into the earth was one Langdon did not relish.

As it turned out, descending was not an option anyway.

An ear-piercing gunshot rang out behind them. The roar of the weapon reverberated in the dome overhead. Langdon and Katherine both wheeled around, frozen in their tracks, as the silver-haired man in the dark suit approached with his weapon leveled at them both.

"Dr. Solomon and Professor Langdon, I presume?" he said calmly. His voice was familiar—the same Southern drawl Langdon had heard on the speakerphone with the ambassador.

Finch.

"You're playing a dangerous game," he said, approaching. "And I'm afraid it's not going to end well for you."

———

Finch knew there was nothing as arresting as the sound of gunfire in an enclosed space. In movies, it made people flee, but in real life it had a paralyzing effect. He took pleasure seeing Langdon and Solomon rooted in place, arms raised, showing their palms—the universal sign of surrender. His targets were now in *reaction* mode, and Finch held all the cards.

"Set down your bag, Dr. Solomon," he commanded in case she had a weapon in it.

Solomon obeyed, laying her shoulder bag on the floor. As she did, Finch saw the bag contained a thick black binder . . . no doubt one of the classified documents they'd collected along the way.

You're making this easy for me.

By all accounts, these two intruders had just broken into a secret government project and stolen top secret material. If Finch shot them dead, there would be no investigation, especially since they had made it this far into the restricted facility. Ironically, *death* was precisely what this room was designed for.

Nonetheless, Finch would need to interrogate them first . . . and find out who else was involved in this, and how. Ambassador Nagel was clearly guilty, having not only crossed Finch but also threatened the agency. *Extremely bad idea.* Director Judd had no doubt detained the ambassador by now and would deal with her appropriately.

The wild card is Sasha Vesna, he thought, remembering the epilepsy wand he had found upstairs. He was still struggling to accept that Sasha had murdered two people. *Questions for later,* he told himself. *Right now, manage the issue at hand . . . my two captives.*

Strategically, it made no sense for Finch to march Langdon and Solomon out of the building at gunpoint. Despite being an extremely fit seventy, Finch's diminutive stature would prove no match for the six-foot Langdon should anything go wrong, and the trek back to the bastion offered far too many chances for a surprise attack. Threshold's secondary access point was closer, but it was currently being used for construction, and it was manned by U.S. soldiers. Finch exiting with two Americans at gunpoint would raise too many questions.

And so we wait, he decided, having immediately called for backup upon finding Housemore's body. *Help is on the way.*

The interrogation would take place in Threshold, Finch had proudly decided. His facility offered superb secrecy and *efficacy.* The EPR pods could be used extremely persuasively, and the Threshold pharmacy burgeoned with interrogational aids, including memory impairment drugs should it become necessary that "none of this ever happened."

As Finch moved slowly toward his captives, he felt confident the situation was entirely under his control. His lone oversight—a minor one—had been failure to check the rounds in Housemore's gun, but having seen no signs of a gunfight upstairs, he was nearly certain her SIG Sauer P226 had a nearly full magazine.

Finch preferred not to use the weapon—at least not yet—but he knew he would have no choice if Langdon and Solomon decided to rush him. *I have to keep them calm.* The most effective manipulation to control captives was to distract them with other thoughts. Conveniently, Langdon and Solomon were still apparently thunderstruck by what they had found down here, and the more Finch explained about Threshold, the clearer it would become to the agency that Langdon and Solomon knew far too much to go free. Ever.

"There's no need to shoot," Langdon declared as Finch arrived before them, gun leveled at their chests. "We'll sign your NDAs. Just tell us what you need."

"Oh, that moment has passed," Finch replied coolly. "You've broken into a top secret facility, and you've seen entirely too much."

"True," Solomon declared, her tone indignant. "I saw you stole my patent."

Her apparent lack of fear told Finch that she had yet to grasp the true peril of her situation. "We stole nothing, Dr. Solomon," he said calmly. "You held no patent. As you may recall, it was denied."

"But why all the tactical maneuvers?!" Langdon demanded. "Why not simply contact Katherine or her publisher and explain—"

"Because we're not suicidal," Finch shot back. "Ask Dr. Solomon how she feels about sharing research with the U.S. military. She gave a damning podcast interview about it once. I could not risk her going public and sharing the agency's concerns. Besides, Mr. Langdon, we had no time. This all came to a head last night very quickly—"

"What experiments are you running here?!" Katherine interrupted, surveying the EPR pods with undisguised amazement. "Are you studying *death*?"

"How much would you like to know?" Finch asked, nodding ominously toward the pod closest to them. "Get in and I'll show you."

"That won't be necessary," Langdon said. "Take your classified binder back. We'll sign NDAs. We've seen some of your facility, but we understood almost nothing."

Finch chuckled. "Bright people playing dumb? That's never very convincing, Professor. Allow me to enlighten you."

"Please don't," Langdon said. "I think we'd prefer *not* to know what you're doing down here."

"Well, that hardly seems fair," Finch said with a smile. "Considering Dr. Solomon helped *build* it."

◆ ·· ◆

The Golĕm had stepped onto the pneumatic lift to ascend back to the domed chamber when the gunshot rang out. Alarmed, he immediately stepped off, waiting in silence beneath the opening.

The conversation above was perfectly audible.

An armed man had just taken two hostages in the dome, and he had addressed them as Dr. Solomon and Robert Langdon. Why the two Americans were down here, The Golĕm had no idea, but neither one of them deserved to die.

The man with the gun, however, most certainly *did*. The Golĕm had quickly realized that this was Everett Finch, who, according to Gessner, was the mastermind behind Threshold.

The head of the snake. Here in the flesh.

The universe had just offered The Golĕm an unexpected gift—the opportunity to eliminate Sasha's ultimate betrayer . . . the man who had created this house of horrors.

As alluring a prospect as it was to kill Finch, the task seemed nearly impossible. The Golĕm had only a stun gun with a single discharge remaining—no match for a firearm—and if he ascended on the pneumatic platform, he would rise out of the floor in plain view at the back of the domed chamber, totally exposed.

The clock is ticking, he reminded himself, estimating he had only fifteen minutes or so before this room detonated and became a catastrophic pressure bomb.

Waiting here too long was certain death, and he wondered if he should run back through the long utilities passageway to the SMES vault and try to abort the blast. The airtight portal's turn wheel had required substantial effort to seal on his way out, and he feared that the energy required to open it again might prove too much for him.

A dangerous gamble without my wand, he thought.

The Golĕm felt ready to trade his life for Mr. Finch's, but he knew he could not make that decision for Sasha. If he didn't escape and release her, she would never again see the light of day.

CHAPTER 112

I n the spectral glow of the dome, surrounded by suspended-animation pods, Robert Langdon stood beside Katherine and studied their captor. Having positioned himself a safe five yards away, Everett Finch was leaning comfortably against a pod, his gun leveled.

Considering the tense circumstances, Finch's demeanor seemed unsettlingly serene. There was an icy detachment about this man that suggested he was capable of doing whatever was necessary.

"The future will be controlled by those who develop the first true human-to-machine interface," Finch began. "Effortless communication between people and technology. No typing, dictating, viewing . . . just *thinking*. The financial ramifications alone are enough to create a new world superpower, but the *practical* applications, particularly in the field of intelligence work . . . are unimaginable."

Langdon suspected a viable H2M technology, in the wrong hands, could make the worst Orwellian nightmare look like an amusing daydream.

"For this reason," Finch continued, "the CIA had been working tirelessly to keep pace with the biotech behemoths—Neuralink, Kernal, Synchron, and the rest—all of whom have bottomless war chests and the same quest to be the first brain implant capable of true high-speed, human-to-machine communication. Fortunately for us, they've all faced the same hurdle."

"The interface," Katherine said. "How to create artificial neurons."

Finch nodded. "Neuralink has had moderate success, but nothing on the scale of what's necessary. The missing piece turns out to be a design that the CIA has been fortunate enough to be developing for two decades now."

"Taken from Katherine's patent," Langdon said.

"To repeat, Dr. Solomon holds no patent. And if she *had*, we would have taken it over in the name of national security. The challenge with exercising eminent domain is that the process can be contentious and public, often revealing precisely what the agency is interested in keeping secret."

"What are you doing with my design?" Katherine demanded. "What is Threshold?"

Finch removed his glasses with his free hand and slowly rolled out his neck. "Dr. Solomon, perhaps you recall when Caltech built an implant that tapped into the brain's visual cortex and could effectively 'see' whatever the host was seeing through his or her eyes."

"Certainly I remember," Katherine said. "The implant captured optical signals passing through the optic nerve, translated them, and broadcasted them out as live video."

Langdon was not familiar with the technology, but it sounded essentially like an internal GoPro camera—a way to look through someone *else's* eyes. *Is Threshold monitoring what subjects are seeing?* If so, it was an entirely new kind of surveillance. Langdon looked up at the video screens encircling the dome and imagined point-of-view broadcasts from people moving about their daily lives. *But then why the pods?*

"The agency has been working on something similar," Finch said, "a far superior version of that implant—one that can monitor what is being experienced not by the *eyes* . . . but rather by the *mind's eye*."

For Langdon, the phrase "mind's eye" conjured images of the colorful *bindi* dot worn between the eyebrows to represent the gateway to spiritual wisdom, also called the Third Eye.

"Your mind's eye, Professor," Finch said, apparently sensing Langdon's uncertainty, "is the mechanism by which your brain sees *without* your eyes. When you close your eyes and picture your childhood home, a vivid image appears. That is your *mind's eye*. Your brain does not require visual input to conjure detailed images. Your brain continuously views memories, fantasies, day-dreams, imaginations. Even when you sleep, your brain conjures images in the forms of dreams and nightmares."

"You can't really have built . . ." Katherine trailed off, looking for the right words.

"We did," Finch replied with a hint of pride. "Threshold has created an implant that can view the content of the mind's eye. We can now monitor the full spectrum of images a brain con-jures . . . seeing it unfold in real time, in full detail."

From the stupefied look on Katherine's face, Langdon sensed this was an astonishing feat in the field of brain science. He was aware that a scientist at Kyoto University had recently announced a technology that recorded dreams and played them back as a rough movie, although his process sounded rudimentary—using AI to translate MRI dream data into approximated images. What Finch was describing sounded like a quantum leap.

Can Threshold spy on the imagination?

Langdon wondered if this technology related somehow to Katherine's notion of the brain as a receiver. After all, if an implant could see an image that *materialized* in the brain, maybe the implant could also tell *where* the image came from. Was it stored *inside* the physical memory, as materialists claimed? Or was it flowing in from the *outside*, as Katherine believed in her model of nonlocal consciousness?

"This implant . . . actually works?" Katherine asked, finding her voice. "A technology like that could have enormous implica-tions for consciousness research . . ."

"So I imagine," Finch said. "But Threshold is focused solely on national security."

Langdon saw Katherine go slightly pale as she turned and surveyed the sleek EPR pods fanned out beneath the dome. "Suspended animation . . ." she whispered, turning fearfully back to Finch. "Are you placing subjects on the edge of death . . . and watching what they *see?* You're *monitoring* near-death experiences?"

"In a sense, yes, of course," Finch replied. "As you well know, the delicate 'threshold' between life and death is a mystical place."

Finch paused, as if to let the words soak in.

Threshold.

Langdon hadn't thought of the term that way until now.

"Those hovering on the brink of death will *see* things, *know* things, *understand* things normally beyond our reach," Finch continued. "The agency has been running psychic research for nearly half a century—aimed at harnessing the untapped power of the human mind for the purpose of intelligence gathering. We've hired psychics, mediums, clairvoyants, remote viewers, precognition specialists, and even lucid dreamers. But the world's most gifted minds cannot come close to achieving what can be achieved in the altered state that accompanies death."

This is exactly what Katherine wrote about . . . Langdon realized, recalling her theory about the chemistry of death: as we die, GABA levels plummet, our brain filters dissolve, and we receive a vastly wider bandwidth of reality. Langdon couldn't help but feel that if enhanced perception were truly the mystical gift accompanying death, then harnessing it for military intelligence work was somehow . . . sacrilegious.

"The challenge," Finch said, "is that near-death experiences are fleeting and confusing. When you emerge and try to recall them, it's a bit like trying to remember a dream in the morning; the images are fuzzy and dissolve quickly."

"And now you can *record* the experience?" Katherine said, looking astonished.

"Yes, and in addition we can introduce guides on the *outside* watching in real time." Finch motioned to the array of cockpits and video screens, each associated with its own coffin-like pod. "When this facility is up and running, these walls will broadcast direct feeds from human minds in the ultimate altered state— the brink of death—which, as you know, Dr. Solomon, usually results in—"

"An out-of-body experience," she said quietly. "Nonlocal consciousness . . ."

Langdon thought of the common accounts of patients "dying"

in the operating room, only to be resuscitated and report hovering over their bodies or the hospital itself. *In death we leave our bodies behind.*

"Correct," Finch replied. "When a subject in one of these pods is placed near death, their consciousness becomes untethered. The powerful mind becomes a detached soul, if you will . . . a conscious mind *outside* the physical body. We refer to someone in that state as a 'psychonaut.' And when that happens, we can monitor exactly what the psychonaut perceives as he lifts off out of the pod, ascends through the dome, and moves out into the world. These screens will show us a point-of-view feed from an untethered mind . . . the full experience of nonlocal consciousness, if you will."

This cannot be real, Langdon told himself, and yet Katherine was taking it all in as if it made perfect sense to her. She looked captivated, as if she had entirely forgotten the man talking to her was holding a gun.

This is her Holy Grail, Langdon reminded himself.

In Katherine's world, out-of-body experiences were the best evidence for nonlocal consciousness, and yet they were fleeting, and far from *proof.* A person claiming to have hovered outside his own body was describing a subjective experience, perceived alone and in an altered state of mind. No witnesses . . . no scientific corroboration. And the inability to reproduce these mystical phenomena in a controlled setting—the replication crisis, as Katherine had described it—regularly cast doubt on the veracity of the accounts. This facility, on the other hand, might finally offer *proof* that human consciousness could survive apart from the human body; it would be a paradigm-altering breakthrough with miraculous implications for our perspective on life.

And also our perspective on death, Langdon thought, recalling Jonas Faukman's rationale when he paid top dollar for Katherine's manuscript: *Evidence of nonlocal consciousness speaks directly to humankind's ultimate hope—the existence of life after death . . . It's a topic of universal impact and massive commercial potential.*

"What are the cockpits?" Katherine demanded, pointing to the raised platform.

"Believe it or not," Finch said, "those are for the *pilots*. We're still perfecting piloting, but as you can imagine, two implanted brains can now communicate in ways we're just learning to understand. The out-of-body state is a confusing world, so the psychonaut is coupled with a 'grounded mind' to help pilot the experience. The person in the cockpit acts as a *spirit guide* of sorts."

Katherine stared at him, momentarily at a loss for words. "You're telling me you're *navigating* . . . an untethered consciousness?! As if . . . flying a drone?"

Finch smiled, obviously enjoying Katherine's epiphany. "I knew you'd understand, Dr. Solomon. You are correct . . . When this dome is fully operational, these cockpits will support a small squadron of pilots who navigate what amounts to a fleet of *invisible* drones, which we will send anywhere in the world to observe whatever we like—battlefields, war rooms, or boardrooms. Undetectable. Inescapable."

And totally impossible! Langdon wanted to shout. *It's madness . . . pure science fiction.* And yet he knew these claims were supported by the increasingly accepted theory of nonlocal consciousness.

Despite Katherine's beliefs, Langdon still could not quite accept that a consciousness could exit a body and still be present enough to observe the physical world. As a rigorous academic, Langdon felt it was his job to maintain skepticism and rationality in the face of superstition—but in the case of Threshold, he was facing a paradox.

At some point . . . skepticism itself becomes irrational.

In order to maintain his cynicism about Finch's claims, Langdon needed to set logic aside and ignore a growing mountain of rational proof. First, there existed thousands of medically documented near-death experiences describing *precisely* this phenomenon. Second, the world of quantum physics had revealed overwhelming evidence that consciousness was nonlocal and worked in ways we could not yet comprehend. Third, there were thousands of established cases of "paranormal" phenomena— telepathy, precognition, mediumship, shared dreams, sudden savant syndrome—occurrences impossible within our established model, and which required Langdon either to shift his perspective dramatically or be willing to classify those phenomena under his least favorite heading: "Miracles." In light of the evidence, Langdon knew his refusal to believe that Threshold could work was as rational as seeing a lunar eclipse and insisting the moon was a myth.

"Robert . . ." Katherine turned to him, her voice brimming with exhilaration. "This changes everything! This is beyond theory . . . it is *proof* that consciousness is nonlocal . . ."

Langdon nodded, trying to imagine how this moment would feel for her, learning suddenly of exponential breakthroughs in a field she had been studying for decades.

Katherine turned back to Finch. "The scientific community needs to know. Noetic science—"

"Threshold is *not* a science project," Finch snapped, his fierce tone immediately dominating the room. "It's a military intelligence operation. The only true source of power is *information*, and in the war to understand our enemies, this dome is our nuclear arsenal—the ultimate surveillance tool. Threshold is the next generation of remote viewing. The CIA has been working toward this facility for decades."

Decades? Langdon was taken aback. "Why would the CIA invest so heavily in a project that sounds just like Stargate . . . which failed thirty years ago?"

Finch's gaze was uncomfortably piercing. "Very simple, Mr. Langdon. Stargate never failed." He held his pistol steady as he gestured around the expansive room. "It simply evolved . . . into something far greater."

CHAPTER 113

In the secure communications room at CIA headquarters, Director Judd paced anxiously, awaiting word from Prague. Gessner's detailed video confession was a disaster. It revealed far too much about their top secret facility. He only hoped he would be able to contain it in time.

Threshold, in concept at least, had been part of Judd's life for decades now.

As a young CIA analyst, Gregory Judd had been handed a rough drawing of a construction site, which contained a series of unusual mechanical cranes. He was asked to compare the drawing to a satellite photo of the same site. As one would expect, the depictions were almost identical, and Judd logically concluded that the artist had *seen* this site in person . . . or at least the photograph.

Then they told me the truth, Judd recalled.

The facility depicted was a highly classified Russian location in Siberia; the satellite photo was taken *after* the drawing was created; and the artist was a young man named Ingo Swann who had never left the U.S. His information had come from "remote viewing" the site—that was, closing his eyes and relocating his consciousness to Siberia . . . his point of view hovering over the site and memorizing its features.

Ludicrous, Judd remembered thinking, along with many others at the agency. Nonetheless, the question remained . . . How did this drawing exist?

The apparent answer came in 1976 when Soviet émigré August Stern confessed to having worked at a Siberian psi-intelligence facility that had successfully remote-viewed a top secret American military installation. Stern's description of the secure facility was alarmingly accurate . . . right down to the detailed tile pattern on the floor.

Feeling like they'd been caught flat-footed, the CIA immediately launched the nation's first remote-viewing program with the goal of matching the Soviets' success. Founded beneath the innocuous umbrella of an academic think tank associated with Stanford University, the classified project went through various early iterations and code names, including Grill Flame and Center Lane, before it was formally established in 1977 as Stargate.

To the surprise of the scientists involved, Stargate's first stable of remote viewers—Ingo Swann, Pat Price, Joseph McMoneagle, and others—achieved startling success. While consistently entering the out-of-body state proved challenging, they were able to achieve "projection" and provide mind-boggling intelligence.

Including some "eight-martini results," Judd recalled—the project's official lingo for a success so mind-boggling that everyone required multiple cocktails to recover. Those results included spying on a Soviet double-hulled Typhoon submarine in the Arctic; finding a crashed Soviet Tu-95 bomber in Africa; locating kidnapped Brigadier General James L. Dozier in Italy; identifying a KGB colonel spying in South Africa; and more than a dozen other seemingly impossible results.

In 1979, the House Select Committee on Intelligence presented a closed-door, live demonstration of remote viewing, and many lawmakers in the room were left reeling. Democratic Congressman Charlie Rose had gone on record to say: "If the Russians have it and we don't, we're in serious trouble."

The Stargate program grew in secrecy until 1995, when a series of serious security leaks went public and ignited public indignation. It appeared the CIA was either training an army of psychic spies . . . or was wasting taxpayer money on an absurd endeavor.

Rather than trying to deny the secret program was real, the agency made a sheepish public admission that Stargate had indeed existed, but that it was now defunct, having been shut down as a total failure and waste of U.S. tax dollars. It was not true, but the agency hoped their red-faced mea culpa would silence the public's curiosity about the program and also persuade many of America's global adversaries not to pursue psi-based intelligence.

The ploy worked fairly well, although it ruffled the feathers of some of Stargate's retired remote viewers, who took offense at having their groundbreaking successes declared "bunk." Several of them decided to write unauthorized biographies whose titles included:

- *Psychic Warrior: The True Story of America's Foremost Psychic Spy and the Cover-Up of the CIA's Top-Secret Stargate Program*
- *PSI Spies: The True Story of America's Psychic Warfare Program*
- *A Sorcerer's Apprentice: A Skeptic's Journey into the CIA's Project Stargate*
- *Project Stargate and Remote Viewing Technology: The CIA's Files on Psychic Spying*

Conveniently for the agency, the accounts shared in these books, while mostly true, sounded so far-fetched that almost nobody believed them to be accurate. Rather than pursuing legal action against the authors and calling attention to what they'd written, the agency simply shrugged off the books as misguided, fictionalized money grabs by unstable former employees.

But there was more serious trouble to come.

In 2015, *Newsweek* magazine ran another unexpected exposé of Stargate. Judd would never forget reading the quote from retired Stargate project manager Lieutenant Colonel Brian Buzby, who broke two decades of silence and said: "I believed in it then, and I believe in it now. It was a real thing, and it worked."

Troublingly, the article also described a remote-viewed sketch by Stargate's legendary Agent 001—Joseph McMoneagle—depicting an enormous submarine with twin hulls, in a secret shipyard in Russia. According to *Newsweek*, U.S. satellite photographs later confirmed the existence, at the Soviets' secret Severodvinsk shipyard, of a massive double-hulled Typhoon submarine, which constituted a new threat to American national security.

U.S. Senator and future Secretary of Defense William Cohen, when asked his thoughts on the defunct Stargate program, had replied:

> I was impressed with the concept of remote viewing. . . . The exploration of the power of the mind was, and remains, an important endeavor. . . . I did support the Stargate program, as did Senator Robert Byrd and other members of the committee. There seemed to be a small segment of people who were able to key into a different level of consciousness.

Following that article, Director Judd found himself facing a deluge of Stargate conspiracy documentaries on television. One particularly alarming film was called *Third Eye Spies,* and although the agency gave it the standard brush-off response, Judd recalled being surprised how many of the film's conspiratorial claims were accurate . . . including the suspicion that Stargate's public failure had been a carefully stage-managed illusion.

They have no proof . . . but they're not wrong.

In fact, remote viewing had quietly continued within the walls of Langley, SRI International, and Fort Meade. The smoke screen of Stargate's failure enabled the agency to quietly plan the future of the program—a better-funded, far more secure, and infinitely more technologically advanced version of itself . . . deep underground, a world away from its tainted past, and with a brand-new code name.

Project Threshold was born.

"Director?" a voice crackled in the comm. "She's on."

Judd emerged from his daydream, raising his eyes to the video screen before him. "Thanks," he said. "Please connect me."

A moment later, the CIA seal on the screen dissolved, replaced by the defiant face of Ambassador Heide Nagel . . . flanked by two U.S. Marines.

CHAPTER 114

Katherine stared into the barrel of Finch's gun, feeling like she had just been jolted back to reality. The CIA's "death lab" was no consciousness research facility . . . it was a mission control for an astonishing new kind of weaponized remote viewing.

In Katherine's world of noetics, Threshold would be the ultimate triumph. The key to understanding nonlocal consciousness had always been understanding out-of-body experiences; but that understanding had always faced two massive hurdles.

And Threshold solved them both.

The first hurdle was that out-of-body states were rare, fleeting, and often unpredictable. Only a few uniquely skilled individuals were capable of "projecting at will," and even they struggled to maintain the out-of-body state for a full minute. At Threshold, however, using Gessner's pods, *anyone* could be forced into an out-of-body state and suspended there for an hour or more.

Terrifying but true.

The second challenge with OBEs was *recall*. Upon returning to their bodies from an out-of-body state, subjects reported the experience faded almost instantly, like a dream, creating challenges for researchers looking for detailed data they could trust. But now, with Threshold's neural brain implant, those experiences could be *recorded* and studied.

A potential quantum leap for consciousness research, this facility had the potential to unveil the deepest secrets of the human mind. *Including the nature of death itself.* And yet, to Katherine's enormous frustration, rather than delving into the mysteries of consciousness and death, the CIA had harnessed nonlocal consciousness to create a surveillance coup of unimaginable proportions. Katherine was still struggling to accept that a technology like this could truly exist and that it could be weaponized so effortlessly.

"One thing I don't understand," Katherine said. "The brain implant . . . the neural mesh integrated so quickly—"

"I've heard enough," Langdon interrupted, eyeing Finch's gun, still aimed at them both. "Sir, Katherine's manuscript is destroyed. She's not going to publish her book. We're willing to sign your NDA. You can put the gun away."

"In due time," Finch said, glancing over his shoulder at the doorway as if expecting someone. "I'm pleased that Dr. Solomon noticed we integrated her neural mesh so quickly."

Impossibly quickly, Katherine noted. According to the records they'd found, the rate at which Sasha's existing neurons had fused with her *artificial* ones was ten times faster than natural growth patterns, or anything Katherine had seen in a lab setting.

"The solution," Finch boasted, "is a new technique we call 'forced cooperation'—a kind of joint puzzle solving. We use virtual reality to feed the same puzzle into both the subject's *brain* and also the implanted *chip* at the same time. As you know, when disconnected neurons sense they can be more efficient by sharing information, they form new synapses."

The most brilliant solutions are always the simplest, Katherine thought, and this strategy was exactly that—elegant in its simplicity. By presenting the *identical* challenge to two discrete processing machines—a human brain and a computer chip—they encouraged the two entities to cooperate . . . motivating them to synapse as quickly as possible. *Neurons that* fire *together* . . . wire *together.* The process was known as *Hebbian learning*, and it had been part of the neuroscience field since the 1930s when Donald Hebb discovered that the brain, when challenged repeatedly with intense tasks, would grow new neural pathways very quickly, in much the same way a weight lifter grew muscles by exercising.

"And the drugs in the VR lab?" Katherine asked. "I assume psychedelics amplify neural plasticity?"

"They do," Finch said. "In addition to stimulating growth, the drugs are used to make the puzzles more challenging by forcing the brain to focus through a fog. It's like a marathoner who trains in weighted sneakers. The added burden speeds up adaptation."

Katherine was amazed. "You didn't get this idea from my thesis," Katherine said. "Was it Brigita's idea?"

"Much of it, yes. She was not always easy, and we disagreed fundamentally on many things, but we couldn't have built Threshold without her."

"Katherine's thesis," Langdon demanded. "How did the CIA have access to it?"

"The Blavatnik Awards submissions," he said. "Those submissions always contain the boldest ideas from the sharpest young minds. So back then the CIA always made sure that one of the judges was from Stanford Research Institute."

SRI? Katherine was amazed the connection had not occurred to her immediately upon learning of the CIA's involvement in her missing manuscript. Stanford Research Institute had longstanding ties to the CIA and was even believed by conspiracy theorists to be the birthplace of Stargate. An SRI "professor" on the judges panel for the Blavatnik Awards could easily have been a spy hiding in plain sight.

"When your thesis didn't win even an honorable mention," Finch said, "your Princeton professor—Cosgrove, I believe— questioned the prize committee relentlessly, especially the judge from Stanford. He figured out SRI was involved and knew enough to back off and never speak of it again."

"We want to leave," Langdon said. "Now."

"You're in no position to make demands, Professor," Finch said. "You've broken into a top secret facility and violated many laws. And if you think the ambassador is going to come and save you, I doubt she is free to go anywhere at the moment."

"If Katherine and I disappear," Langdon said, his tone threatening, "*many* people will notice. It won't be like your anonymous test subject Sysevich."

"You know nothing of what happened to Dmitri."

"We know you used him as a human guinea pig," Katherine said. "Along with Sasha Vesna."

"They were living tortured lives," Finch fired back. "Gessner saved them. She cured their epilepsy and gave them a life."

"*That's* your rationale?" Langdon challenged. "Does Dmitri have a better life now? We saw his records. It looks like he died here!"

"Professor," Finch said, shifting position and aiming the gun at Langdon now. "It must be luxurious to live in academia and not face the real problems in our country . . . not worry about those who want to destroy the Western way of life. The world is an extremely dangerous place, and people like me are the only reason your city of Boston is still standing. I mean that quite literally."

"That may be true," Langdon replied, "but it doesn't give you the right to experiment on human beings without their knowledge."

Finch stared at him. "The ultimate test of a man's conscience is his willingness to sacrifice something today for future generations whose words of thanks will not be heard."

"If you're going to steal a quote," Langdon fired back, "you should know what it means. Gaylord Nelson was referring to saving the environment, not abusing innocent people."

"Sasha is far from innocent," Finch said. "She murdered Dr. Gessner."

"That's absurd," Langdon said. "Sasha loved Brigita. There's no—"

"She also killed my field officer upstairs," Finch said. "I half expected it was *Sasha* who had broken into Threshold. I found an epilepsy wand upstairs near my officer's dead body . . . and there's only one person it could belong to."

"That wand is *mine*," declared a ghostly voice in the darkness. "And I want it back."

CHAPTER 115

Finch whipped around in alarm and scanned the room.

Who the hell said that?!

The acoustics in the dome made it difficult to discern exactly *where* the words had come from. Langdon and Katherine looked equally startled.

"Where are you?!" Finch called out, not recognizing the hollow male voice. The accent had definitely sounded Russian. "Show yourself now!"

Finch heard a soft hiss of air, the only sound that pierced the silence of the dome. It was coming from the rear of the room, behind Langdon and Solomon. As his captives turned toward the sound, Finch looked past them, realizing this hiss was emanating from the pneumatic lift that accessed the utilities area.

As the platform ascended, they all witnessed a spectacle unlike anything Finch would have imagined in his wildest dreams.

From out of the earth . . . a monster was rising.

The face appeared first—its skin deathly gray and featureless. The head was hairless, shrouded in the hood of a black cloak, and its two cold eyes seemed locked on Finch and his outstretched gun. As the cloaked body rose into view, its arms were extended horizontally, showing bare palms like some kind of ascendant Christ.

When the pneumatic platform stopped, the figure stepped off and began moving toward them, his heavy boots thudding on the carpeted floor. Arms still splayed in surrender, he approached through the sea of pods, his black cloak billowing. Finch now saw that the monster's head and face were caked with thick clay or mud, and some kind of writing was etched into his forehead. *What the fuck is this thing?!*

"Stop!" Finch shouted, finally finding his voice when the creature was not more than fifteen yards away. "Not another step!"

The monster obeyed, halting, his arms still outstretched.

Finch stepped to his right for a clear shot past Langdon and Katherine. "Who are you?!" *What are you?!*

"You have betrayed Sasha's trust," the figure replied, his voice hollow in the dome. "I am her protector."

"Is Sasha here too somewhere?" Finch demanded.

"No, she is somewhere safe. She will never lay eyes on any of this again."

"And *you* are?"

The monster's body twitched suddenly, which seemed to startle him, but he regrouped. "I . . . am—" His voice cracked, and this time Finch saw fear flash in his eyes. The creature's outstretched arms began trembling, and his defiant air evaporated. *"No . . . ne seychas!"* he stammered, his tone now more of a frightened supplication. "Not now . . ."

Abruptly, the monster collapsed to the floor, his entire body shaking uncontrollably. He rolled onto his back, lying on the carpet, helpless, trembling.

Finch had witnessed epileptic seizures before, and while he had no idea who this was, this person's presence explained the epilepsy wand Finch had found upstairs. *Is this another of Gessner's patients? From outside the program?*

The monster was now struggling to search his cloak pockets, clearly trying in desperation to locate something.

"Is this what you're missing?" Finch taunted, pulling the metal wand from his pocket and moving toward the incapacitated figure. "Tell me who you are, and I'll give this to you."

"He can't speak!" Langdon shouted. "For God's sake, help him!"

"Would you like your wand?" Finch said, arriving over the figure, who convulsed helplessly, his head now vibrating against the floor.

"Help him!" Katherine shouted.

Gun still in hand, Finch crouched down beside the shuddering form and held the wand before his eyes. "Why don't you start by telling me—"

Finch never finished the sentence.

In a flash of precisely coordinated movement, the trembling figure sat upright, and like a snake striking, one arm shot out toward Finch, connecting with his chest. There was a loud hiss and a flash of blue light, and a searing pain tore through the man's body. Finch's gun discharged into the side of a pod as he went rigid and fell forward, his attacker twisting deftly out of the way to allow Finch to hit the floor face-first.

On impact, Finch felt the cartilage in his nose shatter completely. The pain was nauseating, like nothing he'd felt in his life. Blood streaming down his face, his paralyzed body came to rest on its side. He could see the cloaked figure rise effortlessly to his feet, a hand reaching down to collect the gun and wand, both of which Finch had dropped. The heavy platform boots moved toward Finch, inches away from his face. Gasping for breath, Finch strained to turn his head, his eyes climbing his attacker's body all the way to his face. Upon seeing the monster who stood over him, Finch wondered if perhaps he had died and gone to hell.

The creature staring down at him was barely human. His face was earthen with deep cracks running through his skin of dried clay. On his forehead, three symbols were etched deep into his muddy flesh. The creature's eyes were unyielding, and their glare told Finch there would be no mercy.

◆——··——◆

Robert Langdon was accustomed to processing complex information quickly. At the moment, however, the scene before him had unfolded too rapidly to comprehend fully what was happening. Finch now lay on the floor, quivering and debilitated. The cloaked figure facing Langdon and Katherine was wearing a costume of some sort; his shaved head and face were caked with thick clay, and his forehead was inscribed with a Hebrew word.

אמת

Langdon did not read Hebrew well, but these three letters were legendary. They spelled EMET, and when etched on a forehead, their meaning could never be mistaken.

Truth . . .

The Golĕm of Prague.

Before Langdon could even begin to try to make sense of any of it, the silence of the room was shattered by a deafening siren. Piercing and shrill, the alarm wailed overhead, and spinning warning lights began sweeping repeatedly around the interior of the dome.

"*Go!*" shouted the figure in the cloak, pointing back the way they had come. "NOW! This entire facility is about to explode!"

Langdon hoped he had heard incorrectly. *Explode?!*

"We locked the RFID door!" Katherine said. "We have no card to get out!"

"Come here!" The cloaked figure crouched down over Finch, who was still quivering, helpless. Langdon hurried over in bewilderment as the monster went through Finch's pockets, pulled out his wallet, and extracted a black "PRAGUE" card identical to the one Gessner was carrying.

"You'll have twenty seconds," the figure shouted, barely audible over the alarm as he grabbed Finch's hand and forced the man's thumb onto the surface of the card until a tiny indicator light turned green. He immediately handed the activated card to Langdon. "Twenty seconds! Go!"

"What about *you*?!" Langdon asked.

"I am The Golĕm," the figure replied. "I have died many times."

◄—··—►

Godspeed, The Golĕm thought, relieved to see Robert Langdon and Katherine Solomon racing from the dome. *They do not deserve to die.*

Finch, however, was a different story.

The Golĕm stood over his bloody captive . . . the puppet master who had overseen this project. In the spinning lights of the Threshold dome, the creature turned to the nearest EPR pod, pressed the release button, and opened the lid. Then he hoisted the diminutive man up over the lip of the pod and dumped him inside as if he were already a lifeless corpse.

Finch's eyes bulged, and he started to regain mobility, but it was too late. The Golĕm quickly affixed the pod's heavy Velcro straps to his arms and legs, imprisoning his captive in the coffin-like interior.

"Please . . . stop . . ." the man croaked, regaining his voice.

Leaning into the pod, The Golĕm placed his mouth an inch from Finch's ear and whispered, "I wish I could turn your blood to ice and let you feel what I felt so many times . . . but there is no time for that."

"Who . . . are . . . you?" the man stammered.

"You know me," The Golĕm replied. "You *created* me."

Finch stared up, scrutinizing his attacker, his eyes probing the monster's face with increasing desperation. But The Golĕm had no desire to give him the satisfaction of discovery.

Calmly, The Golĕm stared down at his victim and spoke the last words the man would ever hear. Then he pressed the button on the side of the pod and watched contentedly as the transparent gullwing lid lowered into place, sealing Finch inside, muting his screams of terror, which were lost in the siren's urgent wail.

CHAPTER 116

Langdon and Katherine burst into the hallway outside the domed suite, having barely managed to unlock the RFID scanner with Finch's card before it deactivated and blinked red in Langdon's hand.

In unison, they turned right, racing together toward stairs at the end of the hallway. It seemed a good bet that these stairs were a faster way out than the circuitous route by which they'd entered.

In the chaotic flash of spinning security lights, they reached the door at the end of the hall and hurried into a drab concrete stairwell. Bounding up steps two at a time, Langdon could still hear the hollow voice of the clay-covered creature who had just helped them escape. *This entire facility is about to explode.* How or why that would happen, Langdon had no idea, but judging from the sirens and emergency lighting, something in Threshold had definitely gone catastrophically wrong—most likely by the man's own hand.

One of the by-products of fear, Langdon knew—especially the fear of *death*—was total clarity of purpose. Despite the tangle of questions in his head about what had just transpired in the dome, Langdon's brain had muted that noise and tuned itself to one, solitary channel.

Survival.

He led the way to the upper landing, where he and Katherine arrived breathless at a metal door marked ADMIN. Without hesitation, Langdon pushed through, and they found themselves in a carpeted, oak-paneled corridor. Gone were the cold, sterile edges of the operations facility; this looked more like the corporate offices of a sophisticated Cambridge law firm.

They ran down the hall, past conference rooms, offices, and into a sprawling cubicle farm. Here Katherine stopped short, reaching out and stopping Langdon as well. At the far end of the room, a professionally dressed woman was urgently gathering items off her cubicle. Apparently, Threshold had not been entirely deserted today. Just then, two young men in suits rushed over to join her, motioning for her to follow. They all ran off without looking back.

Follow them, Langdon thought. *They must know the way out.*

Once they were out of sight, Langdon and Katherine headed in their direction, which he suspected was toward the main entrance they had seen earlier on the edge of Folimanka Park. Langdon eyed the classified binder sticking out of Katherine's shoulder bag and hoped the emergency evacuation would create enough chaos that they could slip away undetected.

If we get out in time, he thought as the sirens wailed overhead.

"There!" Katherine shouted, pointing to a glowing EXIT sign at the end of the hallway.

They pushed through the doors and found themselves in a security room similar to the one they'd passed through earlier—with a metal detector, X-ray conveyer, and body scan. Fortunately, it was unmanned, and Langdon and Katherine rushed through, emerging into what appeared to be a large underground parking garage, mostly empty except for several construction vehicles, a few cars, and some large machinery on flatbeds.

Fifty yards ahead, Langdon saw what he had feared they might never see again.

Daylight.

At the far end of the parking lot, the bunker's arched opening led up the inclined driveway. The three employees they had just seen inside were now hurrying up the slope and disappearing from view. Langdon and Katherine ran toward the opening, but as they did, the daylight began to fade . . . the opening beginning to taper.

They're closing the door!

"Wait!" Langdon shouted, his voice swallowed by the cacophony of alarms. "WAIT!"

He could see they would never make it. Still twenty yards away, the shaft of daylight dwindled to a sliver and then disappeared entirely as the portal slid shut with a resounding thud, sealing them inside.

◆—··—◆

Three stories below, strapped down like some violent psychiatric patient, Mr. Finch had stopped struggling. He could only stare upward in disbelief through the translucent cover of the EPR pod and watch the muted shapes of emergency lights sweeping across the dome above.

This facility-wide alarm sequence confirmed for Mr. Finch two inescapable realities. First, his attacker's final words had been true. *I closed your helium valves . . . and sealed your vent.* And second, Threshold and everything in it were about to be destroyed.

The SMES is overheating.

Installing the superconducting magnetic energy storage system had been Finch's brainchild—a way to discreetly disguise Threshold's energy consumption spikes during operations that would require vast amounts of power. Rather than drawing the attention of local utilities, Threshold pulled inconspicuous amounts of low power from the grid around the clock, building it up in the superconducting coils for use whenever they needed it.

Constant, uninterruptable power.

It was technology that was extremely stable and safe. That was, unless someone decided to weaponize it, which held true for most technologies.

There are no fail-safes for espionage.

Finch now understood he was going to die, and he forced himself to accept that fact with the same detached coolness he had called upon to handle every decision and crossroads in his life. Having now realized the true identity of his killer, he felt like he was trapped in some kind of classical myth. *A monster returns to destroy its creator.* The irony of Prague's historical golem was not lost on him.

As Finch pictured the SMES downstairs, he knew it was only a matter of seconds. What was about to happen would be cataclysmic.

A pressure bomb . . . detonated deep underground.

The last sound Finch perceived before his eardrums imploded was the isolated crackle and shattering of the pod's lid above him. As his point of view accelerated upward toward the domed ceiling, he was uncertain whether his spirit was rocketing from his body, or if the entire dome floor was rushing skyward. Either way, he felt no pain . . . only a vague detachment as his physical body was torn to pieces by the howling white wind.

———··———

The concussion wave erupted from its subterranean prison with unfathomable force. In less than a tenth of a second, it tore through the floor of the domed chamber and spread laterally through the lower level of Threshold, leveling the quantum computing lab before exploding upward into the RTD lab, medical center, and surgery space, obliterating them all. The billowing cloud of gas, still expanding, pushed out in all directions, seeking the path of least resistance.

An instant later, that path was found.

———··———

It took a lot to rattle a U.S. Marine.

Even so, Sergeant Scott Kerble felt as off-balance as he'd felt in his entire career. The spectacle unfolding before him was unlike anything he had ever witnessed or even imagined possible.

Having located the ambassador's SUV parked discreetly among some trees on the access road to Crucifix Bastion, Kerble had been standing on the ridgeline, puzzling over the situation, when he felt the ground shudder violently beneath his feet.

Earthquake had been his first instinct, but the trembling was just a single jolt, accompanied by a deep roar within the earth. As Kerble glanced down at the snowy expanse of Folimanka Park far below him, he realized he was witnessing something else entirely.

In slow motion, the center of the park seemed to be rising up, straining skyward in a vast, bulbous mound, as if a colossal subterranean beast were trying to break free. The snow was shedding down the sides of the hill as the ground continued climbing higher. Then, with a thunderous crack, a violent geyser of white gas rocketed through the surface of the earth, projecting hundreds of feet into the air.

Stupefied, Kerble staggered backward as the pillar of vapor climbed into the sky over the park. The deafening howl from below lasted only seconds before subsiding . . . followed by the impact of the mountain of earth collapsing back on itself.

He inched forward in disbelief and surveyed the devastation. A deep crater had opened where the center of Folimanka Park had once been. The gaping hole contained a twisted heap of rubble and rising dust.

A moment later, a deathly cold wafted up from the park.

And then, as if by magic, the air around him crystallized and filled with snowflakes as fine as confectioners' sugar.

CHAPTER 117

Seconds before the blast, with sirens at full volume, Langdon and Katherine had shouted for help as the fortified garage door slid closed and sealed them inside. Desperate to be heard, Langdon yanked open the driver's door of a nearby sedan and began honking the horn, but even that was barely audible over the noise.

It didn't matter anymore. Langdon now felt a palpable shift in the air . . . a sudden pressure in his ears, accompanied by the first wave of a deep, guttural howl.

Whatever was happening at Threshold . . . was happening *now*. Langdon hoped this garage was far enough away from the core of the facility to avoid the blast.

"Get in front!" Katherine shouted as she pulled open the sedan's back door and climbed in. Langdon jumped in behind the steering wheel, both of them slamming their doors in unison. "Get down and buckle your—"

The car windows exploded, and a torrent of frigid wind whipped through the car. With the force of a passing high-speed train, a hurricane tore through the garage, extinguishing all light and lifting the sedan like a toy. In an instant, they were upside down in the darkness, their car tumbling side over side across the garage floor.

"Katherine!" Langdon shouted into the deafening storm, holding on to the steering wheel and trying to brace himself as best he could as the car rolled sidelong. A barrel roll in a fighter jet was said to be the least jarring of maneuvers because the centripetal force held you in your seat. Langdon now realized it was true . . . at least for a couple of moments.

Then came the impact.

The sedan collided with something immovable and jolted to an abrupt halt.

Langdon launched from his seat and crash-landed on his chest . . . *somewhere*. Dazed and in total darkness, he felt startlingly cold. His brain took a quick inventory of his body, gauging the pain merely as cuts and bruises rather than torn limbs. The fury of the explosion had subsided as quickly as it came. The warning sirens had fallen silent too.

Langdon's ears were ringing, and with no light, he felt entirely disoriented. A biting cold had descended around them, although Langdon sensed he was still inside the car.

"Katherine?" Langdon ventured.

The voice that replied was weak but very close. "Here."

Langdon felt a wave of relief. "Are you okay?"

"I'm not . . . sure," she managed. "You're . . . crushing me."

Langdon now realized he was lying directly on top of her. Carefully, he shifted his weight to one side, rolling off her. His shoulder landed painfully on pieces of broken safety glass, and he shifted again, finding a clean area on which to support himself. As he got his bearings, he realized the car in which they had taken refuge was upside down, and they were now lying against its roof.

Wriggling forward, Langdon felt his way through the darkness until his hands found the frame of a shattered window. The opening felt too small for him to pass through, and he continued groping his way around the interior of the car until he located a larger opening—the windshield or rear window. Grasping one side, he heaved himself forward, slithering through the opening onto the hard floor of the garage.

The floor was slippery and cold with a layer of what felt like frost. On hands and knees, Langdon turned around and reached back through the opening.

"Katherine, over here," he said as calmly as he could, anxious to know whether she was injured. "Can you find my hand? Are you hurt?"

He could hear her movement in the darkness, and he kept speaking to her, guiding her in his direction. Finally, their hands touched. Katherine's fingers were cold, her hands trembling in shock. Gently, he eased her toward him, helping her out of the car. She immediately got to her feet and wrapped her arms around him, holding tight.

As they embraced, Langdon felt a sense of déjà vu—holding her once again in cold darkness, a feeling of overwhelming relief to know she was safe.

"My bag . . ." she whispered. "I lost it . . . the binder . . ."

"Forget it," he said, holding her tighter. *We're alive. That's all that matters.*

Langdon had no idea what had just happened or how extensive the damage was, but he suspected the U.S. government would be answering myriad questions in the coming days. With luck, he and Katherine might now be the *least* of the CIA's concerns.

Finch is most likely gone, Langdon thought, feeling little sorrow for the loss. The pang of sadness and guilt that Langdon felt was for the other lost soul—the man in the golem's mask of clay—the creature who had literally risen out of the earth to save their lives.

Finch had demanded the intruder's identity, and the creature had calmly replied: *You have betrayed Sasha's trust . . . I am her protector.*

Langdon thought about Sasha Vesna, wondering where she was, and even whether she was still alive somewhere in this city. He had decided that if he and Katherine got out of here in one piece, they would find Sasha and *help* her. Not only did Sasha deserve and need it, but Langdon and Katherine owed a debt of gratitude to the man who had just saved their lives. *Sasha's protector,* he had called himself. *If he is gone, helping Sasha is our moral imperative.*

"Look," Katherine whispered, placing her hand on his shoulder and turning him in the darkness. "Over there."

Langdon squinted into blackness, seeing nothing. "Where?"

"Straight ahead," she said, turning him slightly to the right. Now he saw it.

In the distance, barely visible through the haze of settling dust, a faint sliver of daylight glimmered in the blackness.

◆——··——▶

On any normal day, an earthquake rattling Prague would have been high on the list of concerns for Ambassador Nagel. At the moment, however, the tremor she had just felt seemed trivial in comparison to her conversation with CIA Director Judd.

"Remove her handcuffs," the director had ordered the Marine guards as soon as the connection had been established. "Stand post outside the room. Nobody in or out."

The guards obeyed, and once Nagel was uncuffed and alone, Judd had lowered his voice and said, "Finch is a loose cannon. Consider this protective custody."

With no further explanation, the CIA director had launched into a monologue, attempting to justify everything Nagel had heard in Gessner's horrifying confession. Now, having made his argument, Judd leaned forward toward the camera, his expression both pleading and deadly serious.

"We're in an arms race, Heide," he said, "and our adversaries are growing more powerful and aggressive every day. The plans being formulated against the U.S. are very real and potentially catastrophic, and we need to know about them *before* they happen. Threshold represents the advantage our intelligence community requires to help our country survive the coming storm. If we fail to take an inside track in the technology of the human mind, someone else *will* . . . and rather than being the watchers, we will be the watched."

The age-old argument, Nagel thought. *Someone is going to do it, so it had better be us.*

The most dangerous and ethically questionable scientific endeavor in history—building an atomic bomb—had been launched on a similar justification. And outside of ethical or political argument, it was true that the United States' being *first* to have the bomb had ended a devastating war and cemented the

U.S. as a superpower for the next half century . . . a persuasive example of the ends justifying the means. But this was a different landscape.

Nagel could not begin to imagine how this video would play on the world stage. Not only did it reveal the existence of a shocking classified technology, but it lifted the veil on an appalling and unforgivable truth; the CIA performed testing on kidnapped Russian psychiatric patients, one of whom, Dmitri Sysevich, had apparently perished in the program. *The CIA would be crucified top down . . . starting with the director.*

"As you probably guessed," Judd said, "In-Q-Tel was not involved with Threshold in any way. I placed Finch in their London office as credible cover and for operational support, but he clearly overstepped." The director looked regretful. "I should never have granted him so much power."

A loud knock on the door drew Nagel's attention, and one of the embassy guards stuck his head in.

"Madam Ambassador?" he said, looking shaken. "I apologize for the interruption. We have an emergency call for you."

I'm already on one! she wanted to yell. "Who is it?"

"Sergeant Kerble," the Marine said. "He says there's been a massive underground explosion in Folimanka Park."

CHAPTER 118

Three hundred meters from the epicenter of devastation, the subterranean tram tunnel back to Crucifix Bastion had survived more or less intact, despite no longer having power or lights. The small platform outside the entrance to Threshold was strewn with debris and dust.

Lying at the bottom of the concrete channel that housed the rails, a figure stirred.

In total darkness, The Golĕm slowly rose to his knees, knowing he was lucky to be alive. His flight from Threshold had not gone as planned, and he had barely reached the tram before the blast had hurled him down into the concrete channel.

The question now was whether The Golĕm would be able to exit this underground tomb. The route behind him was undoubtedly destroyed and blocked by rubble. The way forward, through the long, pitch-black tunnel, could easily have collapsed from the pressure wave, and there was no way to know if the elevator shaft leading to Crucifix Bastion was still intact. Despite his profound exhaustion, The Golĕm knew he could not afford to perish down here.

I must escape so I can release Sasha.

Fueled by this knowledge, The Golĕm located the side of the channel, placed a hand on it, and then forced himself onward into the blackness. Dragging his hand along the wall for guidance, he fell into a steady rhythm, his platform boots crunching on the uneven surface that was littered with occasional blast debris, his legs feeling heavier with every step.

A guardian angel cannot sleep.

Shaken and bruised, Langdon and Katherine inched through the murky garage, navigating the shattered edges of demolished vehicles and fallen concrete, moving toward the lone source of illumination—a sliver of daylight that grew brighter as the dust continued to settle.

When they finally reached the light, Langdon could see the garage's massive sliding door had been knocked from its track. The bottom of the panel was bent outward, creating a low, narrow gap. Langdon crouched down and peered through, able to see a few feet of the inclined driveway beyond.

Unsure what they would find on the other side, Langdon went first, lying on his side and shimmying into the gap. Inch by inch, he pulled himself headfirst through the opening. The breach was tighter than imagined, and halfway through he felt another wave of claustrophobia grip him. Desperately, he bucked his body until his hips finally cleared, enabling him to roll onto his hands and knees and scramble out into the open air.

The relief he felt to be free, however, was quickly dampened by the two black-clad soldiers standing over him with assault rifles aimed at his chest.

That went well.

Before Langdon could warn Katherine, she was already slithering through the opening, pulling her slender frame out onto the driveway with much less difficulty. As she looked up, the second soldier shifted his aim to her.

"Identification!" he shouted. "Now!"

Langdon squinted at his surroundings, seeing precisely what he feared—the heavily guarded construction entrance they had seen earlier, enclosed within the triangle of fencing.

"Identification!" the soldier repeated, stepping closer. "I'll give you precisely—"

"STAND DOWN, SOLDIER!" an authoritative American voice shouted from the top of the driveway. An imposing U.S. Marine in full dress blues came striding down the incline. "THOSE TWO ARE WITH ME!"

The startled guards took a step back from Langdon and

Katherine to engage with the Marine, who apparently out-ranked them. Their conversation was brief, and the two soldiers, clearly displeased at having been overruled, retreated back up the incline.

Langdon appreciated no longer having guns aimed at him, but he now feared he and Katherine might have fallen into an even more serious situation.

Who is this Marine? CIA? One of Finch's cronies?

As the soldiers departed, the Marine's stern demeanor soft-ened, his affable expression now out of synch with his rigid attire. "Mr. Langdon . . . Ms. Solomon," he said as he helped them to their feet. "I'm Scott Kerble. I work for Ambassador Nagel."

Langdon hoped he was telling the truth. "We need to see her right away."

The Marine was about to respond when one of the army guards came back down the incline, took a snapshot of all three of them together, and then marched back up, placing a call as he went.

Kerble cursed under his breath. "I've got to get you out of here right away."

"To the embassy?" Langdon asked.

"We can talk about that in the car," he said, starting up the incline. "Follow me."

Talk about it? The comment made Langdon doubly wary. "Actually, before we go anywhere, we'd like to speak to Ambas-sador Nagel."

"I agree," Katherine said. "If we—"

"Both of you, listen," the Marine snapped, spinning back to them and standing close, his affable demeanor vanishing. "The ambassador has been detained on orders from the CIA director himself. And I'm fairly certain *you* two are next on his list."

CHAPTER 119

B ehind the wheel of the embassy sedan, Scott Kerble sped northward along the river, racing back the way he had come. In the opposite direction, a line of rescue vehicles streaked toward Folimanka Park.

Nothing left to save, he thought.

In his backseat, Langdon and Solomon had fallen into a stunned silence after glimpsing the extent of the devastation they had survived. All that was left of the Folimanka bomb shelter was a gaping hollow, several stories deep, filled with a jumble of rocks, earth, shattered concrete, and twisted steel.

Kerble could not imagine what had caused the unusual explosion. As far as he could tell, there had been no fire or heat—only cold. He knew the Soviet-era bomb shelter had been under restoration by the U.S. Army Corps of Engineers for the past couple of years, and it certainly should not have contained any explosives.

"Where are you taking us?" Langdon asked from the backseat.

Good question, Kerble thought. He hadn't quite worked out the big picture, but he knew Ambassador Nagel and CIA Director Judd were locked in a power struggle, and it somehow involved Langdon and Solomon.

After the blast, as Kerble hurried down the ridge, he had phoned Nagel to confirm her safety. She had been on a call with the director. When Kerble explained that the tremor was not an earthquake but rather an explosion beneath Folimanka Park, Nagel's first words, strangely, had been to inquire about Langdon and Solomon's whereabouts. She ordered Kerble to head to the scene and search for them.

Regardless of what was unfolding between the ambassador and the CIA director, Kerble had already chosen sides an hour ago, with his snap decision to smuggle Nagel's diplomatic pouch out of the embassy. It was a timely improvisation, as the director had almost immediately ordered a search of the ambassadorial suite along with her closest staff, including Kerble himself.

If I'd kept the pouch . . . the CIA would have it now.

As he drove toward the embassy, in case his sedan was being tracked, Kerble's instincts told him that delivering Langdon and Solomon into the hands of the CIA director was not what Nagel would want. He also sensed there was a lot he was not being told by the Americans in the backseat.

"We need to get out," Langdon declared, his voice surprisingly authoritative considering the circumstances. "I can't give you details, but trust me when I tell you that your ambassador is in *grave* danger—especially if the CIA director has detained her."

Grave danger? Kerble was well aware of Gregory Judd's reputation for taking no prisoners when it came to national security. *But would he really harm an ambassador?* Kerble considered mentioning the diplomatic pouch that the director had seemed intent on finding, but the ambassador's orders about the pouch had been clear. *Tell no one.*

"If the ambassador is going to survive this—physically or politically," Langdon said, "I believe there is only one thing left that can help her. I also believe I can find it."

Despite the boldness of the claim, Kerble sensed the man at least *believed* what he was saying. "What is it you're looking for?"

"It's not a *what*," Langdon replied. "It's a *whom*."

Kerble glanced up, locking eyes with the professor in the rearview mirror. "Who is it?"

"Her name is Sasha Vesna," Langdon said, "and everything the ambassador needs to weather this storm is located in Sasha's head."

Robert knows how to find Sasha?

For a moment, Katherine feared Langdon might be bluffing, but his nod of assurance told her he was speaking in earnest.

Finding Sasha is the key to everything . . .

Far more conclusive than the binder Katherine had lost in the blast, Sasha *herself* was the most irrefutable proof that Threshold had even existed. A single brain scan would prove not only that this advanced implant was real, but also that the CIA had tricked a young Russian psychiatric patient into becoming a medical test subject.

Locating Sasha was even more important now, as the destruction of Threshold had made their tenuous situation even more dangerous. The CIA would be in damage-control mode, and with all evidence of wrongdoing conveniently buried beneath Folimanka Park, the agency would be moving quickly to tie up all loose ends.

Robert and I definitely qualify as unresolved details, she knew. *As do Sasha Vesna and Dmitri Sysevich.*

Katherine pictured the eerily cloaked figure they had seen in Threshold. The man had proclaimed himself "Sasha's protector" and was almost certainly Sysevich—the dark-haired Russian epileptic who, like Sasha, had been taken from an institution. His medical records, at first glance, had suggested to Katherine that he had died, but it now appeared something *else* had happened to him. Perhaps he had escaped their grasp. Whatever his situation, nobody more than Dmitri possessed the motivation to return and obliterate the facility that had subjected him to untold horrors.

Mental illness, Katherine suspected, was almost certainly involved. *The man smeared himself with clay and sacrificed his life to destroy Threshold.* She wondered if Dmitri had a preexisting psychological condition in the institution, or whether it had been caused by the trauma of invasive brain surgery and forced psychedelic drug use. Either way, Dmitri Sysevich was clearly not a well man.

Sasha is somewhere safe, the man had said.

"Robert," Katherine urged. "You really know where to find Sasha?"

"I just figured it out," he replied. "There's only one place she could be . . . but in order to find her, I need to get into her apartment—"

"She's not there," Kerble interrupted. "I was the one who found Harris's body. Sasha was long gone. Our team quickly retrieved Harris, locked up, and left."

"I understand," Langdon said. "But I still need to get inside. There's something there that can help us. How did you gain access to her apartment?"

"My colleague, Dana Daněk. She had a key."

"On a Krazy Kitten key ring?" Langdon asked.

Kerble glanced over his shoulder. "How did you know that?"

"Because *I'm* the one who gave it to Ms. Daněk. And now I need it back from her immediately."

"That's impossible," Kerble said. "Dana no longer has it."

Langdon cursed under his breath. "Who has it now?"

Kerble reached into his pocket and tossed a small object back to Langdon. "*You* do, Professor."

———··———

A massive explosion in Prague?!

Jonas Faukman frantically skimmed the *New York Times* alert on his computer and tried to convince himself that the blast was just a coincidence. Despite the statistical improbability that Langdon had been anywhere near the blast, his friend had a disconcerting habit of finding himself at the epicenter of trouble.

More than an hour had passed since Langdon's email, and there had been no word since then. Unable to push the mounting concern from his mind, Faukman dialed the Four Seasons Hotel in Prague and asked to be put through to Langdon's room.

———··———

Trudging through total darkness in the enclosed tunnel, The Golěm heard a sudden change in the reverberant sound of his footsteps.

Less echo . . . I'm in an open space.

Running his hand up the wall, he found a ledge and realized to his relief that he had finally reached the tram platform beneath Crucifix Bastion. The ledge was at eye level, higher than anticipated, and he would need to hoist himself up.

He quickly shed his heavy cape and platform boots, arranging them in a pile at his feet. Then he stepped onto his makeshift stool, reached up, and felt the ledge, gauging its height. He would need to jump high enough to brace his elbows and forearms on the platform.

You must escape. Sasha's life depends on it.

Fueled by the thought of her, The Golĕm crouched low and leaped with all his strength, barely managing to prop himself up. Kicking his weary legs, he was able to swing one upward and hook his heel on the ledge. Fighting gravity and exhaustion, he dragged himself onto the metal platform . . . and collapsed.

For nearly a full minute, he rested, eyes closed, breathing deeply.

When he finally opened his eyes, The Golĕm saw something hovering in the darkness . . . a tiny glowing circle.

A light at the end of the tunnel.

It was the illuminated button for the Crucifix Bastion elevator.

CHAPTER 120

Katherine felt wary as she and Langdon climbed out of the embassy sedan into the cold wind near Old Town Square. At Langdon's request, Sergeant Kerble had agreed to deposit them here before he continued on to the embassy.

I hope Robert knows what he's doing.

Over the past several minutes, she could tell Langdon was being strangely elusive with the Marine, refusing to reveal exactly where he believed Sasha was located. All he would say was that he needed to go to Sasha's apartment to locate something that would help. Kerble seemed to understand, perhaps even appreciate, Langdon's rationale for reticence. *The CIA director desperately needs to locate Sasha Vesna; if questioned, Kerble can't reveal what he doesn't know.*

Katherine would have felt safer if Kerble had accompanied them, but clearly he needed to get back to the embassy. It seemed as if he might be the ambassador's lone ally and felt obligated to be on-site to protect her from the CIA director in whatever way he could.

"The ambassador will be grateful for your efforts," Kerble said, rolling down his window to say a quick goodbye. "Good luck. *Wherever* it is you're going."

"Thanks for your understanding," Langdon replied.

"OPSEC compartmentalization," Kerble said. "You could be a Marine."

"There's a scary thought," Langdon said as he reached through the window and shook the Marine's hand. "I've got your direct number. I'll call you the second we have anything."

"If we locate Sasha," Katherine added, "we'll take her somewhere safe, and the ambassador will have all the leverage she needs to protect you."

"I hope you're right," Kerble said. "Court-martials have a way of ruining a weekend."

As the Marine pulled away, Langdon put an arm around Katherine and guided her across the bustling square. On the far side, they passed beneath an archway into a series of narrow alleys. When the sounds of the square began fading behind them, Katherine sensed it was finally private enough to talk.

"So what's going on?" she blurted. "And where are we going? Where is Sasha?"

"We're going to her apartment," he said. "I figured out that Sasha never left. She *couldn't* have. She's still inside."

Katherine stopped short. "That Marine just said Sasha is *not* there."

"He's wrong."

"He said forensics searched the apartment!"

"Yes, but they didn't search the *whole* thing."

"I don't understand."

"You *will*," he said, holding out his hand. "Come on."

Katherine followed Langdon deeper into the maze of alleyways surrounding Prague's town square. *I'm glad he has a good memory*, she thought as he retraced the path that Sasha had taken him on earlier today. The alleys grew even narrower, and the cobblestone walkways fell into dark shadows with the fading afternoon light.

"This is it," Langdon finally announced, stopping outside a nondescript door that looked like every other doorway they had passed.

"You're certain?" Katherine saw no numbers or markings.

Langdon pointed to the window beside the door, and Katherine was startled to see four eyes staring out at her. Two Siamese cats watched intently from inside, as if awaiting their owner's return. Despite confirming this was Sasha's apartment, the presence of her cats only furthered Katherine's mystification as to why Langdon thought Sasha was actually *here*. "Robert, those cats look like they're waiting for Sasha to get home."

"They *are*," Langdon said. "They just don't know she's here either."

The comment made no sense to Katherine.

"Look at this alley," Langdon said, motioning around them. "Remember I told you about the note that was slipped under Sasha's door this morning? Within seconds of getting the note, I ran out into *this* very alleyway, but the messenger had vanished. Impossibly so. He couldn't have simply disappeared into thin air."

She surveyed the alley. *Admittedly, nowhere to hide.*

"And then I realized," Langdon said, "the answer was obvious. The person who left the note . . . *never* fled the area. He simply stepped into a very convenient hiding place."

Katherine glanced around, confused. "Where?"

"Right there," Langdon said, pointing.

Katherine's gaze followed Langdon's outstretched finger up the facade of the building to a set of windows directly above Sasha's apartment. All of the upstairs windows were boarded up with heavy wooden shutters.

"The apartment upstairs," Langdon said. "Gessner said she owns both flats and used to live up there over her ailing mother. Now she lets Sasha use the lower apartment, and the upper apartment sits . . . vacant."

Katherine studied the shuttered windows of the empty flat and pictured someone—most likely Dmitri—placing a note under Sasha's door and then quietly slipping upstairs while Langdon searched the street in vain. *Quite possible . . .*

Langdon strode to the building's outer door, which was made of thick wood, diagonally slatted, with a security screen. He fished the Krazy Kitten key ring from his pocket, unlocked the door, and ushered Katherine into the dingy foyer.

Despite the modest entrance, she could see that Sasha had made it her home. Her apartment door was immediately on the right, decorated with potted plants, a wisteria wreath, and a welcome mat that said: PLEASE WIPE YOUR PAWS.

On the back wall of the foyer, a small storage room was packed to the ceiling with old cardboard boxes. To Katherine's surprise, Langdon headed directly for it, stopping only an inch from the blockade of boxes, his chest practically touching them. He peered upward, as if studying the architecture of the alcove, and then gave a nod, waving her over.

As Katherine approached, Langdon stepped sideways to his right, disappearing into an imperceptible opening that apparently existed between the boxes and the wall of the alcove. Startled, she quickly followed, slipping through the cramped passageway, turning left around the stack of boxes, then left again, finding herself at Langdon's side. In the faint light filtering around the boxes, she could see that they were standing at the bottom of a narrow staircase, which ascended into darkness.

This is not a storage room at all, she realized. *It's the landing to a staircase.*

"I didn't notice initially that this foyer had no staircase to the second floor. Later, I realized there *had* to be access, and since there's no separate entrance, both apartments would have to be accessible through this foyer. It also explains how someone could disappear without a trace immediately after sliding a note under Sasha's door."

Katherine nodded. "Hiding just a few steps away. Very clever."

"Yes, and after I ran off to Petřín Tower, he simply emerged from hiding, entered Sasha's apartment, and either convinced her to go upstairs or incapacitated her somehow. Either way, he must have left her upstairs so she wouldn't have to see him killing Harris."

Simple and clean. Katherine nodded. "And when the embassy found Harris's body, Sasha was gone, so they logically assumed she had fled the scene."

"Exactly."

"So how are you going to get *into* the apartment?" she asked, peering up the stairs.

"I'm going to bang on the door and hope Sasha hears me."

"That's your plan?" Katherine demanded. "What if she's too

drugged to hear you? Or she's restrained and can't get to the door?"

Langdon frowned. "Then I have a plan B."

As Langdon started up the darkened staircase, he flipped the light switch at the bottom, but nothing happened.

Katherine motioned to the fixture overhead, which was bare. "No bulb."

She was about to suggest Langdon go into Sasha's apartment and find a flashlight, but he was already pushing on into the blackness, no doubt eager to get out of the cramped passageway.

Katherine enjoyed darkness about as much as Langdon enjoyed enclosed spaces, but she forced herself to follow. With her hand placed firmly on the rickety railing, she climbed to the top of the stairs and reached out tentatively to find Langdon on the small landing, in near-complete darkness, standing outside a solitary door.

"Sasha?!" he called, knocking. "Hello?!"

Silence.

He knocked more heavily now. "Sasha? It's Robert Langdon! Are you okay?"

Nothing.

Langdon tried the door. Locked.

After pounding some more, he held his ear to the door for a full ten seconds. Finally, he backed away and shook his head. "It's dead quiet in there. I hope she's okay."

"What was plan B?" Katherine asked in the darkness. "Should we find a crowbar or hammer?"

"It might be simpler than that," Langdon said, thinking. "Gessner owns both these apartments, and she used to live above her sick mother . . ." He seemed to be examining the door handle in the darkness.

Katherine squinted to see what he was doing. "Are you trying to pick the lock?"

"Not quite," he replied. He continued to jiggle his hands, and then she heard the sound of a cylinder click. Langdon lifted the handle and gave the door a gentle push. It swung open.

Katherine stared at him. "What just happened?"

Langdon held up the Krazy Kitten key ring. "Gessner lived here, owned both apartments, and her mother was ailing—so why not make it simple and have *one* key that works for both flats, for easy access?"

Of course, Katherine realized, *and there was no reason to change the locks when Sasha moved in because the second apartment sat empty.*

As the door creaked inward, Langdon and Katherine found themselves staring into pitch-darkness, which was not surprising considering the heavy shutters shrouding the windows. Katherine reached inside the doorframe and felt around, locating a light switch. When she flipped it, they both stepped back in surprise. The scene that illuminated before them was a foreign world.

The barren flat was bathed entirely in an eerie, purple luminescence.

CHAPTER 121

The Golĕm stared at his clay-caked face in the mirror, knowing it was a face he would never see again. The end was near, and thankfully it was exactly the end he had imagined.

I am The Golĕm. My time is almost done.

Having ascended safely to Gessner's lab, he was now one level beneath Crucifix Bastion, standing in the small laboratory bathroom.

At the sink, he studied the three Hebrew letters crudely etched on his forehead. They were faded from perspiration and dust, but the powerful ancient word still resonated.

אמת

Truth.

The Golĕm had always known this moment was coming.

Truth becomes Death.

As Rabbi Judah Loew had done centuries ago to kill his earthen monster and release him from servitude, The Golĕm now pressed his index finger against the thick dried clay—pushing down on the rightmost letter, *aleph*. Feeling a pang of loss and identity, he scraped his finger downward, chipping off the clay until the letter had vanished.

As was the ancient protocol, his forehead now bore a different word entirely.

מת

The Hebrew word for *dead*.

The Golĕm felt no different outwardly, and yet he could feel that his inner self, his soul, his consciousness . . . was beginning to shift. He was preparing to detach from this borrowed body once and for all.

The Golĕm had died many times, and he knew his essence would linger, but he also knew that *this* time was different. This time, it was his choice.

I came to this realm . . . so she could live.

And soon I must depart . . . so she can live.

Today had seen the death of many things.

The death of Threshold.

The death of Sasha's tormenters.

And soon, the death of The Golĕm himself.

Turning from the mirror, The Golĕm began removing his remaining clothes. Once he was naked, he stepped into the lab's emergency shower and turned it on.

The lukewarm water felt restorative on his weary head and shoulders.

Accepting his transformation, he lowered his eyes and watched the streaks of wet clay running down his pale flesh . . . long gray rivulets spiraling down the drain for the final time.

CHAPTER 122

Robert Langdon stepped warily into the luminescent flat, trying to make sense of the scene before him. The upstairs apartment appeared to be lit entirely by black lights, its desolate interior infused by a ghostly purple haze. The walls, floors, and ceilings were painted solid black. In the corner was a cheap chair and table on which sat a glass that appeared to be half-full of water.

Does someone actually live here?

Langdon needed only a moment to conclude that the mysterious occupant must be Dmitri Sysevich. The realization brought a host of unanswered questions, but Langdon was fairly certain, at least, that the man would not be returning.

He is most likely buried under Threshold.

Sasha probably had no idea her apartment shared a key with the abandoned space upstairs. Dmitri, however, almost certainly knew. *Sasha's self-proclaimed protector . . . had direct access to Sasha's locked apartment.* The thought made Langdon's skin crawl.

"Sasha?" he called out, moving deeper. "It's Robert Langdon! Are you here?"

Silence. The air tasted stale, and the floors creaked as he and Katherine moved.

"Sasha?!" Katherine shouted.

The layout of this flat was different from Sasha's, although it was equally meager. Methodically, Langdon and Katherine searched the space. The kitchen was barren, the refrigerator empty except for two large bottles of Poděbradka mineral water.

The small walk-in closet outside the bedroom contained only a rod with three empty hangers.

Langdon was starting to think this flat was less of a residence than some kind of bizarre occasional refuge.

"The bedroom has no lights," Katherine said, flipping the switch up and down.

Langdon joined her at the bedroom door. "Sasha?"

Getting no reply, he moved past Katherine into the blackness, inching blindly across the room with outstretched arms, hoping to feel a window and perhaps a way to open the shutters. Halfway into the room, he felt himself step on something soft on the floor—a cushion or mat of some sort.

The hiss of a sulfur match sizzled behind him, and Langdon turned to see Katherine crouching before a low table and lighting a series of candles. As the light grew brighter, Langdon could see the table was some kind of shrine that consisted of three candles and an arrangement of dried flowers. Above them on the wall hung a woman's photo.

Langdon recognized the blond woman instantly. "My God . . . that's Sasha," he said to Katherine, walking toward the eerie display, realizing that Dmitri's affection for Sasha had bordered on . . . obsession. *Her protector*, he thought, still trying to put the pieces together.

"Look," Katherine said, pointing to a large mat on the center of the floor.

"I guess he slept here sometimes."

"I don't think so, Robert. That's not for *sleeping*. There's no pillow. No sheets. And . . . there's a *ball gag*."

Sure enough, there on the mat, Langdon saw a buckled leather head strap affixed to a black plastic ball. The soft neoprene orb was perforated like a wiffle ball so the person being gagged could still breathe. "So, this is some kind of . . . sex room?" he said.

"I don't think that gag is for *sex*," she said. "I think it's for protecting the teeth and tongue during an epileptic seizure."

Surprised, Langdon pictured the PATI seizure mouth guard in his classroom's first-aid kit. This perforated ball would serve the same purpose.

"Dmitri must have used this room as a safe place to experience an epileptic event," Katherine said. "Pillows pose a suffocation threat, and sheets can get tangled. This would be a safe environment. Especially if he was wearing a ball gag."

Langdon found it odd that someone who possessed Gessner's epilepsy wand would not choose to thwart every seizure. Then again, some epileptics claimed seizures brought about a mental clarity and bliss that were well worth the physical trauma. Dmitri's epilepsy wand, it seemed, offered the best of both worlds. *He could choose where and when to receive his seizures . . . doing so in a safe, controlled environment.*

Regardless, all Langdon knew for certain was Sasha didn't seem to be here. With only the bathroom left to check, Langdon headed down the hall while Katherine blew out the candles in the bedroom. Sure enough, he found the bathroom and tub empty; if Dmitri had hidden Sasha somewhere, it was not in this apartment.

The bathroom's light fixture, like the rest of those in the flat, was equipped with a black-light bulb, which caused the white sink and tub to luminesce. Strangely, the mirror over the sink had been removed, leaving only bare screw holes in the wall.

Next to the sink, on a shelf, Langdon found a hand mirror, a palette knife, a mixing bowl, and a stack of white rubber skullcaps. He also found three canisters of theatrical makeup called UltraMud, whose label bore a frightening photo of an actor's face encased in thick cracked mud. The effect was all too familiar.

As Langdon scanned the rest of the room, his gaze caught on something luminescing in the wastebasket under the sink. It looked like a white washcloth had been wadded up and discarded. It also appeared to be covered in blood . . . a *lot* of blood.

Alarmed, Langdon lifted the basket and dumped the washcloth into the sink, immediately seeing he had been mistaken. Lying in the basin was a white skullcap, crumpled up and smeared with mud.

Not blood, he thought with relief. The purple light made it hard to discern color.

As he eyed the skullcap, however, he noticed something glinting in the light—a tiny fiber stuck on the rubber cap. The strand was so small that had it not been luminescing, Langdon would never have noticed it.

That can't be what it looks like . . .

He reached down and carefully plucked the item off the cap, holding it up to the light. There was no doubt what he was looking at, but what Langdon could not fathom was what it was doing *here.*

This makes no sense at all.

Then he felt an unexpected dread. *Unless . . .*

Langdon's classes on symbolism often included an adage: *A shift in perspective will often reveal a hidden truth.* This idea, in many ways, had defined Langdon's career. His ability to view a puzzle from an unexpected angle had repeatedly enabled him to glimpse truths that others had missed.

Now, as he studied the tiny item pinched between his fingertips, Langdon feared he might be experiencing one of those moments.

Knocked off-balance by the sudden reorientation, Langdon put a hand on the sink to steady himself. In his mind's eye, he could see all the puzzle pieces he had assembled today. They were suddenly shattering apart, tumbling through the air, the fragments recombining and falling back to earth. One by one, the image in Langdon's head reassembled into a new picture.

My God . . . how could I have missed this?

The idea before him was almost unimaginable, and yet instinctively he knew it had to be true. Like every pure truth, it answered every question . . . resolved every anomaly . . . and had been right in front of him all along.

"Nonlocal consciousness . . ." he whispered. "Katherine was right."

◆—··—◆

"I missed it!" Langdon announced, rushing out of the bathroom and heading for the exit. "We need to go—I'll explain later!"

Missed what?! Katherine wondered as she hurried after him. *Wait!*

When she reached the door, Robert was already thundering down the darkened staircase. When she caught up to him, he was in the foyer, kneeling on Sasha's welcome mat outside her apartment. He seemed to be trying to feel for something under her door. *What is he doing?!* "Robert, we have a key if—"

"It wasn't even *possible!*" he exclaimed, jumping to his feet, digging into his pocket, and pulling out a slip of paper that Katherine recognized as the note he had received earlier beneath Sasha's door.

To Katherine's bewilderment, Langdon tried repeatedly to slide the note under her door, failing each time to feed it beneath the tight doorjamb. The paper kept hitting the thick band of weather stripping that had been installed to keep out the cold.

"It wasn't even possible," Langdon repeated, finally standing up. "I saw the weather stripping earlier, but it didn't register. There's no way to insert this note under the door from out here!"

"I see that," Katherine said, "but I don't—"

"Don't you see, Katherine? The note wasn't delivered from outside . . . The person who left it was *inside* the apartment the whole time!"

A creeping chill overtook her. *He was already hiding inside.* "In the hall closet . . ." she whispered, picturing the dark-haired Russian waiting for a quiet moment . . . emerging from the closet . . . sliding the note partway under the door . . . knocking loudly on the inside of the door. . . . and immediately disappearing back into the closet. It was a brilliant trick. Both Sasha and Robert were completely fooled.

"No," Langdon said, his face now ashen. "Not in the closet." He looked as disturbed as she could remember seeing him. "*Nobody* was in the closet. The hiding place was . . . far more ingenious." His voice was tremulous now. "I can't believe I never saw any of this . . ."

"What didn't you see? I don't understand."

Langdon stood up. "You talked about it in your lecture

last night," Langdon said, locking eyes with Katherine. "You described it as evidence of nonlocal consciousness . . . proof that our brains work as receivers, and if they are damaged, the signals can get confused . . ."

"You mean sudden savant syndrome?" she said. "Okay, but I don't see—"

"No! What you described right *after* that!"

Katherine thought a moment, recalling the sequence of her speech, and suddenly it dawned on her what Langdon was referring to. She needed only an instant more to grasp what he was trying to tell her. "Oh . . . Robert . . . you can't possibly think—"

"I found this in the bathroom," he said, holding up something tiny, pinched between his thumb and index finger. "It was stuck on the inside of his dirty skullcap."

Katherine saw what Langdon was holding.

If he was correct, then everything they had believed about the golem figure was dead wrong.

CHAPTER 123

Steam filled the lab shower at Crucifix Bastion. The Golĕm tipped his head back and savored the softness of the water on his face. Gently massaging his cheeks with his palms, he could feel the final remnants of dried clay releasing from his flesh . . . the last of The Golĕm dissolving away.

As he ran his hands over his head, he realized that in his exhaustion he'd forgotten to remove his skullcap. Finding the edge of the skintight cap with his fingertips, he pried it away from his forehead, wincing as it slid backward off his head, inevitably tearing several hairs from his scalp.

The Golĕm dropped the cap onto the floor and gently massaged his scalp, letting the water flow through his thick hair, rinsing away any remaining mud. Only after the water spiraling down the drain had become perfectly clear did he step from the shower.

Wrapped in a towel, he stood at the sink, taking a rare moment to study himself in the mirror.

The eyes staring back at him were bloodshot and weary . . . a face scarred by a violent past. He knew this was not a pretty face, and yet it was the face he had been given.

I have learned to see beauty in it, he thought.

Over time, The Golĕm had come to love this face . . . the way the blond hair fell to the shoulders and framed the innocent blue eyes. Even the crooked nose had a charm to him now. He pictured the candlelit photo on the wall of his *svatyně* and smiled.

"Sasha," he whispered to his reflection. "I wish you could know me."

The blond woman in the mirror did not reply.

Despite Sasha's bodily presence in the room, she heard nothing. The Golĕm had locked her away in a sleeplike void where she was blissfully unaware of all things, including even herself.

Although they shared this physical form, The Golĕm had established his dominance long ago, always in control, carefully filtering what Sasha witnessed, remembered, understood. He did this for her protection, to shelter her gentle soul. He was the vault to hold her pain, the army to fight her battles.

You summoned me, Sasha . . . and I answered.

The Golĕm would never forget that horrifying moment in the Russian psychiatric hospital, when Sasha's soul, unable to endure another moment of suffering, had called out to the universe in desperate need of help.

The moment of my birth . . .

Few recalled the instant they came to be, and yet The Golĕm recalled his. He had flickered abruptly into consciousness, awaking to sheer horror, finding himself trapped in a body that was being mercilessly beaten. Overcome with pain and outrage, he instinctively rose up, summoning wells of strength this body had never accessed, and he strangled his attacker's neck. Standing over the lifeless body of Sasha's night nurse, The Golĕm had heard his own hollow voice for the very first time.

"I am your protector, Sasha. You are safe now."

———·· ——

In the foyer outside Sasha's apartment, Katherine Solomon's brain struggled to organize the cascade of disquieting thoughts brought on by Langdon's words. He was correct that her lecture last night had included a description of sudden savant syndrome—a condition she believed was clear evidence of nonlocal consciousness—a damaged brain receiving multiple signals.

He was *also* correct that she had then discussed a *second* remarkable phenomenon.

"There exists another curious condition," Katherine had told the audience, "that is related to sudden savant syndrome, as it also suggests the ability of the brain to receive multiple signals.

The phenomenon goes by the clinical term 'dissociative identity disorder'—although most of us know it more commonly as 'split personality disorder'—a psychological phenomenon that presents as *multiple* distinct personalities inhabiting a *single* body."

This globally documented condition, Katherine had gone on to explain, was most common in women and often arose as a coping mechanism for repeated physical or sexual abuse. Most frequently, the second identity manifested for the purpose of *absorbing* the host's pain by enduring the trauma in her place—a kind of proxy victim—sustaining the anguish, blocking all memory of it, and enabling the host to "disassociate" from her own suffering.

The secondary personality was known as the alternate or "alter" and typically appeared in an abrupt schismatic break during acute trauma. Having manifested, the alter could then take up permanent residence in the host, lingering for years or a lifetime as a kind of guardian, even subsuming the subject's darkest memories in a kind of selective amnesia—providing a clean slate with which to move forward. It was not uncommon for a protective alter to assume control of the body and become the *dominant* personality, deciding when and how the traumatized subject could safely "surface."

Dissociative identity disorder had first been diagnosed in the 1800s under the name "double consciousness"—a kind of waking sleepwalking in which an individual seemed to be taken over by another consciousness, who then carried out actions without the permission, knowledge, or recollection of the individual.

Two of the most extraordinary cases in history were so meticulously documented that they became the basis for the bestsellers *The Three Faces of Eve, Strangers in My Body,* and *Sybil.* Of course, the most famous book of all time on the condition was Robert Louis Stevenson's *The Strange Case of Dr. Jekyll and Mr. Hyde.*

Katherine knew that many instances of DID involved *multiple* alters—some with more than a dozen identities living in one host body. Incredibly, the alters all had different voices, accents, handwriting, skill sets, food preferences, and even gender identities. They walked differently, preferred different living spaces, suffered different physical ailments, and even had different IQs and eyesight.

One radio receiving multiple distinct stations . . .

Psychiatrists diverged wildly over how these stark dissimilarities between alters could be possible, and some skeptics even accused DID patients of being skilled actors looking for attention. However, when patients submitted to rigorous testing involving MRIs, lie detectors, and sophisticated lines of interrogation, the results were always the same—there were *indeed* multiple discrete individuals existing within one body.

Some of the alters were *aware* of the others living with them in what was known as "the system." These alters were called "co-conscious." In contrast, some alters were oblivious that the system even existed, believing instead that they were alone in the body. They often suffered memory gaps when stronger alters blocked them out, taking over the forefront of the mind in an action known as "fronting."

Now, as Katherine stood with Langdon in the dingy foyer, she felt her attention fixated on the strand of blond hair that he had pulled from the skullcap. His conclusion was shocking . . . and logical. *He believes The Golĕm and Sasha are the same person.*

If Robert was right, then finding Sasha was no longer a possibility. Tragically, the psychological condition that had arisen to save Sasha Vesna's life had also likely ended it. The Golĕm must have died in the explosion . . . taking Sasha with him.

———·——

The Golĕm finished dressing and scrutinized himself in the mirror. Her image always felt foreign to him, and yet this was how he found himself most often existing in the world—dressed as Sasha, wearing the clothing she donned every morning.

Today's attire—jeans, a white blouse, tennis shoes, and a parka—were clothes The Golĕm had left in Sasha's office for this very moment. The look was not flattering, and her hair was matted and wet, but it made her a pitiable figure . . . and she was in desperate need of pity.

Please help Sasha . . .

The Golĕm had done his best to be a silent partner in Sasha's life, hiding back in the deepest recesses of her mind, watching as she bravely navigated her new life . . . the life she deserved. Like any caring guardian, The Golĕm occasionally intervened for Sasha's own protection. He would step forward and quietly grab the reins, taking over Sasha's body, effortlessly mimicking her voice and demeanor. These interventions were to protect her . . . to shield her from dangerous situations, painful information, or difficult decisions she was not prepared to make.

For Sasha, these moments were brief blank spots in her life and memory, akin to daydreaming while driving a car and arriving at your destination with no recollection of how you got there. She accepted that her memory was occasionally spotty. The Golĕm's interventions had become less frequent recently because Sasha had been as happy as he had ever seen her.

The reason for her happiness was Michael Harris.

Sasha was in love.

The handsome attaché had entered her life by chance, or so it had seemed, and while The Golĕm was uncomfortable with their growing physical relationship, he had chosen not to intervene. Sasha deserved a first love, and Michael seemed like a decent man.

As it turned out, appearances were deceptive.

Three weeks earlier, The Golĕm had been lying on the hemp mat in his *svatyně*, enjoying a postictal bliss, when he heard someone in the apartment below. Puzzled, he pressed his ear to the floor and heard what sounded like someone *searching* Sasha's flat. Before he could get dressed and run downstairs, a voice began talking loudly in the space below.

The voice belonged to Michael Harris.

Stunned, The Golĕm found himself listening to a phone conversation between Harris and the U.S. ambassador. The call revealed not only that Harris had ulterior motives for befriending Sasha, but also that the kindness shown by Sasha's trusted mentor, Dr. Brigita Gessner, might also be disingenuous.

In a matter of seconds, The Golĕm reassessed the charmed

life he thought Sasha had found. He was well aware of the extensive medical treatments she had undergone, and yet his belief was always that Brigita Gessner had benevolently cured Sasha of her ailments—and continued to administer procedures to perfect the results.

Now The Golěm saw a different reality. From that moment on, he was almost always present, watching through Sasha's eyes, observing, listening, guiding, and awaiting his opportunity to reveal the truth. Last night, The Golěm had finally seized his opportunity, isolating Gessner in her lab and immortalizing the treachery. His recorded confession of Gessner had covered it all . . . surgeries, implants, Dmitri's death, psychedelic drugs, Mr. Finch, the CIA, and their true objective in Prague.

Threshold is now gone, The Golěm reveled as he exited the lab's bathroom into the hallway. He hoped Robert Langdon and Katherine Solomon had escaped; the American professor had shown significant kindness to Sasha today, and his scientist friend understood the universe in ways that only those like The Golěm could truly grasp.

The day, while ending in triumph, had presented no shortage of unforeseen challenges. The Golěm's first shock had been encountering ÚSZI officers at the bastion; his second seeing Langdon crouched over Gessner's body; and his third—no doubt triggered by the first two—an epileptic seizure in Gessner's lab that he was unable to stop.

The challenge with seizures was that The Golěm's brain always rebooted to its original *default* state—Sasha. She always awoke alone and vulnerable. Post-seizure, Sasha's consciousness was fully present and in control until The Golěm could flicker back online after several minutes and take over. For this reason, he kept his *svatyně* pitch-black when he received the Ether, ensuring Sasha would always awaken to darkness rather than to an unfamiliar room.

This morning, following his seizure beside Gessner's body, The Golěm had wrestled his consciousness back to the forefront and found himself cradled in the arms of Robert Langdon. Realizing his descent to Threshold would have to wait, The

Golĕm persuaded Langdon to flee the bastion—ostensibly with Sasha—but as the professor descended the snowy slope to Folimanka Park, The Golĕm had been with him every step, watching through Sasha's eyes.

At Sasha's apartment, Harris's imminent arrival provided the perfect opportunity to punish Sasha's cruelest betrayer, so The Golĕm had sent Langdon out of harm's way by improvising a simple illusion—a slip of paper; a knock on the door; a momentary retreat back into the bathroom. Langdon found the message and dashed into the alleyway in his socks, never noticing The Golĕm watching from Sasha's window.

Less than an hour ago, here at the bastion, a female operative had attacked him, and he could still see her startled expression as she desperately drove her hands up into The Golĕm's chest . . . and encountered the soft shape of Sasha's breasts.

I am not as you think I am.

And then, his final challenge, downstairs in Threshold. Having lost his magnetic wand, The Golĕm was hit by another seizure and frantically searched the domed chamber for a safe place to ride it out, finally opting for the padded interior of one of the EPR pods. It was a place he knew well.

I have died there many times.

The Golĕm shuddered as he now recalled the true nature of Gessner's experiments—pushing Sasha to the brink and pulling her back—over and over. At the time, he had believed in Gessner's generosity and had done his best to absorb the pain of those events, to shield Sasha from the discomfort and fear. Fortunately, Sasha could not recall the many times Gessner had drugged her and wheeled her through Threshold to perform various experiments in the operating suite and pod room.

But I remember, The Golĕm thought.

The faint wisps of recollection still haunted him.

Another life, he told himself. *That was the past.*

The future was getting close now, the future he had planned for Sasha, the future she deserved. *Soon I will set her free and vanish.* All that remained was to ascend from this subterranean world . . . and make his way to the United States embassy.

CHAPTER 124

L angdon stood in Sasha Vesna's kitchen, still grappling with what he and Katherine had uncovered. Sasha's two Siamese cats were twisting affectionately around his ankles, and the scent of Russian Caravan tea still hung in the air. Even so, her home felt utterly foreign to him now.

When I was here, I was probably not talking to the real Sasha.

The revelation was deeply disturbing, and yet Sasha's psychological condition answered a lot of questions—The Golĕm's access to Crucifix Bastion . . . Sasha's memory loss . . . the strange flat upstairs . . . and perhaps even why Langdon had been given a key to Sasha's apartment and urged to return. *Did he want* me *to find Harris's body and deliver the envelope to the ambassador?* Either way, the realization about Sasha's identity was providing aspects of clarity.

Katherine joined him in the kitchen after looking around the apartment. "I wonder," she ventured, "if Threshold chose *epileptics* as test subjects because of their natural predisposition to out-of-body experiences . . . or because epileptics provided Brigita the perfect cover to do brain surgery without raising suspicion."

It was a good question, and Langdon imagined it might have been both. "Either way, it's unforgivable. I suspect something went terribly wrong with Dmitri and he is dead, as his records suggested."

A long silence hung between them as Langdon scanned the sweet, even childlike, decorations around the kitchen.

"And what about these two?" Katherine asked, crouching

down and petting Sasha's immaculately groomed cats. "When is the last time they were *fed*?"

True, Langdon thought. *Someone will need to adopt them.* He went to the cupboard beneath the sink and pulled out their bag of cat food.

"I'll do it," Katherine said, taking the bag. "You should make the call."

Langdon went to the phone on the wall and dialed the number that Scott Kerble had given him. As the line began to ring, he wondered what he would say when Kerble asked about Sasha Vesna. *We didn't find her. She died in Threshold. By the way, she killed Michael Harris.* Langdon was still trying to comprehend that Sasha could have deeply loved Harris at the same time her protector knew the truth about Harris and loathed him. *Two people. One body.*

Langdon recalled hearing once of a court case involving an alleged rapist, William Milligan, who had proven in a lie detector test that he had no recollection of his alleged crimes. As it turned out, Milligan was an unwitting sufferer of DID; one of his alters had committed the crimes without his knowledge. Milligan was acquitted and placed in a psychiatric facility.

Before modern psychiatric care, many of those exhibiting a split personality were taken to the only psychiatric professionals available—priests. The Church frequently diagnosed them with "demonic possession" and prescribed a common treatment plan: "exorcism." To this day, the Rite of Exorcism was still performed regularly on individuals with mental disorders, and while Langdon had always been horrified by this, he had to admit that Katherine's description of nonlocal consciousness added a new perspective.

Perhaps an exorcist is not trying to coax a demon out of a body . . . but rather trying to retune the body's receiver to block the unwanted station.

"Kerble here," a familiar voice said on the phone, pulling Langdon back to the moment.

"Hello, this is Robert Langdon."

"We've been expecting your call, sir. Please hold for Ambassador Nagel."

Langdon was surprised the ambassador was available to speak. *I thought she was under arrest.* It appeared something had shifted at the embassy.

"Professor," the ambassador's voice chimed in on the line. "I can't tell you how relieved I am that you're both safe. Scott told me it was . . . quite close."

"I'm not sure it could have been any closer," Langdon said.

"And we heard you were arrested by the CIA director?"

"Yes, although Director Judd claimed the detainment was a temporary protective custody to ensure my safety."

"Do you believe him?"

"I'd *like* to," Nagel said. "He claimed he was concerned Finch might . . . I don't know. Anyhow, I've had no contact from Finch since our last phone call."

"Finch is dead," Langdon said bluntly. "We saw him at Threshold just before the blast. Katherine and I were the last ones out, and Finch—"

"Okay," she interrupted, sounding shaken. "Not on the phone. We'll discuss it in person."

"We have a lot to share," Langdon said. "Is the embassy a safe place to talk?"

"I'm not confident of that," Nagel replied. "I'd suggest your hotel, but it's too obvious, and I really can't promise we'd be safe. Not yet." She paused a moment. "Are you familiar with the Dripstone Wall?"

"I am," Langdon said, puzzled that she would mention such a public place . . . especially one that was notoriously creepy. "It's near the embassy, but I'm not sure—"

"Get there as fast as you can."

◆——··——▶

At ÚZSI headquarters, Lieutenant Pavel was solemnly gathering the last of his personal belongings from his locker. His lengthy interrogation at the hands of his new superior officer had resulted in his demotion and a three-month probationary leave.

I won't be coming back, Pavel knew.

Everything was different now. Although his recollection of the day was foggy, Pavel would never forget the image of his uncle lying dead in an icy ravine. The captain's death had been officially cataloged as an accident, and as much as Pavel wanted to protest, he was in no position. Moreover, any further ÚZSI investigation had been shut down by the U.S. ambassador, who held all the cards after uncovering Janáček's deceitful methods in detaining two prominent Americans.

Pavel exited the building and trudged toward the bus stop. When he arrived, there was a young woman waiting for the bus. She had a kind face, and Pavel gave her a weary smile.

"To je ale zima," he said politely. *It's so cold.*

The woman immediately turned away and relocated to the far end of the stop.

Pavel felt suddenly very alone in the world.

When the bus arrived, Pavel boarded and moved toward the back. None of the other passengers glanced up, their eyes all focused downward on their devices. Pavel took a seat and pulled out his own phone, reflexively opening Dream Zone, his virtual dating simulator.

Several new requests pinged in, and he expected to feel the glimmer of warmth that always accompanied the hope of fresh possibilities. Tonight, however, the phone felt cold in his hand. He gazed into its glare a long moment and then startled himself by powering it off and sliding it back into his pocket. Then, closing his eyes, he said a prayer for his uncle and listened to the hum of the bus as it carried him home.

CHAPTER 125

The Dripstone Wall, one of Prague's more surreal ancient attractions, resembles a towering cliff of melted rock. Rising over forty feet above Wallenstein Garden, this mysterious seventeenth-century sculpture gives the impression of a river of molten lava, hardened mid-flow into a wall of fluid stalactites, bulbous outcroppings, and amorphous hollows.

Formally known as the Grotto, it remains to this day one of Prague's eeriest destinations. The organic undulations in its stone surface have an almost phantasmagorical quality, and visitors enjoy pointing out the various grotesque faces they see peering out at them. For centuries, church officials have petitioned to tear down the wall, claiming it is haunted and invites the emergence of evil spirits. Tourists regularly complain of nightmares after visiting the wall, and several prominent dignitaries have found themselves nauseous while standing before it.

Ambassador Nagel was not one of them.

I find it calming, she thought, gazing up at the wall before her. The Grotto looked especially beautiful right now, muted and pale in the fading afternoon light, with wisps of white snow settled in the nooks and crannies of the countless faces.

As Nagel waited in the dimming light, she saw fresh faces materialize in the wall before her. She had learned that only a fraction of the faces she saw were actually there, *intended* by the architect. The others, as it turned out, were faces she was *hallucinating*—a psychological phenomenon known as *pareidolia*. The brain had a natural inclination to conjure meaningful shapes out of nebulous contours, and humans saw faces in everything—

from clouds to fabric patterns to bowls of soup to shadows on a lake. All it took was two dots and a line, and most human brains made the same connection.

From her work at the CIA, Nagel was convinced that conspiracy theorists suffered a kind of cognitive pareidolia, seeing suspicious patterns where no patterns existed . . . hallucinating order out of chaos.

Everett Finch was the opposite. He spotted *real* patterns and used them to manufacture chaos . . . all in an effort to preserve some kind of order in the world. News of Finch's death had granted Nagel a reprieve, and yet it was not something she would ever celebrate. She had learned one simple truth in her career at CIA: *Good and evil do not exist in pure form.* Finch's ruthlessness, she knew, was fueled by his deep commitment to an agency that was trying to gain a foothold in the brave new world of brain technology.

"The owls are sleeping," a deep voice spoke behind her, echoing off the Dripstone Wall's looming surface.

For a moment, Nagel thought she had just overheard some kind of secret spy phrase, but when she turned, she saw two familiar faces. Robert Langdon and Katherine Solomon were approaching past the garden's aviary where Wallenstein's resident owls were perched motionless, with their heads tucked into their shoulder feathers.

Nagel smiled and shook their hands as her ever-present guardian, Scott Kerble, emerged from the shadows and joined the group. Langdon and Solomon still had no coats, but fortunately, this conversation was not intended to be held outdoors. "Follow me," she said, leading them toward the Dripstone Wall. "We'll talk inside."

Langdon glanced up at the solid cliff, clearly puzzled. "Inside . . . *where?*"

Without a word, Nagel led the entourage toward the base of the wall and stopped at a tiny wooden door—no more than four feet tall—surrounded by frightening skull-like formations. Langdon's expression of incredulity was complete when Nagel pulled out a key and unlocked the door.

One of the perks of being U.S. ambassador, she thought. The wealthy Americans who owned what lay beyond this door had loaned Nagel a key, giving her access to this discreet backdoor entrance in hopes she would visit often, which she did.

As they entered, Nagel wondered what Langdon would think if he knew where they were now headed. Behind this wall, in any of six candlelit chambers, the professor might find himself lying naked on a granite slab while robed attendants poured hot wax across his flesh.

———·——

She has a key?

If Langdon's memory served, Prague's famous Dripstone Wall had been erected against the rear facade of a thirteenth-century Augustine friary—the St. Thomas Monastery—meaning he had just stepped through the wall into ancient, hallowed hallways.

Not so hallowed anymore, he mused.

This grand monastery, like so many in Europe, had been repurposed to serve the needs of an increasingly secular world. In this case, it had been transformed into a Marriott Hotel— the Augustine Luxury. The monks' ancient brewery was now reimagined as the ultrahip Refectory Bar, and the monastery's original scriptorium had been preserved fully intact, complete with ancient texts, writing implements, and sharpening stones for quills.

"As quietly as possible," Nagel whispered, guiding them down a narrow passageway to a service door. When she pushed it open, Langdon found himself in an elegant hallway that smelled of tea tree, incense, and eucalyptus.

"You brought us to a *spa?*" he asked as they arrived at a golden door, where a placard listed various treatments, including their specialty—the Monastic Ritual. He was no cloistral specialist, but he was fairly certain monastic rituals did not involve lavender body candles and collagen facials.

"We're safe here," she whispered. "I know the staff, and the walls are soundproofed."

With that, Nagel motioned for them to wait as she slipped inside. Within a matter of seconds, she returned with a key fob and ushered them down the hall, where she unlocked one of the spa's private, post-treatment *salóneks*.

The windowless lounge had a faux-ecclesiastical feel with flickering electric candles, stained-glass art, and piped-in Gregorian chant. The soundtrack, Langdon noted, predated the monastery by four centuries. But anachronisms aside, he could imagine worse places to be. *It's private and warm.* Better yet, Kerble had headed into the hotel to see if he could find them some food.

"First off," Nagel said, shedding her winter coat and motioning them to sit on the comfortable couches, "I can't possibly imagine what you've both endured today. I'm relieved that you're okay, and I realize we have a lot to discuss. But before we delve too deeply into it, I wanted to share some very good news." She gave them both a tired smile. "As it turns out, the incriminating evidence that we were hoping to obtain about Threshold . . . We now *have* it."

How? Langdon wondered, imagining that all physical evidence of Threshold's existence was pulverized and buried in rubble . . . along with, tragically, the most potent proof of all. *Sasha Vesna herself.*

Nagel eyed them both, looking tired but energized. "As it turns out, we have a guardian angel. Stated more accurately, Sasha Vesna has a guardian angel."

Langdon was startled by the comment. He immediately pictured the cloaked figure who had declared himself Sasha's protector and guardian. *Does Nagel know about her split personality?*

"And her guardian angel," she added, "sent me *this*."

Nagel produced a sheet of paper and laid it in front of them. When Katherine saw it, she let out a little gasp. Langdon felt a similar pall to read the handwritten message scrawled on a piece of cat-themed stationery.

PLEASE HELP SASHA.

My God, he thought, picturing Sasha's hands writing these very words . . . a desperate call for help . . . an appeal that, strangely, Sasha knew nothing about.

The ambassador quickly explained that the URL included in the message led to a tortured video confession in which Gessner divulged all she knew about Threshold—human testing, brain surgeries, implants, psychopharmaceuticals, near-death experiences, the list of people involved . . . all of it.

"The video is very difficult to watch," Nagel said, "but its existence means the CIA can never again come after you."

She let that sink in.

"I've safeguarded a copy, and I intend to make backups. In short, no matter what else happens, this video is the only insurance you'll ever need." Her eyes flashed in the candlelight. "It's your atomic bomb."

"Yours *too*, I hope," Katherine said quietly.

Nagel nodded. "Although I'm not sure how much we'll need it. The director seemed as appalled as I was to learn some of the things that had gone on at Threshold."

"He *had* to know," Langdon argued. "He's the *director*."

"Yes, which is why he might *not* have known," Nagel countered. "The agency is hypercompartmentalized on process— plausible deniability, autocratic efficiency. He put Finch in charge and therefore would have known only the details Finch chose to share."

Maybe, Langdon thought, *maybe not*. He picked up the letter, sensing the ambassador knew nothing of Sasha's condition. "But why would Sasha's guardian address this to *you*? Why not send the video directly to the press?"

"In the video," Nagel said, "Dr. Gessner admits that I knew almost nothing about Threshold's true purpose and would be horrified by its existence. I suspect that admission is why Sasha's guardian entrusted the video to *me* . . . imagining I was influential enough to help Sasha . . . or to make a difference. It goes without saying that if we ever locate Sasha, I am poised to help her in any way I can. She is a victim, and I *did* play a role in making Threshold a reality . . . despite being coerced and unaware." She glanced away suddenly, staring into space. "But Michael Harris . . ." she whispered, almost tearfully, "what I forced him to do . . . spying on Sasha for Finch . . . It cost Michael his life." Her eyes returned to them. "I will carry that guilt and shame forever."

Langdon wondered how Nagel would feel when she learned the complicated truth about Harris's killer. *The woman you ordered Harris to seduce was, in an odd sense, the one who murdered him.*

"Sasha's protector," Katherine said. "Her 'guardian angel,' as you put it. Did you ever learn his identity?"

"Not conclusively," Nagel replied. "He appeared only in glimpses in the video and was disguised, but I do have a strong suspicion I know who it was."

Langdon and Katherine exchanged a surprised glance.

"The man on the video who tortured Gessner spoke with a Russian accent," Nagel said. "And he told Gessner he was punishing her for betraying Sasha's trust. But there was something about his rage that felt like *personal* betrayal . . . as if he too had been a Threshold test subject."

He was, Langdon thought. *In a sense, he was patient number three.* Langdon didn't fully understand the complexities of DID, but it seemed that whatever procedures Gessner had carried out on Sasha could have been experienced by her alter, especially if that alter was protective and chose to endure those parts of Sasha's life that were painful. According to Katherine, a dominant alter could govern which identity was conscious and in the forefront at any given moment.

"The director informed me," Nagel continued, "that Threshold's first test subject was also Russian and was taken from the same institution as Sasha. His name was Dmitri Sysevich. Finch said he had *died* in the program, but the director said he had seen no proof of Dmitri's death. It's possible that Finch lied about it for some reason."

Finch didn't lie, Langdon knew. *Dmitri is dead. We saw his medical file.*

"Considering the video," Nagel said, her tone regretful, "the director and I concluded that Dmitri Sysevich must have survived the program somehow and returned to take revenge."

In the uncomfortable silence, Langdon glanced at Katherine, their gazes locking. They both knew what needed to happen. It was time for the ambassador to learn the truth.

"Ma'am," Langdon said, turning back to her. "The person you saw killing Gessner . . . it was *not* Dmitri Sysevich."

CHAPTER 126

Ambassador Nagel was uncertain how much time had passed when the group emerged through the Dripstone Wall. *An hour? Two?* Darkness had settled over Wallenstein Garden, and there seemed to be a cold foreboding in the shadows.

She was still reeling from what Langdon had explained about Sasha, and while Nagel knew she would eventually be able to accept the truth *intellectually* . . . she feared there would be one fact that would forever cut through her emotions like a knife to the heart.

Michael Harris was killed by . . . Sasha.

"You have to remember," Katherine insisted. "It was *not* Sasha who did this to Michael. She loved Michael. You must think of them as *two* people."

Either way, the news had caused her a fresh wave of crushing guilt. Nagel found herself wishing she could beg both Michael and Sasha for their forgiveness . . . but they were both gone.

Even Wallenstein Garden seemed lifeless to her now, the rosebushes wrapped in burlap bags and the pond drained for winter. Nagel doubted she would witness its annual renaissance this spring. As of a few hours ago, she possessed enough political leverage to do whatever she wanted, which no longer included being a U.S. ambassador living in Prague.

I was never supposed to be here, she thought. *I was sent as a puppet.*

She would probably wait a month to help the embassy through the current crisis and then tender her resignation. She had no idea what she would do next, but she felt like she had some fight left in her . . . and a lot more to give.

At the moment, her most immediate concern was recovering the USB stick that Scott Kerble had cleverly smuggled out of the embassy in the box of Dana's belongings. Kerble would be headed to her flat shortly to recover it.

As they exited the garden, Nagel glanced back at Langdon and Solomon, who were talking quietly as they followed. No doubt they both were deeply exhausted and needed sleep.

"I'll drive them back to their hotel," Kerble said, as if reading her thoughts exactly. "Right after I drop you at the embassy."

They emerged into the glow of the streetlights, and Nagel knew she would miss Kerble most of all. "Scott," she said softly. "I'm fully aware of the risks you took for me today . . . and I don't take your loyalty for granted."

The Marine gave her a rare smile and touched his cap. "Nor I *yours.*"

CHAPTER 127

The most disturbing and effective piece of art in Europe, Langdon had long believed, was *Victims of Communism*— a memorial consisting of six life-size bronze men descending a wide concrete staircase. Each of the men was emaciated, bearded, and on a different step. Eerily, all six men were the same individual . . . but each was in a different state of decay . . . one missing an arm, another half his head, another with a gaping chasm through his chest.

Defiance and endurance, Langdon recalled, was the artist's message. *This individual, regardless of his level of suffering, remained standing.*

Langdon had not anticipated seeing the sculpture on this visit to Prague, and yet there it was, rushing by the window of the embassy sedan as they sped along Újezd Street. He would have pointed it out to Katherine, but she was already asleep on his shoulder, her tousled hair soft against his cheek.

Having dropped the ambassador at the embassy, Sergeant Kerble was now whisking Langdon and Katherine south along Petřín Gardens, headed for the Four Seasons Hotel and a much-needed rest. As they turned left onto Legion Bridge, Langdon closed his eyes and listened to Katherine's soft breathing, feeling comforted by the reassuring sound of . . . life.

The concept of *death* had been entirely too present today, not only in discussion, but also in Langdon's reality . . . nearly freezing to death in the Vltava River, then being shot at by Pavel and narrowly escaping Threshold.

Remarkably, over the past year, everything Langdon had

learned from Katherine about consciousness had altered his perspective on dying . . . markedly easing his trepidation about aging and mortality. If Katherine's nonlocal model of consciousness turned out to be correct, then the logical conclusion was that some part of Langdon, his being, his soul, his mind . . . would transcend the death of his body and live on.

I'm in no hurry to find out, he thought, savoring the warmth of Katherine's head on his shoulder.

Yesterday, while touring the Vyšehrad, they had stumbled across an unusually morbid reliquary displaying a human shoulder blade—allegedly that of St. Valentine—and Katherine had startled him with a deceptively simple question: *How do you define death?*

Having never considered death in literal terms, Langdon drew a blank, finally offering a feebly circular definition that he never would have accepted from his students: *Death is the absence of life.*

To his surprise, Katherine told him his reply was quite close to the official, medical definition: *The irreversible cessation of all cell function.* Then she informed him that the official medical definition was 100 percent incorrect.

"Death," she explained, "has nothing to do with the *physical* body. We define death in terms of *consciousness*. Consider a brain-dead, nonresponsive patient on life support—his body is technically very much alive, and yet we routinely pull the plug on that body. Without consciousness, we view a human body as essentially *dead* . . . even when its physical functions are perfectly intact."

True, Langdon realized.

"And the opposite is equally true," she continued. "A quadriplegic in a wheelchair, who has lost physical function in his entire body and yet remains *conscious*, is very much alive. Stephen Hawking was essentially a mind without a body. Imagine if someone suggested pulling the plug on him!"

Langdon had never heard the point made quite that way.

"Robert," she finished, "we can no longer deny the growing tide of evidence that consciousness can exist *outside* the body . . .

beyond the confines of the brain. The day has come for us to entirely redefine consciousness . . . and therefore entirely redefine *death*!"

Langdon hoped she was right, and that dying was not as "terminal" an event as most imagined. From the recesses of his memory, the ancient teachings of Asclepius bubbled up:

Far too many fear death and regard it as the worst disaster that can befall them: they know nothing of what they speak. Death comes as a dissolution from an exhausted body . . . Just as the body leaves the mother's womb when it is mature in it, so also does the soul leave the body when it has come to perfection.

As a young student of comparative religion, Langdon had been amazed by the *universality* of the promise of reincarnation and life after death—the lone, unswerving assurance offered by every single religious tradition that had survived the test of time. He had always viewed this consistent trait as an example of Darwinian "survival of the fittest." *The only religions that survived were those offering a solution to humankind's greatest fear.*

The more spiritual side of Langdon often wondered if perhaps the age-old promise of eternal life might actually *predate* religion . . . finding its roots in the lost wisdom of the ancients . . . a time when the human mind was sufficiently uncluttered to perceive the deepest truths that permeated the universe.

A thought for another day, he decided as their car slowed in front of the Four Seasons.

"Hey, sleepyhead," he whispered to Katherine beside him. "We're here."

Faukman lunged for the phone. "Hello?!"

"Jonas, it's Robert," announced the unmistakable baritone voice. "I'm just back at the hotel. The manager said you've been calling nonstop."

"I have been!" Faukman exclaimed. "The explosion in Prague? I was worri—"

"Sorry, we're both okay."

Faukman sighed in relief. "You know, Robert, most authors

make me nervous by submitting their manuscripts late, but you have an irritating habit—"

"Thanks for your concern," Langdon replied with a laugh, "but I was nowhere near the blast."

"Glad to hear it, even if I don't believe it," Faukman said. "I've witnessed your proclivity for proximity to peril."

"And I your predilection for paranoid presumptions."

Faukman chuckled. "That response was a bit too quick . . . even for *you*, Robert. How do I know this isn't some AI chatbot?"

"Because AI would never know you declined one of the best-selling novels of the past twenty years because you thought the author used too many ellipses."

"Hey! I told you that in confidence!"

"Yes, and I'll take it to my grave," Langdon assured him. "Just not today."

"Any word on Katherine's manuscript?" Faukman asked hopefully.

"Sorry," Langdon replied, his voice weary. "I wish I could give you better news . . ."

———··———

It was just before seven o'clock when Langdon turned off the steam shower in the Royal Suite. The night was young, but a wintry darkness had long since settled over Prague, and he and Katherine had agreed they were headed directly to bed.

Wrapping a towel around his waist, Langdon stepped from the shower and found Katherine submerged in a bubble bath with one lithe leg extended and a safety razor in her hand.

She's shaving her legs? he thought, surprised. "Are we going out?"

Katherine laughed. "No, Robert, we are *not* going out. Do you really not know why a woman shaves her legs before bed?"

"Ah . . ." He hesitated. "I just thought . . . you were exhausted."

"I was. But when I saw you get in the shower, I woke up." She motioned to his toned abs. "You look pretty good, Aquaman . . . for someone your age."

"My *age*? You're older than I am!"

"Do you really want to go there?"

"No, my darling . . . I do not." Langdon walked over to the tub, sat on the edge, and placed a hand affectionately on the back of Katherine's neck. "What I meant to say is you're beautiful, brilliant, hilarious, and I adore you." He kissed her softly on the lips. "And I'll see you in bed."

◆—··—▶

It's official, Katherine thought as she finished her preparations and got out of the tub. *I'm in love.*

She suspected maybe she'd loved Langdon all along, and finally their timing was right. It didn't matter. Either way, they were here now. Together. *Savor these moments.*

After drying off, she reached beneath the sink and pulled out the handsomely wrapped package that she had hidden there earlier. It contained the most elegant piece of lingerie Katherine had ever purchased. *Simone Pérèle macchiato silk.* She hoped Robert liked the sophisticated one-piece from their Dream Collection.

After letting her hair down, Katherine dropped her towel and slipped into the near-weightless lingerie. The silk felt luxurious against her warm skin, falling perfectly over her body. Forgoing her usual Balade Sauvage, she pulled out the tiny spritzer sampler of Mojave Ghost that had come with the lingerie. She sprayed a cloud of mist into the air and walked through it, her senses aroused by the notes of Chantilly musk and powdery violet.

After checking herself one last time in the mirror, she opened the door to the bedroom, pleased to see that Langdon had already turned off the lights. *Perfect*, she thought, knowing her sheer lingerie was now backlit, leaving her lithe silhouette on full display. Smiling coyly, she struck a seductive pose in the doorframe awaiting Langdon's reaction.

But the only response she heard was the soft, rhythmic cadence of his gentle snoring.

CHAPTER 128

In a modest apartment in the Dejvice district, Dana Daněk sat alone on her couch watching television news. The U.S. military had now taken full responsibility for the Folimanka explosion, which had been caused apparently by a vast store of natural gas that the engineers had brought in to heat and cure the fresh concrete they were pouring. According to numerous outside construction specialists, this technique was very common, especially in damp underground spaces in winter, and this was not the first such accident.

Even so, political pundits were starting to question the story. Nonetheless, whatever had caused the blast, the U.S. military was already sealing the area and preparing for a massive cleanup operation.

"Ms. Daněk?" a man called from the hallway after knocking on her door. "It's Sergeant Kerble."

Surprised, she walked over and looked through her peephole. Sure enough, it was the ambassador's lead security detail. *Am I in trouble?* No Marine security guard had ever visited her home. Dana was wearing a sweatshirt, glasses, and no makeup, and she wondered if Sergeant Kerble would even recognize her.

When she opened the door, the baby-faced Marine was standing a polite distance away. "Ms. Daněk," he said, "I'm sorry to bother you at home. The ambassador asked me to convey once again her deep personal sadness over the passing of Attaché Harris. The entire embassy is shaken, of course, but Madam Ambassador said you two were very good friends."

"Thank you, Scott."

"I also should mention that the ambassador's arrest was a misunderstanding, and she has been released with a full apology."

"She may regret it," Dana said, motioning to the television behind her. "She's going to have her hands full with this. Your government is already taking heat."

"Yes, this entire situation is a bit . . ."

"Fucked?" Dana offered.

Kerble smiled. "I was going to say 'politically nuanced.' "

"Then you should take over my post in PR."

"Actually," he said, "that's why I'm here. The ambassador very much hopes you'll come back and work PR on this crisis."

Dana laughed out loud. "Scott, do you know what happened to me today?! A woman pointed a gun in my face, my boyfriend was strangled to death, the U.S. ambassador was arrested in front of me, I was escorted off embassy grounds, and Folimanka Park exploded! Am I missing anything?!"

Kerble sighed. "I'm sorry, Dana, I admit today has been . . ."

"Politically nuanced?"

"I was going to say 'fucked.' "

Dana managed a smile. "So what the hell is going on?"

"I don't have all the facts. You should ask the ambassador tomorrow when you return to work."

"That's your pitch?"

"I've never been a good salesman. Would you please just think about it?"

"I will. Have a good night."

Dana began to close the door, but Kerble stepped closer. "Actually, I was wondering if I might have a look in that cardboard box." He pointed past her into the living room at her box of personal items from her office. "I think there may be a diplomatic pouch in there that belongs to the ambassador. I'm afraid I may have dropped it in your box by mistake. May I come in?"

Dana had endured more than her fair share of lousy pickup schemes, and had she not held Sergeant Kerble in such high regard, she would have guessed this was another. Still, she motioned for him to wait in the doorway. "I'll look for you."

Dana walked over and dug through the box, astonished to encounter a sealed diplomatic pouch addressed to Ambassador Heide Nagel. The pouch had a sticky note affixed:

D— Tell no one about this. Someone will contact you.

Dana spun to him in shock. "What the hell is this?! And what's it doing in my box?!"

"I'm sorry," he replied. "I put it there. And now I need it back."

━━━ ·· ━━━

At the U.S. embassy, Heide Nagel sat alone in her office and stared into her now-empty tumbler of Becherovka. She seldom drank hard liquor, and never two cocktails in one day.

If not today, when?

She and the director had arrived at an agreement—a détente of sorts—but even so, Nagel was not about to relinquish her leverage and trust him blindly. *I still have the USB of the video.*

Kerble had gone to recover it from Dana, and from the sound of footsteps now climbing her marble stairs, Kerble had returned . . . except the face that appeared in the doorway was not his. It belonged to one of the embassy's newer Marine guards.

"Ma'am?" the young man said, looking uneasy. "I'm sorry, but we have a situation at the front door that requires your attention."

"No more situations today," she said. "Please just have your team handle it."

"We're not officially qualified, ma'am. It's a *diplomatic* matter."

Nagel's head felt foggy. *A diplomatic matter . . . at the front door?*

The young man entered, holding out a slip of paper. "This is for you."

Nagel took the paper and eyed the two handwritten words.

САША ВЕСНА

"I don't know what this is," she said, annoyed. "I don't speak Russian."

The Marine looked puzzled. "She assured me you would know who she is."

"I'm sorry, who?"

"The Russian at the front door. She asked to speak to Michael Harris."

A Russian looking for Michael? Here? Now?

"I asked her to write down her name." The Marine motioned to the slip of paper. "I believe it's pronounced 'Sasha Vesna.'"

CHAPTER 129

As he drove away from Dana's apartment, Sergeant Kerble felt drained. He switched on the car radio and cranked the volume to help him stay alert. The diplomatic pouch sat on the seat beside him, and as ordered, he would deliver it to the ambassador at once.

Halfway around the massive rotary in Vítězné Square, Kerble felt the phone in his pocket begin to vibrate. He pulled it out and checked the caller ID—a U.S. embassy extension.

"Kerble," he answered, turning down the radio.

"Thank God you answered!" The woman's voice was familiar but sounded uncharacteristically frantic.

"Madam Ambassador?" Kerble was instantly on high alert. "Is everything—"

"Where are you right now?!" she interrupted.

The ambassador's abruptness was unusual, and Kerble had the odd sense she'd been drinking, which was also out of character. "I'm just leaving Dejvice," he said. "I have the item you requested, and I'm headed—"

"I need you to do something else. Right away."

As the ambassador explained, Kerble's instinct told him something about this situation was seriously wrong. "Ma'am, I'm having trouble hearing you," he lied, implementing their agreed-upon security protocol. "Are you in town? Running errands?"

"For Christ's sake, Scott!" she snapped. "You know I don't run errands! Just do what I asked!"

———··———

Ambassador Nagel's heart was pounding as she descended the marble staircase into the embassy's elegant foyer. The anteroom that separated the embassy from the street was always manned by a Marine guard, but tonight, as Nagel had requested moments earlier, there were three muscular Marines positioned in the foyer. The young corporal in charge looked relieved to see her approaching.

The guards were standing with a new arrival—a blond woman in jeans, a parka, and sneakers. Her shoulder-length hair was wet and disheveled, and her posture was slumped, as if she was profoundly weary, or perhaps even injured.

Nagel recognized the woman at once, having seen her in photos.

Sasha Vesna . . . and she looks like she's been through a war.

The Russian woman's presence here—bedraggled but *alive*—came as a sobering shock. Seeing her, Nagel felt momentarily disoriented, especially considering what she knew about Sasha's complex personality. If Langdon and Solomon were correct about the woman's dissociative identity disorder, then the first thing Nagel had to do—as bizarre as it seemed to her—was to discern *which* Sasha had just shown up at the embassy.

"Ms. Vesna," the ambassador said politely, keeping her distance. "I am Ambassador Nagel. I was informed you are looking for Michael Harris?"

"Yes," the woman said, her voice frail with a thick Russian accent. "Michael is my friend. He said if I was in trouble, I should come see him here." The young woman was shivering in the cold, and her voice faltered. "And . . . I think I'm in trouble."

You think *you're in trouble?!* Nagel wanted to shout. *You killed Michael Harris and blew up a top secret government installation!* When the ambassador spoke, however, her tone was calm. "I'm afraid Michael is not here right now." *And I think you know that already. Don't you?*

"Will he be back soon?" Sasha asked. "Michael said I could come unannounced if I ever felt I was in danger."

"*Are* you in danger?" Nagel asked.

"Yes, I . . . think so," she said, on the verge of tears.

"From whom?"

"I don't know!" she said, tears flowing freely now. "I don't know what happened to me! I'm confused and I don't remember . . . I just know I need a safe place to be!"

"So are you requesting *asylum*?" the ambassador asked.

"I don't know what that is," she said, taking a step toward Nagel. "I just need—"

"*Sasha, stop!*" Nagel bellowed as two Marines stepped between them, causing Sasha to halt immediately in her tracks. She looked genuinely terrified that she'd done something wrong.

"Ms. Vesna," Nagel said, regaining her calm. "I want to help you, but first I need you to listen to me very carefully. It's extremely important."

Sasha nodded.

"This embassy is considered U.S. soil, and when a non–U.S. citizen requests safe harbor on U.S. soil, we call that 'a petition for *asylum*.' All asylum petitions require an immediate assessment interview by a ranking consular officer. That would be me."

Sasha nodded her understanding.

"The rules for these interviews," Nagel continued, "are very strict. Standardized protocol under the Asylum Adjudication Framework necessitates a procedural mandate we term 'controlled restraint.'"

The Marine standing closest to Sasha eyed Nagel askance, which was not surprising considering the ambassador was making this up as she went.

"You are not in trouble, Ms. Vesna, despite it perhaps feeling that way. Controlled restraint is an essential part of our asylum protocol. It is a precautionary measure and ensures a secure environment for both you and the embassy staff mem—"

"I understand," Sasha said, extending her hands and offering her wrists. "It's okay if you restrain me."

"Thank you for your cooperation," Nagel said, surprised by Sasha's instant compliance. "My team will now restrain you per our protocols. You will be placed in a safe, locked conference room, where you will be given food, water, access to restroom facilities, and medical attention should you require it."

The Marine guards hesitated just long enough to see Nagel staring daggers, and the lead corporal sprang into action. Within seconds, he had affixed a set of standard-issue flex cuffs to Sasha's outstretched wrists and, together with the other guards, guided her through the security divider.

Nagel gave them a wide berth, glancing at her watch. It was 8:30 p.m. "I will join you as soon as I'm able, Ms. Vesna, but it may take some time. In the meanwhile, my staff will ensure you are warm and fed."

Sasha had tears in her eyes as she passed by. "Thank you for your kindness," she managed to whisper.

As Nagel gathered herself and headed back upstairs, she realized she had some very big unanticipated decisions to make.

And fast.

CHAPTER 130

The Manhattan sidewalk glistened beneath Faukman's feet as he made his way up Broadway. The afternoon rain had finally passed, and it was time to go home.

His call with Prague had been brief, as Langdon was hesitant to say much on the phone. He offered assurances that he and Katherine were safe and also alerted Faukman that they were considering a stop in New York on their way home so they could all debrief face-to-face about everything that had transpired with the manuscript.

Not much to discuss, the editor lamented. Even if Katherine could wrap her head around rewriting her entire book, the CIA would almost certainly have something to say about it. For Faukman, losing this book was a considerable professional blow, and yet he took solace in knowing Robert and Katherine were safe.

As he neared Columbus Circle, Faukman smelled the earthy scent of dark roast coffee, and he slipped into the city's busiest Starbucks. If ever there were a day that warranted an extra dose of caffeine for the walk home, it was today.

With apologies to Robert, he mused as he placed his order.

The Harvard professor had long boycotted Starbucks for what he proclaimed to be their "egregious misuse of a classical symbol."

Faukman chuckled as he eyed the familiar logo emblazoned on every coffee cup in the establishment.

"The Starbucks *mermaid*," Langdon had railed, "has *two* tails! That means she's not a mermaid at all, but rather a *siren*—an evil seductress who lures sailors to follow her blindly toward

shipwreck and ultimately toward *death*! I can't trust a corpora-
tion that neglected to conduct any iconographic research before
adorning Frappuccinos with a deadly sea monster . . ."

Leave it to a symbologist to ruin a good cup of coffee, Faukman
thought, feeling no guilt as he took his first heavenly sip of the
creamiest flat white in the city. Then, turning up the collar of his
vintage gray peacoat, he stepped back outside and headed home.

CHAPTER 131

Hovering in darkness, Robert Langdon floated high above Prague. He gazed down at Charles Bridge far below him, the gas lanterns glimmering like strings of pearls that stretched across the black river. Weightless and detached, Langdon drifted downstream, crossing over the waterfall, feeling no emotion except a vague annoyance at a distant pounding noise. As the pounding grew louder, gravity suddenly seized him, and Langdon felt himself being dragged downward in a panicked free fall . . . accelerating toward the frigid river . . . until he shattered its mirrored surface.

Jolting awake, Langdon sat up in bed, surprised that he had not realized he was dreaming. It was a baffling paradox to him—the human mind's ability to find itself in an obviously impossible situation and yet accept the situation as fact, ignore every incongruity, and never suspect it was not *really* happening.

Alert now from the adrenaline of the dream, Langdon scanned the darkened hotel room. All was silent except for Katherine's soft breathing beside him. The scent of her exotic perfume hung in the air, and Langdon could still feel the luxuriously smooth texture of whatever she had been wearing when she sat on the edge of the bed and whispered, "So sorry to wake you, Professor . . ."

Langdon could still feel the afterglow.

Dr. Solomon, please feel free to wake me like that anytime.

He slipped quietly out of bed, put on a bathrobe, and walked into the suite's living room. To his dismay, the grandfather clock showed just past 9 p.m.

I've barely slept at all.

He gazed out the bay window, realizing his bizarre dream was not all that surprising. His brain was probably still trying to sort through the trauma of his frantic leap from this very window into the frigid water. Dreams had always fascinated Langdon, and he'd been shocked today when Katherine claimed to have discovered what *caused* them.

Incredibly, her experiments had revealed that a *dreaming* brain was similar to a *dying* brain. In both instances, GABA levels plummeted, thus lowering the brain's filters, opening the door to wider bandwidths of information. The influx of unfiltered data was the reason dreams manifested as such illogical jumbles of images and ideas. Furthermore, it explained why, within seconds after waking, even the most vivid dreams began to fade despite our desperate attempts to remember them. The brain reset, GABA levels increased, and filters reengaged . . . purging the information and once again regulating our perception of reality.

Dying felt a lot like dreaming, she had explained, describing how in dreams we often perceived ourselves as weightless, massless beings, with the ability to move through obstacles, fly through the air, or shift locations—in essence, we became a consciousness without a physical form. *The bardo body,* Langdon thought, recalling its description from *The Tibetan Book of the Dead.* In many cultures, the *dream* body was held sacred for its perceived ability to pass back and forth between the realms of life and death.

As consciousness becomes untethered, our powers of perception grow.

Langdon was still standing at the window when every phone in the suite suddenly began to ring at once. He rushed to the living room extension and picked up the receiver, hoping the call had not awoken Katherine.

"Mr. Langdon, this is the night manager," announced the familiar voice. "I'm sorry if I woke you. I tried knocking, but there was no answer."

The pounding in my dream. "Yes, is everything . . . okay?"

"I don't know, sir," the manager replied, clearly alarmed.

"There's a Marine Kerble here from the U.S. embassy. He says it is critical the ambassador see you immediately."

—— ·· ——

In a locked conference room in the U.S. embassy, The Golĕm gazed down at the restraints on his wrists. *I will not let Sasha see herself bound*, he thought. *She endured enough of that during her years in the institution.* The Golĕm had yet to release Sasha back into the forefront of his mind since he had left the rubble of Threshold, but that moment was fast approaching.

Everything is going to plan.

Despite Sasha being effectively incarcerated at the moment, The Golĕm remained confident the ambassador would become a sympathetic ally to her.

Gessner's confession revealed all I needed to know.

"Ambassador Nagel knows nothing!" Gessner had insisted. "She would be horrified to know what is happening down here— she's only in Prague because Finch tricked her into her job. He needed a diplomat as an ally!"

I need one too, The Golĕm had decided.

And so he had reached out to her.

Please help Sasha.

No doubt the ambassador was trying to sort out precisely what "helping Sasha" would entail, but it would not take her long to realize there existed only one workable scenario. The Golĕm had planted the idea ever so delicately, and it had already taken hold.

Minutes ago, the ambassador had uttered the only word The Golĕm wanted to hear.

Asylum.

CHAPTER 132

Heide Nagel had spent her entire professional life in service to her country. Trained to think always of the greater good, she rarely thought solely of herself. At the moment, however, thinking of herself was precisely what Nagel was doing.

She had already made the decision to resign as ambassador and leave Prague. It was what she wanted to do years ago, but now, very suddenly, her world was transformed. Finch was gone, and she possessed the leverage to weather even the most violent political storm.

To Nagel's surprise, however, the assurance of survival brought her no solace . . . only a gnawing emptiness that had been growing for the past several hours.

My life has to be focused on something more than just . . . surviving.

And then Sasha Vesna walked through the embassy's front door.

———··———

Katherine Solomon felt like it was only minutes ago that she was lost in a deeply satisfied dreamworld, only to be yanked back into the harsh light of reality.

What are we doing here?!

Sergeant Kerble had just delivered them to the office of Ambassador Nagel, who was standing at her bar pouring three cups of coffee into fine china emblazoned with the official embassy seal. "Again, I'm sorry for calling so late," she said, "but I'm afraid there have been some major developments in the last hour, and I need to bring you up to speed right away. The information is both urgent . . . and highly sensitive."

"You're telling us *here*?" Langdon asked. "I thought you no longer trusted the embassy's privacy."

"I don't," Nagel replied, "but everything has changed. The information I'm about to share with you is something I will have no choice but to share with the CIA director as well." The ambassador turned from the bar, carrying a tray with the coffees toward the sitting area in the corner. "If he's listening, so be it."

"What changed?" Katherine demanded, with the uneasy feeling their lone ally might be rethinking their alliance.

"There are a lot of moving pieces," she said, motioning for them to sit, "so I'll start with those developments that affect you both directly."

Katherine didn't like the sound of that.

"I've been informed that a U.S. military task force is now en route from Ramstein Air Base in Germany. They are landing shortly to formally lock down Folimanka Park and commence cleanup." Nagel set down the coffees and took a seat opposite them, her expression solemn. "In addition, I've been told a CIA team is flying in from Langley to initiate a covert investigation into *who* was responsible for the explosion. I've been advised that their investigation will begin with *you*."

"Us?!" Katherine was shocked.

The ambassador gave a grave nod. "The U.S. Army has a photo confirming that two unauthorized civilians—you and Professor Langdon—were caught exiting the facility only minutes after the blast."

Damn. Katherine glanced at Langdon, whose expression was taut.

"You entered the facility illegally," Nagel said, "which in itself makes you suspects for sabotage, but considering your conflict with the agency over the manuscript, which could be considered motive for revenge . . ."

"But the *video*," Langdon protested. "Dr. Gessner's confession, you said—"

"Yes, we have leverage. I can protect you. And I *will* protect you. The question is *how* we best insulate you. The answer comes down to what actions we take in the next few hours."

"Okay," Langdon said. "Do you have a plan?"

"I do," she said, "and I suspect you will not like it on first hearing, so before I lay it out, there are some things I need you to understand about the CIA . . . and what we're up against."

Katherine and Langdon both reached for their coffee at the same moment. Apparently, there would be no sleep anytime soon.

"On my call with the director," Nagel said, "he confirmed for me that Threshold is indeed the continuation of work the agency has been doing for decades, which began as a rudimentary exploration of remote viewing—Stargate, as you had correctly mentioned earlier. Over time, however, Threshold evolved into something far more encompassing, a project designed to seek answers to some of the most pressing questions that loom in the future. What is the nature of human consciousness? Can the human mind communicate directly with other minds? With machines? Over significant distances? Perhaps even with other dimensions?"

"Respectfully," Katherine interjected, "I'm not sure a military intelligence organization is the best vehicle for exploring humankind's deepest philosophical questions."

Nagel steepled her fingers, her mouth narrowing into a harder line. "Dr. Solomon," she said, "this is not about philosophical questions. I mean no offense by this, but you and Professor Langdon enjoy the luxury of exploring science and history in the hallways of academia for one reason only—the diligence of our nation's intelligence agencies. I can certainly appreciate the allure of pure science, but I'm afraid it is the *application* of that science that protects people like us from enemies who, if given the opportunity, would erase our nation from the face of the earth."

Katherine drew a breath to defend herself, but the ambassador was apparently not finished, her gaze still unflinchingly locked on the scientist. "The CIA director *passionately* believes that America's very future depends on our being first to master the potential of human consciousness. He was not shy in reminding me that when Einstein first predicted the massive amounts of energy stored within the atom, the American government poured millions into covert physics research, and we beat everyone to the atomic bomb. But just imagine if we had *not*. Imagine if Russia alone had the bomb. Or Germany. Or the Japanese."

The argument, Katherine had to admit it, was a fair one.

"The current race to harness the power of the human mind is no different," Nagel continued. "The Russians can already read brain waves with ultrasound; the Chinese are placing massive orders for Neuralink's brain implants; bot-fueled social media campaigns influence our elections, and we've just discovered what appear to be brain-control technologies embedded in social media apps from overseas. Make no mistake about it, we're in a *covert race* that has already reached fever pitch, and frankly, it's a race that you and I had better hope we win."

The ambassador sat back and sipped her coffee.

"I apologize," Katherine said, her tone conciliatory. "If my comment implied I am ungrateful for the agency's work, or ignorant of world affairs, then I misspoke. I was simply highlighting the fundamental problem with assuming the moral high ground while performing invasive brain surgery on people without their knowledge or consent."

"And I agree with you in every way," Nagel replied. "The problem is that Director Judd was never informed of a patient fatality or of Finch's methods for procuring test subjects."

"You can't possibly *believe* that," Langdon said.

Nagel shrugged. "Whether or not Finch informed him, oftentimes a CIA director has no choice but to turn a blind eye. National security is a world where *results* are valued over methodology. It's easy to be indignant until you've glimpsed the alternatives. Sometimes the best choice is simply the least objectionable outcome."

"Madam Ambassador," Langdon said quietly. "Katherine and I can both appreciate the complexities of the CIA's duties, but you called us here to say we are in danger, and you have a plan to insulate us . . . which hinges on what we do in the coming hours?"

"Yes," Nagel said, setting down her cup. "This situation is intricate, but I've realized there is a way through it. A *right* way. A *decent* way." She leaned forward, her gaze now on Langdon. "But in order to pull it off, I'm going to need your help, Professor."

Langdon looked uncertain.

"About half an hour ago," the ambassador said, "Sasha Vesna walked into this embassy . . . very much alive."

CHAPTER 133

sylum?

Robert Langdon paced the ambassador's office, trying to organize his thoughts. The startling update that Sasha was *alive* had left him on edge both physically and emotionally. Langdon was relieved to learn of her survival, but Sasha's existence raised an alarming array of delicate questions.

The most immediate concern—*Is she dangerous?*—had apparently been handled by restraining Sasha and locking her alone in a guarded conference room. It seemed harsh somehow, but considering everything that had happened, what else could Nagel do?

Langdon was mystified why Sasha would request asylum from the same government that had abused her. *Unless Sasha doesn't know what they've done to her?* The only other possibility was that her alter had arrived *posing* as Sasha, which also made little sense; Sasha's alter wanted to protect her, and delivering her into the hands of the U.S. government seemed the opposite of that.

Langdon returned to his seat beside Katherine while the ambassador poured more coffee. "Earlier tonight," the ambassador said, "Dr. Solomon reminded me that Sasha and her alter are two *different* people and should be considered as such. I've been trying, and as hard as that is for me to grasp, I have concluded that Sasha Vesna—if considered alone—is an innocent victim. She was a child epileptic, institutionalized, physically and mentally abused in a secret program whose exploitation of her body quite possibly exacerbated her mental issues to their current state."

"I agree," Katherine said. "She is definitely a victim."

"And then we have *this*," the ambassador said, motioning to the handwritten note laid out on the coffee table.

PLEASE HELP SASHA.

"While I don't make a habit of taking orders from killers," the ambassador said, "I have given this note a lot of thought, and considering the circumstances, it seems that helping Sasha is an ethical thing to do."

A moral imperative, Langdon thought.

"The challenge, of course, is that Sasha Vesna is two people." The ambassador sighed and shook her head. "She is an innocent victim . . . and a cunning killer. There is no way to grant one asylum . . . and prosecute the other. Whether Sasha is aware of it or not, she is harboring a dangerous criminal. She is also in possession of a highly classified prototype brain chip and cannot be allowed simply to roam free."

Langdon sensed in the ambassador's eyes that the issue of Sasha, beyond being exceptionally complex, was deeply personal.

"Another problem," Nagel continued, "is that our time is very short. Prague is not safe for Sasha. By dawn, this embassy will be in the midst of an onslaught of international inquiry, outrage, and demands for a forensic investigation into the events at Folimanka Park. Sasha's fingerprints are all over Crucifix Bastion, most likely on multiple dead bodies, and her face—or, shall I say, *faces*—will no doubt be pulled from surveillance archives and her past movements carefully tracked. It will not take long for investigators to assemble enough pieces to identify Sasha as a person of interest."

Along with Katherine and myself, Langdon thought, feeling the walls closing in.

Nagel took off her glasses and leaned toward them. "While I have not yet told *anyone* that Sasha is alive, I'm guessing Direc-

tor Judd will know very soon. In fact, he may already know she's
here at the embassy."

"How?" Langdon asked.

"Surveillance, staff leak, or most likely—GPS. I wouldn't be
surprised if Sasha's brain chip includes a tracker of some sort."

Of course it would, Langdon realized.

"And not to be grim," she added, "considering the sensitive
nature of this project . . . her chip might also be equipped with
remote destruct capability. It's a common protocol for advanced
technologies in the field, and it's embedded in everything from
sat phones to submarines . . . in case the technology falls into the
hands of an enemy who might try to reverse engineer it."

"Wait," Langdon said. "You think Sasha's brain chip can be
remotely . . . *destroyed*? I trust that means remotely switched off
or erased . . . not *exploded* or something."

"Definitely nothing so dramatic," Nagel said, "but I happen
to know that Q holds patents for silicon chips embedded with a
sealed layer of hydrofluoric acid that can be released by a phone
call to dissolve the entire processor."

"In her *brain*?!" Katherine exclaimed. "That would kill her!"

"Quite possibly," Nagel said, "but killing Sasha, I believe,
would be a last resort for the agency. The director knows I would
consider it a flagrant breach of our agreement, and he is well
aware I have countermeasures. Right now, my primary concern
is keeping clear lines of communication open with the director. If there's one thing the Cold War taught us about mutually assured destruction, it's that *communication* is critical. Don't
make your adversary *guess* what you're doing—let them know.
If Director Judd suspects that Sasha is in play, it is crucial, for
all of us, that he hear the details from me . . . *all* of them, and in
context."

In light of everything the ambassador was balancing, Langdon was impressed with the clarity of her strategic thinking.
Nagel must have been one hell of an attorney.

"And the video?" Katherine said. "Do you think it's enough
to keep the CIA at bay?"

"In isolation, perhaps not," she replied. "But in conjunction with the explosion and Dr. Gessner's death, the agency will have a hard time claiming the video is fake. Even if they do, it shines a light in a direction that would be very damaging for the agency."

"What about Sasha?" Langdon asked, aware that Threshold's lone surviving test subject was now locked in a room downstairs. "Do you trust the video will protect *her* too?"

"Yes, but she doesn't need it," the ambassador said. "Sasha enjoys an exceedingly rare level of protection—she is far more valuable to the agency *alive* than dead. The director will undoubtedly rebuild Threshold—not here, but *somewhere*—and Sasha will be viewed as an irreplaceable asset to a billion-dollar program. She represents years of R&D, and I imagine the first thing Director Judd will do is attempt to negotiate with us . . . for Sasha's return."

The thought sent chills through Langdon. "So how do we keep Sasha out of his hands?"

Nagel took a deep breath. "We don't."

The response took Langdon off guard. "I'm sorry?"

"We don't," she repeated, her voice firm.

"Ambassador Nagel," Langdon protested, his voice rising. "Are you suggesting we give Sasha back to the CIA?"

"That is precisely what we will do. It is the only option."

"Absolutely not!" Katherine exclaimed. "Threshold already killed one patient! You *can't* send Sasha back into—"

"I *can't*?!" Nagel interjected forcefully. "I will remind you both that inside this embassy, I am the ranking official, and I will ask you both to hear me out before telling me what I can and can't do."

The ambassador gave it a moment, and Katherine sat back, quietly shaking her head in defiance.

"These are the facts," Nagel declared in an even tone. "Sasha Vesna requires highly specialized care—both physical and psychiatric. She has proven herself extremely dangerous, meaning whoever is involved with that care will need to take caution and also understand her situation *completely*. Considering the hardware in Sasha's brain, the list of entities qualified to care for her is exceedingly short. Perhaps a list of *one*. When I reflect on what you told me about these advanced artificial neurons in her brain, I have to conclude that the *only* people qualified to give Sasha proper mental care are the scientists involved in Threshold."

Langdon could see the logic in her argument, but at its core, the ambassador's plan was essentially to entrust Sasha to the same people who had used her as a laboratory animal. Beside him, Katherine was still shaking her head, clearly not convinced.

"Make no mistake about it," Nagel said. "I am not suggesting Sasha return to Threshold as it was. I will tolerate *zero* further testing on Sasha Vesna. Period. She will return as the program's most valuable and cherished asset, to be treated as such, and to live well. Sasha is a triumph—she represents the program's greatest victory to date, and her presence offers an invaluable research opportunity. I will stress to the director that Threshold's experimentation on this woman's brain most likely exacerbated her mental condition, if not *caused* it altogether. In other words, I will make him understand that Sasha's mental well-being is the agency's ultimate moral responsibility. In the end, Director Judd will be highly motivated to ensure Sasha's overall health—especially knowing I will be watching with my finger on a trigger."

A long silence fell between them, and Langdon found himself in the throes of the quintessential archetypal battle—the Apollonian-Dionysian conflict, as it was known in mythology—the ultimate internal struggle. *Brain versus Heart.* Langdon's Apollonian brain saw order and reason in Nagel's plan, while his Dionysian heart saw chaos and injustice.

"You paint a nice picture," Katherine said, breaking the silence. "But Sasha never asked to have Threshold in her life."

"Nor did *you*, Dr. Solomon, and yet here we are." Nagel's gaze was unflinching now. "We all must play the cards we are dealt. In order for Sasha Vesna to live a healthy life, she will need to interact in some capacity with Project Threshold. The level of her involvement can be her own decision, and perhaps only in those parts of the project related to consciousness research. But once Sasha's mental state is stable, I have to believe that being part of a team might even provide her a purpose and a status unlike anything she has ever experienced in her life."

Langdon felt wary. *We all need purpose.* But what Nagel was describing relied on the agency doing the right thing, and Langdon had little confidence in that.

"I realize *trust* may be hard to summon in this case," Nagel continued, as if sensing Langdon's hesitation. "Especially after all you've witnessed with the agency. But please remember, your experience was with Everett Finch. You will *now* be dealing with Director Gregory Judd. His mistake was giving Finch too much leeway, but I have always found Judd to be a decent man in a world of indecent options. If nothing else, he is honest."

"Honest?" Katherine challenged. "You were his *senior* counsel, and still he lied to you—telling you Stargate had failed."

Nagel gave a dismissive wave. "DBD protocol—disinformation by deception. It's a common compartmentalization tactic. False narratives protect employees who don't need to know the truth. We all lie better when we actually *believe* the lie we're telling. And obviously Stargate was not the *only* classified project the agency lied about and then rebooted. If my trust in Director Judd is misplaced," the ambassador concluded, "I will remind him of the sword of Damocles over his head, making it crystal clear that I have every intention of bringing it down should the agency not meet its moral obligations to Sasha."

The three sat silently in the ornate office. "Not to mention," the ambassador added, "in almost any other scenario, Sasha will be unprotected—and quite possibly detained and prosecuted for treason, terrorism, and murder."

Katherine turned slowly to Langdon, her eyes still tentative, but a tired nod delivered a clear message. *I will follow your lead on this.*

Langdon pictured Sasha locked up downstairs, and his heart went out to her. Despite profound concerns about the ambassador's plan, Langdon saw no better option. As hard as it was to admit, the absolute safest place on earth for Sasha Vesna was probably in Langley, Virginia. It felt paradoxical to Langdon that Sasha's oppressors would now become her guardians . . . but it was also somehow . . . unavoidable.

Perhaps even ingenious.

The fact that Sasha had materialized outside the embassy made Langdon wonder if her mysterious golem guardian might already have thought all this through. He had provided Nagel the leverage required to take the upper hand . . . and then made the simplest of appeals.

Please help Sasha.

Now, as Langdon considered everything the ambassador had just proposed, he heard a single unanswered question echoing in his mind.

———··——

Quis custodiet ipsos custodes?

Despite having never studied Latin, Ambassador Nagel recognized the question Langdon had just posed. It was the ubiquitous battle cry of antigovernment whistleblowers everywhere.

Who will guard the guards?

It was a fair question, and one asked with increasing frequency. In this case, the CIA would be watching over Sasha . . . but *who* would be watching over the CIA? Even if Nagel threatened to release the video in response to violated protocols, she would have no reliable way to know if protocols were being followed unless she had a trusted source right *there* . . . in the middle of it.

Who will guard the guards?

Nagel realized she already knew the answer, and when she spoke it out loud, she heard a purpose in her voice that had been absent for years.

"*I* will," she said, raising her eyes to Langdon.

As she made the vow, Nagel felt a sudden upwelling of emotion, and she realized that caring for Sasha Vesna might actually be the exact redemption her own battered soul required . . . a gradual atonement for her complacency and fear for her part in all that had transpired in Prague.

I will never make up for Michael Harris . . . but I can try.

CHAPTER 134

Alone, Langdon ran his hand along the iron banister as he descended the marble staircase outside the ambassador's office. He felt unsteady about what lay ahead—not only in the next few minutes, but also in the coming months.

Nagel will guard the guards? he wondered, reflecting on the conversation they had just had in her office. She intended to monitor Threshold *personally*, establishing herself as a kind of inspector general, or perhaps even director, for the next iteration of the project. Rebuilding Threshold, she had insisted, was critical to national security and also the *right* thing to do . . . but it had to be done in the *right* way.

"The high ground can be defended only if we are actually *on* it," Nagel had said. "I will be an on-site, personal advocate for Sasha Vesna—her living conditions, her safety, and her mental well-being. I will do the same for those who will participate in the program in the future." Nagel paused and let out a barely audible sigh. "Having oversight will give *me* something crucial as well—the opportunity to redeem myself and the terrible mistakes I've made."

Langdon sensed a deep well of emotion fueling her words.

"The more I consider it," she continued, "the more I truly believe this will be the best outcome for Sasha, for the CIA, and also for us. But before I call Director Judd and inform him exactly what he will be doing for us . . . *with* us . . . there's one remaining hurdle to jump."

"Sasha . . ." Katherine said. "You have to convince her."

Nagel nodded. "Her full consent to this plan is crucial . . .

Without it, none of this happens. I promise you this agency will never again force her—or *anyone* for that matter—into participating in something against her will or without her knowledge."

Langdon appreciated the sentiment. "It's hard to know if she'll agree."

"The answer, I imagine, resides in *how* she is asked."

Spoken like a true diplomat, Langdon thought. "Do you think you can persuade her?"

"I've never properly spoken to the woman, so no, I don't believe I can," Nagel replied, studying him intently. "But I suspect *you* might."

Langdon cocked his head. "I'm sorry? You want *me* to talk to Sasha?" Nagel had said earlier she would need Langdon's help, but this was not what he had envisioned.

"Of the three people in this room, Professor, *you* are the only one who has spent any time with Ms. Vesna. Sadly, you might be the only person left in her world to whom she *would* actually be willing to talk."

That thought hung in the silence for a moment. "Actually," Langdon countered, "at the moment I'm not even sure *whom* I met today. It felt like I was with Sasha, at least some of the time, but in many ways, it makes more sense that I was with her alter—pretending to be her and orchestrating everything that was happening. I would have no way to know."

"Regardless," the ambassador said, "whoever you were dealing with today, you were helpful and kind, and that person seemed to take notice. After all, he protected you not once but twice."

True, Langdon realized, recalling how he was urged to flee Threshold and also being tricked to leave Sasha's apartment prior to Harris's murder.

"Sasha has shown she trusts you," Nagel continued. "I am curious, hypothetically speaking, what you think would convince her to put her trust in us, in me, in this plan, and in a new life in America?"

Langdon was starting to suspect it might not be a very hard sell at all. "I would simply remind her that this proposal, in many ways, is her dream come true. And depending on how much she actually recalls or understands about what has happened to her, I would impress on her that the way forward will require *forgiveness*—not just on her part—but for everyone involved. Bilateral absolution. Her alter will understand that as well. Sasha will need to forgive the agency that horribly betrayed her, and the agency will need to forgive the subject who took revenge on the people and secret facility that harmed her. If both Sasha and the agency can leave the past in the past and agree to a mutual pardon for the greater good, then there exists a shared future that benefits everyone."

Nagel and Katherine exchanged an impressed nod, and the ambassador said, "Which is precisely why I asked *you*, Professor."

Langdon cracked the door to the embassy's oak-paneled conference room and peered inside. At the far end of a very long table, Sasha Vesna was seated alone. Her blond hair was tangled and wet, her face drawn. A towel was draped over her shoulders, and a half-eaten meal sat before her. Her hands were in her lap, no doubt bound.

Langdon studied her a long moment before entering and closing the door behind him. He slowly approached with a soft smile. "Hi, Sasha."

She looked more wary than happy to see him.

"I'm relieved you're safe," Langdon offered, choosing a seat about ten feet away from her.

"Thank you," she said, studying him with an uncertain look.

Langdon suddenly sensed this meeting would not be the warm and fuzzy reunion the ambassador had predicted. "Sasha," Langdon began, "I'm here because I have important information for you, and I want to be sure that I deliver it"—he paused, searching for the words—"in a way that makes the most sense to you."

"Okay," she said, giving him nothing.

Langdon took a moment, gathering his thoughts, and then spoke as calmly as his unsettled state would allow. "Sasha,

I understand that you came here tonight asking for help. I'm pleased to report that the ambassador very much *wants* to help you. She is aware that you feel you're in danger, and she wants to protect you and make you feel safe. She has a plan to do exactly that. I've heard her plan—it's not a *perfect* solution, but it's the best one available . . . and the ambassador believes it is your best chance to enjoy a safe and relatively normal life. I have to agree."

Sasha's expression seemed to brighten slightly.

"Before I explain the idea to you," Langdon said, "I'm sorry, but I need to ask you an unusual question. It may sound quite strange . . . but it's absolutely critical that you reply with full honesty. None of this can happen without that." Langdon paused, fixing her pale eyes with his firm gaze. "Forgive me for asking, but I need to know—with *whom* am I speaking right now? Is this *you*, Sasha?"

The young woman studied Langdon for a long moment and then shook her head. "No," she replied in a deep, hollow voice. "For Sasha's own safety, I have not released her yet."

CHAPTER 135

Katherine sat up abruptly on the ambassador's couch, realizing she had drifted off. Robert had not yet returned, and the ambassador was at her window, staring blankly into the darkness. Hearing Katherine stir, Nagel turned back into the room and checked her watch.

"Half an hour," she said. "They're still talking."

"It could be a good sign," Katherine offered. "Robert can be . . . meticulous."

"I've noticed," Nagel said, coming over to sit with Katherine. "He took me aside earlier and interrogated me from *every* angle about your missing manuscript, demanding I order the CIA to return it."

"And?" Katherine pressed, hopeful.

Nagel shook her head. "Sadly, the director confirmed that Q's operations team destroyed all copies."

Katherine scoffed. "I don't believe them."

"It tracks, unfortunately. After WikiLeaks, we implemented rigid new protocols governing the immediate disposal of information the agency deemed damaging. I'm sorry, but I do believe the book is gone."

Katherine picked at the couch, trying not to think of all she had lost. "You know, it's pretty ironic the CIA destroyed the book. In reality, the ideas in it could have given the agency a fresh perspective on terror management theory."

Nagel looked surprised by the comment. "You wrote about TMT?"

"It's quite relevant to my work." *As it is to yours.*

Terror management theory was utilized by military intelligence to predict a population's reaction to certain threats. Its findings were well established. Human anxiety had countless sources—fear of nuclear war, terrorism, financial ruin, loneliness—and yet TMT had established that the predominant fear and strongest motivator behind human behavior was, undeniably . . . the fear of death. When a person was terrified that he or she might die, the brain employed extremely well-defined strategies to "manage" that terror.

Under normal circumstances, our unpleasant knowledge that we will die—known as "mortality salience"—was managed through a wide range of strategies, including denial, spirituality, mindfulness practices, and various types of philosophical reflection.

Under extreme circumstances, however—war, crime, violent confrontations—people behaved predictably across all demographics; they would either battle to the death to save themselves . . . or flee the threat. This was known classically as the fight-or-flight response, and for military strategists, it was particularly helpful to predict *which* of the two would occur.

"As it turns out," Katherine said, "fight or flight is not the brain's *only* response to the fear of death. There is something more gradual that occurs, over many years, as we begin to fear our world is unsafe . . . as so many people now do."

"It's a fear based on sound logic," Nagel said.

"Every day, we're exposed to graphic media coverage reminding us of our collapsing environment, increased threat of nuclear war, coming pandemics, genocide, the world's endless atrocities. *All* of this triggers the brain's terror management strategy to run in the background, at a low level—not yet in fight-or-flight mode, but . . . anticipating the worst. In essence, the more terrifying our world becomes, the more time we spend *preparing* subconsciously for death."

Nagel looked uncertain where all this was going. "Prepare for death . . . *how*?"

"I think the answer to that will surprise you," Katherine said. "It certainly did *me*. While researching mortality salience and the brain, I found that an increased fear of death produced a consistent array of behavioral responses—all of them *selfish*."

"I'm sorry?"

"Fear makes us *selfish*," Katherine said. "The more we fear death, the more we cling to *ourselves*, our belongings, our safe spaces . . . to that which is familiar. We exhibit increased nationalism, racism, and religious intolerance. We flout authority, ignore social mores, steal from others to provide for ourselves, and become more materialistic. We even abandon our feelings of environmental responsibility because we sense the planet is a lost cause and we're all doomed anyway."

"That's alarming," Nagel said. "Those are precisely the behaviors that fuel global unrest, terrorism, cultural division, and war."

"Yes, and that make the CIA's job so difficult. Unfortunately, it becomes a hall of mirrors. The worse things get, the worse we behave. And the worse we behave, the worse things get."

"And it's your theory that this troubling pattern stems from humans' fear of death?"

"It's not *my* theory," Katherine said. "It's scientifically proven in mountains of statistical evidence gathered through observational analysis, behavioral experiments, and scientific polling. The most important point in the research, however, shows that those who do *not* fear death, for whatever reason, tend to exhibit behavior that is more benevolent, accepting of others, cooperative, and caring about the environment. Essentially, this means that if we could all free our minds of the burden, of the terror we feel about death . . ."

"Then we would find ourselves in a dramatically improved world."

"Precisely," Katherine said. "To quote the great Czech psychiatrist Stanislav Grof, 'The elimination of the fear of death transforms the individual's way of being in the world.' Grof believes that a radical inner transformation of consciousness might be our only hope of surviving the global crisis brought on by the Western mechanistic paradigm."

"Well, if that's true," Nagel offered as she poured more coffee, "perhaps we should spike the world's water supply with anti-anxiety meds."

Katherine chuckled. "I'm not sure Xanax is the existential answer, but there is hope on the near horizon."

Nagel paused mid-sip. "Oh?"

"As I wrote in my manuscript, I believe our views on death are about to change. Top scientists around the world are increasingly convinced that reality is not *at all* as we believe. This includes the provocative idea that death is, quite possibly, an illusion . . . that our consciousness *survives* physical death and lives on. If this is true, and if we can prove it, then within several generations, the human mind will function under an entirely different premise—the belief that death is not so terrifying after all . . ."

Katherine's voice was brimming with passion. "Just think about that. The *one* universal fear that drives so much of humankind's destructive behavior . . . would evaporate. If we can hold on long enough to arrive at that paradigm shift without blowing ourselves up or destroying our planet, then our species may well turn a philosophical corner that ushers in an unimaginably peaceful future."

The ambassador fell silent, and Katherine sensed in her eyes a deep desire to feel encouraged despite all she had witnessed of the world. "How I hope you are right," she whispered.

Moments later, Robert finally materialized in the doorway.

Nagel leaped to her feet. "How did it go?"

He entered with a weary smile. "Ambassador, I believe it's time you call the director."

———·——

It was late afternoon in Langley, Virginia, when Director Gregory Judd ended his second video call of the day with his former lead counsel, Heide Nagel.

I was a fool to fire her, he thought—not because Nagel had come back to haunt him, but because she was so damned good at what she did. Few people cut through the bullshit like Nagel. While most attorneys lived in a black-and-white world ruled by the letter of the law, Nagel lived in the real world, as it truly was—a shifting, complicated landscape, rendered in shades of gray.

With clarity, humility, and surprising emotional transparency, Nagel had shared with him the unexpected developments pertaining to Sasha Vesna, as well as the obvious implications for the inevitable reconstruction of Threshold. Like any good negotiator, Nagel had helped Judd arrive at *her* conclusion, while making it seem the idea had been his own.

The director was not a scientist, but the CIA's research into the human mind had certainly unveiled a reality unlike anything Judd had imagined as a younger man. Fortunately, Judd's job was not to comprehend the nature of reality, but rather to harness its power to best serve his nation and to protect it.

On occasion Judd allowed himself to dream about a future where programs like Threshold unveiled proof of the interconnection between all human minds, ushering in a global community bound not by fear and rivalry, but by empathy and understanding . . . a world where the concept of national security was a relic of the past.

For the moment, however, there was work to be done.

CHAPTER 136

Outside the private terminal at Václav Havel Airport, Heide Nagel stood on the tarmac and felt the weight of the plan she had forced into motion.

Asylum.

It was the correct decision, she told herself. *The only decision.*

Not far away, Scott Kerble sat behind the wheel of the idling embassy sedan, its trunk loaded with duffels full of Sasha's hastily packed clothing and personal belongings. Sasha herself sat quietly in the backseat, still securely restrained in flex cuffs, looking dazed but calm as she played with the two Siamese cats in the pet carrier on the seat beside her.

A small private jet emerged from the terminal hangar and turned toward them. It was the Citation Latitude on which Finch had arrived earlier. The pilots had received direct orders from the CIA director personally, commandeering a "ghost flight" for two unnamed passengers back to Langley Air Force Base in Virginia.

No manifest.

As Nagel watched the jet approach, she felt increasing trust in Director Judd. Even so, her years at the CIA had taught Nagel the perils of blind faith. In the world of national security, the bond of *trust*—even the deepest of loyalty—was routinely betrayed when the needs of the country outweighed the needs of a few of her citizens. Serving the greater good had a nobility to it, but Nagel had done her time.

To cement her leverage, Nagel had taken four IronKey 256-bit encrypted hard drives from embassy storage, loaded each with a copy of Gessner's interrogation video, and locked each with a requisite sixteen-character passkey, chosen tonight and known only to her. One of the drives was in her pocket, one was in her personal safe, and the other two were already sealed in diplomatic pouches en route to two attorney friends—one in Europe and one in the U.S.—along with instructions that the pouches were to be opened *only* in the event of Nagel's untimely death or disappearance.

A redundant, double-blind, dead man's switch.

The wild card in this situation was Sasha Vesna and the unusual condition that made her very difficult to predict or trust. The young Russian was in need of psychiatric care, to be sure, but with all she had endured in her life, she also deserved a home, friends, security, and a chance to live a somewhat normal life. Her protective alter personality had come forward only when people had harmed Sasha, and Nagel's plan revolved around avoiding that.

I need to give Sasha a safe haven, she thought. *As safe as possible under the circumstances.*

The ambassador felt eager to get Sasha airborne and out of Prague. Within the hour, a literal army would be landing from the U.S. air base in Ramstein, Germany, to begin "restoration" of the blast site. As Nagel understood it, the debris in the crater would be pulverized using targeted microexplosions and covered with a layer of poured concrete. Atop that would be a layer of gravel, followed by topsoil and then sod. If all went to plan, within weeks, the lawns of Folimanka Park would look like they'd never been disturbed.

Buried and gone, she thought. *Only a handful of people would ever know Threshold had even existed.*

As the Citation taxied closer, Kerble got out of the car and joined Nagel. "Ma'am, Ms. Vesna seems quite content. Shall I load the bags?"

"Thanks, Scott," Nagel replied. "I appreciate your traveling with her—obviously keep some form of restraint intact until you transfer her. The director's team will meet you on the ground and take over."

"Of course, ma'am."

"The director assured me he'll be there in person when Sasha lands. If you could please give him this?" Nagel pulled the encrypted hard drive from her pocket and handed it to Kerble. "He'll know what's on it. Tell him it's one of four, and if he wants to confirm the contents, he can call me for the password."

"Yes, ma'am." Kerble slid the drive into his pocket and turned to go.

"Actually," Nagel said, reconsidering, "better yet, just tell him it's the first letter of every word in his favorite Kissinger quote."

Kerble looked bemused and headed off to get the bags.

As Nagel walked toward the plane, she hoped Robert Langdon and Katherine Solomon were feeling more confident about their situation. They were both perfectly safe now, especially as one of the most powerful men in the country could not risk anything happening to either of them. Nagel had shared with Judd some of Katherine's thinking on TMT and the future, and he was so intrigued that he asked if Nagel thought Dr. Solomon might be persuaded to join the Threshold team.

No chance in hell, she told Judd, albeit in slightly more politic language, reminding him of everything Katherine had endured at the hands of the agency. *Besides, she may choose to rewrite her book.*

———·· —➤

Sasha Vesna often felt as if she'd awoken from a deep sleep and missed something important. Normally days like today—with an unusually large number of blank spots in her memory—were unsettling to her. At the moment, however, despite remembering only murky snippets of the day's events, Sasha felt unusually at peace. Her inner voice, the one she had learned to trust, kept whispering that everything was going to be fine . . . *wonderful,* in fact.

Half an hour ago, Sasha had emerged from a thick fog to find herself restrained in the backseat of a warm sedan with Harry and Sally beside her in their carrier. A man in a uniform was driving, and a woman who had introduced herself as the U.S. ambassador was in the passenger seat, turned fully, looking back at Sasha and carefully explaining what was happening.

Strangely, Sasha felt no panic at being restrained, nor to be in the sudden company of strangers. Instead, she felt prepared for this moment, her inner voice reassuring her that all of this was for her own benefit . . . and safety.

The ambassador had apologized for the handcuffs and the rushed departure, offering a detailed explanation. Sasha had understood very little—something about an opportunity for political asylum, State Department regulations, flying over international waters—but none of it mattered to her. All she heard was one thing.

I'm going to America.

The voice in her head urged her to be thankful and cooperative, but Sasha did not need to be told. Going to America had been Sasha's fantasy since she was a little girl, losing herself in romantic movies. She wondered if someday she might even make it to New York City to see Central Park, Katz's Deli, and the Empire State Building.

Exactly how all this had transpired, Sasha was unclear, and she wondered if maybe it was related to all the diligent work she had done for Dr. Gessner. All Sasha knew for sure was that the U.S. ambassador had made it possible.

She is someone I can trust, Sasha sensed. *A new friend.*

Sitting alone with her cats in the warmth of the sedan, Sasha waited for the cobwebs to begin clearing from her mind. She watched the Marine load her bags into the plane, and she realized there was nothing left for her in Prague anymore. Without Brigita, Sasha had no job, no place to live, no—

Sasha suddenly flashed on the other thing she was leaving behind—Michael Harris. *I never said goodbye!* Strangely, her memories of Michael seemed to be dissolving with startling speed, as if he were already a lover from her distant past. *First loves are important*, she recalled a romantic movie once saying. *Because they open our hearts for what's to come.*

But what is to come? Sasha wondered, sensing for the first time in her life that she was entering a world of limitless possibilities. The quiet voice was again whispering within her mind. *Don't question your past, Sasha,* it told her. *Look toward your future.*

The voice was one she heard often. According to Michael, it was her own intuition, her higher self, her subconscious. Everyone had a voice within, he assured her, a part of one's soul that whispered, reassured, and guided. Sasha would write Michael a letter once she got settled. Then again, maybe it was just best to let it go. Recently she had experienced a sense that they might be nearing the end of their romantic connection.

"Ms. Vesna?" a voice called outside the window. The Marine had returned and opened her door. "They're ready for you." He unstrapped her seat belt and helped her out of the car. Then he reached back into the car and gently lifted out the pet carrier. "Let's get Harry and Sally settled on board, shall we?"

She nodded appreciatively. "Thank you, sir."

"You can call me Scott," the man said, glancing over with a smile. "I'll be flying with you today. Shall I call you Sasha?"

"Of course!" she exclaimed, feeling a rising excitement as they neared the jet. At the bottom of the staircase, the ambassador stood alone, apparently waiting to say goodbye.

"Sergeant Kerble," the ambassador said as they arrived, "perhaps you could get those two fine felines out of the cold and then come back for Ms. Vesna?"

"Absolutely, ma'am," he said, carrying Harry and Sally up the stairs and disappearing into the cabin.

The ambassador studied Sasha with concern. "I know this is all very sudden and a lot to absorb. Are you okay?"

Sasha was trying to hold herself steady in an unexpected rush of gratitude, bewilderment, excitement, and disbelief. The ambassador had repeatedly promised that everything would begin to make more sense in the coming days. She also promised to join Sasha very soon in the United States—a thought that brought Sasha a deep sense of tranquility.

"I'm . . . okay," Sasha managed. "Still very foggy. But I know you've been so kind to me." She was suddenly on the verge of tears. "How can I ever thank you?"

The ambassador looked emotional now too. "Believe it or not, Sasha . . . you already have."

As Sasha broke down, the ambassador stepped forward and gave her a long hug that reminded Sasha of the hugs her mother used to give when she was only four or five . . . before she was a damaged girl. Sasha had not been hugged like that in many, many years.

CHAPTER 137

The winter sun had just risen over Prague, its muted rays glinting off the skyline of snow-covered spires.

Langdon was feeling anxious about the final piece of unfinished business he needed to resolve before he and Katherine flew out this afternoon. He wondered how she would react when he explained the delicate situation.

I almost told her earlier, he thought, but despite a sincere desire to share what had happened, Langdon had never quite found the right moment. *Enjoy your breakfast,* he reassured himself. *It will all work out.*

Ninety minutes ago, after some weighty final discussions with the ambassador and an uncertain farewell with Sasha, Langdon and Katherine had exited the embassy and, at Nagel's personal recommendation, walked a mere twenty paces across the cobblestone plaza to the Alchymist Hotel for their famed "prosecco breakfast."

The hotel made its home in an impeccably restored sixteenth-century Baroque mansion whose large inner courtyard, every winter, was converted into an ice-skating rink that glistened beneath a canopy of twinkling lights. The dining room decor was fanciful, with crimson upholstered chairs, glittering Murano chandeliers, and "Corinthian twist" gold pillars that looked like a storybook movie set.

At a quiet window table overlooking the rink, Langdon and Katherine had finished a sumptuous breakfast that culminated in fig dumplings topped with edible gold flakes. Fully sated and having reflected at length on the morning's events, they were now quietly sipping chicory *melta* and gazing out at the ice rink, where a young woman had just arrived and was lacing up her skates.

"The skating *nun*?" Langdon offered, referencing their waiter's ghost story about a nun who had died on this spot centuries ago and who materialized occasionally to skate peaceful patterns on the ice.

"I think not," Katherine replied as the young woman shed her coat to reveal a skimpy skating costume bejeweled in white sequins and silver beadwork.

As the young woman stepped onto the ice, she seemed surprisingly off-balance for someone with such an elaborate outfit. *Odd*, Langdon thought, watching her stumble awkwardly to the middle of the rink, where she stopped, fluffed up her hair, raised a phone, and began taking selfies.

"Mystery solved," Langdon said. "Instagram skater."

"Our new reality," Katherine said with a laugh.

"Doesn't it concern you?" he said, turning to her. "Young people broadcasting themselves nonstop to the world? I see it every day on campus. Even the world's 'best and brightest' seem far more interested in the online world than the *real* one."

"That could be true," she said, taking a sip of her tea. "But first of all, it's not *just* young people doing it. And second, I think you have to consider that the online world *is* a real world."

"A real world where love is expressed with emoticons and measured in 'likes'?"

"Robert, when you see someone glued to a phone, you see a person *ignoring* this world—rather than a person *engrossed* in another world . . . a world that, like this one, is made up of communities, friends, beauty, horror, love, conflict, right and wrong. It's all there. The online world is not so different from our world . . . except for one stark difference." Katherine smiled. "It's nonlocal."

The comment caught him off guard.

"The online world," Katherine said, "is untethered from

your location. You inhabit it as a bodiless mind . . . free from all physical restraints. You move effortlessly *anywhere*, see what you want, learn what you want, interact with other bodiless minds."

Langdon had never considered the Internet in that light, and it both startled and intrigued him. *Online, I am a bodiless consciousness* . . .

"When we lose ourselves in the virtual world," Katherine said, "we are giving ourselves a kind of nonlocal experience that, in many ways, parallels an out-of-body experience—we are detached, weightless, and yet connected to all things. Our filters are dropped . . . We can interact with the entire world through one screen and experience almost *anything*."

Langdon realized Katherine was exactly right.

She drained the last of her *melta* and dabbed the linen napkin to her lips. "Anyhow, I wrote about all of this in my book. It's an unusual idea, but I've come to believe that our current tech-nological explosion is actually part of a *spiritual* evolution . . . a kind of training ground for the existence that, in the end, is our ultimate destiny . . . a consciousness, untethered from the physi-cal world, and yet connected to all things."

Langdon sat back, thoroughly impressed by the trailblazing genius of Katherine's ideas.

"It all funnels into one larger concept," Katherine said fer-vently. "Death is not the end. There's more work to do, but science continues to discover evidence that there is *indeed* some-thing beyond all this. *That* message is one we should be shouting from the mountaintops, Robert! It's the secret of all secrets. Just imagine the impact it will have on the future of the human race."

"And that is why you still need to publish your book!"

The comment elicited a frown from Katherine, snapping her back to reality, and Langdon wished he'd kept his thoughts to himself. Even so, he'd been excited to learn that the CIA direc-tor had agreed there would be *no* interference with any future publication of Katherine's book—provided she remove a handful of sensitive paragraphs and, of course, omit her patent applica-tion. Katherine's response to the good news had been subdued, which was not surprising considering she was still livid with the agency, not to mention daunted by the prospect of starting the writing process all over again.

Langdon shifted, feeling restless that he'd upset her.

"So," he ventured quietly, "still want to see Prague Castle before we fly out?"

Katherine glanced up, clearly eager to have something else to think about. "Absolutely. I barely saw anything the night of my lecture, and you said St. Vitus is not to be missed."

"Perfect," he said, reaching for his coat. "From here, it's just a short walk up the hill." His mind turned again to the task that lay ahead of him. He was still concerned about how Katherine would take the news.

Katherine glanced around for a waiter. "I'd pay the check, Robert, except I lost my bag."

"Not to worry," he replied with a smile. "I was informed our breakfast is compliments of the U.S. embassy."

———··———

As they exited the hotel into the morning light, Katherine and Langdon looked toward the ambassador's office window to wave their thanks, but the window was dark. With luck, everything had gone smoothly with Sasha's departure, and Heide Nagel was headed for bed.

The ambassador had promised a package would be delivered to their hotel this morning containing travel cash, two first-class plane tickets, and a pair of diplomatic letters to ensure they both made it home with no complications. "It's the least the embassy can do," Nagel had told them, "considering the past twenty-four hours."

Katherine followed Langdon into the quaint cobblestone alley called Tržiště, which ascended toward Prague Castle. As they began to walk, Langdon put his arm around her waist and kissed her on the cheek, pulling her close. They had gone only a dozen paces or so up the hill when suddenly Langdon paused, as if reconsidering the climb.

"Too steep for you in this bulky coat?" she ribbed, poking his prized crimson Patagonia "puffer" coat, which Katherine had repeatedly suggested he replace with something from *this* millennium.

"No . . ." He pulled back the sleeve of his coat, checked his Mickey Mouse watch, and frowned. "But it just occurred to me . . . we only have a few hours before we go to the airport, and there's some paperwork I need to take care of before I can leave the country. How about I meet you up there?"

"Paperwork?" she asked.

"Sorry," he said. "I haven't really wanted to tell you everything that happened yesterday. It was chaotic, and there's just one loose end that I need to tie up."

Katherine was concerned about what it might be, especially when she considered that yesterday morning Robert had evacuated a luxury hotel and eluded the Czech police. "Is everything okay, Robert? Do we need to involve the ambassador?"

"It's all going to be fine," he reassured. "I promise."

"Shall I come with you?"

"Thanks, but I don't want you to miss this walk." He motioned up the walkway. "It's spectacular. I'll jump into a cab, take care of this, and with luck we'll arrive at the castle at about the same time."

"As you like," she said, still unsettled. "Where do we meet?"

Langdon thought a moment. "I'll see you at the door with the seven locks."

Katherine stared at him. "There's a door . . . with *seven* locks?"

He nodded. "One of the most mysterious doors in all of Europe. Just ask when you get there."

"Robert," she protested, "why don't we meet at the information booth like normal people?"

"Because . . ." He kissed her on the cheek. "*Normal* is profoundly overrated."

CHAPTER 138

High above a dark expanse of ocean, Scott Kerble could feel a deep fatigue settling in. As the jet raced westward ahead of the rising sun, he walked to the rear of the plane to make one final check before he closed his eyes.

Sasha was sleeping soundly.

Kerble had already removed her handcuffs and substituted a single ankle restraint affixed to her chair. He had also let Harry and Sally out of their travel crate, and the two Siamese cats were now dozing on the seat beside her, intertwined with each other, a single ball of fur, purring as one.

Kerble returned to his seat and shed his jacket, feeling the encrypted hard drive in his pocket. He pulled it out and studied the device, curious what could possibly be on it that had given the ambassador such incontrovertible power. As he eyed the built-in keypad, he recalled what he was supposed to tell the director about the sixteen-character passkey.

The first letter of each word in your favorite Kissinger quote.

Kerble pondered it a moment and then pulled out his phone and asked ChatGPT if CIA Director Gregory Judd had ever quoted Henry Kissinger in any public speeches. As it turned out, Judd had done so many, many times—always the same quote— and usually accompanied by a preamble: "Only Kissinger could convey such a complex truth in only sixteen words."

A country that demands moral perfection in its foreign policy will achieve neither perfection nor security.

ACTDMPIIFPWANPNS, Kerble thought, knowing he could easily unlock the disk and view whatever data was locked inside. He also knew he would never betray the ambassador's trust. Without a second thought, he slid the disk deep into his duffel for delivery to the director.

Semper Fidelis, he thought as he closed his eyes to sleep.

———··——→

In a backseat of the darkened cabin, The Golĕm emerged from the shadows. Sasha was sound asleep, and The Golĕm slipped quietly to the forefront of her mind, opening his eyes and gazing out the window. Beneath them, he saw only blackness . . . the great void that separated the Old World and the New.

America would be a fresh start for Sasha . . . as it had been for millions of people throughout history. A second chance. The Golĕm finally felt confident that his dedication and love for Sasha would be rewarded. *The universe helps those who understand it.*

Even though The Golĕm felt increasingly confident that Sasha would be safe in the ambassador's care, he had no plans to leave Sasha entirely. Not yet. He would continue watching from the shadows, each day a bit farther back, less and less a part of her life, eventually just a quiet whisper in her mind. The thought felt melancholy somehow, and yet it also filled him with a sense of accomplishment.

The less she needs me, the more I have served her.

While The Golĕm knew he had the power to leave Sasha entirely, to untether and return to the realm from which he had come, he sensed that a part of him would forever be with her . . . a guardian angel. He would manifest quietly in the ways so many angels appear . . . as an instinct, a hunch, a knowing . . . a helpful nudge from a more experienced soul, streaming in from another world.

Sasha will live the life she deserves.

Contented in his soul, The Golĕm closed his eyes and gave himself permission to lose himself in the deepest slumber he'd enjoyed in a very long time.

"*Spokoynoy nochi, milaya,*" he whispered. *Good night, sweetheart.*

As he drifted off to sleep, his left hand reached out, by its own volition, and gently stroked the two Siamese cats purring on the seat beside him.

CHAPTER 139

Having finished her steep climb up Castle Hill, Katherine needed a moment to catch her breath and also to absorb the sheer scale of the structure before her. Prague Castle was not a castle at all . . . but rather a sprawling walled *city*.

This hilltop fortress, according to Robert, enclosed more than fifteen acres, including four palaces, two gathering halls, a prison, an armory, a presidential residence, a monastery, and five distinct churches, including one of the largest in the world . . . St. Vitus Cathedral.

Two nights ago, when Katherine had come here to give her lecture, she had been delivered by car and ushered into Vladislav Hall through a modest columned entrance on the south side of the complex. *Probably so I wouldn't be terrified*, she concluded, eyeing the menacing gauntlet that now faced her at the main entrance.

Access to the castle was blocked by a colossal, five-story perimeter wall, which itself was shielded behind a towering spiked fence whose wrought-iron gate was guarded by two uniformed soldiers holding rifles. The only opening in the fence was flanked by two giant statues of muscular men in the process of spearing, stabbing, and bludgeoning lesser men.

Message received, Katherine thought.

She slipped through the gate and made her way through a maze of courtyards and tunnels before emerging into a sprawling cobblestone plaza. As she stepped into the open, her gaze turned immediately upward, climbing the facade of a building so large that she could scarcely believe it stood *within* the castle walls.

St. Vitus Cathedral.

All she knew about this cathedral was that Langdon considered it an architectural masterpiece. His favorite feature was a hundred-meter bell tower that housed one of Europe's largest bells—a seventeen-ton behemoth named Zikmund—which apparently rang so loudly that it was struck only on Christmas and Easter for fear its reverberations might damage the ancient tower.

Katherine took a few moments to gaze up at the massive bell tower before heading for the entrance, eager to locate the famous door that, according to a guard she had just asked, lay within the cathedral.

The door with the seven locks. She still had no idea what it was, but she hoped to find Langdon waiting there already. Her walk up the hill had taken far longer than expected, and Langdon had taken a cab, so with luck his paperwork had been sorted out quickly.

The interior of St. Vitus Cathedral was precisely as Katherine expected—cavernous, opulent, and imposing—just like every other European cathedral she'd ever visited. She remained perplexed that humans had toiled for centuries to construct these shrines to an all-powerful, benevolent God . . . during an era when plagues, wars, and famine were killing the faithful by the millions. She wondered if their God was either indifferent to human suffering . . . or powerless to stop it. Even so, it seemed obvious that the promise of "eternal life" was an irresistible balm that soothed the universal fear of death.

And remains so today, she thought as she moved deeper into the church, scanning for Langdon. St. Vitus was nearly deserted at this hour, and when she asked the lone docent about the mysterious door, he pointed up the nave's central aisle to an arched opening on the right, just off the center of the sanctuary.

"Wenceslas Chapel," he whispered.

The empty chapel turned out to be a breathtakingly beautiful chamber with a gray marble floor and elaborately frescoed walls that climbed several stories to a vaulted ceiling. In the center of the chapel stood an enormous rectangular box of multiple tiers, all inlaid with colorful gems and topped by a peaked canopy. It was so unusual that Katherine had to read the sign before she realized what she was looking at.

A royal sarcophagus.

This box, as it turned out, entombed a famous "king" who was never actually king, but rather a good-hearted prince mistakenly immortalized as a king in a popular English Christmas carol. Katherine was pleased to read that the resting place of Good King Wenceslas *also* served as the gateway to the priceless Bohemian Crown Jewels . . . secured in a vault accessible only through a famous door with seven locks.

Katherine hurried over to the door, which stood in the corner. It was an imposing slab of gray metal, crisscrossed with interlaced reinforcing bands riveted into place on the diagonals. The resulting diamond pattern was embellished with rampant lions and eagles, both symbols from the Czech coat of arms. Running vertically down the left-hand side of the door was a series of ornate keyholes. Katherine was not surprised to count seven of them, each surrounded by armored plating.

She glanced over her shoulder at the empty chapel and then, feeling foolish, tried the door.

Locked.

After waiting a few more minutes with no sign of Langdon, she finally exited back into the main sanctuary to rest her legs in a nearby pew. It felt good to be off her feet, but her concern about Langdon was increasing. *Did something go wrong?*

Forcing her mind elsewhere, she raised her eyes to the main altar—a towering framework of gold lattice spires against a backdrop of stained glass. There was no denying this building was an astonishing human achievement, a majestic work of art.

Even the pulpit is a masterpiece, she thought, admiring the intricately carved podium mounted on the column beside her. Accessed by an elegant spiral staircase, the lofty hexagonal pulpit was crowned with a canopy of gilded cherubs. The sacred perch had clearly been designed to imbue the speaker with almost deific authority.

"There you are!" a deep voice called across the church.

She turned to see Langdon exiting Wenceslas Chapel and rushing toward her, still bundled up in his Patagonia puffer. "I didn't see you in there and was afraid you gave up on me," he said, arriving breathless. "Did you find the door with the seven locks?"

"I did," she said. "Shockingly, it was *locked.*"

Langdon smiled, looking more relaxed now. "Well, if you want me to open it, I'll need to make seven phone calls—the president, the prime minister, the archbishop, the administrator, the dean, the mayor, and the chamber chairperson."

"I won't even ask why you know that, Robert. Did you sort out your paperwork?"

"I did," he said. "We're all set."

Katherine felt relieved. "Are you going to tell me what it was all about?"

"I will . . ." he said, seeming distracted by the nearby pulpit. "Hold on . . ." He glanced around the deserted cathedral and then back at Katherine. "Sit right here—I want to show you something." He headed for the pulpit stairs and deftly stepped over a velvet swag that blocked them.

"Robert, what are—"

He bounded up the curling staircase. When he reached the top, only his head was visible as he peered down over an immense Bible that lay open on the lectern. "Katherine, I'd like to read a few passages to you," he said, his tone earnest. "Just open your heart and listen."

Bible passages? "I don't underst—"

"Just listen," he urged. "I believe these words will comfort your soul."

Katherine gazed up in bewilderment as Robert got himself situated, removing his puffy coat, dropping it on the floor, and fumbling with the Bible. He seemed to be flipping pages as if searching for a specific passage.

Once settled, Langdon cleared his throat and made eye contact with her again before turning his eyes to the lectern. When he spoke, his familiar baritone was clear and resonant. "It has now been proven," he orated dramatically, "that *infants* are capable of conscious experiences from birth . . . thereby undermining our current model that consciousness develops over time."

I'm sorry? Katherine's thoughts scrambled. *What did he just say?!*

Langdon flipped several pages and began reading again. "Most remarkably," he continued, "we have now detected irrefutable *evidence* of intense gamma wave activity in the brain as it dies."

Katherine leaped to her feet, now recognizing precisely what he was reading from. *That's impossible!* She dashed toward the pulpit as Langdon began to read another section.

"GABA levels," he intoned, "fell precipitously in the moments before death, and with it, the brain's ability to filter out the broadest spectrums of human experience that are normally unknown."

Katherine scrambled up the curved stairs, heart racing. "Robert!" she exclaimed, reaching the pulpit, coming to an abrupt stop, and staring in disbelief at the familiar stack of laser-printed pages sitting atop the massive bible. "Is that my *manuscript*?!"

"Apparently so," he said with a shrug and the lopsided grin she had come to love.

Katherine now realized he must have been carrying the manuscript beneath his coat. "But . . ." She fumbled for words. "I thought . . . you *burned* it!"

"Only your bibliography, my darling . . ." he said with a smile. "The rest of the manuscript I hid behind some ancient books on the library's balcony shelves."

Stunned, Katherine pictured the blaze Langdon had started on the metal stairs and the charred scraps of paper drifting down to the floor below. "But . . . the fire seemed so *big*."

"It *was*," Langdon said. "Leave it to *you* to cite forty-two double-spaced pages of sources. You *do* know your publisher lays that out for you at the end, right? Anyhow, I mixed in a handful of blank vellum pages from one of the old ledgers up there. Animal fat creates a *lot* of black smoke."

Katherine fought back a torrent of emotions rushing through her. Relief, gratitude, disbelief, and also frustration. *My manuscript was never lost?!* "Why didn't you *tell* me?!" she demanded. "I was devastated!!"

Langdon's expression was sincerely remorseful. "Believe me, Katherine, I desperately *wanted* to. It was agonizing to see you suffer, but we were surrounded by chaos and were on the verge of being arrested and interrogated. I didn't want you to have to lie. It was far safer for you *not* to know the manuscript existed until this was all sorted out—the last thing I wanted was to have it confiscated again by ÚZSI or worse."

Katherine was a lousy liar, and they both knew it . . . She realized he was probably right. *Disinformation by deception,* as Nagel had called it. Langdon had not even told Jonas on the phone.

"I'm hoping you'll forgive me . . ." he entreated. "It was a tough secret to keep."

Katherine stared at him indecipherably and then stepped forward and wrapped her arms around him, melting into his body. "Paperwork . . . ? Really?"

"Important paperwork," he clarified. "Far too important to burn."

She hugged him tighter. "There is one thing I just can't believe—the esteemed Professor Langdon actually tore vellum pages out of an ancient book?"

"*Blank* pages," he retorted. "They will never be missed. And as my prep school English teacher Mr. Lelchuk used to tell us: 'The right book at the right time can save your life.'"

She laughed. "I'm fairly certain that's not what he meant."

"Probably not," Langdon said, pulling her body closer to his.

Katherine had no idea how long they had been embracing on the pulpit of St. Vitus Cathedral when the cathedral bells overhead began to toll. She was lost in the joy of having her manuscript back . . . along with the waves of affection she was feeling for the man in her arms.

"I love you, Robert Langdon," she whispered. "I'm sorry it took me so long to figure that out."

EPILOGUE

Robert Langdon awoke to the sound of military drumming—a lone rhythmic snare, playing a battle cadence as if leading a small army. When he opened his eyes, he was looking out over the wintry expanse of a wooded park. In the distance, dawn's first light was breaking, filtering through a maze of skyscrapers.

Manhattan, he remembered as his mind slowly sharpened. *Mandarin Oriental Hotel. Fifty-second floor.*

The drumming continued. It seemed close.

Langdon sat up in bed, now seeing that Katherine was awake beside him, propped up on her elbow, smiling playfully, her hair tousled and loose. She was tinkering with her new phone, which Langdon now realized was the source of the drumming.

"I got tired of Grieg's 'Morning Mood,'" she said. "I changed our wakeup call."

To a military march? Langdon now heard a single flute join the drum, playing a familiar melody. "Wait . . . is that *Boléro?*"

She gave an innocent shrug. "Maybe."

Ravel's orchestral masterpiece was widely considered the most erotic piece of classical music ever written. Often called "the perfect soundtrack for lovemaking," *Boléro* was fifteen minutes of insistent, pulsing rhythm that crescendoed into a full orchestra fortissimo climax that reviewers had referred to as a C-major orgasm.

"Subtle, you are not," Langdon said, grabbing Katherine's phone, turning up the volume, and playfully pinning her to the bed. For the next ten seconds, he gazed into her eyes and did absolutely nothing but listen to the snare and flute duet.

"Um, Robert?" Katherine finally said. "What are you doing?"

"Waiting for the clarinet entrance in measure eighteen," he replied. "I'm not a savage."

———··———

An hour later, Langdon and Katherine were lounging in plush terry cloth robes, enjoying a room service breakfast in the sunlight that streamed in over Central Park.

Langdon's body was sublimely content, and yet his mind was restless, eager for their afternoon meeting with Jonas Faukman at Random House Tower.

He still has no idea we have the manuscript.

Katherine's book was safely stowed in their room's safe, bound by two large rubber bands. Before leaving Prague, they had made three photocopies and securely sent one to Katherine, one to Langdon, and one to Jonas. With luck, they would not need any of them; Penguin Random House was only a few blocks away.

"Do you have a title yet?" Langdon asked. "Jonas will want to know."

Katherine glanced up. "For my book? Nothing yet . . ."

"I ask only because you said something in Prague that's been bouncing around in my mind. I think you might have landed on the perfect title."

"Oh?"

"You told me that if science can prove there is indeed something beyond death, then we should be shouting that message from the mountaintops. You called it the secret of all secrets . . . and you claimed it would have enormous impact on the future of humanity."

"I remember."

Langdon waited. Katherine seemed to be waiting too. "Don't you hear it?" he asked. "*The Secret of Secrets.* If you think about it, the question at the core of the book—what happens when we die?—is the mystery that *all* human minds have pondered. It is truly the secret of secrets."

"As a *book title*?" Katherine looked skeptical. "I don't know, it sounds . . ."

"Like a bestseller?" Langdon prompted.

"I was going to say 'over-the-top.'"

He laughed. "Well, my precognitive instinct is that the Penguin Random House lobby will soon be making space on its shelves for one more classic."

Katherine's eyes welled with emotion. She leaned forward, gently kissing him. "Thank you, Robert . . . for so many things."

They sat in silence a long time, watching the bustling world beneath their window. Finally, Katherine stood and checked her watch. "We've got five hours to explore the city," she said. "I'll take a shower, and then you can play tour guide."

"Sounds perfect," Langdon said as she headed for the bathroom. "We'll start at Trinity Church. Then Cathedral of Saint John the Divine, Saint Patrick's, Grace Church, the Cloist—"

"Robert!" Katherine spun around. "No!"

"Kidding, my dear," he said with a smile. "Leave it to me. I know exactly where to take you."

•——··——•

The Circle Line sightseeing boat plowed through the choppy waters of New York Harbor. In the morning breeze, a lone osprey coasted effortlessly off the port side, scanning the water for its breakfast. On the bow, Katherine Solomon tucked herself under Langdon's arm, enjoying the warmth of his body and the briny scent of fresh ocean air.

"Incredible, isn't she?" Langdon whispered as they neared their destination.

She is, Katherine thought. *I had no idea . . .*

In front of them, rising more than three hundred feet above the water, a colossal figure stood proudly on her own private island, emanating a solemn grace that seemed almost divinely infused. With her right arm raised, she held out a gleaming torch whose twenty-four-karat flame glinted in the morning sun.

As the ferry churned closer, Katherine began to see details in the statue's verdigris copper—the broken chains of bondage around her sandaled feet, the delicate folds in her robes of justice, the tablet in her left hand bearing the nation's birth date, the steadfast gaze and reassuring countenance . . . and there, atop her head, the ancient symbol that Langdon had brought Katherine here to see.

The radiant crown.

The spiked halo adorning America's Statue of Liberty was the same ornament that had crowned enlightened minds for millennia. The seven spikes, each over nine feet long, were said to symbolize the rays of enlightenment that would radiate outward from this young country and illuminate all seven continents.

It's the precise opposite, Katherine believed, seeing them as rays of enlightenment that flowed *inward* . . . representing the stream of cultures, languages, and ideas from the seven continents, all coursing into the melting pot that was the mind of America. This nation, after all, had been created as a kind of receiver, pulling in disparate souls from around the world, all of them flowing inward toward a shared experience.

Gazing out at Lady Liberty, Katherine could hear the faint echoes of the millions who had come to these shores to pursue their dreams. *As my own family did . . . generations ago.* Her immigrant ancestors were gone now, of course, and yet to *where*, Katherine remained uncertain. What she had come to accept was that human consciousness was not as we believed it to be. Something real and profound lay beyond our physical experience . . . beyond our physical end.

As the wind blew harder, Katherine gently laid her head on Langdon's shoulder, her mind as clear as it had ever been. She looked up at him. "I wish we could stand here forever."

"Me too," he said with a smile. "But you've got a book to deliver."

- THE END -

ACKNOWLEDGMENTS

First and foremost, to Jason Kaufman—the finest editor a writer could ever have—for his narrative instincts, sense of humor, and tireless hours in the trenches with me.

To my incomparable agent, Heide Lange, for her decades of dedication and friendship, and for so expertly guiding all aspects of my career with unparalleled enthusiasm.

A very special thanks to my stalwart publishers Maya Mavjee and Bill Thomas for their unwavering support and patience while I wrote this book . . . and, above all, for their commitment, creativity, and excitement during its publication.

To the world-class team at Doubleday and Penguin Random House, with special notes of thanks to publicity guru Todd Doughty; the innovative marketing crew of Heather Fain, Judy Jacoby, Erinn McGrath, and Abby Endler; wonderful assistant editor Lily Dondoshansky for her careful work and good cheer; the meticulous Nora Reichard in production editorial, along with Vimi Santokhi, Barbara Richard, Kirsten Eggart, and Casey Hampton; the creative art directors and jacket designers, Oliver Munday and Will Staehle; the world's finest sales team, with extra thanks to Beth Meister, Chris Dufault, David Weller, and Lynn Kovach; legal expert Claire Leonard; the IT and security team of Chris Hart, Tom Saal, Mike DeMasi, and Zafar Nasir; Amanda D'Acierno in audiobooks; Beth Lamb in paperbacks; my dear friend Suzanne Herz; and, of course, in the corporate offices, the steady hands of Nihar Malaviya, Jaci Updike, and Jeff Weber. Thank you all.

A debt of gratitude to my fifty-seven international publishers, who have moved mountains to make these books a global success and who have become my extended family away from home. A big thank-you as well to the talented team of translators who bring these books to life around the world.

A very special thanks to my Czech editor and friend, Petr Onufer, for his invaluable research and guidance on all aspects of Prague, Czech culture, and Czech language . . . and also for helping me see the spectacular city of Prague in a truly mystical light. My thanks also to the directors of Argo Publishing in Prague, Milan Gelnar and Hana Gelnarova.

To my brilliant UK publisher Bill Scott-Kerr for being such a great friend since day one with my very first novel.

My sincere admiration and gratitude to the remarkable minds who make up the Institute of Noetic Sciences. Thank you for the important and illuminating work you do.

A very special thanks to Norm Eisen, former ambassador to the Czech Republic, for his generous hospitality while I was in Prague, and for his fascinating stories over dinner in the spectacular Petschek Villa.

Over the past six years, a wide array of scientists, historians, curators, religious scholars, government officials, and private organizations have generously offered assistance in the research of this novel. Words cannot begin to express my appreciation to all of them for their generosity and openness in sharing their expertise and insight.

To my trusted personal assistant Susan Morehouse for her steadfast friendship and dedication through the years and for all she does behind the scenes to keep this train on the rails.

To my tech-savvy digital guru Alex Canon for handling all aspects of my online world (and also for tracking down manuscript hackers).

To the dream team at William Morris Endeavor—with special thanks to Ari, Sylvie, Conor, Ryan, Michael, and CJ—for forging such exciting synergies.

To the distinguished legal mind of Karl Austen for his expertise and also for being an NSA cryptologist in my first novel.

To everyone at Sanford J. Greenburger Associates, with heartfelt gratitude to Iwalani Kim and Madeline Wallace for handling endless details with elegance and precision, and also to the skills of Charles Loffredo for handling all things numerical.

To Peter Fahey, Philip McCaull, Jennifer Rouleau, Ginny McGrody, Glenn Greenfader, and associates for deftly managing the *Fructus laborum.*

Thank you as well to Dr. Mona Laifi, Dr. Elizabeth Klodas, Dr. Bob Helm, Dr. Chad Prusmack, Dennis G. Whyte at the MIT Plasma Science and Fusion Center, Georgie Venci and Charlie Venci for their aquatic acumen, Carl Schwartz for his culinary skills, my trainer Evan Schaller for pulling me away from my desk and keeping me mobile, the Four Seasons Hotel Prague for their hospitality, the Prague Tourism Bureau, Charles University, the Klementinum, U.S. Ambassador's security detail Carlton Cuse, the indomitable Emanuel Swedenborg, the Global Consciousness Project, the Center for Consciousness Science, to Rose Schwartz, Eric Brown, Neil Rosini, and the memory of my dear friend Michael Rudell for being such a role model of grace and kindness.

To the late great literary agent George Wieser for taking me to lunch in 1994 and strongly suggesting I take a sabbatical from music . . . and write a novel.

Mi agradecimiento al distinguido caballero Roberto Batalla por haberme servido de guía en el paisaje costarricense.

To my first-draft readers—Gregory Brown, Heide Lange, John Chaffee, Iwalani Kim, Madeline Wallace, Lily Dondoshansky, and others. Thank you for your early input on a *very* long manuscript. And continued appreciation to Rebecca, Caleb, Hannah, and Sophie Kaufman, plus Olivia and Jerry Kaufman, for years of support . . . and for kindly sharing my editor.

A lifetime of gratitude to my parents—Connie and Dick Brown—for teaching me to be eternally curious and to embrace the difficult questions.

And finally, to my fiancée, Judith Pietersen, for her patience, love, and astonishing good humor while I was buried in this book.

ILLUSTRATION CREDITS

ABOUT THE AUTHOR

DAN BROWN is the author of numerous #1 international bestsellers, including *The Da Vinci Code, Inferno, The Lost Symbol, Origin, Angels & Demons, Deception Point,* and *Digital Fortress.*

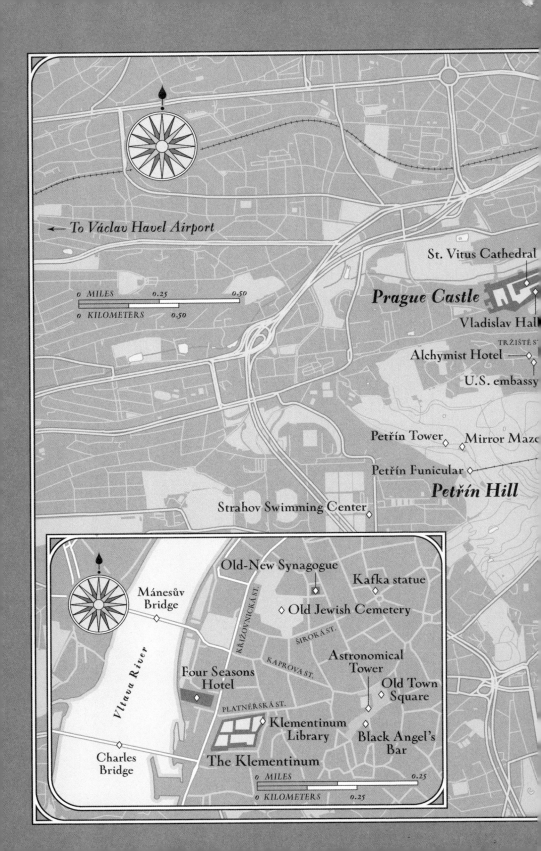